THE
MANDIE
COLLECTION

VOLUME TWO

Books by Lois Gladys Leppard

FROM BETHANY HOUSE PUBLISHERS

The Mandie Collection: Volume One (Books 1–5)
The Mandie Collection: Volume Two (Books 6–10)
The Mandie Collection: Volume Three (Books 11–15)
The Mandie Collection: Volume Four (Books 16–20)
The Mandie Collection: Volume Five (Books 21–23)
The Mandie Collection: Volume Six (Books 24–26)
The Mandie Collection: Volume Seven (Books 27–29)
The Mandie Collection: Volume Eight (Books 30–32)
The Mandie Collection: Volume Nine (Books 33–35)
The Mandie Collection: Volume Ten (Books 36–38)
The Mandie Collection: Volume Eleven (Books 39–40 plus 2
holiday adventures)

MANDIE: HER COLLEGE DAYS

New Horizons

THE
MANDIE
COLLECTION

VOLUME TWO

LOIS GLADYS LEPPARD

BETHANYHOUSE

a division of Baker Publishing Group
Minneapolis, Minnesota

© 1986, 1987, 1988 by Lois Gladys Leppard

Published by Bethany House Publishers
11400 Hampshire Avenue South
Bloomington, Minnesota 55438
www.bethanyhouse.com

Bethany House Publishers is a division of
Baker Publishing Group, Grand Rapids, Michigan.

Printed in the United States of America by Bethany Press International, Bloomington, MN.

ISBN   978-0-7642-0538-5

Previously published in five separate volumes:
Mandie and the Medicine Man © 1986
Mandie and the Charleston Phantom © 1986
Mandie and the Abandoned Mine © 1987
Mandie and the Hidden Treasure © 1987
Mandie and the Mysterious Bells © 1988

MANDIE® and SNOWBALL® are registered trademarks of Lois Gladys Leppard

The Library of Congress has cataloged Volume One of this collection as follows:
 Leppard, Lois Gladys.
       The Mandie collection / Lois Gladys Leppard.
          v. <1–   > cm.
       Summary: A collection of tales featuring Mandie, an orphan, and her friends as they solve mysteries together in turn-of-the-century North Carolina.
       Contents: v. 1. Mandie and the secret tunnel ; Mandie and the Cherokee legend ; Mandie and the ghost bandits ; Mandie and the forbidden attic ; Mandie and the trunk's secret —
       ISBN–13: 978-0-7642-0446-3 (pbk.)
       ISBN–10: 0-7642-0446-7 (pbk.)
       1. Children's stories, American. [1. Family life—North Carolina—Fiction. 2. Orphans—Fiction. 3. Christian life—Fiction. 4. North Carolina—History—20th century—Fiction. 5. Mystery and detective stories.] I. Title.
 PZ7.L556May   2007
 [Fic]—dc22   2007023752

Cover illustration by Chris Wold Dyrud

21   22   23   24   15   14   13   12

ABOUT THE AUTHOR

LOIS GLADYS LEPPARD worked in Federal Intelligence for thirteen years in various countries around the world. She now makes her home in South Carolina.

The stories of her own mother's childhood as an orphan in western North Carolina are the basis for many of the incidents incorporated in this series.

Visit her Web site: *www.Mandie.com*.

MANDIE'S TRAVELS

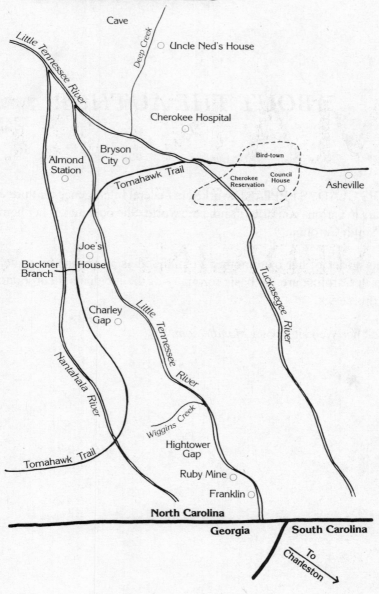

Cave

Deep Creek

Uncle Ned's House

Little Tennessee River

Cherokee Hospital

Bryson City

Almond Station

Tomahawk Trail

Bird-town

Cherokee Reservation

Council House

Asheville

Joe's House

Buckner Branch

Charley Gap

Little Tennessee River

Tuckasegee River

Nantahala River

Tomahawk Trail

Wiggins Creek

Hightower Gap

Ruby Mine

Franklin

North Carolina

Georgia

South Carolina

To Charleston

MANDIE

AND THE
MEDICINE MAN

For My Mother,
Bessie A. Wilson Leppard,
and
In Memory of Her Sister,
Lillie Margaret Ann Wilson Frady, Orphans of North Carolina
Who Outgrew the Sufferings of Childhood

CONTENTS

MANDIE AND THE MEDICINE MAN

With love to all those wonderful readers
who have written to me, including:

Angela

Julia Batson

Amanda Berl

Katie Bolding

Amy, Robyn & Angel Booth

Stephanie Brock

Michelle & Malissa Burns

Christy Cook

Danielle & Deeann Cowan

Melanie Cox

Aaron Crabb

Heather & Jennifer Crowe

Deanne Devlin

Linda D'Hoore

Colleen Dorr

Renee Fowler

Megan Frahm

Karen Garner

Anna Gilbertson

Kristi Gosnell

Carolyn Grant

Ashley Hall

Krista, Alicia & Sara Hanson

Jennifer Hinson

Mary Hoffman

Melissa Holden

Amanda Howard

Mariah Hutchison

Samara & Nicky Ibanez

Julie Jackson

Amy Karcich

L. Vande Krol

Krista Kulp

Cindy & Candy Leapord

Lisa Lee

Jennifer Lewis

Jennifer Little

Margaret Long

Christi Mc Croskey

Lashon & Sonya Miner

Melissa Mitchell

Kelly Morris

Mandy Nesbitt

Ruby Newton

Lisa Nygren

Jennifer Owens

Kimberly Reeves

Nancy Pafford-Reifenstein

Jessica Robinson

Tobey Roethler

Karin Schorr

Michael Schroeder

Ella Severs

Georgia Shelton

Sandra & Stephanie Springer

Malinda Stiver

Barbie Stufflebeam

Nellie Suber

Debbie Summerall

Anne Telker

Rochelle TerMaat

Tanya Turcotte

Michelle Van Mill

Angie Wallace

Gretchen Walters

Margaret Watson

Jackie Wessels

Mindy Wilson

"Now faith is the substance of things hoped for,
the evidence of things not seen."
Hebrews 11:1

CHAPTER ONE

OFF FOR THE HOLIDAYS

"I wish you could come home with me," Mandie told Celia as they packed their trunks.

All the students at Misses Heathwood's School for Girls in Asheville, North Carolina, were getting ready to leave for their first holidays of the school year.

"I wanted you to go to Charleston with us." Mandie's blue eyes sparkled. "I can't wait to see the ocean!"

"Mandie, you know I'm torn between this wonderful trip you have planned and going home to see my mother," Celia answered. She folded a dress and laid it in the open trunk. "It would be nice if I could do both, but I can't. You know I haven't seen my mother since I came to school here. I've just got to go home."

Mandie straightened up from the trunk she was packing and studied her friend with the sad green eyes and thick, curly auburn hair. "I know," she agreed. "That's what you should do. This will be a short holiday anyway. Just one week. Maybe you can come home with me for Thanksgiving. We'll get two whole weeks then."

"I'll see," Celia replied. "My Aunt Rebecca should be here pretty soon. She'll spend the night here at the school, and we'll leave tomorrow morning to go home to Richmond. It'll be good to get home again, see my mother, and the horses, and my dog, Prickles."

"I'm glad my mother took Snowball home with her when she and Uncle John were here last week. It has been nice having my kitten right here in town at my grandmother's house. But since Grandmother is going away on a long trip, Snowball wouldn't be able to stay there any longer," Mandie said.

"When do you leave?" Celia asked.

"Mother and Uncle John ought to be here early tomorrow morning, and then we'll leave on the train," Mandie replied. "We'll spend tomorrow night at home in Franklin, and then the next day we'll start out for Charleston. I'm so glad Tommy Patton's parents invited us to his home there. I can't believe that the time has finally come to go."

Suddenly there was a knock at the door of their room. When Mandie opened the door, Aunt Phoebe, the old Negro who worked for the school, was standing there.

"Missy, Miz Hope want you down to de office," the black woman told Mandie.

"Miss Hope? Oh, goodness! What have I done now?" Mandie gasped, dropping the skirt she held. "Aunt Phoebe, what does she want?"

"Don't you be gittin' all flustered, Missy," said Aunt Phoebe. "Miz Hope, she don't seem upset 'tall. De doctuh man, he be in huh office."

"Dr. Woodard? He's in Miss Hope's office? Goodness, I'd better go see what she wants!" Mandie exclaimed.

As Mandie ran out the door, Celia called to her. "Hurry back and tell me what's going on."

Mandie quickly made her way to Miss Hope's office on the main floor. The door was open. Dr. Woodard sat in front of Miss Hope's desk. Miss Hope, smoothing back a stray lock of faded auburn hair, smiled at Mandie as she entered.

"Dr. Woodard, is anything wrong?" Mandie asked anxiously.

"No, no, Amanda. Nothing serious," Miss Hope told her quietly. "Sit down for a minute."

Mandie sat in the other chair and looked from Miss Hope to the doctor.

Dr. Woodard cleared his throat. "Amanda, your mother and your Uncle John will not be coming for you tomorrow—" he began.

"Not coming for me?" Mandie broke in quickly.

"No. You see, I had to come here to Asheville to see some patients and will be going home myself on the train tomorrow," the doctor explained, "so you're to go back with me to Franklin."

"Oh, that's great! I was afraid something was wrong," Mandie responded, a smile lighting up her blue eyes.

"Well, there is a little change in plans," the doctor said slowly. "You see, you probably won't be going on to Charleston the next day."

Tears filled Mandie's eyes. "We aren't going to Charleston, Dr. Woodard? Why not? Tommy's family is expecting us."

"Amanda, please let Dr. Woodard explain without any more interruptions," Miss Hope reprimanded her.

"I'm sorry, Miss Hope, Dr. Woodard," Mandie apologized.

Dr. Woodard looked at her with concern. "We're having some trouble at the hospital," he said.

"Oh, no!" Mandie gasped.

"Someone is tearing down the walls of the hospital as fast as they're being put up," the doctor explained. "So far, we have no idea who would do such a thing, but I told your Uncle John you'd want to come and help solve the mystery, isn't that right?"

"Well, yes, Dr. Woodard." Mandie hesitated. "But I would like to go to Charleston, too."

"Your Uncle John said that as soon as this matter is cleared up, you will all go on to Charleston as planned. Maybe it won't take long. We've already put guards around the place," he said.

Miss Hope sat forward. "This is the hospital for the Cherokees that is being built with the gold you and your friends found in a cave, isn't it, Amanda?" she asked.

"Yes, ma'am," Mandie replied. "The great Cherokee warrior, Tsali, left the gold in a cave. After we found the gold, the Cherokees refused to have anything to do with it. They said it would cause bad luck. So they put me in charge of the gold, asking me to use it for whatever I saw fit. I knew they needed a hospital, so we're building one for them."

"That is a big job for a twelve-year-old girl, but it's a sensible thing for you to do, Amanda," the school-mistress told her. "I do hope you get all this straightened out."

"I hope it won't take long." Amanda looked at Dr. Woodard, pleading. "I want to go to Charleston. I've never seen the ocean, and I've been so excited about this trip," she said.

"We'll all pitch in, Amanda," Dr. Woodard promised. "The Cherokees will help us solve this thing, and I'm sure you'll get to Charleston." He stood and patted her blonde head. "Just be sure you're ready when I call for you tomorrow morning so we can make the train on time."

"I'll be ready." Mandie got up and hurried to the door. "I'd better finish my packing. See you in the morning, Dr. Woodard."

Racing up the steps to the room she shared with Celia Hamilton on the third floor, Mandie burst through the door. Celia stopped packing and looked up.

"I'm going home with Dr. Woodard tomorrow," Mandie told her friend. "Somebody is tearing down the Cherokees' hospital as fast as it's being built. I have to go home and stop them."

Celia smiled. "You? Stop them?"

"Sure. Joe, and Sallie, and Dimar will all help me. When we work on a mystery we always solve it one way or another." Mandie laughed, walking around the room. "Of course it usually takes some grown-ups to help. But we'll have to hurry and solve this mystery so we can go on to Charleston before we use up all the holidays."

"I do hope you're able to visit Charleston," Celia said. "I know how much you want to go."

There was another knock at the door. Aunt Phoebe once again brought a message.

"Message fo' you dis time, Missy Celia," said the old woman. "Dat ahnt of yours be waitin' downstairs wid Miz Hope. She say fo' you to git right down."

"Thanks, Aunt Phoebe," Celia said, following her into the hallway. "I'll be right back, Mandie."

Mandie continued packing. In a few minutes Celia was back, bringing a tiny dark-haired lady with her.

"Aunt Rebecca, this is Amanda Shaw—Mandie I call her. She's my best friend," Celia introduced them. "Mandie, this is my Aunt Rebecca."

"How do you do, Miss . . . ah . . . Miss . . ." Mandie stopped and smiled at the woman. Turning to Celia, she asked, "Well, what is her name? I can't call her Aunt Rebecca, you know."

The woman reached out and took Mandie's small hand in hers. "Of course you can, dear," the lady said. "My name is Rebecca Hamilton. I'm Celia's father's sister. I've heard so much about you from letters Celia has written to her mother. I feel I know you. Now, what can I do to help you girls get finished?"

"Nothing, Aunt Rebecca. Just sit over there in that chair and talk to us while we get done." Celia motioned toward the only empty chair in the littered room. "How is Mother? I was hoping she could come with you so she could meet Mandie and see the school."

"I know, dear, but she wasn't feeling up to the trip. I doubt that the school has changed much since she was a student here," Aunt Rebecca said, relaxing in the chair. She turned to Mandie. "I know she would like to meet Elizabeth's daughter, however. She told me that your mother went to school here with her."

"My mother is not coming either," Mandie said. "Dr. Woodard is in town, and I'll be going home to Franklin as he goes tomorrow." She told Aunt Rebecca what was happening at the hospital.

"I think it's wonderful for you to do such a thing, building a hospital for those poor Indians," the woman replied.

"Well, after all, they are my kinpeople. My grandmother was full-blooded Cherokee," Mandie explained, continuing to fill her trunk.

"Yes, I believe I remember hearing about that. Your father died and then your mother married his brother, John Shaw, didn't she?" Aunt Rebecca asked.

"Yes, ma'am," Mandie said sadly as she pushed back her long blonde hair. "My father was a wonderful man. I loved him so much. Of course I love Uncle John, too, but no one can replace my father."

"I know that from experience, Amanda," Aunt Rebecca replied. "My father died when I was small. My mother never remarried."

"I can just barely remember Grandmother Hamilton," Celia said. "Mandie, you're lucky your Grandmother Taft is still living. My mother and Aunt Rebecca are all the close relatives I have left."

"I have lots of Cherokee relatives. There must be dozens and dozens of them. But then the Indians claim kinship with each other whether they're really blood related or not," Mandie explained.

Aunt Rebecca smiled. "In a sense that's true, isn't it? God made us all. We're really all brothers and sisters," she said.

17

Mandie and Celia nodded thoughtfully.

"So, now you're going home and then on to see your Cherokee relatives before you make this trip to Charleston. I wish you a lot of luck with the hospital. I hope they catch whoever is responsible for such vandalism."

The bell in the backyard rang loudly for supper, and the girls stopped working.

"Aunt Rebecca, let me show you to the guest room downstairs," Celia said. "We have only about ten minutes before we have to be in the dining room, and I know you want to freshen up. Be right back, Mandie."

"I'll see you downstairs, Miss—Aunt Rebecca." Mandie smiled.

"Yes, dear," the lady replied, hurrying out the door with Celia.

In a couple of minutes Celia was back, and the girls rushed to the bathroom down the hall to wash their hands. As they came back out into the hallway, they almost ran into April Snow.

Mandie looked up into the tall girl's face. "April, I'm sorry you won't be able to go home for the holidays," she said kindly.

"Whether I go home or not is my own business," April snapped. "Just be sure and remember that."

Mandie and Celia looked at each other as April rushed on down the hallway.

"She just won't let anyone be nice to her," Mandie said.

Celia frowned. "April's not very nice to be nice to," she said. "That girl is always making trouble. You know that as well as I do."

"I sure do," Mandie agreed. "But don't forget. The Bible says to return good for evil."

"It'd sure take a whole lot of good to even things out with her evil," Celia said.

"We should keep on trying though," Mandie reminded her.

After the evening meal, the girls hurriedly left the dining room.

Just outside the door, April Snow stepped in front of them. "Enjoy your holidays because you might not enjoy coming back," she sneered. Turning quickly, she disappeared down the hallway.

"Now, what on earth can she be talking about?" Mandie asked in surprise.

"She's talking about making trouble, and we are her target," Celia replied.

"Well, we'll see about that," said Mandie.

Back in their room the two girls thought the night would never end. Excited about their forthcoming trips, they talked most of the night away. Then before daylight they got up, dressed, and waited for the bell to ring for breakfast.

The morning meal with Miss Prudence, the head schoolmistress, watching over them seemed to take longer than usual. Neither Mandie nor Celia could eat much.

When it was time to leave, Uncle Cal, Aunt Phoebe's husband, brought the girls' trunks downstairs and loaded them into the school rig. While they waited on the veranda, Dr. Woodard arrived, and Mandie introduced him to Aunt Rebecca.

The two adults stood chatting while Mandie and Celia went back inside to bid Miss Hope good-bye.

"We are leaving now, Miss Hope," Mandie said as they stood before the schoolmistress's desk.

"You're both leaving?" Miss Hope looked surprised. "But you are going in opposite directions, Amanda."

"Dr. Woodard said we'd just all go to the depot together," Mandie explained. "Celia's train will come through about thirty minutes ahead of ours. So we can save Uncle Cal another trip to the station."

Miss Hope stood up, walked around the desk, and put an arm around each girl. "I know it's just for a few days, but I'm going to miss you both," she said. "Be good girls and tell me about your trips when you get back."

"We will, Miss Hope," they promised.

April Snow caught up with the two girls in the hallway. She stepped in front of them, blocking their way to the front door.

"Just remember what I said," April threatened. "Enjoy your trips because you might not enjoy coming back."

"Just what do you mean?" Mandie asked.

"Just what I said," April replied. "You'll see when you get back."

Stepping around them, April headed down the hallway in the other direction.

Mandie and Celia looked at each other in exasperation.

"I wish she wouldn't act like that," Mandie complained. "It sort of puts a damper on things. Now I'll be wondering the whole time I'm gone what she's talking about."

"Me, too," Celia agreed.

When Mandie and Celia rejoined Dr. Woodard and Aunt Rebecca on the veranda, Uncle Cal was waiting for them in the rig. Climbing aboard, the girls began talking excitedly about being free for a whole week.

Not long after they arrived at the depot, a big, noisy train came whistling up the track. The girls looked at each other.

"I'm going to miss you, Celia, but I hope you have a nice time at home with your mother," Mandie said, giving her friend a hug.

"I'll be thinking about you, Mandie, and wondering how your trip is turning out," Celia replied. "I hope you catch those culprits real fast so you can go to Charleston."

The train came to a halt and sat there puffing.

"Come, Celia. Good-bye, Amanda," Aunt Rebecca called to them. She turned to board the train, letting Celia go ahead of her. "Good day, Dr. Woodard. It was nice meeting you."

"My pleasure, ma'am," said Dr. Woodard, removing his hat. "Give my regards to Celia's mother."

Celia quickly found a seat near an open window and waved to Mandie. As the train hustled on its way, the wind blew Celia's auburn curls around her bonnet.

Mandie waved until the train disappeared down the track. Then she turned to Dr. Woodard. "I hope our train isn't late. I'm in a hurry to get home and catch those crooks," she said. "If it takes too long, I won't be able to go to Charleston. And I've just got to see the ocean."

"Don't worry, Amanda. I think you'll make it," Dr. Woodard told her. "We'll all help."

The train was on time. Mandie and Dr. Woodard were soon on their way to Franklin.

There, on the veranda, everyone was waiting for her: Aunt Lou, the housekeeper, her enormous black face beaming, Liza, the young Negro maid who was also Mandie's friend, Jennie, the cook, Jason Bond, the caretaker, and of course her mother and Uncle John.

Snowball, her white kitten, bounded toward her, meowing loudly. Mandie grabbed him and broke into a run to the porch, pulling off her bonnet as she ran.

She embraced each one amid their welcoming remarks.

"My child, I'se so glad to see you back," said Aunt Lou, smoothing Mandie's long blonde hair.

"Aunt Lou, I've missed you so much," Mandie told her. She turned to Jennie. "I sure hope you've got something good cooked. That school food is not half as good as yours, Jennie."

"I got a lil' bit o' ev'ything all hot and waitin,' " Jennie replied.

"Mr. Jason, I hope you haven't let anyone into our secret tunnel," said Mandie to the caretaker.

"It's locked up and I'm the one that's got the key," said Jason Bond, his gray eyes twinkling.

Mandie grabbed Liza's hand. "Liza, just wait till you hear about that school!" she exclaimed.

"Is it dat bad, Missy?" the Negro girl asked.

Mandie glanced at her mother, then bent forward and whispered in the girl's ear. "I'll tell you how bad later."

Liza grinned and danced around the porch.

"Mother, Uncle John, it's so good to be home," Mandie said, embracing her mother and tiptoeing to kiss her uncle's cheek.

"Enjoy it, dear," Elizabeth Shaw told her daughter. "We have to leave early tomorrow morning to go to Deep Creek."

"Deep Creek? Are we going to stay at Uncle Ned's house?" Mandie asked.

"Yes, the hospital site is nearer his house than the others," said Uncle John, "and he's expecting us."

"Good." Mandie grinned. "That means I'll get to see Sallie and Morning Star."

"Right now I think we'd better get inside and finish things up for our journey," her mother said.

Joe stepped to Mandie's side. "I'm going with you to Uncle Ned's," he said.

"And I'll be along out there later after I make some calls here in Franklin," Dr. Woodard added.

Mandie could hardly contain her excitement. "This is going to be a great trip," she said, swinging her bonnet by its ribbon.

Mandie spent a happy evening with her family and friends. When she told Liza about the "uppity" school she was attending, Liza laughed till her sides hurt.

"Lawsy mercy, Missy," Liza gasped, dancing around Mandie's bedroom. "Why don' you come home and go to school with yo' own kind o' people? Whut good all dat fancy schoolin' gonna do you when you gonna wind up marryin' dat Joe boy?"

Mandie blushed. "Liza! My mother went to that school, and she married my father who was half Cherokee. And Uncle John is half Cherokee, too, of course, since he's my father's brother."

"Well, maybe Joe boy will git to be a rich man somehow," Liza said. "But he don' need no money if he marries you 'cause yo' uncle de richest man dis side o' Richmond. And lawsy mercy, dey say yo' mother got money to burn."

"Better not let Aunt Lou hear you say that. Remember?" Mandie warned her. "She won't like you discussing people's business."

"Whut she don't know can't hurt her," Liza laughed. "Well, anyhow I gotta go. See you in de mornin.'"

"Good night, Liza," said Mandie.

"Night, Missy," Liza replied. "I knows you gonna sleep good in yo' own bed."

"You bet." Mandie hopped into bed as Liza slipped out into the hallway.

The world was going around in Mandie's pretty blonde head as it touched the pillow. So much was happening. And she didn't want to sleep too much of her holidays away.

Morning came and Elizabeth was shaking her to wake up.

"Darling, it's time to get up," Elizabeth told her.

Startled awake, Mandie sat up and looked around for a second before she realized where she was. Then she jumped quickly out of bed, dumping Snowball onto the floor from his place at the foot of her bed.

"Good morning, Mother. I'm so glad to be home," Mandie said, stretching and yawning. .

"I'm glad to have you home with us for a while," Elizabeth told her, giving her a quick hug. "Now wear some serviceable clothes on the road, dear. It'll be a long, dusty journey. You've been there before. You know how it is."

"Yes, ma'am," Mandie replied. "I'll wear my red calico and take the blue gingham."

"That'll be fine. Now hurry and dress," her mother urged.

"Mother, would you mind if I took Sallie and Morning Star some presents?" Mandie asked.

"Why, no, dear. That would be nice," Elizabeth replied. "What would you like to give them?"

Reaching into a bureau drawer where she had unpacked her things, Mandie pulled out an ivory fan. "How about this for Morning Star?" she asked.

"Well, I suppose so. I don't know whether she'd have any use for it, but give it to her if you like," Elizabeth told her.

Then Mandie held up a small velvet-covered Bible. "And this for Sallie? I bought it in Asheville for myself, but I have the Bible that you gave me. I don't really need this one, too."

"I know Sallie would appreciate that," her mother agreed. "Now do hurry, dear."

"I will, Mother," Mandie promised. "The sooner we get to Deep Creek, the sooner we'll get our job done, and the sooner we can go to Charleston."

Elizabeth laughed. "I suppose that makes sense," she said, leaving the room.

As soon as they all finished breakfast, Dr. Woodard left to make his calls, and Mandie, Elizabeth, Uncle John, and Joe climbed into the big covered wagon. All the others gathered on the veranda to see them off.

Mandie carefully tucked her presents for Sallie and Morning Star into a bag and then sat down beside Joe at the back of the wagon.

Snowball curled up in Mandie's lap as they traveled quickly down the rocky dirt road. The mountainous terrain bounced the wagon around, uphill and downhill. As the wagon swayed far to the right and then far to the left, Mandie and Joe held on to the side rails of the wagon. Snowball sank his claws into Mandie's apron to keep from sliding around.

When Mandie and Joe tried to talk, their voices trembled from the vibration of the rough road.

After a long time the road became parallel to the Tuckasegee River. Then they crossed an old wooden bridge and traveled along the rocky banks of Deep Creek. The glistening water flowed over hundreds of rocks on the clear bottom.

"Look!" Mandie cried, pointing to the creek. "Wouldn't I—"

"Don't say it!" Joe interrupted. "I know you'd like to get in that water, but remember the last time we traveled along this road and you decided to put your feet in the water?"

"I know, I know," Mandie replied. "I remember that awful panther staring at me! And Tsa'ni wouldn't help me. If Uncle Ned hadn't come along right then, I might not be here now to tell about it. That panther was ready to come after me."

Joe reached for her hand. "I don't understand Tsa'ni," he said. "He's your cousin, but he tries to see how mean he can be."

"That's because he's full Cherokee and I'm only one-fourth." Mandie sighed. "And he doesn't like white people," she added.

"Well, he'd better behave himself this time," Joe said. "Or I'll see to it that he wishes he had."

Mandie looked at Joe and didn't answer. She remembered all the trouble Tsa'ni had caused on their other trip to Deep Creek.

Cornfields with bare dried-up stalks began appearing along the way. Harvest came early in the North Carolina mountains. The odor of food cooking over wood fires filled their nostrils.

The wagon rounded a sharp bend in the road. Several log cabins came into view.

"We're here!" Mandie cried, trying to lean out and see ahead of the wagon. Snowball fell off her lap. He stretched and started washing his white fur.

Joe grabbed the edge of Mandie's apron. "Mandie, be careful! You'll fall out!" he warned her.

Mandie sat down quickly. "Oh, well, we're almost to Uncle Ned's house anyway."

CHAPTER THREE

VISIT WITH UNCLE NED

John Shaw slowed the wagon in front of the largest cabin. The house looked very similar to the one in which Mandie had lived with her father until he died. The old cabin was made of logs chinked together and had a huge rock chimney at one end. The door stood open. Horses grazed behind a split-rail fence.

After the wagon came to a halt by the barn, John helped Elizabeth down. Mandie, with Snowball on her shoulder, jumped off the wagon with Joe.

Her father's Indian friend, Uncle Ned, and his wife, Morning Star, and their granddaughter, Sallie, stood waiting by the open door to greet them.

"Welcome!" said Uncle Ned with a big smile.

"Hello, Uncle Ned," Mandie replied, reaching up to hug his neck. Then she embraced the old Indian woman who stood beside him, grinning. "Morning Star, I'm so glad to see you." Reaching out to their granddaughter, she cried excitely, "Oh, Sallie, I have so much to tell you!"

"And I have things to tell you," Sallie replied, pushing her long black hair back with a toss of her head.

"Come," Uncle Ned said, leading them all into the cabin.

Joe quickly helped Uncle John bring the bags in from the wagon, and Mandie retrieved the presents she had brought.

Inside, Morning Star removed a cloth from a long, rough, wooden table, revealing dishes piled high with steaming, delicious-smelling food, all ready for supper.

Mandie looked around. Everything was the same. At the far end of the room were several beds built into the wall and covered with cornshuck mattresses. Curtains hanging between the beds could be pulled around each one for privacy. Over in the other corner stood a spinning wheel and a loom. And against the wall was a ladder going upstairs, where there were more beds in the two rooms there.

Mandie walked over to Morning Star with the ivory fan in her hand. "Morning Star, I brought you a present," Mandie told her. Spreading the fan wide, she fanned herself with it, and then handed it, closed, to the old woman.

Morning Star looked at the fan, puzzled. Then she managed to open it and stood there fanning her smiling face.

"Good!" Morning Star grunted. She couldn't speak English, but she could understand some things.

Mandie turned to Sallie and handed her the velvet-covered Bible.

Sallie fingered it excitedly. "This is for me?" she asked.

"Yes, I bought it in Asheville," Mandie told her.

"Thank you, thank you, Mandie!" Sallie cried, hugging her friend. Sallie showed the Bible to Morning Star, talking rapidly in Cherokee.

Then Morning Star gave Mandie a big hug, fanning herself all the while with her new ivory fan.

"She thanks you," Sallie explained. "She hopes we soon find the crooks who are tearing down the hospital."

"Thank you," Mandie told the old woman.

Uncle Ned, standing nearby, seemed proud to have the white people in his house. He and Morning Star had once lived in the house of Mandie's grandparents, and he tried hard to do things the way his guests expected.

"Wash! Eat!" Uncle Ned said loudly. "Food get cold."

John and Elizabeth headed for the washpan on the shelf. A clean towel hung on a nail beside it. A bucketful of fresh drinking water sat nearby with a gourd dipper hanging on a nail above it. As soon as John and Elizabeth washed their faces and hands, Joe and Mandie did likewise.

"Come on, Joe," Sallie said, leading him to the side of the table opposite where the adults were seated. "I will sit between you and Mandie so I can talk to both of you."

"I sure hope you're not having owl stew again," Joe moaned as he sat down.

"Why, Joe, I thought you liked owl stew," Mandie teased.

Sallie smiled. "You are lucky; my grandmother has cooked ham tonight. Can you not smell it?" the Indian girl asked, straightening her full, red flowered skirt as she sat down.

"Hmm," Joe sniffed. "Well, yeh, but I was afraid it was something else that might smell like ham. And I'm so hungry I could eat almost anything—except owl stew."

Uncle Ned stood at the head of the table and tapped his tin plate. "John Shaw will thank Big God for food," the old Indian announced.

They all bowed their heads as John returned thanks.

"Thank you, dear God, for the privilege of being with our dear friends again, and for the good food you have supplied for this meal that we are about to partake of. And, dear God, please lead us and guide us in our search for those who are tearing down the hospital the Cherokees so badly need. And, dear God, please give us the courage and strength to follow through with this and get the hospital built. We ask your blessing on everyone present at this table. Amen."

Joe looked at the two girls. "Now, that's what we came for. We've got to get that hospital built," he said as the adults began their own conversation.

"You are right, Joe," Sallie agreed. "We must find out who is tearing down the walls and put a stop to it."

"Yes, Sallie," Mandie said. "We're all going to see what's being done there. I haven't even seen the land cleared for it, much less the building, because I've been away at that silly school."

Sallie passed Joe a big platter of ham. "Please, tell me about your school, Mandie," she begged. "Why do you call it silly?"

Joe took several large slices of ham, then helped himself to the potatoes sitting in front of him and passed the bowl to the girls.

Mandie, helping herself, explained. "They teach you to be what they call *a lady*. It's a lot of put-on and silly stuff. You learn how to walk with a book balanced on your head so you'll be straight. You learn how to stoop and pick up something without sticking your bottom up in the air. You learn how to talk quietly, in what they call a *well-modulated voice*. I call it leaving all the fun out of living."

Mandie looked up as Morning Star placed a plate of hot bread in front of them. "Eat," said Morning Star loudly.

"Thank you," Mandie said. "You eat, too." After each of the young people had taken some bread, Mandie handed the plate back to Morning Star.

Joe started to get up. "Let me carry the plate back for you."

Morning Star stepped back. "Sit! I take," she said sternly. Carrying the plate around the table she sat down next to Uncle Ned and helped herself.

Joe looked puzzled. "Did I make her angry?" he asked.

"You are our guest," Sallie told him. "She must serve you. You must not serve her."

"Sorry," Joe apologized. "I forgot she has a different way of doing things."

"Have you been to see this silly school that Mandie goes to, Joe?" Sallie asked, returning to the previous subject.

Joe grinned and swung his feet under the table.

"You bet I've been to that school. I've helped Mandie and her friend Celia solve some pretty baffling mysteries around that place," he said.

"Mysteries around the school?" Sallie questioned.

Joe looked at Mandie, waiting for her to explain as he dug into the food heaped on his plate.

"We heard a mysterious noise in the attic when I first went there. We got that solved and then we found a terrible secret in an old trunk in the attic," Mandie explained between bites of food. "It's a terribly long story."

At that moment Mandie's great uncle, Wirt Pindar, from Bird-town, came through the open doorway, followed by his grandson, Tsa'ni. Uncle Ned motioned for them to sit at the table.

"Sit. Eat," Uncle Ned told them.

As they sat down, Morning Star got up, gave them plates, and passed the food.

"Hello, Uncle Wirt, Tsa'ni," Mandie greeted them across the table.

"Glad to see Papoose." Uncle Wirt beamed. "And doctor boy."

"How are you, sir," Joe replied.

Tsa'ni nodded his head at Mandie but did not smile or speak.

As the adults began discussing the hospital, the young people listened.

"Walls torn down every day," Uncle Wirt told them. "Every day work done is torn down."

"And nobody has seen anyone around there?" Uncle John asked.

"Moongo, she come back after many, many years. Married to Catawba man, Running Fire. Two big sons, live near to hospital. See nothing, hear nothing," Uncle Wirt replied.

"Moongo? I remember her from when I was a small boy. She must be old by now," Uncle John said. "So she finally came back. Where do they live, Uncle Wirt? I don't remember any cabin anywhere near the hospital."

"Live in old horse barn near creek," Uncle Wirt explained. "We put man to guard hospital tonight."

"Moongo and her family are that close but don't ever hear anything going on? That's strange," Uncle John mused.

"I haven't even seen the hospital yet," Mandie put in. "How much have they got done?"

"Rock on ground for bottom," Uncle Wirt told her. "Wood for floor. All still there. But when walls made, walls get torn down."

"Uncle John, when are we going to see it?" Mandie asked.

"We'll go early tomorrow morning," Uncle John replied. "I think one of us ought to stay with the guard every night after the workmen leave."

Uncle Ned spoke up. "Dimar say he watch."

"Dimar?" Mandie and Joe said together.

"Dimar say he wait for us at hospital tomorrow," Uncle Wirt answered.

"I'm so glad we're going to get to see Dimar," Mandie remarked.

Joe looked at her with a hint of jealousy in his eyes. "Yes, we will all be glad to see Dimar," he said.

"Remember how you and Dimar caught those thieves who set fire to my grandfather's barn?" Sallie asked Joe.

"Yeh, and I think Dimar and I can catch whoever is tearing down the hospital," Joe replied. "Mr. Shaw, may I have your permission to help Dimar guard the hospital tomorrow night?"

"Well, I suppose so, but your father should be here before tomorrow night. You'll have to ask him, of course," Uncle John said. "You boys will have to promise not to let anyone see you. They could harm you. All we want you to do is watch, and when you see someone doing this malicious work, you hurry and get us men. Is that understood?"

"But I'm almost fourteen," Joe protested. "And so is Dimar. We could put up a pretty good fight."

"No, no, that won't ever do. You might get hurt," Uncle John told him. "The only way I'll let you stay out there is under the conditions I've mentioned."

"Well, all right, sir. I'll do whatever you say," Joe gave in.

Mandie turned to Joe. "You and Dimar will see all the excitement. Sallie and I will miss out on that," she protested.

"You'll find out what's going on when we come back to tell Mr. Shaw that there's someone there," Joe told her.

"*If* you come back," Mandie replied. "I know you."

Tsa'ni sat through the whole conversation without saying a word. He listened and took it all in.

CHAPTER FOUR

THE TORN-DOWN HOSPITAL

The first bright rays of sunshine the next morning peeped through the upstairs window and played around on Mandie's face. Opening her eyes and squinting in the light, Mandie looked around bewildered. Then she saw Sallie sleeping next to her on the cornshuck mattress and she remembered that she was in Uncle Ned's house. Also, her friend Joe was sleeping on the other side of the rough wall dividing the attic into two rooms. And today was the day she was to finally see the hospital being built.

Slipping out of bed, trying not to wake Sallie, she quickly pulled her cotton nightgown over her tousled blonde curls. Snowball jumped down and rubbed around her legs as he meowed. Hastily grabbing the dress hanging on a nail near the bed, she pulled it over her head and buttoned the waist.

Sallie sat up, rubbed her eyes and smiled at her friend. She rolled out of bed.

"You are up early this morning," Sallie said, exchanging her gown for her red flowered skirt and white waist.

"I don't want to waste a minute. We're going to see the hospital, remember?" Mandie told her, quickly brushing her long hair and braiding it into one long plait down her back.

"Hey, wait for me!" Joe called from the other side of the partition.

"I'll meet you downstairs," Mandie yelled back at him, tying her apron over her blue gingham dress.

"I smell coffee," Joe called from the other side.

"My grandmother is already up. She gets up before daylight every morning," Sallie said loudly to Joe. She hurriedly tied her dark hair back with a red ribbon.

The three of them scrambled for the ladder to go downstairs. Joe managed to get down first and stood there waiting for the girls. Mandie had to carry Snowball down. He refused to go down the ladder.

"Aren't y'all pokey this morning?" Joe teased, standing with his long legs spread apart and his hands on his thin hips.

"You won because your legs are longer than ours. It wasn't a fair race," Mandie told him, setting Snowball on the floor and straightening the skirt of her dress.

Joe, laughing, told them, "Come on. Let's see who gets to the wash-pan first." He turned to run across the room, Sallie and Mandie following. The girls lined up behind Joe to wash their faces and hands.

Morning Star, Uncle Ned, Elizabeth and Uncle John, sitting at the table, looked at them in surprise.

"What's the big hurry?" Uncle John asked.

Mandie's blue eyes sparkled. "We want to go to the hospital."

"But it isn't far from here," said Uncle John. "We don't have to hurry that much."

Elizabeth smiled. "She wants to hurry up and get this thing settled so we can go to Charleston," she explained.

"You are going to Charleston?" Sallie's eyes grew wide.

"Yes, if we can straighten everything out here, we're going to Charleston to see the ocean," Mandie told her.

"You mean you're going to see some boy you met at that school in Asheville," Joe retorted, sitting down at the table.

Elizabeth and John looked at each other with raised eyebrows.

"Joe Woodard, hush up," said Mandie, as she and Sallie sat down next to him. "We're just going to stay at his parents' home."

"Well, that's going to see him, isn't it?" Joe sounded angry.

Elizabeth interrupted. "Yes, Joe, we are going to visit Thomas Patton and his parents. Amanda met Thomas while she was at school. My family

34

has known the Pattons for years. So we're going to visit them, and also give Amanda an opportunity to see the ocean for the first time."

Joe meekly bowed his head. "Yes, ma'am, I understand," he said.

Uncle Ned spoke up, "Thank Big God, John Shaw."

John gave thanks and when he had finished, the old Indian said loudly, "Eat!"

Morning Star ladled out the hot mush.

As they ate and talked, Uncle Wirt and Tsa'ni came in and joined them at the table. Tsa'ni remained silent but listened to every word of the excited conversation.

Before long, everyone except Morning Star piled into Uncle Ned's big wagon and they were on their way. In a short while they rounded a bend in the dirt road. Through the branches of the trees and bushes, Mandie caught her first glimpse of the structure that would be the hospital for the Cherokees.

She was breathless. "Look!" she cried.

Uncle Ned stopped the wagon a little farther down the road, and Mandie jumped down. As she ran around the building, she saw the splintered planks all around that had evidently been part of the walls. Then something caught her eye. Hastening to look behind the building site, she found a man gagged and blindfolded, tied up and lying on the ground. She screamed to the others.

When Uncle Wirt arrived, he stooped to untie the man. "This Kent, man who watch last night."

As the man was released from all the ropes, he took a deep breath and managed to sit up.

Uncle John squatted down beside Kent. "What happened?" he asked.

"I don't rightly know," said the man, trying to wet his parched lips with his tongue. "I was walkin' 'round, lookin,' and all of a sudden somethin' hit me hard on the noggin. That's all I 'member. I wakes up, can't see, can't move."

Elizabeth brought water from the barrel that Uncle Ned kept in his wagon. She offered a dipperful to the man. He greedily swallowed it and stood up, stretching his cramped limbs.

"Are you all right?" Uncle John asked. "I'm sorry about this. We'll just have to post another guard with you. They won't be able to surprise two at one time."

"Sorry, mister, but I don't want the job," Kent said. "You see, I'm one of the carpenters tryin' to build this thing. I just wanted to make a little extry money stayin' at night, but it ain't worth it. I'll keep on workin' in the daytime with the others, but no more night work for me."

Uncle Ned pointed to the road. "Men come to work," he said as a group of white men arrived in a wagon loaded with lumber and tools.

The workmen got off the wagon and advanced toward the group. Looking around they shook their heads in disgust when they saw their previous day's work lying in ruins.

"Mornin,' Mr. Shaw," said the leader. "Sure glad that you come to do somethin' about this. If that ain't the beatin'est thing I ever heerd of. Fast as we'uns builds it, summins else is atearin' it down."

As the workers stood staring at the mess, Uncle John called to Mandie, and she came to his side. "Amanda, this is Mr. Green," said Uncle John. "He's in charge of building this hospital. Mr. Green, this is my niece, Amanda Shaw, who discovered the Cherokees' gold and is responsible for this hospital being built in the first place," he said proudly.

Mandie stepped forward, holding out her small white hand. "How do you do, Mr. Green," she said, shaking his big rough hand. "I know it's frustrating to you to have your work undone every night, but we are here to do something about it. And I think we can find a way to stop it."

"Yes, ma'am," Mr. Green said, in awe of the well-spoken young girl who had such a great responsibility. He had heard the whole story.

Suddenly Mandie saw Dimar emerge from the bushes. His great admiration for her gleamed in his eyes. Mandie immediately dropped her ladylike air as she raced to meet him.

"Dimar!" she cried, catching his brown hand in hers. "I'm so glad to see you. It's been so long."

"Yes, it has been a long time," Dimar replied, transfixed by her friendly greeting. He withdrew his hand and stepped toward the others. Mandie walked by his side.

"Good morning," he said to the waiting group. "Either you are early or I am late."

"We not here long," said Uncle Ned as Sallie and Joe greeted the boy.

"Dimar, it's a pleasure to see you again," Uncle John told him.

"You just missed the excitement," said Mandie. "Last night someone tied up Kent, over there, and just left him. We found him just a few minutes ago."

"I promise to stay tonight and watch," said Dimar. "I will not let them tie me up."

"I have permission to stay with you, Dimar," Joe told him.

"Between the two of us nothing will happen tonight," Dimar said.

Sallie smiled at Tsa'ni, who was standing nearby. "Tsa'ni, are you staying with Joe and Dimar also?" she asked.

Everyone grew silent, waiting for his reply.

Tsa'ni rubbed the toe of his moccasin in the dirt. "No, I do not wish to stay," he said.

The others pretended they had heard nothing and went on discussing the forthcoming night.

"All right, Mr. Green, we will be back before you quit work at five o'clock," said Uncle John. "And we'll do everything possible to catch these vandals tonight."

"It sho' is disgustin' to do all that hard work and then have somebody tear it all down," Mr. Green replied. "I sho' hope you catch 'em, and I hope the punishment ain't too mild."

"I can assure you it will be quite severe," Uncle John promised.

Uncle Ned examined the splintered boards scattered all around. "No piece of wall good. Must have new boards," he said, stooping and tossing the wood around.

"We got a load of boards in the wagon, and we got 'nother one comin,' " Mr. Green said. "Sho' is a waste of money to buy all them boards and have 'em split up that way."

Mandie was not worried about the money. The supply of gold seemed endless. "It's a waste of time, too," she said. "This hospital needs to be finished so it can be used."

"Used?" Joe queried. "Who's sick?"

"Joe," Mandie said with irritation, "your father will be coming here at least once a month to keep up with everyone's health. Besides, we're going to hire a nurse who will stay here all the time."

"This is a wonderful thing for the Cherokees," Sallie told her.

"Humph!" Tsa'ni grunted.

Dimar frowned at Tsa'ni. "The Cherokees do get sick once in a while, and they need a doctor just like everyone else," he said. "Remember the last time these people visited, when you hurt your foot in that trap and had to have a doctor?"

Tsa'ni silently turned on his heel and walked away toward Uncle Ned's wagon.

"If he need doctor, he be glad hospital here," Uncle Wirt said.

Joe looked longingly at the workmen. "Could I stay here all day and help the men work?" he asked John Shaw.

"I would like to help, too," said Dimar.

Uncle John looked thoughtful for a moment. "No, that's impossible," he said. "You don't have anything with you to eat, and you wouldn't have any way to get back to Uncle Ned's. Let's go back now, and after we have our noon meal, you and Dimar can ride two of the horses back out here. How's that?"

"Thanks, Mr. Shaw," Joe said, smiling.

"Thank you, sir," Dimar added.

"Before we go, Uncle John," Mandie began, "tell me something about the hospital, please."

"What do you want to know, Amanda?" Uncle John asked.

Mandie turned, walked up the steps, and paced the floor of the building. Sallie followed.

"How is it to be arranged?" Mandie asked. "You know, how many beds will it hold and how many rooms, and all that?"

Uncle John joined them. "You see all those posts standing up around here?" he said. "They are called studs. They will be covered with boards to make the interior walls and divide the hospital into rooms. The studs will be four feet apart around each room, and then you have to allow four feet for the doors. So if you'll just walk around and look at the studs you can figure out how many rooms there will be and how big each one will be."

The two girls walked about and counted the posts.

"Here's one big room," Mandie said, pointing to one section. "There's another smaller room, and another, and another, and then here's a long narrow room, too narrow for beds, I think. What is this room for?"

"That is the office," he told her. "The records will be kept there. Dr. Woodard will use it, and when you come to visit, Amanda, that will be your office."

"Me? An office? What for, Uncle John?" Mandie asked in surprise.

"You told your mother and me that you would like to know what's going on with the money since you are responsible for it, so we thought we'd just make you a little office right here," he teased.

"Oh, I don't need an office. I depend on you to keep up with things, especially while I'm away at school," Mandie told him. "That will have to be your office and Dr. Woodard's."

"Anyway, we need an office for records," he told her.

Mandie looked across the other side of the building. "That big room looks like it would hold about ten single beds," she calculated. "How many windows will it have?"

"One on each end and two on the side, I believe," Uncle John replied. "Why? Are you planning on making the curtains for it?"

"That's a good idea!" Mandie exclaimed. "Sallie, could you make some of them and I'll make some?"

Elizabeth called to her, "Amanda, don't forget you'll be away at school. You won't have time to make curtains."

"I suppose not," she decided. "I'll just have to get Aunt Lou to make them. She can make anything, Sallie. You'll have to come to visit us in Franklin again."

"I hope to someday," Sallie assured her. "I would like to get up there."

"Oh, yes, you've got to," Mandie agreed.

"Right now, girls, I think we'd better see Morning Star. She probably has a good hot meal waiting," Uncle John reminded them.

"Yeh, let's hurry so Dimar and I can come back and do some work," Joe put in.

When they returned to Uncle Ned's house, Morning Star had the table set and food waiting. Dr. Woodard was just pulling up in his buggy, and Joe ran out to take the horse for him.

"Mr. Shaw is having the hospital guarded at night, Dad," Joe informed his father. "Dimar has volunteered to stay all night, and Mr. Shaw said I could, too, with your permission." He held up his hand. "Before you protest, we aren't going to let anyone see us," he said, helping unhitch the horse and buggy. "If someone comes around, we're going to hightail it back to Uncle Ned's and get the men. Is it all right if I stay? Please, Dad?"

"I suppose so, provided you don't try to defend the place. Leave that to the men," Dr. Woodard told him. "If you see anyone around, you get out of there. People of that nature could be dangerous."

"Thanks, Dad," Joe said. "I promise."

After hurrying through dinner, Joe and Dimar asked to be excused, then ran to the barn to saddle two horses.

Mandie and Sallie waved good-bye to them.

"Joe, please catch those crooks tonight, but be careful. You, too, Dimar," Mandie called to the boys.

"Yes, please be careful," Sallie added.

"We know your Uncle John's orders," Joe called to them. "If we see or hear anything, we are not to let them see us, and we are to come back immediately for help."

"That's right, boys," Uncle John told them.

Tsa'ni stood by, watching and saying nothing.

"So they are off," Sallie said as the boys disappeared in a cloud of dust down the road.

She and Mandie sat down on an old log.

"I think that we should ask God to watch over them," said Mandie, her brow furrowed with concern.

"I agree," Sallie replied.

Taking the Indian girl's dark hand in her white one, Mandie looked toward the sky. "Dear God," she said, "please take care of Joe and Dimar and keep them from harm. And please help us catch those crooks. Thank you, dear God. Amen."

"Amen," Sallie echoed.

The girls didn't realize then how badly Joe and Dimar would need help.

CHAPTER FIVE

JOE DISAPPEARS

Mandie and Sallie spent the afternoon under a huge chestnut tree in Uncle Ned's yard talking about Mandie's school, its strange rules, and its strict headmistresses, Miss Prudence and Miss Hope. The Indian girl was fascinated with Mandie's stories about her friend Celia Hamilton, and the school troublemaker, April Snow.

"Your grandfather, Uncle Ned, comes to visit me at the school, you know," Mandie told her.

"Yes, I know that. He promised your father he would watch over you, so he keeps his promise. But he never tells me anything about your school. He just says you are all right and you send your love, and all that."

"He has never been inside the school," Mandie explained. "When he comes to see me, he always waits for me under the magnolia trees after the ten o'clock bell has rung at night. By then everyone is supposed to be in bed."

"Why are you not also in bed then?" Sallie asked.

"Because I've always been afraid to ask permission to see him. You see, Miss Prudence would probably forbid it," Mandie replied.

"Why? Why would she forbid you to see my grandfather?"

Mandie looked at her friend, trying to soften her explanation. "Sallie, you haven't been out into the big world, like at the school,"

Mandie began. "You see, some white people just don't like Indians. I didn't know that either until my father died and I had to leave Charley Gap."

"You mean they don't like some people just because they are a different color, a different kind of people?" Sallie asked, puzzled.

"You know how Tsa'ni is always making remarks against the white people? That's the way some white people are about Indians," Mandie explained. "Even though God made us all, some white people would have you think Indians were just . . . just . . . trash or something."

"Do these white people know you are one-fourth Cherokee?" the Indian girl asked.

"They know. There was a big ruckus one day when April Snow spread the word that I was part Indian. But Miss Prudence put a stop to that real fast," Mandie said.

Sallie looked confused. "But you said these people at the school do not like Indians."

"Even though I'm part Indian, Miss Prudence wouldn't dare treat me differently. You see, my Grandmother Taft is a terror sometimes." She laughed. "She has a lot of influence among the rich people who send their daughters to the school. Miss Prudence wouldn't want to get on the wrong side of my grandmother."

"I agree that this is a very silly school you are in," said Sallie. "They do not seem to be honest. They let wealth decide who to be nice to."

"You're exactly right, Sallie," Mandie replied. "I wish I could live with my Cherokee kinpeople. There is such a difference."

"Maybe someday you can," Sallie said. "But your mother wants you to be educated at that school, so you must do what she says."

"Yes, I know," Mandie replied. "I miss my father so much. If he had lived longer, maybe he and my mother would have gotten back together again."

"But your father was married to that other woman," Sallie reminded her.

"I know, but things could have been different if my mother had known about me, that I didn't really die when I was born, and that her mother, my Grandmother Taft, told my father that my mother didn't love him anymore."

"Your grandmother told your mother that you died when you were born and made your father take you away so your mother would not try to find your father or you. Your grandmother thought she was doing the best thing for everyone," Sallie said.

"I suppose she did," Mandie said with a big sigh.

"Do you dislike your grandmother because she separated your mother and your father and you?" Sallie asked.

"No, I don't dislike her. In fact, she's my friend. At first she wouldn't have anything to do with me. But then after my mother married Uncle John, and I came to school in Asheville where she lives, I finally got to know her."

"Does Joe let you know what is going on at Charley Gap since you left there?"

"As much as he can find out," Mandie replied. Looking into her friend's dark eyes she added, "Joe promised to get my father's house back for me when he gets old enough."

"And how is he going to do that?" Sallie asked.

Mandie laughed. "I'm not sure. He just said leave it to him. Joe wants to be a lawyer, you know."

"Then he will learn how to get the house back," Sallie assured her. "Joe is a brave boy."

Mandie looked at her in surprise. "You think so?"

"Yes, look what he is doing right now. He is risking his life to save the hospital for you," Sallie replied.

"I know it's dangerous," said Mandie, "but we have asked God to take care of them. We must trust God."

Meanwhile Joe and Dimar were working hard with the men, replacing wall boards at the hospital. When the workmen left for the day at five o'clock, all the walls were up around the structure.

Joe and Dimar washed their faces and hands in the nearby creek, then sat down on the hospital steps to eat their supper.

Uncovering the basket Morning Star had packed, Joe examined its contents. "Can you tell what this is?" he asked. "Is it fried chicken, rabbit, or what?"

Dimar laughed. "Now, you know that is fried chicken," he said. "Can you not smell it?"

Joe spread the cloth on the steps and laid out the food. "I guess so, but I just plain don't like some of those other things that Morning Star cooks up. I'm not used to it," Joe told him.

"Like we Cherokees are not used to some things that the white people eat." Dimar laughed. "But I think we both like fried chicken, and Morning Star knows that."

"Do you think she notices when there are some things I don't eat at her house?" Joe asked, alarmed.

"Yes, she notices, and she understands. So she tries to please you," Dimar explained.

"Goodness. I guess I'm a lot of trouble then," Joe said.

"No more than anyone else," Dimar assured him.

Joe hungrily ate the chicken with his fingers, cramming in a bite of biscuit now and then, and drinking a little coffee to wash it all down.

"I suppose one of us ought to stay at the front of the building and the other one at the back. That way it would be easier to see anyone who comes up," Joe suggested.

"Yes, I will stay at the back, and you stay here at the front," Dimar agreed. "But we must stay far enough back in the bushes so no one will see us."

Joe looked concerned. "I hope they don't see the horses."

"I do not think they will if the horses will just be contented to stay quietly down by the creek," the Indian boy said. "If one of us sees someone coming here to do damage, we must let the other one know. Then one of us will ride quickly to get Mr. Shaw and the others."

So it was agreed. The two boys walked quietly back and forth in the bushes, keeping an eye on the building. Now and then they would meet each other and turn back. They talked very little and then only in low whispers.

It grew dark. The birds settled down for the night. Frogs began croaking along the creek. Here and there lightning bugs flashed their lights. The scent of clean creek water drifted into the air. The horses seemed to be well satisfied as they continued to graze in the darkness. The two boys grew bored and weary.

Joe stopped Dimar as they met in the bushes on one of their patrols. "How about some of that sweetcake and coffee that we've got left?" he whispered softly.

"That sounds good," said Dimar.

"I'll get it," Joe volunteered. Groping his way through the bushes to the basket they had hung on a tree limb near the horses, he took it down and hurried back uphill.

Sitting down by Dimar, who sat waiting in the woods, Joe uncovered the basket.

"It's so dark, I can't see too well," Joe told him. "But take what you want and then I'll get mine." He held out the basket.

"Here is a piece of the cake," said Dimar, feeling around in the dark basket. "And I think this is the jar of coffee I was drinking out of before."

"And I'll have the same," Joe said, reaching inside. He took a big bite of cake. "Mmm, this is good," he said.

"It will help us stay awake and alert," the Indian boy said.

"I can—" Joe began to speak and then stopped, motioning Dimar to silence. "Listen," he whispered.

Someone was walking through the brush. The boys dropped their cake back into the basket and rose to their feet. The footsteps came closer.

"There is more than one person," Dimar whispered in Joe's ear.

Then there was a loud bang as something crashed against the wooden walls of the hospital.

"Quick! You go for the men! You ride faster than I do," Joe told Dimar in a low whisper. "I'll stay here and watch."

"Do not let them see you," Dimar warned as he ran for one of the horses nearby.

Joe stood frozen to the spot. Dimar was so quiet that Joe didn't hear him lead the horse away before mounting. Joe's heartbeat quickened in anger at the thought of someone tearing down the walls. He edged closer to the structure. He could hear talking, but it was too low to be understood. As he moved still closer, he could see three men with axes standing by the hospital. In the darkness he could not tell whether they were Indians or white men. He moved just a little closer. A dry twig cracked loudly under his foot.

The three men turned in his direction and listened. Then they moved forward quietly to investigate.

Joe stood motionless, hoping they wouldn't hear him breathing. Suddenly the three men came at him.

As Joe tried to flee, the men spread out and surrounded him. In the scuffle, they caught him by his shirt and tore it off him. Then they pulled Joe closer for a better look.

"Nobody we know," one man said. The other two agreed.

Quickly the men pulled out rope and handkerchiefs from their pockets. Even though Joe put up a good fight, they managed to gag and bind him.

After carrying Joe away from the hospital, the three men picked up their axes and completely wrecked the walls. Satisfied with their destruction, they pulled Joe to his feet and pushed him ahead as they tromped off into the woods.

As Dimar arrived back at Uncle Ned's house, he called to the men for help. Within minutes Uncle Ned, Uncle John, Uncle Wirt, and Dr. Woodard had dressed and saddled horses to return with the boy to the hospital. Tsa'ni had already gone home.

When the girls heard the commotion, they hurriedly dressed enough to get downstairs before the men left. Elizabeth and Morning Star were there, too.

"Dimar, is Joe all right?" Mandie asked anxiously. "You left him alone with those crooks."

"He is all right, Mandie. He is not with the crooks. I left him hidden in the bushes," the Indian boy told her.

"Please hurry, Dimar," Sallie urged him. "And be careful."

"I will," the boy promised. Hurrying outside, he rode quietly off into the night with the men.

"Amanda, Sallie, if you're staying up, we might as well have some tea," Elizabeth told the girls. "Morning Star is getting it ready."

"I couldn't go to bed with all this going on," Mandie told her mother.

Mandie and Sallie pulled chairs over in front of the huge fireplace. Morning Star poked at the fire and soon had a nice blaze going.

Mandie shivered. "I'm so excited, I'm cold."

"So am I," Sallie admitted.

"I know it gets cold in these mountains at night, but it's partly nerves, too," Elizabeth told them. "The tea will help."

Sallie looked around the room. "Mandie, where is Snowball?" she asked.

Mandie jumped up to look for him. Then she laughed as she saw the white kitten perched at the top of the attic ladder. He looked down at them, whining. Climbing the ladder, Mandie picked up her kitten and brought him down.

"Snowball, you've got to learn to come down the ladder, you silly cat," she said.

When she set him down in front of the fire, he curled up and began purring while the women and girls drank hot tea and discussed the chances of catching the crooks.

Before the men got very close to the hospital, they dismounted to avoid being heard.

"Must be quiet," Uncle Ned told the others as he led the way on foot.

Silently, they crept through the bushes. As they came within sight of the hospital, the clouds uncovered the moon. The men stopped in horror when they saw the destruction. Circling around, they found no one.

"They're gone," Uncle John said.

Dr. Woodard looked around for his son. "Where is Joe, Dimar?"

"We were in the bushes down this way," Dimar said, leading them into the woods. "Joe," he called out, "it is Dimar. Joe, where are you?"

There wasn't a sound except for the restless horse that Joe had left down by the creek.

"Did you remind him not to let anyone see him?" Uncle John asked.

"Yes, sir," Dimar replied. "He said he would stay out of sight."

As Uncle Ned scoured the bushes, he found Joe's torn shirt.

"Here, boy shirt," Uncle Ned said, holding it up for everyone to see. "Torn."

Dr. Woodard stepped forward and took the shirt. "Looks like he might have been in a fight," he said.

"I sure hope the boy is all right," Uncle John said.

"We find. We follow feet marks," Uncle Wirt assured him, bending to search the ground.

Then the moon went back under the clouds, and it was too dark to find anything.

"It shouldn't be too long till daylight," Uncle John said. "We'll just have to stay here and wait until we can see."

Dr. Woodard sat down on the hospital steps. "We're in a bigger mess now than ever," he said. "The crooks not only got away with their vandalism, but they've evidently kidnapped my boy."

"I am sorry, sir," Dimar said.

"I'm not blaming anyone but Joe," Dr. Woodard replied. "He's headstrong sometimes, and he probably got excited and let them see him."

"We find doctor boy, and we find crooks," Uncle Ned told him.

"We find," Uncle Wirt echoed.

"Yes," said Uncle John. "And this destruction is disgusting. We've got to put a stop to it somehow."

At the first crack of dawn the search began. The old Indians were able to pick up a trail, but it seemed to circle around and then disappear into the creek. They spread out and combed every inch of the surrounding bushes without success.

When the sun came up, the workmen came to the hospital site and looked around angrily.

"Done it agin, heh? We's expectin' it," Mr. Green called to Uncle John. " 'Bout par for the course."

"That's not all they did this time," Uncle John told him. "They've evidently kidnapped one of the boys who stood guard last night."

The other workmen gathered around.

Mr. Green whistled. "You don't say! What are you goin' to do?"

"Since you are here, I think we might as well go home, eat a bite, and break the news to the women. Then we'll come back for an all-day search," said Uncle John.

The others agreed, and within minutes they had mounted their horses and were heading back to Uncle Ned's house.

When Mandie and Sallie heard them coming, they ran to the door. Mandie looked around quickly. "Where's Joe?" she asked.

Uncle John came into the room, put his arm around her shoulders, and led her over to the warmth of the fireplace. "I'm afraid we don't know where Joe is right now," he said. "He seems to have disappeared."

"Disappeared? Oh, Uncle John, where is he?" Mandie demanded, her eyes filling with tears. "Where is he?"

Dr. Woodard walked over to Mandie and took her hand. "We'll find him, Amanda," he assured her. "You know Joe. He likes to go off and do things on his own. He—"

"Dr. Woodard!" Mandie interrupted, spying Joe's shirt under the doctor's arm. She snatched it from him and sank into a chair in shock. "Oh, please, dear God," Mandie cried, "don't let anything happen to Joe! Please send him back to us. Please, dear God!"

Tears filled every eye in the room.

CHAPTER SIX

THE SEARCH

Dimar and the men hurriedly ate a good hot meal, but no one said much. They were all worried about Joe. Mandie couldn't speak a word without breaking into tears, and Sallie stayed right by her side. Dimar kept blaming himself. Although Dr. Woodard tried to keep his emotions under control, it was obvious that he, too, was very worried.

Just as the men were about to leave, Tsa'ni appeared in the doorway.

Uncle Wirt frowned at his grandson. "Where you been?" he asked roughly.

"I have been home. I came to help you search for Joe," Tsa'ni replied, his gaze never wavering from his grandfather's angry, wrinkled face.

"Joe?" Mandie spoke up. "How did you know about Joe?"

Everyone stared at Tsa'ni. No one outside their own group knew about Joe's disappearance.

Uncle Wirt grabbed Tsa'ni by the shoulder. "How you know? How?" the old man demanded.

Tsa'ni dropped his eyes and stuttered, "Why . . . I . . . I . . . I came by the hospital. The men working there told me."

"I don't believe you, Tsa'ni," Mandie said. "I don't believe you at all."

"What you do at hospital?" Uncle Wirt asked, still holding the boy's shoulder.

"I . . . I . . ." Tsa'ni stammered again, looking at the floor.

"Why *did* you come by the hospital?" Mandie interrupted, moving closer. "You wouldn't even volunteer to stand guard with Dimar and Joe last night."

Uncle John put his arm around Mandie's shoulder. "Amanda, please—" he said, trying to calm her. Mandie didn't want to be calmed. "Tsa'ni, I suppose you already know who the crooks are. That's why you didn't want to help out last night."

Tsa'ni stared at her. "They are not crooks who tear down the hospital," he said firmly. "They are the spirits of the Cherokee. They do not believe in the white man's medicine."

"Spirits of the Cherokee?" Mandie echoed.

"No such thing," grunted Uncle Wirt, angrily.

Uncle Ned stepped forward. "The spirits of our Cherokee do not do bad things," he said. "Tsa'ni, *you* bad Cherokee."

Morning Star stood near the fireplace, obviously confused about what was happening. Uncle Ned turned to her and explained rapidly in Cherokee. The old woman suddenly grabbed the homemade broom from the hearth and ran toward Tsa'ni, screaming in Cherokee.

Uncle Wirt let go of Tsa'ni's shoulder and pushed him toward the angry woman waving the broom.

Tsa'ni jumped backward toward the door. "Just wait. You will see!" he yelled at Mandie as he turned and quickly ran out the doorway.

Mandie walked over to Uncle Ned. "What does Tsa'ni mean?" she asked, looking up into the old man's face. "What is he talking about?"

Uncle Ned took her small white hand in his old, wrinkled one. "Papoose, not worry," he said. "Tsa'ni bad Cherokee. Speak wash hog."

Mandie looked at him questioningly. Then a little smile played on her face. "You mean *hogwash,* Uncle Ned."

Uncle Ned smiled too. "Story hogwash," he said. "Do not believe."

"I don't believe him. But where in the world did he get such an idea?" Mandie asked.

The old Indian touched his forehead with his finger. "Here," he said. "Tsa'ni have crazy thoughts here. Papoose not listen to him. We find Joe. We find crooks."

Mandie turned to her mother and Uncle. "I'm going with you, Uncle John," she declared.

"No, Amanda," Elizabeth told her. "You must stay here with Morning Star and Sallie. The men can do a better job without us. Besides, you didn't get much sleep last night, waiting for them to come back."

"But, Mother, that's Joe we're looking for. If it was me lost somewhere, Joe would be right along in the search. I have to go, Mother. Please?" Mandie begged.

"I said no, Amanda," Elizabeth replied firmly.

"Mother, please let me go," Mandie tried again. Then, turning to Uncle John and looking at him with tear-filled blue eyes, she asked, "Please, Uncle John, may I go?"

"Amanda," Elizabeth said sharply.

"Well," Uncle John hesitated. He could never refuse those blue eyes anything. "Elizabeth, I think she'd be all right with us."

"Please, Mother?" Mandie pleaded. "I couldn't bear to sit here and wait all that time. Please let me go."

"Well, Elizabeth?" Uncle John waited for a reply.

"Oh, John, you two always win out," Elizabeth said, giving up. "But, Amanda, you must promise me to be careful and to stay with the men at all times. No wandering off alone."

"Yes, ma'am. I promise." Mandie moved to her mother's side and squeezed her hand. "Thank you, Mother."

Sallie looked at her grandfather. "May I go, too?" she asked.

Uncle Ned grunted and then spoke to Morning Star in Cherokee.

The old squaw smiled at Sallie and rattled off something in their native language.

Sallie's eyes sparkled as she answered in Cherokee, then turned to Mandie, who waited breathlessly for the verdict. "My grandmother says I may go, too. But I also have to stay near the men."

"I'm glad, Sallie. I was afraid to ask if you could go, too," Mandie said.

Dr. Woodard stood up from the table. "Well, if y'all are ready, I say let's hit the road."

Uncle John nodded. "Yes, I think we're all ready now." He turned to kiss Elizabeth. "Pray for us, dear."

"I will," Elizabeth promised. "And Dr. Woodard, my heart goes out to you. I hope you come back with Joe."

"Thank you, dear," the doctor replied, patting Elizabeth's shoulder. "I sure hope so too."

They all went outside where the horses were saddled and waiting.

"Must get more horses for Papooses," Uncle Ned said, walking toward the fenced pasture where the animals grazed.

Dimar followed him. "I will help," he said.

When they brought out two ponies for the girls, everyone mounted and waved good-bye to Morning Star and Elizabeth. Mandie balanced Snowball on her shoulder, and they galloped off down the road.

The search was tiresome. They left the horses at the creek in the woods by the hospital, hoping to return before the workmen left for the day. Then they invaded the bushes, searching and calling Joe's name.

As they walked along the creek bank, it became an uphill climb, and Mandie looked around, sensing something familiar. "Sallie, isn't this the way to the cave?" she asked her friend.

"Yes, it is," Sallie replied.

Mandie spoke to Uncle Ned, just ahead of them. "Are we going to the cave where we found the gold, Uncle Ned?"

The old man turned around. "Cave fell in, remember? All closed up now. Rockslide," he said. "We pass it soon, Papoose. We look in mountain for doctor boy."

"And we will stop by my house to rest and eat," Dimar spoke up from behind Mandie. "My mother will have food ready."

"It will be nice to see your mother again," Mandie told him.

The group tramped on through the bushes, climbing the steep mountainside. Soon they came within sight of the waterfalls that had hidden the doorway to the old cave.

Mandie stopped and stared. "Look!" she exclaimed. "The waterfalls have changed, haven't they? Aren't they a little lopsided?" Snowball jumped down from her shoulder.

Everyone stopped to look.

"Rocks slide down, make different shape when cave fell in," Uncle Wirt said.

Dr. Woodard stood by Mandie and put his hand gently on her shoulder. "So that's the cave where you, and Sallie, and Joe found the gold," he said to her. "You know I've never been up through these mountains before."

"Yes, this is it," said Mandie. "I thought everyone knew about this place. You see, you had to walk under the waterfalls to get to the opening in the rock. When you went through that opening, there was a huge dark cave, lots of rooms, and also lots of bats. We frightened them one time, and they went wild, flying all around us."

"And the gold we found was in one of those dark rooms," Sallie added.

"As soon as Uncle Ned and Uncle Wirt took the gold out, the whole cave fell in," Mandie explained. "Rocks came sliding down every which way."

"Joe told me about that," Dr. Woodard said, still staring at the waterfalls. He cleared his throat and moved forward. "Guess we'd better keep on going, so we can find him before dark."

"Yes, we'll have to hurry to cover all this area and get back out before dark catches us," said Uncle John.

The old Indians kept alert as they led the search party. There was no clue or any sign of a trail. Snowball followed Mandie until he became tired and meowed for her to let him ride on her shoulder again.

Finally they came to Dimar's house, a neat log cabin set deep in the woods by a small stream. When the young people spotted the cabin, they hurried ahead, and arrived at the door before the others.

Jerusha Walkingstick, Dimar's mother, stood in the doorway, waiting for them. She embraced the two girls.

"Come! Eat!" she told them, leading the way back into the cabin. Then returning to the door, she beckoned the others.

After they had all gathered around a long table full of food, Uncle Wirt thanked God for their lunch and asked for help finding Joe.

As they ate, Snowball wandered out the open door into the yard. A few moments later there was a loud shot, and a bullet hit a tree near the front door. The kitten came bouncing back into the cabin, his fur ruffled.

The men jumped up, grabbed their rifles, and ran outside. The girls followed. But since there was no one in sight, the men split up, heading different directions toward the surrounding woods.

"You girls stay there with Jerusha," Uncle John called back. "Dimar, you keep watch with them. Back in the house at once, all of you."

The girls obeyed, and Dimar stationed himself at the doorway with his rifle. Standing by the window with Jerusha, Mandie and Sallie watched the men vanish into the woods.

"Dimar, does anyone else live around here?" Mandie asked.

Dimar didn't take his eyes off the yard outside. "No one who would shoot at us," he replied. "There are only friends."

Sallie spoke up. "Then maybe it is someone who does not live in the woods."

"But why would anyone shoot at Dimar's house?" asked Mandie.

"I do not know, but we will find out," Dimar assured her.

After a while the men returned. They stopped to study the tree the bullet hit and then came inside the house.

"There is no one out there," Uncle John said, standing his rifle by the chair where he sat.

Uncle Wirt and Uncle Ned warmed themselves by the fireplace while Dr. Woodard sat back down at the table.

"Did you see anything?" Mandie asked.

"Nothing, Amanda," Dr. Woodard replied.

"But there was a gunshot. I saw the bullet strike the tree," Sallie insisted.

"Yes, there was a gunshot, Sallie, but whoever was shooting got away before we could catch them," said Uncle John.

"We find feet marks. Go in creek," Uncle Ned muttered.

"And we catch," Uncle Wirt added.

Uncle John stood. "If everyone is finished eating, I think we'd better get on our way."

Everyone stood and got ready to leave.

"Thank you, Mrs. Walkingstick, for the food and everything," Dr. Woodard told the woman.

"Yes, we appreciate it, Jerusha," Uncle John said as the two Indian men echoed their thanks.

Jerusha smiled. "Always welcome," she said.

Mandie and Sallie put their arms around the Indian woman. "Thank you," they said in unison.

Jerusha squeezed them tight.

The men started out the doorway, and the girls hurried to catch up.

"Must be careful," Jerusha called after them from the doorway.

"We will," the girls called back. They waved and went on their way.

Again they walked and they walked, through bushes, briars, weeds, and swinging tree limbs, but they could find no trail or clue. They met no one and heard nothing.

Although Mandie was soon exhausted, she did not complain. After the fright of the gunshot, Snowball clung to Mandie's shoulder, content to be carried along.

Walking through an open meadow between Dimar and Sallie, Mandie turned to the Indian boy and said, "Dimar, you said Joe was all right when you left him at the hospital after the men came. If he promised to stay out of sight, how could he have gotten into trouble?"

"Perhaps the crooks came through the bushes and found him," Sallie suggested.

"Perhaps," Dimar agreed. "But I think whoever shot at the tree by my house is one of the crooks who tore down the walls of the hospital."

"You do? Why?" Mandie asked quickly.

"Because whoever it was, went into the creek so we could not follow his footprints," Dimar observed. "The crooks at the hospital also went into the creek so we could not follow their footprints."

"You are absolutely right," Mandie agreed.

Sallie looked puzzled. "But why would the crooks follow us all the way to your house?"

"I do not know but I intend finding out," said Dimar.

After hours of walking, the tired band of searchers finally got back to the hospital. It was late. The workmen had already left for the day. And again their entire day's work had been torn down.

Gasping in anger, Mandie ran ahead. Then she spied a large piece of cardboard nailed to a post that was left standing. "Look!" she cried, pointing. Hurrying closer, she read out loud, "White man, go home!"

Everyone crowded around.

Uncle Ned grunted loudly. "Crooks are Indians. We stop. Call pow-wow at council house."

"That is a good idea," said Uncle John.

Uncle Wirt looked very angry. "We tell all Cherokee help find doctor boy. Stop tearing down walls," he said loudly.

They made their plans to call all the Cherokees in the Eastern Nation to the council house the next day.

CHAPTER SEVEN

CHEROKEE POWWOW

After mounting up with the others, Mandie sadly turned her pony back onto the trail to Uncle Ned's house. They still had not found Joe, not even a trace of him.

Mandie was worried. Joe could be in danger somewhere, and there was no way for her to help. They had traveled miles and miles that day to no avail. He had to be somewhere. And those crooks had to be somewhere, too. Why couldn't they find Joe or the crooks? *Please, dear God,* she prayed silently as her pony clopped down the trail with the others. *Let them be found. Please let Joe be all right.*

Elizabeth and Morning Star waited for them at the doorway of Uncle Ned's cabin when they returned. The two women silently looked among the group, and when they didn't see Joe, they said nothing.

Mandie jumped down from her pony and ran to her mother's arms. Elizabeth hugged Mandie tightly, smoothing her daughter's tangled blonde hair. Tears flooded Mandie's worried blue eyes. She couldn't control the sobs.

"Darling," her mother whispered, looking over Mandie's head at John.

John shook his head sadly.

Dr. Woodard came over to Mandie and took her in his arms. "Look now, Amanda dear, we've not given up hope yet," he said. "Remember, where there's a will there's a way. So we've got to keep that will in order to find a way."

Mandie looked up at his worried face. "I'm sorry, Dr. Woodard," she sobbed. "I know you are worried about Joe, your own son, but you're trying not to show it."

"We have to trust in the Lord to help us. We can't just give up, Amanda," Dr. Woodard said. "You're worn out. That was quite a trip for a young girl. Why don't you get prettied up a bit, eat some good hot food, and get some rest?"

"I'll try, Dr. Woodard," Mandie said.

"You'd better try real hard, young lady. That's doctor's orders," he said, trying to smile.

Sallie, standing nearby, came to her friend's side. "Come on, Mandie. Let's get washed so we can eat."

Mandie followed her to the washpan at the other end of the big room. After everyone had washed and gathered around the table for prayer, Elizabeth and Morning Star silently dished up hot food.

No one seemed to want to talk about the day's fruitless search. Uncle Ned finally broke the silence. "We send word. All Cherokees powwow in council house when sun comes up tomorrow," he said.

"I will spread the word," Dimar volunteered.

"And I find young braves to help," Uncle Wirt added.

"All Cherokees, every one, must come to council house," Uncle Ned emphasized.

Dr. Woodard looked surprised. "Is it possible to gather all the Cherokees in such a short time?" he asked.

"Oh, yes, it has been done before," Uncle John told him. "One Cherokee tells another, and the next one tells another, on down the line. It works pretty good."

"Is there any way I can help, Uncle Ned?" Mandie asked.

Uncle Ned shook his head. "Papoose must stay here. Only braves do this job."

"May I go to the council house for the meeting?" Mandie asked.

"Yes. Papoose Cherokee, too. Must go to powwow," Uncle Ned replied.

Mandie smiled. "Thank you, Uncle Ned."

"I guess I'm the only outsider," Elizabeth remarked.

"Mother of papoose go, watch but not talk or vote," said Uncle Ned.

"I appreciate that," Elizabeth answered.

"Oh, but you forgot. I am also an outsider," Dr. Woodard spoke up.

Uncle Ned said, "Doctor must go, too. Doctor father of lost boy."

"So we will all go to the meeting," Uncle John declared.

After hurriedly finishing their meal, Uncle Wirt and Dimar left to relay the message to all the Cherokees. Mandie and Sallie, exhausted from all the walking, climbed up to the attic room with Snowball and crawled into bed.

Mandie was so worn out that in spite of her worry she soon fell asleep.

The next morning after breakfast, Uncle Wirt and Dimar arrived to ride with the others to the big Cherokee powwow.

In the excitement of getting ready to leave, Uncle John took charge. "You young people ride in the wagon with Uncle Ned," he said. "The rest of us will go with Uncle Wirt."

Outside, Dimar helped Morning Star onto the seat of Uncle Ned's wagon, and then crawled into the back. Uncle Ned took his place next to Morning Star, and the others got into Uncle Wirt's wagon.

As they rode down the dirt road, Mandie smiled at Dimar. "I hope you had time to get some sleep last night."

"I did," Dimar replied. His dark eyes reflected his admiration for her. "It did not take long to get the message line going."

"Do you think Tsa'ni will be there?" Sallie asked.

"He had better be. This is a meeting for all Cherokees," Dimar said.

"Dimar, do you think all the Cherokees will help look for Joe?" Mandie asked.

"They will be glad to help. Some of them know Joe, and they know he is your friend," Dimar replied as the wagon bounced on down the road.

"But where will they look? We covered so much territory yesterday. I don't see how there could be anywhere else to look," Mandie said.

"They will go over the same area again, and they will also search everyone's house," Dimar answered.

Mandie frowned. "Search everyone's house? Don't they trust each other?"

"Yes, but since it was an Indian who put that note on the hospital wall, there has to be a bad Indian somewhere, and they will not stop until they find the traitor," Dimar explained.

"What will they do when they catch him?" Mandie asked.

"He will be brought before a council meeting," said Dimar. "The council will decide the punishment. It will be severe, too, for kidnapping someone and damaging Cherokee property," the boy told her.

Sallie spoke up. "I have never heard of a Cherokee doing such a bad thing. They all know the Cherokee laws."

"I hate to see anyone punished, but in this case I think it is right. The crook should have to pay for his bad deeds," Mandie said.

As the young people talked on, the sun climbed higher in the sky and birds sang cheery greetings along the way. Now and then stray pigs ran along the road with chickens cackling and flying out of their way.

Soon the seven-sided, dome-roofed council house came into view. Hundreds of Cherokees were already milling about, laughing and talking with each other. Most of the women had red kerchiefs tied around their heads. The young girls, dressed in their finest, shyly chatted with the young Indian men. There was a festival air about the meeting.

Uncle Ned pulled into a vacant spot along the road and unhitched the horses. Uncle Wirt stopped his wagon right behind them.

As they all walked to the council house, Elizabeth spoke to Uncle Ned. "Am I supposed to wait outside?" she asked.

"No, sit in backside. Wait there," he said.

"Thank you," Elizabeth replied.

The Indians standing around the entrance smiled at Mandie, then moved aside as Uncle Ned led the way into the building.

Mandie looked around. She had been here once before, but the place still interested her. There were wooden benches to sit on. Huge log poles held up the dome-shaped thatched roof. The symbols of the various clans adorned the posts. The place of the sacred fire was directly ahead as they entered. The six leaders of the clans sat behind the fire.

Uncle Ned motioned for everyone to sit near the front, and then he went to stand behind the fire with the leaders. As he did, all the Cherokees quickly took their seats and became silent.

Mandie sat between Dimar and Sallie. She turned slightly to look behind her. The council house was full. She saw Tsa'ni come down the aisle with two other boys and sit down nearby. Tsa'ni looked directly at Mandie but did not speak.

One of the men behind the fire stood and began waving his arms and chanting loudly in the Cherokee language. Mandie looked at Dimar questioningly.

"He is praying," Dimar whispered.

Mandie smiled and watched as the man sat down. Then Uncle Ned began his speech in Cherokee. His voice was angry and demanding, but Mandie could not understand a thing he was saying.

Dimar leaned toward her and whispered, "He is telling the Cherokees what a disgrace it is that an Indian would kidnap a white boy who is our guest. He also says it is a bad crime to destroy the hospital—Cherokee property."

Sallie helped with the translation, too. "He is telling the Cherokees that every man, woman, and child must stop whatever he is doing and join the search," she whispered. "Nothing else is to be done until Joe is found."

Mandie silently looked around the council house. The Cherokees were listening to every word and nodding in agreement.

Uncle Ned concluded his speech with some loud, angry words. The Cherokees rose to their feet and echoed whatever he had said. As they sat back down, Uncle Ned beckoned to Mandie to come forward.

Her heart beat rapidly. Must she go up there before all these people? She had done it once before but she was so frightened, she could hardly speak. She hesitated, but Uncle Ned called loudly, "Come, Papoose."

Sallie and Dimar pulled her to her feet and pushed her out into the aisle.

"But what does he want with me?" she whispered.

"He wants you to speak to your people," Sallie replied.

"Go. He is waiting," Dimar urged.

Uncle Ned stepped down from the platform to meet Mandie on the way. Taking her small white trembling hand in his old wrinkled one, he led her up on the platform by his side.

"Must tell Cherokees you want their help," Uncle Ned said softly.

Mandie looked at him and smiled. She could do that.

"My people," she began in a weak, shaky voice. "Please help me find my dear friend, Joe Woodard. The same terrible people who have been tearing down the walls of your hospital have taken my friend." Her voice grew stronger as she continued. "We must find Joe first, and then catch the crooks. We must put a stop to their destructive work and get the hospital built before someone really needs it. Will you help me, please?"

She paused, and Uncle Ned translated her speech into Cherokee. Instantly, the Indians stood and applauded wildly, stomping their feet and chanting.

Tears glistened in Mandie's eyes as she smiled and motioned for them to sit down.

"Thank you, my people, thank you!" she cried. "I know some of y'all know Dr. Woodard, Joe's father, but I want him to come up here and let everyone meet him. Dr. Woodard?"

While Uncle Ned translated, Mandie motioned for Dr. Woodard to join her. Dr. Woodard looked startled, but after an awkward silence, he got to his feet and walked rapidly to the platform.

"I know a white man is not supposed to speak at a council meeting, but Dr. Woodard is no ordinary white man," Mandie began again, pausing after every few words for Uncle Ned to translate. "First of all, he's Joe's father and he is the best friend the Cherokees ever had. Without his doctoring, many Cherokees would have died. And he will be in charge of the hospital when it is finished. Now, here he is," she said.

When Uncle Ned finished translating, the crowd again stood, this time to welcome the doctor. Then they sat back down.

Beads of sweat formed on Dr. Woodard's brow as he stepped forward nervously. "Thank you, my dear friends," he said loudly. Uncle Ned translated again. "I know you will do everything possible to find my son, Joe. I have faith in you. And when the person or persons responsible for destroying the hospital walls is caught, I hope you mete out a stiff punishment. Thank you."

As the crowd again clapped, and stomped, and beat on the boards of the benches, Mandie turned to Uncle Ned. "May we sit down now?" she asked.

"Go, sit, Papoose. Doctor, sit," he said, smiling.

When Mandie and Dr. Woodard had returned to their seats, Uncle Ned quieted the crowd. "Now we vote to find Joe," he said in both Cherokee and English, obviously wanting everyone present to know what was happening. "Everyone who say yes raise hand."

It looked as though all the Cherokees in the audience raised their hands except Tsa'ni and the boys with him.

"Now everyone who say no raise hand," the old man said.

There was complete silence. Mandie turned slightly and gasped as Tsa'ni and the two boys raised their hands.

Uncle Ned looked directly at the boys in disgust. "Why you raise hand no?" he asked.

The three stood up.

Tsa'ni spoke in English. "We think the Cherokee gods are tearing down the hospital and would not like our interference."

Everyone stared at him in silence.

"No Cherokee gods," Uncle Ned said angrily. "Only one God, Big God. You know that."

"That is what the white man wants you to believe," Tsa'ni replied. "Do not forget the Big God is the white man's God."

Mandie jumped up. "That is not so, Tsa'ni, and you know it!" she yelled. "There is only one God. You are just trying to confuse things. I think you are the one who is tearing down the walls. And I believe you also know what happened to Joe."

"I am not tearing down walls," Tsa'ni argued. "But if I knew who it was, I would help them destroy the white man's building. And Joe got lost somewhere because he is not man enough to take care of himself," the Indian boy scoffed.

Trembling with anger, Uncle Ned yelled at Tsa'ni in Cherokee. Mandie couldn't understand but Tsa'ni did. He plopped down on the bench and said no more.

Mandie sat down and looked at Sallie. "What did Uncle Ned say to him?" she asked.

"He said unless Tsa'ni repents and believes in the Big God, his soul will burn in hell forever," Sallie explained. "And if he is involved in this crime in any way, he will be severely punished."

As Uncle Ned continued to speak in Cherokee, Dimar told her that Uncle Ned was explaining how to go about the search.

Finally Uncle Ned stepped to the edge of the platform and raised his hand. He said something softly in Cherokee, and the crowd stood. Looking toward Mandie and then the sky, he said loudly in English, "Big God, we ask help to find doctor boy and to stop crook." Then he began praying in Cherokee so the people could understand him.

They all raised their faces upward.

Mandie squeezed Sallie's hand on one side and Dimar's on the other as she prayed silently, *Dear God, please help us find Joe. Guide our footsteps in the right direction, and help us stop the crooks from tearing down the hospital. I know you will help us. You always do. I love you, dear God. Amen.*

As the meeting broke up, Mandie felt a heavy burden lift from her heart. She knew God would answer her prayers. She didn't know how, but she knew she could depend on Him.

CHAPTER EIGHT

TROUBLE FOR MANDIE AND SALLIE

Just as Mandie came out of the council house, Uncle Wirt grabbed Tsa'ni by the shoulders and shook him so hard his head wobbled. The whole time he was screaming at his grandson in Cherokee.

Everyone stood back watching. No one spoke.

Uncle Ned stepped forward and laid a hand on Uncle Wirt's arm. "Must go now," Uncle Ned told him. "Go search."

Uncle Wirt dropped his hands and nodded in assent. Tsa'ni quickly turned to leave.

"Tsa'ni," Mandie called to him. "I still believe you know where Joe is, and if you don't tell us, you're going to be awfully sorry."

"Ask your Big God where he is. You say He knows everything," Tsa'ni called back, disappearing into the crowd.

"He is a bad Cherokee," Sallie repeated.

"He does not like white people," Dimar said. "He is afraid they will change the way of life for the Cherokees. He does not realize the Cherokees must learn better ways of living."

"I think the hospital will be the best thing that ever happened to the Cherokees," Sallie said.

"We'll get it built in spite of all this trouble," Mandie assured them. "God will help us."

Elizabeth caught up with Mandie as the young people walked toward Uncle Ned's wagon. "I am proud of you, Amanda," Elizabeth told her daughter. "That was an impressive speech you made. I know the Cherokees will find Joe, wherever he is."

"Thank you, Mother," Mandie said, smiling up at her. "May I go with the Cherokees on their search?"

"I don't think they will want you to, Amanda. Your Uncle John says that the men will begin first, and if necessary the women will join in later, and then maybe the children," her mother said.

"But, Mother, when the women join in, I should also help," Mandie argued.

"We'll talk about it later, dear," said Elizabeth, starting toward Uncle Wirt's wagon.

Mandie followed her mother and climbed into Uncle Ned's wagon with Sallie and Dimar. As she sat down, Mandie let out a big sigh.

Sallie patted Mandie's hand. "I know you are disappointed, Mandie, but it is better this way," Sallie tried to comfort her friend.

"The men can move faster without the women," Dimar added. "And I promise to let you know the minute we find Joe."

"You're going with Uncle Ned and the men?" Mandie asked.

"Yes. As soon as we take y'all home, we will meet the other men at the hospital and start searching from there," the Indian boy explained.

"But you aren't really a full-grown man, Dimar," Mandie teased.

"The Cherokees consider me a man. I am now thirteen years old," Dimar said solemnly.

Just then Uncle Ned came and helped Morning Star onto the seat of the wagon. Then he harnessed his horses.

Climbing into the wagon, he looked at the young people. "We hurry now. We go home," he said. Picking up the reins, he turned the wagon onto the road.

Mandie was sitting in the wagon bed behind Uncle Ned. "Thank you, Uncle Ned," she called to him. "Thank you for asking all the Cherokees to join in the search for Joe."

"Doctor boy friend of Papoose. I promise Jim Shaw I watch over Papoose when he go to happy hunting ground," the old man explained. "We find doctor boy for sad Papoose."

Mandie smiled. "Thank you, Uncle Ned. I love every one of those Cherokee people. After all, they are my people, too."

Sallie gave Mandie a hug. "We all love you, too, Mandie."

Dimar smiled at her. "Yes, we do."

Mandie blushed. Dimar was good-looking and awfully nice. She looked down.

Dimar sensed her discomfort. "We will find Joe for you," he promised. "And the crooks, too."

"Thank you, Dimar. You are truly a friend," Mandie said.

"If I am in the group that finds Joe, I will let you know myself, I promise," he said.

Uncle Ned looked back at Mandie. "If I find doctor boy *I* bring him to Papoose," he called to her over the rattle of the wagon. "We hurry fast." He whipped the reins, and the horses sped off down the road.

When they reached Uncle Ned's house, Morning Star ran into the cabin and quickly began packing food for the men.

Uncle Ned was already unharnessing the horses by the time Uncle Wirt and his wagonload had arrived. Elizabeth went inside to help Morning Star, and the girls stood around in the way, not knowing what to do.

Dimar brought fresh horses from the pasture for the three men and himself and tethered them at the door. The girls went outside to wait with him until the men came outside and prepared to leave.

"Please be careful," Mandie called to them as they mounted their horses.

"We will," Uncle John promised.

Elizabeth stood with Morning Star in the doorway. "I wish you all Godspeed," she said, waving to them.

"Dr. Woodard," Mandie called, "I'll be praying that you find Joe soon and that he is all right."

"Bless you, Amanda," the doctor answered.

Uncle Ned took command. "We go now. We find Joe. "Find crooks," he said. And with that, the four were off, riding quickly down the dirt road.

The women and girls watched until the men were out of sight and all they could see was a cloud of dust. Then they went back into the cabin to wait.

The day dragged by for the girls. They ate the noon meal. They helped with the chores. They wandered listlessly around the yard until late afternoon. Then they sat on a fallen log under the big chestnut tree.

"I wish they would hurry back so we'd know something," Mandie said.

"You know they will return just as soon as they find Joe," Sallie replied.

Mandie sighed. "I know, but I wish I could do something."

"Would you like to pick some wild flowers?" Sallie asked.

"Sure." Mandie stood. "But I'll have to ask Mother first."

They ran for the cabin and found Elizabeth peeling potatoes. Morning Star was stirring several pots over the fire in the fireplace.

"Mother, why are you cooking so much food?" Mandie asked.

"We don't know when the men will return, Amanda," Elizabeth replied, "or how many there will be, so we have to cook a lot of food and have it ready for them."

"You don't need us, do you?" Mandie asked.

"No, dear. Morning Star and I have everything under control," her mother said.

"Then could Sallie and I go out and pick some wild flowers?" Mandie asked.

"If you promise not to be gone too long," Elizabeth consented. "It's not long till suppertime."

"We won't," Mandie promised.

"Come on, Mandie," Sallie said after talking to Morning Star. "I have permission to go."

As the girls hurried outdoors and started down the road, Snowball followed.

"We can go to the woods," Sallie suggested. "It is not very far."

"Are there a lot of flowers there?" Mandie asked.

"Yes, everywhere. All kinds," Sallie told her.

At the bend in the road, the girls walked off into the woods. Sallie was right. As they went along, they found more and more flowers.

Pulling their aprons up to hold the flowers, they kept going, not realizing how late it was getting.

Then Sallie stopped suddenly and looked around. "Mandie, we are a long way into the woods. We are almost to the hospital," Sallie said.

"We are?" said Mandie. "But it took a long time to get there on the road."

"It is much shorter through the woods," Sallie said. "But since we—" she paused, listening. "Mandie, do you hear something?"

Mandie held her breath to listen for a moment. "I hear pounding," she said.

"Yes, it sounds like someone chopping wood," Sallie added.

"Chopping wood? And we are near the hospital? Could it be the workmen who are building the hospital?" Mandie asked.

"We will go find out," Sallie replied.

The two girls hurried on through the woods, still holding their flowers in their aprons. The noise grew louder, and then it suddenly ceased. The girls stopped and looked at each other. The sound of footsteps came toward them through the brush.

"Quick! Behind those big trees!" said Sallie, running for cover.

Mandie followed. Together they stood there, holding their breath, waiting to see who came along. Mandie's heart beat wildly. The footsteps grew louder. Three men carrying axes passed in front of them, then walked on out of sight.

The girls, shaking with fright, came out from behind the trees.

"Who was that?" Mandie asked.

"That was the Catawba man, Running Fire, and his sons. He is the husband of Moongo, the old Cherokee woman who came back not long ago. She had been gone many, many years, but they now live in an old barn near here," Sallie explained.

"Oh, yes," Mandie replied. "Uncle Ned told us about them. But they were all three carrying axes, and the chopping noise stopped just before they came by here," Mandie observed. "Come on! Hurry! Let's check the hospital."

"This way," Sallie told her, quickly running ahead.

When they came to the hospital clearing, they were panting for breath. They stared at the hospital, then at each other. The workmen were gone, and the walls had all been chopped down.

"Sallie, let's follow them!" Mandie urged her friend. Turning back the way they had come, Mandie held Snowball tightly as they ran. Since the men weren't walking very fast, the girls quickly caught up with them.

Angrily Mandie ran up to Running Fire and stood in front of him, blocking his path.

"You tore down the walls to the hospital, didn't you?" she cried. "Why did you do that? Why?" she demanded, tears choking her voice.

"Move!" Running Fire demanded.

Mandie stepped closer. "You also kidnapped Joe, didn't you? Where is he? Where is he?" Mandie screamed, dropping her apron and spilling the flowers to the ground.

Sallie also dropped her flowers and grabbed Mandie's arm. "Come, Mandie," she said.

Mandie ignored her friend.

"Well, you won't get away with it!" she shouted. "We have the whole Cherokee nation out looking for you."

The Catawba man reached out and grabbed her long blonde braid. "We take you, too," he said. Then pointing to Sallie, he told his sons, "Get her!"

The two younger men snatched Sallie and held her tight.

"Go," ordered Running Fire, pushing Mandie ahead of him. "We take you where white boy is."

The other two men pushed Sallie along with them.

Mandie held Snowball tightly. "You don't have to shove. We'll go," said Mandie. "If you're taking us to Joe, we'll go."

"Shut up!" snapped Running Fire.

Without another word, the girls went along with the three men to the old barn where the Catawba man lived.

"Stop here!" Running Fire ordered. Then turning to one of his sons, he said, "Open."

The younger man, after waiting to be sure his brother had a secure hold on Sallie, walked to a mound of straw and kicked it aside. Beneath the straw was a wooden door made flat into the ground. He removed a large boulder sitting on the door, then pulled the door open.

The girls watched in amazement. No wonder no one had been able to find Joe if he was in there.

Running Fire motioned to the girls. "Get in!" he ordered, shoving Mandie toward the opening in the ground.

The son pushed Sallie forward.

Mandie looked down into the dark hole and saw an old ladder hanging down inside.

"Get in!" Running Fire shouted again, giving Mandie a sharp push.

Trembling with fear and anger, Mandie stooped down, put Snowball on her shoulder, and then carefully made her way down the ladder into the storm cellar. Sallie was forced to follow.

At the bottom, when Mandie's feet touched ground, she peered around the semidarkness. Someone groaned. Over in the corner Joe lay on the ground, gagged and tied up. Mandie ran to him, and Sallie quickly joined her.

"Joe!" Mandie cried, fumbling to untie him. "Joe! It's me, Mandie!"

The boy only groaned.

The girls looked him over. He was bruised, and beaten, and evidently very ill, almost unconscious.

Overhead, Running Fire closed the wooden door, and the girls heard the stone being pushed back over it.

Mandie bent over Joe compassionately. "Sallie, what are we going to do?" she cried. "Joe is sick."

"He is cold, too," Sallie said. "It is cold in here."

Mandie stood up. "Let's use our aprons to cover him up a little," she told Sallie.

The two girls quickly removed their big, full aprons and carefully covered the boy as well as they could.

With the door closed, it was almost completely dark in the storm cellar.

Mandie shivered. "Sallie, we must pray. Joe is sick, and if he doesn't get help soon, he may die," she said with tears in her eyes. "He's been gone since night before last."

The two girls quietly knelt beside Joe and looked upward.

"Dear God, please, please get us out of here," Mandie prayed aloud. "Let somebody find us before it's too late for Joe. Please don't let him die, dear God, please." Mandie's voice broke. She took a deep breath and repeated her favorite prayer from the Bible. "What time I am afraid, I will trust in Thee." She began to sob.

"Yes, dear God, please do not wait too long," Sallie begged.

Sallie put her arm around her friend. "Mandie, remember what Dr. Woodard said. We must not give up. We must not!" the Indian girl told her.

Mandie rubbed her sleeve across her wet eyes and straightened up. "We won't give up. Never!" Mandie determined. "Someone will find us. I know they will."

"Yes, someone will find us," Sallie agreed.

Mandie sat quietly for a moment, thinking. "Sallie, I've just realized something awful," she said.

"What?"

"I'm afraid I have wrongly accused Tsa'ni," Mandie cried. "He was not the one who was tearing down the walls."

"You can straighten things out with Tsa'ni later," the Indian girl replied.

"But I accused him in the council house in front of all our people," Mandie reminded her. "He'll never forgive me. I just hope God will."

"If you ask God to forgive you, I think Tsa'ni will, too," Sallie comforted her. "But we must get out of this place first."

"I hope it is soon," Mandie replied.

CHAPTER NINE

TSA'NI TELLS A LIE

The day was beginning to fade away. Elizabeth and Morning Star sat near the open doorway where they could watch for the others to return.

Elizabeth fidgeted nervously. "Morning Star, I know you can't understand much of what I say, but I have to talk to someone," she said. "I am worried. Amanda and Sallie should have been back long ago. They only went to pick flowers. And someone in the search party should have let us know something by now. Do you understand what I am saying, Morning Star?"

Morning Star grunted and nodded her head. "Late," she said, frowning.

"That's right. You do understand some things," said Elizabeth, a little relieved. "I don't know which way they went, but even if I went to look for them they might come back a different way." She pulled out a handkerchief and dabbed at her eyes. "Oh, why did I give Amanda permission to pick flowers? There is so much danger around with Joe missing and the hospital vandalism."

Morning Star listened intently. To Elizabeth's surprise, the old Indian squaw stood up and said, "We find. We go."

"No, Morning Star," Elizabeth objected. "We don't know which way they went."

"Flowers, woods," Morning Star tried to explain.

"You mean they went into the woods to pick flowers? Is that where they went?"

The old woman nodded.

"But the woods are—"

"We go," Morning Star repeated.

"Wait," Elizabeth said. "I must leave a note in case someone comes before we get back."

She walked across the room and rummaged in her travel bag for a piece of paper and a pencil. Morning Star watched her in puzzlement.

As Elizabeth sat down at the table to write the note, a shadow blocked the light from the doorway. Elizabeth looked up to see Tsa'ni standing there.

Tsa'ni stared at her without speaking.

When Morning Star saw him, she began talking rapidly to him in Cherokee. Tsa'ni listened in surprise as Elizabeth sat and watched. Evidently the old woman was telling him about the girls.

Tsa'ni looked at Elizabeth. "Mrs. Shaw, Morning Star says Mandie and Sallie went out to pick flowers and have not come back."

Elizabeth got up and walked toward the boy. "Yes, Tsa'ni, that is true. We are worried sick. Something must have happened to them," Elizabeth said.

Impatiently, Morning Star rushed over to the boy and shook him, obviously scolding him harshly in Cherokee.

Elizabeth waited to see what the vile-tempered boy would do.

Tsa'ni said something to the old squaw then turned back to Elizabeth. "She wants me to go hunt them," he said belligerently.

"Oh, Tsa'ni, would you?" Elizabeth pleaded. "Morning Star and I were about to go and look for them when you came in, but we don't know where to look. Morning Star said they went into the woods. You probably know this area better than she does, and I know nothing at all about it. Will you go?" she repeated.

Tsa'ni scuffed the toe of his moccasin on the rough floor and lowered his eyes. Elizabeth Shaw had always been kind to him, even when all the others were not. He could promise to look for them, but it didn't matter to him whether he found them or not. If he found the girls he would tell them to go home. If he didn't find them, he would just keep on going. He had only come by Uncle Ned's house to see if his grandfather had returned.

"I will look for them," he told Elizabeth. Turning to Morning Star, he spoke rapidly in Cherokee.

The old woman smiled.

"Tsa'ni, thank you. I appreciate it," Elizabeth said sincerely. "I certainly hope you find them. And, please, don't you get lost, too."

"I have never been lost. I know every tree in the woods," the boy bragged. "I will go now."

He hurried out into the yard and started down the road. The women watched him until he was out of sight.

Tsa'ni took his time tramping through the woods. He headed straight for the hospital building, looked around there, and then circled out away from it. Enlarging the circle as he walked, he came nearer and nearer the Catawba man's house.

Then noticing something white through the bushes, he made his way through the brush and found the two piles of flowers the girls had dropped. He bent down, examining the flowers and the tracks around them. Evidently there had been three men here besides the girls. His heartbeat quickened. Three men were more than he wanted to take on. He stood up, looked around, and continued on through the woods. He would just go on home. It was getting late.

As Tsa'ni walked quickly through the deepest part of the woods, he suddenly spotted his grandfather's search party through the trees. Tsa'ni tried to escape notice, but the old Indian saw him.

"Come!" Uncle Wirt called to him.

Knowing he had to obey, Tsa'ni slowly walked over to his grandfather. The others in the party heard Uncle Wirt's shout and came to join him.

"Where you go?" his grandfather demanded.

"Home," Tsa'ni replied.

"Where been?" the old Indian persisted.

Tsa'ni hesitated.

Uncle Ned stepped forward. "To my house?" he asked.

"Yes," the boy answered.

"Why?" Uncle Wirt asked.

"To see if you had come back," Tsa'ni replied. "For what other reason would I go there?"

John Shaw looked concerned. "Was everyone there all right?" he asked.

"Yes," the boy said sharply.

Dimar looked at Tsa'ni with suspicion. He didn't appear to believe anything Tsa'ni said.

"Did you see anyone else in the woods?" Dr. Woodard asked.

Tsa'ni looked at the doctor coldly and then answered, "Of course not."

"We go back," Uncle Ned told them. "Crooks not this way. Crooks that way." He pointed toward the trail to the hospital.

"You're right, Uncle Ned," John agreed. "If they had come this way we would have seen them."

Dimar looked over at Dr. Woodard. The old man was tired and worried about his son. "Dr. Woodard, when we find the crooks, I am sure we will find Joe," he said. "I think the crooks hid Joe somewhere."

"Yes, Dimar, that's what I've been thinking, too," the doctor answered.

As Uncle Ned led the way back to the hospital site, the other men followed. Tsa'ni stood there watching them for a minute, then continued on his way home.

When the sky became dark and Tsa'ni didn't return to Uncle Ned's cabin, Elizabeth and Morning Star paced the floor frantically. Evidently the girls had not been found.

CHAPTER TEN

SNOWBALL HELPS

Mandie and Sallie huddled together in the storm cellar, trying to comfort one another while they watched over Joe. How they wished someone would come and rescue them!

Suddenly there was a noise overhead. The girls quickly jumped up, and Snowball slid off Mandie's lap.

"I heard something," Mandie whispered.

"Someone is at the door overhead," Sallie replied.

"I'm going to climb the ladder and surprise them when they open the door," Mandie said softly.

"Please be careful," Sallie pleaded. "We do not know if it is the crooks or our people."

Mandie climbed the ladder and stopped near the door above. Slowly the door was opened a crack, and Running Fire's face appeared in the opening. His beady eyes looked at her, then glanced down at Sallie and Joe.

"Mister, please let us out of here," Mandie begged. "My friend Joe is sick. He needs a doctor bad."

"No," the Catawba man snapped. "We wait. We catch white men."

"Please don't harm anyone else," Mandie said. "We don't even know why you hate us so."

"White man must go home. Leave us alone," said Running Fire. "Hospital not good for Indian."

"But the Cherokees all want the hospital to be built," Mandie argued, hanging on to the ladder. "They want to be able to take their sick there."

"No!" Running Fire stormed. "No! Hospital not be built! Not need white man's doctor. I am medicine man. I heal sick Indians. Not need white man. No, no, no!"

Sallie called to him from below. "You are a medicine man for the Catawbas. Cherokees do not want a Catawba medicine man. We want a white doctor who knows how to heal."

"No, no, no!" Running Fire shook with anger as he perched over the doorway. "Medicine man doctor all Indians."

"So you are a medicine man. Now I understand what's been going on," Mandie said. "You are angry because the Cherokees do not believe in medicine men anymore. They have seen white doctors heal their sick. They do not need you."

"Hush up!" the Catawba man cried. "I come down and hush you up."

As he fumbled trying to close the door, Mandie spied a good-sized rock lying near the top of the ladder. Grabbing the rock quickly, she stuck it under the door just as Running Fire shut it. The rock let a crack of dim light into the dark cellar. Mandie listened. Running Fire rolled the boulder on top of the cellar entrance again, but the rock held the door open a crack.

Mandie slid down the ladder. "Look, Sallie!' she whispered. "I put a rock under the door so it wouldn't shut tight."

Sallie glanced upward. "That was fast thinking. Now we have a little light and air in here. But it will soon be dark outside and then it will be pitch black in here again," she said.

Mandie bent over Joe in the faint light from above. His face was all bloody and bruised. Their aprons still covered his motionless body.

"Joe has not moved an inch," Mandie said.

"He is still breathing though," Sallie replied.

Mandie picked up his limp, cold hand and rubbed it with hers. "Sallie, we've got to get him out of here before it's too late," she cried.

"I wish I could think of a way," Sallie replied.

Snowball rubbed around Mandie's legs and meowed loudly. Evidently he was hungry.

Picking him up, Mandie rubbed his soft white fur and put his cold nose against her cheek. "Snowball, I'm sorry you're hungry. Come to think of it, I am, too," she told the kitten.

"So am I," Sallie said. "My grandmother and your mother must have supper ready by now. I know they are worried about us."

"I imagine Mother is walking the floor," Mandie told her friend.

"My grandmother is probably out looking for us," Sallie said.

Mandie thought for a moment. "You're right. Mother and Morning Star are both out looking for us, I'm sure," Mandie said. "Oh, will my mother be angry with me!"

"I think they will be too glad to see us to be angry with us," Sallie told her.

"I hope you're right," Mandie replied. "I'm going up the ladder again to see if I can see anything through that crack," Mandie said, putting Snowball on her shoulder.

Climbing the rungs of the ladder, Mandie got as close to the crack as she could and tried to see outside. But the crack was at an angle, so she couldn't see much.

Snowball jumped onto the ledge under the door and began scratching at the dirt around the crack.

Mandie reached for him. "Snowball, come back here," she scolded.

Snowball only scratched harder, kicking dust in Mandie's eyes.

That gave Mandie an idea. "Sallie," she called to her friend. "If we could scratch enough dirt away, we could poke Snowball through the hole. Then maybe he would go home."

Sallie stood up. "That is a good idea. Is the ladder strong enough to hold both of us?"

"I think so," Mandie said. "It didn't shake when I came up. Here, I'll move over to one side."

As Mandie moved over, Sallie carefully climbed the ladder. It did not even sway.

Arriving at the top, Sallie looked at the crack where Snowball was still scratching. "Yes, I think we can make the hole larger so Snowball can get through," she agreed. "But there is nothing to dig with."

Pushing the kitten aside on the ledge, Mandie and Sallie went to work on the dirt with their bare hands. They broke their fingernails and scratched their hands, but they kept digging. The hole slowly grew a little larger. The girls stopped and listened now and then to be sure no one was around to hear them.

"Whew!" Mandie sighed. "My fingers are bleeding."

Sallie looked at her own hands. "Mine, too," she said. "But now the hole is almost large enough for Snowball to go through."

Leaning back, Mandie looked at the hole and then at Snowball. "Come here, Snowball," she called, reaching out to him. She held him up next to the hole and looked at Sallie. "It's large enough."

"Are you sure? Do not force him through. It might hurt him," Sallie cautioned.

Mandie looked again. "Maybe just a little bit more."

The girls dug more dirt out until the hole finally looked large enough.

"Now!" Mandie declared.

"Yes," Sallie agreed.

Mandie picked up Snowball and started to push him through the hole. Then she stopped suddenly. "I have an idea," she cried. "Let's tie our hair ribbons around Snowball. Then whoever finds him might figure out that we are not able to come home."

"That is a good idea," Sallie said, quickly pulling the red ribbon from her long, straight black hair.

Mandie untied the blue ribbon from her blonde braid and started to tie it around Snowball's neck.

Sallie stopped her. "No, no," she said. "He might get caught on something and the ribbon would choke him. Tie it around his belly."

"Will it stay?"

"If you tie it like this it will," Sallie said, showing Mandie how to crisscross it behind Snowball's front legs.

"Perfect," said Mandie, tying her ribbon as Sallie had shown her.

Snowball thought it was a game. Meowing, he rolled over on his back, trying to reach the ribbons with his claws.

"No, silly cat," Mandie scolded him. "Don't pull it off. You've got to be our messenger to get us out of here."

She picked him up and tried to push him through the hole. Snowball didn't like that at all, and Sallie had to help. Then when he got outside, he tried to come back in. Mandie quickly stuffed a rock in the hole to make it too small for him to get through. But Snowball didn't leave. He just sat outside and meowed loudly.

"Goodness!" Mandie exclaimed. "He'll alarm the whole neighborhood. Those crooks will hear him and come to see what's going on."

"Maybe we could get him back inside," Sallie suggested.

"Let's try," Mandie agreed.

Removing the rock, they tried to coax the kitten inside. But he only sniffed at their hands and meowed louder.

"Well, I guess we'll just have to wait and see who hears him," Mandie said, disappointed.

"Yes, that is all we can do," Sallie agreed. "I am going back down. I want to sit for a while.

"I'll stay up here and listen," Mandie told her friend.

While Sallie kept watch over Joe, Mandie listened at the cellar door. Someone was sure to come soon. Snowball wouldn't quit meowing.

CHAPTER ELEVEN

RESCUE

Tsa'ni was almost home when he decided to go back. If he circled far enough out, he could bypass his grandfather's search party and get back to Uncle Ned's cabin. He might as well tell the women he didn't find the girls. He wouldn't mention that he had met the search party.

As Tsa'ni tried to sneak past the Catawba man's house, he suddenly heard Snowball crying. Silently he moved closer to see the kitten. There was Snowball, sitting by the barn, decorated with ribbons, howling for no apparent reason. Tsa'ni decided that the cat must have gotten lost.

When Snowball saw Tsa'ni approaching, he hunched up, ruffled his fur, and hissed at the boy.

Tsa'ni quickly jumped back. He had never touched that cat before, and he didn't intend to now.

As Tsa'ni turned and quietly continued on his way, Mandie stood at the top of the cellar ladder, holding her breath.

"Sallie, there was someone outside just now," she whispered. "Snowball stopped his meowing and began hissing at somebody. It must have been somebody he didn't like."

"Yes, I heard," Sallie called softly from below. "But whoever it was must have left. Snowball is meowing again."

As Tsa'ni headed for Uncle Ned's cabin, he began making up the tale he would tell the women.

Elizabeth and Morning Star saw him approaching and stood in the doorway to wait.

"I saw no one in the woods," he told them as he entered the cabin. "No one at all." He repeated it in Cherokee to Morning Star.

"Oh dear!" Elizabeth exclaimed.

Morning Star began screaming at the boy in Cherokee, but Tsa'ni just stood there with a sly grin on his face.

Elizabeth watched, trying to understand. "What did Morning Star say?" she asked as the squaw stomped over to the table and began wrapping up some food.

"She told me I should have found them. She said that I am no good, so she is going to find them," Tsa'ni told Elizabeth.

Elizabeth walked over to Morning Star, watching her put some food into a basket.

"I am going with you," Elizabeth announced. "Tsa'ni, will you go with us?"

Tsa'ni hesitated. "Yes," he said. "I will go with you. I will get the lantern and the matches. It will be dark soon."

"I need to get a coat," said Elizabeth. "Tsa'ni, will you please tell Morning Star to get a coat or something warm. It will be cold before long. And tell her that you and I are going with her."

Tsa'ni walked over to Morning Star and spoke quickly in Cherokee. Morning Star replied but kept wrapping food to fill the basket. Then she reached for a jar, filled it with water, and set it up straight in the basket so it wouldn't spill.

Tsa'ni took a lantern from the nail where it hung by the door and put some matches in his pocket.

Elizabeth finished the note she had started writing earlier, and placed it in the middle of the long table. The three left the cabin and walked down the road toward the woods.

Silently, Elizabeth again prayed that the girls were safe and asked God's help in finding them.

Morning Star, sensing that Elizabeth was praying, raised her eyes toward the sky and said her prayer in Cherokee.

In the meantime, Uncle Ned had led the search party back into the woods. Although it was getting dark, they didn't light their lanterns for fear the crooks would see the light. They all walked quietly. Only occasionally was there a sound of a twig breaking under someone's foot.

Uncle Ned stopped for a moment, pointing ahead to the left. "Near Catawba man's house," he muttered softly.

"Let's see if anyone is home," John suggested.

"Yes, but quiet," Uncle Ned reminded them, stealthily leading the group forward.

The old barn came into view when they reached the clearing. The men slowly slipped around the makeshift house and peered through the open window.

"No one is home," Dr. Woodard whispered.

"I go inside," said Uncle Wirt.

"I suppose we should search every conceivable place," John agreed. "They could have hidden Joe anywhere."

Uncle Wirt quietly opened the sagging door and slipped inside. The others watched through the window as the old man searched the room. He looked under everything and behind everything. There wasn't much furniture in the old one-room barn.

"We go around," Uncle Ned said, waving his arms to indicate searching the surrounding area.

As the men fanned out in various directions, Uncle Ned headed straight toward the storm cellar. The old Indian heard a noise and stopped to listen. He walked a little farther. It sounded like someone crying. Uncle Ned hurried forward and found Snowball sitting there, meowing.

He looked around quickly, then stooped and picked up the white kitten. Snowball immediately hushed and started purring. Uncle Ned examined the ribbons tied around the kitten.

"Snowball, where Papoose? What you do in woods?" the old man talked to the kitten, smoothing its white fur.

Although there wasn't much light and the Catawbas had camouflaged the storm cellar door, Uncle Ned's sharp eyes noticed the small hole in the ground. He stooped to look closer.

Hovering over the hole, he once again talked to the kitten. "Snowball, hole there," he said, setting the kitten down. He kicked at the mound of straw and found the wooden door to the storm cellar.

Mandie's heart beat wildly. "Someone is outside, Sallie," she whispered.

Sallie quickly climbed up the ladder and stood beside her friend.

Uncle Ned stooped to move the boulder on top of the door. "Move, Snowball," he said, giving the boulder a push.

Instantly Mandie and Sallie recognized the voice.

"Uncle Ned!" Mandie cried.

"Grandfather!" called Sallie.

Uncle Ned realized who was inside. "Papooses, what you do in there?" he shouted.

Standing up, he signalled the other men with a shrill bird whistle, then struggled to pull the cellar door open.

Uncle John, Dr. Woodard, Uncle Wirt, and Dimar came running at his call.

"Papooses in there," Uncle Ned told them.

"Papooses? Amanda and Sallie?" Uncle John asked.

When the door finally came open, the girls were clinging to the top of the ladder. Everyone started talking at once.

Mandie grabbed the doctor's sleeve. "Dr. Woodard, Joe is down there. He's sick—bad," she said as she and Sallie climbed out.

Dimar quickly jumped into the cellar, and Dr. Woodard made his way down the ladder.

"Joe, at last," Uncle John said with relief. He called down to Dr. Woodard. "Need me to help, or would I be in the way?"

"We will manage," Dr. Woodard called back.

In a few minutes Dimar appeared on the ladder with Joe's limp body slung over his shoulder. Dr. Woodard came right behind him, carrying the girls' aprons. Reaching the top, they laid Joe on the ground, and again covered him with the aprons.

"Go get blanket," Uncle Ned directed Dimar, pointing back toward Running Fire's house.

Dimar hurried off, and Uncle Wirt followed in case he had any trouble.

As Dr. Woodard examined his unconscious son, Mandie and Sallie explained how they got there.

Mandie clung to Uncle John, while Sallie hugged her grandfather.

"The Catawba man, Running Fire, is the one who has been tearing down the hospital," Mandie told them. "He's a medicine man."

"That explains a lot of things," said Dr. Woodard.

Mandie knelt beside Joe, watching the doctor work. "Will he be all right, Dr. Woodard?" she asked, trembling. In the dim light, she could again see the dried blood and bruises on Joe's ashen face.

A tired, worried frown creased the doctor's forehead. "We'll see," he said. "We must get him in a warm bed at once."

Dimar and Uncle Wirt returned with two heavy blankets.

"We make bed," Uncle Ned told them. Laying one blanket on the ground, he waited for Dr. Woodard to move Joe onto it. Uncle Ned covered Joe with the other blanket, then motioned to Uncle Wirt, Uncle John, and Dimar to help him pick up the corners to form a hammock-like bed for carrying Joe.

Dr. Woodard protested being left out of the operation. "I could carry one corner," he said.

"No, it's better you stay right alongside him," Uncle John replied as the party started off through the woods, carrying the sick boy to Uncle Ned's house.

CHAPTER TWELVE

CAPTURED!

Tsa'ni carried the lantern as he led Morning Star and Elizabeth to the hospital site. They met no one and heard nothing. Now and then they stopped to call the girls' names, but received no answer.

Elizabeth was becoming frantic. She wished she knew how to contact John to get his help.

While Tsa'ni and the women were searching the woods, the men arrived at Uncle Ned's house with Joe. When they entered the cabin, they looked around but found no one home.

"Where is Elizabeth? And Morning Star?" Uncle John said. "Elizabeth! Elizabeth!" he called up the ladder to the attic room. No answer. "Now, don't tell me they've disappeared, too," he said.

Mandie quickly climbed the ladder, looked around, and came back down. Then she saw the note on the table. She ran to pick it up. "Uncle John, they've gone to look for Sallie and me," she said, handing him the note.

"Of all things," said Uncle John, reading the note. "We can't seem to get all of us together. It's dark out there now. There's no telling where they are."

Uncle Ned helped Dr. Woodard put Joe in one of the beds near the fireplace, then stirred up the fire. "Morning Star know woods. Not get lost," he said.

"But it's getting late, Uncle Ned. We'd better go find them," Uncle John said.

"Yes, we find," Uncle Wirt spoke up.

"I will go, too," Dimar volunteered.

"Amanda, you and Sallie be sure you stay right here with Dr. Woodard," said Uncle John. "Don't set foot out of this house for any reason at all. Do you hear me?"

"Yes, sir, I understand," Mandie replied meekly. "I'm sorry we caused so much trouble. We won't ever go looking for flowers again."

"I am sorry, too," Sallie added.

"Dr. Woodard may need your help with Joe anyway," said Uncle John. "We'll be back as soon as we find your mother and Morning Star."

Uncle Wirt gave Dr. Woodard a rifle. "Catawba man come, you shoot," he said.

"Well, I'll sure slow him up with this if he comes messing around here," Dr. Woodard replied. He stood the rifle by the bed and turned back to Joe. "Girls, will you get me a pan of hot water?"

"Sure, Dr. Woodard," Mandie answered, quickly obeying.

As Uncle John and the others left, Sallie closed the door behind them and put the crossbar in place.

When Mandie returned with the hot water, Dr. Woodard bathed his son's wounds and applied some medicine. Then he placed a hot brick at the bottom of Joe's bed to keep his feet warm.

Joe remained unconscious, and Dr. Woodard stayed right by the bed.

The men hadn't been gone long when they spotted a lighted lantern ahead.

"That must be them," said Uncle John. "No one else would be going around with a lighted lantern when we've all been trying to catch up with those crooks."

As the men moved closer, they saw the two women and Tsa'ni searching the bushes.

"Tsa'ni told us he was going home when we saw him," Uncle John said, confused.

"Tsa'ni!" Uncle Wirt called.

Tsa'ni and the women stopped and looked around. The men quickly came within the light of the lantern.

Elizabeth ran to John, and he eagerly wrapped his arms around her.

"Oh, John," she sobbed, "Amanda and Sallie are missing."

"No, they aren't. We just took them home, along with Joe," John told her, smoothing her soft, blonde hair.

"Thank the Lord!" Elizabeth cried.

When John explained what had happened, the women were joyous, eager to get back to the house. Tsa'ni said nothing.

As they started back to Uncle Ned's house, by way of the hospital site, Tsa'ni took the lead, carrying the lighted lantern. When they came around the corner of the hospital, they almost tripped over Running Fire and his two sons, who were dozing under a nearby tree in the darkness.

Startled, the three troublesome Indians grabbed their guns and jumped to their feet.

Uncle John and Uncle Ned quickly stepped in front of the women and drew their rifles. Everyone was silent, waiting for the other to make the first move.

"We know all about you," Uncle John warned the three.

"Drop gun or we shoot!" Uncle Wirt yelled at them.

Running Fire took one step forward. "*You* drop gun or *we* shoot," he snarled.

Uncle Ned's eyes flashed with anger. "You, Catawba man, drop that gun. Cherokees all about in woods."

Tsa'ni quietly slipped behind a tree trunk and blew out the lantern. In the pitch-black darkness he quickly jumped on top of Running Fire.

The other men realized what he was doing, and also made a dive for the strangers. The Catawba men were outnumbered, and Uncle Ned's party soon had them under control. As Uncle Wirt quickly tied their hands, Dimar took their rifles.

Uncle John approached Running Fire.

The Catawba man cringed.

"Do not touch me, white man!" he yelled. "I am Running Fire, the medicine man for all Catawbas."

"I know who you are," Uncle John replied. "And I won't touch you. You're too filthy for me to dirty my hands on. But let me tell you this. If you and your family are not long gone by sunup, you will wish you were. Every Cherokee in the nation will be hunting you. And they will do more serious things to you than we are."

"Dirty crook!" Uncle Ned spat at the old man. "Hurt doctor boy. Hide Papooses."

Uncle Wirt shook his big hands at them. "You here sunup I take you apart."

Dimar spoke up. "And I will help. I am young and I am strong."

Tsa'ni stood silently listening. Then he stepped forward and pushed the three strangers.

"Get! Now!" he yelled at them.

The Catawbas, anxiously glancing behind them, ran through the woods with their hands still tied together and disappeared.

Uncle John turned to Uncle Ned and asked, "Do you think they will leave?"

"If they do not leave, we make them leave," Uncle Ned assured him. "Must get message to other Cherokees now to watch and see they leave. Also tell Cherokees Joe found."

"I will spread the word," Dimar offered.

Tsa'ni stepped forward, saying, "And I will help."

Everyone turned in surprise. Tsa'ni was finally volunteering. The two boys hurried off into the woods on their mission.

Uncle Ned, Uncle Wirt, and Uncle John trudged back through the woods to Uncle Ned's house, with the women carefully surrounded.

What would they find at Uncle Ned's house? Would Joe be all right? Would anyone else have disappeared?

CHAPTER THIRTEEN

TOMORROW . . .

Dr. Woodard was still sitting beside Joe's bed when the others returned. Mandie and Sallie sat nearby on the floor. They jumped when Uncle Ned knocked on the door.

"Let us in," he called. "We home."

The girls raced to the door and removed the crossbar. Mandie ran to her mother's arms while Sallie embraced her grandmother.

As they all gathered around the warm fire, the men told how they had met Running Fire and his sons in the woods and ordered them to leave Cherokee territory, and the girls related their adventures to Elizabeth and Morning Star.

Suddenly, in the midst of the excitement, Joe opened his eyes. "What's going on?" he asked weakly.

Everyone gathered around his bed, grateful that he had regained consciousness.

His father gripped his hand and smiled. "Well, it's like this, son. We brought you back here to Uncle Ned's house, the crooks have been caught, and everything seems to be under control," said Dr. Woodard, wiping the perspiration from his brow.

Mandie ran over to Joe, knelt by the bed, and took his hand. "Oh, Joe!" she cried. "I'm so glad you're getting well."

Joe smiled at her. "I have to get well," he said in a stronger voice. "Remember, we're going to get married when we get grown."

Tears welled up in Mandie's eyes, and she buried her face in the covers.

Joe patted her blonde head. "Now, please get me some food, woman. I'm hungry. And not any of that owl stew stuff either," Joe teased.

"Now I know you're better!" Mandie cried. Getting to her feet, she went to see what Morning Star had cooked that day.

Morning Star had understood Joe's request and was already ladling soup from the big black iron pot into a bowl. She handed it to Mandie with a smile. Mandie took it and hurried back to the bed.

"Can you sit up to eat this?" she asked.

"No, you're going to have to feed me," Joe said with a sly grin.

His father looked at him disapprovingly. "Now, Joe, come on," he said. "I'll prop you up on the pillows. Here." He smiled as he tried to make the bed more comfortable.

"I'll hold the bowl," Mandie offered. "You use the spoon and eat this good soup."

Joe propped himself up on one elbow and began to eat the soup slowly. He seemed to revive as the hot broth went down. When he had eaten all he could, he moved a little to stretch. "Oh, I'm sore!" he said. "Those men beat me up."

"We know," said Uncle John, "but they won't be bothering you or anyone else around here. They were ordered out of the territory and the Cherokees are all watching to make sure they leave."

Everyone joined in a garbled explanation of what had happened since the Catawba men took Joe.

Joe was furious when he heard that Mandie and Sallie had also been kidnapped. "It's good they will be gone by the time I can get out of this bed. I'd like to take care of them myself," he said.

Just then Tsa'ni and Dimar came in, having relayed their message to the other Cherokees.

When Mandie saw Tsa'ni, she knew she had to ease her guilty conscience. Embarrassed, she slowly walked over to him. "Tsa'ni, I must beg your forgiveness," she began, clearing her throat nervously. She never knew what reaction she would get from the Indian boy.

"For what?" Tsa'ni asked sullenly.

"I wrongly accused you of tearing down the hospital walls and of knowing where Joe was. I know now that I was wrong, very wrong. I'm sorry, Tsa'ni. I ask you to forgive me," she said.

The others listened silently.

"You will get your hospital built," Tsa'ni replied. "I know now that the hospital is necessary for the advancement of the Cherokees. We must catch up with and pass the white man. For many, many years the Cherokees have been held back and had no chance to improve. No more. The hospital will be built," Tsa'ni declared.

"But, Tsa'ni, will you forgive me?" Mandie repeated.

"Accusations of the white man do not matter to me because—" Tsa'ni paused. He hung his head and then straightened up to look Mandie in the eye. "I cannot be angry with you because, after all, you are my cousin. I am sorry, too." He grinned and held out his hand.

Mandie gripped his hand tightly and looked upward. *Dear God,* she prayed silently, *please forgive me.* Looking back at Tsa'ni, she smiled. "Thank you, Tsa'ni, for forgiving me. I love you, my cousin."

Tsa'ni stuck his hand in his pocket and sauntered off to the other side of the room.

Uncle Ned put his arm around Mandie's shoulders and steered her to another corner of the room. "Papoose must think with head," he said softly. "Think before Papoose does things. Over and over Papoose do something then think. Backward way. Must think first. Must remember. Think first. Think first."

Mandie reached up to grasp his hand on her shoulder. "I will try, Uncle Ned. I will try real hard," she promised.

"Big Book say not judge," the old Indian reminded her.

"I know. 'Judge not, that ye be not judged,'" she quoted the Bible verse. "I'm going to do my best, and I hope you'll help me," she said, smiling up at him.

"I help," said Uncle Ned. "I promise Jim Shaw I watch over Papoose when he go to happy hunting ground. I keep promise."

"I love you, Uncle Ned," said Mandie as they embraced.

A few minutes later, Mandie turned her attention back to Joe and his father. "Dr. Woodard, how long will it take Joe to recover?" she asked.

"He should be well enough to go home in a day or two," the doctor replied.

"Oh, that's wonderful!" said Mandie. Relieved that Joe was going to be all right, she looked over at her mother and Uncle John. "Can we still go to Charleston?" she asked hopefully.

"I don't see any reason why we can't leave first thing in the morning," Uncle John replied.

Mandie could hardly contain her excitement. At last she would get to see the great big ocean!

MANDIE

AND THE
CHARLESTON
PHANTOM

With Thanks
to
J.M.B.

CONTENTS

MANDIE AND THE CHARLESTON PHANTOM

"Be ye angry, and sin not:
let not the sun go down upon your wrath."
Ephesians 4:26

CHAPTER ONE

MEAN WORDS, HURT FEELINGS

Mandie Shaw stared at her friend Joe in disbelief. "Why shouldn't I go to Charleston?" she asked, rocking her Uncle John's porch swing back and forth in irritation.

"Because you're *my* friend," Joe insisted, "and I don't think it's proper for you to go visiting another boy when you promised to marry me someday," he said, slapping his knees with his thin, long-fingered hands for emphasis.

"Joe!" Mandie exclaimed. "I never knew you could be so selfish! I may have promised to marry you, but I was a lot younger then. It will be a long time before we will be grown up enough to get married. I can't promise to never talk to another boy. I don't mind if you talk to other girls."

"Oh, you don't, huh? Well, what about that time you got jealous of Polly Cornwallis because I was nice to her?"

"I didn't get jealous!" Mandie protested, her blue eyes flashing.

"Oh, yes you did," Joe argued.

Mandie's temper rose out of control. She stood up and shook her long skirt. "Joe Woodard, you are the most stupid, selfish, pigheaded boy I've ever met. If you want to get mad because I am going to Charleston to visit Tommy Patton's family and to see the ocean, then you can just get mad!" she yelled. "I *am* going. I don't care what you say!" She whirled angrily and disappeared inside the house.

Pausing in the hallway, she took a deep breath. Just who did Joe think he was, trying to order her around that way? He wasn't going to run her life and tell her what she could and couldn't do. She took another deep breath and ran up the staircase to her room. Her white kitten, Snowball, followed.

In her room, Mandie picked up Snowball and flopped across the blue silk bedspread on her bed. Before, she had been excited about the opportunity to travel with her mother and Uncle John (who was also her stepfather) to Charleston, South Carolina. This was her chance to see the ocean for the first time. Why did Joe have to put a damper on her mood like that? After all, she was only twelve years old, not old enough to make a marriage commitment!

I'll just ignore him if that's the way he wants to be, she thought. I've been waiting for this trip too long to let him spoil it. I'm going to have a good time with Tommy and his family and forget all about Joe Woodard, she decided.

Mandie had first met Tommy Patton when the boys from his school came to visit her school in Asheville, North Carolina. But Tommy's parents had been friends of Elizabeth (Mandie's mother) and Uncle John for many years, and they invited the Shaws to come to Charleston for a visit.

Unfortunately, their stay would have to be a lot shorter than they had planned because Mandie's family, Joe, and his father, Dr. Woodard, had just arrived in Franklin, North Carolina, that afternoon from investigating some vandalism at the Cherokee hospital construction site.

Some time earlier, while exploring an old cave, Mandie and her friends had found a fortune in gold that belonged to the Cherokee Indians. That gold was paying for the Cherokees' hospital.

After they all returned to Franklin, Dr. Woodard had immediately left to make his rounds in the town. Medical doctors were scarce in western North Carolina around the year 1900, and the doctor covered a lot of territory to take care of the sick.

As Mandie lay on her bed, the blue-flowered ceramic clock on the mantelpiece struck six. Mandie jumped up. She glanced in the floor-length mirror and straightened her rumpled pink organdy dress. Then smoothing her long blonde braid, she hurried downstairs to the dining room and met Liza just inside the French doors.

The young Negro girl, hurrying toward the table with a bowl of steaming corn on the cob, stopped and gasped. "Lawsy mercy, Missy, I done forgot," she said. "I'se s'posed to tell you dat yo' ma say fo' you to be in de parlor at six o'clock, and it already be six o'clock, ain't it?"

"That's all right, Liza. I'll go to the parlor right away," Mandie said, turning back into the long, wide hallway.

Hurrying through the double sliding doors, Mandie found her mother and Uncle John on a settee talking to Dr. Woodard. Out of the corner of her eye she saw Joe sulking in a big chair in the corner. Ignoring his stares, Mandie walked toward her mother.

"Amanda, we wanted to talk a little before we go in to eat," Elizabeth Shaw told her daughter. "Sit down for a minute, dear. Dr. Woodard has been telling us about his visit with Hilda this afternoon."

Mandie perched on the edge of a nearby chair and leaned forward. "You saw Hilda, Dr. Woodard?" She felt goosebumps rise on her arms as she remembered the excitement of finding the frightened young girl hiding in the school attic.

"Yes," the doctor nodded slowly. "I went by the sanatorium to see how she was. I thought you might like to know she actually asked for you," Dr. Woodard told her.

"You mean she is talking now?" Mandie cried. "Oh, Dr. Woodard, she has been healed. I've been hoping and praying she would be able to talk soon."

"Well, I wouldn't say she is completely healed. She still needs a lot of loving care, but she is improving. And the doctors at the sanatorium are thinking about letting her leave soon if they can find just the right family to take care of her. Her parents simply are not willing or able to care for her properly."

Mandie's eyes grew wide in excitement. "Imagine! Hilda talking!"

"Yes," the doctor replied. "In fact, her exact words were, 'Where is Mandie? When will she bring me another new dress?' "

Mandie laughed. "She is better! Just think of how she was when we found her—all frightened, couldn't say a word. But she did love my dresses! Dr. Woodard, would you take her one for me?"

"I'll be glad to, Amanda," the doctor said.

"Thank you, Dr. Woodard. After supper, I'll pick one out," Mandie told him. "And as soon as we get back to Asheville, I'll go see her."

"You may not have time, dear," Elizabeth reminded her. "We've been delayed already because of the vandalism at the hospital. Even with the extra days Miss Prudence allowed you, we'll have to push to return you to school on time."

"Maybe y'all shouldn't go to Charleston," Joe said from his corner.

Everyone turned to look at him.

Uncle John frowned. "Joe, you know this trip was planned quite a while ago," he said.

Mandie opened her mouth to speak but thought better of it. She said nothing.

"Yes, sir," Joe replied meekly.

Aunt Lou, the enormous Negro housekeeper, appeared in the doorway. A big white apron covered a plain dark house dress. "Miz 'Lizbeth, de dinner be on de table," she announced.

"We're coming, Aunt Lou. Thank you," Elizabeth said, rising. "Has Mr. Bond returned yet?"

"Yessum, he done brought de tickets back from de depot. He waitin' in de kitchen fo' y'all," the old Negro woman replied.

"Tell him we'll meet him in the dining room, please, Aunt Lou," Elizabeth said.

Jason Bond, caretaker at the Shaws' home, met them at the table. He smiled at Mandie. "Well, all you have to do now is go down and get on the train tomorrow."

Mandie grinned back at him and took her place across the table from Joe. "I'm so excited. I won't sleep tonight!" she exclaimed. "Mr. Jason, I wish you could go with us."

"I'm a mountain man. Don't care about all that water out there at the edge of the country," Mr. Bond said, shaking his head. "Never had no desire to see it."

Liza hurried in with a tray of hot biscuits and placed them next to Mandie. Bending slightly forward, she whispered, "I knows somethin' you don't knows." She rolled her eyes and glanced at the others.

"What?" Mandie whispered back. "Tell you latuh," Liza whispered. Then she danced out of the room.

Mandie hurried through dinner. She couldn't wait to find out what Liza's mysterious message was.

CHAPTER TWO

LIZA'S SECRET

After dinner, Liza was helping Aunt Lou clean up in the kitchen.

"Liza, git dem dishes from de table now," Aunt Lou ordered. "They's all done an' we's got to git movin.' "

With a wink at Mandie, Liza grabbed the large dishpan and hurried into the empty dining room.

Mandie followed right behind her. "What do you know, Liza?" Mandie asked the girl.

"Well, it's like dis," Liza said, beginning to collect the dirty dishes from the table. "I overheerd somethin' you might jes' want to know about."

"Liza, what is it?" Mandie persisted. "Tell me."

"Promise you won't be tellin' I said so?" Liza asked, sticking her finger into the chocolate pudding Joe left untouched by his plate. "Mmm, dat's good!" She took another taste.

"I promise I won't tell that you told me whatever it is you know," Mandie said. "Now what is it, Liza? Mother will be looking for me. We have to finish packing."

Liza's eyes widened. "I sees Missy Polly nextdo' talkin' to de doctuh boy in de yard a while ago," she teased.

"Polly talking to Joe? What were they talking about?"

"It seem Missy Polly gwine to have him over fo' dinnuh when y'all leaves tomorruh," Liza replied.

Mandie looked at the Negro girl questioningly. "Are you sure, Liza?" she asked, feeling her anger return.

"Sho I be sho. Aftuh all, I knows Missy likes de doctuh boy, and I has to watch out fo' Missy's innerests. Now if I wuz you, I'd walk right up to de doctuh boy an' ask him where he gwine to eat dinnuh tomorruh," the girl advised.

Mandie struggled with her thoughts. Joe was jealous about Tommy, yet here he was, planning to have dinner with Polly.

"That's all right, Liza," she said after a moment. "I've decided to forget about Joe and just have a good time while I'm gone. If he wants to eat dinner with Polly and keep it a secret from me, then I might just do something and keep it a secret from him."

"Now, Missy, don't you be goin' doin' things you gwine to regret," Liza warned. "I knows de doctuh boy be sweet on you. But I also knows Missy Polly she be sweet on de doctuh boy, and she don't want you should know."

"Thank you for telling me, Liza, but I'm not going to let it worry me," Mandie assured her. "Nothing is going to spoil this trip."

Aunt Lou thrust her head through the doorway from the kitchen. "Liza! Git dem dishes in heah! Right now!" the old woman yelled.

Liza almost dropped the dishpan but hurried along, gathering up dirty dishes from the table.

"Thanks, Liza," Mandie called as her friend scurried into the kitchen.

So, Mandie thought to herself, *as soon as I'm out of sight, Joe is chasing Polly, huh?* She went up to her room to get the dress for Hilda. Well, not exactly chasing Polly, she admitted, but allowing Polly to chase him. Yet he was throwing a fit because she was going to visit Tommy and his family.

Taking a lavender organdy dress from its hanger, she hurried back downstairs to the parlor, where everyone sat quietly talking.

Mandie sighed as she entered the room. She had thought she could get away from Joe for the evening, but he sat slouched in the corner chair again.

She turned to her mother. "May I give this dress to Hilda?" she asked.

"Yes, that will be fine," Elizabeth said.

Mandie handed the dress to Dr. Woodard and sat down in a big chair in the opposite corner from Joe. He glared at her, but she pretended not to see him.

Uncle John was talking to Dr. Woodard. "You and Joe are welcome to stay here as long as you wish, of course," he said.

"I know that, John, but I reckon we'll be heading home tomorrow," Dr. Woodard replied. "We've been gone long enough."

Joe sat up straight and scowled. "We're going home tomorrow? But I figured we wouldn't be leaving until the day after tomorrow."

"That's what I thought, too, son, but I finished all my calls today except one. I have to see Mrs. Gaines early tomorrow morning, and then we'll leave," he replied.

"We will?" Joe looked pale.

Mandie smiled inwardly. So he would miss having dinner with Polly.

"In that case I'd better get my things together," Joe said, jumping to his feet.

Elizabeth smiled at him. "We'll see you in the morning, Joe. We have to get back to our packing, too, in a few minutes," she said.

"Yes, ma'am," Joe replied. "Good night, everybody." He hurried out of the room.

Mandie rose slowly from her chair. "I think I'll go finish my packing, too."

"I'll be with you in a few minutes, dear," Elizabeth told her.

Mandie ran upstairs. Inside her room, she blew out the oil lamp and watched from the window. In a minute she saw Joe slip out into the yard and head for the Cornwallises' house. She laughed when she saw Liza sneaking along behind him.

It was funny. Joe's plans had been changed but hers would go ahead as scheduled.

When Mandie heard her mother coming up the stairs, she hastily relighted the oil lamp and turned to the open trunk at the foot of the bed.

Elizabeth entered the bedroom and looked around. "It looks like you're almost ready, but be sure you take your parasols, dear. It's always much warmer in Charleston than it is here, and we don't want the sun to make freckles pop out on that pretty nose, do we?" Elizabeth said, putting her arm around her daughter.

"Oh, I wouldn't mind if I had one or two. It'd be something different, Mother," Mandie said, laughing.

"Well, I mind, dear. Freckles would spoil your face, so just be sure you pack enough sun bonnets and parasols."

"Yes, Mother," Mandie promised, her mind occupied with what Joe was doing.

"I guess I'll say good-night to you now. When you finish, you had better go right to bed and get plenty of rest." Her mother started to leave the room. "I'll wake you early in the morning. Good night, dear."

"I'll probably be awake before you are, Mother. In fact, I probably won't sleep all night," Mandie replied.

As soon as her mother closed the door, Mandie blew out the lamp again and huddled on the window seat to watch for Joe to return. But as tired as she was from the other trip, she soon fell asleep. Awakening later in the night, she stumbled sleepily into bed and went right back to sleep.

Morning came sunshiny and bright. But everyone was up before daylight, bustling about until it was time to go to the depot. Throughout all the preparations, Mandie had managed to avoid Joe, but she couldn't get Liza alone until the last minute.

"I saw you last night, Liza," Mandie whispered to the Negro maid as they started down the stairway together. Snowball snuggled on Mandie's shoulder.

"I follow de doctuh boy. He tell Missy Polly his pa say he got to go home today and he can't have no dinnuh wid huh," Liza whispered.

"I thought so," Mandie answered softly.

"But he also say he gwine to have dinnuh wid huh next time he come to town," Liza added.

Mandie stopped in her tracks. Well, how do you like that? she thought. He does plan to have dinner with Polly eventually.

"Amanda," Elizabeth called from the downstairs hall.

"You have a good time, Missy," Liza told her as they reached the bottom of the stairs.

"Thank you, Liza. You keep watch for me while I'm gone."

Liza grinned and nodded.

"Amanda," Elizabeth said, "I do hope the Pattons don't mind our bringing Snowball with us. Some people don't like cats, you know."

"They won't mind, Mother. Snowball isn't like most cats. He's smart," Mandie said, following her out onto the porch.

Mr. Bond waited in the rig to take the Shaws to the train depot. Dr. Woodard and all of the servants lined up along the bannister to say goodbye, but Joe sat in the porch swing alone.

"Goodbye, everybody!" Mandie called out quickly, running to board the rig. She waved her hand around in the air to include everyone, but she avoided looking at Joe.

A chorus of goodbyes rang out as Elizabeth and John hurried down the porch steps to join her.

Out of the corner of her eye, Mandie saw Joe just sitting there on the swing, his arms folded. She sat back and settled Snowball in her lap as Mr. Bond whipped up the horse.

Uncle John winked at Mandie. "Well, we're on our way," he said.

"Yes, we're finally on our way, and I intend to have a wonderful time!" Mandie exclaimed, stroking Snowball's soft fur. She squared her shoulders and lifted her head, trying to put Joe out of her mind. *I'm going to forget all about everything here and enjoy my trip,* she determined.

But in her stomach, she felt a little quake at the thought of Joe's silent parting.

CHAPTER THREE

TO CHARLESTON AT LAST!

The journey to Charleston was long. Mandie excitedly wished the time away until she would finally get there. Although they had a layover in the city of Columbia, the capital of South Carolina, there was not enough time to see the town.

After they again boarded the train for the second part of their journey, Elizabeth put her arm on Mandie's shoulder. "This is our last stop, Amanda. We'll go straight to Charleston on this train."

Mandie quickly took a seat by the window in front of her mother and Uncle John. Giving Snowball a little squeeze, she smiled. "Then we'll soon see the ocean," she said with a sigh.

"No, actually we won't be able to see the ocean from the train on the way into Charleston," Uncle John explained. "The Pattons will probably be waiting for us at the depot, and we'll go to their house first."

The train jerked forward, picked up speed, and began a steady roaring motion.

"Then we'll just ask them to take us to see it," Mandie said. "I hope this train goes faster than the one we were just on."

But the train didn't seem any faster. In fact it seemed to crawl at first. Then the landscape began to change, and Mandie became interested in the scenery. There were huge forests of tall pines. Then the land gave way to swamps. Pools of stagnant water stood everywhere alongside the railroad tracks. Water lilies grew in some places, and sometimes the train traveled on a trestle high above the swampland.

Mandie noticed something growing on the trees. "Look! What is that on those trees?" she exclaimed, turning to look back at her mother and Uncle John. "It's a funny gray color, and it looks like giant spiderwebs."

"That's Spanish moss, Amanda," Uncle John told her.

"It sure looks like it must grow awfully fast. It's everywhere," Mandie replied. She leaned against the half-open window for a closer look as the train chugged along through the eerie-looking scene.

"It does grow fast," said Uncle John. "You might want to take a piece of it back home and see if it'll grow on a tree there. Sometimes you can get it to hang on for a while before it shrivels and dies. Our climate at home gets too cold for it."

"No thanks!" Mandie suddenly shoved the window down. "Whew! It smells awful out there!" she exclaimed, holding her nose.

"That's the sulphur in the swamps that you smell, Amanda," her mother explained. "Charleston will definitely have a different odor than our fresh, clean mountain air at home."

"Don't tell me it's going to smell bad the whole time we're there!" Mandie moaned.

"It's a different smell, but after you've been there for a few hours, you won't even notice it," Elizabeth said. "Besides, you'll have too much to see to bother about what you smell."

Mandie laughed. "Tommy never told me about the odor. He just told me the nice things about his hometown."

"He probably thought you wouldn't notice it." Uncle John chuckled. "He'll keep you entertained so well you'll never realize that things don't smell exactly like they do back home."

"I hope so," Mandie said.

After what seemed an eternity, a huge body of water came into view. Mandie quickly pushed the window back up to see out. "Look at all that water!" she cried.

"That's the Ashley River, dear," Elizabeth told her. "We'll also see the Cooper River on our left as we get closer."

"It sure is a big river," Mandie exclaimed.

"It's actually a lot bigger than what you can see right here," Uncle John said. "In fact, after we get to the Pattons' home, we'll take a ferryboat across the Cooper River to the Isle of Palms. The Isle of Palms is on the Atlantic Ocean."

"Oh, I just can't wait to get my first look at the ocean!" Mandie squealed.

"I'm afraid you're going to have to wait," Elizabeth teased.

Soon the bare, swampy landscape gave way to farms, and buildings, and houses—they were approaching the city of Charleston.

Mandie had never seen such a big city with so many, many houses and buildings. Palm trees grew everywhere. She sat motionless as her big blue eyes took it all in.

Finally, the train crawled to a stop in the depot, and Mandie spied Tommy waiting with his family on the platform. "There's Tommy, right there, Mother," she said, pointing.

"Yes, dear, now get your bag and let's go to meet them," Elizabeth said, taking her own bag down from the rack above. Uncle John carried the two largest bags.

Mandie quickly pushed her long blonde hair back under her bonnet and smoothed the long skirt of her wine-colored traveling suit. She felt self-conscious meeting Tommy face-to-face in his own territory.

Holding Snowball securely, she hung her purse on her arm and picked up her small traveling bag. She followed her mother and Uncle John out onto the platform of the train and down the steps to greet the waiting Pattons.

The tall, nicely dressed man and elegant woman standing beside Tommy came forward, followed by a young girl with glasses.

"Lucille! George! It's so good to see you again," Elizabeth said as she set down her bag and gave the woman a tight squeeze.

"You look wonderful, Elizabeth," Lucille Patton replied. "You, too, John."

"Thanks, Lucille," Uncle John said. "How are you, George?"

George Patton shook John's hand. "We're glad y'all could come," he said. Turning, he looked at Mandie. "So this is Amanda. Welcome to Charleston and the great big ocean, young lady." He reached out to rub Snowball's head as the cat clung to Mandie's shoulder. "I see you brought your cat," he said, a little uncertainly. "Tommy has told us all about Snowball."

"Thank you for having us, sir," Mandie said, smiling up at him.

Mr. Patton was about the tallest man Mandie had ever seen. *No wonder Tommy is so tall,* she thought. Mr. Patton had a friendly smile and Mandie liked him at once.

"We're glad to have you with us." Lucille Patton repeated the welcome but seemed to shy away from the cat. "We hope you enjoy your visit."

"Thank you, ma'am. I know I shall," Mandie replied in her best ladylike language. Apparently there was some use for the silly things she was learning at the Misses Heathwood's School for Girls in Asheville, North Carolina. She supposed it was for people like this.

Tommy stepped forward and looked at Mandie with admiration. "May I add my own hello?" he asked. "I haven't seen you since last month, and I've never met your parents."

Mandie smiled at Tommy, still feeling a little self-conscious.

"By the way," Tommy added, "this is my sister, Josephine." He motioned to the nearsighted girl beside him.

Josephine looked like she was about the same age as Mandie, perhaps a year older. She was skinny and almost as tall as her brother. Her long, straight dark brown hair fell over her shoulders as she merely nodded at the introduction. Her black eyes seemed magnified by her thick wire-rim glasses, which kept slipping down on her nose.

For some reason, Mandie instantly disliked the girl, and the feeling seemed mutual.

When they all boarded the Pattons' phaeton nearby, Mandie noticed that Josephine walked with a slight limp. Tommy made sure he sat beside Mandie in the open carriage.

As the Pattons' two horses drew the four-wheeled carriage through the city streets, Tommy pointed out landmarks while the adults visited up front. Josephine sat across from Mandie, squinting at her in spite of her thick glasses.

Mandie studied her surroundings carefully. "Everything is so big, and so old, and so close together," she observed. "And so beautiful," she added as they passed St. Philip's Church.

"Of course," Josephine taunted. "This is a big city, not a hicktown like Asheville."

"Josephine!" Tommy scowled at her. "Asheville isn't a hicktown. It's a good-sized city. Besides, you can't compare the two. Charleston is much older and therefore has had more time to grow and expand." He turned to Mandie. "Charleston was the capital of South Carolina until Columbia was built in 1789," he explained.

"That's interesting," Mandie said, "but when am I going to see the ocean?"

"I think my parents are planning on taking you there as soon as we eat," Tommy replied.

"Thank goodness I don't have to wait too long," Mandie said.

"I'm sure you'll be disappointed," Josephine told her. "It's nothing but a huge body of water moving around like somebody was whipping cake batter."

"Josephine, will you please stop deflating everything for Mandie?" Tommy pleaded.

"I'm not deflating anything. I'm only stating facts so she isn't disappointed," his sister replied. "There are two sides to everything. If you're going to build things up, then I have to try to bring them back down into perspective."

Mandie looked from one to the other. Josephine was ruining everything. Since Mandie was the Pattons' guest, she must behave herself and ignore Josephine's rude remarks. But she wished she could talk to Tommy alone.

CHAPTER FOUR

THE GREAT BIG WONDERFUL OCEAN!

Finally the phaeton stopped in front of a huge three-story brick building behind a high wall. Mandie stared through the gate.

"Home at last," Tommy said.

Mandie looked at him in disbelief. "Don't tell me this is your house."

"It's the house we live in when we're in the city," Tommy explained as everyone began leaving the carriage. "Most of the time we live at the rice plantation. You'll see that, too, before you leave. It's way out on the Ashley River. We also have a small house on the beach, and we'll spend some time there with you, as well."

"Three houses!" Mandie exclaimed.

Tommy laughed and gathered up the bags.

Josephine leaned close to Mandie. "Yes, three houses," she whispered, "and they're all haunted!"

"What?" Mandie asked sharply.

But the girl ran ahead, ignoring her.

A uniformed servant came from the house to help with the baggage.

As Mandie entered the mansion, she felt as if she were in a dreamland. She had thought her Uncle John's house was a mansion, but it was nothing compared with this.

The entry hall had a marble floor and a marble staircase rising out of sight to the upper stories. Gold and silver sparkled everywhere she looked. Velvet and silk draped the windows and upholstered the chairs. There was nothing inexpensive. Old portraits lined the wallpapered walls.

Mandie stopped to gaze at the painting of a beautiful young lady with long black hair and blue eyes who was wearing a low-cut, frilly pink gown trimmed with lace. In one hand she held a fan made of pink feathers.

Josephine noticed Mandie's interest and limped up beside her. "That is Melissa Patton," she whispered. "She was murdered in this very house. When the moon is full, she can be seen pacing the widow's walk. That's where she was pushed to her death."

Mandie's blue eyes grew round as she listened, holding Snowball tightly.

Tommy saw the two girls talking and stepped forward. "Josephine, you're not telling Mandie any stories, are you?" he asked.

"I'm only telling the truth," Josephine replied.

"The truth is that no one knows what actually happened to Melissa," Tommy said.

Josephine turned and limped quickly up the staircase.

"Josephine, wait!" Mrs. Patton called, stifling a sneeze. "I want you to show Amanda to her room."

Josephine paused on the stairs. "Yes, Mama," she said in a sarcastic tone. "And I know, help her feel at home."

Mrs. Patton looked at her daughter sharply, then smiled at Mandie reassuringly. "She will show you upstairs, dear. After you have refreshed yourself, come back down and we'll have a bite to eat." Taking a lacy handkerchief from her pocket, she dabbed her watering eyes. "Then I think we'll get the ferryboat and take you to see the ocean." Her nose began to twitch, and she sneezed daintily into her handkerchief.

"God bless you," Mandie said. Then her face broke into a big smile. "We really get to go to the ocean soon? Oh, thank you, ma'am. Thank you. I'll hurry!" She put Snowball down and hurried after Josephine with Snowball at her heels.

Josephine led the way along the second floor hallway. "You are to stay in the blue room, which is next door to mine," she said. "We'll be far away from the other rooms." Josephine stopped to push open a door at the end of the hallway.

Mandie looked inside. It was truly a blue room. All the furnishings were in various shades of blue. Even the wallpaper had a blue tint. She clasped her hands in delight and just stood there, admiring the beautiful room.

"Well, are you going in or not?" Josephine asked, squinting through her glasses. "I see Rouster has already put your things in here."

"Thank you, Josephine," Mandie said uncertainly. For some reason, she didn't trust Tommy's sister. "I think I can find the way back by myself. I'll see you downstairs in a few minutes." Mandie stepped inside and shut the door.

Snowball immediately jumped onto the bed. Mandie took off her bonnet and started to look for her hairbrush in her bag.

Suddenly the door opened. Mandie jumped.

"I forgot to tell you where the bathroom is," Josephine said with a laugh. "It's through that door over there across the hall. We share it," she said, quickly shutting the door again.

Mandie was worn out from her trip, but she was also jumpy because of Josephine's remark about their houses being haunted. She didn't want to be left alone in this isolated part of the big house. Hurrying into the bathroom, she washed her face and hands.

Leaving her purse in her room, she called to Snowball, and he followed her down the long hallway to the staircase. At the foot of the stairs Mandie encountered a very small Negro girl in a maid's uniform. The girl didn't look old enough to be a maid.

"Hello," Mandie said.

"They all be in de drawing room. Last door on de right," the girl told her. "Let me take dat kitty and feed him." The girl picked up Snowball, and he didn't protest.

"Thank you." Mandie continued down the first-floor hallway toward the huge ornate door the girl had pointed to. Just inside the doorway, Mandie stood and stared. The drawing room looked as though it belonged in a palace. Mandie had never seen such finery. The furniture was upholstered in peach-and-gray silk brocade. The draperies were a darker shade of gray with golden tassels. The carpet, which covered much of the parqueted floor, was so thick her little heels sank in deeply.

Everyone was sitting around a gray stone fireplace that covered almost an entire wall. Mandie was drawn to the portrait hanging over the fireplace. She felt sure it was a duplicate of the one of Melissa Patton in the hallway. At closer inspection, she could see it wasn't the same girl, but there was a strong resemblance. This girl was also dressed in pink, but she was definitely older, and her eyes were brown.

Tommy came to her side. "That's Melissa Patton, too, only this Melissa is the other one's mother," he told her. "This one was my father's grandmother."

"It's nice to have your ancestors' portraits hanging around where you can see them," Mandie said, smiling. "Where I come from, we're lucky to have an old tintype."

Uncle John heard the remark and looked up. "You know, Amanda, we do have some tintypes of your father that could possibly be made into a portrait by a good artist," he said.

Mandie's heart beat faster. "Pictures of my father? Honest? Please let me see them when we go home."

"Of course, Amanda. We'll go through all the old pictures we have packed away," her uncle promised.

Mandie again studied the portrait of Melissa Patton over the fireplace. "Her face reminds me a little bit of Hilda," she said, hardly realizing she had spoken the words aloud.

"Who's Hilda?" Tommy asked.

Just then Josephine came into the room followed by one of the maids. The maid cleared her throat. "Everything be ready," she announced.

"Thank you, Tizzy," said Mrs. Patton. Then gracefully rising from her chair, she turned to the others in the room. "Shall we eat?" she asked, leading the way into the dining room.

"I'll tell you about Hilda later," Mandie whispered to Tommy.

Inside the elegant dining room, again Mandie could only stare. She felt as though she had stepped into another world. Having been born and raised for most of her young life in a log cabin in the western

North Carolina mountains, she still couldn't get used to such finery. She felt uncomfortable trying to act like a young lady all the time. Even Tommy seemed more reserved. When he had visited her at school, he had always seemed a happy-go-lucky boy who enjoyed breaking staid customs.

At the long table that would have easily seated thirty people, Mandie found herself next to Tommy, across from Josephine. Snowball rubbed around Mandie's ankles under the table.

After Mr. Patton asked the blessing and everyone began eating, Tommy asked Mandie about Hilda.

"It's really a long story, but to make it short, Hilda is a girl about my age whom Celia and I found—" Mandie interrupted herself. "You remember Celia from school, don't you?"

Tommy nodded.

"Well," Mandie continued, "Celia and I found this girl, Hilda, hiding in the school attic."

"Really?" Tommy exclaimed. "What was she doing there?"

Suddenly everyone at the table was listening as Mandie related the story about hearing clinking noises in the attic at night. "I must admit that at one point we thought it was a ghost," Mandie said with a laugh. "But I don't think I believe in ghosts anymore." She stared directly at Josephine.

Josephine looked away and continued eating in silence.

"What was making the noise?" Mrs. Patton asked from the other end of the table. "I didn't hear."

"This poor, scared girl named Hilda," Mandie replied. "She had run away from home and hid in the school attic. By the time we found her, she was sick, she was *very* hungry, and she was unable to talk. It turns out that her parents thought she was insane and had kept her locked up at home."

"Oh, the poor dear," Mrs. Patton's face clouded with concern.

Mr. Patton sat forward with interest. "What happened to her?" he asked.

Mandie smiled. "Our friend Dr. Woodard got her into the sanatorium and she's doing much better. He told me she's even talking a little bit now, and they might let her leave soon if they can find a good family to take care of her."

Lucille Patton's eyes twinkled. She turned to her husband. "Did you hear that, George?"

"Sounds interesting, doesn't it?" her husband replied.

Josephine pushed her glasses up on her nose and squirmed around in her seat.

Suddenly, Mrs. Patton began sneezing repeatedly.

"Mother, are you catching cold?" Josephine asked.

"Oh, excuse me," she apologized, getting up to leave. "Sometimes I just get these sneezing spells . . ."

Just then, Snowball ran out from under the table and finding Mandie, hopped up on her lap.

"Especially around cats." Mrs. Patton covered her nose with her handkerchief and hurried out of the room, sneezing over and over.

Elizabeth looked at her daughter. "Amanda, I wondered about bringing Snowball."

"Nonsense," Mr. Patton said. "We love having Snowball here. Lucille will just have to avoid getting too close. That kitten is important to Amanda, so he is certainly welcome."

The rest of the meal didn't last long because everyone was in a hurry to get to the ferryboat.

The boat ride across the Cooper River was refreshing and exciting to Mandie. She was glad she had left Snowball back at the house so she didn't have to keep track of him.

As the boat moved slowly forward, she and Tommy stood at the rail, staring at the swirling water below. The adults sat talking nearby, and Josephine squinted through her thick glasses and limped about, curiously taking in all the sights on the crowded ferry.

After they docked at the river side of the Isle of Palms, Mr. Patton excused himself to find a rig that would take them over to the ocean side.

While the others waited, Mandie bent down and picked up some sand, allowing it to trickle through her gloved fingers. "What beautiful sand! It's so white!" she exclaimed. Hastily removing her gloves, she did it again. This time she laughed. "It feels so nice and soft and warm."

Tommy's dark brown eyes twinkled as he watched her. "Yes, it does," he said. "Just wait till you get to the other side."

As they rode across the island in the rig, at everyone's insistence, Mandie sat on the front seat so she could see the ocean as soon as it came into view.

In a little while, they rounded a curve, and through a clump of palm trees Mandie caught her first glimpse of the huge body of water. Before the rig completely stopped, she jumped down. Tommy immediately followed, keeping her from falling. Racing across the wet sand of the beach, they stopped at the edge of the water and watched as the big waves lapped inward.

Tears of joy filled Mandie's blue eyes. "Oh, what a wonderful thing God created!" she cried. "How beautiful! I never imagined it could be this great!" She had to yell above the sound of the water crashing around.

"You must get your feet wet to really enjoy it," Tommy told her.

"My feet wet?" Mandie frowned up at him. "My mother would never allow that."

Elizabeth and Uncle John came up behind them.

"I imagine your mother would allow that this one time," Elizabeth told her daughter.

"Really, Mother?" Mandie's eyes grew wide in amazement.

"Sit down in the rig and remove your shoes and stockings. Be sure to tuck up your skirt so it doesn't get wet," Elizabeth instructed.

"Like Tommy says," Uncle John added, "you've got to get your feet wet to fully understand what it's all about."

"Oh, thank you!" Mandie cried, racing back toward the rig.

In only a minute, she ran barefooted back down to the water's edge, holding her skirt high.

Tommy had already removed his shoes and rolled up his pants legs. Taking her hand, he led her into the water.

Mandie squealed with delight. The cool, wet sand squished between her toes, and the waves swirled around her legs. She giggled and swished about with Tommy holding her hand to keep her from falling.

Mandie knew the adults were standing on the beach, laughing at her antics, but she didn't care. She was having fun. At least she wasn't like Josephine, standing alone and brooding.

Finally, Elizabeth called to Mandie. "We must go now, Amanda. It's getting late."

"Do we have to, Mother?" Mandie called back above the roar of the water.

"Yes, I'm sorry, but we do," her mother answered.

"That's all right," Tommy told her. "We're going to our house on the beach tomorrow."

"We are?" Mandie asked.

Tommy led her out of the water and up the beach. "Mother wanted to spend the first night in the city so you could see the town," Tommy explained. "Tomorrow morning we're going to show you around. Then in the afternoon we're all going to the beach house."

"I'm so glad you asked me to Charleston, Tommy," Mandie said.

"And I'm glad you could come," he replied.

Again Elizabeth called to her. "Go ahead and get your things on, Amanda," she said. "We'll be there in a minute."

Mandie hurried to the rig and brushed the wet sand from her feet. Josephine followed her.

While Mandie was putting on her silk stockings and slippers, Josephine leaned down and spoke to her quietly. "Just wait till you get to the beach house tomorrow," she said. "We always have lots of fun out there with all the ghosts that inhabit the place."

"I don't believe one word of what you say, Josephine Patton," Mandie replied, standing up to stomp her foot into her shoe. "I think you're addled in the head."

"Just wait and see," Josephine said. Then seeing the adults and her brother approaching the rig, she fell silent and quickly took a seat.

Mandie didn't know whether to believe the girl or not. Josephine seemed to think there were ghosts everywhere. Mandie still wasn't sure she believed in ghosts.

Joe had told her there were no such things. Joe—his memory brought a sudden sadness into Mandie's thoughts. Was he still angry with her? She shouldn't have left angry. What if he never forgave her?

CHAPTER FIVE

THE SCARY WIDOW'S WALK

That night an enormous dinner was laid out in the formal dining room. It seemed like a hundred people could have been seated at the long table. Tizzy and her daughter, Cheechee, were among the uniformed servants who waited on them attentively throughout the meal.

Mandie quickly became friends with Tizzy. She reminded Mandie somewhat of Liza except that Tizzy evidently had some education. The little Negro girl Mandie had met earlier was Tizzy's ten-year-old daughter, Cheechee, who worked in the kitchen. Cheechee had taken a liking to Snowball, and she was constantly feeding him and keeping him out of Mrs. Patton's way.

At the table, Mandie sat next to Tommy again. Tommy played the perfect gentleman, pulling out her chair for her and seeing that her plate was piled high. Josephine sat across the table, squinting and listening to their conversation.

After the blessing was asked, Mandie turned to Tommy. "I just remembered something you told me back at the school," she remarked. "You told me you had a collection of sand dollars. Where are they?"

"Oh, the sand dollars are all out at the beach house. That's where I found most of them—on that beach," Tommy replied. "When we get there, I'll help you find some to take back home with you."

"Thank you, Tommy," Mandie said. "I hope I find enough to take one back to Liza and Celia and—" she paused. She was about to add Joe's name to her list but decided not to. She was determined to block him out of her mind and enjoy her trip.

Tommy smiled as he cut his steak. "Maybe you'd like to see our flower garden after dinner. It's supposed to be one of the showplaces in Charleston. The outdoor gaslights will be lit and there's a full moon tonight, so it'll be light enough to see."

Mandie looked at him, startled. "The moon is full tonight?" she questioned, glancing across the table at Josephine.

Josephine grinned. "It sure is," she said. "It's time!"

Mandie understood. It was at the time of a full moon that the supposed ghost of Melissa Patton came out. *I wonder where the widow's walk is in relation to the room I'm using?* she thought. At least if she were sleeping on the second floor of the three-story house, there would be another floor between her and the walkway around the roof.

Tommy missed Josephine's remark. "We could also go up to the widow's walk so you could see the ships in the harbor. You can see for miles from up there."

"Oh, really?" Mandie said weakly, not wanting Josephine to know she was bothered by the ghost tales. She smiled at Tommy. "I'd like to go up there. I've never heard of a widow's walk, much less seen one."

"It gets its name from the old days when the women would walk around up there, watching for their husbands to come home from the sea," Tommy explained. "And some of the sailing men who were lost at sea left widows who never gave up watching and hoping their husbands would come home." Tommy took a drink from his water glass and continued. "This house is about a hundred and fifty years old," he said. "The father of my great, great grandmother—the woman whose portrait hangs over the mantlepiece in the drawing room—built this house. He was a sea captain and owned a fleet of ships."

"Does your family still own ships?" Mandie asked, grateful for the change of topic.

"No, business declined down through the generations. My father owns one merchant ship that runs between here and England," he explained.

"Then he owns a store?" Mandie asked.

"No, he wholesales the goods off the ship to the local merchants who in turn sell it in their stores," Tommy said.

"And your family owns a rice plantation, too," Mandie remembered. "Busy family."

Josephine proudly sat up straight. "My father is a lawyer, too," she added. "He has so many different businesses going I don't see how he keeps up with things. What did your father do before he died?"

"My father was a farmer in Swain County, North Carolina, and we lived in a log cabin," Mandie told her. "His family had a lot of money from mining, but he left home after a disagreement with my Uncle John when they were young. He didn't want any of the money."

"Money isn't everything," Tommy said quietly, buttering a hot biscuit. "To me, other things are more important—like faith, hope, and love."

Mandie smiled. "Money can't buy those things," she agreed.

"But you've got to have money to live," Josephine insisted. "You wouldn't want to be poor and have no money, would you?"

"I suppose I was poor until I found Uncle John after my father died," Mandie told her.

Josephine looked shocked. "Really poor?" she asked.

"Yes, really poor. When my father died, I had to quit school and go live as a servant in another family's house," Mandie said.

"You? A servant?" Josephine laughed. "But your mother is rich. How come your father was poor?"

"Josephine," Tommy scolded, "please stop asking so many questions about things that don't concern you."

"I'm just curious," his sister pouted.

"That's all right," Mandie said with a sigh. "It's a long story, but you see, my Grandmother Taft didn't like my father, so when I was born, she told my mother I had died. And she told my father that Mother didn't want to see him or me again. Father took me and went to farm in Swain County where he married a widow woman with a really mean daughter named Irene. I thought that woman was my mother until after Father died." Mandie looked up to see if Josephine was following her story.

The girl pushed her glasses back up on her nose and motioned for her to go on.

"My father's old Indian friend, Uncle Ned, promised him that he would watch over me after Father died," Mandie continued. "So Uncle Ned helped me get to Uncle John's house. I didn't even know I had an uncle until then. Uncle John found my mother for me, and not long after that, they got married," Mandie explained. She took a deep breath.

Tommy was caught up in the story. "But why didn't your grandmother like your father?" he asked.

"My father's mother was a full-blooded Cherokee, and Grandmother Taft didn't want her daughter to marry anyone who was half Indian. But when they got married anyway and had me, my grandmother invented these tales to drive them apart," Mandie explained.

"Your other grandmother was a Cherokee?" Josephine taunted. "Then you are . . . one-fourth Indian," she quickly figured. "Humph!"

"You really are?" Tommy asked in surprise. "How interesting."

"Yes, and my Uncle John is one-half Cherokee, same as my father was," Mandie told them.

Josephine gasped. "We are entertaining Indians?"

"Josephine! That will do," Tommy reprimanded. "If you don't apologize to Mandie right this instant, I will see to it that Mother hears about your conduct toward our guest."

Josephine gave him a mean look. "I was only stating facts. We are entertaining Indians. Mandie herself just told us she and her uncle are part Indian."

"You may be stating facts, but your tone of voice says otherwise," Tommy said. "Now if you don't apologize, Mother will make you wish you had."

Josephine started to take a bite of her food. She squinted at her brother. "I don't see why I—"

"Forget about it, Tommy," Mandie interrupted. "I don't think she said anything wrong. I am part Cherokee and proud of it. That's the way God made me." Turning to Josephine, she asked, "And did He make your foot lame?"

Josephine's face reddened and Mandie immediately regretted what she had said.

Josephine quickly laid down her fork and spoke angrily. "No, He didn't make me lame. I'm not lame! I merely broke my ankle when I fell three years ago."

"I'm sorry," Mandie apologized. "I didn't mean it that way. I—"

"I don't care what you meant," Josephine said hatefully. "You have no right to ask such a question. It's not nice at all."

Tommy shot his mother a helpless look.

Mrs. Patton had been watching from the end of the table but apparently hadn't been able to hear the conversation. As she looked around the table, everyone seemed to be finished with the meal, so she stood up. "Shall we go into the drawing room and have our coffee there?" she asked.

Everyone rose and followed her down the hallway into the drawing room.

Mandie found Elizabeth and walked beside her. "Mother, Tommy wants to show me the flower garden," she said with a question in her voice.

"All right, dear, but don't be too long. We need a good night's sleep tonight after that long journey," Elizabeth replied.

"Yes, Mother," Mandie said, rejoining Tommy as they entered the drawing room.

Snowball came bounding into the room and rubbed around his mistress's ankles. Mandie picked him up. "Guess we'll have to take him, too," she told Tommy. "He needs some fresh air."

"All right, let's go," Tommy agreed.

"Are you coming, Josephine?" Mandie asked, trying to be nice to the girl.

"No, thank you. I've seen it before," Josephine said sarcastically.

Ignoring the snide remark, Mandie put Snowball on her shoulder and followed Tommy outside through a pair of tall French doors. The air smelled different from the North Carolina mountains, but it was still refreshing after being inside.

Snowball wiggled to get down.

"If I let you down, Snowball, you won't run off, will you?" Mandie said to her kitten, smoothing his fur.

"I think we can keep up with him. The whole yard is closed in with the wall," Tommy said.

"But he's a cat. He can climb walls and fences," Mandie reminded him.

"So can I." Tommy laughed. "We'll watch him."

Mandie bent to set the kitten down, and Snowball immediately took off, sniffing among the flowers. It was not quite dark, but the gas lamps were already lighted. The full moon hung in the sky just above the horizon.

Mandie surveyed the many flowers of various colors all growing in neatly planned beds. "How beautiful!" she exclaimed. "I don't even know what most of these are."

"Those are marigolds and old maids," Tommy said, pointing to clusters of gold and pink. "I'm pretty sure I've seen some of those in North Carolina. It's really the wrong time of year for a lot of our flowers to be in bloom. Those are crepe myrtle trees along the fence and azaleas around the house. You should see them blossom in the spring. And these red flowers right in front of us are camelias," he added. Then changing the subject abruptly, he said, "I really just wanted to talk to you away from Josephine."

Mandie suddenly blushed. "You did?" she managed to say, not daring to look up into her tall friend's face. Her heartbeat quickened.

"Yes, I wanted to apologize for my sister's behavior," he said.

Mandie instantly felt relieved. "You don't have to apologize for her," she said. "I can be pretty mean myself sometimes, and I don't have a brother to apologize for me."

Tommy laughed and took her hand. "I don't believe there's a mean bone in you, Amanda Shaw."

"Well, Thomas Patton, you don't really know me." She giggled.

"I know you all right," Tommy said. He stopped walking and looked down into her upturned face. "I think you are beautiful, and you are the nicest girl I've ever met."

Mandie blushed again, suddenly realizing she was trembling.

Tommy looked at her curiously. "Are you cold, Mandie? Do you want my jacket?"

It took all Mandie's willpower to steady her voice. "I'm not cold," she replied. "I just never had a boy say things like that to me before."

"Honest?" Tommy teased. He cleared his throat. "Well, then all the others must be blind or something," he added.

"All the others," Mandie corrected, "would only be Joe. He's the only boy I've ever really known except for you. And Joe is—well, I guess he's just practical or something. He never says fancy things."

Tommy laughed again and turned back toward the house. "Come on. Let's go up on the widow's walk."

A hint of fear gnawed at Mandie's stomach at the mention of the widow's walk. "Wait, I have to catch Snowball," she said. "Snowball, where are you?" She looked around in the flowerbeds. After a few moments she found him chasing a cricket among the vines. She picked him up. "We've got to go, Snowball. Be still."

The kitten climbed onto her shoulder and began purring as Tommy led Mandie to the side door of the house and up the stairs. When they reached the third floor, he opened the door to a small room. Inside, a narrow spiral staircase led up to the roof.

Mandie looked up and panicked. "You mean we've got to climb up those steps?"

"Sure. Nothing to it. You go first, and I'll stay right behind you just in case you slip or something. When you get to the landing up there, just stand still until I catch up with you," Tommy instructed, helping her up on the first step.

Mandie cautiously made her way up the narrow steps, never daring to look down. Snowball clung tightly to the shoulder of her dress. Tommy stayed right behind her. At the top, Mandie stepped onto a small landing and waited. Tommy slipped past her, and taking a key from a nail on the wall, he opened a small door. As Mandie looked out, the doorway seemed to open to nothing but the darkening sky.

"Come on, it's safe out here," Tommy told her. Taking her hand, he led her out onto the roof.

Mandie looked around and realized that they were standing on a small, narrow walkway that ran around the edge of the roof. The height made Mandie dizzy for a minute. She stood still and closed her eyes.

"If you look over that way, you can see the ships in the harbor," Tommy said.

Mandie reluctantly peeked at where he was pointing. Then her eyes grew wide. He was right. Off to the left lay a beautiful harbor with various ships docked there—some big, some little. Between the

Pattons' house and the harbor were dozens of rooftops everywhere, and along the avenues, stately palm trees lined the way.

"I've never been up so high in my life." She gasped for air, clutching her equally frightened kitten. "Imagine walking all the way around this roof. I think I'd get dizzy-headed and fall off."

"No, you wouldn't after you got used to it. You see, the women who came up here to watch for their husbands probably did this every day. The height didn't bother them because they were watching the water for signs of their husbands' ships coming into port," Tommy explained. "Let's walk over to the railing. It's safe."

Mandie shrank back. "Sorry, but I can't do that. Maybe next time I'll be more used to it as you say." She looked around the roof. "And this is where the ghost of Melissa Patton supposedly walks?"

"Don't believe all of Josephine's stories," Tommy warned. "She likes to make things up."

"But Melissa Patton really was killed up here, wasn't she?" Mandie asked, hovering near the doorway to the inside.

"There are old rumors in the family that she either committed suicide by jumping off the roof, or else she was pushed," Tommy said. "Anyhow, she died a long, long time ago."

"Do you mind if we go back downstairs?" Mandie asked in a small voice.

"I suppose we'd better," Tommy replied.

Mandie practically ran down the stairs until she reached the first floor. Tommy came right behind. At the foot of the steps Mandie ran into Josephine.

"Did Tommy show you where Melissa Patton went through the railing?" Josephine asked.

"Josephine!" Tommy spoke sharply.

"No, and I don't want to see it," Mandie said, rushing past the girl. On her way to the drawing room, Mandie hoped she could just bid everyone good night and hurry up to bed. She only wanted to snuggle up in a nice soft bed and forget about the dead lady.

CHAPTER SIX

NIGHT NOISES
AND GHOST STORIES

When Mandie and Tommy reached the drawing room, however, Mrs. Patton quickly stood. "Oh, Amanda," she said, "I'm glad you're back. We want to talk to you."

"Me?" Mandie asked.

"Yes. Mr. Patton and I have been talking to your mother and Uncle John about something," she explained. "Sit down, dear. We would like your opinion as well."

Mandie looked at her mother, who smiled and nodded. Mandie tried to remember her ladylike manners as she eased into the peach-colored settee next to Mrs. Patton and spread her skirt out wide. *What on earth could a bunch of adults want my opinion about?* she wondered.

Tommy stood beside Mandie, leaning against the settee, and Josephine glared at her from across the room.

"Now then, Amanda," Mrs. Patton began, "we've been thinking about your friend at the sanatorium."

"Hilda?" Mandie asked, not understanding.

"Yes," Mr. Patton replied. "You said they might release her if they found a loving family who could care for her, didn't you?"

"Well, yes, that's what Dr. Woodard said, but—"

"Do you think Hilda would like it here with us?" Mrs. Patton asked eagerly. "We certainly have the room."

"You mean you would be willing to have Hilda come to live with you?" Mandie asked.

Mrs. Patton's eyes twinkled. "We could certainly give her a great deal more love and attention than she could get in the sanatorium," she said. "And there are such good doctors here in Charleston."

"We would have to go through proper channels, of course," George Patton added thoughtfully, "but I love the idea of another youngster around the house." He beamed.

Mandie felt like she would burst with excitement. "If you really mean it," she said, "I think it would be wonderful!"

Uncle John sat forward. "I can talk to Dr. Woodard about it as soon as we get back," he offered. "He can find out what the procedures would be."

"Thank you, John," Mr. Patton replied. "That would be great!"

As the conversation turned to other topics, Mandie excused herself and headed for her room.

Finding her nightgown laid out and the bedcovers turned down, she quickly got ready for bed. As she slid beneath the silky sheets, she set Snowball on top of the covers. Closing her eyes, she thought about Hilda coming to live with the Pattons. Tommy's parents were such nice people. Although Josephine seemed a little strange, Tommy was very kind. Mandie felt sure he would watch over Hilda.

Somehow the idea of Hilda living in such fine surroundings eased Mandie's mind. The Pattons could certainly afford any medical care Hilda needed. Yes, Mandie was sure of it. Hilda would be genuinely loved and well cared for.

Mandie grew more sleepy, but thoughts of her busy day still whirled in her head. She remembered the nice things Tommy had said to her in the garden. Why didn't Joe ever say things like that, especially since he was so certain she was going to marry him when they grew up?

On the other hand, why did she even have to think of Joe? Although she tried desperately to enjoy her visit, she couldn't help having a heavy heart about their argument.

Sometime later, after Mandie dozed off, a sudden noise woke her. At first she couldn't figure out where she was. Then, getting her bearings, she realized the noise must have been right above her room. She lay completely still and listened, her heart beating loudly in her ears.

Through the stillness of the night, there was a faint moan and a crash overhead. Mandie jumped out of the bed and tried to lock the door. She remembered seeing a key in the lock before, but now the key was gone!

She heard Snowball outside her room. How had he gotten out into the hallway? Cracking the door just enough to let him in, she looked around the room for something to bar the door. All she could find was the pitcher and bowl on the washstand. As Snowball sniffed around the room, Mandie set the big bowl on the floor against the closed door and put the pitcher in the bowl, hoping they would at least make a noise if someone tried to come in.

Grabbing Snowball, Mandie jumped back into bed. She looked toward the sky through the window. "What time I am afraid," she whispered as her heart thumped loudly, "I will put my trust in Thee, dear God."

She lay there listening, determined to stay awake, but when nothing else happened, she finally drifted off to sleep.

The next morning, Mandie had already dressed and put the bowl and pitcher back on the washstand when Josephine barged into the room. Mandie stood in front of the mirror brushing her long blonde hair. Still nervous from the noises during the night, she turned quickly to see who it was.

"Did you hear her?" Josephine asked excitedly.

Mandie stopped brushing her hair and stared at the girl. "Hear who? What are you talking about?" she asked.

"Melissa Patton was up there walking around last night. Didn't you hear her? I told you she appeared when it was a full moon."

"You're talking nonsense, Josephine," Mandie said, trying to keep her voice steady. But as she started brushing again, she could hardly keep her hand from shaking.

"You may think it's nonsense, but I know it isn't," Josephine insisted. "She was up there last night on the widow's walk. Didn't you hear that loud bang when she shut the door?"

"How can a ghost close a door?" Mandie asked.

"I don't know but they can," Josephine declared.

Mandie yanked hard on her hairbrush. "Phooey, you probably heard someone in the house closing a door."

"I went up there just now to see," Josephine said. "The door was unlocked."

"So what? Tommy and I went up there last night, and I'm not sure he locked it," Mandie told her. "Besides, anybody could unlock or lock it. The key is hanging right there."

"The key was gone and the door was unlocked," Josephine insisted. She held out a fragment of a pink feather. "I found this on the roof."

"What is it?" Mandie tried to appear unconcerned, but she knew what Josephine was going to claim.

"It must have fallen off the fan Melissa was holding in the portrait," Josephine said.

"Now how could a piece of feather from a portrait made generations ago suddenly appear on the roof?" Mandie put down her brush and tied her long blonde hair back with a blue ribbon to match her dress.

Josephine squinted at Mandie eerily. "They say that the outfit she has on in the portrait was the same one she was wearing when she was murdered—pink feather fan and all."

Just then someone knocked on Mandie's door and she jumped. "Come in," she called.

Cheechee, the little maid, opened the door apologetically. "I comes to tell you breakfas' is ready, Missy. And Missy Josephine, yo' ma waitin' fo' you, too."

Josephine held out the piece of pink feather. "Look at this, Cheechee," she taunted. "Melissa Patton was on the widow's walk last night. She left a piece of the feather from her fan."

Cheechee screamed. "No, no, no! Don't you touch me wid dat. I don't want nothin' to do wid no ghost. May the Lawd rest huh soul." The Negro girl ran from the room.

Mandie pretended to be calm as she turned to follow her. Letting Snowball out into the hallway, she said, "You heard her. Breakfast is waiting."

Since Mandie had no idea where breakfast would be served, she let Josephine lead her downstairs to a beautiful glass-enclosed sunroom. A sideboard at one end of the room was weighed down with eggs, bacon, ham, grits, hotcakes, sausage, hot biscuits, preserves, milk, coffee and juice. The others in the house were already helping themselves.

Mrs. Patton greeted Mandie sweetly. "Come on in, dear. Breakfast is very informal. We just help ourselves to whatever we want. And I do hope there is something over there that you like."

"Yes, ma'am," Mandie replied, helping herself.

Elizabeth greeted her daughter as Mandie took her plate and sat down. "I hope you slept well, dear."

Mandie smiled weakly. "Well, it's always hard to get used to another house, but I slept all right once I got to sleep," she said, noticing that Tommy and his father had just entered the room.

Mr. Patton took a plate from the stack at the end of the sideboard and let his son go ahead of him.

Tommy looked over at Mandie. "Good morning," he said with a smile.

"Hello, Tommy," she replied, still a little embarrassed by the sweet way he looked at her.

Mr. Patton rested his hand on his son's shoulder. "Let's hurry so we can show our guests the city," he urged.

Mandie expected Josephine to mention the so-called ghost noises, but the girl didn't say a word to anyone about it during breakfast.

CHAPTER SEVEN

THE MYSTERIOUS APPEARANCE

Within the next hour they were all riding through the city in the Patton's rig, stopping here and there for the Shaws to investigate some place of interest.

Although Mandie had brought Snowball with her, she soon regretted it.

While the two families were looking around outside historic St. Michael's Episcopal Church, Mr. Patton acted as a tour guide. "This is the oldest church in the city," he told them. "George Washington worshiped here in 1791, when he toured the southern part of the country. These church bells have rung for over two hundred years."

Mandie looked up at the 186-foot steeple, topped with a gilt ball and above that a weather vane.

"That ball on top," Mr. Patton continued, "was blown down to the street in the cyclone of August 1885. A year later, it had just been restored to its place when the earthquake shattered the church. The ball is now eight inches nearer the ground, due to the sinking of the steeple in that earthquake."

"Earthquake?" Mandie questioned. "You had an earthquake here in Charleston?"

"Yes, dear, just fourteen years ago," Mrs. Patton put in. "And I hope I never experience another one."

Mr. Patton led the group through the door into the dimly lighted interior of the church. Mandie became so interested in the various plaques on the walls that she didn't notice when everyone else started leaving.

All of a sudden Snowball jumped down from her shoulder and scuttled away.

"Snowball, come back here!" Mandie called, stooping to look for him under various pews. "Snowball, Snowball!"

Suddenly she heard a weird clanking noise. She looked up. A strange, headless, robed figure moved slowly toward her in the semidarkness. She caught her breath. The thing sounded like it was made of metal. It clanged and moved nearer.

Mandie froze.

The figure quickened its pace.

Out of the corner of her eye, Mandie saw Snowball under the next pew. She grabbed him and started to run out of the church.

Then she noticed it. The figure was limping! Mandie turned quickly and snatched at the robe. "Josephine, you are disgusting!" Mandie told her. "Why don't you grow up?"

"I had you scared all right!" The girl dropped the robe on a pew and set down the metal collection plates she was holding.

At that moment Tommy appeared in the doorway. "We must have lost you somehow. Come on," he said.

"Snowball ran away and I had to find him," Mandie explained. She was tempted to tell Tommy about Josephine's prank, but she decided against it. She would just have to watch out for Josephine from now on.

The two families explored other historic places, including the oldest public building in Charleston, one of America's first playhouses, and the first fireproof building erected in the United States.

"Whew! I've had some history lesson today!" Mandie exclaimed as they rode back to the Patton house.

Tommy laughed. "We don't really expect you to remember all we told you," he said.

"I won't remember all of it, but I think I'll know enough to turn in a good paper for my history class when I get back to school," Mandie replied, stroking her sleeping kitten. "Will we be going to your beach house now?" she asked.

"As soon as we eat and get our things together," Tommy replied. "That shouldn't take long. I can't wait to show you the sun rising over the ocean tomorrow morning."

"I can't wait to see everything," Mandie said.

Later that afternoon the Pattons' rig pulled up in front of the beach house. It was an impressive frame structure built up on stilts over the beach. The Pattons had sent servants on ahead, including Tizzy and Cheechee, to prepare for the guests.

As they were about to leave the rig, Mandie turned to Tommy. "Why is the house built on stilts?" she asked.

"You'll see when the tide comes in," Tommy said, helping her down from the rig. "The water normally comes up almost to the base of the stilts. But in case there's an unusually high tide, the water would just pass through under the house."

"The tide?" Mandie questioned.

"Some of the water in the ocean washes up high onto the beach at certain intervals—twice a day, as a matter of fact," Tommy explained. "That is what you call the tide coming in. Then the water washes back out to sea, and that's what you call the tide going out." Tommy took a couple bags from the rig and started inside. "Wait till you see it. It's really a sight to see."

Mandie followed. "You love the beach, don't you?"

"The beach has always been my life, like the mountains are to you," Tommy replied. "I miss the beach when I'm at that stuffy old school in Asheville."

"I know what you mean," Mandie replied.

Inside, Mandie marvelled at the rich furnishings of the beach house, but she was appalled to find out she had to share a bedroom with Josephine.

"You take the bed by the windows so you can see out," Josephine told her as they dropped their bags in their room. "I'll take this one over here by the door."

"Thank you," Mandie replied, suspicious of anything Josephine said now.

After an informal supper, everyone sat outside on the veranda, which overlooked the ocean. While the adults talked leisurely, Mandie stood transfixed, watching the motion of the waves. So when Tommy asked her if she wanted to take a walk on the beach, she gladly accepted.

Tommy had shown Mandie his sand dollar collection shortly after they arrived, and she wanted to find some for herself. Snowball hopped and skipped along over the sand, trying to follow.

Time passed quickly, and Tommy and Mandie found quite a few sunbleached sand dollars of various sizes. But as dusk settled over the beach, the two couldn't see much.

"Well, I guess that's it." Tommy handed her one more sand dollar he had uncovered, shuffling along in the sand. "After the tide comes in and goes back out, we'll look again. Morning is the best time to find them—and shells, too."

Mandie took off her sunbonnet, and as they strolled along, she paused now and then to stare out at the water.

Finally, Tommy showed her the pier where they fished sometimes. It was a long, high walkway, which extended far out over the ocean. As the two walked out on it, Mandie became dizzy and had to close her eyes.

"This thing is moving," she cried.

"No it isn't." Tommy laughed, taking her hand to steady her. "You're just not used to the movement of the water. It's only the water that is moving, not the pier," he said. "Just stand perfectly still for a minute, then look down at the water and you'll see what I mean."

Mandie did what he said, and then smiled. "You're right," she admitted.

"I think we'd better head back now," Tommy suggested. "It's getting late."

Mandie picked up Snowball, and they started back for the house. When they arrived, no one was on the veranda.

"Everyone must have gone inside," Mandie observed. "Let's go sit in the sand down there for a few minutes and listen to the water before we go in," she suggested.

Tommy agreed and led the way down toward the water.

"Here," Mandie said, plopping down into the warm sand.

Tommy sat beside her. "It's nice to have a holiday from school isn't it?"

"It certainly is. I don't care too much about the Misses Heathwood's School for Girls anyhow. They teach too many silly, useless things," Mandie replied.

"So does our school," he said. "I'll never need half the things they are teaching me."

"Are you planning to go into business with your father someday?" Mandie asked, pushing back her long blonde hair.

"I haven't decided yet," he said. "I might go to Europe for a while first."

"To Europe? That would be wonderful!" Mandie exclaimed. "I'd love to see the rest of the world."

Tommy turned to look at her. "Maybe you will someday."

"I'm not holding my breath," Mandie laughed. "You and I live in different worlds. Now that I've visited your home and your town, I can see that."

Tommy's eyes twinkled. "Don't be so sure. I understand your mother was the belle of the season before she married your father. And your grandmother definitely moves in social circles."

"Yes, Grandmother Taft could move in any circles she pleased," Mandie agreed. "She really knows how to get what she wants."

"That's what I've heard," Tommy said knowingly. "But you have years before—"

"Look!" Mandie jumped up. "What's that?"

Tommy sprang to his feet beside her. The two stood in shock as a phantom-like apparition rose into the air near the pier. Then it dropped into the ocean and disappeared, making an eerie sound.

Mandie shivered. "Was that a g-ghost?" she asked.

Tommy seemed more in control. "A ghost? No, I don't think so, but it certainly did look like something supernatural, didn't it?" he said. "Let's walk back down that way and see if we can find anything."

Mandie followed him somewhat reluctantly. "It looked like a bundle of filmy, wispy white something or other," she said.

Walking back to the pier, they found nothing.

Mandie sighed in frustration. "Tommy, please do me a favor and don't tell anyone about this," she said.

"You mean like Josephine?" he teased.

"Yes. She would be just too pleased that we actually saw a ghost or whatever it was."

"I understand. I won't mention it. But it certainly is strange. There's nothing here, and I can't see anyone else around," he said. "I guess we'd better get back to the house. They'll be worried about us. But we'll come back down in the morning to see the tide."

Later that night, lying in her bed with Josephine nearby, Mandie kept thinking of the eerie white thing they had seen near the pier. Was there really such a thing as a ghost? If only Joe were here . . . He always helped her solve her mysteries. Oh, why had she been so unkind? She wished she could just see him and tell him she was sorry. She had to make things right.

As she lay thinking, the rhythmic sound of the waves lapping on the beach lulled her to sleep. She dreamed about Joe.

CHAPTER EIGHT

THE PHANTOM
IN THE MOONLIGHT

Before daylight, Mandie awakened to a gentle touch on the shoulder. She opened her eyes and saw her mother standing beside her bed.

"Amanda," Elizabeth whispered, trying not to wake Josephine. "Tommy is waiting for you to go down and watch the tide."

"It can't be time to get up, Mother," Mandie protested. "It isn't even daylight."

"No, but the tide won't wait for daylight. It'll be gone if you don't hurry," Elizabeth whispered. "After you watch the tide, you can stay and watch the sun rise over the ocean."

Half asleep, Mandie tumbled out of bed and quickly dressed with Elizabeth's help.

"Now you're ready, dear." Her mother handed her a shawl and urged her out the door. "Tommy's in the kitchen. Leave Snowball here, and please be quiet so you won't wake anyone."

Mandie found Tommy wide awake and drinking orange juice in the kitchen. Mandie rubbed her eyes and yawned. "I hope it's worth it," she mumbled.

"Here, this will wake you up," Tommy said, handing her a small glass of orange juice. "I've been up a long time. I like to rise early."

"I do, too, at home, but somehow the ocean has made me sleepy," Mandie said. She started drinking the juice.

"You were just tired after your long journey and all that sightseeing we did yesterday," he told her.

"I'm awake now. Let's go," she said, putting down the empty glass.

"We're only going out on the porch until the tide goes out," Tommy said, leading the way. "Then later, we'll go down on the beach and look for sand dollars and shells."

As Mandie followed him out onto the veranda, the roar of the ocean waves was deafening. She was glad her mother had insisted she take a shawl. It was cool outside. Huddling on a bench by the railing in the dim predawn light, she looked out over the ocean in amazement. The entire beach was covered with water.

Mandie got close enough to Tommy to yell in his ear. "Will it come on up to the house?" she asked, above the roar.

"No, it has come just about as far as it ever does," Tommy yelled back.

Then the water's motion reversed and little by little it began moving back out to sea. Mandie watched the slow process as the waves grew more calm and the sand reappeared, looking much smoother after being washed by the high tide.

"I think we can go down there now," Tommy said. "But it's going to be awfully squishy. You'll ruin your shoes."

"That's all right. These are my old shoes. Mother had me bring them just for the beach," Mandie told him.

The two walked along the beach, picking up numerous sand dollars and shells of various shapes and sizes. They put them all in a cloth bag Tommy had brought. Stepping over piles of debris which had washed up with the tide, they found a small fish, live and wiggling in the sand. Tommy picked it up and tossed it back into the water so it wouldn't die.

As the first streaks of dawn finally appeared in the sky, Tommy suggested that they go out on the pier to watch the sunrise. "Come on. We'll have to hurry because the sun doesn't waste any time when it comes up," Tommy said, taking her hand.

Hurrying out to the end of the pier, they stood against the railing to watch. Instantly, the sun began peeping up over the water's edge. Then it splashed its golden rays out over the ocean like a huge spotlight, illuminating everything between them and the sun.

Mandie caught her breath as the sun moved upward. "Oh, how beautiful!" she cried in delight. "God created some wonderful things, didn't He?"

"Yes, and I never get tired of watching. When we're at the beach house, I come down here every morning and wait for the sun," Tommy told her.

"I just can't believe such a glorious thing is happening. The water looks like it's on fire," Mandie cried. "Do you mind if I come with you to watch the sun every morning while we're here?"

"I was hoping you'd want to," Tommy said, smiling. "I love to watch you enjoy things. You make it all seem new to me."

Mandie blushed. She was beginning to realize how much she liked Tommy. The things he said to her made her feel special. Yet even while she was with him, the memory of Joe's hurt face stayed with her.

As she watched the sun rise, she felt closer to God and silently asked Him to forgive her for arguing with Joe.

"Hey, you haven't gone back to sleep, have you?" Tommy jostled her out of her reverie.

Mandie turned. "I'm sorry. I was just doing some thinking," she told him.

"Thinking? This early in the morning?" Tommy teased. "I can't think until I've had breakfast. Let's go get some. Tizzy ought to have it ready by now."

"Great idea!" Mandie agreed.

They hurried back across the beach, not taking time to look for any more sand dollars or shells. They had the whole day ahead of them to search the sand.

Mandie enjoyed the lazy pace of the day. The only things scheduled were mealtimes. While the adults sat around talking, Mandie and Tommy spent most of their time on the beach. Mandie was never quite sure what Josephine was doing.

After supper that night Tommy and Mandie went for another walk out to the pier. Mandie liked this time of day. Because the sun was almost out of sight, she could take off her bonnet without worry-ing about getting freckles. The constant cool breeze felt good on her face. And since her mother found out what bad shape Mandie's shoes were in from the wet sand, she allowed Mandie to go barefooted for a while.

After sitting out on the pier, talking until after dark, Mandie and Tommy strolled back toward the house. Suddenly an eerie scream pierced the air. They whirled. The ghostly apparition floated in the moonlight for a few seconds and then disappeared into the water near the pier again.

Mandie moved closer to Tommy.

"There has to be an explanation for that thing, whatever it is," Tommy declared calmly.

"It must be a ghost!" Mandie's voice trembled.

"I don't think ghosts can swim, Mandie," Tommy said, "and evi-dently that thing must know how to swim because it lands in the water."

For several minutes they stood there, staring at the pier.

"I think I'd like to go back to the house," Mandie said.

"Let's go then," Tommy agreed.

Taking a short cut under the house, Tommy almost tripped on Jo-sephine, who was huddling there in the dark.

"What are you doing here?" Tommy asked.

Josephine jumped up, brushing the sand from her skirt. "What are y'all doing under here?" Josephine tossed back at him.

"What does it look like we're doing?" Tommy asked. "We've been on the beach, and now we're coming back to the house. What are you up to?"

"I don't have to account for anything to you," Josephine told him.

"Maybe not, but you'll have to explain it to Mother if I tell her," Tommy reminded.

"Go ahead. I'll just tell on you and Mandie going off in the dark on the beach. I know for a fact that Mandie didn't ask permission," Josephine retorted.

"Come on, Tommy. Let's go inside," Mandie urged. "I don't want to get mixed up in a quarrel."

"I'm sorry, Mandie. Of course we'll go inside," Tommy said.

Josephine sneered at them and plopped back in the sand as Mandie and Tommy climbed the steps to the house.

"Josephine was outside," Mandie said softly. "I wonder if she saw the ghost."

"I don't imagine she did or she'd be talking about it," he replied.

"Let's keep it our secret and not tell anyone else. Maybe we can find out what it was," Mandie whispered.

"I don't think we have much to tell anyone, anyway," he whispered back. "No one would believe us."

As they approached the door, Elizabeth came out onto the porch. "Oh, there you are, Amanda," she said. "I didn't know where you had gone."

"I'm sorry, Mother. I should have asked. Tommy and I have been walking on the beach," Mandie explained.

"You should let me know where you are when it gets dark, Amanda," Elizabeth said.

"I'm sorry, too, Mrs. Shaw," Tommy apologized. "I asked Mandie to walk on the beach but forgot to ask your permission. We will next time," he promised.

"All right, Tommy. And you remember that, too, Amanda," Elizabeth said. "By the way, we just got word that Uncle Ned will be here tomorrow."

Mandie clasped her hands in excitement. "I'm so glad he's coming. I was hoping he could make it."

Elizabeth looked amused. "Amanda, you know he goes everywhere you go. He promised your father he would watch over you, and he keeps that promise," she said. "I appreciate his loyalty."

"I'd sure like to meet him," Tommy said. "I've heard so much about Mandie's great protector, but I've never seen him."

"You'll love Uncle Ned. He's a dear old man," Mandie said.

"Yes, he is," Elizabeth agreed, starting back into the house.

"And he has helped me out of a lot of trouble," Mandie added.

"I'm going back inside," Elizabeth called over her shoulder. "You won't go wandering off down the beach anymore tonight, will you, Amanda?"

"No, Mother," Mandie replied, plopping down on a soft-cushioned bench on the veranda. She looked up at Tommy. "Let's just sit here for a while and smell the water and listen to its roar."

"Sounds like a good idea to me," Tommy said, sitting beside her.

Just then Snowball wandered out onto the porch. Mandie picked him up and put him on her lap, stroking his soft, white fur. "Maybe Uncle Ned can help us solve the mystery about that thing we saw," Mandie said. "He always helps out when I get involved in something."

"But we're not really involved in anything," Tommy reminded her.

"Not yet, but I'd like to find out what it was that we saw," Mandie insisted.

"I'd like to know, too," Tommy said. "I just hope Josephine doesn't find out about it. She's bad enough already with all her ghost stories."

They didn't know it, but Josephine had crept under the porch and had heard every word they said.

CHAPTER NINE

TROUBLE ON THE PIER

The next morning Mandie and Tommy stood at the railing of the pier again. As they watched, the sun burst over the far horizon like a great fiery red ball. And as it rose, the red color faded into gold. The sky lightened to a bright blue, and all that stretched out before them was water and sky.

"It's such a beautiful sight. I just won't be able to describe it to my friends back home," Mandie said in awe.

"Bring them all with you next time," Tommy invited.

Mandie looked at him to see if he were joking. "You don't mean that, do you?"

"I certainly do," Tommy replied, hopping up on the top rail of the pier. "As you can tell, my mother loves company, and we have plenty of room. Maybe that's why my parents are thinking about helping your friend, Hilda." Tommy paused as if trying to adjust to the idea.

"Oh, that would be wonderful for Hilda," Mandie said. "I think I might even be a little jealous." Instantly she regretted using that word.

Fortunately, Tommy didn't seem to notice.

Mandie hurriedly continued. "How do you feel about Hilda coming to live with your family?"

"I don't know exactly," Tommy replied. "I wouldn't really mind, I guess. It just takes some getting used to. But I guess, to be honest, if we're going to add another member to the family, I'd rather have a brother than another sister." He swung his legs freely from the railing where he sat. "I think having your friend Hilda around would be very good for my mother, though," he said. "She has a kind heart and loves to do things for other people. But when I'm away at school in Asheville, Mother is often alone here. My father is away on business a lot, and my sister isn't much company. Josephine likes to be by herself. She's been known to disappear for hours at a time, and no one knows where she goes."

Tommy jumped down from the railing. "Are you hungry?" He changed the subject abruptly. "I imagine Tizzy has breakfast ready for us."

"I'm starving as usual," Mandie replied.

As they started back down the long pier, Mandie caught sight of someone hurrying down the beach. She stopped for a moment and then yanked excitedly at Tommy's hand. "Come on. That's Uncle Ned!" she exclaimed, pointing toward the tall, thin figure in the distance.

"At last I get to meet him," Tommy said, running with her.

Jumping down off the pier onto the beach, Mandie held her skirt high and ran awkwardly through the thick, loose sand. Tommy held her hand to keep her from falling as they ran.

Uncle Ned quickened his pace, and they met halfway up the beach.

Mandie reached out to squeeze the old man's hand. "Uncle Ned!" she called, out of breath from running.

"Papoose must not run in soft dirt. Fall, get hurt," the old Indian scolded.

Mandie plopped down on the beach. "Sorry . . . but I have to . . . sit down . . . right here," she said, still trying to catch her breath. "Sit down, Uncle Ned. This is Tommy Patton. He goes to Mr. Chadwick's . . . School for Boys in Asheville. Tommy, this is my dearest friend . . . and my father's friend, Uncle Ned."

"How do you do, sir." Tommy was only a little winded as he greeted the old Indian. The two shook hands and crouched down in the sand beside Mandie.

"Papoose tell me about Tommy Boy. I thank Tommy Boy to let Papoose see Big Water." He waved his old wrinkled hand toward the ocean.

"It's a great pleasure to meet you, sir," Tommy said. "Mandie has told me so much about you. And you're the first real Indian I've ever met. I'm honored that you have come to visit my family."

Uncle Ned grinned and nodded.

"Have you been to the house yet, Uncle Ned?" Tommy asked.

"I see mother of Papoose. She tell me go where you are," he answered.

"Uncle Ned, I'm glad you're here—for more reasons than one," Mandie told him. "We've got something we need to solve. Tommy and I have been seeing some kind of phantom or ghost or something by the pier."

"Ghost?" Uncle Ned questioned.

"Well, we don't know exactly what it is, but we'd like to find out," Mandie explained. "This thing comes floating through the air and then plops into the water. It's all white and wispy-looking, and when it lands in the water, it makes a real spooky sound."

"Where? We go look." Uncle Ned rose to his feet.

Mandie and Tommy jumped up, brushing the sand off their clothes.

"Come this way," Mandie said, leading the way to the pier. The three of them searched all around the tall pilings under the pier and found no clue.

"Let's go up on top," Mandie suggested. Hurrying ahead of the others, she had almost reached the end of the structure when suddenly a large board in the flooring flipped up.

Instantly she fell through the boards and plunged into the water below. "Help!" she screamed, thrashing around in the deep water. "I can't swim!"

Uncle Ned dove off the pier. "Papoose! Ned coming!" he called, swimming powerfully toward her.

Tommy jumped in after him. When Uncle Ned and Tommy reached Mandie, her body was rigid with fright, and she was choking violently.

Uncle Ned grabbed her in his arms and held her head above the waves as he swam to shore.

Pulling her onto the beach, he motioned for Tommy to help. "Quick!" he said. Together they turned Mandie upside down and shook her hard. She coughed up water and went limp with relief.

Uncle Ned sat down on the sand and held her in his arms like a baby, smoothing her wet hair and crooning in Cherokee.

Tommy sat by his side, drenched as Uncle Ned was, and exhausted. He leaned forward. "Are you all right, Mandie?"

Mandie nodded. "I'll be fine in a minute," she said shakily, "Thank you, Uncle Ned.

The old Indian smiled at her. "Tommy Boy, he help too."

"Yes, I know. Thank you, Tommy," she said. "I can't swim a lick."

"I can't understand how you fell through," Tommy said, looking toward the pier. "We were up there before Uncle Ned came, and the board wasn't loose then."

"I know, Tommy, but I don't think we walked by that exact spot. Remember, we didn't go all the way out on the pier this time," Mandie reminded him.

"I'm going to take a look." Tommy stood to his feet and shook his wet clothes. "You stay here and get your breath, Mandie, so we can take you back to the house to change. Are you cold?"

"No, the sun is hot," Mandie replied. "It feels good."

Tommy walked out the long pier. When he came to the loose plank, he stooped to examine the flooring.

Mandie tried to squeeze the water out of her heavy clothes. Then with Uncle Ned close by her side, she walked beneath the pier to the edge of the water. She looked up. Where the plank hung down over the water, something white caught her eye.

"Look, Tommy!" Mandie exclaimed, pointing. "There's something white hanging beneath the floor where you are. I don't know why we didn't see it before."

"Where?" Tommy asked, stooping to look around.

"It looks like it's attached to the loose plank," Mandie called, still pointing.

"I see it but I can't reach it from up here," Tommy called back.

Uncle Ned strode over to the water's edge. "I get," he said. Swimming out into the water, he stopped at the piling near the loose plank, then climbed up the tall post. Reaching out his long arm, he jerked the white material from the board.

As he came back to shore, Tommy hurried down to investigate.

Uncle Ned held up a long strip of soft white silk material. "Just piece of cloth," he mumbled.

Mandie reached for it and examined it thoroughly. "It must belong to the ghost. What is it?"

"Like Uncle Ned said, it's just an old piece of cloth," Tommy replied.

"But that thing we've been seeing looked like it had some long trailing white material around it," Mandie insisted. "And isn't this about where we've seen that thing floating through the air?"

"It could be," Tommy said, taking the material from Mandie. "I'd like to know how that plank got loose. It's a perfectly good board. It just looks like the nail was pulled out of it. There's something fishy about the whole thing."

"Hand of human make board loose, not ghost," Uncle Ned agreed.

"But who?" Mandie asked.

"I don't know who, but I'd like to find out," Tommy said.

CHAPTER TEN

HOW MUCH DOES JOSEPHINE KNOW?

As the three wet figures approached the house, Elizabeth ran to the top of the porch steps in alarm. "What happened?" she gasped.

"I fell into the water, Mother," Mandie told her. "Uncle Ned and Tommy helped me out."

"Fell in the water? How could you do that?" Elizabeth scowled.

"I'm sorry, Mrs. Shaw, but a board on the floor of the pier was loose and Mandie fell through," Tommy explained.

Elizabeth put her arms around her daughter. "Are you all right, Amanda?" Her scowl melted into concern.

"I think so."

"You must try to be more careful, dear," her mother warned. "I'm not trying to make you feel bad, but I love you and I simply don't want anything to happen to you."

"I know, and I love you, too, Mother," Mandie replied.

"Well, if you're sure you're all right, why don't you go inside and change your clothes, dear," Elizabeth told her. "We don't want you to catch cold. But be quiet, Amanda. Everyone else is still asleep except the servants."

As Mandie went inside, she heard her mother say, "Thank goodness you were there, Uncle Ned."

A little while later, Tommy and Uncle Ned arrived in the sunroom just as Mandie did. Mandie felt much better with dry clothes and shoes on. She had brushed out her long blonde hair into a cascade of tiny, wet ringlets down her back. Tommy smiled at her approvingly.

In the sunroom, sparkling white breakfast dishes were already laid out on the table.

"Sit down, Uncle Ned. Make yourself at home," Tommy said. Politely pulling out a chair for Mandie, he nodded for her to sit in it.

As they all sat down at the table, Tizzy hurried into the room with a huge tray and set the hot food on the table before them.

"Tizzy, you timed it just right. How did you know we were in here?" Tommy teased the maid.

"I heerd that loud mouth of yours, Mistuh Tommy," Tizzy replied, "and I knows I gotta shut it up wid some good hot food." She stopped and stared at Uncle Ned. "Mistuh Injun Man, does you eats what we eats?"

Uncle Ned smiled at her. "I eat same."

"Oh, thank goodness," she replied. "I'se 'fraid I'se gonna have to cook some snakes or somethin' fo' you."

"Tizzy!" Tommy scolded. "Where did you get such an idea? Nobody eats snakes. Gruesome thought!"

Mandie sat forward. "Sometimes Morning Star cooks up a pot of owl stew."

"Mornin' Star?" Tizzy questioned.

"She's Uncle Ned's wife," Mandie explained. "She cooked owl stew one time when Joe and I were visiting. Joe almost gagged on it when he found out what he was eating, but I thought it was pretty good."

Tizzy stood there in astonishment.

Uncle Ned smiled at Mandie. "Morning Star see Joe not like. Not cook owl stew now when Joe visit."

"You ate owl stew, Missy?" Tizzy couldn't believe it.

"I ate a whole bowlful of it. After all, I'm part Cherokee, too," Mandie boasted.

"You is? Which part?"

"Which part?" Mandie repeated. She grinned. "My grandmother's part of me. She was full-blooded Cherokee."

"Lawsy mercy!" Tizzy exclaimed, leaving the room.

"Now she's going to be afraid of me, I reckon," Mandie said.

"No, she's being silly," Tommy assured her. "You and Uncle Ned are just a little different. She has never met an Indian before. She was born and raised on our rice plantation and has never been outside of Charleston. Most of the Negroes around here are suspicious of outsiders, regardless of who they are or where they come from. They are worse than the old-timers who come from a long line of Charlestonians."

"Someday," Uncle Ned spoke up, "white man, black man, and Indian man all be friends."

Mandie reached over and patted the old man's hand. "I hope so, Uncle Ned," she said. "God made us all, and in that way we are all His children."

Uncle Ned smiled and squeezed her hand.

Tommy nodded. "Some people want to forget that, or they overlook it on purpose," he observed.

Mandie pushed back her damp hair. "Whew! What a deep subject," she said, signaling an end to that topic of conversation.

After they gave thanks for their food, Mandie turned to Tommy. "What did you do with that piece of material?" she asked, helping herself to the delicious-looking food in front of her. The others did the same.

"It's safe," Tommy answered. "I stuck it under my mattress."

"What are we going to do about it?" Mandie took a bite of her scrambled eggs.

"What *can* we do about it? It's just a piece of old cloth," Tommy said.

"We should find out how it got there and who it belongs to," Mandie insisted.

"And who make board loose, make Papoose fall in water," Uncle Ned added.

"I'd sure like to know that," Tommy said, passing the biscuits. "I'd fix them all right. You could have been seriously injured, falling like that."

"I probably wouldn't have fallen through if I hadn't been running," Mandie said. "I would have seen it in time."

"Must find who make plank loose," Uncle Ned repeated, taking a sip of hot coffee.

"But how are we going to find the ghost?" Mandie asked.

"We watch, we wait," the old Indian told her.

"Uncle Ned, you don't really believe it's a ghost we've been seeing, do you?" Tommy asked.

Uncle Ned thought for a minute. "Maybe not," he replied.

"What would a ghost be doing up there on the pier, anyway?" Tommy asked.

"Whatever a ghost would be doing anywhere," Mandie answered.

"A ghost couldn't pull that board loose," Tommy protested. "Besides, what would a ghost want with that piece of cloth?"

"Ghost may be human," Uncle Ned suggested.

Mandie laughed. "Then it wouldn't be a ghost."

At that moment Josephine entered the room and everyone immediately hushed.

"What wouldn't be a ghost?" Josephine asked, sitting down at the table.

"Why don't you get your mind off ghosts?" Tommy chided.

"I distinctly heard the word when I opened the door. Is it all right for y'all to talk about ghosts but not for me?" Josephine asked.

No one answered.

Josephine looked around the table. "Mandie, your hair is all wet. Did you wash it this early in the morning?" she asked, reaching for a biscuit.

Tizzy came into the room again and placed more food on the table.

Mandie evaded Josephine's question. "Is there something wrong with washing your hair early in the morning?"

"A person usually waits till up in the day so the sunshine can dry it," Josephine replied. She squinted at Uncle Ned. "I haven't met your Indian friend yet."

"I'm sorry, Josephine. This is Uncle Ned," Mandie told her.

Uncle Ned smiled at the girl.

Josephine frowned. "He isn't my uncle. It wouldn't be proper for me to call him Uncle Ned," she objected.

"In that case, he is Mr. Sweetwater to you," Mandie corrected. "Uncle Ned, this is Miss Josephine Patton, Tommy's sister."

"What an unusual name. How do you do, Mr. Sweetwater." Josephine nodded.

"I do fine, Miss Josephine," Uncle Ned replied.

"Are you staying with us long, Mr. Sweetwater?" Josephine asked.

"Josephine!" Tommy scolded. "Uncle Ned is our guest for as long as he wishes to stay."

"I only asked because we are all moving out to the plantation house this afternoon, and I was wondering if he was going with us to Mossy Manor," Josephine defended herself.

"Yes, he is going with us," Tommy told her. "And you'd better hope Mother lets you go after I tell her how you've been misbehaving."

Mandie put her hand on Tommy's arm. "Please, Tommy, don't cause Josephine any trouble."

"I won't tell Mother if you don't want me to, but I can sure give her trouble if she doesn't straighten up," Tommy said.

Josephine got up to leave the room. "Trouble? Don't forget I have the ghosts on my side," Josephine called over her shoulder. "They can cause you trouble for me."

Mandie, Tommy, and Uncle Ned all looked at each other.

Uncle Ned spoke first. "Missy Josephine know Papoose fall in water?"

"She sure acted like she did," Tommy replied.

"We'll just have to keep one step ahead of her and find that phantom," Mandie said with determination. "Then everything will be explained."

"I hope so," Tommy admitted.

Suddenly Mandie's face clouded with concern. "I just realized what Josephine said. She said we're all moving out to the plantation house this afternoon. How are we going to solve the mystery on the pier if we aren't here?" she asked.

"We'll be back before you go home," Tommy replied. "In the meantime we'll have fun at the plantation."

"Uncle Ned, you *are* going with us, aren't you?" Mandie asked.

"Yes, Papoose. Mother of Missy Josephine ask me go," the old Indian answered. "I watch over Papoose. No harm come."

"Thank you, Uncle Ned," Mandie said.

"First, I need powwow with Papoose. Old problem to clean up."

Mandie looked at Tommy and then back at Uncle Ned. She knew very well what the problem was. She also knew that Uncle Ned had come to talk to her privately about Joe. And she had better have some answers.

CHAPTER ELEVEN

MOSSY MANOR

A little while later, Mandie and Uncle Ned silently spread a blanket on the beach and sat on it.

Mandie opened her parasol and twirled it over her shoulder. "I love the ocean, Uncle Ned." She was nervous, anticipating what was coming.

Uncle Ned only nodded.

"All right, Uncle Ned, I know you are going to give me a lecture, so let's get on with it," she said, staring out over the ocean.

Uncle Ned came straight to the point as usual. "Papoose," he said, "doctor son hurt in heart. Papoose do bad thing."

Mandie tried to keep her voice from trembling as she remembered the terrible, angry words that she and Joe had said to each other. "I'm sorry if Joe was hurt by our argument, Uncle Ned, but he hurt me, too."

"Doctor son say he sorry. He ask Big God to forgive," the old Indian explained. "Papoose must ask Big God forgive."

"I have, Uncle Ned," Mandie told him. "I already asked God's forgiveness for anything I might have done wrong."

Uncle Ned leaned forward. "Papoose has done wrong!" he said vehemently. "Big Book say not let it get dark time while angry. Papoose see many darktimes since fuss with doctor son. Big God not like angry people. I not like angry people. Jim Shaw watch from happy hunting ground and not like Papoose angry."

Mandie looked into the old man's wrinkled face, and her blue eyes began to fill with tears. Silently, she closed her parasol and set it down beside her in the sand. Her lips trembled, and she leaned her head on Uncle Ned's shoulder.

He put an arm around her and smoothed her damp blonde hair.

"I'm sorry, Uncle Ned," Mandie confessed, haltingly. "I know I've been bad. I'm sorry."

"Papoose must tell doctor son sorry," Uncle Ned told her.

Mandie tilted her head back to look up into his face. "I will, Uncle Ned, as soon as we go home. I promise. I thought I could just go away, and have a good time, and forget about it. But I've been miserable about this ever since I left home. I know I've done wrong, and I am truly sorry."

"Must not hurt others with mean words," the old man told her. "Papoose must remember. Anger stab heart like arrow. Hurt bad. Real bad. Hard to heal."

"But Joe got angry and hurt me, too, so I kept saying mean things to hurt him back," Mandie said. "Just a few little angry words can sure cause a big hurt."

"Papoose must remember. Say no more mean words," Uncle Ned said. "Papoose growing up big now. Must act more like big person."

"But what can I do to control my temper, Uncle Ned?"

"Papoose must think before saying mean words," he said. "God give brain to think. Papoose get angry, must take deep breath, blow it out. Mean words come out with it and go away. Must not hurt other people with mean words."

"I know that now," Mandie admitted. "Do you think Joe will forgive me?"

Uncle Ned nodded slowly. "Doctor son say he sorry to hurt Papoose. He forgive. But Papoose must ask doctor son to forgive—ask Big God to forgive. Papoose not let darktime come on anger again."

Mandie reached for Uncle Ned's hand. "Thank you for always helping me," she said. Then looking toward the bright blue sky as she always did when she prayed, she said, "Dear God, please forgive me and help me to be more careful what I say. I know You will."

Uncle Ned also turned his face toward heaven. "Big God," he prayed, "Papoose truly sorry. Please forgive. Make her better Papoose."

Mandie smiled at her old friend. "Remember the Bible verse that says, 'Be ye angry, and sin not; let not the sun go down upon your wrath'?"

Uncle Ned nodded.

"I guess I memorized it but didn't really learn it very well, did I?"

The old Indian smiled back at her.

"I'm going to write that down and put it somewhere to remind me to control my temper." She paused, staring out at the ocean waves rolling into shore. "I feel better now. I can't wait to get home so I can talk to Joe. What a relief that will be!"

"Must go back to house now." Uncle Ned rose to his feet. "We go to rice fields."

Mandie jumped up. "Yes, I need to help my mother get things ready," she said.

Together, they shook the sand off the blanket and folded it. Mandie picked up her parasol and opened it as Uncle Ned threw the blanket over his shoulder. Then taking her small white hand in his old wrinkled one, he led Mandie back to the beach house.

"Thank you again, Uncle Ned. I love you," she said.

"Love make people do good things." The old Indian smiled down at her.

When they reached the porch, Mr. Patton was standing there, looking out over the ocean. "It never gets old," he said with a chuckle. "I still love to watch the waves roll in."

Uncle Ned stopped to talk with him, but Mandie hurried inside in search of her mother. Elizabeth and John were in their room, packing for the move to the plantation house.

When Mandie entered the room, Elizabeth looked up from her packing. "Hello, dear. Did you have a nice visit with Uncle Ned on the beach?"

"Uncle Ned always helps me sort things out and do what's right," Mandie answered, not wanting to explain the whole problem again.

"Uncle Ned has been a good friend to all of us," Uncle John said without looking up.

"But I think we'd better get busy here so we will be ready when the Pattons want to leave. Amanda, have you put your things back into your traveling bag?" Elizabeth asked.

"Yes, ma'am, but I need to find Snowball," Mandie said, turning toward the door. For a moment she lingered, watching her mother and Uncle John pack their bags.

Elizabeth noticed her standing there. "What is it, Amanda?" she asked.

"I guess I'm just homesick," Mandie replied. "I love the ocean, and I'm eager to see the rice plantation, but I'll sure be glad when we get back home."

Elizabeth and John looked at her in amazement.

"Is something wrong?" Uncle John asked.

"No, not really," Mandie answered. "I'll go find Snowball now," she said, leaving the room.

Mandie was unusually quiet during the journey to the plantation. First they rode in the rig to the dock. Then they boarded a large boat on the Ashley River.

In the beginning Mandie had trouble standing up in the rocking boat, and Snowball clung to her shoulder in fear. But after a while, she became used to the rocking motion and began to relax a little.

Tommy tried to start a conversation with Mandie as they stood at the boat's railing. But he seemed to sense that her mind was miles away. He gave up and they rode in silence.

Josephine was the one who wouldn't shut up. "You'd better learn how to swim, Mandie," she teased. "You have to if you're around this much water. You never know what's going to happen."

Mandie looked at her without a word. So she had seen the incident.

"If your Indian friend and Tommy hadn't been with you when you fell into the ocean this morning, you might not be here to tell about it now," Josephine continued.

Mandie still didn't say anything, and Tommy didn't reprimand his sister as he usually did.

"What's the matter with you? Have you forgotten how to talk?" Josephine asked.

"Josephine!" Tommy finally said, exasperated.

Uncle Ned stood nearby, watching and listening. He smiled.

Taking a deep breath to cool her rising temper, Mandie smiled back at him. She turned to Tommy. "Let's walk around to the other side of the boat," she suggested.

As they walked away, out of the corner of her eye, Mandie saw Uncle Ned move toward Josephine. *She is about to get a lecture,* Mandie thought. *A gentle one, of course, but maybe he can put some sense into her head.*

As Mandie and Tommy strolled across the deck, the fresh ocean air revived Mandie's spirits. Other boats passed up and down the river. Sometimes Tommy recognized someone and waved. Elizabeth and John sat with the Pattons in the small cabin, but they kept a constant eye on the young people through the glass windows.

Tommy and Mandie stopped by the rail on the other side of the boat. Huge cypress trees, draped with Spanish moss, stood in swamps along the way. The motionless black water was dotted with lilies, but the heavy odor from the stagnant swamps became almost unbearable.

Mandie wondered if the plantation house would be situated in an area like this. "What is Mossy Manor like?" she asked Tommy.

"It's a huge old house surrounded by acres and acres of woods and open fields," he said proudly. "The nearest neighbor is five miles down the road. We have a lot of animals there—cows, pigs, chickens, and horses. And the woods are full of deer and wild turkeys."

"You have horses?" Mandie exclaimed.

"Do you ride?" Tommy asked.

"I have my own pony at home," she said, "but I think it's about time to graduate to a full-size horse. After all, I am twelve years old now. I love to ride."

"Good, then I can show you the place on horseback," Tommy said. "We have acres and acres to ride over. You know, this house is even older than the one in town," he continued. "The Pattons built Mossy Manor first when they came to the United States from Holland in the seventeenth century. And there have been Pattons here ever since—some good ones, some bad ones," he said with a laugh. "Everything from a United States Senator to a pirate."

Suddenly Josephine came up behind them. "We're almost there," she said, limping up to Mandie. "Just wait till you see it. I'll bet you don't have such places back up there in the North Carolina mountains."

"Of course not, Josephine," Tommy put in. "You couldn't grow rice in that climate."

"What I meant was that mountain people would never have the money to build such a place," the girl said.

Just then Uncle Ned joined them, and Mandie sighed with relief. The conversation was starting to get out of hand.

"Uncle Ned, Josephine says we're almost there," Mandie said.

"I go help with baggage," the old man said, turning to leave.

Tommy put a hand on Uncle Ned's arm. "No, sir," he said kindly. "You don't have to help. We pay our servants to do things like that. You are our guest, sir. Stay with us."

Uncle Ned smiled. "I never see rice fields before. I been to Charleston City, never see rice."

"It's not such a big thing anymore," Tommy said. "The War of Northern Aggression spoiled all the big plantations, but it's just as well. Times change and some things for the better."

"Look!" Josephine cried, pointing ahead as they came around a bend in the river. "There's the dock."

At a large loading dock ahead, nearly a dozen strong-looking men scurried around, loading and unloading the boats that were tied there. On the shore, a little distance from the dock, stood a cluster of brick buildings.

"Looks like a busy place," Mandie remarked.

"They're bringing in supplies," Tommy said. "And they're probably loading merchandise for the markets."

"Just wait till you see the house!" Josephine told Mandie. "You'll probably get lost in it. We need ten house servants to take care of it when we use the whole house."

As their boat turned toward the dock, Mandie could see a rig waiting.

"Isn't that your rig from town?" Mandie asked.

"Right," Tommy replied. "Rouster brought the other servants from town in the rig after he took us to the boat. There's a road from the beach house to the plantation, but Mother thought you'd enjoy the boat ride. We usually come by water anyway. It's not as dusty, and it's smoother riding."

As their boat docked, they all disembarked and piled into the waiting rig.

"But where is the house?" Mandie looked around, holding Snowball.

"It's up the road apiece," Tommy answered. "The house is built away from the water in case of flooding."

After riding through a thickly wooded area, they suddenly came into a clearing. There stood Mossy Manor. Made of handmade brick, it rose three stories high behind big round white columns that supported a two-story porch. Balconies lined the outside of the third floor. Shrubbery grew thick around the house, and Spanish moss dripped from the giant oak trees. Peacocks strutted possessively around the grounds.

Mandie was awestruck. She glanced at Uncle Ned. He, too, looked speechless.

As the rig stopped at the wide front steps, uniformed house servants came to greet them and to unload the baggage.

Josephine jerked on Mandie's hand. "Come on. I'll show you the house." She jumped down from the rig and Mandie followed reluctantly.

"I'll catch up with you later," Tommy called as Josephine hurried Mandie into the house ahead of the others.

Inside, Mandie put Snowball down and looked around. The huge entry hall was filled with priceless antiques. The richness had an old, mellow look about it. Josephine hurried her through double doors into another smaller hallway.

"Come on. First, I'll show you where the ghosts stay," Josephine said.

Mandie tried to pull away, but the girl's grip was firm. "Josephine, please don't start that ghost nonsense again," she protested.

"You can at least let me show you and listen to what I have to say," Josephine insisted.

Mandie drew a deep breath and allowed herself to be pulled up a narrow staircase. "All right, but I'm not going to believe a word you say."

Yet Mandie wondered if there really were such things as ghosts. And why did Josephine talk about them so much?

Mandie had to find some answers.

CHAPTER TWELVE

GHOSTS FROM THE PAST

Josephine led Mandie all the way up the stairs to the third floor. "These are the servants' stairs," Josephine told her. "But they're nearer to what I want to show you."

At the top of the stairs, the two girls stepped into a dark, narrow hallway.

"These are the servants' quarters over here," Josephine explained. "Not all of the rooms are occupied because we don't need as many servants as my ancestors did when they built this house. Come on, down this way," she said, taking the lead.

As they walked down the hall, they passed rows of open doors revealing neat interiors, some furnished with expensive antiques. Josephine stopped at the doorway of one of the rooms.

"These don't look like servants' rooms," Mandie remarked. "Look at all the antiques."

"I know, but the antiques were willed or given to servants down through time. These things have all been passed down to the present owners. You see, we still have descendants of slaves working for us, but they're on a salary now since the war. Some of these people have never even been off the plantation except to go in to Charleston. They are born here, marry someone else here, raise their children here, and then die here. The slaves' cemetery has a lot more graves in it than the white cemetery does."

At the end of the hallway was a door. Josephine opened it. "I'll go first, but be careful," she warned. "It's so dark in here you can't see where you're going." She stepped inside and Mandie followed, her heart beating faster as she groped in the darkness.

"There are steps here," Josephine told her. "They're steep, and winding, and narrow. Hold onto the bannister."

"Where in the world are we going?" Mandie demanded.

"You'll see." Josephine started to climb the narrow steps.

Still suspicious, Mandie followed, cautiously moving one foot and then the next to the steps above her. She certainly didn't want to fall in this dark place with only Josephine to help her.

When Josephine reached the top, she opened another door. Instantly, light flooded the stairway, and Mandie could see that she was in a round tower room of some kind with stairs that spiraled to the ceiling. Josephine waited for her at the top.

Stepping off the last step, Mandie looked around her. The door opened into a circular hallway with windows all around it.

"This is the watchtower," Josephine explained. "It has been used to watch for all kinds of things—ships, pirates, whatever."

A narrow window seat ran almost all the way around the room, and there was still another door at the far side. Josephine unlocked the door, and when she had opened it, Mandie could see an outside walk on the roof similar to the one on the house in Charleston.

Mandie followed her outside. The height made her dizzy. Trying not to let Josephine know this, she turned around to look at the inside, rather than out into open space.

"Is this what you wanted to show me?" Mandie asked. "Just an old tower with a walkway around it?"

"Call it an old tower if you want to, but it's more than that," Josephine replied. "It's haunted. Years and years ago, before anybody living today was even born, the master of the plantation was an old decrepit snob named Nathaniel Patton, and he had a beautiful young wife named Ophelia. Well, Ophelia was having her portrait done by Alonzo de Bussy. She was posing outside here on the walkway."

"Way up here? Why?"

"I don't know," Josephine said impatiently. "But anyway, Nathaniel was a jealous, suspicious old codger, and he spied on them. When he found the artist brushing Ophelia's hair back from her face, and straightening her gown, Nathaniel thought that was just too intimate. In a fit of rage, he drew his sword, and without a word, he stabbed Ophelia."

"He killed his own wife? Oh, how awful," Mandie said in disbelief. "Why wouldn't he kill the artist instead?"

"He tried," Josephine said in a cocky sort of way. "After he killed Ophelia, he turned to Alonzo. But Alonzo was much younger and stronger, and he managed to escape. He left Nathaniel lying unconscious on the walkway there." Josephine pointed a short distance away. "All that time, Ophelia's maid, who was acting as chaperone, hovered around the corner during the fracas. By the time the old man came to, the maid was long gone. She told the other servants her terrifying story, took a horse, and ran away. She was never heard from again."

Mandie looked at Josephine skeptically. "Is this really true?"

Josephine nodded. "Of course it's true. Alonzo was nearly finished with the portrait when Nathaniel went after Ophelia with his sword. The painting got splattered with Ophelia's blood. I found the portrait one day. I'll show it to you. It still has bloodstains on it." Josephine watched for Mandie's reaction.

Mandie's eyes grew wide, and she shivered in spite of herself. "Oh, how horrible!" she exclaimed.

"Well, that's not all," Josephine continued. "Sometimes the door here is found unlocked and standing wide open."

"Maybe a servant comes up here," Mandie suggested.

"Oh, no, there's never been a servant in the house who would come up here after what happened. They're afraid of the place. But sometimes you can hear the outside door banging, like it was being opened and shut real hard," Josephine said. Then in a spooky voice she added, "I've even heard Ophelia's screams."

Mandie cleared her throat. "Well, someone has to be doing it."

"Someone who is dead," Josephine insisted. "It's the ghost of Ophelia who is trying to come back alive. Ophelia died too young."

Mandie wrinkled her nose in disbelief. "Whatever happened to Nathaniel? Did they try him for murder?"

"Of course not," Josephine replied. "He was the lord of the manor and did what he pleased. He reported that when he found his wife and Alonzo alone together, the artist grabbed his sword and in trying to stab him, Alonzo accidentally stabbed Ophelia and ran away. So that was the end of it. The servants all knew better, but they didn't dare speak up."

"If they didn't speak up, then how did anyone know what happened?" Mandie asked.

"Nathaniel died soon after that and the information became common knowledge," Josephine explained.

Mandie shook her head sadly. "And just think, the poor woman died for no reason."

Josephine walked over to the window seat and raised the lid. She pulled out a large portrait and stood it up on the seat. "There she is. See the bloodstains?" Josephine pointed to several dark brown spots on a corner of the portrait.

Mandie looked at the woman in the painting. She was a small-looking blonde with curls piled high on her head and sparkling green eyes. She wore a lacy white gown and was seated on a bench on the walkway outside the tower room. Emeralds circled her slender neck and adorned her ears. She held a red rosebud in her left hand. Mandie moved closer to inspect the picture.

"What is it?" Josephine asked, watching Mandie.

"She was married, but she doesn't have on a wedding band," Mandie observed.

"I know. She must have removed it for the picture. Maybe Nathaniel noticed that, too."

"Are you sure this is Ophelia's portrait?" Mandie asked.

"Of course I'm sure. The family has talked about it for years. Besides"—Josephine pointed—"there is blood on it."

"How do you know that's blood?" Mandie asked, looking closer at the brown spots on the portrait. "It could be paint, or mold, or something else."

"Don't you understand? The family knows all about this portrait," Josephine said, exasperated. "I know this is Ophelia."

"But you said you found it. Didn't anyone else know where it was?"

"Not until I found it in the window seat there. No one living had ever seen the portrait until I found it. But the story has been in the family for generations," Josephine said. "Ophelia does haunt this room up here. I've heard her scream, and I've also seen the door to the outside walk slam shut with no one near it."

"You saw the door close with no one around?"

"Yes, look!" Josephine moved the creaking door back and forth. "See? The door drags a little on the bottom. It could never swing by itself, and it could never be blown shut either."

Josephine was right. Could her story really be true? Did the dead woman's ghost really haunt the tower?

"Now that I've told you about Ophelia, let's go downstairs and I'll show you her room," Josephine said, locking the outside door. "I'll wait till you get down the stairs before I shut this door, so you'll have light to see. But for goodness sakes, please hurry."

Mandie quickly ran down the curving stairs. When she was about halfway down she thought she saw something white moving below. Then as she got nearer the bottom, the door to the hallway slammed shut with a loud bang. Her heart thumped wildly. Her legs felt as if they wouldn't hold her up. She bit her lip, tightened her grip on the bannister, and kept going.

"What was that?" Josephine called from above. "Is someone else down there?"

"No, the door just blew shut, that's all," Mandie replied, trying to keep her voice from quavering.

"I'm closing the door up here. Hurry and open that one down there," Josephine called.

Mandie quickly felt her way down and pushed the hallway door open.

Josephine ran down the stairs. "Come on. We'll go this way," she said, reaching the bottom.

"Where is this room you want me to see?" Mandie asked without moving.

"It's on this floor," Josephine told her. "But if you don't come on, I'll leave you standing there all by yourself."

At that threat Mandie quickly followed Josephine down the hallway and through a door into a much larger hallway.

"This is the wing that Ophelia and Nathaniel used when they lived here. It's all closed up now," Josephine said.

As Mandie silently walked behind Josephine, she noticed the fine old draperies on the windows in the hallway and the antique chairs, chests, and tables along the way. It looked like a museum.

Josephine stopped in front of a door at the corner of the hallway. "Prepare yourself! This is it!" she exclaimed dramatically. She flung open the heavy, ornate door.

Mandie stood still, not knowing what to expect. Josephine stepped ahead of her inside the room, blocking her view and waiting for her.

Mandie hesitantly followed. She caught her breath. The room was beautifully decorated in green and white. In the center stood a high four-poster bed, complete with canopy and curtains, and a small green-upholstered footstool for climbing into bed.

Over a huge fireplace, which took up half of one wall, hung a portrait. Was the woman in the painting the same woman in the tower-room portrait? Mandie wondered. In this picture the blonde woman wore an emerald green gown with diamond jewelry around her neck and on her ears, fingers, and wrists. She also had a wedding band on her left hand.

"You see, Ophelia did wear a wedding band," Josephine said, noticing Mandie's attention to this.

"But how do you know this is Ophelia?" Mandie asked.

"Can't you see that's the same woman in the portrait upstairs?" Josephine tapped her foot impatiently.

"It could be two different women, like the two Melissas at your home in town," Mandie suggested.

"Oh, no, it can't." Josephine walked over to the portrait. "You see that little mole right there on her left cheek? Well, the portrait upstairs shows the same thing in the exact same spot."

"Is that how you figured this must be her room?" Mandie asked.

"In a way," Josephine said. "But the servants still tell tales about Ophelia, and none of them will come up to this part of the house. So one day I did some exploring, trying to figure out what it was that frightened them. The other rooms are used for storage, but this room is special."

Mandie looked around at the well-kept furnishings. "If the servants won't come up here, who keeps this room clean?"

"That I can't tell you, but I don't know of a servant on this plantation who will come here. They all know Ophelia's story," Josephine said.

I'd never come here either after all the tales Josephine tells, Mandie thought.

Josephine stepped over in front of a large, ornately carved dresser with an oval-shaped mirror. "Look, even her jewelry box still plays," she said, picking up a small gold box with a metal rose on top. She turned the key and opened the box to reveal a beautiful strand of pearls. As the music began to play, Mandie recognized the tune—The Blue Danube waltz.

Mandie stepped closer to look. "Are those her pearls in there?"

"I suppose so," Josephine said, picking up the strand and then dropping it back inside. Closing the music box, she stepped over to a huge matching wardrobe and opened the doors. "Even her clothes are still in here," she said.

Mandie walked slowly toward the wardrobe in awe. It was filled with expensive-looking gowns, every one of which was either green or white. "Didn't she ever wear anything besides green and white?"

"Evidently not," Josephine replied, running her hand across the hanging gowns. She took a green dress from its hanger and held it out for Mandie to see. "This is the one she had on in that picture, see?"

Mandie looked at the dress and then at the portrait. Impossible, she thought. How could a dress survive all these years and be in such good shape? Yet it did seem to be exactly like the green dress in the portrait. It was all a mystery.

Suddenly, Mandie became nervous. "Don't you think we'd better go back downstairs? Everyone will be wondering where we are."

"I suppose so," Josephine said, hanging the dress back in the wardrobe. "I'll show you the rest of the house later. Come on. I know a different way to get back downstairs."

Josephine closed the door behind them, then led Mandie to a wide, curving staircase.

At the first landing, which was the second story, Josephine paused. "You'll be using a room right down that hallway." She pointed to the right.

Mandie looked where she pointed, wondering if that part of the house were deserted, too.

Josephine must have guessed what she was thinking. She laughed. "Don't worry. My room is right next to yours. Your parents are nearby, and Tommy's room is down at the end of the hall."

Just then Tommy appeared at the foot of the stairs in the first-floor hallway. "I've been looking everywhere for you two," he called. "Mandie, I want to show you around outside."

"Oh, thank you, Tommy," Mandie said, hurrying down to join him.

What a relief to be rescued from Josephine and her ghosts! Maybe the story Josephine told was true and maybe not. Or maybe part of it was true, and the girl added to it. Anyway, Mandie didn't want anything more to do with ghosts. One ghost at the beach house was enough to have to investigate!

CHAPTER THIRTEEN

RICE FIELDS

Tommy led the way outside into the backyard. "I want you to see the field hands reaping the rice," he said as they walked by the toolshed. "It's something you'll never forget."

"I've never seen rice growing," Mandie said excitedly.

Tommy paused by the stables. "It's a long way. Should we ride?"

"Let's walk. I love to walk," Mandie told him.

It was a long trek along a well-worn path. Before they got to the rice fields, Mandie heard someone singing. "Where is that coming from?" she asked.

"The field hands. They always sing while they reap the rice—an old custom passed down through generations," Tommy explained. "They also know we'll be giving them a party when they finish, so I guess they're happy about it."

The trees began to thin out, and suddenly Mandie stopped to stare. There before her lay a golden sea of rice plants as far as she could see.

Dozens of Negro field hands sang as they clipped the top ends of the plants, making indentations in the fields as they waded through.

Tommy and Mandie walked on, stopping at the edge of the field.

"That is rice?" Mandie exclaimed. "How beautiful!"

Tommy smiled at her. "They are clipping off the heads because that's where the rice is. But you'll notice they are leaving the heads lying on the stalks. That's so it will dry out. Tomorrow another group will follow this one's path and collect the rice heads."

"Then what happens?" Mandie couldn't take her eyes off the fields.

"Each sheaf, or handful, is wrapped with a wisp of the plant and stored in cocks. Cocks are cone-shaped piles of straw," Tommy explained. "Then it's ready for shipment."

"Where do you ship it?"

"Lots of places. A great deal of it is sold in the United States, but a lot of it also goes to Europe."

"It sounds easy," Mandie commented as she watched the workers.

"It takes a great deal of work just getting it this far," Tommy told her. "The fields have to be drained, and you hope a hurricane won't come and destroy the crop before you can bring it in. Some years the whole crop is damaged and you lose money. Then again, good years like this one bring in a lot of money."

"What do these rice plants grow from? Where do you get them?"

"From seed. Some of this crop will be saved for seed to plant next year. The seed rice is beat out of the sheaves by hand so it won't be damaged. That's called flailing."

"Is that how you get it out to cook and eat, too?" Mandie asked.

Tommy laughed. "No, that's another stage. The rice kernels are covered with husks. These have to be removed by pounding. Then after you get all the husks off, the rice is ready to cook and eat."

"Are we going to eat some of your rice while we're here?"

"We sure are," Tommy replied. "We have rice every night— with other things, of course. It's like eating bread. Rice goes with everything."

"At home, we eat potatoes like that," Mandie said.

"Talking about eating, I imagine we have tea waiting for us at the house by now," Tommy said, turning to go.

"Come to think of it, I'm starving," Mandie laughed.

As they walked back through the woods to the house, they suddenly came face-to-face with Josephine.

She was obviously out of breath from running. "Mother sent me to—"

"I know, tea is ready," Tommy interrupted her. "We're on our way back."

"Then you'd better hurry. Mrs. Shaw . . . has asked me three times . . . if I knew where Mandie was," Josephine said, still out of breath. "Of course I didn't tell her."

"Why not?" Mandie asked.

"Mandie, I don't know about where you come from, but in this part of the country a young girl doesn't go off into the woods with a boy unchaperoned," Josephine told her.

"But we just went for a walk," Mandie protested.

"The adults think they can't trust us," Josephine said.

"Fortunately, that old custom is rapidly becoming obsolete," Tommy added. "But I do hope your mother isn't angry with me for taking you off to the rice fields."

"I don't think she will be," Mandie replied. "She trusts me."

When the three arrived at the manor house, everyone was in the parlor having tea and cakes.

Elizabeth immediately stood up. "Amanda!" Her face showed relief. "You must let me know where you are going. This place is too big. You might get lost."

Uncle John, who was usually more lenient with Mandie, nodded in agreement. "Yes, Amanda, you should keep us better informed."

"I'm sorry," Mandie apologized. She walked over to her mother. "I promise I'll ask permission next time, but I just had to see the rice fields."

Tommy looked a little embarrassed. "I'm afraid it was all my fault, Mrs. Shaw," he said. "The rice is being reaped, and I was so eager to show it to Mandie that I didn't stop to think. I'm sorry."

"I appreciate your showing Amanda around, Thomas, but I'm afraid I find it difficult to keep up with her whereabouts sometimes," Elizabeth said with a little laugh. She turned back to Mandie. "I'm not requiring you to ask permission for every move, Amanda, but I would like to know where you are."

Mrs. Patton sat forward. "You're absolutely right, Elizabeth. This is a huge place, and Amanda could very well become lost," she said.

"Thomas, you and Josephine must make sure one of you accompanies her around outside so she won't get lost."

"You might include the inside of the house as well, Lucille," Mr. Patton added. "This old house is so big and built in such a jumble it would be easy to wander around lost in it for hours."

"I've already been showing her around the house," Josephine spoke up. "It was Tommy's idea to go to the rice fields," she tattled.

Mrs. Patton frowned at her daughter. "He already told us that," she said, obviously displeased.

Uncle John tried to smooth over the situation. "And what did you think of the rice fields, Amanda?" he asked.

"Oh, they're beautiful!" Mandie exclaimed. "Just think, the rice we eat comes out of those great, golden fields. I had never even thought about where rice came from before."

Elizabeth patted her daughter's hand. "This trip has been quite educational for you, hasn't it, Amanda?"

Mandie nodded.

"I'm glad you are enjoying yourself, dear. Now please sit down and have some tea," her mother instructed.

As Mandie started to sit down, she looked around the room, frowning. "Where is Uncle Ned, Mother?" she asked.

"He took one of the horses and went riding to get a little fresh air," her mother replied.

Pleased that Uncle Ned felt at home, Mandie sat down across the room near Josephine and Tommy. Tizzy was waiting to serve her.

"Thank you, Tizzy," she said to the maid, accepting a cup of tea and a dainty chocolate cake.

"You see, your mother doesn't trust you," Josephine whispered so the adults would not hear.

"Yes, she does," Mandie disagreed. "We love each other a lot. And she wants to be sure nothing happens to me, that's all."

"Now what could happen to you here?" Josephine asked.

Tommy nudged Mandie lightly. "Let's take our tea and sit on the veranda," he suggested.

Mandie stood up and looked across the room to her mother. "Tommy and I are going to sit on the veranda," she said.

"All right, dear," Elizabeth answered.

On the huge porch, there were several dark green wooden rocking chairs. Tommy led the way to the far corner where they sat down.

"This is the best place to sit. From here you can see all the flowers around the corner. You can also see where everyone is going because the servants' entrance is around there," he said, pointing to the side of the house.

"Is that the servants' entrance that goes up to the third floor?" Mandie asked, sipping her tea.

"Well, yes, but how did you know?" Tommy asked.

"Because Josephine took me up there. That's where we had been when we ran into you this afternoon."

"Why in the world did she take you up there?"

"To show me the watch tower and tell me about Ophelia."

"Ophelia?"

"You know, Ophelia, the woman who was married to Nathaniel Patton until he murdered her," Mandie answered.

"She told you about that?" Tommy asked, surprised.

"Yes, why? Is it a family secret?" Mandie asked.

"Oh, no, nothing like that," Tommy said quickly. "It's just that no one actually knows the whole story."

"But Josephine seemed to know everything," Mandie said, relating Josephine's story.

"I don't know what we're going to do with my sister. She embroiders the truth about everything, and sometimes I think she lives in a fantasy world," Tommy said. "No one knows what actually happened to Ophelia. It's all rumor."

"Is that really her portrait up there in the window seat?" Mandie asked.

Tommy shrugged. "It might be, but no one knows for sure."

"And I suppose that beautiful room with the wardrobe full of green and white dresses was not really hers either, was it?"

"The corner room was Ophelia's," Tommy replied, "but I have no idea what's in it. I didn't even know it was kept clean. Maybe I should ask Mother about it."

"Please don't, Tommy," Mandie pleaded. "Let's keep this talk a secret between the two of us, like our secret about the phantom at the beach."

"I'm sure there is some explanation for that thing, too," he said. "We'll find out what it is when we go back."

"I've heard so much about ghosts, I'm beginning to believe in them." Mandie laughed, but she kept wondering if Tommy was passing lightly over all the ghost business so that she wouldn't be scared.

"Oh, don't start believing in ghosts now," Tommy chided, "because when we find out the truth, your belief is going to be badly shaken."

"I'm sure we'll be able to solve the mystery at the beach with Uncle Ned's help," Mandie agreed. "Let's go find him so we can talk a while."

Tommy stood up. "All right. I'll saddle two horses. Come on."

After checking with her mother, Mandie followed Tommy to the stables. She looked forward to seeing Uncle Ned. In these strange surroundings, she found herself secretly wishing away the time until she would be on her way home. But in the meantime, maybe Uncle Ned could help her solve all these mysteries.

CHAPTER FOURTEEN

THE DESERTED CABINS

In the stables, Tommy introduced Mandie to the Negro stable boy.

"Is that really your name? Udunit?" Mandie asked.

"Sho is 'cause I done done it," the boy replied, laughing.

"You've done what?" she asked.

"I done done ebrything—dat's whut my ma say," Udunit told her.

Tommy smiled. "Well, let's see what you can do to find Mandie a horse that isn't too fast, Udunit," he said, walking among the stalls. Then looking at Mandie, he asked, "Are you sure you want a horse to ride? We have a pony here."

"I am twelve years old," Mandie reminded him. "It's time to leave the ponies behind. Just don't pick out one that's too big."

Tommy laughed and opened the door of one of the stalls to reveal a young horse, not quite grown. "How about Slowpoke here?"

"Is that the horse's name?" Mandie asked.

"Not exactly, but he's so slow somebody gave him that nickname," Tommy explained.

"All right, as long as I can keep up with you," Mandie said.

Tommy and the stable boy saddled Slowpoke and then brought out a light brown horse with a beautiful chestnut mane.

"Oh! Is that horse yours?" Mandie squealed, reaching out to touch the silky mane.

"Yes, he's mine. His name is Cyclone," Tommy said.

"Why Cyclone?"

"He rides through anything and smashes everything in his way. I'll let you ride him sometime."

"I think I'll have to work up to that," Mandie laughed. Holding Slowpoke's reins, she started talking to him and patting his nose.

The horse immediately rubbed his head against her arm, thoroughly delighting her.

"Oh, Slowpoke, you're a sweet doll. You behave for me, and I'll get you some sugar when we get back."

Slowpoke snorted and rubbed her arm again.

"Ready?" Tommy asked, leading his horse outside.

"Ready." Mandie brought her horse alongside his.

With a little help from Udunit and Tommy, Mandie mounted Slowpoke from the stepping block. She grasped the reins and held her breath. This was a great experience for her, her first time on a real horse. Everything on the ground seemed so far away.

"Please be careful," Tommy cautioned her as he mounted Cyclone. "I'll lead the way, but I won't go fast."

"Thanks," Mandie said with a smile. "Let's go."

Slowpoke *was* a slowpoke. Tommy had to keep reining in his horse for Mandie to keep up with him. Following a different path from the one they had taken to the rice fields, Tommy led the way along the edge of the woods. Rounding a bend in the path, they came upon a settlement of cabins in the woods. Here and there Negro children played in the yards.

"These must be the field hands' homes," Mandie called to Tommy.

Tommy reined in his horse and waited for her to come alongside of him. "They used to be slaves' cabins, but now they are part of the pay the hands receive. They're not all occupied. That whole row down there is vacant," he said, pointing down by the creek.

Mandie turned to look at the tumbled-down shacks. The deserted houses somehow looked mysterious and intriguing. "Let's go closer," Mandie said, starting toward the abandoned cabins.

At that moment, one of the Negro men on horseback called to Tommy and rode quickly toward him. Tommy waited for the man he greeted as Uncle Luke, and the two talked for a while.

All of a sudden, as Mandie reached one of the cabins, Slowpoke bolted and ran off with her. Mandie screamed. In panic she held the reins tightly and yelled for the horse to slow down. But he wouldn't. "Help!" she hollered.

"Hang on, Mandie!" Tommy called to her. "I'm coming!"

Mandie's fingers hurt so badly that she could hardly hang on anymore. If she were thrown, she could be seriously injured or even killed. "Dear God, help me!" she cried.

In seconds, Mandie caught a glimpse of Uncle Ned. He was racing toward her on horseback from a clump of trees nearby. Then suddenly Mandie felt herself being snatched from the saddle. She almost collapsed with relief.

When Uncle Ned slowed down enough to set her on the ground, her legs were so wobbly she could hardly stand up.

Uncle Ned threw his arms around Mandie. She buried her head on his shoulder. The old Indian gave Mandie a big hug. "Do not cry, Papoose," he begged. "Things all right now."

"Thank you, Uncle Ned," Mandie said.

Tommy, catching up with them, dismounted. "Are you all right, Mandie?" he asked in genuine concern.

Mandie nodded. "But what about the horse?" she asked.

"Don't worry about the horse," Tommy said. "Uncle Luke will catch him."

Mandie watched as the old Negro galloped at full speed, quickly turning this way and that. Finally Uncle Luke managed to intercept the runaway horse. He grabbed Slowpoke's reins. "Mastuh Tommy!" he called, waiting as Tommy quickly mounted and raced over to him.

The old Negro looked worried. "Mastuh Tommy, Slowpoke ain't no slowpoke no mo,' " he said. "Sumpin' spoofed dat hoss sho' as I'se asittin' heah."

"Thanks, Uncle Luke," Tommy said. "It looks like he's quieted down now. Would you take him back to the stables for me?"

"Sho, Mastuh Tommy. I takes him," the old man said, leading the horse away.

Tommy joined Mandie and Uncle Ned and again dismounted. "What happened, Mandie?" he asked.

"I don't know." Mandie's voice was still shaky. "Just as we passed that third cabin, Slowpoke suddenly snorted and bucked. I thought he was going to throw me, but then he took off aflying. And just as I was about to fall, that's when Uncle Ned came along."

"I'm thankful you're not hurt." Tommy sighed with relief. "Let's go look at that cabin."

The three walked back up the slight hill to the long row of shacks. The buildings had not been kept up, but the grounds were clean.

"It was this one," Mandie said, indicating the third from the end. "I didn't see anything, but that horse sure got frightened when we passed this house."

"You stay here. I'll have a look inside," Tommy told her.

Mandie stood still while Tommy stepped inside the open doorway.

Uncle Ned bent to look closely at the ground, making his way around to the back of the cabin.

In a minute Tommy came back outside. "I didn't see a thing but some old rags," he told her.

Then Uncle Ned came out through the front, too. "Feet marks at back. Go out into field," he reported. Leading the way to the back, he showed them some faint feet marks in the dirt.

"But Uncle Ned, those were probably made by some of the children playing up there." Tommy pointed to the cabins where the field hands and their families lived.

"Big feet marks," Uncle Ned insisted.

"Well, maybe some of the adults came down here. I don't know," Tommy said in frustration. "But I think we'd better get back to the house."

"I think so, too," Mandie agreed. She looked up into Uncle Ned's face. "We came to find you and it's a good thing we did."

"I watch over Papoose," Uncle Ned said, smoothing her long blonde hair. He smiled.

"Well, we only have two horses left, Mandie," Tommy said. "Do you want to ride with Uncle Ned or with me?"

Mandie sighed. "It's not too far, is it? I think I'd like to walk if y'all don't mind."

"I don't blame you for not wanting to get on another horse," Tommy told her.

"It's not that, Tommy. It's just easier to talk if we're walking," she said.

"Walk good for legs," Uncle Ned agreed.

Leading the two horses, they started back toward the house.

"We'll be going back to the beach house tomorrow," Tommy remarked as they strolled along.

"I hope we can find out what that phantom is that we saw at the pier," Mandie said.

"No ghost. We find no ghost," Uncle Ned said.

"Right," Tommy agreed. "There's just no such thing."

"Then what was that thing?" Mandie persisted.

"We find out." Uncle Ned nodded.

After taking the horses to the stables, they walked on to the house. Mandie's mother and Uncle John were sitting on the porch talking to the Pattons. Snowball jumped down from the porch and ran to meet Mandie.

Picking him up, Mandie hugged him tightly. "I might as well tell you, Mother," Mandie began as she came up the steps. "I—almost had an accident, but—"

"Accident!" Elizabeth interrupted. "What happened?"

"Well, I talked Tommy into letting me ride a horse for the first time, and he gave me Slowpoke to ride. He's supposed to be the slowest of all the horses, but he suddenly ran away with me down by the deserted cabins."

"Amanda!" Elizabeth gasped.

Suddenly everyone was talking at once.

"Are you all right?" Uncle John asked.

"Yes, I'm all right." Mandie nodded. "I had lots of help," she said, relating the story of the rescue.

"I'm glad Tommy and Uncle Ned were there to help," Mrs. Patton told Mandie. "What could have spooked the horse?"

"It was probably a snake or rat," Mr. Patton answered. "We try to keep the place cleaned off down there, but it grows up in spite of everything."

"No snake. No rat," said Uncle Ned. "Feet marks."

"Footprints?" Uncle John questioned.

"Big ones," Uncle Ned replied.

"I thought they might have been made by some of the field hands," Tommy suggested. "They probably roam around all over the place down there."

"Regardless of what it was, Amanda," Elizabeth told her daughter, "you'll have to promise not to ride any strange horses again. Just think of what could have happened to you!"

"I promise, Mother," Mandie said. She bent to give her mother a little hug then followed Tommy to the other end of the porch where Josephine was sitting alone.

As Mandie approached, Josephine looked up. "Those weren't the footprints of any field hands," she whispered. "The field hands are all afraid to go near the deserted cabins. Those old shacks are haunted by murdered slaves."

"What!" Mandie sank down into a nearby chair.

Tommy sat down next to her and spoke to his sister. "Josephine, you've got to stop all this ghost nonsense."

"Well, there were slaves murdered down there. You know it as well as I do," Josephine insisted.

"We will talk about something else," Tommy said firmly. Turning to Mandie, he changed the subject. "It will be suppertime before long, and we're having rice. In fact, the whole meal will be products from our plantation."

"I think that's wonderful," Mandie replied. But her mind wasn't on supper. *Josephine knows something about murdered slaves that Tommy doesn't want me to hear,* she thought. He always seemed to be trying to protect her. There were too many strange things going on here.

CHAPTER FIFTEEN

THE MYSTERY OF THE PHANTOM

The evening meal was served in the huge formal dining room, and everyone dressed up for the occasion.

Mandie looked around the table. Even Uncle Ned wore a dark suit. Mandie had never seen him dressed like that before. All through the meal he looked terribly uncomfortable. He didn't say a word but just listened to the young people's conversation, smiling at Mandie across the table.

Mandie returned his smile with a quiet sigh. Her mother and Uncle John looked right at home here in this finery, yet Mandie couldn't help but think of her father. He wouldn't have been comfortable here. He was such a down-to-earth person, enjoying the simple things of life. She had been so happy with him back in their log cabin.

Tears of sadness suddenly filled her eyes. She quietly put down her fork and raised a finger to wipe the tears away. When she looked up, Tommy was watching her.

He leaned toward her. "Are you all right, Mandie?" he asked softly.

"Yes." Mandie tried to laugh but her voice caught in her throat. "I'm all right. Just tired and upset after that wild ride this afternoon."

"You'll probably feel better after we get back to the beach house tomorrow," he said. "This house is so big and old it's not comfortable to live in. I don't see how our ancestors ever spent their entire lives here. My favorite place is the beach house. I'd live there all the time if it were up to me."

"That would be nice, I suppose, but I'm just a mountain country girl."

Josephine smirked.

Mandie pretended not to notice. She, too, was looking forward to returning to the beach house—and then home!

During a lull in the young people's conversation, Mandie again heard the adults discussing Hilda.

"We would, of course, have to redecorate one of the rooms here for her," Mrs. Patton told her husband. "But that would be quite a pleasant undertaking."

"You wouldn't have to redecorate," Mandie spoke up. "Why couldn't you use O—" Suddenly she felt a sharp kick on her leg. She looked up to see Josephine scowling at her.

"What's that, dear?" Elizabeth asked.

"Never mind," Mandie replied. She reached down to rub her leg where Josephine had kicked her. "Dumb idea." Mandie glared at Josephine and the adults resumed their conversation.

Later that night, as Mandie lay in bed, she kept thinking of all the spooky things Josephine had told her about the old house. The night seemed awfully long. She kept hearing strange noises, and every time the house creaked, she jumped.

She held tightly onto Snowball, who purred contentedly beside her for a while, then got up to walk about in circles on the bed before returning to curl up at her side again.

With all the mysterious things that had been happening here, Mandie kept wishing she could get back to her own kind of people. A twinge of guilt wrenched her heart at the thought of how angry she had been with Joe. She had known him all her life, and they had never had such an argument before. She promised herself that it would never happen again.

As Mandie grew sleepier, her mind wandered to thoughts of the beach and the phantom at the pier. The way it rose in the air and then fell into the water, how could it be anything other than a ghost? But what about the piece of white material they had found? Maybe some of Josephine's tales were true. No matter what Tommy said, Mandie was becoming more and more convinced that there was a ghost at the beach house.

Suddenly a door slammed. Mandie grabbed Snowball and sat up in bed. She held her breath and listened for a long time, but nothing else happened. Reluctantly, she lay back down, but the night was far spent before she finally fell asleep.

A knock on the door in the early morning woke Mandie. She sat up, rubbed her eyes, and looked around. "Come in," she called.

The door opened and Cheechee entered. "Breakfas' ready, Missy," the Negro girl told her. "We'se all agittin' ready to go back to de beach."

"Thank you, Cheechee," Mandie replied, jumping out of bed. "I'll be down in a minute."

Cheechee started out the door, then turned back. "I done forgot." She giggled. "You is to git yo' things togethuh, Missy," she said, hastily disappearing out the door.

Mandie grabbed Snowball and danced around the room in her long nightgown. "We're leaving, Snowball. We're leaving," she cried. "We're going back to the ocean, and then tomorrow we're going home!"

Snowball was used to his mistress's moods and merely reached out with his tongue to lick her face.

Mandie hurriedly dressed and crammed her belongings into her traveling bag. Snowball sat on the bed and watched.

"You're lucky, Snowball. You don't have to get dressed and pack up clothes and things," Mandie told the white kitten.

As she quickly brushed her long blonde hair, and tied it back with a ribbon, she heard voices in the room next to hers. Although she couldn't understand what they were saying, it sounded like Josephine was arguing with someone.

Mandie tiptoed to her door and listened. Just then a nearby door slammed and Mandie heard someone running down the stairs.

What on earth is happening around here? she wondered.

"Let's go eat, Snowball. Maybe I can find out what's going on." Mandie picked up the kitten and hurriedly left the room.

At the foot of the stairs she ran into Tizzy, who took Snowball into the kitchen for some food. Mandie joined the others in the breakfast room. Everyone else, including Josephine, was already seated at the table. Mandie took a place next to Uncle Ned, who looked much happier now, wearing his deerskin jacket and trousers.

"Oh, it'll be good to get back to Franklin tomorrow, Uncle Ned," Mandie said softly to him. "You know why."

Josephine looked up. "Why do you want to leave us so badly, Mandie?" she sneered. "Did you hear Ophelia's ghost slam that door last night?"

Mandie glared at her in silence.

"I know you heard it because I did, and your room is next to mine," Josephine told her.

"Oh, I heard something." Mandie tried to act nonchalant. "I thought it was probably someone going to bed late."

Josephine pushed her glasses up on her nose. "I don't know whether ghosts go to bed or not. I suppose they would have to rest sometime." She continued eating but never took her eyes off Mandie.

The adults, sitting at the far end of the table, stood up to leave. As Elizabeth passed Mandie's chair, she said, "Meet me at the front door in half and hour, Amanda, and be ready to leave, dear."

Mrs. Patton spoke to Tommy and Josephine. "You, too," she said.

Josephine got up and left the table quickly.

Mandie turned to Uncle Ned beside her. "And you, too, Uncle Ned," she said, laughing.

Uncle Ned smiled. "Me do," he replied, remaining seated with Tommy and Mandie.

As soon as the other adults were out the door, Tommy spoke up. "I'm sorry I banged that door so hard last night. I slipped down to the kitchen to get something to eat. I tried to be quiet, but that door to my room is hard to shut. I had to push it hard."

Mandie looked at him curiously. He's trying a little too hard to discredit Josephine's ghost story, she thought.

As soon as Mandie finished her meal, she jumped up from the table. "I have to go get Snowball. I'll see y'all later," she said.

"Be careful not to leave anything," Tommy called to her, taking one more helping of eggs.

"I'll try not to leave anything of mine, but I'll sure leave Josephine's ghosts here," she called back.

Mandie looked for Snowball in the kitchen first, but neither Tizzy nor Cheechee had seen the kitten for a while. After searching the entire first and second floors, Mandie started up the stairway to the third floor.

At the top of the stairs, she heard someone talking. Mandie's heart began to pound. She didn't think anyone would be up here, except maybe Snowball.

Hardly daring to breathe, she tiptoed down the hall toward the sound of the voice. *I haven't been in this part of the house before. Wait. Yes, I have.* There, at the end of the hall in the corner was a familiar ornately carved door. It was Ophelia's room. The door stood partially open. Could that be where the voice was coming from? Was she about to meet her first ghost?

Mandie crept quietly along the hall. Her heart was beating so loudly she hoped whoever or whatever was in that room couldn't hear it.

Just outside the beautiful green-and-white room, she hid behind the open door and peered around it. She gasped.

There in front of the huge dresser's oval-shaped mirror stood a young woman with long dark hair, and she was dressed in the emerald green gown Ophelia wore in her portrait!

Mandie almost screamed but quickly covered her mouth with her hand. *Wait,* Mandie told herself. *Ophelia had blonde hair.* She looked again. There on the dresser lay a pair of wire-rimmed glasses just like . . . That was Josephine standing before the mirror! And she was talking to herself as though she were a woman of high society carrying on a conversation with a dear friend.

Mandie stood outside the door for several minutes, watching.

Josephine smoothed her dark hair and smiled into the mirror. "Well, I suppose I ought to be going now," she said. "George and Lucille will be calling for me any minute."

Mandie turned quickly and tiptoed back downstairs. *Tommy is right,* she thought. *Josephine does live in a fantasy world.*

When Mandie got down to the first floor, Cheechee emerged from the kitchen, carrying Snowball.

"I done foun' him outside, Missy," Cheechee explained. "Musta got out whilst we wasn't lookin.'"

Mandie took Snowball from the girl. "Thanks, Cheechee."

"Yo' ma and Miz Patton, they be hoppin' mad, wonderin' where y'all be," Cheechee warned. "Best git out theah."

"I'm going right now," Mandie assured her, "and I think Josephine will be downstairs in a minute. Thanks."

A short time later, as everyone waited and talked in the rig, Josephine came running out of the house. "Sorry," she said, out of breath.

Her parents frowned at her but said nothing. Tommy shook his head.

Mandie wanted to tell him what she had seen, yet she felt that somehow it wasn't any of her business.

As soon as they arrived back at the beach house that morning, Mr. and Mrs. Patton made plans to cook the evening meal outside on the beach.

"We're going to build up a huge fire down there tonight and roast chicken," Tommy told Mandie as they stood on the veranda overlooking the beach. "The servants are all coming to join in, and Rouster will play his fiddle."

Mandie smiled. "Then you do mix with your servants and treat them like people—I mean not just like servants, you know what I mean?"

"I think so," Tommy said. "I know you must think we're all stiff and formal about everything, but we do break down every now and then and enjoy living."

Mandie laughed. "I suppose I just stay broken down all the time," she said.

"I wouldn't say you're broken down," Tommy teased. "But I would say you really enjoy life, every minute of it."

"Every minute of every day," Mandie admitted. "I just can't stand to sit still and do nothing."

"Let's don't just sit then. Let's go down on the beach," Tommy suggested.

The two strolled along, stopping every now and then to watch the waves. They found a few sand dollars and shells.

When the sun dropped low behind the horizon, the servants scurried about, moving a long wooden table to the beach.

Rouster piled up wood and started a huge fire. Tizzy and Cheechee brought chicken from the house and placed it on the spits Rouster had improvised over the fire. As darkness came, the servants lighted torches and placed them around in pots to light the area.

"That chicken sure smells good," Mandie told Tommy as Uncle Ned helped them spread blankets all around for everyone to sit on.

"Salt water air make Papoose hungry," Uncle Ned said.

"Makes me raving hungry," Tommy laughed. "Won't be long now till we can eat."

At last the sumptuous dinner, which was prepared entirely on the beach, was spread out on the long table. They all gathered around and helped themselves, taking their heaping plates and glasses of iced tea with them as they went back to sit on the blankets.

Rouster played his fiddle, and from time to time they all would clap their hands in time to the music.

As Mandie ate and talked with Tommy and Uncle Ned, she noticed that Josephine was sitting by herself on a blanket not far away. Mandie stared at the girl. "This is our last night to catch the phantom," she said.

"I know," Tommy agreed. "I hope it appears so we can find out what it is."

"We find," Uncle Ned said confidently. "But no ghost."

"We'll stay out here and watch after everyone eats and goes back to the house," Tommy said. "I just hope Josephine doesn't hang around."

But the phantom didn't wait for the adults to go back to the house. After the fire had died down and everyone had finished eating, Tommy carried one of the lighted torches while he, and Mandie, and Uncle Ned wandered down toward the pier.

Suddenly they heard that familiar eerie scream. The white filmy thing sailed through the air from the pier.

Tommy instantly threw the torch at it. He missed, but there was a scream of fright, and the phantom fell into the water beneath the pier.

Uncle Ned quickly jumped into the water after it. All the others ran to the pier and crowded around, asking questions. The old Indian surfaced in a minute and pulled a shaking, screaming young girl, black skin shining wetly, to the shore. As he set her down on the wet sand, Mandie and Tommy stared in disbelief.

It was Cheechee, wearing a thin white dress full of ruffles and lace!

Tizzy ran over to her daughter. But instead of comforting her, she started slapping her. "You no good fool!" Tizzy screamed. "You ain't no 'count atall!"

"Tizzy!" Mrs. Patton spoke firmly. "Stop that. I think it's time we get to the bottom of this."

Rouster took Tizzy by the arm and pulled her away from the girl.

Lucille Patton's face showed concern. "Is she hurt, Uncle Ned?"

"No, not hurt. Scared," the old Indian replied.

Mrs. Patton sighed loudly. Her jaw became firm. "Well, she'd sure better be scared. I want to know what this is all about, Cheechee. Get up! Get to your feet instantly!" she demanded.

Cheechee stood up but then bolted and ran away up the beach before anyone could stop her.

Tommy started to go after her, but Mrs. Patton grabbed his arm. "No, Thomas, let her go." She turned to her guests. "I'm sorry," she apologized. "I have no idea what this is all about."

George Patton came to his wife's side. "Why don't we all go back to the house?" he suggested.

While the others headed in, Mandie, Tommy, and a drenched Uncle Ned stayed behind. Uncle Ned warmed himself by the fire while Tommy stirred it up with left-over branches. Josephine was nowhere in sight.

"You see, I told you it wasn't a ghost," Tommy said.

Mandie laughed. "What a disappointment. But why on earth was she doing things like that?"

"I don't know, but I'd sure like to find out," Tommy said.

"Cheechee must come home," Uncle Ned observed. "Then we find out."

"I hope she gets back before we have to leave tomorrow," Mandie said.

"She'll have to so she can go back with us to the house in town," Tommy reminded her.

Mandie sighed. "So now we know what or who the phantom was, but we still have to solve the mystery of why Cheechee was doing it," she said in exasperation.

CHAPTER SIXTEEN

THE TRUTH COMES OUT

The next morning, when Tommy and Mandie returned from watching the sunrise, the others had already eaten breakfast and were finishing their packing.

Just as Tommy and Mandie entered the breakfast room and were about to help themselves to the food spread out on the sideboard, they heard a commotion in the kitchen and the sound of Tizzy's angry voice.

"I should've knowed you'd come back fo' food, you fool child!" Tizzy yelled.

Tommy and Mandie glanced at each other and ran into the kitchen. Tizzy grasped Cheechee's shoulders and was shaking the young girl unmercifully.

Tommy rushed forward. "That's enough, Tizzy," he ordered.

Tizzy meekly took her hands from her daughter's shoulders. "Cheechee done sneaked back heah jes to git sumpin' to eat," the maid explained. Her face was twisted with anger.

"I'm glad she came back," Tommy said, taking control. "We would like to ask her about some strange things that have been going on around here."

Both Tizzy and Cheechee hung their heads.

"I don' want no trouble." Cheechee shook her head from side to side. "I'se jes doin' what Missy Josephine done tol' me," she said quickly.

Just then, Uncle Ned entered the breakfast room, and Mandie motioned for him to join them in the kitchen. "Cheechee says she was only doing what Josephine told her," she repeated to her Indian friend. "Come to think of it, I haven't seen Josephine yet this morning."

"Me go find. Find others, too," Uncle Ned said gravely. "End big mystery."

In a few moments, Uncle Ned returned with Josephine and her parents, as well as Elizabeth and Uncle John.

Mr. Patton looked at Tommy curiously as the entire group crowded into the kitchen. "What is going on, son?" he asked.

"Cheechee says that Josephine put her up to her phantom stunt last night, and I have a feeling she was behind the other strange ghost appearances during Mandie's stay, including the runaway horse. Isn't that right, Josephine?"

"She's lying," Josephine accused. "How could I make her do anything like that?"

Mandie thought for a moment then looked at Cheechee. "I heard Josephine arguing with someone the other morning. Was that you, Cheechee? Did that have anything to do with this?"

"Yessum," Cheechee admitted readily. "Missy Josephine, she done catched me doin' sumpin' I shouldn't, and she say she tell my ma and Miz Patton if'n I doesn't help huh wid huh plan. I didn't wanna do it no more, but she get real mad."

Josephine squinted angrily at Cheechee but said nothing.

"What plan?" Tommy asked.

"Missy Josephine she say she don't want Missy Mandie aroun',' so she aks me to play lahk I'se a ghost so's to skeer Missy Mandie away."

"Why would I want to do that?" Josephine shifted nervously from one foot to the other.

Suddenly, Mandie had an idea. "Were you afraid of Hilda coming?" she asked.

Josephine pushed her glasses up on her nose but didn't reply.

"That's it, isn't it? You were afraid your parents would give Hilda the room that Ophelia used to have."

Mrs. Patton put her arm around Josephine. "Why would that bother you, dear?"

Josephine's hard exterior began to melt. A tear ran down her cheek. "That's *my* special room," she explained.

Mr. and Mrs. Patton looked at her, confused.

"I think I'm starting to understand," Mandie told them. "The other morning, when I was looking for Snowball, I found her in that room. She didn't even know I was there. She had taken her glasses off and put on one of Ophelia's dresses. She stood in front of the mirror, primping and talking to an imaginary friend."

A strange look came into Josephine's eyes. "I like to pretend that I'm Ophelia," she said in a dreamy-sounding voice. "When I stand in front of her mirror without my glasses on, that's the only time I feel pretty. You can't take my special place from me. You can't give it to some little girl who can't even talk right," she cried.

Mr. Patton took Josephine into his arms and hugged her tightly. "Josephine, we had no idea how you felt about the room or about Hilda," he said gently. "It was wrong for you to behave hatefully toward Mandie. You should have told us how you felt." He stroked his daughter's long dark hair.

"Perhaps we can find another room for Hilda," Mrs. Patton suggested. "But if it's at all possible, we do want to give her a place in our home. I believe she already has a place in our hearts—just like we once found a place for *you* in our hearts."

Josephine looked up at her questioningly.

"Yes, dear," her mother replied. "I suppose we should have told you long before this, but when you were less than a year old, your mother died, so we adopted you—made you a regular part of our family."

Tears filled Josephine's eyes as she realized what her mother was saying. "I'm adopted?" Her voice quavered as she said the words.

Mr. Patton gave her a big hug. "Yes, Josephine, but we love you just as much as if you were born to us," he assured her. "And we'd like to keep sharing our love by reaching out to Hilda just like we reached out in love to you. Do you understand?"

Josephine buried her head in her father's chest and cried uncontrollably. "Oh, I'm so sorry," she sobbed. "I wish I could . . ."

"Hush, now," her father consoled. "Perhaps we've all grown a bit because of this whole incident."

Josephine looked up at Mandie. "I'm sorry, Mandie. I didn't know."

Mandie took a deep breath and blew it out, battling the angry feelings she had had toward Josephine. "I guess I understand," she said.

After the young people finished breakfast, the Pattons took the Shaws and Uncle Ned directly to the depot in town in order to get the train on time. As they pulled up in the rig, the train was already waiting, so goodbyes were short.

Elizabeth singled out Tommy. "Thomas, you must visit us while you're in school in Asheville. Let us know when, and we'll come and get you and Mandie for a weekend."

"Thank you, ma'am. I will," Tommy promised. He turned to Mandie and squeezed her hand. "See you back in Asheville next time our two schools do something together."

"Thanks for everything, Tommy," Mandie said. "This is one trip I'll never forget." She tightened her grip on Snowball and boarded the train.

The Shaws and Uncle Ned all found seats together, and Mandie flopped down with a sigh of relief. She slept most of the way, and before she knew it, the journey had ended. They were home at last!

Jason Bond met them at the depot with their rig, and as they approached the house, Mandie's heart beat faster. Dr. Woodard's buggy was at their gate.

"Is Dr. Woodard visiting us?" she asked Jason Bond.

"Sure is. His boy, too." Mr. Bond winked. "They just got here today."

Mandie turned to look at Uncle Ned, who was sitting behind her. The old Indian smiled knowingly. He was waiting to see if she apologized to Joe.

As the rig came to a halt, the front door of the house burst open and Joe raced down the walkway to meet them. "I'll help carry the baggage," he said excitedly to Uncle John. He glanced at Mandie.

In spite of her good intentions, Mandie suddenly was afraid to speak to Joe. She jumped out of the rig and ran up to the house. Calling hellos to everyone she met inside, she quickly went to her room, set Snowball down, and plopped down on the bed. As she threw off her bonnet and gloves, she berated herself. *Now, why did I act like that?* she wondered. *Joe obviously made the first move and I didn't even meet him halfway.*

In a few minutes Liza danced into the room. "Dat doctuh boy send word he waitin' fo' you on de veranda," she announced. "And he been good boy since you left. Ain't said 'nother word to Missy Polly. Not one."

Mandie bristled as she thought about Polly inviting Joe to dinner. "He hasn't?" she asked.

"No, 'cause he ain't been heah till today. And if he ain't heah, he cain't talk to huh. And now she done gone back to huh school, so you's got him all by yo'self," Liza explained.

"You say he's on the porch?" Mandie repeated.

"Sho is. Waitin' fo' you," the maid replied.

"See you later," Mandie said, hurriedly leaving the room.

Mandie looked around quickly as she opened the front screen door.

Joe was sitting in the swing, and when he saw her, he hurried across the porch to meet her. "Mandie, I'd like to say I'm sorry," he said, holding out his hand.

"I wanted to tell *you* I'm sorry, Joe," Mandie said at almost the same time.

Joe took her hand and led her to the swing where they sat down.

Mandie blinked back her tears. "Oh, Joe, I've been miserable ever since I left. All I've done is think about how I hurt you—"

"I hurt *you,* Mandie," Joe interrupted. "And I'm truly sorry." He looked down. "I promise I won't ever act like that again. Am I forgiven?"

"Of course, Joe. Will you forgive me?" Mandie asked.

"I forgave you the day after you left," he assured her.

Mandie sighed with relief. "Whew! I'm sure glad that's taken care of," she said. "You know, the Bible says, 'Let not the sun go down upon your wrath.' But I did let the sun go down on my wrath *many* times before I could come back and ask your forgiveness. I think that's why I was so miserable."

At that moment Aunt Lou, the enormous Negro housekeeper, stuck her head out the front door. "You chilluns is wanted in de parluh," she called to them. "Tea done been served."

As Mandie and Joe entered the parlor together, Uncle Ned nodded at them. They each took a piece of cake from Liza and walked to the far side of the room where Uncle John and Dr. Woodard were talking.

Dr. Woodard looked up at them and smiled, then continued. "So, John, you think the Pattons are serious about taking Hilda into their home?"

"Yes," Uncle John replied. "They asked me to talk to you about it—to ask you to help them go through the proper channels."

"I'll certainly help where I can, but I don't think they'll have any trouble," Dr. Woodard said. "I've known George Patton for years. He's highly respected as a businessman as well as an attorney, and he has made sizeable contributions to various hospitals and institutions in the area. That man has a heart of gold and so does his wife. I think the Pattons would be the perfect couple to care for Hilda." He looked up at Mandie. "What do you think, Amanda?"

"I like them a lot." Mandie nodded. "I think Hilda would love being in their home—homes," she corrected herself. "Especially the beach house."

Dr. Woodard laughed. "Well then, it's settled as far as I'm concerned. I'll start things rolling at the sanatorium, and by the time all the legal business is worked out, I'm sure Hilda will be well enough to leave." He looked up. "She loved the new dress, Amanda. She even told me to thank you. Yes, indeed, she's making progress."

Mandie felt good inside, knowing Hilda liked the dress.

Dr. Woodard smiled and took a drink of his tea. "By the way, John," he said, "what I really came for was to tell you that Jake Burns is interested in buying that old mine you've got over there at Rose Creek."

Uncle John looked surprised. "Why, that old mine's been shut up for years. I don't know what he wants with it. All the rubies have been dug out long ago."

"Well, maybe he'd like to try anyway," Dr. Woodard replied.

"But it's been neglected so long it's probably falling in," Uncle John protested.

Mandie and Joe exchanged glances, then leaned forward to listen.

"You own an old abandoned mine, Uncle John?" Mandie asked.

"The ruby mine we're talking about, Amanda, belonged to my father," Uncle John explained. "It has been closed since I was young."

"Oh, Uncle John, please don't sell it until we can see it," Mandie begged.

"Please, sir," Joe added.

Uncle John looked at Dr. Woodard and smiled. "Looks like we've started something here."

"We might find one little teeny ruby if we look hard," Mandie persisted.

Uncle John chuckled. "I'm sure you won't find any, but I guess I can wait to sell it until you have had time to check it out."

"Thank you, Uncle John," Mandie replied, clapping her hands. "We will find out whether there are any rubies left in it, won't we, Joe?"

"We sure will," the boy agreed.

"And when is that going to be?" Dr. Woodard asked.

"The next holidays I get from school, we'll go explore it," Mandie promised.

"Yes, we will if my father gives me permission," Joe said, sending his father a pleading look.

"Oh, I suppose so, if Amanda is allowed to go," Dr. Woodard agreed.

"Thanks, Dad," Joe said excitedly.

"If that mine has any rubies in it at all, I'll bet we'll find them, Dr. Woodard," she promised.

Mandie's blue eyes twinkled brightly. Somehow, going back to school tomorrow didn't seem so bad, knowing that one day soon she and Joe could explore that old abandoned ruby mine!

MANDIE

AND THE
ABANDONED
MINE

With love,
to my granddaughter,

Natalie Rae Leppard,

that precious blue-eyed, blonde-haired darling,
not yet old enough
to read about Mandie,
but old enough to love books.

CONTENTS

MANDIE AND THE ABANDONED MINE

CHAPTER ONE

A SAD, BAD MINE

"Is this what a ruby mine looks like?" Mandie Shaw asked her Uncle John as she stared in surprise. All she could see was what looked like a plank floor covering the ground, going down the hill out of sight toward Rose Creek, a branch of the Little Tennessee River. The sound of voices and hammering came from beneath the boards.

Uncle John dismounted and offered his hand to help twelve-year-old Mandie down from her pony. Her white kitten, Snowball, squirmed in her arms as she slid down.

"Well, this is not exactly a typical mine for western North Carolina," he explained. "Most ruby mines don't go underneath the ground like this one. You see, Amanda, the dirt has to be dug away until you reach the gravel. Instead of digging a tunnel, you just scrape the dirt off the top. The rubies are in the gravel."

Mandie's long-time friend Joe stood nearby with his father, Dr. Woodard, listening. "Then why is this one underground?" Joe asked.

"Probably because this mine is about nineteen feet deep, and the depth of the dirt was so great that it made a huge crater when they dug it away. When they closed the mine years ago, they must have had to cover it with boards to keep people and animals from falling in," Uncle John explained.

"Why was it closed, John?" Dr. Woodard asked. "Was it mined dry?"

"No, I don't think so. I don't remember ever seeing it worked. I was small when my father closed it. It must have been nearly fifty years ago, around 1850. I remember hearing that there had been some special reason for closing it, but I don't remember what. In fact, I was forbidden to go near it when I was a child," Uncle John told them.

"How do we get under there to look for rubies?" Mandie asked, flipping her long blonde braid behind her back.

"As soon as the workmen shore up the timbers, we'll be able to go down inside," her uncle replied.

"But how? I don't see any entrance," Mandie said, looking around.

Uncle John pointed to an opening in the boards. "There are steps going down over there. The opening was covered over with the planks, so the workmen had to hunt for it. We were surprised to find it in fairly good shape, considering how many years it has been closed."

"Is this where our family got all its money?" Mandie asked, holding Snowball tighter as he tried again to get down.

"Part of it," Uncle John replied. "My grandfather, who was your great-grandfather, was in on the gold rush when gold was discovered here in our state at Concord in 1799. Most people don't know that the first gold discovered in the United States was found there. There was so much of it that the government had to open a mint in Charlotte about 1837 to take care of it."

"You mean the original gold rush was here in North Carolina and not in California?" Joe asked.

"Yes, it was some fifty years before the California discovery. Not only that, but gold was also found on Cherokee land before the rush to California. That was the main reason the white people moved the Indians out," John reminded him.

"Gold can do terrible things to people," Dr. Woodard remarked.

"Why does everybody have to be so money crazy?" Mandie sighed. "Was my great-grandfather money crazy?"

"No, Amanda, I can honestly say he wasn't. It just happened that gold was found on land he owned, and also emeralds, sapphires, garnets, and the rubies here, and mica. It just happened that way. He didn't go looking for it," Uncle John explained.

"Are all those other mines closed now?" Joe asked.

"No, not all of them," Uncle John answered. "We have a large mica mine over near Sylva, and we have a couple of other gem mines here in Macon County. They seem to be full of stones."

"If the rubies are in the gravel, how do you go about finding them? Do you just get down and dig through to the gravel?" Mandie asked.

Uncle John laughed. "No, dear, that would take forever. You have to remove the topsoil, and you need a water trough and a sieve. The loose dirt and fine gravel filter through the sieve and wash away, leaving the larger pieces of gravel in the sieve. Then you have to examine what's left to see if there are any rubies in it. Once in a while you'll find a ruby stuck in a rock left in the gravel."

"That sounds easy enough," Mandie said.

"Oh, but it takes time, lots of time, to do this and really come up with anything worthwhile. The rubies are few and far between," her uncle stated.

"And even though it sounds like fun, it's wet, dirty, backbreaking work," Dr. Woodard told her.

"But it'll be fun anyway," Joe remarked.

"Yes, I can't wait to get started. Are you getting us a water trough and a sieve, Uncle John?" Mandie asked.

"There's a trough already down there with a hand pump to bring the water through, and we've got sieves back at the house," Uncle John said. "While one of you dips the sieve in the water, the other one will have to be sure the water is pumping through."

"By the way, Amanda," Dr. Woodard warned, "the rubies you may find won't look like the setting in a ring. They'll be a dull, dirty-looking dark red. They have to be polished and cut before they are used in jewelry."

"That's right," Uncle John agreed. "You have to look very closely. Some of them might look just like old rocks."

"I'll be sure to examine every little particle," Mandie replied. "That way I'm sure I'll find some rubies."

"And if you do find one, what are you going to do with it?" her uncle asked.

Mandie's blue eyes sparkled as she thought for a moment and then answered, "Why, I'll have it polished and cut like Dr. Woodard said, and I'll have it made into something for my mother. That would make a nice Christmas present for her, wouldn't it?"

"It sure would. But in the meantime, I think you'd better plan on an alternate present, because you might not find a single one, you know," Uncle John said.

"If there are any rubies down there, I'm sure Joe and I will find them," Mandie replied, smiling.

"And what do you plan to do with any you find, Joe?" Uncle John asked.

"Me? You mean I can keep whatever I find?" Joe inquired.

"You certainly may. If you're going to do all that work, you're welcome to keep whatever you find," Uncle John told him.

"Well, thanks, Mr. Shaw. I'll just . . . uh . . . uh . . . keep them until I decide what to do with them, I suppose," the boy said, glancing shyly at Mandie.

"And don't you two forget," Uncle John reminded them, "I may be selling this mine to Jake Burns soon, so you'll have to work fast."

"When Sallie and Dimar get here, we'll have plenty of help," Mandie stated.

Just then one of the workmen stuck his head out of the opening to the mine. "Mr. Shaw," he called, "I reckon we'll have this thing safe and sound some time tomorrow."

"That's good, Boyd," John Shaw called back. "Then we'll let the kids explore it tomorrow." He walked on down to talk further with Boyd.

Mandie clasped her hands in delight, releasing Snowball onto her shoulder. He immediately jumped down and ran toward the workman.

"Thank goodness, it's not taking long to get it ready." Mandie turned to chase Snowball, and her bonnet fell back. "Snowball, come back here. Don't you go inside."

"I won't let him in, Missy," Boyd called to her as the white kitten raced on toward him.

Joe hurried to help. Together they cornered Snowball as he stopped to sniff at the workman. Mandie picked up the kitten and turned back up the hill. Joe followed.

"Snowball, you've got to learn to stop running away like that. One of these days you might get lost," Mandie reprimanded the kitten as she cuddled him in her arms.

"And then we'll have to waste time looking for him," Joe added.

"I know, and we don't have any time to waste. We have to go back to school after Thanksgiving, so we've got to hurry," Mandie agreed.

Dr. Woodard called to them as they came up the hill. "Do you see what I see?" He pointed to the trees behind him.

Mandie looked up the hill and then began running with Joe right beside her. Uncle Ned, Mandie's old Indian friend, was riding toward them on his horse.

As the old Cherokee dismounted and tied his horse to a tree, Mandie grabbed his wrinkled hand. "Uncle Ned, I'm so glad you got here. Did you bring Morning Star and everyone?" she asked excitedly.

Uncle Ned stooped to embrace the small girl. "Papoose, do not make talk so fast," he laughed. "Sallie and Dimar come with me. Morning Star come Thanksgiving Day. Needed in village now."

"I'm so glad you're here," Mandie said. She turned to Uncle John, who was coming up the hill with Dr. Woodard. "Are we going home now, Uncle John?"

"I suppose we are, Amanda," Uncle John told her. He extended his hand to the old Indian. "How are you, Uncle Ned?"

"Good," Uncle Ned replied.

Dr. Woodard shook hands with the Indian. "Glad to see you," he said.

Uncle John pointed to the opening in the mine. "Looks like we'll have it open tomorrow, Uncle Ned."

"Bad to open," the old Indian grunted. "Ruby mine bad place."

Mandie and Joe looked at him and frowned.

"The workmen are making sure the timbers are solid and everything is safe," Uncle John assured him.

"No good mine. Your papa close. Bad to open," Uncle Ned insisted.

"What do you mean by bad?" Dr. Woodard asked.

"Your papa close mine because bad things happen. Bad to open mine," the Indian replied, adjusting the sling over his shoulder holding his bow and arrows.

"But why is it bad to open the mine?" Uncle John wanted to know.

"You no remember?"

"No, I was too young. What do you remember about it?" John persisted.

"I put away memory. Best not to open mine," Uncle Ned repeated.

"If you won't tell me why you think it shouldn't be opened, I don't see any reason not to," John said, exasperated.

Mandie took the old Indian's hand and gave it a slight jerk. "Please, Uncle Ned, tell us whatever you know."

"I watch over Papoose. I promise Jim Shaw when he go to happy hunting ground I watch over Papoose. When Papoose go in ruby mine I watch," he told the girl.

"My father would be proud of you, Uncle Ned, if he could know how well you've kept your promise since he died," Mandie responded.

Dr. Woodard cleared his throat. "All this talk of the mine being bad sounds awfully mysterious to me, Uncle Ned," he said. "Is it safe for the young people to go inside?"

"I keep watch." Uncle Ned untied his horse. "Sallie and Dimar wait at house of John Shaw. They say hurry."

The others all looked at each other as the Indian mounted his horse and rode off. Then Mandie and Joe laughed loudly.

"We sure didn't get a straight answer from him," Mandie cried as she turned to get her pony. "Depend on Uncle Ned to keep a secret!"

"Yep, if anybody can keep a secret, he can," Joe added.

"Well, there's nothing left for us to do but go back to the house," Uncle John said to Dr. Woodard.

"Whatever was bothering Uncle Ned probably wasn't very important," Dr. Woodard agreed.

Uncle Ned was already out of sight by the time the others mounted. It wasn't far to John Shaw's house in the city of Franklin, and Mandie and Joe excitedly rushed ahead of the men.

As they approached the huge white house, they saw Sallie and Dimar sitting on the front porch waiting for them. Uncle Ned's horse stood at the gate, but the old Indian wasn't in sight. The young people quickly dismounted, tied up their ponies, and ran up the long walkway.

"Sallie! Dimar!" Mandie cried. "You finally got here!" She embraced Sallie Sweetwater, who was Uncle Ned's granddaughter, and turned to shake Dimar's hand. Dimar was a neighbor of the Sweetwaters.

"I am so excited." Sallie laughed. "This is so different from where we live in Deep Creek."

"I know how you feel. I remember when Uncle Ned helped me get here to Uncle John's house after my father died. I had never been away from our log cabin at Charley Gap." Mandie sat down beside Sallie in the swing. "But you have been here before."

"Yes, but it is exciting," the Indian girl said, smoothing her long black skirt.

Dimar cast an admiring glance at Mandie. "I am glad to see you, Mandie—and Joe, too," he said, sitting with Joe on a bench near the swing.

"Dimar, wait till you see the mine where we're going to hunt for rubies," Joe told him.

Mandie's blue eyes sparkled. "That's where we've just been. It'll be ready for us to go inside some time tomorrow."

"Inside?" the Indian boy questioned. "Ruby mines do not have an inside."

"This one does," Mandie replied. "Uncle John says the dirt was so deep they had to dig about nineteen feet down before they got to the gravel. We have to walk down some steps to get inside."

"Oh, I see," Dimar replied. "Then it will be interesting."

"According to Uncle Ned, it will be *bad,* but he wouldn't tell us what he meant by that," Joe added.

"Where is he?" Mandie asked. "He rode off ahead of us in a big hurry."

"He went inside the house," Sally answered. "He said that it is a bad mine and it should not be opened again."

"He would not tell us why," Dimar said.

Mandie rose from the swing. "Oh, well, Uncle John is getting it opened anyway. Let's go inside the house now."

Liza, the young Negro servant girl, appeared at the front door. "Y'all wanted in de parlor," she said. "Ev'ry one of y'all."

"Thank you, Liza. We were just coming in," Mandie replied.

Liza stared at the two young Indians as the group entered the house and went through the big double doors into the parlor. She noticed every little detail as they passed her. Sallie, a little taller than Mandie, had black hair and black eyes. She had a red scarf tied around her hair, and shell beads jangled around the neck of her white blouse. Dimar wore a deerskin jacket like Uncle Ned's. He was not quite as tall as Joe, but he was handsome.

Mandie gave her mother a hug, spoke to Mrs. Woodard, and then sat down beside Uncle Ned. The others seated themselves in comfortable chairs around the room.

"I'm so glad you invited our friends for Thanksgiving," Mandie said to her mother. She looked up as Uncle John and Dr. Woodard entered the room.

Her mother smiled. "Your Grandmother Taft and Celia Hamilton will be here tomorrow," she said. "We will have a wonderful time."

Liza had followed the young people into the parlor and stood just inside the door, staring.

Elizabeth, Mandie's mother, noticed the servant girl and spoke to her. "Liza, would you please pass the little cakes for me while I pour the tea?"

"Yessum, Miz Shaw," Liza said, stepping forward to take the plate from her.

Elizabeth filled teacups and passed them around as Liza moved from one to another with the plate of sweetcakes. When she came to the Indians, she stood back and held out the plate.

"Liza, what's the matter with you?" Mandie asked. "You know all these people."

"Yessum, Missy. I jest ain't seed 'em in a long time," the Negro girl replied, quickly bringing the plate to Mandie.

"Liza, I think Aunt Lou needs your help getting the dinner table set. Why don't you go and see?" Elizabeth said.

"Yessum, yessum, Miz Shaw. I sho' bet she does," Liza replied quickly. She almost ran out the door.

Mrs. Woodard laughed. "That Liza is a strange one, isn't she, Elizabeth?"

"In a way. You know, she was born and raised here in this house and has never been anywhere else much."

"And she was already working here when you married John, wasn't she?" Mrs. Woodard asked.

"Yes, all the servants were here. I didn't make any staff changes when John and I got married. I just left everything the way it was. Aunt Lou is the best housekeeper anyone could ask for, and she keeps a rein on Liza and Jenny, the cook."

Uncle John took a sip of his tea and spoke to Elizabeth. "The mine will be ready to open tomorrow," he said.

Uncle Ned grunted, and everyone looked at him.

"Uncle Ned doesn't want us to open the mine at all," Mandie told her mother.

"Why not?" Elizabeth asked.

The old Indian merely shook his head.

"He said it's a bad mine," Mandie answered.

"A sad, bad mine," Uncle Ned corrected her.

"But why, Uncle Ned? What's wrong?" Elizabeth asked.

Uncle Ned crossed his arms and remained silent.

Elizabeth tried again. "Is it dangerous?"

When Uncle Ned didn't answer, John said, "I know it's safe. The workmen have been very careful to examine everything."

Mandie stood by Uncle Ned's chair and put her small white hand on the shoulder of his deerskin jacket. "Please tell us why you say the mine is a sad, bad mine," she begged.

Uncle Ned looked into her blue eyes and reached for her hand. "Papoose be all right. I watch over Papoose," he told her.

"And you won't tell us whatever you know?" Uncle John asked.

"You find out," the old Indian said.

Everyone fell silent, contemplating what the Indian had said. There was something very mysterious about the mine, and Mandie was determined to find out what it was.

CHAPTER TWO

THE STORE-BOUGHT DRESS

When Uncle John and Dr. Woodard escorted the young people back to the mine the next day, Uncle Ned refused to come. He said they were only going to look inside and that when they really settled down to prospecting, then he would watch over Mandie and her friends.

The workmen were still at the mine when the group rode up.

Boyd came to meet John Shaw. "We had a little trouble getting some new posts cut just the right height, Mr. Shaw," he said. "So I guess it'll be a while yet before we're through. I'm sorry."

"That's all right, Boyd. Take time to be sure it's positively safe. Don't rush and cut corners," John Shaw told him.

"That's why we've been this long getting it open. I know how important it is to know without a doubt that it's safe for the young people," Boyd said.

Dimar sat forward on his pony and smiled at Mandie. "Now I understand why you said it had an inside, Mandie," he said.

"Uncle John said it's probably nineteen feet deep under there," Mandie explained.

The Indian boy looked around. "The dirt from uphill there has probably washed down this way for a hundred years or more. That is why the gravel was so far down."

Sallie followed his gaze. "I see a chimney over there," she said, pointing off through the dense trees that were beginning to lose their leaves. "Does someone live there?"

"Let's go see while we're waiting for them to get finished," Mandie said. She called to Uncle John and Dr. Woodard, who were still talking to Boyd. "We're going to ride over there through the trees." She pointed.

"Don't go too far away," Uncle John called back.

"And don't be gone too long," Dr. Woodard added.

The young people promised they wouldn't and rode off through the trees in the direction of the chimney.

Coming into a clearing a few hundred yards away, they found an old abandoned farmhouse, standing on tall stone pillars. The shutters hung haphazardly from the windows, and the front door stood half open. Tall weeds surrounded the house.

Joe slid off his pony beside the sagging front porch. "Looks like nobody lives here," he remarked.

The others dismounted and joined him as he carefully stepped up the shaky front porch steps.

"I wonder if this house is on Uncle John's property," Mandie said as she and the two young Indians followed.

"It is so near the mine it probably belongs to your Uncle John," Dimar said, looking back the direction they had come.

"This is a very old, very worn-out house. We must be careful. Something may fall in," Sallie cautioned the others as she looked about.

Joe stepped up to the front door, which was slightly ajar, and pushed it open. "The inside seems to be all right." He walked into the long front room of the house. At one end rose the huge fireplace for the chimney they had seen.

The others followed Joe inside. Mandie stepped through the doorway into another room. There was something hanging on the far wall. She walked over to it. "Look what I've found!" she exclaimed. "A lady's dress! And it must be store-bought! Look!"

She took the garment from the nail and held it up for all to see. It was a light blue gingham dress with white frills and buttons. Around the waist was a wide sash.

Sallie held the material up to her nose. "It is new," she said. "I can smell the starch in the new cloth."

"It looks just like something in the Sears Roebuck catalogue," Joe said, watching the girls examine the dress.

Dimar laughed. "Yes, it must be a white lady's dress. No Cherokee could afford a store-bought dress like that."

Mandie puzzled over the matter. "Who do you suppose would leave a pretty, new dress in this old falling-down house?"

"Maybe whoever lived here last," Joe suggested.

"I do not think so," Sallie said. "This house looks like it has been deserted a long time, and that dress is fresh and new."

Joe climbed the ladder and stuck his head into the attic room. "Nothing up here," he called down to the others. "When the people moved out of here, whoever they were, they sure didn't leave anything behind."

The others looked around downstairs.

Dimar walked over to the huge open fireplace. "There are not even any ashes left in the fireplace," he said.

"What should we do with this dress?" Mandie asked, still holding it in her arms.

"Leave it where you found it," Joe said, coming back down the ladder. "It's not ours."

"It seems a shame to leave such a pretty dress in this dirty old house, but I suppose you're right," Mandie reluctantly agreed. She turned to hang the dress and sash back on the nail.

"Whoever left it here will be sure to return to get it," Dimar stated.

"I know, and we'll never know whose it is," Mandie said, regretfully.

Joe walked over and stood in front of Mandie. He drew himself up to his full gangly height and snapped his galluses with his thumbs. "Mandie, this dress is none of our business. Now please don't go off on one of your investigating adventures, because I won't help you," he told her.

"Joe Woodard, you think l make a mystery out of everything. Well, I don't," Mandie replied, stomping her foot.

Sallie, always the peacemaker, spoke up quickly. "I think we should go," she said. "Your uncle will be looking for us if we are gone too long. Besides, they may have the mine open by now."

"You're right, Sallie. We'd better get back," Mandie agreed, hurrying toward the door.

Without another word the young people rode back to join Uncle John and Dr. Woodard at the mine.

"Boyd needs the rest of the day to get the new posts in," Uncle John told them.

The four moaned in protest.

"I know you are all disappointed, but at least we'll know the place is safe once Boyd gets done with it," Uncle John said. "He should be finished tomorrow."

"I sure hope so," Mandie said.

"Yeah, our holidays are going away fast," Joe added. He paused for a moment, then looked up at Mandie's uncle. "Mr. Shaw, how long has it been since someone lived in that old house over there?"

"Why, I don't remember. It seems like someone lived there when I was a child, but I'm not sure," John replied.

"Does that house belong to you, Uncle John?" Mandie asked.

"It's on our land. We have several hundred acres through here," Uncle John answered. "Why? Did you see someone over there?"

"No, sir," Mandie said. "But we found a brand-new dress hanging on a nail in one of the rooms of that house."

John Shaw and Dr. Woodard looked at each other in surprise.

"You found a new dress in there?" Uncle John questioned. "That's strange."

"Maybe someone is using the house, John," Dr. Woodard suggested.

"No, sir, it's completely empty, not even any ashes in the fireplace," Joe put in.

"Did you leave the dress where you found it?" Uncle John asked.

"Yes, sir. I put it back on the nail," Mandie replied.

"Well, it's not hurting anything, so we'll just leave it where it is," Uncle John told the young people. "Now we'd better get home and see if the rest of our company has arrived."

The young people raced their ponies ahead of the men and pulled up in front of John Shaw's house. Mandie's heart beat wildly as she recognized her Grandmother Taft's carriage parked at the gate. Mandie and her friends quickly tied up their ponies at the hitching post and rushed up the front steps.

"Celia!" Mandie cried, embracing the auburn-haired girl on the porch as though she hadn't seen her in months. Actually, they had parted only the week before at the Misses Heathwood's School in Asheville. The school closed for the Thanksgiving holidays. Celia had gone home to Richmond. Then her mother had brought her back to Mrs. Taft's house in Asheville so Celia could go on to Mandie's house in Franklin with Mrs. Taft.

Mandie turned to the boys. "Joe, will you and Dimar wait for us in the sunroom? We'll take Celia upstairs so she can get freshened up. Mother and the others are probably in the parlor."

The boys agreed and the girls rushed up the stairs to Mandie's bedroom where another bed had been moved in so that Mandie, Sallie, and Celia could share a room. There in the middle of Mandie's bed was Snowball, curled up asleep. He opened his blue eyes sleepily and stood up, stretching. He sat there washing his face and watching the girls.

Celia pulled off her bonnet and gloves that matched her brown traveling suit. She danced about the room, looking at everything. "Oh, I love your Uncle John's house," she said. "It's beautiful. And Sallie, I'm so glad to finally get a chance to know you. Mandie talks about you all the time at that school we go to in Asheville."

"And I am glad to make your acquaintance, Celia. Mandie talks about you a lot, too. Mandie is my dearest friend, and I hope she will soon be able to visit us for a long stay. Every time she visits they do not have much time. Maybe next summer when school is out, you could come with Mandie for a long visit," Sallie invited.

"I'd love to, Sallie. Let's plan on it, provided my mother gives me permission," Celia replied. Looking around, she spied her luggage in a corner. "Let me take off this traveling outfit and put on some more comfortable clothes." She opened the nearest bag and pulled out a green calico dress.

"I'll help you hang your things in the wardrobe with Sallie's and mine," Mandie offered, stooping to unpack while Celia changed clothes.

With Sallie's help, they were soon finished, and the three girls hurried downstairs again.

Mandie began to laugh. "I just realized something," she said. "I got so excited about seeing you, Celia, that I forgot to even say hello to my Grandmother Taft."

The other girls giggled with her. At the bottom of the steps, they ran into Aunt Lou, the robust Negro housekeeper, who at that moment was wiping her round face on her big white apron.

Mandie started to introduce Celia. "Aunt Lou, this is–

"Slow down, my chile," the black woman scolded with a twinkle in her eye. "I bet you don't know who be in de parlor."

"Yes, I do, Aunt Lou," Mandie replied in a teasing voice. "It's Grandmother Taft."

Aunt Lou pouted. "Yo' Gramma Taft and who else?" she teased back.

Mandie's eyes grew wide. "I don't know, Aunt Lou. Who is it'?"

The Negro woman looked up at the ceiling. "Some girl whut ain't got a lick o' sense," she replied.

"Hilda?" Mandie grabbed Celia's and Sallie's hands. "Come on!" She led the way into the parlor and ran to hug her grandmother. There on the settee beside Mrs. Taft sat Hilda Edney, the poor girl Mandie and Celia had found hiding in the attic of their school. But now here she was, dressed like a millionaire's daughter.

Joe and Dimar in the sunroom heard the commotion and came into the room. Everyone started to talk at once.

Hilda, seeing Mandie, jumped up, stood right in front of her, and extended her hand, smiling. "I . . . love . . . you." She enunciated each word slowly.

"Oh, Hilda, I love you, too," Mandie said, putting her arms around the girl. "And you are talking more and more."

Hilda burst into tears and clung to Mandie.

Mrs. Taft stood and patted Hilda on the shoulder. "There, there, now. What is it, dear?"

The dark-haired girl just kept crying and wouldn't let go of Mandie.

"Hilda," Mandie tried to scold the girl gently. "Let's sit down over there. There's nothing to cry about. Young ladies don't cry in front of other people."

Hilda allowed herself to be led to the settee, and she sat down beside Mandie.

Mrs. Taft looked concerned. "I think Hilda is afraid she won't ever see you again if the Pattons adopt her. She seems frightened of them."

"Hilda, the Pattons are real nice people. And they live down in Charleston where you can see the ocean," Mandie told her.

"No." Hilda sobbed. "No." She reached for Mandie's hand and squeezed it tightly.

"Grandmother, how did you happen to bring Hilda here?" Mandie asked.

"Dear, when the Pattons came to get Hilda from the sanitorium, she was gone. They couldn't find her anywhere. Then Aunt Phoebe at your school sent word to me that Hilda was at their home," Mrs. Taft explained. "I had to go get her, and when I tried to take her back to the sanitorium, she became wild. So I thought I would just bring her here to see you. Since she loves you so much, maybe you can talk some sense into her head."

"I doubt if I can, Grandmother. Hilda doesn't understand everything we say," Mandie said.

Dr. Woodard cleared his throat. "She understands more than you think she does. And she is improving all the time. After being shut away in that room by herself most of her life simply because she couldn't talk, I think she is doing well."

Hilda had hushed and was listening carefully to Dr. Woodard. He visited her often at the sanitorium, and she seemed to like him.

Mandie turned to Hilda, smiling. "Just wait until you see the ruby mine Uncle John owns," she said, changing the subject abruptly. "He's going to let us dig in it and look for rubies. And you can help if you don't cry anymore."

Hilda brushed the back of her hand across her wet eyes. Mrs. Taft handed her a handkerchief, and Hilda wiped her eyes with it. Straightening, she smiled at Mandie. "Help. I help," she said, though not seemingly aware of what the conversation was all about.

Mandie smiled back at her and then fingered Hilda's lovely lavender silk dress. "Where did you get the pretty dress?" she asked.

Hilda looked down, then quickly stood up to shake out her long full skirt. Her brown eyes shone as she tossed her long dark hair. "Gramma," she said, pointing to Mrs. Taft. "Gramma."

Mandie looked at her Grandmother Taft.

"Yes, dear, I had to get her some clothes to take with her to the Pattons. I've been her benefactor ever since you and Celia found her," Mrs. Taft reminded Mandie.

Sallie drew in a deep breath and whispered to Celia, "So this is the girl you and Mandie found hiding in the attic at your school."

"Yes, isn't she pretty?" Celia replied.

"She is," Sallie agreed.

"What are you going to do about her, Mrs. Taft?" Dr. Woodard asked. "You know how much the Pattons want to take her into their home."

"I know, but if she's frightened, maybe she could stay with me in my home for a while," Mrs. Taft told him. "As you know, I have plenty of room."

"Hilda? Staying with you, Mother?" Elizabeth spoke up.

"Why, yes, what's wrong with that?" Mrs. Taft asked.

"Nothing, except that you like to travel all over, and you're not used to having a young person around," Elizabeth replied.

"Well, I did have a young person around when you were growing up," Mrs. Taft said. "If I can teach her some manners, maybe I'll take her with me on some of my other travels."

Everyone looked at one another and then at Hilda, who was silently examining the material of her dress.

Suddenly Mandie laughed loudly. "Oh, Grandmother! If anyone could teach her some manners, you could! You always end up doing the impossible."

"We'll see," Mrs. Taft said. "Besides, when you and Celia go back to school, you can spend a lot of time over at my house helping me teach her."

"I'll be glad to help, Mrs. Taft," Celia offered.

"I'm so glad you live in Asheville, Grandmother," Mandie said. "That's the only good part about going to that school so far from home."

"And I'm glad you're near me during school, dear," Mrs. Taft said with a mischievous smile. "Now, what about this ruby mine y'all are going to explore?"

Mandie's eyes lit up. "It's going to be fun," she said. "It's a big hole in the ground, and I'm sure there are still rubies in it. Uncle John's going to show us how to look for them, and he says we can keep any rubies we find!"

"That does sound like fun," Mrs. Taft replied.

"It would be nice of you to take Hilda with y'all when you go to dig in the mine," Dr. Woodard said. "I know she'll be fascinated by it."

"Do you think it'll be all right for Hilda to go?" Uncle John asked. "Mightn't she get into something and get hurt?"

"No, I think Mandie will be able to control her," Dr. Woodard replied.

"Tell me about the mine, please," Celia begged.

"It's just a great big hole in the ground," Joe teased.

"Are you sure the mine is safe?" Mrs. Taft asked.

"I'm having workmen go over every inch of it before the young people will be allowed inside," John assured her.

Elizabeth bristled. "Mother, you know John and I would never allow Amanda to go if it weren't safe."

"Yes, of course, dear," Mrs. Taft replied.

Later that night, when Elizabeth told the girls it was time to go to bed, Mandie didn't protest.

"All right, Mother." She yawned. "I guess it has been a long day." She turned to Hilda. "You are to sleep in the room with Celia, Sallie, and me," she said. "Let's go upstairs."

Saying good-night to everyone, the girls went up to Mandie's room. Mandie pulled a trundle bed out from under her bed and showed it to Hilda. "You sleep on this," she said.

Hilda stood watching, not saying a word. It took a lot of coaxing from the other three girls to get Hilda to undress for bed. When they finally got her to lie down in the trundle bed, Hilda held onto the covers and watched every move the others made as they finished getting ready for bed.

"Do you think she'll stay there to sleep?" Sallie asked doubtfully.

"I think so. Anyway, I'll hear her if she gets up during the night," Mandie answered.

But Mandie slept soundly that night and didn't hear a thing.

CHAPTER THREE

WAITING

Mandie awoke early, just about dawn, and when she opened her eyes, the trundle bed was empty. She sat up quickly, disturbing Snowball who was sleeping at her feet.

Where was Hilda?

Sallie stirred in her bed and sat up.

"Hilda is gone!" Mandie whispered.

Sallie blinked her eyes a few times and looked around the room. "We must find her," the Indian girl said, swinging her feet out of bed onto the floor.

Mandie crawled over the trundle bed and stood up. "There's no telling where Hilda is," she said, pulling her robe on over her long nightgown. "Come on," she whispered in order not to wake Celia.

Snowball jumped down from the bed and stretched, watching his mistress.

Sallie quickly threw on her robe and slippers, and the two girls started toward the door.

Suddenly the door came open and Hilda walked in, followed by Liza.

"Case y'all been lookin' fo' dis Hilda girl, she been sleepin' in my bed," Liza told them.

Taking one look at Mandie, Hilda went straight to the trundle bed and jumped in, pulling the covers over her.

"In *your* bed, Liza?" Mandie asked, astonished.

"In de middle o' de night I heerd somethin,' and here she wuz gittin' in de other side o' my bed. She didn't say a word, jes' got under de covers and went straight to sleep," Liza explained.

"I wonder how she knew where Liza was," Sallie said.

"I don't rightly know, Missy," Liza told them. "I told her she had to come back up here 'cause I has to git down to de kitchen."

"I'm sorry, Liza. I'll try to keep her here tonight," Mandie said.

"Dat's all right, Missy. I don't care if she wants to sleep in my bed, long as she don't kick," Liza said.

Mandie and Sallie laughed.

Celia awoke and sat up, rubbing her eyes and looking around. "As long as who doesn't kick?" she asked, yawning sleepily.

"Hilda sneaked off during the night and slept with Liza," Mandie explained.

"I gotta go, Missy. Gotta help git breakfus'," Liza said, dancing over to the door. "I knows she don't know no better, so don't y'all be mean to her." Liza rushed out of the room.

"Sorry we woke you, Celia," Mandie apologized.

Celia swung her feet onto the carpet and stood up, stretching. "That's all right. I'm hungry anyway, and Liza said she was going to cook breakfast," she replied. "I don't want to miss that."

"All right, let's get dressed and go down to the kitchen," Mandie suggested.

"That is a good idea," Sallie agreed. "But what about Hilda?"

The girls looked at Hilda in the trundle bed. She was either fast asleep or was making a good pretense of it.

"Let's just leave her here," Mandie said. "I don't think she wants to get up right now."

The three girls washed their faces quickly and slipped into their dresses, being careful not to disturb Hilda. After they brushed their hair, Mandie picked up Snowball, and they tiptoed out of the room.

As Celia silently closed the door behind them, Hilda opened one eye to see that they were gone, then jumped up and quickly put on her dress and shoes. Taking Mandie's shawl from the wardrobe, she threw it around her shoulders, opened the door, and listened. Hearing nothing, she stepped into the hallway and paused again. Then she tiptoed down the servants' stairway at the end of the hallway. Making her way through the dimly lighted hallway downstairs, she found the back door, opened it, and ran out into the yard and off through the shrubbery.

Although Mandie and her two friends stood right inside the kitchen near the back door, they didn't hear her leave.

Aunt Lou was stacking plates on the table while Jenny, the cook, tended something on the big black cookstove and Liza folded napkins.

"Whut fo' you girls done got up so early?" Aunt Lou asked them.

"Please, Aunt Lou, let us eat here in the kitchen," Mandie begged. "It'll be a long time before the grownups get up, and we're starving to death."

"And I s'pose dem boys dey'll be comin' to de kitchen, too," Aunt Lou fussed.

"I don't know whether they're awake yet or not," Mandie told her.

"They are," came a loud voice behind them. "We're hungry, too."

The girls turned to find Joe and Dimar standing just inside the doorway, listening to their conversation.

"Now, my chile, I ain't said y'all could eat in here," Aunt Lou said, " 'cause y'all ain't told me why y'all got up so early."

"It was because of Hilda," Celia volunteered.

Aunt Lou put her hands on her broad hips as she straightened up. "Dat Hilda girl?"

"Yes. Hilda slept in Liza's bed last night," Mandie said. "She slipped out of my room after we went to sleep."

Aunt Lou looked from Mandie to Liza, who grinned and kept on with her task. "Liza, why didn't you make dat girl go back where she belong?" Aunt Lou asked.

"She ain't right in de haid so I didn't wanta be mean to huh," Liza replied.

"She ain't right in de haid 'cause nobody don't try to teach huh no sense," Aunt Lou said.

"We've been trying to, Aunt Lou," Mandie said. "She's learning. It's slow, but she is learning."

"Dr. Woodard says she is brighter than we think she is," Sallie added.

"That's right," Joe agreed.

"And where be dat Hilda girl now?" Aunt Lou asked.

"Liza brought her back to my room a while ago. She's asleep on the trundle bed," Mandie explained.

Aunt Lou shook her head. "I still cain't let y'all eat yet, 'cause breakfus' ain't ready," she said, exasperated. "Y'all find somethin' else to do till we's ready."

Mandie looked at her friends. "What shall we do until breakfast?" she asked them.

"I haven't seen the tunnel yet," Celia said. "You've always talked about the tunnel in this house. I'd like to see it."

"We could do that this morning," Mandie said. "I know the rest of you have been through it, but it won't take long to show it to Celia."

The others agreed enthusiastically, and Mandie led them out of the kitchen and down the hall toward the stairs. As they passed the parlor, Mandie heard a noise and peeked in. There sat Uncle John, quietly reading the newspaper by the window. She went in to speak to him, and the others followed.

"Why are you up so early, Uncle John?" she asked.

"I don't know," he said. "Something woke me before dawn, and I couldn't get back to sleep. What are you all up to already?"

"We want to show Celia the secret tunnel," Mandie answered.

Uncle John's face grew sober, and he stood up. He folded the newspaper and laid it on the table. "I'd like to talk to you alone, Amanda, before you go through the tunnel," Uncle John told her.

Everyone looked at Mandie, questioningly.

"This is a personal matter between Amanda and me. It won't take long," he said.

"All right, Uncle John," Mandie replied. "Will the rest of you wait for me here in the parlor for a few minutes?"

They all nodded.

What have I done now? she wondered. If Uncle John needed to have a private conversation with her, it must be something bad, she reasoned.

Uncle John laughed. "Don't look so worried, Amanda. I'm not going to spank you."

Everyone laughed. Mandie drew a breath of relief.

"Let's go upstairs," Uncle John suggested as they started to leave the parlor.

Mandie followed her uncle from the room. "Upstairs?" she questioned.

He led her up the steps to the door of the third floor library. There he paused with his hand on the doorknob. "I don't know whether I ever told you or not, but this room was my mother's favorite place in this house. She came here to think and solve problems, and to read all our many wonderful books," he said.

"You told me she was a beautiful young Indian girl when your father married her," Mandie replied.

Uncle John slowly opened the door. "Yes, she never lived to grow old," he said sadly, pushing the door open wide.

Immediately in front of them, across the length of the room was a huge fireplace. Over that hung a portrait that had not been there before.

Mandie rushed forward. "My Grandmother Shaw!" she cried. "Oh, she was so beautiful!"

Tears moistened Mandie's blue eyes as she stared at the likeness of a beautiful Indian girl looking down at her. The girl was dressed in red silk, her thick black hair piled high on her head. Indian beads sparkled on her ears, and at her throat they were entwined with a red ribbon.

"She looks as though she could see us and could speak," Mandie said softly.

Uncle John nodded and put an arm around his stepdaughter. "I had told you this portrait was in Asheville getting the frame refinished, remember? I just got it back last week, and I wanted you to see it alone with me," he told her.

Mandie reached up to grasp his hand on her shoulder. "Thank you, Uncle John, for knowing how important this moment is to me. I wish I could have known her," she said with a quiver in her voice.

"Yes, well, even your father was too young to remember her. She died when Jim was only a few months old, but since I was fifteen years older than your father, I can remember her well. She was beautiful, always happy, full of life, always doing things for other people. And she and my father were so much in love. After she died, my father just wasted away. He died in 1868, as you know, when your father was only five years old."

Mandie turned to face him. "And my father died so young, Uncle John. He was just barely thirty-seven years old."

Uncle John tightened his arm around her. "I know, dear. Only God knows the answer to our sorrows."

Mandie wiped tears from her eyes with the back of her hand and looked up at her uncle. "I thank God every night in my prayers for helping me to find you and my real mother after my father died," Mandie said. "And I would never have agreed to anyone but you marrying my mother and becoming my stepfather."

"Yes, I suppose you would have given an unwanted stepfather a bad time," Uncle John teased her, smoothing her long blonde hair.

"You know me!" Mandie laughed.

"Now I think you'd better get back to your friends. I've left the door unlocked over there for you," Uncle John told her, pointing to a small door at one side of the room. "I knew you would want to show Celia the tunnel."

"Thanks, Uncle John. I love you," Mandie said. Squeezing his hand tightly, she hurried back to the other young people and found them impatiently waiting for her in the parlor. Snowball was curled up in the middle of the carpet.

"Are you ready now?" Mandie asked.

"Are *you* ready'?" Joe laughed.

"Yes, I had a nice surprise just now. I'll show you when we get up there," Mandie promised.

"Step this way, ladies and gent," Joe teased as he rose to lead the way. "We've all been there before except Celia, so you know the way."

Celia, Sallie, and Dimar followed Joe and Mandie up the stairs to the third floor. They hurried down the long hallway to the door to the library where Mandie had just been.

As they stepped into the room, Mandie pointed to the portrait. "That's what Uncle John wanted to show me," she told her friends. "He just got it back from being refinished. I had never seen it before. It's my Grandmother Shaw—my father's mother, and Uncle John's mother, too, of course."

The group paused to admire the portrait.

Mandie turned toward the small door that Uncle John had left unlocked. "Joe, would you please carry that lamp over there?" she asked.

Joe picked up the lamp from a nearby table and lighted it.

As Mandie opened the door, Celia stood directly behind her. "It looks just like a closet with a paneled wall, doesn't it?" Mandie stood to one side to let Celia look closely. Then Mandie continued. "Watch what happens when I push this." She pushed the latch, and the paneled wall swung around, making a doorway.

Celia caught her breath in astonishment.

"Now we go right through here," Joe said as he stepped through the doorway into the tunnel.

Celia held onto Mandie's hand as they walked down a dark hallway illuminated only by the oil lamp. The others followed. They went down, down, down the dark stairs to a short hallway below where there were more stairs and another door.

They kept on through doors and down stairways until Joe stopped at a door at the end of a hallway.

"Whew!" Celia gasped. "This is something!"

"My great-grandfather built this house about the time the Cherokees were being moved out of North Carolina. He didn't believe in the white people's cruelty toward the Indians, and he hid dozens of the Cherokees in this tunnel and fed and clothed them until about 1842, when it was safe for them to go out and set up living quarters elsewhere," Mandie explained. "That was the way my grandfather met my grandmother. He was twenty-eight, and she was just eighteen. She was a beautiful young Indian girl, as you can tell from that portrait in the library."

"What a love story!" Celia exclaimed.

"Sallie's grandfather, whom we all call Uncle Ned, knew all about this tunnel and never told me about it," said Mandie. "One day I accidentally stumbled into the wall upstairs with Polly, my friend next-door, when the wall opened up and we found the tunnel."

"My grandfather can keep a secret," remarked Sallie. "He never told me about the tunnel, either."

"This is unbelievable," Celia said, shaking her auburn curls. "Imagine having to live in this tunnel for such a long time. It must have been terrible!"

"Yes, for a Cherokee to have to be confined must have been almost like death," Dimar said. "The Cherokee likes to be free as a bird with no cage."

"And now when I open this door, Celia," Joe teased, "you will be surprised to see what awaits you." Reaching for the key on a nail, he inserted it in the lock, turned it, and pulled the door open, deliberately slow.

There, outside the door, stood Hilda, just as surprised as the rest of the young people.

"That's n-not what I had in mind," Joe stammered. "I meant the outdoors."

"Hilda! What are you doing out here?" Mandie asked, stepping out into the sunshine. She squinted her eyes to adjust to the brightness.

"We thought you were upstairs in bed," Sallie said. "How did you get out here?"

"She has a mind of her own," Dimar observed.

As the others stepped out of the tunnel, they shivered in the chilly morning air.

"Brrrr! I am cold!" Celia rubbed her arms lightly. "Hilda is smarter than we are. She is at least wearing a shawl."

"Yes, my shawl," Mandie laughed.

Joe shuffled through the newly fallen leaves near the tunnel entrance. "It's getting on toward wintertime," he said.

"Come on, Hilda," Mandie urged. "It's time to eat."

Hilda smiled at Mandie. "Eat," she repeated.

"She is learning," Dimar said.

"We just have to keep teaching her," Mandie replied.

"I think we should go around the outside of the house to take her inside," Joe suggested. "That dark tunnel might scare her."

The others agreed.

"I'll run back through the tunnel and lock it so I can leave the lamp upstairs. I'll catch up with you," Joe said.

Joe disappeared inside and the others hurried through the back door.

Liza stood near the sideboard, ready to pour coffee. She grinned when they entered the breakfast room with Hilda. "What fun!" She laughed.

"Yeah, fun, before breakfast," grumbled Joe as he picked up a plate. "Umm! Everything smells so good!"

Mandie removed the shawl from Hilda's shoulders and placed it on a chair at the table.

"Now, Hilda, come and get yourself a plate and fill it up with food," Mandie told the girl. Leading her to the stack of china, she handed Hilda a plate.

Hilda looked at the empty plate and started to hand it back.

"No!" Mandie commanded, taking a plate for herself. "You fill it up like this." Mandie began putting food on her own plate, then reached to put some on Hilda's.

The girl seemed to understand. She immediately started piling food on her plate.

"Not too much of one thing," Mandie told her. "The plate won't hold so much. You see, you take a little of whatever you want now, and then you can come back and get more if you want it."

"Little." Hilda repeated the word, then began taking a very small amount of grits.

"That's the way." Mandie guided her down the length of the sideboard as they both took a small portion of various foods.

Joe watched the two of them for a few minutes, then whispered to Mandie, "You plan to take her along with us to the mine? Can you imagine how much trouble she'll be?"

"That's the only way to teach her anything. We have to let her participate in whatever we do," Mandie replied.

"Just remember that it was your idea," Joe remarked.

Suddenly Hilda grabbed Dimar's hand. "Come!" she said, pulling him toward the table. She balanced her plate precariously with her other hand.

Dimar looked confused, but since he had already filled his plate, he let her lead him.

Everyone looked at each other.

"She seems to like you, Dimar," Joe teased.

"She can't say much, but she knows how to let you know when she likes something," Mandie said.

"Maybe I can teach her to speak Cherokee," Dimar said, sitting down at the table with Hilda.

The others stood still for a moment, then everyone burst out laughing. This was going to be interesting.

CHAPTER FOUR

ANOTHER SECRET TUNNEL

"I'm not going with y'all, this afternoon," Uncle John told the young people at the noontime meal later that day. "We grown folks are all going over to visit the Hadleys, and we won't be back until time for supper. I trust you all to behave and not to do anything you shouldn't. The men should be already gone from the mine, and you may go inside to look, but you'll have to wait to search for rubies until I can show you how."

Mandie looked down the long dining table at her old Indian friend. "Uncle Ned, aren't you going with us?" she asked.

"No, Papoose. John Shaw want me see Hadleys," the Indian replied.

"You may take Liza if you think you need help in looking after Hilda," Elizabeth said.

"I will look after Hilda," Dimar offered. "I am teaching her Cherokee."

Mandie, Celia, and Sallie looked at each other and smiled. Joe nudged Dimar and grinned.

"Please don't let her get away from you, Dimar," Elizabeth cautioned. "She likes to run away at times."

"We know," the girls said in unison, giggling.

"She will not run away from me," Dimar replied.

As everyone rose from the table, the old Indian stopped the young people.

"Papooses be good," Uncle Ned told the girls. "Boys, behave."

"We will," they all promised.

"I'm sure these nice young people will be fine," said Grandmother Taft. "I'd say there's not a bad one in the lot. But just in case you need us, Amanda, you know where the Hadleys live on the other side of town."

"No, Grandmother, I don't know the Hadleys," Mandie replied. "I'm at school in Asheville so much that I don't know many people in Franklin."

"I know where they live," Joe said. "I go over there with my father sometimes when they need doctoring. They're older people."

"Well, that's where we will be," Mrs. Taft said.

"All right. Let's go." Joe urged.

"Goodbye, Mother," Mandie called as the young people left the room.

Jason Bond had brought ponies to the gate for them and was waiting with lanterns and matches. "Here. You'll be needin' these." He handed the lanterns to the boys and gave the matches to the girls. "Y'all be careful now. Just leave the ponies here when you come back, and I'll put them away."

"Thank you, Mr. Jason." Mandie put Snowball on her shoulder. "Don't you want to come with us?" she asked the caretaker.

"Nope. I'm not interested in that hole in the ground," he said.

"But there may be rubies in it," Joe told him.

"There may be and there may not be. It's not worth all that hard work to find out for sure," the caretaker replied. "I'll be here when you get back."

The young people waved goodbye and rushed to the mine. Dimar rode close to Hilda, who seemed to be enjoying the journey.

Mandie looked at Joe. "Let's go by the old house first and show everybody that dress," she suggested, turning her pony in that direction.

The others followed. At the front steps of the old farmhouse, they all dismounted except Hilda. Since she refused to get down from her pony, Dimar stayed outside with her.

"Whose house is this?" Celia asked, following the others inside.

"It belongs to Uncle John, but no one has lived in it for a long, long time," Mandie told her friend. She rushed into the next room to look for the dress.

"It's gone!" cried Mandie and Sallie together, staring at the nail where the dress had hung.

"I told you whoever it belonged to would come back and get it," Joe reminded them.

"Was it a pretty dress? What color was it?" Celia asked.

"It was pretty–" Mandie answered, shifting Snowball from one shoulder to the other, "–a blue gingham, store-bought dress with a sash."

"Well, don't worry about that dress," Joe said. "Let's get on over to the mine." He led the way out of the house and back to their ponies.

As they approached the mine, Celia pointed to the planks covering the ground. "What are all those boards doing there?" she asked.

"They make a roof for the mine," Mandie said. "Come on." She jumped down from her pony and tied him to a branch. "The steps are over here." Taking the lead, she gave Joe and Dimar the matches. "You'd better light the lanterns. It's probably dark down there."

"I'm sure it is. There aren't any windows, you know," Joe replied, lighting the lantern. "Let me go first with the light."

"Then I'll light mine and follow behind," said Dimar.

The others followed Joe down the steep steps into the underground cavern. Hilda clung to Dimar's hand, not understanding what was going on.

Joe flashed the lantern around as they inspected the place. There was a water trough descending through one side. The ground was uneven, mostly gravel and rocks. A number of shovels, hoes, and picks stood in one corner.

"Everything is neat and in order," Sallie remarked.

"Yes, the men did a good job of cleaning up the place," Mandie agreed, setting Snowball down. "Now don't run away, Snowball. I don't think there's anywhere to go down here except back up the steps."

The kitten played around with the bristles of a home-made broom leaning against a nearby post in the corner.

"Well, where are the rubies?" Celia asked.

"You have to dig for them," Joe told her.

"Dig?" she questioned.

"Of course. They aren't just laying around loose in plain sight," Mandie replied.

The young people looked around for several minutes; then suddenly Sallie spoke up. "Where is Snowball?" she asked. "I do not see him anywhere."

Immediately everyone scrambled around, looking for the white kitten.

"He must have gone up the steps," Mandie said, starting toward the steps where Dimar and Hilda were standing.

"He did not go up there. I would have seen him," Dimar said.

"But that's the only way out of here, and I sure don't see him anywhere else," Joe said, flashing the lantern around.

Dimar carefully searched around the posts.

"Snowball was playing with that broom, remember?" Celia said, walking toward the corner. Mandie and Sallie followed her.

Sallie stopped short, pointing. "Look! There is a passageway going out of here," she said.

Joe and Dimar came quickly with the lanterns and lit up the area. Sallie was right. There was a corridor leading into the darkness beyond. A pile of timbers lay nearby.

"Then Snowball must have gone that way," Mandie said. "Come on with the lanterns. I'm going to look for him."

Joe led the way into the tunnel, lighting it with the lantern. It seemed to be a narrow dirt tunnel with posts here and there holding it up.

"Snowball! Here kitty, kitty!" Mandie called as she went along.

The others followed, and Hilda clung to Dimar in fright as he led her into the tunnel.

"Oh, what places y'all can get involved in." Celia gasped.

"Where do you suppose this tunnel goes?" Dimar asked, holding his lantern a little higher.

"I don't know. Uncle John didn't mention this tunnel," Mandie replied. "Snowball! Here, kitty!" She strained her eyes to look for the kitten in the dim light.

As they turned a bend in the tunnel, Joe called back to the others. "I see daylight ahead!" he exclaimed, hurrying forward.

The others rushed to keep up with him. As they approached the opening at the end of the tunnel, Joe blew out his lantern and Dimar did likewise. Rose Creek, a branch of the Little Tennessee River, ran a short distance from the tunnel, and there, playing near the water, was Snowball.

Mandie ran and snatched up the kitten. "Snowball, you've been bad." she scolded. "You know you aren't supposed to run away!" She held him up to look into his face.

Snowball meowed in reply and reached for her shoulder with his tiny paws.

"Ah, Snowball, you're full of stickers," she cried. Then gently and carefully she began removing the briars, stroking his fur as she worked. As she did that, Mandie caught sight of something blue laying on the ground nearby. She quickly picked it up.

"Look!" she cried, holding up what she had found.

"A sash." Sallie exclaimed.

"It's the sash to that dress we found in the farmhouse," Mandie explained to the others.

"I wonder how it got here," Joe said, looking around the edge of the water.

"I wonder where the dress is," Sallie said.

"Someone probably put it on and wore it," Dimar ventured.

"And lost the sash," Celia added. "How could anyone lose a sash and not know it?"

"That would be easy if it came untied and you didn't know." Mandie held Snowball tightly with one hand while she put the sash in her apron pocket.

Joe looked puzzled. "I wonder why your Uncle John didn't mention this tunnel."

"He said he hadn't been in the mine—that it was closed when he was a child, and he hired those men to open it. So he wouldn't have known it was here," Mandie replied.

"But the workmen would," Dimar surmised.

"And they would have thought Mr. Shaw knew it was there," Joe reasoned.

"Yes," Hilda agreed.

Surprised, everyone turned to look at her. The girl smiled and hung her head as she clung to Dimar's hand.

"Hilda, you are improving all the time," Mandie told her.

"That is because I am teaching her," Dimar said with a smile.

"Then you'd better keep on teaching her," Joe stated.

"I plan to," Dimar replied.

"Whew! I'm starving!" Celia announced. "And I ate a big meal at noon."

"Me too," Mandie said, heading back toward the tunnel. "Let's go to the house and get something to eat. It must be time for tea by now."

"Are we going back through that tunnel?" Celia asked.

"Sure. We came through it all right, didn't we?" Mandie walked to the entrance.

Joe pointed to his left. "Look! There's a pile of timbers behind those bushes over there."

The others stopped to look.

Dimar examined the boards. "It does not look like new wood," he remarked.

"No, it's probably been here a long time," Mandie agreed.

"All right. Is everybody ready?" Joe lighted the lantern again to go back through the tunnel, and Dimar did the same.

Back inside the mine, Mandie stooped to pick up a handful of gravel and let it trickle through her fingers. "As soon as Uncle John shows us how to do it, we'll begin looking for rubies," she said. "It's hard to believe that such beautiful gems hide in dirt like this."

Her friends all stooped to examine the gravel beneath their feet.

"But that is where they come from," Dimar said. "This man who wants to buy the mine from your uncle must think there are rubies in this mine."

"Yes, I suppose he does, but I don't know anything about him. I think when he was a boy he used to work here with his father," Mandie replied.

"I've been thinking about that, too, Mandie," Joe said, running his fingers through the dirt. "That man must know something about this mine. He must think that it's valuable in some way, or he wouldn't be wanting to put out good money to buy it."

"I know, but Uncle John hasn't told me anything about his dealings with him," Mandie replied.

"He might have already been here and found some rubies," Sallie suggested.

"I don't see how he could. It has been boarded up all these years," Mandie replied.

"It is easy to tear down boards," said Dimar.

"Oh, you're all making it a big mystery," Celia said, sounding a little frightened. "Maybe there's nothing to it."

"Does the man live near here?" Sallie asked.

"I don't know. All I know about him is what I said, that he used to work here when he was real young. Maybe he just wants the land to build on or something," Mandie said.

"I do not think anyone would want to build on top of land that might have rubies in it," stated Dimar, "but I am sure Mandie's uncle knows what he is doing."

"You're right, Dimar," Celia agreed. "All I know right now is that I'm hungry."

"Me too," said Joe. "Let's go." As he led the way up the steps with the lantern, the others followed, and they raced back to the house on their ponies. Dimar, even though he was leading Hilda's pony, won the race, and Hilda seemed to enjoy the wild ride. Dimar grinned at the others as they caught up with him and Hilda at the gate to the Shaws' house.

"Dimar, we promised we would behave," Mandie reminded him. "It's a wonder Hilda didn't fall off her pony, you were going so fast."

Dimar gently helped Hilda down. "It was not so bad. I am teaching her to ride like a Cherokee."

"Come on. Let's find the food," Joe said, heading up the long walkway to the front door.

Liza, hearing them approaching, opened the door and waited for them.

"De tea, it be ready," she told them. "Did y'all find any rubies?"

"No, Liza, we didn't even look. Uncle John has to show us how," Mandie replied. "None of the grownups are here. Let's have tea in the sunroom."

"All you has to do is dig in de dirt, and I'm sho' you knows how to dig in de dirt," Liza insisted, following them to the sunroom.

Mandie thought for a moment and said, "I guess you're right, Liza. If the rubies are in the dirt, all we have to do is dig."

Aunt Lou appeared at the doorway. "Liza, come here, git dis food," she called.

Liza obeyed and came back with two large platters loaded with sweetcakes and other goodies. Setting it in the middle of the tea table, she went out and returned with the steaming teapot and cups and saucers.

The Negro girl stood back and surveyed the table as the young people poured the tea and quickly cleaned off the platters. "If dat ain't 'nuff to eat, I can git Jenny to send in mo,' " Liza teased.

Everyone laughed.

"I think we'll be doing good to eat all this, Liza," Mandie said. "After all, we have to save room for supper."

"It certainly is a lot of food," Sallie agreed.

"Dat's whut comes from bein' de richest man dis side o' Richmond. It means you kin have anything you wants to eat," Liza said, dancing out of the room.

Everyone looked at each other and laughed.

"Let's go back to the mine after we eat and see if we can find some rubies in that dirt," Celia suggested. "Like Liza said, all we have to do is dig."

"All right," Mandie agreed. "Whoever that dress belongs to might show up, too, looking for the sash." She patted her apron pocket where she had put it.

"I refuse to get involved in another one of your adventures, Mandie," Joe said. "I'll go back to the mine but only to look for rubies."

"Well, that's what we're all going for," Mandie insisted.

As soon as all the food was gone, the group rode back to the mine. They decided to enter by way of the tunnel they had found on their last trip. Riding around to the river side of the tunnel, they dismounted and looked for the entrance. They found it, but it was all boarded up.

"Now, how could that be?" Joe asked, exasperated. He beat on the timbers nailed over the tunnel entrance.

"I don't see how anyone could have closed that up so fast," Mandie said.

"And who would do such a thing?" Sallie asked.

"Maybe it was the person that dress belonged to," Mandie answered.

"Mandie! Stop that!" Joe sputtered. "That dress was in the farm-house and not in this mine."

"But we found the sash here, remember?" Celia defended her friend.

"Well, anyway, we'll have to go around to the other entrance to get inside the mine unless we want to tear all this down," Joe decided.

"We have no tools for that," Dimar reminded him.

"You're right, Dimar. We'll go around to the front."

Riding around to the other entrance, they tied up their ponies, lighted the two lanterns and descended into the mine.

After the boys used the tools to loosen the dirt, they all scratched around in it for a long time, but they couldn't find anything that they thought might be rubies.

Tired and dirty, they returned to the house just in time to get cleaned up for supper. The adults had already come back.

Mandie related the day's events at the table. "Uncle John, did you know there was a tunnel in the mine that comes out by Rose Creek?" she asked.

Why, no, I don't know anything about a tunnel," Uncle John replied.

Mandie related how they found the tunnel in the first place and then later found it all boarded up.

"Evidently someone else knows about it, too, if it was open to begin with and then closed when they returned," Dr. Woodard remarked.

Uncle John turned to Uncle Ned. "Do you know anything about this?" he asked.

"Sad, bad mine," the old Indian grunted. Then he went right on eating.

"Uncle Ned, I wish you would tell us whatever you know about the mine," Uncle John told him.

"Put memory away," Uncle Ned insisted.

Uncle John sighed and turned to Mrs. Taft. "You were living here in Franklin when I was a boy. Did you ever know anything about this mine?"

Mrs. Taft cleared her throat. "Nothing that I can think of, John." She, too, went right on eating.

"I don't know what to think," Uncle John said to Dr. Woodard.

"I don't either," the doctor replied, "but I suppose the important thing is to get these young people started on their gem hunting and get it over with."

"You're right," Uncle John agreed. Turning to the young people, he said, "Tomorrow morning we'll take you to the mine and get you started on this mining expedition."

Excited, the young people all spoke at once.

"But you are to be on constant watch for any strangers. Do you all understand that?" Uncle John asked.

"Yes, sir," they chorused.

"John," Elizabeth said quickly, "do you think they'll be safe there without any adults? With all these strange happenings, I'm not sure we should allow them to stay there without an adult present."

"Well, since there are six of them, I imagine there is safety in numbers." John winked at the young people. "I know I'd hate to come up against the lot of them."

"I still don't know," Elizabeth said uncertainly.

CHAPTER FIVE

THE WOMAN
WITH THE DRESS

"Now, this is how you go about it," Uncle John told the young people as they stood about in the ruby mine the next morning. "You have to get this pump going, like this, in order to get water into the trough." He pumped the handle up and down, flooding the trough with water.

"Will the water stay in the trough?" Mandie asked, watching closely.

"For a while. It slowly runs out the end down there." Uncle John pointed. "But it will stay long enough for you to get a sieveful of gravel washed. Then, if you pump like this, you will notice that the water flows back through the trough. In other words, you are reusing part of the water. Part of it is lost into that trench over there, which becomes a stream as you fill it with water, and then it will flow out to Rose Creek and into the river."

Uncle Ned stood by, silently disapproving of the whole operation.

Dr. Woodard watched. "And you must not pump too fast or the trough will overflow, and you'll get all wet," he reminded them.

"What about the gravel? Won't the trough get full of gravel when we wash a lot of it?" Joe asked.

"No, not if you do it right," Uncle John replied. "You see, you fill the sieve only partially full of gravel, like this, and dip it into the water without turning it sideways so you won't tilt the gravel out into the trough. The water comes up into the sieve through the bottom and washes the gravel. The tiny particles that are small enough to go through the wire in the bottom of the sieve will go on into the water. But those aren't important. They will all wash away. If you find any rubies, they will be in larger pieces."

"Joe, dig some gravel to put in the sieve," Dr. Woodard told his son.

Joe took the shovel and loosened some dirt and gravel as the others watched.

Uncle John held out the sieve. "Now put enough in this sieve to fill it about half full," he instructed.

Joe did as he was told.

Uncle John turned back to the water trough with the sieve and lowered it straight down into the water without tilting it. The water washed over the gravel, and the tiny particles floated away. He shook the sieve and then set it on the edge of the trough. Running his fingers through the washed gravel, he stirred it around.

The young people watched breathlessly.

"Any rubies?" Celia asked.

"I'm afraid not. It's all rock," Uncle John replied, looking closely at what was left. Then he straightened up. "That's all there is to it," he said.

"But what do we do with what's left in the sieve?" Mandie asked.

"Oh, that. You just dump it over there somewhere away from wherever you want to dig. Otherwise, you'll be digging up the same gravel again," he explained.

"This is going to be a very interesting experience," Dimar remarked. "Perhaps I will find a ruby."

"Remember to look at everything very closely," Dr. Woodard cautioned. "I've told you what a ruby should look like. It will be dark and rough, and you could easily mistake it for an ordinary rock," he said.

"Are we staying all day?" Celia asked.

"No, you must come home to eat at noon. That way we'll know you are all right," Uncle John replied.

"But we can come back here after we eat, can't we?" Mandie asked.

"I suppose so—if you're not too tired after all the work you're going to do," Uncle John teased. "Whoever does the digging is going to be worn out."

"We can all do our own digging. There are enough tools over there for all of us," Mandie decided.

Uncle John took a step backward. "Dr. Woodard, Uncle Ned, and I have somewhere we have to go," he informed them. "We're going to leave you here, so please be careful. Don't get too close to each other when you're digging or someone could be hit," he warned. "I'm depending on you all to act like the intelligent young people I know you to be."

"Thank you, Mr. Shaw," said Dimar.

"We will be careful," Sallie assured him.

As the men started to leave, Uncle Ned took Mandie's hand. "Papoose, be careful," he cautioned.

"I will, Uncle Ned," Mandie promised. Then turning to Uncle John, she said, "We'll bring home all the rubies we find." She laughed.

Uncle John winked. "Yes, you be sure to do that."

As the men left, the young people made a dash for the tools.

"I think I'll use a hoe," Mandie stated, taking a long-handled one. "It might be easier to handle than a pick."

The others chose various hoes, shovels, and picks and scattered about in the mine, beginning their task.

Dimar took Hilda over to the far side and showed her how to use a hoe. "Dig. Like this," he explained, digging into the dirt.

Hilda watched and then took the hoe to imitate him. She laughed and kept digging away.

Dimar moved away from her for fear of being hit and began his own search.

They all rushed to see who could get a sieve of gravel to wash first. Uncle John had provided sieves for each of them, and there was a lot of splashing and excitement as they washed the gravel and searched for something that might look like a ruby.

"Oh! Is this one?" Celia cried, holding up a dark-colored rock she had washed.

The others crowded close to examine it.

"It looks like just an old rock to me," Mandie said.

"Yeah, it's just a rock," Joe agreed.

"Oh well, there are lots more," Celia said, dumping the contents of her sieve in the pile of discarded gravel in the corner.

"Yes, there are more than we can ever sift through," Sallie remarked as she continued digging.

"I wish it was summertime and school was out, so we could have more time. We might find something then," said Mandie.

"But your Uncle John will be selling the mine by then," Celia reminded her.

"Yes, and that other man may be getting a rich mine. We will never know because we do not have time to do much," Dimar said as he looked over at Hilda digging away in the corner.

"Hey, less talk and more work, or we'll never get done," Joe called loudly.

"Joe is right. We must concentrate on what we are doing, or we may overlook a ruby," Sallie agreed, bending to fill her sieve.

Hilda stopped digging and stooped to examine the gravel, jabbering incoherently.

Everyone looked over at her.

"What is it, Hilda?" Mandie asked, hurrying to her side.

Hilda pointed to what looked like a piece of broken pottery sticking out of the ground. Mandie bent to pick it up, but Hilda snatched it and quickly put it in her apron pocket. When the others crowded around, Hilda kept her hand tightly over her pocket and backed away.

"What is it, Mandie?" Celia asked.

"It looked like a piece of broken pottery, but it was so dirty I'm not sure," Mandie replied.

"Hilda, will you let us see what you found?" Dimar asked, approaching her cautiously.

Hilda backed away quickly and kept her hand over her pocket.

"It's all right, Hilda. Go ahead and dig. You may find something else," Mandie told the girl.

As the others went back to their digging, Hilda finally picked up her hoe and moved over to a corner by herself to resume digging.

"Well, at least someone found something," Joe said.

The morning slipped away rapidly, and no one else found anything. But the girls' aprons had become very soiled, and everyone's shoes were full of dirt.

'Whew!" Mandie said, standing on one foot to empty the dirt out of her shoe. "It must be time to go eat."

"Not tired, are you?" Joe asked, pausing to wipe a dirty hand across his face.

"Not until I stop," Mandie said. "As long as I am digging, I don't think about being tired."

Celia tried to shake the dirt off her apron. "I sure need a bath," she said.

"Do you think we can get cleaned up enough to be allowed to sit at the table and eat?" Sallie laughed.

"I think so," Mandie replied.

"Maybe this afternoon we will find a ruby," Dimar remarked. "Maybe we will find several rubies."

"Yes," Hilda spoke up.

When they returned for the noon meal, Elizabeth met them at the door and quickly looked them over. "I suppose you're not as dirty as I thought you would be," she said. "Get washed now and get to the table."

"Oh, what fun it was, Mother!" Mandie exclaimed as the young people filed into the hallway.

"But no rubies yet," Joe added.

"Of course not." Uncle John spoke up from the doorway to the parlor. "You couldn't have that much luck," he laughed.

"Hilda did find something," Celia said, turning to the girl who was hovering at the edge of the group. "Show us what you found, Hilda."

Hilda backed off, keeping her hand on the pocket of her apron.

"I think it was only a piece of a broken bowl," Mandie said.

"All right. Get washed, all of you—and hurry," Elizabeth told them.

As they scampered in different directions to wash, Mandie took charge of Hilda. "Come on, Hilda. We've got to wash so we can eat," she said.

When they all returned to the dining room, the young people ate as though they were starved to death. The morning's exercise had whetted their appetites.

Mrs. Taft stopped eating and watched them. "You all must be in a big hurry to get back to that digging," she said.

"Oh, yes, Grandmother," Mandie replied.

Hilda shook her head violently.

Dimar spoke to her gently. "Do you not want to go back to the mine and dig with us?" he asked.

Hilda shook her head again.

Grandmother Taft smiled at Hilda. "That's all right," she said. "She can stay here with us older folks this time."

Mandie wondered why Hilda suddenly didn't want to go back, but she also felt a little relieved. "Are you going this afternoon, Uncle Ned?" she asked the Indian, who had been silent during the meal.

"Not today. Later," he replied.

"We have guests coming this afternoon," Uncle John explained, "and we want Uncle Ned to meet them."

"That's all right. We'll be fine," Mandie assured the old Indian. But she continued watching him. He seemed to be in bad spirits and wasn't joining in the conversation. Actually, Grandmother Taft acted as though she had a secret, too. Perhaps they were involved in some kind of conspiracy. Mandie was anxious to find out what it was.

Elizabeth looked around the table and saw that all the young people had finished eating. "You may go now," she said. "But please be careful."

"And remember. You must all be back here before the sun goes down," Mrs. Woodard reminded them.

The young people scrambled to their feet.

"I wish you could go, Uncle Ned," Mandie urged, stopping by his chair as she left the room.

"Later, Papoose. I promise," Uncle Ned said, squeezing her hand. "If Papoose get in trouble, I will go."

Mandie didn't understand what he meant, but since the others were leaving, she released Uncle Ned's wrinkled hand and hurried from the room.

As they guided their ponies back toward the mine, Mandie called to the others, "Let's go down by the river first and see if that tunnel is still closed."

"I was going to suggest the same thing," Joe called back.

They carefully made their way through the underbrush toward Rose Creek. As they came within sight of the end of the tunnel, they were amazed to see a man and a woman, carrying heavy bags, get into a boat.

"The dress! That woman is wearing that dress!" Mandie cried as she raced her pony forward. She squinted but she couldn't see their faces. By the time the young people got to the creek bank, the man and woman had rowed far out into the water.

Mandie put her hands on her hips. "Of all things! Get this close and still not close enough!"

"They probably are carrying gems from your uncle's mine in those bags," said Dimar.

Joe laughed. "In those bags? We dug all morning and couldn't find a single stone, and you think they had bags full of them?"

"Of course. That is why we cannot find any. They got them all," Dimar replied.

Joe laughed again.

"I wonder who they are," Sallie said as the boat moved out of sight around a bend. "Do you suppose the dress belongs to that woman or do you think she just found it in the farmhouse and put it on?"

"I sure would like to know. I still have the sash," Mandie said, patting her apron pocket.

"Now we do have a mystery, don't we?" Celia said.

"And as far as I'm concerned, it's going to remain an unsolved mystery," Joe declared. "Come on. Let's get busy."

The entrance to the tunnel was still closed, so Joe led the way around to the front entrance of the mine. There they tied up their ponies and went down in to continue their work.

Although they worked hard that afternoon, digging and sifting gravel, they didn't find a single interesting thing. They checked the tunnel entrance several times to be sure the man and woman had not returned, but there was no sign of them.

The young people got home in plenty of time to bathe and change clothes before sundown.

As they all sat down to supper, Mandie could hardly wait to share her news about the strangers. "Uncle John, we saw a woman wearing that dress we found in your old house," she began excitedly. "And there was a man with her. They got into a boat down by the end of the tunnel and disappeared."

Elizabeth put down her fork. "What!" she exclaimed.

"You saw a woman wearing the dress you found?" Uncle John questioned her. "What did she look like?"

"We couldn't get close enough to tell. They were carrying some heavy bags. And the back entrance to the tunnel is still closed."

"Seems like some shenanigans are going on down at that mine," Dr. Woodard said.

Uncle Ned and Mrs. Taft leaned forward to listen.

Elizabeth looked worried. "Strangers at the mine? John, what is going on?" she asked.

"I don't know, dear," he replied. "Something strange for sure." Turning back to the young people, he asked, "Did none of you get close enough to see who they were, or what they looked like?"

There was a chorus of no's as the young people shook their heads.

"You'd better not go back to that mine again unless an adult is with you," Elizabeth instructed. "We don't know who these people are."

"Why get worried over a couple of strangers, Elizabeth?" Mrs. Taft asked. "There are strangers everywhere that we don't know."

"Elizabeth is right," John said. "It will be safer if they don't go back unless one of us is with them. That place is more or less isolated."

Mandie turned to Uncle Ned, who had not said a word. "Uncle Ned, will you go with us tomorrow? Please?" Mandie begged.

The old Indian shook his head. "Sad, bad mine. Better Papoose not go."

She looked at her uncle. "Uncle John, please go with us so we can go back tomorrow."

"I can't tomorrow morning. I have something else to do. Maybe I can tomorrow afternoon," he said.

"I am beginning to wonder if you should go back there at all, even with someone with you," Mrs. Woodard cautioned. "We don't know who those people are."

"I think it will be safe if we go with them," Dr. Woodard replied.

"We'll be back before noon tomorrow, Mandie, and we'll go to the mine right after we eat," Uncle John promised.

Mandie sighed. "Well, then, I suppose we'll have to wait until tomorrow afternoon," she said, not realizing what lay ahead.

CHAPTER SIX

MANDIE AND JOE IN TROUBLE

The next morning was cool and cloudy, and when Mandie, Celia, and Sallie awoke, Hilda wasn't in her bed. Dressing quickly, the three girls ran down to Liza's room to see if Hilda was there. But Liza was already up, helping in the kitchen. There was no sign of Hilda.

"Liza, did Hilda sleep in your room last night?" Mandie asked as the girls entered the kitchen.

"Not so's I'd notice," Liza replied. "Is dat girl missin' agin?"

"Yes," said Sallie. "Do you know where she might be?"

"Dat girl might be anywheres," Liza answered with a sigh. "Guess we better start huntin.' "

"Huntin' for what?" asked Joe as he and Dimar joined the girls in the kitchen."

"For Hilda," Mandie replied.

"She's missing again," Celia added.

Joe shook his head. "I know you care a lot about her, Mandie, but sometimes . . ."

"I know what you mean," Mandie admitted.

"We should look for her in the house first," Dimar suggested.

"Right," said Joe. "The five of us could search the whole house in a short time if we split up."

In less than a half hour, the five young people had searched all three floors of the house, the secret tunnel, the stables, and everywhere else they could think of. But there was no sign of Hilda anywhere.

When they started questioning the servants, the servants all said they hadn't seen her since the night before—all except Jason Bond. He remembered seeing her very early that morning standing out by the gate.

"What was she doing out there?" Dimar asked.

"Just starin' into space," the caretaker responded. "That's all."

The men had already left for the morning, so when the young people told Elizabeth about Hilda's disappearance, she called the servants together and asked for their help in finding the girl.

"Oh, I feel so responsible," said Mrs. Taft after the servants left on their search. "Maybe I shouldn't have brought her here."

"Nonsense, Mother," Elizabeth replied. "The servants will check with all the neighbors and some of our friends in town, and I even asked Jason Bond to see if she might have tried to find her way back to the mine."

"I do not think she would be there," Dimar offered.

"Dimar's right," Mandie agreed. "I don't think she liked that place. She wouldn't go back with us yesterday."

"Perhaps not," Elizabeth said, "but we must look everywhere. Why don't you young people search the house and grounds again. Maybe she's hiding somewhere."

"Hilda's good at hiding, isn't she, Mandie?" Celia laughed.

"Yes, she sure is," Mandie nodded. "She was hiding in that attic at school a long time before we found her. Come on, everybody," she said to her friends, "let's stay together this time and search real good. We've got to find her before Uncle John gets back."

But after another long, careful search, they still couldn't find Hilda or any clue to where she might be. About mid-morning they joined Elizabeth and Mrs. Taft and Mrs. Woodard in the parlor.

"No success?" asked Grandmother Taft.

The young people shook their heads silently.

Just then Liza rushed into the parlor, out of breath. " 'Scuse me, Miz Shaw," she said, panting. "We done found her, but she won't come. I'se sorry, ma'am. I don't know what's wrong wid her."

"Found her where?" Elizabeth asked.

"Over t' the Hadleys, Miz Shaw," Liza replied.

"Way over there?" Elizabeth exclaimed.

"I'll go get her, Mother," Mandie offered. "She'll come back for me."

"But you don't know where the Hadleys live, dear," Elizabeth said.

"I do, Mrs. Shaw," Joe spoke up. "I've been there on calls with my father. I'll go after her."

"She doesn't know you very well, Joe, but she would come for me. Mrs. Woodard, couldn't Joe go with me to get her?" Mandie asked.

"Of course, dear," Mrs. Woodard replied. "You mustn't go by yourself."

Elizabeth looked relieved. "You may go if you promise to go straight there and back," she agreed. "And if she won't come back with you, you are to return immediately. We'll figure out some other way to get her."

"Yes, Mother," said Mandie. "I promise."

Elizabeth turned to Joe. "Now, Joe, please be careful. Hilda is so unpredictable, and I'm counting on you to keep Amanda out of trouble."

"I will," Joe agreed.

Instantly the other young people clamored to go along.

"No, no," Elizabeth told them. "It will be easier for them to handle Hilda if you all stay here."

The others reluctantly agreed.

Elizabeth gave her daughter a hug. "Now you two get on out to the stable. Jason Bond took the rig out looking for Hilda, and he isn't back yet, so you can ride your ponies," Elizabeth explained. "And remember, straight there and back, no loitering along the way. Now, make haste."

"Yes, ma'am," Mandie replied, picking up Snowball.

"Yes, ma'am," Joe echoed.

Within minutes Mandie and Joe were headed in the direction of the Hadleys' house with Snowball clinging to Mandie's shoulder.

"I don't know why you had to bring that cat," Joe grumbled.

"Snowball needs some outdoor air," Mandie defended herself. "Besides, Hilda is fascinated by him. I may be able to entice her to leave by letting her hold him."

"I hope we can get her to come back," said Joe.

"Where do the Hadleys live?" Mandie asked.

"Not too far," he answered, "but we have to go near the mine."

Mandie perked up. "We do?"

"The road goes pretty close," Joe said as they trotted on.

"Do you think we could just go down the road that runs by the mine on our way to the Hadleys?" Mandie asked.

"What for?"

"Just to look at it as we go by," she said. "If we're going to be that close to it, I don't see why we can't just ride by and look."

Joe thought for a moment. "Well, all right," he agreed. "But remember, we will not stop, no matter what excuse you think up," he stated.

Mandie smiled. "Thanks, Joe," she said as the wind blew her bonnet back from her long blonde hair.

At a fork in the road Joe turned left and Mandie followed. She soon recognized the road as the one they had traveled to the mine from a different direction.

As they came within sight of the mine, Mandie suddenly pulled up the reins on her pony. "Look, Joe! There are two horses tied over there in the trees," she called to him.

Joe slowed his pony to a leisurely walk. "I wonder who they belong to," he said.

They both stopped in the road near the mine, and Mandie stayed at Joe's side. "We could just go down there long enough to see who's there," she suggested.

"You promised your mother you wouldn't go anywhere except straight to the Hadleys and back, remember?" Joe reminded her.

"Well, it wouldn't hurt anything if we just looked to see who it is," Mandie argued.

"But there's no one in sight. Someone must have just left the horses there for some reason," Joe objected.

Suddenly they heard the sound of hammering coming from the mine, and then the noise of planks being moved around. The two looked at each other in alarm.

"Joe?" Mandie gripped Snowball with one hand and slid down from her pony.

"Just remember, you started this," he said, dismounting.

"All right, I'm guilty," Mandie admitted.

They quickly tied their ponies out of sight and then softly made their way toward the mine. Stopping behind two huge tree trunks, they watched the entrance to the mine as Snowball clung silently to the shoulder of Mandie's dress.

Then the noise stopped.

The two were so intent upon watching the entrance of the mine that they didn't see or hear anyone behind them.

Suddenly two pairs of strong hands grabbed them.

Mandie gasped and looked up into the face of an old woman. Joe swung around just as a big, burly man threw a rope around him, tying his arms and hands.

Mandie trembled with fear. "Who are you? What do you want?" she managed to ask as she held Snowball tightly.

Then all of a sudden she realized that the woman was wearing the blue gingham dress. And there on the ground by the strangers' feet lay two big, heavy canvas bags.

"I know where you got that dress," Mandie told the old woman. "I saw it in the farmhouse over there on the other side of the trees. What was it doing there? Did you steal it?"

The old woman grabbed Mandie's hand and gave it a hard jerk. Mandie winced with pain.

"Ain't none of your business," the old woman said.

Joe tried to free himself but the huge man was too strong for him. "Let me go!" Joe demanded.

"Why? So you can go spread the word that we've been here? Never!" the man replied, holding tightly to the rope.

"What are we goin' to do with 'em?" the woman asked.

"That depends," the man replied. "Could be a right serious situation, you know."

"Long as they don't know what we's got in them bags we'll be all right," the woman argued.

"What do you have in those bags?" Mandie asked.

"You shore ain't gonna find out," the man said. "Else you could suffer some bad consequences."

"Let me loose," Joe demanded. "Are you going to stand there all day doing nothing? We've got somewhere we've got to go."

"You ain't goin' nowhere, so don't git your dander up," the old man told him. "That is, nowhere without us."

"You mean you're going to take us with you?" Mandie asked.

The old woman looked sharply at her companion. "That ain't necessary, is it?"

"I think so. Jest long enough for us to be on our way," the man said.

Joe tried to free his hands as the man tightened the rope around him. "Where are we going?" he asked.

The man ignored him.

"I suppose you stole whatever is in the bags, and now you're running away," Mandie said.

"Now, you listen here, you young squirt," the old man said angrily. "What's in them bags ain't none of your business, and you'd better shet up about it, or you'll wish you had."

"Let's git on our way. I don't care whether we take these two or not, but I want to git goin,' " the woman said.

"All right, we'll go. I'll hold on to the girl while you untie the horses and shoo them off. We'll take the boat." The man reached for Mandie's hand and gripped it in his big fist.

"What'll we do when we git back. The horses'll be gone," the woman protested.

"Don't worry 'bout them horses. We'll find a way," the man said. "Now hurry up and do what I told you to."

The old woman hurried over to the two horses, untied them, and slapped them with the reins. The horses neighed and took off running through the woods.

Mandie held her breath, hoping the ponies, which were tethered out of sight, wouldn't make a sound to call attention to themselves.

The woman came back and grabbed Mandie's hand again, and the man pushed Joe forward.

"Into the mine," the old man ordered.

The woman pushed and pulled Mandie along with her, and Snowball dug his claws into Mandie's shoulder.

"Are you leavin' the bags?" the woman asked her partner.

"Nope. I'll git 'em soon as I tie these two up," he said.

The strangers marched the young people through the mine and the tunnel, and on to Rose Creek where there was a boat tied up.

"You'll get in trouble for doing this," Mandie told them.

"And it'll be big trouble. Don't you know who she is?" Joe asked, nodding to Mandie.

"Don't make no difference," the man said,

"It does, too. She is John Shaw's niece, and he owns this mine!" Joe yelled as the old man shoved him toward a tree.

The woman brought Mandie near, and the man quickly wrapped the rope around the two, pinning them to the tree.

"I said it don't make no difference who she is," the old man repeated. He turned to the woman. "You watch 'em so they can't git loose," he commanded. "I'll git the bags."

The woman did as she was told, and the man hurried back through the tunnel.

"Don't you see you're making unnecessary trouble for yourself?" Mandie asked the woman. "We were on the way to the Hadleys, and if you'll just let us loose, we'll go on our way."

"That's easier said than done," the old woman said.

"And we won't even tell anyone that we saw you," Joe added.

"He's the boss," the old woman said.

"But if you do what he says, you'll be in trouble, too," Mandie told her.

"That's right. They call that a conspiracy, I think. They can arrest you for being an accessory to the fact," Joe told her.

The woman just looked at him, not understanding what he was talking about.

"Who are you, anyway?" Mandie asked. "And where are you going with those bags?"

"I ain't tellin' you no more. Them bags ain't none of your business," the woman replied. "Now shet up about it." She slapped Mandie on the cheek, leaving a red handprint.

Tears filled Mandie's eyes at the pain, but she tried to keep calm.

"Stop that." Joe scolded the woman. "Don't do that anymore, or I'll see that you pay for it."

"You ain't the boss," the woman said. "He is." She nodded at the man emerging from the tunnel, carrying the two heavy bags. He threw the bags into the boat.

"That woman slapped Mandie for no reason at all, and I don't like it," Joe protested.

The man glanced at Mandie and then at his companion. "Behave yourself, woman." he snapped. "I'm in charge of this."

The woman looked away.

"Now hold on to that girl," he ordered. "I'm goin' to untie them so we can git them into the boat." He turned to untie the knots.

As the rope came loose, the woman grabbed Mandie's hand.

The man shoved Joe, still partly tied up, toward the boat. "Git in!" he shouted.

"Where are we going?" Joe demanded.

"I said git in that boat," the man repeated, giving the boy a shove. Joe stumbled and almost fell head over heels into the boat.

Mandie's heart raced as she realized they were being taken away somewhere down the river. She had to leave some kind of a clue. Quickly putting Snowball on her shoulder, she reached surreptitiously into her apron pocket, pulled out the light blue sash she had found, and dropped it behind her as the woman shoved her forward.

The man rowed the boat out into deeper water. "You can untie the rest of the ropes now. I don't think they'll try to jump overboard and swim from here."

"I can't swim anyway," Mandie informed him.

"That's good. If your friend can swim, he wouldn't try to git away without you, I'm sure." He laughed.

The man rowed farther and farther down Rose Creek toward the wide open Little Tennessee River. The sky was still cloudy and a light fog started forming over the water.

Mandie looked at her captors, feeling a mixture of fear and anger. "I'm sure you have stolen something out of our mine, haven't you?"

"Ain't nothin' in these here bags out of your mine," the man argued.

"But you're stealing something," Mandie said angrily. "You're still breaking one of the Ten Commandments—'Thou shalt not steal'—and that is a terrible thing to do."

"Listen, miss, mind your own business," the man replied.

Then the woman spoke up. "We ain't the only ones that's been stealin,' " she said.

"I knew you had stolen something," Mandie declared.

"Woman, shet your mouth!" the man yelled.

"You've made one good step. You've admitted your sin, that you have stolen something," Mandie said shakily. "But you must ask forgiveness from God and try to make amends for what you've done."

The woman stared at her in silence, but the man just ignored Mandie.

"What you steal will never do you any good," Joe put in.

"No, it won't, because it will bother your conscience," Mandie told the woman, feeling a little more bold. "I will help you pray for forgiveness if you want me to."

"I don't need no forgiveness for nothin,' " the woman muttered.

"Yes, you do. You need our forgiveness for what you're doing to us," Mandie said. "It's a sin to hold things against people when they do you wrong. You might not exactly like what they do to you, but Christians have to forgive other people." Mandie swallowed hard. "I forgive y'all for what you've done to us. Won't you ask God to forgive you?"

With Snowball curled up in her lap, Mandie fearfully reached across to the woman and put her small hand over an old wrinkled one. She searched the woman's tired eyes.

The woman quickly pulled her hand away and wouldn't look at Mandie.

"Your daddy a preacher or somethin'?" the old man asked.

"No, my daddy is in heaven with God," Mandie said sadly, "but he was a good man. He taught me that God loves us and will forgive us for our sins if we'll tell Him we're sorry."

The woman just stared at Mandie again.

"If you think you can persuade us to let you go with that kind of talk, you might as well shet up, because it won't work," the old man said. "If there's a God up there, He shore has forsaken us. I done give up on that stuff a long time ago."

As they traveled downstream, Joe looked all around. "Where are we going?" he ventured to ask. His voice was a little shaky.

"That I ain't tellin' neither," the man said.

"I reckon I'll see when we get there then," Joe replied.

The man pulled hard on the oars as they swept through a strong current. "We may not be goin' to the same place," he said.

Mandie and Joe glanced at each other. What were these people up to, anyway? And how would anyone ever find them? No one could track them in the water. Was there no way to get to these people's hearts?

Mandie tried again. "Do y'all have any children?"

The old woman shook her head while the man ignored the question.

"I am my mother's only child," Mandie said. "She loves me an awful lot, and I love her more than anything. She's going to be worried about me when I don't get back home on time," Mandie said. "You see, my grandmother didn't like my father because he was half Cherokee. After I was born, she made my father take me and leave. I wasn't reunited with my mother until after my father died. You see, his old Indian friend, Uncle Ned, helped me get to my Uncle John Shaw's house in Frank—"

"Shet up!" the man shouted. "What's all that got to do with us?"

"Maybe you didn't catch what Mandie said," Joe answered bravely. "She is part Cherokee, and the Cherokees will come looking for her when she doesn't show up back at the house. I'd sure hate to come up against those Indians when one of their kin has been wronged. "

"Indians?" the woman echoed.

"That's what he said," the man told her. "Don't you remember all that hullabaloo about the Indians and that mine?"

"I suppose so. Seems like I remember somethin,' " the woman said.

Mandie and Joe exchanged glances.

"What about the Indians and that mine?" Mandie asked.

"Nothin' you need to know," the man said.

"I *am* part Cherokee," Mandie admitted," "but I wouldn't ask the Cherokees to harm you in any way. Most of my Cherokee kinpeople are Christians, and they believe like I do, that we must forgive each other. They wouldn't carry off any white children for no reason at all. They know God sees and hears everything, and they want to live by His Word. But if you harm us, they will see that you are punished."

The old woman fidgeted with her blue gingham dress. "Maybe we's doin' somethin' we shouldn't–"

"Keep your trap shet, woman." the man yelled. "Don't you see what they's tryin' to do? They think they can sweet-talk us into lettin' 'em go, and then they'll go straight to John Shaw with a tale and–"

"We wouldn't cause you any trouble, mister," Mandie interrupted. "Just let us go home. My mother must be awfully worried by now."

Suddenly the man turned the boat toward the creek bank. Mandie's heart leaped in anticipation. Maybe he was going to set them free.

"Grab a bag, woman," the man ordered as he brought the boat near the bank.

Mandie and Joe silently looked at each other. Could they make a run for it? But the man quickly threw the bags on the bank as the woman jumped out onto the sand. Then the man gave the boat a sharp push with the oars as he jumped out, taking the oars with him.

Joe tried to jump out, but the man hit him hard with an oar, knocking him down into the boat.

Mandie held Snowball tightly as the boat rocked and swirled about, floating swiftly down Rose Creek toward the river. She bent over Joe. He looked lifeless. "Joe! Joe! Wake up!" she cried, tears streaming down her pale cheeks.

Fearfully, she watched the man and woman pick up their bags and hurry off into the woods without looking back. "Help us, please," Mandie yelled. "Joe is hurt."

Pushing Joe's hair back from his forehead, she gently touched his cheek. Then she took his limp hands in hers and rubbed them. He didn't move or open his eyes.

As the boat drifted free in the swift current, Mandie sat up on the seat. Gripping Snowball with one hand, she held on to the side of the boat and looked toward the sky. The sun had come out. "Dear God, please help us!" she prayed. "Please! Please don't let Joe die!"

Snowball meowed, protesting the tight grip she had on him, and Mandie held him up to her face to cuddle him. "Snowball, I love you!" she whispered through her tears. "I didn't mean to squeeze you so hard. It's just that I'm so scared. Joe is hurt and the boat is drifting away We may all be drowned!"

She took a deep breath and wiped her sleeve across her tear-stained face as the boat bumped and swirled.

"Now that's not the way to act at all," she scolded herself. She looked toward the sky again and began quoting her favorite verse: " 'What time I am afraid I will put my trust in Thee.' Oh, God," she prayed, "I know you'll take care of us, but please hurry!"

CHAPTER SEVEN

THE SEARCH BEGINS

When John, Uncle Ned, and Dr. Woodard returned home a little before noon, they found the worried women sitting by the window in the parlor. Elizabeth and Mrs. Woodard told them about Hilda's disappearance and about sending Mandie and Joe to get her.

"But they should have returned long before now," Mrs. Woodard said.

Elizabeth rose from her chair and clutched her husband's arm. "Amanda promised to go straight to the Hadleys and back without stopping anywhere," she told him.

"You know Amanda as well as I do," John said with a smile. "She probably found something interesting on the way."

"But Joe was with her, and I'm sure he would have reminded her that they were to go there and back without any delay," Elizabeth replied.

"We find," Uncle Ned said, putting a hand on Elizabeth's shoulder. "Do not worry. We go to Hadleys now."

"Yes, we'll go right now," Dr. Woodard agreed.

John Shaw put his arm around his wife. "Don't worry, dear. With Uncle Ned's help I'm sure we'll find them."

Elizabeth dabbed at her eyes with her handkerchief. "You know how I love Amanda," she said. "If anything ever happened to her, I'd never get over it."

Mrs. Taft looked up from her needlework. "Elizabeth, you don't give Amanda credit for having any sense. She knows how much she means to you. I'm sure she has just been delayed at the Hadleys. Maybe she couldn't get Hilda to come back with her."

"In that case, they were to come on back without her," Elizabeth replied.

"Come back to your needlework, dear," said Mrs. Taft. "The men will find Arnanda and Joe, I am sure."

"That's right," Dr. Woodard said. "We'll find them."

"Where are the other young people?" John asked.

"Probably out in the kitchen worrying Jenny for goodies," Elizabeth said, managing a smile. "But you will go right now, won't you?"

"Yes, dear. We'll leave right now." John kissed his wife on the forehead and started outside with Uncle Ned and Dr. Woodard.

Quickly mounting their horses, the men rode over to the Hadleys. As they approached the huge old house, their eyes quickly searched the grounds for Mandie's and Joe's ponies. There was only one pony at the hitching post, and it was not familiar to them.

"Either they have already come and gone, or they never got here at all," John said.

"I'd say you're right about that," Dr. Woodard agreed.

"We find," Uncle Ned grunted.

They dismounted and walked up to the front door. As John Shaw reached up to use the knocker, the door opened, and there stood Hilda.

The men looked at her in astonishment. Hilda reached to take Dr. Woodard's hand and tried to lead him back down the walkway.

"Home," she said, smiling.

"Wait," Dr. Woodard told her.

Mrs. Hadley appeared in the doorway with her walking cane. "John, I am so glad to see you," she said. "This poor girl just appeared on our doorstep this morning, and she wouldn't go home when Liza came for her. She has been sitting in the parlor all morning, never saying a word, just smiling at me." The elderly woman looked bewildered.

"I'm sorry, ma'am," John replied. "Elizabeth sent Amanda and Joe after her, but evidently they never got here."

"Why, no. I haven't seen another soul all day," Mrs. Hadley said.

The men exchanged glances.

"We find," Uncle Ned insisted.

"Well, I do hope you find them right away," said Mrs. Hadley. "They mustn't be out too late. The days are getting shorter, you know. It will be dark early."

"Evidently Hilda is in the mood to go home. Why don't I take her back to your house while you and Uncle Ned ride around looking for them?" Dr. Woodard offered.

"That's a good idea," agreed John. "You go ahead with her. Uncle Ned and I will work our way back toward the mine. That's the only place I can imagine they went."

After they bade Mrs. Hadley goodbye, Dr. Woodard helped Hilda onto his horse with him, giving her stern instructions to hang on tightly all the way back to John Shaw's house. Apparently she understood, and they started off down the road.

Uncle Ned and John mounted their horses.

"Two roads go to mine," Uncle Ned stated.

"That's right. There are two ways to get there from here. Why don't you go that way?" John said, indicating the road to the right. "I'll take the other road, and we'll meet at the mine."

Uncle Ned nodded. "We meet," he replied.

The old Indian rode off to the right, carefully watching the road for tracks. John Shaw went the other way.

When Dr. Woodard and Hilda arrived at John Shaw's house, Elizabeth greeted them at the door.

"Amanda and Joe weren't at the Hadleys?" she asked.

"Mrs. Hadley had not seen them," Dr. Woodard told her. "But Hilda came with me readily enough."

Elizabeth put her hand on Hilda's arm to keep her from running off somewhere again. "Hilda, we will find Liza to entertain you awhile," she told the girl. Turning back to Dr. Woodard, she asked. "Where are John and Uncle Ned?"

"They're coming back by the mine. That's the only place we could figure the two might have stopped," Dr. Woodard answered. "If they don't find them there, John or Uncle Ned will come back here to get me to help search."

Elizabeth sighed. "Where, oh where can those two be?"

"I'm afraid only the Lord knows that right now, Elizabeth," Dr. Woodard replied.

"Go on into the dining room. We decided to start eating since we didn't know how long you all would be gone," Elizabeth said. "Come on, Hilda, we will eat and then we will find Liza."

The girl smiled and followed Elizabeth and Dr. Woodard into the dining room. Then spying Dimar, she plopped down in the chair next to him. Immediately, all the young people at the table bombarded Dr. Woodard with questions.

"Did you find Amanda and Joe?" Mrs. Woodard asked.

Dr. Woodard shook his head.

"Weren't they at the Hadleys?" Celia dabbed her lips with her linen napkin.

The doctor held a chair for Elizabeth, then sat down on the other side of the table. "No, they haven't been there," he answered.

"We have decided that they went to the mine," Dimar volunteered.

"Why is that?" Elizabeth asked.

"Because Mandie is so enthralled by the place, and there is a mystery about it," Dimar replied.

"A mystery?" Elizabeth questioned.

"A mystery about why the mine was closed and why Uncle Ned won't talk about it," Celia put in.

"There is no mystery about that," Mrs. Taft spoke up. "John's father just decided to close the mine years ago, and that's that."

"My grandfather knows something that we do not know about the mine," Sallie said.

"You really believe that, don't you?" returned Mrs. Woodard.

"Yes, we all believe it. There is something he is not telling about the mine, and Mandie would like to find out what it is," Sallie explained.

"Amanda had better get that out of her head because there is no mystery," Mrs. Taft said.

Elizabeth sat forward. "Mother, you know Uncle Ned has been acting mysterious about the mine. He won't talk about it."

"And he keeps saying it is a sad, bad mine," Sallie added.

"You can remember that far back, Mother," Elizabeth prodded. "What was the reason for closing the mine?"

Mrs. Taft looked around the table. "I have forgotten, dear. That was so long ago. What difference does it make now?"

"I don't know what difference it makes now because I don't know why it was closed," Elizabeth persisted.

Hilda, having listened to the conversation around her, turned to Dimar. "Sad, bad mine!" she exclaimed.

Everyone laughed.

"Hilda has learned to say that, too," Sallie said.

Hilda's face clouded in anger. With tears in her big brown eyes, she banged her fist on the table and yelled, "Do not laugh! Sad, bad mine."

Dimar reached for her hand and spoke softly to her. "Yes, it is a sad, bad mine."

Hilda sighed and picked up her fork to resume eating.

"I think we have said enough for now. Let's eat," Elizabeth said. "We don't want to upset anyone. "

"John and Uncle Ned should be along soon," Dr. Woodard remarked. "They've had time to go by the mine."

"I hope they have Amanda and Joe with them," Elizabeth said.

Just then Liza trudged into the dining room and spoke to Elizabeth. "Mistuh Shaw and dat Mistuh Injun man comin' up de road. Got two ponies wid 'em," she informed them.

They all started to leave the table, but Elizabeth stopped them with a wave of her hand. "Please don't get up," she said. "They will be hungry. They can join us here at the table."

The others sat back down and waited. In a minute John Shaw and Uncle Ned, dejected and tired, entered the room.

"We might as well eat, Uncle Ned," John said, taking a place and indicating one for Uncle Ned. "Well, Elizabeth, Mrs. Woodard, we haven't found them yet. They had been at the mine. Their ponies were tied up near there, but since we couldn't find Joe and Amanda, we brought their ponies home. As soon as we eat a bite, we'll look some more."

Mrs. Woodard took a deep breath and said nothing.

Elizabeth's blue eyes filled with tears. "John, where can they be?" she asked.

"I have no idea. We thought that with Dimar's help, we would spread out from the mine and keep looking," John replied, helping himself to the food on the table in front of him.

"I will be glad to help, Mr. Shaw," Dimar responded.

Elizabeth sighed. "Oh, if only Amanda hadn't disobeyed . . ."

Everyone was silent for a moment.

"Tunnel in mine open," Uncle Ned stated at last.

"It is?" Celia gasped.

"But it was closed with boards when we left!" Sallie exclaimed.

"Do you think Amanda and Joe might have removed the boards?" Dr. Woodard asked.

"They could have if they had had a hammer, but there was no hammer at the mine when we were there, only hoes, shovels, and picks," Dimar replied. "I do not think they could have torn down the boards with those."

"Then someone else must have done it," John concluded. "Didn't you say it was open when you first found it, and the next time you went it was boarded up?"

"Yes, Snowball went through the tunnel to the outdoors. That is how we happened to notice it," Sallie explained.

"And it was still closed when we saw the man and woman leave in a boat," Dimar added.

"Someone is messing around at that mine, John, and they could be dangerous," Elizabeth said nervously.

"I know," John agreed. "Well, Dimar, we should be on our way soon."

"Mr. Shaw, couldn't I go, too?" Celia asked.

"No, Celia," Uncle John replied. "Dimar knows how to get around in the woods. I'm afraid you'd get lost. Then we would have to go looking for you, too." He smiled.

"I would be glad to help find my friends," Sallie volunteered.

"Thanks, Sallie, but I believe Dimar will be enough help, along with Uncle Ned and Dr. Woodard," John replied, smiling at the girl. "I appreciate the concern of all you young people. If we do need you girls later, we'll let you know."

Hilda looked bewildered as she silently listened to the conversation.

Elizabeth rose from the table. "Perhaps we should pray first," she said. Bowing her head, she committed the search party to the Lord, asking Him to guide them and to bring Amanda and Joe safely home. When she finished, a chorus of amens echoed around the table.

"I'll get the lanterns," John stated.

"You know, John, I've been thinking about those ponies," Dr. Woodard said. "Don't you think we ought to take them back with us in case we find Joe and Amanda?"

"Well, yes, I guess you're right," John agreed.

"We find," Uncle Ned nodded. "Not come back till we find."

Bidding the others goodbye, the search party rode directly to the mine and tied up the ponies where they had found them. The men had hastily scanned the place on their previous search, but now they began looking more closely for clues.

"Let's go inside first and comb every inch of it," John suggested. "If there's nothing there, we'll search the tunnel and continue on through to the outside."

"I stay out here. Look for feet marks," Uncle Ned offered.

"All right, Uncle Ned. The rest of us will go inside," John decided.

After descending the steps into the mine, John, Dr. Woodard, and Dimar divided up the area and carefully searched by lantern light for any evidence that the missing young people had been there.

Suddenly Dimar straightened up. "I just remembered something," he said. "Mandie took that white cat with her. There may be paw prints."

"Amanda took Snowball with her? Her mother didn't mention that," Dr. Woodard said, stooping to inspect the dirt.

"You might know she would take Snowball. He goes with her almost everywhere except to church. And I have an idea she would like to take him to church if she thought she could get away with it." John Shaw laughed.

"But what good is it to look for footprints, really?" asked Dr. Woodard. "All of you young people were here earlier, including Snowball."

"Here!" exclaimed Dimar, pointing ahead of him in the direction of the tunnel. "Footprints going into the tunnel. Big footprints."

John and Dr. Woodard hurried to look.

"You're right," John said. "I can see the print of Mandie's boots right there."

"And Joe's are right there." Dr. Woodard pointed. "But there are two sets of larger footprints right next to theirs as well. So they must be fresh footprints."

"Evidently a man and a woman," John observed.

"They must belong to the strange man and woman we saw leaving here," Dimar said. "They left in a boat outside the tunnel."

"Lead the way, Dimar. You're better at this than I am," John told the boy.

Dimar walked slowly through the tunnel, holding his lantern low in order to see the ground. As they came out into the daylight, they extinguished their lanterns and looked around. "The footprints continue this way," he said, bending low to look at the ground as he moved forward.

Something blue in a nearby bush caught his attention. He straightened up and started toward it. The men looked as he held up the blue sash.

"This is the sash to that dress they saw in the farmhouse. Mandie found this sash when we first went through the tunnel, and she has kept it in her apron pocket ever since," Dimar explained, handing it to John.

John and Dr. Woodard examined it. It did seem to be a sash to a lady's dress.

"That means Amanda dropped it here, probably on purpose if she was carrying it in her apron pocket," John surmised.

"As an indication that she had been here," Dimar agreed.

Uncle Ned had worked his way around the mine and met up with the others. John showed him the sash and explained.

The old Indian quickly scanned the ground. "This way. To water," he told the others, slowly leading the way down to Rose Creek. Uncle Ned pointed out across the water. "Go in boat. No more feet marks," he said.

The search party stood at the edge of the creek, not sure what to do next. It would be almost impossible to trace a boat.

CHAPTER EIGHT

ADRIFT IN THE RIVER

Mandie clutched both sides of the boat as it swirled this way and that, drifting out of Rose Creek into the mainstream of the Little Tennessee River. All the while, she tried to keep an eye on Joe, who was in the bottom of the boat, still not moving.

Snowball meowed and meowed as he was thrown around. Every time Mandie tried to catch him, the boat would swerve, and Snowball would fall beyond her reach.

Mandie kept praying. "Dear God," she said, "please don't let Joe die. Please help him. And dear God, please calm the water so we don't get upset and drown. I'm so scared that we'll all fall out or the boat will wreck. Please help us! Please!"

As the wind continued to blow, the boat turned sharply and Snowball landed at Mandie's feet. She released one hand from the side of the boat and quickly snatched him up.

"Oh, Snowball, pretty kitty. I'm sorry you're so frightened," she whispered to the kitten as she buried her face in his soft white fur. "I'm scared, too, but we must trust God to save us, Snowball, because we sure can't save ourselves."

Above the sound of the water Mandie heard a groan behind her. She quickly managed to twist around enough to see Joe shake his head and try to sit up. "Joe! Joe! Are you all right now'?" Mandie cried.

"You mean we aren't drowned yet?" he asked.

"Joe, what a thing to say," Mandie said, as inch by inch she managed to turn completely around, facing him. "Are you really all right?"

Joe sat up and rubbed a hand across his face as he held on to the side of the boat with the other hand. "I suppose I'm all right, considering the situation we're in," the boy told her. "Are you all right?"

"Yes, now that I realize there is nothing I can do about it except trust God to save us," Mandie answered, holding tightly to Snowball with one hand.

"Is Snowball all right?" Joe asked, leaning forward to look at the frightened kitten.

"He's all right. He's just scared," Mandie replied.

"The last I remember, those people pushed us back into the boat and then shoved the boat out into the water and took the oars. What else happened?" he asked.

"You must have been knocked out. I was afraid you were going to die before we got rescued," she said solemnly. "What a terrible thing I have done. I caused all this trouble just by disobeying my mother."

Joe looked at her in silence for a moment. "I know we shouldn't have stopped at the mine, but I think we're getting enough punishment right now. I'm sure our parents will forgive us," he assured. "They'll be glad just to have us home in one piece—if we make it," he added.

Just then a big wave sloshed over the side of the boat, spraying them both as the boat rocked wildly.

"Oh, Joe," Mandie cried, "nobody will ever find us way out here in the middle of this river."

"I wish you could swim," said Joe. "We could probably jump out of this boat and swim to the bank."

"I am going to learn how to swim," Mandie firmly stated. "If I don't drown in this river, I am going to learn how to swim."

"It's about time. Most girls know how to swim by the time they're twelve years old," Joe teased.

Mandie ignored the jest. "I made the mistake of letting those mean people know I can't swim. Otherwise they might have at least left us on land somewhere," she said regretfully.

"I doubt that. They wanted us out of their way for a while, and this was the easiest way to do it," Joe said.

"What do you imagine they had in those bags?"

"I have no idea, but whatever it was, it must have been awfully valuable or important for them to go to all this trouble," Joe replied.

"They must have figured it was more valuable than our lives. They don't know but what we got drowned in this river with no oars to control the boat," Mandie said. "Who do you suppose they were?"

"They knew your uncle's name and that he owned the mine, so they must be from around Franklin somewhere," Joe answered. "I'd like to go after them and make them pay for this."

"No, Joe, we have to forgive them. You know that," Mandie reminded him.

"Well, anyway, I hope we never see them again," he muttered.

"Br-r-r-r!" Mandie shivered as she cuddled Snowball to her, still clutching to one side of the boat. "It's cold out here on this river. I'm getting chilled through and through."

"If we could sit together, we might be warmer. Maybe we could gradually move closer," he suggested. But when he started to get up, the boat rocked dangerously.

Mandie's heart pounded. "No." she cried. "Don't stand up! The boat might turn over!"

Joe looked disappointed. "I'm sorry, Mandie. I wish I had a coat to give you."

"That's all right," Mandie replied. I don't think I'll freeze to death. By the way, where are we headed?"

"This river flows north from Georgia and then northwest right into Tennessee, where it goes into the Tennessee River," he told her. "So we might just end up in Tennessee if we keep on going."

"But that would take an awfully long time, wouldn't it? We aren't actually moving forward very fast. It's mostly the wiggly boat that makes it seem that way, don't you think?"

"I'd say it'd take quite a while to get there, but what else can we do but go on to Tennessee? We can't stop this boat and turn it around or even dock it at a riverbank."

"We can pray," Mandie suggested. "Prayer changes things, you know."

"We haven't said our verse," Joe reminded her.

"I did while you were knocked out, but we can say it again," Mandie offered.

Joe nodded.

Together they looked toward the sky and repeated, " 'What time I am afraid, I will put my trust in Thee.' "

"God will help us," Mandie assured her friend.

"I know. I just hope it's soon. I'm hungry," Joe moaned.

Suddenly the boat lurched and turned toward the riverbank, picking up speed. Then it slammed into the brush growing on the bank by the water.

"Grab something! Quick!" Joe cried. He stood up to snatch at the bushes. The boat almost turned over.

Mandie dropped Snowball in the bottom of the boat and tried to reach the limbs, ignoring the wobbling boat beneath her feet.

The boat kept swirling. Every time Mandie and Joe tried to grab the bushes, the boat would suddenly move too far away. Finally Joe managed to get a limb in his hand, but it was dead and broke right off the bush. Mandie snatched at the leaves on another branch, and the dead leaves crumbled away.

"Keep trying!" Joe yelled.

"I can't reach far enough to get hold of anything!" Mandie yelled back.

The boat moved a little nearer the bank. Then suddenly it whirled back out into the current. Mandie and Joe, thrown off balance by the quick movement, fell onto the seat together. The boat continued on down the river.

Joe bent to scoop up Snowball and handed him to Mandie.

"Oh, Joe, what a shame! We were so close to the bush but we couldn't reach it," Mandie said, her voice quivering.

"Maybe the boat will do that again," Joe encouraged. "And maybe next time we'll have better luck."

The boat continued on its way. So many trees grew along the riverbanks that it was impossible to see whether there were any houses or anyone who might happen to see them and come to their rescue. The leaves were turning yellow, orange, red, and brown but were not yet falling from the trees. The two young people clung to the boat as the current swerved it about on the river.

"I didn't realize there were so many curves in this river," Mandie remarked as they rounded a big bend.

"That's probably because you've never been out on it before," Joe said.

"I hope this is the last time," Mandie replied as Snowball snuggled under her arm in fright.

When the river straightened out again, Joe suddenly pointed toward the trees. "Look." he cried. "There's a man over there."

Mandie looked up. She tried waving but the rocking boat made it impossible for her to take her hand from the side. "Help! Help us!" she yelled as loudly as she could. But her cry was lost in the wind. The man didn't seem to notice, and the boat quickly moved on by.

"I don't think he heard you," Joe said.

"I know," Mandie replied. "We've got to do something. We can't just keep on going like this. We may be thrown out of the boat!"

"I know, but what can we do?" Joe asked, frustrated.

"We can pray again," Mandie suggested.

"You pray," Joe urged.

"Dear God, please help us!" Mandie began, looking toward the sky. "Please forgive me for all the trouble I've caused. I'm so sorry. Please help us get back to our parents. I know they're worried to death by now. Please forgive me, and please help us!"

"Amen," Joe added.

The wind blew strongly in their faces, and Mandie shivered a little.

"We'll be all right, Joe. I know God will help us," Mandie said.

As Mandie spoke, the boat slowed down and stopped wobbling, but it was still in the middle of the big river.

Mandie looked up into the sky. "Thank you, Lord! Thank you! Every little bit helps!"

Mandie looked at Joe. "I believe we're going to get out of this predicament somehow," she said.

"I think you're right, but I'm getting awfully hungry," Joe said.

At that moment the boat hit another strong current. It picked up speed and slammed around in the river.

Mandie gasped.

"Hold on!" Joe shouted.

The boat swirled and headed for the riverbank again.

"Grab something when we hit the bank!" Joe yelled.

"I'll try." Mandie yelled back.

When the boat came close to the riverbank, the two waited for a chance to grab some of the bushes growing along the edge. The boat slowed down and hovered just out of reach of the limbs.

Mandie scanned the bushes. "I hear a dog, Joe. Listen."

The sound of barking rapidly grew louder.

"I hope someone is with the dog," Joe said, watching closely.

Just then a huge black-and-white shaggy dog jumped out of the bushes and sat on the edge of the riverbank, barking.

"Help! Help us!" Joe shouted.

The dog just sat there, barking. No one came to investigate.

Then the boat quickly turned and was pulled by the current out into the middle of the river again, causing Joe and Mandie to fall back down on the seat. Mandie grabbed the frightened kitten by the tail and pulled him onto her lap.

As the runaway boat raced down the river, Mandie and Joe looked at each other.

"God will save us," Mandie insisted in a nervous voice.

"It's just not time yet I guess," Joe surmised.

They smiled bravely, but the two grew colder and hungrier as they floated on down the river. Snowball never stopped meowing and hours seemed to go by.

Then all of a sudden, what they feared most happened! The boat slammed toward the riverbank again, striking an old dead limb sticking out into the water.

There was no time to think. The boat overturned, throwing Mandie and Joe into the water. Snowball leaped out, landing on the dead limb.

Mandie began to sink. "Help me." Mandie coughed as she got a mouthful of water.

Joe, an expert swimmer, quickly swam to her side, grabbed hold of her, and tried to swim toward land.

"Get Snowball!" Mandie cried, pointing to the kitten perched on the dead limb.

When Joe tried to reach him, Snowball dashed up the log, hopped onto the land, and disappeared into the bushes.

"At least we know he didn't drown!" Joe yelled above the slosh of the water as he tried to tow Mandie to safety.

The overturned boat bounced around them and then suddenly struck them both hard. Both Joe and Mandie were stunned for a moment. Joe shook the water out of his eyes, held on to Mandie, and tried to make his way toward solid ground.

When they finally reached the safety of the bank, they found the dirt so slippery that they had trouble climbing out of the water.

"I'll push you up," Joe offered. "Grab whatever you can up there so you won't fall back down."

Mandie nodded as Joe grabbed her firmly around the waist and shoved her upward. Mandie grasped at the weeds on the bank, but they came uprooted in her hands, and she fell back down into the water.

"Sorry, Joe," she gasped.

"Try again," Joe urged, giving her another boost.

Mandie reached again but could not catch hold of a thing. She started crying and slid back down, floundering in the water.

"I'm going to drown!" she screamed, becoming hysterical.

"No!" Joe slapped her cheek with a wet hand.

Mandie instantly stopped crying and stared at him.

"I'm sorry, but I had to do that. Now grab something this time— anything. Just grab something," Joe commanded.

Mandie took a deep breath and nodded.

Joe pushed her up out of the water again. This time Mandie grasped the strong limb of a bush and managed to scramble up the slippery bank, slipping and falling in the wet mud. Joe pulled himself up out of the water and the two worked their way up to firm ground where they fell, exhausted and chilled to the bone.

"Thank you, dear God," Mandie whispered as she passed out right there in the weeds.

Gasping for breath, Joe, too, lost consciousness.

The wind blew hard, and the air became colder, but the two young people didn't feel a thing. As the sky dimmed, the overturned boat floated downstream and finally sank.

Mandie and Joe did not stir.

CHAPTER NINE

FORGIVENESS

The men were still at the mine, debating what to do next after Uncle Ned had assured them the footprints led directly to a boat.

"Why don't we split up?" John Shaw suggested. "Dr. Woodard, can you whistle really loud?"

Dr. Woodard placed two fingers in his mouth and answered with a loud, piercing whistle.

"Fine," said Uncle John. "Would you stay here at the mine in case Joe and Amanda come back. You can give us a whistle, and we'll be back in a flash."

Dr. Woodard agreed.

"Uncle Ned, maybe you can search upstream and Dimar can come with me," John continued. "We'll go in opposite directions along the banks of the river to see if we can spot a boat."

"Take lanterns," Uncle Ned suggested, picking up one of the lanterns by the mine.

"Good idea," John replied. "It's not dark yet, but it might be before we get back, so we'll divide up the lanterns among us."

Dimar picked up one and left the third for Dr. Woodard. "I will carry this one for us," Dimar offered.

"I'll be glad to stay here and wait for Joe and Amanda," Dr. Woodard said. "Since they left their ponies, maybe they will come back here—if they can." There was a slight tremor in his voice as he spoke.

"We find them," Uncle Ned assured the doctor.

"I'd say that we should turn back when the sun starts to go down," John suggested. "By that time we will have walked a good distance, and if we don't find them by then, we'll get a boat and go out on the river."

"You don't have a boat around here anywhere, do you?" Dr. Woodard asked.

"No, we'll have to ride a long way down the river to the dock where I keep one. It's too far to walk right now," John replied.

Uncle Ned handed Dr. Woodard his rifle. "Take gun," he said.

Dr. Woodard started to refuse.

"Uncle Ned is right," John assured him. "We don't know what kind of people we're dealing with. You may have to use it."

"But I don't think I could—"

"Have the rifle ready anyway, just in case," John stated. "It is loaded, isn't it?"

Uncle Ned nodded. "Ready," he said.

"I hope that's not necessary," John replied. "If you see or hear anything at all, Doctor, give us your whistle."

Dr. Woodard agreed.

" 'Nuff talk. Go! Make haste!" Uncle Ned headed upstream.

"Come on, Dimar," said Uncle John. "We're on our way."

Dimar nodded and took the lead through the bushes. As he and John walked downstream, they checked the bank all along the way for signs of a boat. It was slowgoing. The brush was thick, and there was a constant scurrying and chirping as rabbits, squirrels, and chipmunks evaded them. The birds flew high up into the trees to fuss at the men invading their domain.

John looked around overhead and laughed. "With all that noise, we certainly couldn't slip up on anyone, could we?"

"I will tell them to be quiet," Dimar said. He stopped and gave several different kinds of whistles.

To John's amazement the birds hushed. He could no longer hear the animals moving about. "You are a gifted person, Dimar. They wouldn't have done that for me."

Dimar shrugged his shoulders. "I only told them that we must be quiet."

John looked sharply at the boy. "You told them that?"

"I spoke in their language. I have learned the different sounds they use," Dimar explained, walking on.

"That is a remarkable achievement," John said "Don't ever lose it."

Dimar smiled.

After they had walked quite a distance, the Indian boy stopped to listen. John stopped also, watching Dimar. He, too, heard something. It sounded like a dog barking in the distance.

"It is coming from up ahead," said Dimar.

As they walked on, the sound grew louder. It was definitely a dog barking. It sounded like a big dog.

Dimar stopped again and peered through the bushes, with John looking over his shoulder. A big black-and-white shaggy dog was sitting there, barking at the trunk of a large chestnut tree. The two looked around. There was no one in sight.

Seeing the people, the dog ran downstream through the bushes, still barking loudly, causing a great commotion among the animals and birds in the forest.

"He must have treed a squirrel," John said.

"Crazy dog to run away from us and to keep on barking," Dimar decided.

Little did they know that downstream, Amanda and Joe were lying unconscious on the bank, oblivious to the frantic search for them.

As Uncle Ned searched the creek bank upstream, he carefully combed the bushes for any clue to the missing young people. Nothing would escape Uncle Ned's keen observation. But there was no sign of anyone or any other clue.

"I promise Jim Shaw I watch over Papoose," he fumed to himself. "Papoose lost. Must find."

He checked his arrows in the sling to be sure he was prepared for any trouble that might arise, then stopped to look at the sun to judge the time of day.

Uncle Ned had not agreed with John that they should walk the banks, but he had not expressed his disagreement. The young people were not on the riverbanks. They had left by boat. The more he thought about it, the more he was sure they should call for help from the Cherokees. If he, and John, and Dimar didn't find them soon, he would talk to John about getting the Cherokees' help.

Mandie and Joe still lay on the riverbank miles downstream. Though the wind had partially dried their clothes and hair, it had also chilled their bodies more. But they were so exhausted, they weren't aware of anything—least of all that someone else was pursuing them.

The man and woman who had set them adrift rode on horseback, the horses having found their way home.

As the couple carefully scanned the river for the two young people, the woman said, "I'm glad you changed your mind. It ain't right to do such a thing to younguns what ain't done nothin' to us. I jest hope they's all right."

"Yeah, I s'pose we did act a little hasty," the man agreed, riding alongside her.

"We's both brung up better than that and you know it," the woman said. "The Lord Almighty is goin' to have a hard time forgivin' us, I can guarantee you that."

"We told Him we's sorry. I ain't done that in coon's ages," the man said.

"Yeah, and now we gotta find them younguns and make sure they's all right."

"I s'pose you're right, Woman. I can look back now and see whut we been doin' ain't done us no good, so we might as well try it t'other way—fer a while anyway."

"Not jest for a while, but from here on," the woman argued. "If you don't straighten up with me and try to do right, I ain't havin' nothin' else to do with you. The Lord don't require a woman to live with a man that jest won't live right."

"Woman, don't you talk that way. You been my wife for purty nigh forty years," the man said.

"And that's goin' to be purty nigh forty years long 'nuff if you don't change your way of livin,' " the woman replied.

The man frowned at her. "You don't care nothin' 'bout me no more?"

"It ain't that atall," she responded. "But we's gittin' old, and one day we's gotta go meet our Maker. If we don't start doin' better, we ain't gonna see Him. We'll be goin' t'other way. I hope you been thinkin' 'bout that."

"Yep, s'pose I have," the old man said. "And I do still love ya, so I s'pose I'll hafta change my ways. To tell you the truth, I'm glad you got on this path of righteousness. I couldn't uh done it by myself."

"If we hadn't met up with that sweet little girl, I don't think I'd uh been thinkin' 'bout our way of livin.' She jest made me realize what a terrible hole we's got ourselves into," the woman said. "I sure hope we find them younguns and they's all right. I won't never be able to forgive myself if they's not."

They traveled on, searching along the riverbank. The wrecked boat was already beneath the water downstream, but as they rounded a bend, they spotted the young people lying on the ground in the weeds ahead.

The woman gasped and jumped down from her horse before the animal had completely stopped. She rushed to the young people, and the man followed.

"Thank the Lord, they're alive!" exclaimed the woman, bending over Mandie. "They don't seem to be hurt none. I think they's jest asleep."

Hearing someone talking above her, Mandie forced her eyes open. Seeing the man and woman standing over her, she was afraid to speak. Unable to tell whether the old people had come to do more harm or what, she only stared at them and tried to straighten her cold, stiff arms. She shivered from the penetrating cold. Just then Joe opened his eyes and sat up quickly as he saw the old couple. "Now what do you want?" he demanded, moving protectively to Mandie's side.

"We want somethin' from you," the old man said, looking down at his feet.

"Something from us?" Mandie questioned.

"We want your forgiveness," the woman said sadly. "We's sorry, truly sorry, for what we's done, and we want to ask your forgiveness."

Mandie and Joe looked at each other, unbelieving.

"Why?" Joe demanded.

"Because like this here young lady told us, we gotta forgive and ask for forgiveness if we wanna git through them pearly gates up there," the woman replied. "My pa was a preacher. He learnt his children what he knowed 'bout the Bible. He'd be ashamed of me right now. It jest seemed so easy to stray from the straight and narrow path."

Mandie reached for the woman's hand and squeezed it. "I know what you mean. That's how we got into all this trouble. I strayed down the wrong path and broke a promise to my mother. I'm awfully ashamed of myself," Mandie told her.

"Well, are you younguns willin' to forgive us?" the man asked.

"Of course," Joe said. "We have to."

"Have to?" the man questioned.

"Joe means that the Bible says if we don't forgive others, our heavenly Father won't forgive us. And we sure have a lot of trespasses ourselves to be forgiven for," Mandie explained. "I told you when you left us that we forgave you, and we really do."

"Yes, we do," Joe added.

The woman took Mandie in her arms, and the man firmly grasped Joe's shoulder.

"We thank you for givin' us a chance to live better," the man said. "We was afraid you'd really make it hard for us. You had a right to."

"What can we do 'bout gittin' you younguns home now?" the old woman asked.

"We left our ponies back at the mine," Mandie told them.

"They may still be there, but I imagine everyone is out looking for us by now," said Joe as he noticed the sun sinking in the sky.

"Yes, I'm surprised Uncle Ned hasn't found us yet," Mandie said, trying to stand. "Oh, I'm so cold I can't stand up."

Joe managed to get to his feet and helped her stand.

Suddenly Mandie gasped. "Where is Snowball?" she cried, looking around. "Snowball, where are you? Kitty! Kitty! Where are you?"

Joe helped her search the bushes, and the old couple joined in the search, too. But the white kitten was nowhere to be found.

"Mandie, I think we'd better go home and get some help to find him," Joe said. "That way our parents will know we're safe."

"I guess you're right, Joe, but l hate to leave here without finding him," Mandie said with tears in her eyes.

"We'll come back," Joe promised. "Besides, maybe Snowball went home. You know he's a smart cat. He could find the way home."

Mandie smiled at Joe. "If he's able, he'll find the way home," she said.

"Come on," the woman said to Mandie, "you're cold. We's got blankets on the horses. You ride with me. The boy can ride with him."

"Oh, will I be glad to get home again!" Mandie exclaimed as the woman helped her up on the horse with her.

The woman wrapped a warm blanket around Mandie, and the man did likewise for Joe. Then they were on their way.

As they rode along, Mandie's curiosity grew. "Why did you do what you did to us?" she asked.

"It's really a bad mixed-up mess," the woman began. "We cain't make no livin' no more. Jest ain't no way to do it. We worked the land long as we could. Nuthin' wouldn't grow. We jest plain didn't have nuthin' to eat and nowheres to git it," the woman said.

"I wish I had known," Mandie said. "I'd have seen to it that you had something to eat."

"Well, I don't know whut a youngun like you could do, but anyway, we figured the only way we could keep from starvin' to death was jest to take 'nuff to live on. And that's all we's been takin,' jest 'nuff to live on," she repeated.

"From where?" Mandie asked, huddling within the warm blanket.

"To begin with, we'd jest take a pig here and a few things there, from various places, like I said—jest barely 'nuff to stay alive. And then we found out 'bout that gold mine over in Buncombe County. So we went over there and took out a little gold when nobody was watchin,' " the woman explained.

"You've been stealing gold?" Mandie questioned.

"Guess you'd call it that, even though we was only takin' 'nuff to buy somethin' to eat," the old woman said. "Anyhow we still got it in the bags. We ain't made 'way with it." She patted the bags hanging across the horse.

"Then you must return it," Mandie told her. "The Bible says, 'Thou shalt not steal.' That's one of the Ten Commandments."

"I know all 'bout that, but when you git so hungry your stomach seems like it's stuck to your backbone, you're liable to do anythin' to git somethin' to eat," she tried to explain.

Mandie patted the woman's hand. "I'm sorry you've been hungry when we have so much to eat," she said. "Y'all just come home with us. I know my Uncle John will see to it that y'all have something to eat from now on."

Joe was asking similar questions of the old man, but the man was more proud, more reluctant to divulge his personal affairs. Yet at Joe's insistence, he finally told all.

"Couldn't you find any work to do'?" Joe asked.

"Naw, too old. Nobody don't want old men like me when they kin git young able-bodied workers," the man said.

"That's not fair. You have to eat the same as the young men," Joe protested. "If you and your wife will go back to Mandie's uncle's house with us, I think my father and her uncle can find something honest for y'all to do."

"I know John Shaw," the old man told him. "But I ain't never had to ask a favor from nobody in my life."

"It's better to ask a favor and be honest than to go doing things like y'all have been doing," Joe told him.

"We'll see," the man replied.

The sky was dimming as they rode up to the mine. The surrounding trees made it darker there than in the wide open spaces.

But when they reached the mine, they were greeted by Dr. Woodard, pointing a rifle at them and giving a loud whistle.

"Don't shoot! It's us!" Joe cried, quickly slipping down from the man's horse. He ran to his father's side.

Dr. Woodard, surprised, hugged his son with one arm. "Where have you and Amanda been?" he asked as Mandie jumped down from the woman's horse and joined him.

"Everything is all right now," Joe told him.

"Yes, Dr. Woodard, we've come to get our ponies," Mandie explained. "These people need help. They'll be going home with us."

"Amanda, don't you know who these people are?" Dr. Woodard asked. "This is Jake Burns and his wife."

"Jake Burns? The man who is going to buy the mine from uncle John?" Mandie asked.

Dr. Woodard nodded, never taking his eyes off the couple.

Mandie turned to the man. "But you said you don't even have enough to eat. How can you have the money to buy this mine?"

"I know it don't make no sense," Jake replied. "We figured we'd have 'nuff gold to buy this mine and that old farmhouse over there in the trees. This is good farming land. We could make a living here without even minin.' "

"But you stole that gold and you must return it," Mandie insisted.

"I know. You're right," Jake said, hanging his head.

Dr. Woodard cleared his throat. "Jake Burns, I'm going to see to it that you get what's coming to—"

"No, Dr. Woodard," Mandie interrupted. "We know they've been bad, but we promised them forgiveness," she said quickly.

"We will see," Dr. Woodard replied, finally lowering the rifle. "Your Uncle John is going to have something to say about this."

"Then let's go home," Mandie said.

"We'll wait for John and the others first," said Dr. Woodard.

In a moment John and Dimar came hurrying through the bushes from one direction and Uncle Ned from the other.

"We were on the way back when we heard your whistle," John said, seeing Joe and Mandie and the old couple. "Mandie, Joe, are you all right?"

"Yes, sir," Mandie said, running into his waiting arms.

"Thank Big God Papoose not hurt," Uncle Ned declared.

John Shaw looked confused. "Jake, Ludie, how did you get here?"

"That's a long story, Uncle John. We'll explain when we get home," Mandie told him.

"Well, let's get going," he said.

Uncle Ned was the last to mount. "Jake Burns bad man. Must punish," he mumbled.

CHAPTER TEN

EXPLANATIONS

Jason Bond had been constantly on the lookout for the search party to return, so when he saw them coming, he hurried to assist with the horses and ponies as they stopped at the gate.

The caretaker smiled at Mandie and reached to help her dismount. "I reckon I'm awfully glad to see you home, Missy. And you, too, young fella," he said, grinning at Joe.

"You just don't know how glad we are to be back," Mandie said, painfully dismounting her pony. Her arms and legs were bruised from being knocked around in the boat, and she ached all over.

"At one point we kinda doubted that we'd ever get back," Joe said, handing his pony's reins to Mr. Bond.

Elizabeth, hearing the horses' hoofs and the voices, came running to the front door. Everyone in the house crowded behind her to wait for the group coming up the walkway.

Mandie ran straight to her mother's arms, and Joe, who was always reserved, went straight to his mother and put his arm around her.

"Amanda, we've been praying for y'all to get home safely. Are you all right?" Elizabeth asked with tears in her eyes. She hugged her daughter tightly. "Where on earth have you been, darling?"

"I'm sorry, Mother. I have a lot of forgiveness to ask," Mandie admitted. She looked up at Celia and Sallie. "Has Snowball come home?" she asked.

"No, I don't think so," Celia replied. "Has anyone seen him?"

As a chorus of no's came from the group, Mandie's blue eyes filled with tears. "Oh, Mother, I've lost Snowball. I couldn't find him in the woods."

Realizing the condition her daughter was in, Elizabeth delayed any more talk. "There, there, Amanda," she said, patting her daughter on the back. "Straight to the bathtub and then some hot food. After that we'll sit down and talk this whole thing out."

"I go help," Liza spoke up from behind Elizabeth.

With a heavy heart, Mandie trudged up the stairs as Liza followed.

"You, too, Joe," Mrs. Woodard told her son, tousling his windblown hair.

Dimar volunteered to go with Joe, and Joe seemed grateful. "This is going to be a big job to get back in shape again," he said.

Mandie was so worn out and hungry that she almost fell into her room when Liza opened the door for her.

The Negro girl caught her by the arm and led her over to the bed to sit down. "First we git dis here fire goin,' " Liza said, lighting the wood in the fireplace. Then she turned back to Mandie. "Now off wid dese filthy, wet clothes, Missy," she ordered.

As Liza helped the girl get undressed, Mandie gave a big sigh. "I could just curl up in bed. I'm so tired," she told Liza.

"Now you finish takin' off dem clothes whilst I fix de water fo' you," said Liza. "And don't you go to sleep. Git dem other things off." She hurried into the bathroom to prepare the bath.

As Mandie limply finished undressing, Liza rushed back, snatched a robe from a hanger, put it around Mandie, and hurried her into the bathroom.

The warm water revived Mandie, and she agreed to let Liza wash her dirty, tangled hair.

Liza helped her into clean clothes and sat her down by the fireplace. Then while Liza gently brushed Mandie's long blonde hair, Mandie began to talk. She told the girl everything that had happened since she and Joe had left that morning.

Liza related the day's events at the house. "Yo' ma, and dat doctuh's wife, dey been wringin' der hands all dis day long," she told Mandie. "And everybody else been sittin' 'round like somebody died. After de men went to de Hadleys and come back wid dat Hilda girl and no sign of y'all, things been awful here."

"Liza, isn't my hair dry enough to go downstairs?" Mandie asked impatiently. "I'm starving to death. We haven't had a bite to eat since breakfast."

"I 'spect so, Missy, if we don't braid it up. Let's jest tie it back wid a ribbon so's it kin finish dryin,' " she suggested, reaching for a ribbon and tying the heavy, long blonde hair back.

Mandie went downstairs and as she entered the parlor, Joe called to her from the settee. "Come over here," Mandie. He patted the seat next to him. The young people were all hovering around Joe, asking him questions.

"Ah, Mandie," Celia said, "Joe has told us what happened. You must be exhausted."

Mandie looked around the room. Hilda was huddled in a corner, watching and listening, Sallie sat in a plush chair nearby, and Jake and his wife seemed to be in serious conversation with Uncle John and the other adults.

As Mandie sat down, Elizabeth came over to them. "Aunt Lou has food on the table for you two," she said. "Everyone else has already eaten. Go on in to the dining room. I'll be in before you get finished."

"Yes, ma'am," Mandie and Joe replied together. They rose and did as they were told.

Aunt Lou hovered over them, making sure that they ate a hearty meal. "My chile, you got to eat up. You gonna be sick if you don't after all dat trouble out on dat river, gittin' wet and cold and all dat," the big old Negro woman told Mandie. "And you, too, young man. I don't want no sick people on my hands."

Mandie swallowed a mouthful of mashed potatoes and laughed at her concern. "Aunt Lou, Joe's father is a doctor, remember? If we get sick, he will doctor us. You won't have to worry about it."

"Now, my chile, you know I hafta look after you. I took you for my chile dat fust day when you come here, all poor and hungry from dat cabin out in de country." Aunt Lou walked around behind the girl and reached to put more potatoes on her plate.

Mandie protested. "Aunt Lou, I can't eat any more potatoes. Please don't stuff me. I'll have nightmares."

The Negro woman turned to Joe and put the spoonful of potatoes on his plate. "You gotta eat, too," she told him. "Git some mo' of dat beefstew. Jenny made it jest right." She pulled the big bowl closer to Joe and stood there while he spooned a big helping onto his plate.

Joe looked up at her mischievously. "Is that enough?"

"Maybe fo' now," Aunt Lou said. "Both of you drink up dat milk. It'll make you sleep good."

Mandie sighed and picked up her glass. "I'd really rather go to bed than eat," she said.

"Too early to go to bed," the old woman said. "Git yo' sleepin' hours all mixed up and git up too early. 'Sides, you got guests to see to."

"I think we've already entertained them enough today," Joe spoke up. "With all that's happened, it's time to rest."

Mandie laid down her fork. "Aunt Lou, I just can't eat any more," she said with a quiver in her voice. "I've been thinking about Snowball. He's lost somewhere, and he's probably hungry."

Aunt Lou immediately put her big arm around the girl, and Mandie buried her face in the woman's apron, bursting into tears.

Joe jumped up and came around the table to take Mandie's hand in his. "Don't cry, Mandie. I know how much Snowball means to you. We'll find him somehow," he assured her.

"There's no way to find him," she sobbed as Aunt Lou stroked Mandie's thick blonde hair.

When Elizabeth entered the room, she rushed to Mandie's side. Mandie released Aunt Lou, and Joe handed her his handkerchief.

"What's wrong, dear?" Elizabeth asked, putting an arm around her daughter's shaking shoulders.

Mandie took a deep breath, trying to control her voice. "I've lost Snowball for good, and it's all my fault." she cried.

Joe stepped back, and Elizabeth pulled out a chair to sit next to Mandie. Joe quietly slipped out the door, and Aunt Lou followed.

"We'll search for him tomorrow, dear," Elizabeth said.

"Mother, I know you're angry with me for disobeying you," Mandie cried. "If I hadn't disobeyed, none of these terrible things would have happened. I'm so sorry. I've asked God to forgive me, too."

"I'm not angry with you, Amanda," Elizabeth said. "I'm hurt because you didn't keep your promise to go straight to the Hadleys and back without stopping anywhere. But hurt and anger are two different things." Elizabeth gave her daughter a hug. "Oh, Amanda, I just love you so much, it hurts me to see you getting into trouble."

Mandie looked into her mother's blue eyes, so much like her own. "I'm sorry, Mother. I don't want to ever hurt you. It's just that we saw some horses tied up by the mine, and I asked Joe if we could stop and see who was there. He didn't want to, but he finally agreed. I didn't know it was going to turn into such a terrible thing. Please forgive me, Mother."

"I do forgive you, Amanda," Elizabeth said. "But please, please try a little harder to act more mature. You must learn to think twice when you're tempted to break promises and disobey."

"I'll really try hard," Mandie said, reaching up to embrace her mother.

"To help you remember," Elizabeth continued, "I have decided to confine you to the house for the rest of the holidays unless an adult is with you. You will not be going anywhere with your friends unless there is a grownup who can go with you. Is that understood?"

"Yes, Mother. I understand," Mandie replied.

"That is rather mild punishment for what you've done, but I can guarantee you that if you disobey me again, the punishment will be much worse," Elizabeth warned. "Those people have told us all about what happened. I'm thankful that you and Joe weren't harmed more than you were."

Mandie looked up into her mother's face with concern. "You and Uncle John will help those people, won't you?"

Elizabeth answered slowly. "That's the Christian thing to do, of course, but they will have to prove that they are sincere about changing their way of living."

Mandie smiled. "Thanks, Mother. I told them you would help."

"Now, if you're finished eating, I think we should go back to the parlor. Your friends are waiting for you," Elizabeth said, rising from her chair.

Mandie followed her mother back to the parlor. As she entered the room Uncle John called to Mandie, "Come over here for a minute, Amanda."

Mandie walked past the group of young people to the other end of the room where the adults and Joe sat talking. "Yes, sir?" she responded.

"Sit down, Amanda. We need to talk a little while," Uncle John told her, indicating a nearby chair. "Jake and his wife, Ludie, have been telling us what went on today," Uncle John began as Mandie sat down.

Mandie turned to the couple sitting next to Uncle John. "Did you tell them everything?"

"Everything that was necessary," Jake answered.

"But everything was necessary," Mandie insisted.

"We didn't think it was necessary to tell him about our personal affairs," Jake said.

"But you must tell him everything, Mr. Burns," Mandie replied. "If you don't, then I will. Uncle John needs to know."

"Amanda!" Uncle John rebuked her for her sharp words. "They told us about finding you and Joe at the mine and leaving you in that boat, and then coming back to rescue you. They said you and Joe had forgiven them, so what else could I do but forgive them. It just better not happen again."

Dr. Woodard agreed. "I guess I feel the same way," he said reluctantly.

"Did you tell Uncle John about the gold?" Mandie asked Ludie.

Ludie looked down at her wrinkled hands. "No, we can take care of returnin' that ourselves," she replied.

"I know you can return it yourselves, but what are you going to do for a living?" Mandie asked.

"You don't have the money to buy the mine," Joe reminded them.

The couple sat humbled in front of John Shaw and Dr. Woodard. Uncle Ned silently watched them with a sullen expression on his face.

"We'll jest have to trust in the Lord," Ludie said. "He won't let us starve."

Uncle John spoke up. "Are you not planning to buy the mine now, Jake?" he asked.

Jake shuffled his thread-worn boots on the carpet. "Ain't got no money now," he replied, avoiding John's gaze.

"Ain't no use beatin' 'round the bush 'bout it, Jake," Ludie said. "We've gotta be honest 'bout everythin.' " She turned to John. "He's taken 'nuff gold from another mine to pay for your mine, Mr. Shaw. But now we's realized the sin we's committed, so we's gotta return the gold to its rightful owner."

John looked from Jake to Ludie in surprise. "You mean you just took gold out of someone's mine?"

"That's jest what we did," Ludie replied. "And after these here younguns showed us the error of our ways, we's decided we'd better straighten up and try to live right. So we's gonna return the gold."

"My goodness, Jake." Uncle John exclaimed. "I had no idea you didn't have the money to buy the mine when you asked about it."

"And that's not all, Mr. Shaw," Joe added. "They don't even have any money to live on or any way to make a living."

"They've been going hungry," Mandie added. "Joe and I thought maybe you and Dr. Woodard could figure out some way to help them."

Dr. Woodard looked concerned. "John, there must be some way we can help."

"Jake, why didn't you come to me and let me know you were so hard up?" John asked. "Your father was a loyal worker for my father in that ruby mine, and you helped, too, I believe. You must know I'd do anything I can for you and your wife. You don't have to go taking other people's gold as long as I'm around."

Mandie and Joe looked at each other and smiled. Everything was working out just the way they wanted it to.

"I ain't never had to ask a favor of no man," Jake grumbled.

"That wouldn't be asking a favor. It would be giving me a chance to return my appreciation for your father's work," John said. He looked at Dr. Woodard. "Now, what can we arrange?"

Dr. Woodard thought for a moment. "Where do y'all live now?" he asked.

"We ain't got no home right now. We was rentin' the old Tittle farm, but we couldn't make a livin' off it, much less pay the rent," Ludie said.

John and Dr. Woodard exchanged glances.

Mandie's eyes sparkled. "What about the old farmhouse you own, Uncle John, over near the mine—the one where we found the dress? No one lives there."

"That's a good idea, Amanda, except we've got to find some work for these people so they can make a living," Uncle John agreed.

"They told us the land around the mine was good farming land. That was why they wanted to buy the mine, just to get the land to farm," Joe spoke up.

Uncle John turned to Jake. "Do you really think that land is any good to grow anything?"

"It sure is, John. It's fertile land. It oughta grow some good corn, and beans, and a few other things," Jake replied.

"What about the mine, Uncle John?" Mandie asked. "Couldn't they work the mine for you, too, after we get through with it?"

"Is the mine worth working, Jake?" Uncle John asked. "You ought to know. You were there when it was closed."

Uncle Ned gave a loud grunt, and Jake stirred uneasily in his chair.

"I really don't know, John. We's been going through your mine lately, but we didn't disturb nothin,' so I don't know," Jake answered.

"Well, why don't we try it and see?" Uncle John asked. "I've already had it opened and had all the necessary repairs made."

"We should make a list of things we need to do," Dr. Woodard said, pulling a notepad and fountain pen from his vest pocket. "The house needs repairing." He began to write.

"Jake can paint and repair it in place of paying rent to begin with. I'll give him the paint and whatever he needs," Uncle John said.

"Does it have any furniture in it?" Dr. Woodard wanted to know. "They said they don't have anything."

"No, there's not a stick of anything in it," Mandie spoke up. "Uncle John, you've got a whole lot of furniture in the attic that you don't use. Could we take some of it to their house?"

"I'll help," Joe volunteered.

Uncle John smiled at the young people's concern. "That's exactly what we'll do. And Jake, I'll see that you get some pigs, and chickens, and feed, and seed. Now don't protest. We'll work things out so y'all can do enough work to cover everything. Don't think this is charity."

The old couple looked at each other, speechless, with tears in their eyes.

Ludie reached for Mandie's hand. "The Lord will take care of us, won't He?" she said to Mandie. "Soon as we trusted in Him, He started taking care of us."

"That's right, Mrs. Burns." Mandie smiled. "I'm so glad you and Mr. Burns decided to change your way of living. We'll do all we can to help you. I'll even ask Aunt Lou to make you a new dress."

"Oh, my! This dress I have on!" the old woman exclaimed, looking down at the blue gingham she was wearing. "It ain't rightly mine."

"Where did you get it?" Mandie asked.

"We took one little piece of the gold to buy it. I ain't never had a store-bought dress in my life. And I ain't had a new dress in twenty years. But then, I guess I don't have one now, neither, 'cause this dress ain't rightly mine, is it?" the woman rambled on.

"Whose mine did you get that gold out of?" Uncle John asked.

"The Tittles' mine. You see, they moved out of their old place when they discovered that gold, and they built a big new house. We was rentin' the old one," Jake replied.

"When we take the gold back, I do hope they don't put us in jail," said Ludie.

"They could," Uncle John told her. "But I'll go with y'all to take it back, and we'll see what we can work out. I know Ed Tittle."

"But what about the dress?" Ludie asked.

"I don't imagine they'd want to take your dress, Mrs. Burns," Mandie assured her.

"But it was bought with their gold," Ludie said.

"I'll pay Ed Tittle for it, and you can work to pay that off, too," John said. "Now you can stay in this house long enough for us to get that farmhouse in livable condition."

Ludie's eyes grew wide in disbelief. "Live here?" she asked, looking around at all the Shaws' finery.

"We'll get some livestock," Uncle John continued, "and then we'll get the mine working. And come to think of it, Ludie, I believe we could use some extra help about the house with all the company we have right now."

"Thank you, Mr. Shaw. From the bottom of my heart, I thank you," Ludie said. "Jest tell me what you want done. I'll be more than glad to do anything you say."

Uncle Ned shook his head and grunted to himself. "Sad, bad mine. Jake Burns know it."

Mandie thought she heard the old Indian speak, and she turned to look at him. "Uncle Ned, you must have known Mr. Burns back when the mine was open," she said.

"Ummm," Uncle Ned grunted, giving Jake a mean look. "Father of Jake Burns close mine for father of John Shaw. No good to open."

Uncle John frowned at the old Indian. "Uncle Ned, I do wish you'd tell me what you've got against opening that mine."

Uncle Ned shook his head again. "Jake Burns there. He know why mine closed."

Jake shuffled his feet and wouldn't look at the Indian.

"Do you know why it was closed, Jake?" Uncle John asked. "Was it mined dry? Is that the secret?"

"Well, no. I didn't know everythin' that was goin' on," Jake replied. "I was only a boy at that time."

"All right, then. We'll work it and see if it yields anything," John said. Turning to Mandie, he asked, "Would you please ask Aunt Lou to get a room ready for these people and to let me know when she's finished. Then you and Joe can go back to your friends over there. I know they're all waiting to hear more about the day's events."

Mandie and Joe jumped up.

"Yes, sir, Uncle John," Mandie said as she and Joe rushed out of the room.

They found Aunt Lou in the dining room overseeing Liza as the girl cleaned off the table.

"Aunt Lou, Uncle John says to ask you to get a room opened up for Mr. and Mrs. Burns. They're going to be staying here until we get the old farmhouse by the mine fixed up for them to live in," she explained.

Aunt Lou thought for a moment. "Well now, it'll have to be de third flo,' " she said. "Wid all dis comp'ny and everything, de second flo' is plum filled up, and de third flo' ain't too fancy."

"That's all right, Aunt Lou. They're going to work for Uncle John. He said Ludie could help here in the house, so I suppose he'll talk to you about that later," Mandie replied. Then catching hold of the big black woman's hand, she asked, "Aunt Lou, could you please make a new dress for Mrs. Burns? She hasn't had a new dress in twenty years."

"Ain't had a new dress in twenty years? My chile, whut in dis world she been wearin'?"

Mandie and Joe glanced at each other, and Joe replied, "She's wearing a borrowed dress right now. They're poor people."

"I guess I could make a plain one, but she'll hafta help," Aunt Lou said. Then she saw Liza leaning against the wall, listening. "Liza, git a move on!" she scolded. "We's gotta go find a room for dem Burns people and air it out."

"Thank you, Aunt Lou," Mandie said, squeezing the woman's dark hand.

"Git out o' here, my chile. Git back to yo' comp'ny," Aunt Lou said. "I'se got work to do."

As Mandie and Joe returned to the parlor, they were immediately surrounded by the other young people. Hilda was still sitting quietly, listening and watching.

Once again Joe and Mandie had to relate the day's events to their friends, covering every detail, even though by now everyone knew what had happened.

"I wish I could have been with you in that boat, Mandie," Celia said.

"Well, I wouldn't have," Sallie said.

"They could have been drowned," Dimar added.

"What are you going to do about Snowball?" Celia asked,

Mandie's face crumpled as she replied in a low, shaky voice, "I don't know. I guess I've lost him."

"We will find him," Sallie told her.

"But I haven't seen him since we got out of the water when the boat wrecked. He ran off into the bushes. We looked and looked, and we couldn't find any sign of him. I thought maybe he would come home, but . . ."

"He's got to be somewhere," Celia said.

"We will go and look for him tomorrow, Mandie," Dimar promised.

That night as Mandie said her prayers with Celia and Sallie, she pleaded with God. "Please send Snowball home to me, and let him be all right. Please, dear God, take care of him and send him home. Please!"

"Please!" Sallie echoed.

"Yes, please!" Celia added.

And in the darkness of the bedroom Hilda repeated, "Yes, please!"

CHAPTER ELEVEN

A MYSTERIOUS FIND

Everyone pitched in the next day to help Jake and Ludie Burns get settled. The boys helped the men hammer and repair the old farmhouse and then paint the inside. The girls donned aprons, tied scarves over their hair, and had a glorious time going through all the dusty old furniture in the attic, choosing which pieces they would take to the Burnses' house.

"We can pick whatever we want to give them," Mandie said. "But Mother says Uncle John will have to approve anything we give away. Some of the furniture up here is old and valuable."

"This is a great idea," Celia exclaimed as she rummaged through the drawers of an old chest. "It's like having our own house and filling it with the furniture of our choice."

Sallie bent over an opened trunk containing books. "How much are we allowed to give them?" she asked.

"I suppose they'll need enough to fill up the house," Mandie said as she pulled old dresses out of a chifferobe. "Y'all saw it. There's one big room and a good-sized kitchen downstairs. Then the attic will probably need at least one bed in case they have company overnight."

"Everything seems to have something in it," Celia observed. "Are we supposed to unload whatever we're giving them? And where do we put the stuff?" she asked, looking around the crowded attic.

"Now, that's a good question," Mandie said, glancing about. "Why don't we just open and shut everything as we go, and see what we can find that is empty' We can't just throw everything out onto the floor. We'll have to find some empty furniture to put it in."

Hilda silently joined the others as they moved about looking for empty drawers, trunks, or wardrobes, but she constantly held her hand over her apron pocket, protecting the object she had dug out of the mine.

All the furniture they went through was crammed full of clothes or other things, until the girls got to the far corner of the attic. Then they opened drawer after drawer and door after door and found them all empty.

"That's funny," Mandie remarked. "Everything is full and running over except right here, and there's not even a string or a hairpin in the furniture in this corner."

"Maybe this is the last stuff put up here and someone emptied it all out," Celia suggested, surveying the jumble of chairs, beds, chifferobes, tables, and trunks.

"I do not think so," Sallie said. "This corner is the farthest from the door. I think it would be the first to be filled up."

"You're right, Sallie," Mandie agreed, turning around. "Look at the pile between here and the door. It would have been impossible to bring this stuff over here through all that mess."

"Then I wonder why all this furniture is empty," Celia said.

"Maybe Uncle John knows. We can ask him. Anyway, if all this furniture is the oldest, it is probably the most valuable, so we might as well pick out something else," Mandie said, going over to a huge wardrobe near the window.

Celia and Sallie followed her. Hilda stayed among the empty furniture, opening and closing drawers as she hummed to herself.

When Mandie opened the wardrobe, to everyone's surprise, there were dolls, dolls, and more dolls—of all sizes, and dressed in various costumes.

"Look!" Mandie cried, reaching for one of them. It was a beautiful doll with a porcelain head, arms, hands, and feet, dressed in white silk, embroidered with blue. "How beautiful!"

The other two girls each took a doll from the wardrobe. Celia got a boy clown—all red, white, and blue. Sallie caressed a beautiful blonde doll dressed in blue organdy.

Hilda, who was watching them from a distance, came running to the wardrobe and quickly seized a doll for herself. She chose a tall, dark-haired bride with a flowing veil, and hugged the doll to herself, humming.

"Where do you suppose all these dolls came from?" Celia gasped. "I never saw so many in my life."

"And they are all so beautiful!" Sallie added.

"We'll certainly have to ask Uncle John about these," Mandie told the girls. "Let's keep out the ones we have and take them downstairs when we go."

"Do you think it will be all right?" Sallie asked, still admiring the doll she held.

"I don't see what harm it could do to take them downstairs," Mandie replied. Then, although she didn't hear anything, she suddenly sensed someone behind them. She turned to see Uncle Ned standing in the doorway of the attic. "Come in, Uncle Ned, and see all these beautiful dolls we found."

Uncle Ned rushed to the wardrobe. "Put back! Put back!" he ordered.

The girls looked at him in astonishment and just stood there with the dolls in their arms.

The old Indian reached for the doll Mandie was holding. Reluctantly, Mandie handed it to him. "But, Uncle Ned, we aren't hurting them," she said. "Who put them in here, anyway? Where did they come from?"

Uncle Ned silently took the dolls from Celia and Sallie and quickly replaced them in the wardrobe. Hilda turned and ran down the stairs with the one she was holding.

"Get doll!" Uncle Ned shouted as Hilda disappeared down the stairway.

Mandie raised her eyebrows and hurried after Hilda, catching her in the hall. It was all she could do to pry the doll away from her. When Mandie finally got it free and started back up the stairs with it, Hilda stomped her feet and screamed. Mandie ignored her and hurried to give Uncle Ned the doll.

"Must not open again," Uncle Ned told the puzzled girls as he closed the doors of the wardrobe.

"But why, Uncle Ned? Who owns all these?" Mandie asked.

"It's a shame to shut all those beautiful dolls in that old wardrobe," Celia said.

Sallie watched her grandfather silently for a while. Finally she spoke. "My grandfather, you know something about these dolls. Please tell us why they are so special."

"My granddaughter, that is not for you to know," the old Indian replied.

"Uncle Ned, you have become so secretive about everything lately," Mandie said. "I share my secrets with you. Please, won't you share yours with me?"

Uncle Ned put an arm around Mandie's shoulders. "Papoose, everything not for telling," he said. "Some things must be secret."

"But why, Uncle Ned? Why can't you tell us about these dolls?" Mandie insisted.

"I made promise," Uncle Ned replied.

"Promise? You promised who?" Mandie asked.

"It happen long ago, Papoose. Sad story," the old Indian told her. Then, making sure the doors of the wardrobe were closed tightly, he spoke to all the girls. "No lock. You promise not to open?"

They nodded.

"I will ask Uncle John about the dolls, Uncle Ned," Mandie said.

"John Shaw say it time to look for Snowball. I come get you," the Indian said.

"Oh, let's go," Mandie said, quickly leading the way down the stairs, removing her scarf from her hair as she went. "Wait for us, Uncle Ned. We've got to get our bonnets."

But as the girls ran to Mandie's room and put on their shawls and bonnets, they completely forgot about Hilda.

Outside, Jason Bond had the girls' ponies waiting alongside Uncle Ned's horse.

Mandie and Joe had told Uncle Ned where they had been washed onto the bank, and Uncle Ned led the way.

"Where are Joe and Dimar?" Mandie asked as she rode alongside the old Indian.

"Still at farmhouse. Will go to mine after meal. We hurry. Must be back to eat," Uncle Ned told her.

When they arrived at the place on the riverbank where Snowball had disappeared, Mandie explained again what had happened. "He jumped out of the boat when it hit that old limb out there. And he ran straight into the bushes. We know he didn't get lost in the river."

"We walk," Uncle Ned told the girls as they all dismounted. He tied the animals to a nearby tree. "We call. We look," he said. "We stay together. Do not get out of sight."

Mandie stooped low to peer into the bushes as she went. "Snowball! Snowball!" she called. "Here, kitty, kitty."

"Pretty kitty," Sallie joined in.

"Where are you, Snowball?" Celia called.

Uncle Ned walked along, tapping the bushes with a long stick to shoo the kitten out if he was hiding.

Sallie looked carefully for paw prints along the water's edge.

Mandie called to her. "You're wasting your time, Sallie. He didn't walk along the bank. He landed on that old dead limb out there in the water, and he leaped from the limb onto dry land."

"Then I will look on dry land," Sallie said, coming back inland to continue looking.

"Kittens don't make tracks in dry dirt, do they?" Celia asked.

"Yes, sometimes there is an impression in loose, dry soil," Sallie replied.

After what seemed like hours of backbreaking bending and stooping, Uncle Ned called an end to the search. "Snowball not here," he told the girls. "We go back."

Tears filled Mandie's blue eyes as she realized the impact of those words.

"But, Uncle Ned, he was here," Mandie argued.

"Gone somewhere else," Uncle Ned declared. "Come." He started toward his horse, and the girls followed.

Mandie slowly brought up the rear. "Uncle Ned, can't I stay here awhile? He might come back," she begged.

"John Shaw say no one out of my sight." Uncle Ned turned to look at Mandie. Seeing the tears streaming down her cheeks, he bent to put his arm around her. "Do not cry, Papoose," he said. "I will ask Cherokees to find lost kitten."

Mandie brightened. "Oh, will you, Uncle Ned? I know the Cherokees can find him."

"We see. Now we go," the old Indian said, helping the girls onto their ponies.

When they arrived back at John Shaw's house, the other men and the boys were already there, and it was time for the noon meal.

Everyone was in the parlor except John. They all looked at Mandie when she and the girls entered the room. They knew without a word that the search for the kitten had been unsuccessful.

Joe stepped forward and took Mandie's hand. "Don't give up. We'll look again," he promised her.

"He'll starve to death if we don't find him soon," Mandie said with a catch in her voice.

Just then Mandie heard someone hurrying down the stairs outside the doorway. Uncle John stopped at the door of the parlor and frowned. "Where in the world did all those dolls come from?" he asked. "They're all over the steps from the third floor going up to the attic."

The girls looked at each other in surprise.

"All over the steps, Uncle John?" Mandie inquired.

"Yes, there must be dozens of them. Whom do they belong to?" he asked.

Sallie looked again at Mandie. "Where's Hilda?"

"Why, I thought Hilda was with you girls," said Elizabeth from the settee. "I hope to goodness she's not wandered off somewhere again."

Elizabeth got up and started toward the stairs, but Mandie stopped her. "Never mind, Mother," she said. "We'll go find her. She's upstairs somewhere."

Celia gasped. "Hilda put all those dolls on the steps because you took that one away from her!"

Uncle Ned looked upset as he listened to the conversation. "Dolls must go back," he stated, looking at John.

"Go back where? Uncle Ned, what do you know about those dolls?" John asked.

"I promise long ago," Uncle Ned replied. "Must keep promise."

"Promised what?" John asked.

"I promise keep dolls safe," the old Indian finally answered.

"Then you do know something about these dolls. Where did they come from?" Uncle John asked.

The old Indian hesitated, looking around. "We talk. Private," he said, turning to lead the way out of the room.

Mandie rushed over to him, placing a restraining hand on his arm. "Uncle Ned, may I go, too? Please," she begged.

Uncle Ned thought for a moment. "Yes, you and John Shaw," he replied.

Mandie and John followed the old Indian into the sunroom down the hallway. Sitting down, they waited for Uncle Ned to speak.

"Long ago, father of John Shaw marry Talitha Pindar in this house," Uncle Ned began, not seeming to know how to start. "Much love."

Mandie and her uncle silently waited.

"Have papooses, John and Jim," the Indian continued.

"We know all this, Uncle Ned," John reminded him.

"But John Shaw not know they have girl papoose," Uncle Ned replied.

"A girl?" John asked quickly.

"My father had a sister?" Mandie could hardly believe it.

"Name Ruby, for rubies in mine," Uncle Ned continued. "Born 1840, eight years before John come."

"Where is she? What happened to her? Why didn't anyone ever tell me about her?" John was full of questions.

"Big God come down and take her home. Accident when Ruby ten years old. John Shaw two years old, not remember her," Uncle Ned explained.

John drew a deep breath. "I don't understand why no one ever told me about her."

"Father and mother of John Shaw broken hearts. Not talk about Ruby," Uncle Ned explained.

"So no one else talked about it, either," John said. "What kind of an accident was it, Uncle Ned? How did she die?"

"Bad accident," the old Indian replied. "Fall off pony. Break neck."

Mandie flinched. "Then all the dolls in the wardrobe belonged to Ruby, didn't they?"

"Yes, I promise mother and father of John Shaw I take care of dolls always," the old Indian said sadly.

Mandie explained to Uncle John how they had found the dolls in the wardrobe in the attic that morning. "And it was probably Hilda who put them all over the stairs," she added.

"Must be." Uncle Ned nodded his head.

"Where is Ruby buried, Uncle Ned?" John asked. "I don't remember ever seeing a grave with that name on it in the family cemetery across the street."

"Ruby there. Stone damaged by Yankee soldiers in war," Uncle Ned explained. "I show John Shaw where."

"After we eat, let's walk over there for a minute, Uncle Ned, and you show me where the grave is," John said.

"May I come, too?" Mandie asked.

"Why, yes, Amanda, but I'd say we shouldn't discuss this in front of the others until after we go over there," Uncle John said. "Now run and see if you can find Hilda so we can eat."

Mandie found Hilda in the attic, sitting on the floor, surrounded by dolls, and carefully examining each one.

"Come on, Hilda. It's time to eat," Mandie told the girl.

Hilda shied away from Mandie, clutching a doll in her arms and holding her other hand over her apron pocket. "No!" the girl refused.

Mandie reached for her hand. "Yes!" she insisted. "It's all right. You can hold that doll, but we have to put all the others back as soon as we eat. Now we'll go by my room, and you can put that doll on the bed so it can sleep until we come back."

Hilda just sat there silently.

"You don't have to keep holding your pocket. I'm not going to take whatever you found at the mine," Mandie assured her. "Now come on. Let's go."

Hilda reluctantly agreed, bringing the bride doll with her.

As they stopped by Mandie's room, she coaxed Hilda to leave the doll on the bed. Hilda carefully covered it with a shawl, humming to it.

At the noon meal, the conversation centered around Jake and Ludie Burns, They looked extremely happy, as if they couldn't believe everything that was happening to them.

"We went through the furniture in the attic this morning, Mrs. Burns," said Mandie. "As soon as Uncle John looks it over, we'll start taking it over to your house."

"The paint won't be dry enough until tomorrow," Dr. Woodard reminded her.

"Besides, we're going mining this afternoon, remember?" Celia remarked.

Elizabeth looked at Mandie sternly. "Not unless an adult goes along and stays with you all every minute," she said.

"That's a good idea," Mrs. Woodard said.

Mandie glanced around the table. "Well, who is going with us?"

"If you young people are going to the mine, then we men will go finish Jake and Ludie's house," Uncle John said.

Mandie looked over at Uncle Ned but didn't say anything.

The old Indian smiled at her. "I will go with Papoose. I watch over Papoose and friends."

"Thank you, Uncle Ned," Mandie said, smiling back at him.

"Thank you, my grandfather," Sallie echoed.

"Before y'all rush off to the mine," John said, rising, "Mandie and I have an errand with Uncle Ned. It won't take more than fifteen minutes. Y'all just stay here at the table and eat. We'll be right back."

A slight frown creased Elizabeth's forehead. "Where are you going?"

"I'll explain later, dear. It's important," John told her. He bent to kiss her cheek as he headed outside with Uncle Ned and Mandie.

The three crossed the road in front of the house and entered the walled-in cemetery behind the church. Uncle Ned led the way, walking directly to a monument with an angel on top of it. The inscription was cracked and illegible. There was a huge piece of the stone missing. Mandie and John stooped down to look closer.

"All I can make out is 1850," John informed them, squinting at the broken marble.

"Ruby die 1850," Uncle Ned said.

"There!" Mandie exclaimed, pointing to one line. "That says Ruby, but the b is missing."

John looked closer. "It certainly does, and I believe the next part says Beloved Daughter, although some of those letters are missing, too."

"Uncle John, there is the name Shaw right beneath the angel," Mandie told him. "It's all cracked, but I'm sure it is Shaw."

"I believe you're right, Amanda," John said, standing up. "Uncle Ned, do you remember which stone mason put this monument up? He might have a copy of the inscription. We could have a new marker made."

"Words on paper in wardrobe with dolls," Uncle Ned told him. "Tom Gentry put up stone. Die many years ago."

"I know where the wardrobe is in the attic, Uncle John," Mandie said. "Come on. I'll show you."

The three of them went up to the attic while the others were still waiting in the dining room.

Stepping between the dolls on the stairs, Uncle John said, "Amanda, you'll get these dolls off the steps, won't you? Someone could trip on them."

"I will, Uncle John," Mandie said, hurrying ahead. "Here's the wardrobe." She opened it for her uncle. "Where's the paper, Uncle Ned?"

The Indian stepped forward and pulled out the big drawer across the bottom. It was filled with papers. He picked up a large brown envelope and handed it to John.

John Shaw sat down in an old rocker behind him and pulled out the contents of the envelope. Mandie leaned over his shoulder.

"My goodness, here's my mother and father's marriage license! I've never seen that before!" John exclaimed, holding up a paper with a seal on it for Mandie to see. "And here is Ruby's baptismal certificate. Let's see. Ruby May Shaw, born May 6, 1840, in this house. Parents—John Shaw, Sr., and Talitha Pindar Shaw. Now, let's see what else is here."

Mandie was reading over his shoulder, itching to get her hands on the papers. "There it is, Uncle John. That paper right there has the name Tom Gentry on it," Mandie said, pointing.

John opened the half-folded paper and found the inscription as given to Tom Gentry by John's father. He read from it. " 'An angel Sent to John and Talitha Shaw on May 6, 1840, and Returned to God on May 1, 1850. Ruby May, Beloved Daughter. We Will Meet You In The Morning,' " Uncle John's voice quivered a little at the end, and he took a deep breath.

Mandie wiped a tear from her eye. "How sad," she whispered.

"Yes, and to think no one ever told me I had a sister," John said. He looked up at Uncle Ned. "Who else was here when this happened besides you and Morning Star? Was Aunt Lou here?"

"No. She come after," Uncle Ned replied. "Just Morning Star and me. All others dead now."

Uncle John seemed puzzled. "I'm trying to figure out some dates," he said. "I was two when she died. Jim wasn't born until I was almost fifteen, and my mother died when Jim was a few months old. But my father didn't die until about five years after that. I don't understand why he never told me about my sister."

"Broke his heart. Not talk to anybody about Ruby. Not allowed to say her name," Uncle Ned stated.

John Shaw placed the papers back inside the envelope, stood up, and dropped the envelope inside the open drawer. "Right now we have to get back to the dining room. I'll go through those papers later," he said.

"Are we going to put up a new monument for Ruby?" Mandie asked.

"I'd much rather recut or repair the original stone because my father put it there, but if that can't be done, then we'll get a new one," Uncle John decided. "The War Between the States was over three years before he died. I don't see why he didn't replace it or have it repaired. He certainly had the money to do it."

"Refused to go to cemetery. Never went to look at grave. Not know it broken. He say, 'My Ruby not dead. She well and happy with Big God,' " Uncle Ned told them.

"Well, let's go," Uncle John said, leading the way. "Amanda, can you get the girls to help you put those dolls back in the wardrobe before you go to the mine?"

"I'm sure they'll help," Mandie replied. "It won't take but a couple of minutes, because everyone is anxious to dig for rubies."

John put his hand on Uncle Ned's shoulder. "Please don't let these young people out of your sight for one minute," he cautioned. "You know how fast Amanda can get into trouble."

Mandie looked up at her uncle. "I promise to be real good this time," she said. "And Uncle Ned will be there to make sure I am."

Uncle Ned grunted. "Papoose will keep promise this time. I see to that."

CHAPTER TWELVE

THE SECRET OF THE MINE

Since there were six young people going to the mine, Uncle Ned took them in his wagon.

"I keep all together better," he explained as they piled in for the ride.

"And this way we'll have something to bring back all those rubies in that we're going to find," Joe joked.

"So far, Hilda is the only one who has found anything. And she won't take it out of her apron pocket, whatever it is," Mandie said, glancing over at her.

Hilda immediately put her hand over her pocket and smiled at Mandie.

"I don't think that would be considered finding anything," Celia concluded, "if it was just a piece of broken pottery."

"But she is proud of it," Dimar added. "And she is afraid we will take it away from her, so she keeps it hidden."

"She does not know all of us well," Sallie said.

Uncle Ned drew up near the entrance to the mine. "Go. Dig," he told them. "I wait here. Watch." He waved them on.

The boys lighted the lanterns, and the young people quickly scrambled down from the wagon to race for the entrance.

Inside, they grabbed tools and began to work. Joe pumped the water to get it going into the trough.

Hilda picked up a hoe and went over to a corner by herself. She began to dig in one spot.

"I'm glad we got all the work done that we could do, so we didn't have to go back to the farmhouse with the men," Joe remarked.

"It is nice to get a chance to dig for rubies," Dimar agreed. "Especially with so many pretty girls," he added with a twinkle in his eye.

"I'm glad you fellas could come with us. There's no telling what we might need you for," Mandie teased. "And Jake Burns is going to take over this mine soon, so we need to dig all we can."

Celia straightened up from her digging for a moment. "Your uncle is being awfully nice to them after what they did to you and Joe," she remarked.

"Uncle John believes that we should return good for evil," Mandie said. "And so do I. We also believe that Mr. and Mrs. Burns are truly sorry for what they did. Uncle John and I talked about it."

"Is that why he took you out of the dining room with him this morning?" Celia asked.

"No," Mandie said, leaning on her hoe. "It seems that my father and Uncle John had a sister a long time ago that they didn't know about."

Everyone stopped to listen as Mandie told them the story of Ruby May.

"And you say she had an accident on her pony and was killed?" Joe said. "I wonder where that happened."

"I didn't even think to ask Uncle Ned about that. You see, he and Morning Star were living with Uncle John and his family when it happened," Mandie explained.

"I told you my grandfather could keep a secret," Sallie said.

"Oh!" Mandie said excitedly. "I forgot to tell you something about Ruby May. All those dolls on the stairs belonged to her. Can you imagine one girl owning that many dolls?"

"Well, if you're rich—and you like dolls," Joe surmised. "Where'd the dolls come from?"

Mandie explained to the boys about the wardrobe in the attic.

"I'm glad you don't still play with dolls," Joe said.

"Me? Why?" Mandie asked.

"Because that is a waste of time," Joe replied. "There are so many other things that a girl should learn about—boys, too, for that matter—before they grow up," Joe replied.

"Such as what? Mandie asked.

"Such as—"

Suddenly there was a loud scream from Hilda in the corner. She stood still, staring at a place where she had been digging.

The others rushed over to her. At first everyone stared silently at the dirt. Then Celia screamed, and Sallie backed off.

"What is it?" Mandie gasped, bending to inspect.

"Do not touch it!" Dimar warned. "Now we know. This is an Indian burial ground we are digging in!"

Uncle Ned, having heard the screams, came to see what it was all about.

When Mandie saw him, she called to him. "Uncle Ned, come see what Hilda has dug up."

The old Indian walked quickly to the spot. Without inspecting the ground, he said sadly, "I know. It is the burying ground of my ancestors."

Tears moistened Mandie's eyes. "Oh, Uncle Ned, we're sorry. We didn't know."

"Someone should have told us," Joe added.

"I knew there was something funny about this place, the way you and Mrs. Taft and that Jake Burns have been acting," Celia said to Uncle Ned. "They knew all the time, didn't they?"

Uncle Ned nodded. "Cherokee tradition say you dig here, you disturb spirits of ancestors. In past, we worship Cherokee ancestors. We Christians now. Know this wrong. Worship only Big God. But must respect burying ground."

Dimar stepped forward. "We will cover it back up," he told him, picking up his hoe.

"Cover what up?" Uncle John asked as he came down the steps with Dr. Woodard and Jake Burns.

"Uncle John, we've uncovered an Indian burial ground," Mandie explained, tears glistening in her eyes.

John Shaw and Dr. Woodard stepped forward to look while Jake Burns stayed in the background. Turning to Jake, John asked, "Do you know anything about this?"

Jake stuttered as he answered. "A l-l-little."

"Well, what do you know about it?" John asked firmly.

"That is the reason this mine was closed," Jake admitted, hanging his head. "Uncle Ned knew about that. But only that part of the mine over there is a burial ground. If you turn back this way, it's all clear."

John shook his head slowly. "Now, Uncle Ned, I see why you called this a sad, bad mine," he said. Then he looked back at Jake. "When you agreed to work it for us, were you planning to dig right through the graves under here?"

"Why, no," Jake said. "Like I said, I knew about the burial ground. I was plannin' to expand in the other direction. I wasn't goin' to disturb the graves over that way."

"I'm sorry, Uncle Ned," John said. "If you had only spoken up and let us know about this, we never would have opened this mine again."

"White man not understand Cherokee ways," Uncle Ned replied.

Mandie took hold of her old Indian friend's hand. "But, Uncle Ned, we're part Cherokee," she said. "We would have understood."

Jake stepped forward hesitantly. "That's not the only reason this here mine was closed up," he said.

"What do you mean by that?" Dr. Woodard asked.

"My pa was killed here after he closed the mine. Nobody could ever figure out how or who did it, but the Cherokees claimed it was their ancestors takin' revenge on the white men who disturbed their spirits."

"Did my father believe that?" John asked.

"Your pa didn't, but your ma did. Remember, she was full-blooded Cherokee," Jake reminded him.

John Shaw turned to look at Uncle Ned.

The old Indian finally spoke up. "Cherokees have many superstitions about mine," he acknowledged. "Ruby come here. She ride pony. Pony go wild and throw her. Your father close mine. Say it never be opened again."

"I wish somebody had told me about all this," John sighed. "I wouldn't have opened the mine for anything."

"I not tell you what do, John Shaw. Your mine," Uncle Ned told him.

"That's right, John. It's yours to do what you like," Jake said.

"Uncle John, couldn't we go on with what Mr. Burns was planning?" Mandie asked. "We could put a wall around this side and close it off, and then work in the other direction."

"Would that be agreeable to you, Uncle Ned?" John asked. "I don't want to do anything to hurt you. These are your ancestors buried here, and this place is as sacred as our own family cemetery."

Uncle Ned thought for a moment. All the young people silently waited for his answer.

"Agree. Do not disturb graves of ancestors," the old Indian murmured faintly.

"Thanks, Uncle Ned." Mandie squeezed his hand hard.

Everyone breathed a sigh of relief.

"All right, Jake, you heard the agreement," John said. "This area is to be walled off and not disturbed."

"Yes, sir," Jake replied. "We'll find more rubies in the other direction anyway."

Hilda, who had been crouching in a corner away from the others, walked slowly toward them. Putting her hand in her pocket, Hilda took out the object she had been hiding and handed it to Mandie.

The other young people quickly crowded around to see what it was.

Mandie looked in her hand, then shivered and tossed the object to Joe.

He caught it in midair. "Oh, no!" he cried.

"What is it?" Celia asked.

Joe examined it more closely. "I think it is part of one of Uncle Ned's ancestors," he said.

The other young people stepped back. Joe handed the small bone to the old Indian, who inspected it closely. Walking over to the opening where Hilda had dug, Uncle Ned knelt down and laid the bone in the ground with the other pieces of the skeleton. Reaching for the hoe, he silently pushed the loose dirt back over the opening.

Sallie and Dimar knelt by Uncle Ned beside the freshly covered grave. Then as the old Indian raised his voice in Cherokee prayer, they all fell silent and bowed their heads.

When the Indians rose, Hilda stepped toward them and said, "Rest in peace."

Everyone looked at her in amazement.

"How did Hilda know what they were saying?" Joe asked. "Does Hilda speak Cherokee?"

Dr. Woodard cleared his throat. "I'm beginning to wonder if Hilda is part Cherokee," he speculated.

"Dimar said he was teaching her the Cherokee language," Mandie told him.

"But I have not been able to teach her much," Dimar stated. "I did not teach her those words."

Hilda looked over at Dimar and smiled. "Cher'kee," she said softly.

"You know, John, maybe that's our trouble with Hilda. She may not understand English," Dr. Woodard said.

"But you said you met her parents. They weren't Cherokee, were they?" John asked.

"They spoke English, but they did look like they could have been Indian, come to think of it," Dr. Woodard concluded. "I'll have to check that out."

"I think we should all call it a day and go home now," Uncle John decided.

The young people groaned in disappointment.

"Could I get just one more sieveful?" Joe asked. "Please?"

"All right, just one more sieve each, and then we'll go," Uncle John agreed.

The young people rushed to fill their sieves and then hurried to the water trough. But again they each groaned as they emptied the gravel—all except Joe.

Joe suddenly called to John as he held his sieve over the water. "Mr. Shaw, please come and see what I have here."

John picked up the object Joe had in the sieve, turned it over and over, and held it next to the lantern. "Looks like you've got a good-sized ruby there," he stated, handing the stone back to him.

"A real ruby?" Joe exclaimed.

"An honest-to-goodness ruby, Joe," John answered.

There was so much excitement among the young people that Uncle John finally allowed one more sieve each, but no one came up with anything but gravel and rocks.

As the group climbed back into Uncle Ned's wagon, Mandie sat next to Joe. "What are you going to do with your ruby, Joe?" she asked.

"I guess I'll get it cut and polished like you're supposed to do," he replied, turning the stone over and over in his hand. "I can't believe I found a real ruby."

"After you get it cut and polished, what are you going to do with it?" Celia wanted to know.

"I'll—uh—I'll just—I'll just keep it," Joe said, glancing at Mandie.

But Mandie wasn't listening anymore. She was thinking of her lost kitten. She couldn't wait to get home to find out if he had come back.

When they all got back to the house, Liza let them in.

"Liza, has Snowball come home?" Mandie asked immediately.

"Missy, I ain't seed hide nor hair of dat white cat," Liza told her.

"I'm afraid he's lost and can't find the way home," Mandie said. "Just in case you happen to see him, will you let me know right that minute?"

"I sho' will, Missy," Liza said sympathetically. "Supper bein' put on de table. Hurry now."

After they all cleaned up and gathered at the dining table for the evening meal, the young people excitedly told the women about what had happened at the mine. The ladies were horrified at the thought of digging up graves.

"John, you're not going to let people go in there and dig now that we know about the burial ground, are you?" Elizabeth asked.

"No, of course not, Elizabeth," John replied. "We're closing off that part."

"May we go back and dig in the other part again before we go back to school?" Mandie asked.

"If you have time," Uncle John said. "Tomorrow is Thanksgiving. Morning Star will be here in the morning. We thought if everybody got together then, we could get all the furniture moved into Jake and Ludie's house while the dinner is cooking. It would be a nice Thanksgiving gesture."

Everyone approved the plan, and bright and early the next morning, Morning Star arrived and they gathered in the attic. Piece by piece, Uncle John approved the furniture that they were taking to the Burns's house.

Ludie, standing nearby, gasped when she saw what she was being given. "Mr. Shaw," she said, "we couldn't possibly take all that nice furniture. It cost too much."

"Ludie, don't worry about it. You and Jake will be working for it. Besides, I don't know that we'll ever need it. No sense in letting it sit here and rot," John argued.

The men pushed a huge sideboard forward to take downstairs.

As Mandie and the other girls stepped back, Mandie spied a paper tacked to the back of the sideboard. She ran forward to get a closer look. "Stop!" she yelled excitedly. "Wait! I've found something!"

Joe, standing nearby, quickly looked to see what it was. "Looks like a map to some hidden treasure," he said.

"Treasure?" the young people echoed.

"What's this all about?" John Shaw asked, stooping behind the sideboard. He looked closely at the large piece of old crumbling paper tacked there, then carefully pulled out the tacks holding it. He straightened up with the drawing in his hands. "Tigris has my sister Ruby's name on it," he said, laying it down on top of the sideboard.

Everyone crowded around to look.

The drawing, dimmed by time, was labeled: My House, River, Rose Creek, Ruby Mine, Your House, Rhododendron Bush, Persimmon Tree, Rock Pile, and the Path to Hezekiah's House.

"Look! It has directions, too!" Mandie exclaimed, pointing to the printing at the bottom. She read aloud: " 'Go down the path to Hezekiah's House. Turn left and go 936 feet to Rock Pile. Go right 572 feet to Persimmon Tree. Then go left 333 feet to Rhododendron Bush. Dig three feet under Rhododendron Bush. That is where Treasure is buried.' " Mandie looked up. "I wonder where all this is," she said.

"The My House would have to be this house if Ruby drew it," Celia reasoned.

"And there is the ruby mine," Sallie pointed.

"But who is Hezekiah?" Dimar asked.

"Do you know who Hezekiah is, Uncle John?" Mandie asked.

"I don't remember ever knowing anyone by that name. But then if you will notice, this map was drawn April 30, 1850," John replied. "I was only two years old then."

"That was the day before she died. What a coincidence," Mandie said in wonderment.

"It certainly was," Uncle John agreed. He turned to Jake. "Did you ever know anyone around here named Hezekiah?"

"No, John. Don't believe I do," Jake replied. "You see, when I was growing up, we lived in an old house right across the river from the mine. I wasn't allowed to go anywhere but to the mine and back. Then, too, we wouldn't have had the same friends as your family."

Dimar leaned forward. "The place called Your House on this map looks like it might be the old farmhouse we are fixing up for Mr. and Mrs. Burns," he said.

"Yeah, it might be," Jake agreed.

"I wonder what the treasure was?" Ludie said.

"Was? I hope it still is because I am going to find it," Mandie declared. "Who wants to go with me?"

"You are not going anywhere, young lady—not until we finish moving these things for Mr. and Mrs. Burns. And by that time the Thanksgiving turkey will be done," Uncle John said. "Now let's get back to work here."

"May I take the map, Uncle John?" Mandie asked.

"I think we'd better put it in that drawer with the other papers over there until we get time to look into it," Uncle John replied. "It might be valuable." He winked at her and smiled.

Reluctantly, Mandie crossed the room to the old wardrobe with the dolls and carefully added the map to the papers in the drawer.

The treasure map was the topic of conversation all morning. The girls helped as much as they could, taking turns going downstairs to open the front door for the men carrying the heavy furniture.

As Uncle Ned was tugging a huge chair through the attic doorway, Mandie came to help.

"I'll open the front door for you, Uncle Ned," she offered, walking ahead of him down the three flights of steps.

In the front hallway, she paused with her hand on the doorknob as Uncle Ned set the chair down for a minute to get his breath. "I think you should have had some help bringing that thing down the stairs," she said.

"Not heavy. Open door now," the old Indian told her.

Mandie flung the door wide and stared out onto the porch in disbelief. There, huddled on the doormat, sat Snowball, meowing weakly.

"Snowball!" Mandie cried as the kitten limped toward her. "Oh, your foot is hurt!" She picked him up and hugged him tightly.

Suddenly his disheveled, dirty body went limp.

Mandie panicked. "Dear God," she prayed, "please don't let Snowball die." Tears trickled down her cheeks as she sat down in the middle of the porch, holding the kitten. Uncle Ned bent over her to look.

The white kitten's dirty fur was covered with briars. Uncle Ned rubbed his hand across the kitten's face. The kitten didn't move. "Do not hold too tight," he said. "Snowball weak, not eat."

Mandie loosened her hold on the kitten and held him up to her face. "Please don't let him die, dear God, please!" she cried again.

At that moment Snowball perked up and lifted his head, then meowed and snuggled against her shoulder.

Mandie was so happy that it was all she could do to keep from squeezing the kitten to death. "Thank you, dear God! Thank you!" she cried.

Uncle Ned sat down on the porch beside her and took her hand in his. "Papoose see what trouble disobedience cause," the old man said. "Must learn to obey. Keep promises."

"You're right, Uncle Ned," Mandie admitted, squeezing his hand. "Let's thank God for sending Snowball home."

The two sat there and looked toward the sky.

"Dear God," Mandie began with tears in her eyes. "Thank you for sending Snowball home. I love him so much. Thank you again for forgiving me for causing trouble. Help me to think before I do things. Thank you, dear God."

"Thank you, Big God," Uncle Ned added.

Mandie cuddled the kitten as she stood up. "I've got to get Snowball something to eat and see what's wrong with his little paw," she said.

"Me see paw," Uncle Ned stated, rising. He examined the kitten. "Here. Thorn in paw. We get out. Hold."

Mandie held the hurt little paw while Uncle Ned worked on it. Snowball meowed weakly and tried to pull his paw away, but uncle Ned held it firm and pulled out the thorn.

"Must get medicine now," the Indian told her.

"Thank you, Uncle Ned," Mandie said. "I'll go bathe it and put some medicine on it."

"Papoose not going to look for treasure?" he asked.

Mandie grinned at him. "Not yet, Uncle Ned. You see, I stopped to think first. I'll go when Uncle John gives me permission. Right now I'll go doctor Snowball."

"Good girl." Uncle Ned smiled back. "Ruby good girl, too. I hope you find Ruby's treasure."

"I will," Mandie promised. "All in good time."

MANDIE

AND THE
HIDDEN
TREASURE

With Thanks to

W. Harold Christian, Jr.,
who has so many talents and
who so willingly shares them.

CONTENTS

MANDIE AND THE HIDDEN TREASURE

"For unto whomsoever much is given,
of him shall be much required."
Luke 12:48

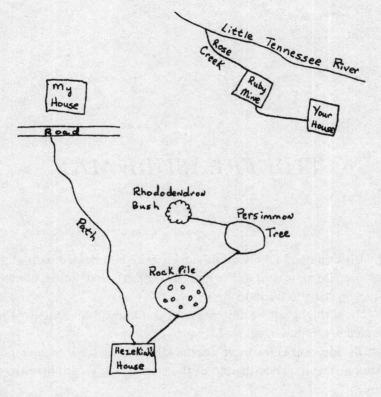

Go down the path to Hezekiah's House. Turn left and go 936 feet to Rockpile. Go right 572 feet to Persimmon Tree. Then go left 333 feet to Rhododendron Bush. Dig three feet under Rhododendron Bush. That is where Treasure is buried.

Drawn by Ruby May Shaw
April 30, 1850

CHAPTER ONE

THE TREASURE MAP

"I wish Celia and Dimar could have stayed and helped us find the treasure," Mandie said as she and her Indian friend, Sallie, climbed the steep stairs to the attic.

"There might not be any treasure, you know," Joe Woodard reminded her, following close behind.

"Oh, Joe, you know there's some kind of treasure," Mandie protested as they reached the top of the stairs. "We've got the map to prove it."

Snowball, Mandie's white kitten, ran ahead of them as Mandie pushed open the door to the attic.

The three stepped over crates and trunks and made their way through a maze of abandoned chairs, dressers, and other discarded furniture to get to the huge old wardrobe standing at the far side of the attic.

"Just because we found a map is no reason to say there really is a treasure," Joe argued. "Someone might have found it a long time ago. That map's about fifty years old. By now, someone could have taken whatever was there."

Mandie bent to open the big drawer on the bottom of the wardrobe and took out the treasure map they had found a few days earlier. As they sat down on the floor of the attic, she spread the map out before them.

"I'm going to look anyway," Mandie told him. "Since Ruby got killed the day after she drew this map, I don't imagine she took the treasure out of its hiding place. And since we found the map tacked to the back side of that old sideboard, I don't believe anyone else ever found it."

"I think as you do, Mandie," Sallie said. "We must explore the places shown on the map and see what we can find."

"Oh, I'll go along with you girls and help look, but I really don't think there will be anything to find," Joe said.

Mandie ignored his remark this time. She read the directions on the map. "It says, 'Go down the path to Hezekiah's House. Turn left and go 936 feet to Rock Pile. Go right 572 feet to Persimmon Tree. Then go left 333 feet to Rhododendron Bush. Dig three feet under Rhododendron Bush. That is where the Treasure is buried." Mandie looked up. "I'm sure Ruby buried something," she said emphatically.

Joe leaned forward, pointing to the drawing. "We've already decided the 'My House' on the map must be this house we're in," he said, "because Ruby was your father's sister, and this was your grandparents' house. Then there is a path drawn to 'Hezekiah's House' right there."

"And we go 936 feet to a rock pile, 572 feet to a persimmon tree, and 333 feet to a rhododendron bush," Sallie added, studying the map.

Mandie nodded. "There's the Little Tennessee River, the ruby mine, and a place marked 'Your House.' It's all right here in Franklin, North Carolina," she said. "But I don't know anything about that path that goes to Hezekiah's House."

"I don't think we can begin in the middle or at the end of this map," Joe told them. "We'll have to start at the beginning and find the path to Hezekiah's house. It looks to me like that path must go right next to the cemetery across the road from here."

"Yes, it does," Mandie agreed.

"The 'Your House' might be the old house where Jake and Ludie Burns are living now," Sallie suggested.

"It probably is," Mandie agreed. "And if it is, then this rhododendron bush, the persimmon tree, and the rock pile must be between our house and the house the Burnses are living in."

"Well, we're not going to find it sitting here in the attic," Joe told the girls.

Mandie picked up the map and turned the front of it around to show Joe and Sallie. "Don't y'all think these things are between here and the Burnses?" She glanced down at the back of the paper map. "Wait! Here's something on the back. Look!" She laid the map upside down for the others to see. "I believe it says, 'It's about'—something—" She shook her head. " '—to Hezekiah's House.' "

" 'One mile,' " Sallie filled in, squinting closely at the writing.

"So it's about one mile to Hezekiah's house," Joe agreed. "Do y'all see anything else written on the back?"

The three of them carefully inspected every inch of the faded paper but found nothing else.

"I guess we've got all the information there is on the map." Mandie sighed. "What do y'all suppose the treasure is?"

"Some silly kid thing," Joe said. "Ruby was only ten years old when she drew this map."

"Lacking five days," Mandie corrected him. "She was born May 6, 1840, and she died on May 1, 1850, five days before her tenth birthday, according to her tombstone."

"Oh, well, nine years and three hundred and sixty days if you want to be exact," Joe grumbled.

"Ten years old is not such a dumb age, Joe," Mandie said. "I'm only twelve myself, and you're not quite two years older than I am."

"And I am almost one year older than you, Mandie," Sallie added. "My grandfather said that Ruby was a sensible, mature little girl. I think she probably hid something valuable."

"It might have been considered valuable by a ten-year-old," Joe said.

"Maybe it was money," Sallie suggested.

"Or jewelry," Mandie said. She lifted the map from the floor, and a small fragment fell off the corner where the tack had made a hole. "This map is so old it is beginning to crumble," she said, pointing to the corner.

"Then we must hurry and find the treasure," Sallie said.

"Where do we begin?" Mandie asked the others.

"We should find the path by the cemetery," Joe stated.

"Or we could talk to my grandfather," Sallie said. "He was living here then with your grandparents, remember?"

"Let's do both," Mandie agreed, getting up from the floor. "Let's find your grandfather and see what he knows, and then we can go to the cemetery across the road." As she held the map, another corner crumbled from the paper.

Sallie gasped. "The map is disintegrating!"

"Why don't we make a copy and put this one back in the drawer?" Mandie suggested. "If this falls apart before we find the treasure, we might not be able to piece it together again. Joe, you can draw better than I can. Will you copy it for us?"

Joe smiled. "Where is the pencil and paper?"

"I'll run down to my room and get some. I'll be right back." Mandie handed him the map and wove her way through the old furniture again.

On the way down the stairs, Mandie met Sallie's grandfather coming up the steps. "Uncle Ned, I'm glad you're coming up to the attic. We have lots of questions we want to ask you," she told him. "I have to go to my room for something. I'll be back up in a minute. Sallie and Joe are up there now."

Uncle Ned smiled at the blonde-haired, blue-eyed girl and continued his way up. "I wait in attic, Papoose."

Mandie rushed into her room, grabbed paper and pencil from her desk, and ran back up the steps, close behind the old Indian. "Here, Joe," she said, holding out the supplies.

"I'll draw right here," Joe said. He knelt to use the top of an old trunk for a table and spread out the map and his supplies. Snowball hopped upon the trunk to watch. "Sit down, Snowball," Joe ordered him. The kitten perched on the edge of one corner.

"Joe is making a copy of the map because the old one is crumbling," Mandie explained to Uncle Ned. "You might as well sit down because we've got lots of questions to ask you."

Uncle Ned smiled and sat on top of another old trunk nearby. Mandie and Sallie sat down on a dusty, faded settee near him.

"Now, Papoose, question," the old Indian said.

"Did you ever know of anyone named Hezekiah?" Mandie asked.

"Hezzie—ky?" the old man asked, unable to pronounce the name. "No, Papoose, I not know."

"Look here on the map." Mandie jumped up and pointed over Joe's shoulder. "You see, it says, 'My House' there, and then it shows a path to Hezekiah's house. It goes across the road, and it must run right next to the cemetery. Do you know if there's a path like that?"

Uncle Ned shook his head. "Not know, Papoose. May be. Not remember."

Sallie moved closer. "My grandfather, do you know whether the 'Your House' on the map is the same house the Burnses live in?"

"My granddaughter, people live in that house long ago, work for father of John Shaw in mines, plant crops. Same house Jake Burns live in now," Uncle Ned replied.

"Who were they, Uncle Ned?" Mandie asked eagerly.

"Not remember." The old Indian frowned for a moment as if trying to recall. "Man called Scoot," he said after a moment.

Joe looked up from his drawing. "But why would Ruby put that house on her map?"

"Daughter of Scoot same age Ruby. Good friends. Ride ponies together," Uncle Ned told them.

"Then I'd say that whoever the girl was, she must have known about Ruby's map and probably about the treasure, too, whatever it is," Mandie said.

"Yeh, and she could have dug it up years and years ago," Joe reminded her.

Uncle Ned shook his head. "No, no, no. Mine close when Ruby die. Scoot move far away."

Mandie looked down at the map Joe was copying. "What about all these other things—the rock pile, the persimmon tree, and the rhododendron bush?" she asked. "Do you know where they are?"

The old Indian laughed and said, "Papoose, on this land find many, many trees, bushes, rocks."

"If we only knew where Hezekiah's house was, then we could count the feet from there," Sallie said.

Just then Mandie looked up. There in the doorway stood Polly Cornwallis, Mandie's next-door neighbor. Polly's long, dark hair was neatly tied back with ribbons, and she was wearing an expensive-looking pink silk dress.

"Hello, everybody," Polly greeted them. "Mandie, your mother told me y'all were up here looking for treasure."

Mandie sighed. "No, Polly," she replied, "we are not looking for treasure up here. We have an old map we found that we're trying to decipher."

Polly squeezed through the furniture maze to look over Joe's shoulder. He looked up at her without speaking, then continued drawing.

"That map?" Polly questioned. "Hey, that looks awfully interesting. Can I help y'all find the treasure on it?"

The other three young people looked at each other.

Mandie hesitated. "Sure, Polly, but I warn you. It may be a tiresome, dirty job, and I know you don't like to get dirty."

"Oh, that's all right. I don't have anything else to do until I go back to school Monday," Polly told her, smoothing her fancy dress.

Mandie caught Uncle Ned's eye and he smiled. Mandie smiled back. Uncle Ned knew Mandie didn't especially like Polly because Polly was forever trying to be too friendly with Joe. He also knew it had taken a lot of self-control for Mandie to include Polly in the treasure hunt.

"You must go home and put on an old dress," Sallie told Polly. "We will be searching through weeds and bushes."

"Never mind about my dress. If I ruin it, I have lots of others," Polly said, twirling her full skirt. "When do we start?"

"You mean where do we start, Polly," Joe said. He turned to Mandie. "How are we going to get started on this silly adventure, anyway?"

"It's silly, is it? Then why did you beg your parents to let you stay over the rest of the weekend to help Sallie and me look for whatever this treasure is?" Mandie asked.

Joe grinned. "Because I have to be here to get you out of all the silly messes you get into."

"Joe Woodard!" Mandie exclaimed. "I can take care of myself!"

"But it always helps to have a boy along," Sallie spoke up. "Remember, Mandie, we have met up with some dangerous people before."

Polly gasped. "Are there any dangerous people involved in this search for the treasure?"

"Who knows? We don't even know how to start on this yet," Mandie said. "If we only knew who Hezekiah was and where he lived. . . . Uncle Ned, is there anybody still living around town who was here back then?"

Uncle Ned thought for a moment. "Me, Morning Star live in this house with father of John Shaw. Long ago. Long, long ago."

Polly looked at the map again and saw the date. "April 30, 1850!" she exclaimed. "My goodness! You mean the map is that old? Why, my mother wasn't even born then!"

Mandie told her all about finding the map tacked to the back of the sideboard, where it had been hidden all these years.

Then Uncle Ned continued his recollections. "People named Massey live in house next to father of John Shaw."

"My house," Polly agreed. "And my mother bought the house from them after my father died. I was just a little baby then."

"What happened to them? Are they still living in Franklin?" Mandie asked.

The old Indian shook his head. "No, move way up north."

"Is there no one at all in Franklin who lived here back then?" Mandie asked.

"Hadleys," Uncle Ned said. "Hadleys live here then. Same house they live in now. Papoose go see Hadleys."

"The Hadleys? Where that strange girl Hilda ran away to? Away over beyond the ruby mine?" Joe asked.

Mandie shot Joe a look of disapproval for talking that way about the disturbed young girl Mandie and her friend Celia had found hiding in the school attic.

Uncle Ned nodded. "Yes," he replied. "Maybe Hadleys know this Hezzie—ky for you."

"I know where they live. May I go with y'all?" Polly asked quickly.

"I know where they live, too," Joe replied. "I've been there with my father when he had to doctor them for one thing or another."

"When are you going?" Polly was insistent.

"Whenever my mother gives us permission, Polly. Don't you ever have to get permission from your mother to do things like going on this search with us? Your mother might not want you to do that." Mandie secretly hoped that Polly would not be allowed to go.

"No, most of the time Mother lets me do whatever I want," Polly said. "She says I'm growing up and should learn to make decisions for myself. I don't think she'll mind if I go with y'all."

"You will have to ask her first, Polly. We don't want you going off with us unless your mother agrees," Joe spoke up.

"I'll ask her. Just tell me when you're planning to go," Polly said.

"I'll let you know. Right now, Joe has to finish copying the map before we can go anywhere," Mandie told her.

A moment later, Joe stood up, waving his new map in the air. "Here it is. All done."

Mandie and Sallie looked at it and agreed he had done a good job.

Carefully picking up the old map, Mandie returned it to the drawer in the bottom of the wardrobe. "Uncle Ned, are you going with us to the Hadleys?" she asked.

"We see," the old man said, standing up.

"Please do, Uncle Ned," Mandie pleaded, taking his old wrinkled hand in her small white one. "Remember, my mother said I couldn't go anywhere without an adult for the rest of my holidays at home because I disobeyed her and got in trouble at the mine."

Uncle Ned smiled down at her. "We see, Papoose."

"Must be time to eat. I'm hungry," Joe said.

Sallie laughed. "You are always ready to eat, Joe, whether it is time or not."

"It's about noon," Polly said. "I'll go home and eat, and ask my mother if I can go with y'all. Then I'll come back and let you know. You won't go until I get back, will you?"

"Not if you don't take too long," Mandie told her. "I'll ask Mother if we can go just as soon as we eat. We're going to the Hadleys first of all. And Polly, please wear something sensible."

"All right. I'll hurry," Polly called back. She ran out the door and disappeared down the steps.

"Let's go," Mandie said, picking up Snowball and leading the way down the stairs. "I suppose we'll have to eat since Joe is hungry."

In the parlor they found Elizabeth, Mandie's beautiful, blonde-haired mother, and John Shaw, Mandie's uncle, who had married Elizabeth after Mandie's father died.

Uncle John laughed when he saw them. "I knew you'd be along soon," he said. "The wonderful aroma from that chicken Jenny is frying is all over the house."

"Fried chicken!" Joe exclaimed. "Mmm!"

Uncle Ned sat down near John Shaw while the young people gathered on the settee.

"Have you figured out the map yet?" Elizabeth asked.

"Some of it, Mother," Mandie replied. "Uncle Ned said we should go talk to the Hadleys to see if they know who Hezekiah was and where he lived."

"Why the Hadleys, Amanda?" Elizabeth asked.

"They're the only people Uncle Ned can think of that were living here when Ruby made the map," Mandie explained.

"And we need to ask them some questions," Joe put in.

"Amanda, you know I told you that you couldn't go off anywhere without an adult with you. Who is going with you?"

"Me go," Uncle Ned volunteered. "Me go with Papoose after eat."

"We'd appreciate that, Uncle Ned," John said. "I know we can always depend on you to keep things under control."

"Like when John Shaw little brave." The old Indian's black eyes twinkled.

"Yes, like when I was little," Uncle John agreed. "You did a good job of looking after me and my brother, Jim, when we were growing up. I don't know what we'd have done without you and Morning Star to get us out of our scrapes." He chuckled.

"John and Jim not bad braves," Uncle Ned replied.

Mandie went over and gave her old Indian friend a hug. "Thank you, Uncle Ned, for saying you'll go with us," she said. "We'll be good and not get into any trouble. I don't know about Polly, but the three of us will behave."

"Polly? Is she going with y'all?" Elizabeth asked.

"If her mother lets her," Mandie said with a big sigh. "I just wish we could have slipped off without her finding out what we're doing. She's not much fun to be around."

"Amanda!" Elizabeth scolded.

Liza, the young Negro maid, appeared in the doorway.

Elizabeth looked up. "Yes, Liza?"

"Dat Missy Polly, she done sent huh cook over heah to say wait fo' huh 'cause huh ma say she kin go," Liza announced.

"Thank you, Liza." Elizabeth smiled. "They'll wait for Polly."

"Yessum," Liza replied, still standing in the doorway. "And Miz 'Lizbeth, Aunt Lou she say de dinnuh on de table."

As they rose and went to the dining room, Mandie whispered to Sallie, "We'll just have to pretend Polly's not there."

"That may be hard to do," Sallie whispered back.

CHAPTER TWO

OLD NEWSPAPERS

Jason Bond, the Shaws' caretaker, had ponies saddled and waiting for the young people at the gate when they finished their noon meal. Uncle Ned's horse was also at the hitching post.

As the young people gathered in the front hall, preparing to leave, Mandie stood in front of the mirror on the hall tree, tying her bonnet.

Suddenly Polly burst through the front door. "I made it!" she exclaimed, out of breath. "And I tied my pony out in front with the others."

Mandie silently looked the girl over. At least she had changed into a gingham dress and was carrying a bonnet and a shawl.

"Mandie, Sallie, take these." Elizabeth handed them the shawls from the pegs on the hall tree. "It's cool outside. And remember, Polly, you must obey Uncle Ned the same as the others have promised."

"Yes, ma'am," Polly agreed. She looked at Mandie. "Who's got the map?"

"I have it," Joe called to her from the doorway as he buttoned his jacket. He held up the rolled-up piece of paper for her to see.

Uncle Ned came into the hallway wearing his buckskin jacket and headed for the front door. "Go!" he said.

Amid reminders from Elizabeth and John Shaw to behave, the young people rushed down the walkway to their ponies.

When Mandie got to the gate, Liza was standing there, waiting for her. Taking Mandie by the arm, she whispered, "Hurry, Missy, git on yo' pony and git 'side dat doctuh son. Dis heah Missy Polly, she got eyes fo' him."

Mandie mounted her pony. "I know," she said with a sigh.

As the group headed out, Mandie tried to ride beside Joe, but Polly kept crowding the road with her pony, and Mandie would be forced to hurry forward toward Sallie and Uncle Ned.

Sallie dropped back to ride beside Mandie. "If the Hadleys did know Hezekiah, what will we do next?" she asked, trying to distract Mandie from watching Polly.

"I hope they remember Hezekiah. Who knows? Maybe we could find him and talk to him. He must have been a friend of Ruby's, don't you think?"

"He probably was," Sallie agreed.

"If we hurry, maybe we can find the treasure before we have to go back to school. I wish I didn't have to keep going to that silly school in Asheville," Mandie said.

"But your mother went to the Misses Heathwood's School for Girls, and she wants you to get educated there also," Sallie reminded her.

"They'll never educate me—not what I call educate. They teach so many silly things that I will never use. I'd like to learn mathematics and finance like the boys do. That would be more useful to me when I grow up," Mandie said as they rode along behind Uncle Ned.

"I do not know where you can learn those things except at a boys' school, and I do not think they would allow you to attend there." Sallie giggled. "I agree that you should learn mathematics and finance, because someday you will inherit your uncle's and your mother's fortunes. But then, most girls just get married and let their husbands worry about that kind of thing."

"Not me," Mandie said quickly. "I would want to know what goes on in my own business affairs. No man is going to tell me how to spend my money when I grow up."

"Not even Joe?" Sallie teased.

Mandie hesitated. "Not even Joe," she said uneasily. "But I don't think Joe would be like that when he grows up. He always treats me like an equal. He encourages me to learn sensible things."

Mandie turned slightly on her pony to look over her shoulder. Polly was riding close beside Joe and seemed to be doing most of the talking.

Looking back at her friend, Mandie said, "Besides, who knows how the future will turn out. Joe and I may outgrow each other someday."

"Yes, you are right," Sallie agreed. She changed the subject. "Are we almost to the Hadleys?"

"It's not much farther," Mandie said, tightening her grip on the reins. "Let's get ahead of Uncle Ned. I know the way."

"But my grandfather is supposed to be watching over us," Sallie objected.

"We'll stay within sight of him. Let's just ride ahead." Mandie urged her pony past Uncle Ned, and Sallie followed.

The old Indian raised his hand to them. "Do not go far ahead," he called.

"We won't," the girls called back.

As they rounded a bend in the road, the Hadleys' huge two-story house came into sight. Everyone hurried forward.

They tied up the animals at the hitching post and rushed to the front porch. Mandie knocked, and a moment later the door was opened by a uniformed maid.

"Are Mr. and Mrs. Hadley at home?" Mandie asked the woman.

The maid looked over the group standing on the porch and asked, "Who is calling?"

Mandie waved her hands around to her friends and replied, "I'm Mandie Shaw. This is Joe Woodard and that's Uncle Ned and Sallie and Polly."

"Just a moment," said the woman and disappeared inside. She returned in a minute and showed them into the parlor where Mr. and Mrs. Hadley were sitting.

Mr. Hadley rose slowly and stepped forward to offer Uncle Ned his hand. "How are you, Uncle Ned?" he said. "I see you have brought us some company." The two men shook hands.

"Papoose of Jim Shaw want to ask questions," Uncle Ned said, taking a seat indicated by Mr. Hadley.

Mr. Hadley spoke to Mandie. "So you are Jim Shaw's daughter. He was a good man, my dear. A good man." He put his arm around Mandie's shoulders.

"Thank you, sir." Mandie's voice trembled. "I'm so glad to finally get to meet you and Mrs. Hadley."

"Sit down. Sit down. Make yourselves at home," Mrs. Hadley told them.

The young people found seats around the room, and Mandie told the Hadleys about her father's sister, Ruby, and the treasure map she had left. She showed them the copy of the map that Joe was carrying.

The Hadleys listened attentively.

"What we would like to know, Mrs. Hadley, and Mr. Hadley, is whether you all were living here back then," Mandie said.

"Yes, my dear, we were here," Mrs. Hadley answered. "I was born and raised in this house, and after my parents died, I married Mr. Hadley. And we've continued living here ever since. I have never lived anywhere else."

"Did you know Ruby Shaw?" Joe asked impatiently.

Mrs. Hadley nodded her head slowly. "Yes, we knew Ruby. We were just a young, newly married couple when that terrible accident happened. Mandie, your grandparents suffered so much, especially your grandfather. He would never allow anyone to mention Ruby's name after she died. He could not bear to talk about it."

"If you were living here then, did you know someone named Hezekiah who lived in that house on the map?" Mandie asked.

Mr. and Mrs. Hadley looked at the map again. They thought for a moment.

"Hezekiah?" Mr. Hadley mulled over the name.

"I can't figure out where that house would be, dear," Mrs. Hadley said.

Joe leaned forward. "Did you ever know anyone at all named Hezekiah?" he persisted.

"I don't believe so," Mr. Hadley answered.

"No, I'm sure I never knew anyone with that name," Mrs. Hadley said.

The young people sighed in disappointment.

Uncle Ned frowned thoughtfully. "Map say Hezzie—ky not far from house of John Shaw." He bent forward to point at the place on the map.

"About one mile, according to the back of the original map. This one is a copy that Joe made because the other one is crumbling," Mandie explained.

"I am sorry, dear," said Mrs. Hadley, "but I just can't seem to place this house on the map. I didn't know your grandparents well."

"I have an idea that might help," Mr. Hadley offered. "I used to own the local newspaper. When I retired a few years ago, I just closed it down. Someone else started the newspaper we have now. But there are hundreds of old newspapers in my old building. They date back to about 1845. Maybe you could find some kind of information in them, at least the story about Ruby's death."

"Oh, could we look at them?" Mandie said excitedly.

The other young people leaned forward.

"All I ask is that you don't take any papers out of the building, and that you leave them as you found them," Mr. Hadley said. "I'll go get the key. Uncle Ned, you know where the building is, I'm sure."

"Yes," the old Indian agreed.

Mr. Hadley went to get the key, and when he returned, he handed it to Uncle Ned. "I'll trust you to return it to me when they're finished looking."

"Thanks so much, Mr. Hadley and Mrs. Hadley," Mandie said, rising to go.

The young people all expressed their thanks.

Mrs. Hadley hobbled to her feet with her cane and raised her hand to them. "Wait!" she called. "There is one promise I'd like from y'all."

Everyone turned to listen.

"Promise me you'll let me know what the treasure is when you find it. This is something I would like to have done when I was your age," she told them. "It sounds so exciting."

"We promise," the young people said in unison.

The Hadleys followed them to the front door.

"Good luck!" Mrs. Hadley called with a twinkle in her eyes.

The young people excitedly mounted their ponies and waited for Uncle Ned to catch up with them.

"Can we go there right now, Uncle Ned?" Mandie asked excitedly.

Uncle Ned untied his horse, smiled, and looked at the sky. "We have time," he replied.

"Thank you, Uncle Ned, for helping us and everything," Joe said.

The old Indian smiled again. "Must hurry before doctor son get hungry."

Everyone laughed as they rode off down the road toward the downtown part of Franklin.

On Main Street Uncle Ned stopped in front of an old two-story building, badly in need of paint. A rotting sign over the doorway with fading letters read: Franklin News.

The young people jumped down and tied their ponies at the edge of the road alongside Uncle Ned's horse. Then they followed him to the front door of the building.

After much turning and shaking, Uncle Ned finally got the door unlocked and pushed it open for the young people to enter. "I wait here," he told them, sitting down on the front step.

As they went inside, they looked around the dark, dusty hallway. Long-unused printing presses stood in a large room with dirty windows on their right. On the left was a room stacked almost to the ceiling with newspapers. One large window high in the wall dimly lit the room. At the back of the hallway, a long flight of steps led upstairs.

Mandie surveyed the piles of newspapers. "What a mess!" she exclaimed.

Joe walked over to the papers and looked for dates on them. "I don't think these are very old," he said.

"Let's see what's upstairs," Mandie suggested, heading up the steps.

Joe followed, the rickety boards creaking at every step.

Polly shrank back. "Are y'all really going up those dark steps?"

"Come on, Polly," Sallie said, offering her hand.

Polly reluctantly gave Sallie one hand and held up her long skirts with the other. They slowly climbed the dark stairway.

As they came to the landing at the top, Polly shivered. "There may be rats in here," she said.

"If there are, they will be frightened of us and run away," Sallie assured her.

The upstairs was one big room, almost completely filled with copies of old newspapers. The only light for the room came from a large skylight covered with grime.

Mandie and Joe looked about and began searching for dates on the papers. Sallie let go of Polly's hand and joined them.

"We are looking for 1850 newspapers," Mandie said. As she pulled the top paper off one stack, a cloud of dust assailed them, and Polly backed off, sneezing.

Over in one corner, Sallie began reading dates aloud. "This says 1845, these are 1849, and these are 1845 again."

As they explored the stacks and moved the papers about, the room became clouded with dust. Their hands got black with newspaper print, and dirt settled in their hair and on their clothes. Polly stayed at the top of the stairs, watching the others and holding her handkerchief to her nose.

"Here they are!" Joe called from the far side of the room. As he attempted to pull out a newspaper sticking out of a huge stack, the entire pile came tumbling down on top of him, sliding this way and that.

Rushing to see what Joe had found, Mandie and Sallie got caught in the avalanche of newspapers. As they looked at each other among the mountain of papers, the three suddenly laughed hysterically and then started sneezing from the dust.

"You're all dirty, Mandie," Joe told her as he worked his way out of the mess.

"So are you, Joe," Mandie said.

"We are all a mess!" Sallie gasped, trying to help Joe extricate himself from the newspapers.

"Remember, Mr. Hadley said to leave the papers as you found them," Polly reminded them as she watched from the top of the steps.

The other three looked at each other in exasperation.

"How can we ever get those papers back like we found them?" Mandie asked.

"We don't know what order they were in when they fell," Joe remarked.

Sallie picked up a few of the papers in front of her. "I think if we just stack them neatly, it will be all right," she suggested.

"Good idea, Sallie. That's all we can do," Mandie agreed.

"But we'd better read as we stack," Joe warned. "Otherwise, we'll have to take the stack apart again."

"Let's just sit down here and look through them." Mandie plopped down in the middle of the scattered papers and picked up one issue at a time.

"I can't find the 1850 copies I spotted before the pile fell in," Joe murmured as he continued shifting papers.

"Here is one dated the week of Monday, March 4, 1850," Sallie said.

Mandie looked up. "See if you can find one for later. Ruby died May first, remember?"

"We should stack the papers as we look at them, to get them out of our way," Sallie said.

"Right!" Joe agreed.

Mandie pushed the fallen papers away from the corner. "Let's make a pile right here." She began a new stack with the paper she had just checked.

"Are y'all going to read all those dirty old newspapers?" Polly called to them, keeping her distance.

"Maybe. Don't you want to help?" Joe asked.

"No, thank you. I'm dirty enough from all the dust y'all stirred up," Polly answered, still holding her handkerchief over her nose and mouth.

As Mandie looked over at Polly, she noticed a door near where Polly was standing on the landing. "Hey, Polly!" she called. "Open that door behind you and see what's in there."

Polly quickly turned around. She looked at the door with the ceramic doorknob and shrank away from it. "No!" she cried. "It's—it's probably—dark in there, whatever it is."

Sallie jumped up. "I will open it."

As Sallie approached, Polly moved down a couple of steps, away from the door. Mandie and Joe watched across the room as Sallie tried to push the door open. When it finally gave way, there was a terrible noise from inside the room. It sounded like someone beating on things and throwing things around, and there were creepy moans among it all.

Joe and Mandie raced to Sallie's side as she stood back, afraid to enter the room.

"It's dark as pitch in there!" Joe exclaimed.

"What is all that noise? I can't see a thing," Mandie cried.

"It's probably rats," Joe decided.

"Rats do not whine like that," Sallie protested.

"Hand me that yardstick over there. I'll poke it inside," Joe told the girls.

Mandie got the yardstick and handed it to Joe. He gradually pushed the stick inside the dark room. Then getting braver, he stepped one foot inside and whacked the yardstick around, hitting something and causing a greater commotion.

Mandie, standing close behind him, jerked back. "Something cold touched my head!" she cried.

Joe backed out with her, but when he did, something touched his head also. Reaching up to fight it off, whatever it was, he realized he was banging at a chain dangling from above. He pulled hard on it, and suddenly the room was flooded with light.

Looking up, they saw an old skylight opened by the chain. At the same instant, there was a great fluttering sound and dozens of birds flew out the opening. It was just an empty room with one small, dirty, broken window.

"Pigeons!" Mandie gasped.

"What a relief!" Joe exclaimed.

"We should have recognized their sound," Sallie said.

Polly, still watching from the steps, called to them. "At least it wasn't rats."

At that moment a huge field rat ran out of the room, scurried past Polly within inches of her feet, and disappeared into a hole in the floor.

Polly screamed, grabbed up her skirts, and ran down the stairs. She ran all the way out the front door and joined Uncle Ned to wait for the others.

The other three young people laughed until their sides hurt.

"We'd really better get busy," Mandie finally managed to say. "Uncle Ned will be saying it's time to go home pretty soon."

Sallie and Joe agreed.

In a short time Mandie had located the newspaper for the week of Monday, April 29, 1850. "This is the paper for the week Ruby died," she said excitedly. Sitting in the middle of the floor, she spread the paper out as Sallie and Joe joined her.

They read the whole eight-page paper but found nothing at all about the Shaws or anyone named Hezekiah.

"Wait. We are looking at the wrong paper," Sallie told them. "If Ruby did not die until May first, it would not have been in this newspaper at all. It would be in the one for the next week."

"That's right, Sallie," Mandie said.

Joe scrambled for more papers, and in a few minutes he had located the one for the week of Monday, May 6, 1850. He laid it out on the floor before them.

The three anxiously combed the pages of the newspaper and finally found an account of Ruby's death.

Mandie read aloud with a quiver in her voice. " 'Little Miss Ruby May Shaw, nine-year-old daughter of John and Talitha Shaw, died Wednesday, May 1, evidently thrown from her pony near her father's mine. Mine workers say she was well and happy when she mounted her pony after a visit with them that day. A young Negro boy found her lying in the bushes halfway between the mine and her home. She was already dead. Her pony was grazing nearby. The town will mourn the loss of this bright, friendly little lady who knew no strangers. She was buried in the church cemetery on Thursday, May 2, across the road from her home. Today would have been her tenth birthday.' "

Mandie, Joe, and Sallie looked at each other.

"So sad!" Sallie whispered.

"Terrible!" Joe agreed in a husky voice.

Mandie wiped a tear from her eye. "I wish I could have known her," she said.

"I wonder who the Negro boy was. They don't even give his name," Joe puzzled.

"Maybe my grandfather knows," Sallie suggested.

"Let's get these newspapers stacked back up so we can leave," Mandie said.

Soon everything was back in shape. They looked around, closed the skylight in the empty room, closed that door, and hurried downstairs to find Uncle Ned.

The old Indian was sitting alone on the front step.

"Where is Polly?" Mandie asked, looking about.

"Home," Uncle Ned replied. "Her cook come down road in wagon. Polly get her pony and follow home."

Mandie breathed a sigh of relief.

"Papooses all dirty," Uncle Ned said as he stood up to survey the group. "Doctor son, too." He shook his head slowly. "Mother of Papoose not like dirt."

The three young people looked down at themselves guiltily.

Joe shrugged. "We found the newspaper with the story about Ruby's death in it. It was near the bottom of a huge pile, and when I tried to pull it out, everything caved in on top of me," he explained. "And the girls got dirty trying to help me get out."

Uncle Ned just shook his head again.

"The newspaper said a young Negro boy found Ruby lying in the bushes after her pony had thrown her," Mandie said. "Do you remember who he was?"

"No, Papoose," Uncle Ned answered. "I in Deep Creek, doing business things when Ruby die."

"Didn't anyone ever discuss it or say anything about the boy afterward?" Joe asked.

"Father of Ruby Shaw not allow it. Family, servants, not speak of it ever," the old Indian said.

"But I imagine people in town talked about it, didn't they?" Joe asked.

"Yes, there was much talk. But Father of Ruby know boy not guilty," Uncle Ned replied.

"Was the mine closed the same day that Ruby died?" Sallie asked.

"Yes. Father of Ruby say sad, bad mine," the old Indian said.

"Maybe the Hadleys would remember who the boy was," Mandie suggested. "They had the story in their newspaper. They must have known."

"No more today. Go home. Wash," Uncle Ned told them. Motioning for them to get on their ponies, he strode over to his horse and mounted.

"Will you go back to the Hadleys with us tomorrow, Uncle Ned?" Mandie begged. "Please!"

"We have to return the key to them anyway," Sallie reminded him.

"We could go with you when you return the key," Joe said.

"We see," Uncle Ned grunted.

"I hope they can remember who the boy was," Mandie said as they rode off toward home.

CHAPTER THREE

CEMETERY PATH

"Come in. Come in. Make yourselves at home," Mr. Hadley greeted the group the next morning, opening his front door wide.

"Morning," the young people chorused, following their host and Uncle Ned into the parlor.

"Thank you for key," Uncle Ned said, handing it to him.

"You are very welcome," Mr. Hadley replied. "Sit down. Sit down," he invited. "I am sorry Mrs. Hadley is a little under the weather this morning. Well, what did you find in the old newspapers?"

The three young people perched on a settee nearby.

"We thank you, Mr. Hadley, for letting us look at your old papers," Mandie said. "We found the story about Ruby's death. It said a young Negro boy found her after the accident. Do you remember who he was?"

"A young Negro boy?" Mr. Hadley repeated. He scratched his thick gray hair. "Well now, I don't believe I remember. In fact, I don't think anyone ever said who he was. He was probably just someone who happened to be passing by."

"Did the authorities investigate the accident?" Joe asked.

"I don't think so. You see, it was taken for granted that her pony had thrown her," Mr. Hadley explained. "Besides, as we told you before, her father wouldn't talk to anyone about it. Even the funeral was private."

"Do you know of anyone else who was living here when it happened, someone who is still living here in Franklin?" Mandie asked.

Mr. Hadley thought for a moment. "I don't believe I do. Most of our friends are dead now."

Sallie spoke up. "Is the funeral man still living?"

"The funeral man? Oh, the undertaker," Mr. Hadley answered. "Why, yes, I believe the current undertaker was in business back then, or at least it was the same family."

"Where is the funeral parlor?" Mandie asked.

"Right down on Main Street below our newspaper building. It's called Hudson's Undertakers," Mr. Hadley said. "I don't know whether they kept any records back then or not, but someone there might have some kind of information."

"Thank you, Mr. Hadley," Mandie replied as the young people rose to go.

"I hope Mrs. Hadley will be feeling better," Sallie said.

"We appreciate your help," Joe added.

Outside, as they mounted their ponies, Mandie spoke to Uncle Ned. "Mother won't let us go to the undertakers without an adult . . ." she began.

"It would only take a few minutes to stop by there, Uncle Ned," Joe said.

Sallie smiled as she watched her friends try to convince her grandfather to take them.

"Not this day," Uncle Ned insisted as they rode off. "Later."

When they arrived at Mandie's house, they hurried up the walkway in search of Uncle John. They found him in the library bent over a lot of papers on his desk.

"Uncle John," Mandie began as the young people gathered around him. "Uncle Ned can't go with us to the undertakers, and Mother won't let us go anywhere without an adult. Will you please take us?" she begged.

"The undertakers? What are you talking about?" Uncle John laid down his pen and straightened in the big chair.

Mandie quickly explained.

Uncle John shook his head. "I'm sorry, Amanda. I can't go anywhere today. There's a businessman coming to see me in a little while, and he'll probably be here all afternoon."

"Oh, shucks!" Mandie exclaimed.

"Why don't y'all go do something else for the time being? Go measure some of the distances on the map or something," Uncle John suggested. "But you must stay within sight of the house."

"That's a good idea," Joe said.

"I do have to get back to my work here," Uncle John said. "Maybe tomorrow I'll have time to help you."

The young people went outside and strolled across the road to the cemetery.

"Now how are we going to measure the distances? We don't have anything to measure with," Joe said as they stood at the iron gate to the cemetery.

"First, we should find the pathway next to the cemetery shown on the map because we'll have to measure from the house on down that pathway," Mandie said. "Or would you like to see Ruby's grave first?"

"Yes, let's do that. Come on," Joe said, lifting the latch to open the gate.

The girls followed him inside the walled-in cemetery, and they walked quietly among the tombstones.

"Here is Ruby's grave," Mandie said, kneeling by the broken tombstone. "You see, it's all cracked up with pieces missing. Uncle John is going to have it repaired if possible. If not, he's going to have a new one put up."

Joe pointed to a huge double monument nearby. "And here are your grandparents' graves," he said.

Mandie got up to look and then went on to the next plot. "And here are the graves of my great-grandparents," she said, stopping at the next two individual stones. "I wish my father had been buried here so I could put flowers on his grave." She looked up at Joe. "Do you ever go to the graveyard back home at Charley Gap?" Tears swam in her blue eyes.

Joe patted her hand. "I do, Mandie. Every once in a while I take flowers up there and put them on your father's grave, just like I promised."

"Thank you, Joe." Mandie cleared her throat.

"Do you not think your father would rather have been buried in the mountains he loved so much?" Sallie asked.

"I guess so." Mandie quickly changed the subject. "We need to find that path now." She started to leave, but Joe kept looking around.

"Hey, there's another gate!" he said excitedly, hurrying toward the back corner to investigate.

Mandie and Sallie caught up with him. The big iron gate was just like the one at the front.

Mandie stood on tiptoe to see over the wall to the outside. "There's a pathway outside!" she exclaimed. "We've found it." She reached up to lift the rusty latch on the gate. It wouldn't budge.

"Let me try," Joe said.

"This latch must not have been used in a long time," Sallie observed.

"I'm afraid we're going to have to get a hammer or something to knock it open," Joe finally said.

"Let's just go around," Mandie suggested.

When they assembled again on the other side of the cemetery wall, Mandie looked down the faint path that seemed to start at the back corner of the cemetery. "This path is really overgrown. I didn't even know it was here," she said.

"Well, at least we found it," Joe remarked. "Now we must decide how to measure the distances on the map."

Mandie thought for a moment. "Let's go find Abraham and see if he has anything to measure with," she suggested.

They found the old Negro gardener working among the Shaws' beautiful flower beds.

"Abraham," Mandie began, "do you have anything we can measure with?"

Abraham stopped his work and leaned on his hoe. "What y'all want to measure?" he asked.

"We're hunting for buried treasure, and we've got a map and everything," Mandie said with a twinkle in her eye. She hoped he wouldn't take her seriously. She didn't want to have to go through all the explanations again.

"And how fur might dat be?" Abraham asked.

"About a mile or so," Mandie said.

"A mile or so," the old man repeated. "De longest measure I'se got be dat rope hangin' on de fence over dere. It be one hundred foot long."

Joe went to pick it up and said, "This is just what we need, if you'll let us borrow it."

"Sho, go ahaid," the old man said.

"Thanks, Abraham. Let's start at our front porch," Mandie said, turning to lead the way. Then she stopped and turned back to the gardener. "Abraham, how long have you lived here?" she asked.

"I live here years and years, Missy," the old Negro said. His smile showed quite a few teeth missing.

"Were you living here in 1850?" Joe asked.

"In 1850? No, I guess not. My fambly moved to Noo Yawk City in 1847, when I be eight year old," the Negro said.

"But you came back sometime or other because you're here now," Mandie reminded him.

"Missy, I comes back when I be sixteen year old and go to work for yo' grandpa. Mistuh John, he be 'bout seven year old den," the old man explained.

Mandie quickly calculated the dates. "You came back about 1855 then?"

"I reckon. I don't knows, Missy. I'se born in 1839. I knows dat," the old man said.

"So you left in 1847, if you were eight years old. Did you know Mandie's grandparents before you moved to New York?" Joe asked.

"No, I'se a lil' child den. Didn't know much folks dat I kin 'member," Abraham replied. "My ma and pa die in Noo Yawk City. My uncle asks old Mistuh Shaw if he could hep me out. He kindly gives me work and a place to live back here in Franklin. Been here ever since."

"Guess we're out of luck there," Joe told Mandie.

"He couldn't have known Ruby, and he certainly wasn't here when she died." Mandie turned to walk toward the porch. "Now, to get down to business. The map says it's one mile to Hezekiah's house."

"And there are 5,280 feet in a mile, so if we stretch the rope between us, and the last one keeps moving forward, it won't take long," Joe said.

"Yes, and we can do this standing up as we walk," Mandie agreed.

The old Negro gardener wandered over to watch them stretch the rope and move forward.

They were almost even with the back gate of the cemetery when they heard Liza calling. They looked up to see her standing beside Abraham at the front gate to the house.

"Eatin' time!" the Negro girl yelled. "Eatin' time!"

"Of all times to call us to eat!" Mandie sighed.

"We'll have to remember where we stopped, or we'll have to measure it all over again," Joe said.

"How many is that?" Mandie asked.

"Five rope lengths," Sallie announced.

"Right," Joe agreed. "That's 500 feet."

"But we still have a long way to go." Mandie sighed again.

"Eatin' time," Liza called again from across the road.

"Coming!" Mandie yelled as they started back.

When they came to the house gate, Liza asked, "What y'all be doin' by dat graveyard?"

"Dey's lookin' for buried treasure, Liza," Abraham teased.

"Buried treasure? Ain't no buried treasure in dat graveyard," she replied. "Nuthin' but buried daid folks."

"You're right, Liza," Mandie agreed.

"Come on. Time to eat," the Negro girl said as she turned to go back to the house. Looking back at the three straggling young people, she added, "Like Aunt Lou say, git a move on!" She danced on across the yard.

"I'll leave the rope on the fence, Abraham," Joe said as he draped it over.

Laughing, Mandie, Sallie, and Joe turned to say good-bye to Abraham. At that moment a horse and buggy pulled up at the hitching post, and they stopped to see who it was. Liza also stopped to watch.

A huge Negro man in a fine dress suit jumped down and spoke to the gardener. "Abraham, how are you?" he asked, holding out his hand.

Abraham's eyes grew big, and he reached to put an arm around the big man. "Samuel!" he cried. "Where y'all come from? Noo Yawk City a long way off from here!"

"I came to visit my brother. He's been under the weather lately, and I thought I'd better come down and check him over," the man said, glancing at the young people.

Abraham proudly turned to the young people and said, "I wants y'all to meet my very best friend from Noo Yawk City, Mistuh Doctuh Samuel H. Plumbley."

The three stepped forward to shake hands, greeting the man.

"I'm Mandie Shaw," Mandie said, introducing her friends, as well.

"How do you do, Missy?" the doctor replied. "Pleased to make your acquaintance, all of you."

"Glad to meet you," Joe said. "My father is also a doctor."

"Is that right? Does he live here in Franklin?" the man asked.

"No, we live over in Swain County in the mountains, but he doctors people all around," Joe replied.

"I'm glad to hear that there is a physician practicing around here," the doctor said.

Aunt Lou appeared on the front porch. "You younguns git in here!" she yelled across the yard. "Food's on de table, and you keepin' it waitin.'"

Liza ran around the house to the back door to avoid Aunt Lou.

"Yes, Aunt Lou. We're coming," Mandie answered. She turned back to the doctor and said, "I'm glad to have met you, Dr. Plumbley, but we have to go eat now. Bye."

"Good-bye, Missy," the doctor replied.

The three rushed into the house, leaving Dr. Plumbley and Abraham standing in the yard.

"He sounds awfully educated," Sallie remarked.

"Yes, he does," Mandie agreed. "But then I suppose all the people in New York are educated. They have so much money up there that nobody should be poor."

"Oh, Mandie," Joe protested. "That's not so at all. Every place has its rich and its poor. You need to travel around the country and get better educated about these things."

"Just give me time, Joe Woodard!" Mandie snapped.

CHAPTER FOUR

ABRAHAM'S SECRET

"Uncle John, we met a doctor who is visiting Abraham," Mandie remarked as they all sat down to the noon meal.

"Doctor? What doctor? Is Abraham sick?" Uncle John questioned her.

"Oh, no. He's a friend of Abraham's from New York," Mandie explained.

"Yes, Abraham did live in New York years ago," Uncle John replied, passing the bowl of green beans to Joe.

"Abraham let us use his rope to measure the distances on the map," Joe said, helping himself to the beans.

"But we did not get finished," Sallie said.

"Because we had to stop and come and eat," Mandie added, reaching for a piece of hot corn bread.

"Measuring what?" Elizabeth asked.

"We've been trying to figure out some distances on the map Ruby made. And the path to Hezekiah's house, whoever he was, seems to go right next to the graveyard," Mandie explained.

"But, dear, if you don't know who this Hezekiah was or where he lived, how are you going to find his house?" Elizabeth asked.

"I don't know, but we'll find it somehow because we have to count the feet from his house to other things on the map in order to find the treasure," Mandie said.

Uncle Ned was sitting near Uncle John. "Papoose will find. Always." He smiled.

"If you say we will, then we will." Mandie grinned at the old Indian.

Joe turned to Mandie. "I was just thinking," he said. "I wonder if Abraham's doctor friend ever lived here in Franklin."

"We didn't even ask, did we? Why don't we go find out?" Mandie suggested.

"What's the man's name?" Uncle John asked, sipping his coffee.

"Abraham introduced him to us as Mister Doctor Samuel H. Plumbley," Mandie replied, laughing.

"Plumbley? I don't believe I ever knew anyone here named Plumbley," Uncle John said. "Did you, Elizabeth?"

"No, that's not a familiar name," his wife replied. "What does he look like?"

"He's a big Negro man," Mandie said, "and real friendly."

"He is an older man, but not as old as my grandfather," Sallie added.

"A Negro man?" Uncle John asked. "Uncle Ned, did you ever know a Negro doctor here in Franklin?"

Uncle Ned shook his head. "No such doctor ever here."

"Come to think of it, he has a brother in town," Joe said. "He told us his brother had been sick, and he came down from New York to check him over."

"That's right," Mandie agreed.

"We should go ask Abraham more questions," Sallie said.

John and Elizabeth looked at each other, puzzled.

"Let us know what you find out," Uncle John told the young people.

"We will," Mandie promised.

As soon as they could finish the meal, the young people asked to be excused from the table. They hurried to the front door, and looked out at the gate to see if the horse and buggy were still there.

"Oh, he's gone!" Mandie whined.

"Let's go see Abraham anyway. Maybe he knows something." Joe led the way down the front steps and around the house to the gardener's cottage.

Abraham was sitting in a rocking chair on his front porch with a cup of coffee in his hand. The young people crowded around the chair.

"Where is your doctor friend, Abraham?" Mandie asked.

"Oh, he done gone back to his brother's house," Abraham said.

"Abraham, did your doctor friend ever live in Franklin?" Joe asked.

"Samuel? Why, he sho' did—"

Instantly Abraham was bombarded by questions from all three at once.

"Whoa, there! I ain't got but one set of ears. I cain't hear but one question at a time."

Everyone laughed.

"We're sorry," Mandie apologized. "When did he live here?"

"Well now, I reckon he lived wid his grandparents out yonder in de country. Dey die and he go live wid kinfolks in Noo Yawk City," the old man explained.

"When did he leave Franklin? About what year?" Joe asked.

"Well, it's like dis here. My ma and pa, dey buy their freedom and move to Noo Yawk City to find work 'cause Samuel's kinfolks live up there and tell 'em 'bout it," Abraham began. "Den when I be 'bout thirteen year old, Samuel's grandma and grandpa dey die, and he come live wid kinfolks in Noo Yawk City near where we live."

"When were you thirteen?" Joe began figuring. "That would have been in 1852."

"In 1852!" Mandie repeated quickly. "Then he was here!"

"Yes, he would have been living here in 1850," Sallie agreed.

"Abraham, we've got to talk to him. Where does his brother live?" Mandie asked excitedly.

"His brother, he live 'bout ten mile from here," the old man said.

"Ten miles! Mandie, we can't go that far," Joe said. "Is he coming back to see you, Abraham?"

"He sho' is."

"When?" Sallie asked.

"Soon as he gits done doctorin' dat brother of his," Abraham assured them, taking a drink of his coffee.

"Do you think he might have known my grandfather?" Mandie asked.

"Yo' grandpa? Don't imagine so. I didn't know de Shaws 'til I comes back from Noo Yawk City. You see, me and Samuel, we's just younguns back den. We didn't know no grownup white folks," the old man said.

"You don't have any idea when Dr. Plumbley will be back to see you?" Mandie persisted.

"Like I done tol' you, he come back when he git done doctorin' dat brother of his," he said. "Den y'all come back and talk all you wants wid him."

"Would you please knock on the kitchen door and ask Jenny to let us know when he comes back?" Mandie asked.

Abraham shook his head quickly. "No, Missy, I don't talk to dat Jenny."

"You don't talk to Jenny?" Joe asked. "What do you mean?"

"Well, it be like dis here," the old man explained. " 'Bout forty year ago, me and dat Jenny, we gits hitched by de travelin' preacher. Den three days later I ketch her makin' eyes at dat Willie what work in de stables on Main Street, and I say to her, you gits out of my house right heah and now."

The young people listened, fascinated by his tale.

"And she got out?" Joe asked.

"She sho' did, bag and baggage," Abraham said.

"Where did she go?" Sallie asked.

"Why, Missy heah," he said, indicating Mandie, "her grandpa give Jenny a room up there on de third flo' of de big house where she been ever since."

"You mean you and Jenny have been married for forty years and haven't lived together but three days?" Mandie gasped.

"And you haven't even spoken to each other in all that time?" Joe asked.

"Dat's what I been tellin' y'all. Don't you listen to what I say?" Abraham rocked back and forth quickly in the rocking chair.

"You and Jenny must run into each other, living and working around here," Sallie said.

Abraham looked out from the porch toward his beautiful flowers. "Jenny cook fo' de big house and live there. I garden de flowers and live out heah," he replied. "Missy's grandpa, he give me dis house fo' long as I live. We don't see each other. If we does, she run quick her way, and I goes quick my way."

"But Abraham, she's your wife. You must have loved her, or you wouldn't have married her," Mandie said.

"Jes' wife accordin' to de law only," Abraham said. "She don't love me. Never did. She go cuttin' eyes at dat Willie when our weddin' wuz jes' three day old."

"Has she been makin' eyes at that Willie all this time?" Joe asked.

"Nope. Dat Willie cut his eyes on another woman. He be married since four days after we did," Abraham said.

"This all sounds like you and Jenny just had some kind of misunderstanding," Mandie said. "Maybe you misunderstood things, Abraham, or maybe she did."

"I ain't misunderstood nothin.' I seed her and she ain't misunderstood. She gits out when I say git out," the gardener replied.

"But you said Willie got married four days after y'all did. If he'd been interested in Jenny, he wouldn't have married another woman, would he?" Joe asked.

"No matter what he innerested in. Dat Jenny got innerested in him after she done married to me," he insisted.

"Abraham, the Bible says we must forgive others for any wrong they do us," Mandie reminded him.

"I knows what de Bible say. I done read it cover to cover. But I ain't never goin' to fo'give her fo' actin' like dat.

"So y'all might as well go on back to yo' measurin.' Cain't no-body change my mind," the old man said as he rose from the rocking chair.

"How will we know when your friend comes back?" Joe asked.

"You kin git dat Mistuh Jason Bond to watch out fo' him. He let you know. Now go on back to yo' measurin,' " he said, opening his front door to go inside.

"All right. I'll go ask Mr. Jason to let us know," Mandie said.

The gardener went inside the house.

"I'll go find Jason Bond and ask him. Wait here." Joe ran across the yard and through the back door of the house, then came running back a minute later. "I was lucky. He was in the kitchen. He'll watch for us. Let's go," he told the girls.

Mandie picked up a hoe leaning against the end of Abraham's porch.

"We might need this," she said.

"All right but it'll be a nuisance to carry along," Joe said, as he took the rope from the fence where they had left it.

They hurried across the road to continue measuring.

"Do you all believe Abraham told us the truth?" Sallie asked as they approached the cemetery.

Joe and Mandie stopped to look at the Indian girl.

"The truth?" Joe asked.

"About what, Jenny or the doctor?" Mandie asked.

"I think the truth is that Abraham still loves Jenny, and all these forty years he has not known how to tell her so," Sallie answered.

"I sorta thought that, too," Joe said.

"Do you think Jenny still loves him?" Mandie asked as they walked on toward the spot where they quit measuring.

"I do not know Jenny well," Sallie replied.

"I know she cooks wonderful food, and they say the way to a man's heart is through his stomach," Joe said, laughing.

"Abraham doesn't eat her cooking," Mandie reminded him. "He lives all alone in his house and does all his own housekeeping, and cooking, and everything. But if Jenny has never been interested in another man in all these years, I'd say she still loves him. I have an idea. . . ."

"No interfering with other people's quarrels!" Joe warned.

Mandie put her hands on her hips. "I'm not planning to interfere, Joe Woodard! You could at least let me finish before you jump to conclusions. I was going to suggest that we talk to Aunt Lou about Abraham and Jenny. She has been here forever, and she would know everything."

"What good would that do?" Joe asked. "We are not going to butt into other people's business!"

"There's no harm in finding out all the facts," Mandie retorted.

Sallie spoke up. "I would like to know more about it. It is too bad if two people are in love and stay apart because of anger."

"All right, you girls talk to Aunt Lou. I won't have anything to do with it. I'll just keep measuring." Joe leaned against the wall at the back corner of the cemetery. "Are you two going to help or not?"

"Of course we're going to help. You're not going to find the hidden treasure all by yourself," Mandie told him.

"This is where we stopped," Sallie said, patting the corner of the brick wall with the palm of her hand. "We had already measured five hundred feet from the porch to here, remember?"

"Yes, and we have just 4,780 feet left to make a mile," Joe replied.

"Do you still have the map in your apron pocket, Mandie?" Sallie asked.

"Yes, but it seems like that path curves around behind the cemetery. Once we get back there, we'll be out of sight of the house. Uncle John warned us to stay within sight of the house unless an adult is with us. I'll run ask my mother if Liza can come."

"Liza's not an adult! She's only a couple years older than you are," Joe reminded her.

"We've run out of adults right now," Mandie argued. "Maybe my mother will let Liza come since no adult is available. I'll be back in a minute." She ran toward the house, disappearing inside the front door.

Elizabeth, who was walking down the hallway at the time, turned to see who was coming through the front door in such a big hurry. "What's wrong?" she asked quickly.

"Nothing, Mother," Mandie said, breathless from running.

"I came to ask you if Liza could go with us on down the path behind the cemetery. We'll be out of sight of the house then, and all the grownups are busy."

"Down the path behind the cemetery?"

Mandie pulled the map out of her pocket again and showed her mother where they had been measuring to find the path to Hezekiah's house. "We've measured all the way to here, and we need to measure on down the pathway that goes behind the cemetery," she explained.

"What do you want with Liza?" Elizabeth asked.

"We just wanted her to go with us in place of an adult, so you'd let us go on with our search," Mandie said. "Please, Mother."

"Every time you get out of my sight you get into trouble, Amanda," Elizabeth replied.

"I promise I'll behave and won't get into anything bad. Please, Mother. Time is running out. We all have to go back to school next week," Mandie pleaded.

"I know that," Elizabeth replied. "Do you promise to obey Liza?" she asked. "I'll caution her to keep you in her sight."

"Yes, ma'am. I promise. I'll do whatever you say."

"All right, let's find her. I think she's in the kitchen." Elizabeth turned down the hallway.

Mandie followed. "Thank you, Mother."

Elizabeth explained to Liza that she was to go with the young people and make sure they did not get out of her sight. Liza didn't like the idea much until she found out they didn't have to go through the cemetery.

Liza stepped into the pantry and took down a large container of cookies from a nearby shelf. Opening it, Liza started rolling up some of the cookies in a dish towel.

"What are you doing?" Mandie asked.

"We's got to have some food for tea time. I'll jes' stick some of dese in dis towel and bring 'em along," Liza told her. "You go on now. I'll meet you outside in a minute."

"All right, but hurry. We'll be at the back gate."

"I'se on my way, Missy," Liza replied.

"But where is Liza? Isn't she going with us?" Sallie asked, as Mandie caught up with her and Joe.

"Here she comes," Mandie said, watching the Negro girl run out of the house, swinging the towel tied in knots to hold the cookies.

"Where we goin,' Missy?" Liza asked as she approached.

"Down this way." Mandie pointed down the dirt pathway ahead of them. "Now we have to measure how long it is, so you'll have to help us count."

"I don't know how to measure," Liza protested.

"We'll do the measuring. You just carry the hoe," Joe said.

"How much y'all gwine t' count?" Liza took the hoe.

"Four thousand, seven hundred and eighty feet," Joe replied. "But we've already got a good start."

"Lawsy mercy, dat's gwine t' take all day and all night!" Liza exclaimed. "Good I brung dese heah cookies." She patted the towel.

"Oh, good! Food!" Joe laughed. "But we have to work first."

"It goes fast, Liza," Sallie told her.

"Anyway, we have to be back in time for supper," Mandie said.

"I gits out of heppin' dat Jenny cook de supper! Ha! ha!" Liza laughed, merrily dancing around.

As they stretched the rope, Mandie asked, "Liza, what is Abraham's last name?"

"Abraham? Why, he be known as Mistuh Davis," Liza replied, looking at Mandie curiously. "Why you want to know dat, Missy?"

"Davis," Mandie repeated. "Liza, did you know that Jenny and Abraham are married—"

"Mandie!" Joe interrupted. "You're starting something!"

"No, I'm not," Mandie said, turning back to Liza. "They've been married forty years. Did you know that, Liza?"

"Lawsy mercy! No, Missy. Who say dey married?" Liza asked, her black eyes growing round in amazement. "I ain't never heerd dat."

"Abraham told us," Mandie said.

She explained the story to Liza as they began moving forward with the rope.

"Well, bust my buttons! Ain't dat a crazy tale!" Liza exclaimed. "I always wondered why dat Jenny ain't never been sweet on no man. Now I knows. She sweet on Abraham!"

"Do you think so, Liza?" Sallie asked.

"I knows so," Liza said. "I ain't never seed dat woman even look at another man in my life, and I'se almos' fifteen years old."

"Are you sure, Liza?" Mandie asked.

"I knows everything dat woman does. She cook, wash dishes, eat, and sleep. She don't go nowheres, not even to church wid de rest of us. And she save ebry bit o' dat money what yo' uncle pay her to work."

"Does Abraham go to church with y'all?" Mandie asked.

"He sho' do, every Sunday, and sometimes fo' prayer meetin,' " Liza replied.

"Then that's why she won't go—because he does," Mandie said.

"Oh, come on, Mandie. Pay attention to the measuring, or we'll never get done," Joe said.

The narrow path wound through bushes and weeds. It was hard work but they continued on. After measuring four thousand feet they rounded a bend and came to a dead end. The trees and bushes before them were so thick that there was no sign of the path continuing.

Mandie looked around. "Don't tell me this is the end!"

"I can't see any more of a path," Joe said.

"Remember, it has been about fifty years since Ruby made that map. Trees and bushes grow big in that length of time. They may have completely covered the path," Sallie reminded them.

Liza plopped down on a nearby log. "Lawsy mercy, Missy!" she exclaimed. "I'se tired. Ain't y'all? Let's jes' git a lil' rest and have our tea time." She unrolled the towel.

The others joined her on the log and sat munching on the cookies Liza had brought.

"What are we gwine t' do after we runs out of cookies?" Liza asked.

"We're going to have to search the woods all around here to find the path," Joe replied.

"And it's going to be an awful job trying to measure through all that stuff growing around here," Mandie added.

"We can do it," Sallie said confidently.

But Mandie was not so sure about that.

CHAPTER FIVE

FINE FOOD SINCE 1852

As soon as the last cookie crumb was swallowed, the young people were ready to continue their search for the rest of the path.

"Sallie, you know more about this kind of thing than we do. Tell us how to go about finding the rest of the path," Mandie asked her friend.

"If there is any more of it," Joe added.

"Yes, there was more at one time," Sallie said, peering through the bushes. "You see the shortest, youngest trees and bushes there? Those have grown up since the other ones that were already along the side of the path."

"I see what you mean. If the path was not used, and trees and things grew up in the middle of it, they would all be smaller and newer than the others," Mandie said.

Joe was poking among the bushes, bending things this way and that in order to look about underneath.

"I see a lot of small rocks and gravel under this bush," Joe said, bending things out of his way.

Sallie came to look. "You are right. That is part of the path."

Joe began beating the bushes with the hoe to clear the path.

"Y'all gwine t'walk through all dat stuff?" Liza asked, watching Joe.

"We have to follow the old pathway, or road, whatever it was," Mandie told her.

"I ain't so sho' I'm gwine t' follow y'all," Liza replied.

Joe was several feet into the bushes when he called to them. "Hey, this goes into a clearing. Come on."

Sallie immediately followed him, but Liza stayed back.

Mandie turned to her. "Come on, Liza," she said.

"Y'all go ahaid. I'll jes' wait here fo' you," the Negro girl replied.

"No, you have to go with us," Mandie said. Stepping back to take the girl's hand, she pulled her forward. "You promised my mother you would stay with us. Remember, you got out of helping Jenny cook supper by coming with us."

"But I didn't bargain for no wilderness like dat," Liza protested, trying to pull her hand free.

"If you don't come with us, Liza, we'll all have to go home. Please come," Mandie pleaded.

Sallie stepped back out of the bushes. "Come on, Liza. Look, Joe has already made a path through there. You can see through to the clearing on the other side. Come on." She bent the remaining bushes back so Liza could see.

Liza peered ahead and finally allowed Mandie to hold her hand. Mandie slowly urged her forward. As they got to the middle of the broken-down bushes, a playful squirrel romped through underfoot. Liza screamed and rushed forward to where Joe was standing in the clearing.

"What happened?" Joe asked the girls.

"Nothing. A squirrel ran through and brushed against our legs," Mandie explained.

Liza held her sides in fright. "Dat wudn't no squirrel. Dat be a snake."

"No, Liza. I saw it," Sallie said. "It was a squirrel."

"Let's git goin' befo' it come back," Liza said, walking forward down the open pathway. "I ain't used to no sech things. I stay home where I belongs. I don't go trampin' 'round de world like y'all does."

"I'm sorry," Mandie said, catching up with the girl.

"You jes' go yo' way. I'se stayin' up here next to de doctuh son. He protect me."

"Wait a minute," Joe said. "We've got to measure the distance through the bushes I chopped down."

They backtracked enough to add the distance to their calculated total while Liza, shivering with fright, stood in the opening, waiting.

All of a sudden something white came bouncing out of the bushes and rubbed around Liza's ankles. She screamed, and the others came running.

"Snowball! Where did you come from?" Mandie rushed forward to grab her kitten. "Look, Liza, it's only Snowball. Look."

The Negro girl finally hushed and opened her eyes. She stared at the white kitten. "You mean dat Snowball come runnin' over my feet?" Liza asked shakily.

"That's right. Here he is," Mandie said, rubbing the kitten's fur.

"How he git here?"

"I don't know. He must have been following us all the way here," Mandie replied. "Do you want to carry him for me?"

Liza took the kitten and cuddled him in her arms. "Snowball, you bad kitten, scaring lil' ol' Liza like dat," she scolded.

Snowball purred and reached up to lick her throat.

"That cat!" Joe said, exasperated.

"Joe, you know he always goes with me everywhere," Mandie said. "This time I left him in the house because I didn't want to have to stop measuring to go find him when he decided to run off."

"He got out somehow," Joe said. "Maybe he'll keep Liza entertained so she'll quit that screaming every time we turn around."

Sallie looked ahead. "It looks like the path goes on out of sight without anything else blocking it."

"Let's work fast while the path is clear," Mandie said, as they moved forward with the rope stretched between them.

They walked on quickly down the path without finding any more obstructions. Then suddenly they came to the end of it.

"The path ends up at that main road ahead. Look!" Joe quickened his strides.

In seconds they all stood on the main road.

"Look!" Mandie pointed to a big house directly in front of them across the main road.

"How many feet have we gone now?" Sallie asked.

"A little more than 5000 feet," Joe calculated.

"Then that must be Hezekiah's house," Mandie cried. "Come on. Let's go over there!"

They ran across the road and stopped at the edge to look at the house. There was a sign across the front door: Fine Food Since 1852.

"A restaurant!" Mandie exclaimed.

"Probably a boardinghouse," Joe said.

"It has been in business since two years after Ruby died," Sallie noted.

"Don't look like no bidness to me. Look like somebody's house," Liza muttered, holding Snowball tightly.

"Let's go knock on the door," Mandie suggested.

They walked up the long front yard, and as they approached the porch, two people came out the door.

As the door swung open, Joe peeked inside. "Looks like a store inside to me. I don't think we should knock. You don't knock on a store door. You just go in," he said, pushing the door inward.

The girls followed close behind. The inside did look like a variety store, but there was also the strong, wonderful aroma of food cooking.

"Food!" Joe whispered.

The girls smiled at him.

Behind a counter stood a short, fat, bald-headed man, and Joe led the way toward him.

"How do you do, sir?" Joe began, introducing himself and the others, including Snowball.

The man looked up and smiled. "What can I do for y'all?"

"We're looking for a house where a man named Hezekiah lived about fifty years ago," Mandie said.

"Fifty years ago? Hezekiah?" the man asked in amazement.

"Yes, sir. How long have you lived here?" Joe asked.

"We've been here about thirty-five years," the man said.

"Thirty-five years," Sallie repeated, a little disappointed.

"Do you know who lived here before you?" Mandie asked.

"Nobody. We built this here house ourselves," the man replied.

"But your sign says Fine Food Since 1852," Sallie objected. "That would be forty-eight years ago."

"Oh, that's because the other owners didn't have much of a house. The roof fell in when a heavy snow came one winter. They sold it to us and we built a new house," the man explained.

"And they owned a store and a restaurant, too?" Joe asked.

"This here is a boardinghouse, young fella, and a store," the man replied. "That's what they had, too, so we just kept their sign to put on our door."

"Do you know who the other people were?" Mandie asked.

"No, don't recollect who they was," the man said. "You see, it was my grandpa that bought it from them, and he handed it down to my pa, and he gave it to me, and they're all dead now."

"Do you remember anyone having the name Hezekiah, or ever hearing anyone mention the name?" Joe asked.

"Don't believe I do. Only thing I remember for sure was that these other owners had built their house on the site where an old house had burned down many years ago," the man told them.

"Has there ever been any other house near here?" Mandie asked.

"Not that I can remember," the man said. "Where you younguns from? Are you looking for long-lost relatives or something?"

Mandie and Joe looked at each other. It wouldn't do to let anyone know there was supposed to be buried treasure somewhere near here.

"I live in town with my Uncle John Shaw and my mother," Mandie replied. "We were just walking around and thought we'd see if we could find some old property of some of their friends from long ago."

"Oh, yes, I know John Shaw when I see him. Sorry I can't help you." He shook his head. "I've got to go in the back now and see how the cooking is coming along for supper," he said, starting to leave.

"That's all right, sir," Joe said. "But I don't believe I got your name."

The man stopped. "Name's Jud Jenkinson. Y'all come back."

The young people turned and went out the front door. Once outside, they stopped to talk in the yard.

"This has got to be Hezekiah's house, or where it used to be," Mandie said. "I just know it is."

"It probably is," Sallie agreed.

"I don't know." Joe looked skeptical.

"Well, y'all hurry and decide whose house it be, so's we kin go home. Must be time to eat," Liza said, cuddling Snowball in her arms.

"You're right, Liza. It must be nearing suppertime," Mandie said. "Do y'all think we have time to measure the other distances from here?" She pulled the map out of her pocket. "It says it's 936 feet to a rock pile, but that's in a different direction from the way we came."

"I think we'd better head home," Joe said. "If we're late for supper, your mother may not let us go out again tomorrow."

"Besides, that doctor friend of Abraham's was supposed to come back," Sallie reminded them.

Mandie gasped. "Oh, I forgot all about him! Let's hurry! He may be there by now."

" 'Bout time to hurry home, ain't it, Snowball?" Liza grumbled, holding the kitten tightly.

When they got back to the house, Jason Bond, the caretaker, was sitting on the front porch waiting for them. "Where in tarnation have y'all been?" he asked. "You tell me to let you know when that doctor comes back to Abraham's house, and then you go off and don't even let me know where you are. And everybody else is gone off, too."

"Mr. Jason, I'm sorry. Has the doctor been back to see Abraham?" Mandie asked.

"Yep. Been and gone," the caretaker told her.

"Gone? Oh, shucks!" Mandie cried.

"Well, we can't be in two places at one time," Joe said.

"And he might not know anything anyway," Sallie added.

"Has dat Jenny got supper cooked wid out me?" Liza asked.

"I believe so. Everything is waiting for Mr. and Mrs. Shaw and Uncle Ned to come back," Jason Bond replied.

"In dat case, I'll jes' go on in," Liza said. Opening the screen door, she took Snowball with her inside the house.

"Where has everybody gone?" Mandie asked.

"I don't rightly know, Missy. Said they'd be back in time for supper," the caretaker replied. "I reckon they'll be here any minute now."

Aunt Lou appeared in the doorway and stood listening to the conversation.

"Let's go ask Abraham if Dr. Plumbley has left town or if he's coming back," Mandie said.

"Yes, he might be back," Sallie said.

"Come on." Joe led the way down the front steps.

"Don't go nowhere now," Aunt Lou called to them as they hurried around the house. "Git in here and git washed up for suppuh."

Ignoring Aunt Lou, they found Abraham on the front porch again, rocking and drinking coffee.

"Here's your rope and your hoe," Joe said, laying them on the end of the porch.

"Done missed him," Abraham said as they walked up the steps.

"I know. Mr. Bond told us," Mandie said. "Is he coming back again?"

"Maybe tomorruh or de next day," Abraham replied. "He has to doctor his brother. He be good and sick."

"I'm glad Dr. Plumbley's coming back, but I'm sorry his brother is so sick," Mandie said.

"Tomorrow or the next day," Joe repeated. "You know what tomorrow and the next day are, don't you, Mandie? Tomorrow is Sunday and the next day is Monday. Sallie and I both have to leave on Monday to go back to school."

"Maybe he'll come back tomorrow," Mandie said.

"We need to spend the day tomorrow measuring off the other distances on the map to see if we can find anything else," Sallie said.

"Ain't y'all got nuthin' to do but go 'round measurin' things?" Abraham asked. "Y'all ain't even stayin' home long 'nuff to have comp'ny."

"Company?" Mandie asked. "We're not expecting any company. All our company has left except Uncle Ned, Joe, and Sallie."

"Dat lil' girl what live next do,' she been over heah two time dis afternoon lookin' fo' y'all," the gardener said.

"You mean Polly?" Joe asked.

"Dat her," Abraham replied. "I heah her come over two times and aks Aunt Lou where you at."

Mandie sighed. "Aunt Lou didn't know where we were. But, anyway, I guess Polly will come back later."

"I think we had better go get washed up before your mother gets home, Mandie," Sallie warned.

"Abraham, just in case your doctor friend happens to come back tonight unexpectedly, will you please come and let us know?" Mandie asked.

"He won't be back tonight. Too far," Abraham replied. "But I let you know when he do come back."

The young people went through the back door of the house. As they entered the long hallway inside, the kitchen door was open, and they could see Jenny stirring pots and moving about, getting the meal ready.

"Let's go through the kitchen," Mandie said, quickly entering the room.

"Something smells good!" Joe exclaimed. He tried to look into the pots on the big iron cookstove.

"Outta dem pots, boy!" Jenny scolded. "Ain't done yet nohow!"

"Oh, Jenny, can't I even look?" Joe teased.

"Nope," Jenny said, shaking a spoon at him. "Git!"

"All right, we'll git . . . Mrs. Davis," Mandie said slyly.

Jenny dropped the spoon she was holding and turned to look at Mandie. "You talkin' to me, Missy?" She picked up the spoon, took it to the sink, and rinsed it off.

"You are Mrs. Davis, aren't you?" Mandie replied.

Joe stood by, tightening his lips.

"What you talkin' 'bout, Missy? My name Jenny," the Negro woman said.

"I know. Your name is Jenny Davis," Mandie said. "Abraham told us."

"Who dis Abraham?" Jenny turned back to the stove.

"Jenny," Mandie chided, "we know Abraham, the gardener, is your husband. Why won't you go back and live with him? You do still love him, don't you?"

Jenny stood there, speechless.

"Mandie, I think we had better hurry and wash up," Sallie prodded.

"Yes, let's go," Joe said, walking toward the door.

Mandie stepped up close to Jenny. "Abraham still loves you," she whispered quickly.

Jenny's eyes filled with tears, and she dropped the spoon down into the big pot.

In the hallway Joe waited for Mandie. "You shouldn't go messing in other people's business, Mandie," he scolded.

Mandie smiled. "I'm not messing in anybody's business. I'm just trying to fix things up a little."

"I know about your kind of fixing up," Joe replied. He bounded up the stairs ahead of the girls to clean up.

"Do you think Abraham and Jenny will ever get back together again?" Sallie asked as they walked slowly to Mandie's room.

"If I can figure out how to finagle things around, they will." Mandie laughed. As she walked by the full-length mirror in the corner of the room, she shrieked. "Oh, I have to change dresses. I'm filthy!" she cried.

"So am I. We had better hurry," Sallie said.

They quickly washed up and changed clothes and were back downstairs shortly after Joe came down and the adults returned.

At the supper table the young people told the adults about their afternoon measuring.

"We found a house that I know must have been Hezekiah's," Mandie said.

"You mean it may be where Hezekiah's house might have been," Joe corrected her.

"Where is this?" Uncle John asked, looking up from the ham he was slicing.

"It's down on a main road about a mile from here," Mandie replied. "We traced an old dirt path by the cemetery down to this road, and there was the house. A man named Jud Jenkinson owns it, and he said he knows you, Uncle John."

"Jud Jenkinson? Yes, he owns a boardinghouse. Is that the house you're talking about?" Uncle John asked.

Mandie nodded, then proceeded to tell her uncle about the 1852 sign and the previous house.

Uncle Ned looked up. "House burn down," he said. "Old people die."

"You remember it, Uncle Ned?" Mandie asked excitedly. "Who were the people? Was one of them named Hezekiah?"

Uncle Ned shook his head. "No remember name," he said. "Old man, old woman. Die."

"Probably Hezekiah is dead. That is why we cannot find anyone who knew him," Sallie said.

"Does Mr. Jenkinson not know who lived there before his family, dear?" Elizabeth asked.

"No. He said his grandfather bought the place from the previous owners, and then his father owned it, and now he owns it. All the others are dead," Mandie said, biting into a hot buttered biscuit.

"What are you all planning to do next?" Uncle John asked, passing the sliced ham. "Are you going to keep on looking for clues on the map?"

"We thought we'd go back to that house and then measure off the 936 feet to the rock pile if we can find it. And then on to the other places Ruby put on the map," Mandie replied.

"You know you will have to take someone with you again, Amanda, if you're going that far away," Elizabeth reminded her.

"Not Liza, please," Joe muttered under his breath.

"Tomorrow is Sunday, so we'll all go to church in the morning," Uncle John said. "Then after the noon meal, you young people can get back to your prospecting."

"On Sunday, John?" Elizabeth asked. "They should stay home and respect the Lord's Day."

"I don't think this once will hurt. They have to go back to school next week, and I do believe they have been exceptionally well-behaved lately," Uncle John said, winking at Mandie.

"Just this one time," Elizabeth conceded.

"Thank you," the young people said.

Mandie smiled at Uncle John. "Who is going with us?" she asked.

"We are having Mr. and Mrs. Turner over tomorrow afternoon, dear, so I suppose you'll have to take Liza with you again," Elizabeth told her.

"Liza!" Joe exclaimed.

"Well, I guess she'll do if nobody else can go." Mandie sighed.

"What do you mean by that, Amanda?" Uncle John asked.

"She's afraid of everything. Snowball found us somehow and nearly scared the daylights out of her," Mandie said, laughing.

Liza had stepped into the room and stood by the door, listening. She danced up to the table with a platter of hot biscuits. "Dat's right,

Missy," she said. "Dat white kitten skeered me good. I ain't goin' no place like dat wilderness no mo.' No, I ain't!"

"Liza, Mother just said you'd go with us tomorrow so we can keep on with our search," Mandie told the girl.

Liza picked up the empty platter from the table and replaced it with the one of hot biscuits. She glared at Mandie. "I'd druther stay heah and hep Jenny cook."

"Liza, we have to have somebody go with us, and you're the only one not busy," Mandie said.

"Not busy? I stays busy all de time. I does," Liza insisted.

"If you would rather stay here and serve tea tomorrow afternoon for our guests, that will be all right, Liza. The Turners are coming," Elizabeth told her.

Liza's eyes grew wide. "De Turners? You say de Turners is comin'? No, ma'am. I go wid Missy," she said, quickly leaving the room.

Joe laughed. "What's wrong with the Turners?"

"The last time they were here, Liza accidentally spilled a cup of tea, and it splashed on Mrs. Turner's dress," Elizabeth explained with an amused look on her face. "Mrs. Turner naturally was quite upset, and she yelled at Liza. Now Liza is afraid of the woman."

"For our sakes, I'm glad she is," Mandie teased.

"So we will continue our search tomorrow after church, and Liza will go with us," Sallie summed it all up.

"Yes, and we're going to have to hurry. Time's running out," Joe warned.

CHAPTER SIX

THE OLD HOUSE ON THE ROCK PILE

As soon as the young people could finish eating their noon meal after church services the next day, they took Liza with them and went to Abraham's house in the backyard. He was inside having his own meal, and they had to knock. Joe picked up the rope and the hoe still on the porch.

Abraham opened the door. "I'se eatin' my dinnuh now. What y'all wants?" he asked.

"We want to tell you we're going back down that dirt path behind the cemetery to measure some more. If your doctor friend comes while we're gone, would you please tell him we want to see him?" Mandie asked.

"Measurin' on Sunday? Dis de Lawd's day. Y'all s'posed to sit and read de good book," Abraham reproved them.

"We know that, Abraham, but Mr. and Mrs. Shaw made this one exception for today because we have to leave tomorrow to go back to school," Joe explained.

"Measurin'! Cain't find nuthin' else to do?" the old gardener grumbled. "I'll tell Samuel, but if he's in a hurry, he won't wait fo' you to come back."

"Thanks, Abraham," Mandie said. "We'll hurry."

"Git on yo' way. I'se got to finish my dinnuh," Abraham told them, closing the door.

"For goodness sakes, does Abraham never get in a good mood? He's always fussing," Joe mumbled.

"If you'd lost your wife a few days after you were married and you had to live alone when she lived right next door, you'd be fussy, too," Mandie remarked.

They headed out the front gate.

"I'd have better sense than to lose her in the first place," Joe said. "There's just no excuse for them to live apart."

"Maybe it's bettuh to live apart than to live together and fuss," Liza said, picking up Snowball who was following.

"Maybe, Liza, but how do we know they would fuss at each other if they lived together, anyway?" Mandie asked.

"I don't know about them, but when I marry you, Mandie, we are not going to ever fuss," Joe stated firmly.

"It is a long time until you grow up," Sallie said. "Everything may change by then. You may not want to marry each other. I do not think I would like to plan so far ahead."

Mandie blushed slightly.

"Right now we need to hurry and find this hidden treasure before we all have to go back to school," she reminded them.

The four of them hurried down the dirt path to its end at the main road.

"It didn't take long dis time, did it?" Liza said as they stood looking across the road at Mr. Jenkinson's boardinghouse.

"That's because we didn't have to worry about measuring and counting and digging out paths to get through," Mandie replied. She pulled the map out of her apron pocket and unfolded it.

"Y'all ain't plannin' on goin' into no mo' wilderness, are you?" the Negro girl asked.

"That depends," Joe replied, looking at the map over Mandie's shoulder. "You see, we have to find a rock pile that is 936 feet from here."

"A rock pile? Lawsy mercy, what in dis world you want wid a rock pile?" Liza asked.

"We don't really want the rock pile, Liza. We just have to find it and then measure 572 feet from it to find a persimmon tree," Mandie explained.

" 'Simmon tree?" Liza questioned. "You ain't plannin' on eatin' no 'simmons, are you? Dey taste sumpin' awful."

Sallie smiled. "We know, Liza, but we are not going to eat any."

Joe looked at the map again. "And from the persimmon tree we have to measure 333 feet to a rhododendron bush," he said.

"Now, what fo' y'all has to measure to find a 'dendrum bush when there's piles of 'em growin' in de yard at home?" Liza asked, puzzled.

"But this one is special," Mandie said. "There's something special about it that we have to find out."

"Special? Humph! I s'pose it blooms green or sumpin.' "

Joe glanced up from the map, looking back the way they had come. "Do you see what I see?" he asked.

Everyone turned to look. Darting in and out of the bushes, Snowball bounced along, trying to catch up with them.

"Dat white kitten! Y'all went off and left it. De po' lil' thing done walked all dis way," Liza said. She ran to pick him up. "Come here, you po' lil' tired kitten. I'se gwine t' carry you de rest o' de way, I is."

Snowball curled up in Liza's arms and purred.

"I know I shut him up in the kitchen." Mandie sighed.

"That's not a good place to leave him. So many people go in and out of the kitchen, he's sure to get out," Joe said.

"He wants to go everywhere you do, Mandie," Sallie observed.

"I wish he had stayed home this time," Mandie said. "Liza, if you get tired of carrying Snowball, I'll take him. I don't think we'd better let him down. He may get lost."

"I carries dis po' lil' kitten. He be tired," Liza said. "Y'all jes' git on wid yo' measurin' rock piles and 'simmon trees and such. I'll take care o' Snowball."

"Thank you, Liza. I'm sure Snowball appreciates it," Mandie said.

Joe studied the map again. "If that's the place where Hezekiah's house used to be—across the road there—then according to the map, when we turn around, we should angle back to our right to find the rock pile," he concluded.

"But the path to Hezekiah's house on the map doesn't show a big road like this one. It must have been made since then," Mandie said.

"Even if the road was not there, the rock pile should be back in the direction Joe says," Sallie agreed.

"We do have to measure from that house though," Mandie said.

"And measure across the road backtracking to the right," Joe explained.

"The road is about fifty feet wide, and it's about fifty feet from the road to the house, so that's one hundred feet to here," Joe said, indicating the edge of the road.

"At least it's clear land for a while," Mandie said as the group surveyed the area ahead.

"So now we go 836 feet to the rock pile," Sallie said.

"Here we go," Joe said. He started off at an angle to their right. The girls helped stretch the rope between the three of them. Liza followed.

"Where we gwine now?" Liza asked.

"We're aiming right straight to those woods down yonder." Mandie pointed.

"Woods? I ain't gwine through no briary woods," Liza grumbled, holding Snowball closely.

"Remember, Liza, you have to go with us wherever we go. We can't leave you standing here, and my mother told you not to let us out of your sight," Mandie reminded her. "Of course if you'd rather go home and serve tea to the Turners—"

"I ain't gwine home," Liza interrupted. "I go wid you."

As Joe led the way, the girls counted aloud in unison. It was about five hundred feet to the woods, and there they had trouble.

"There are so many trees here, Joe, how can we measure in a straight line?" Mandie asked.

They all just stood there, staring at the thick woods in front of them.

"We'll just have to step around the trees and hope we figure right," Joe said.

"We only have about 336 feet more before we get to the rock pile," Mandie reminded them, "so maybe it won't take long to get through these trees."

"Chiggers! Dat's what y'all gwine to git," Liza muttered.

"We'll have to take that chance," Joe told the Negro girl. "Let's go."

Liza followed along, carefully holding her long skirts against her with one hand and clutching Snowball with the other.

When they finally came into a clearing, they stood there for a moment, looking around.

"It was 300 feet through the woods. That leaves about 36 feet to the rock pile," Mandie calculated. "We'll have to guess at 36 feet because the rope is one hundred feet long. 36 feet would be a tiny bit more than one-third of the rope."

"Does anybody see a rock pile?" Joe asked.

They all looked about. There was an old house across the clearing, but they couldn't see a rock pile.

"I wonder if anyone lives in that house over yonder," Sallie said.

"If someone does, I hope we're not on their property," Joe replied.

As they walked on, they kept looking for a rock pile, but there was nothing but dirt and weeds.

They were within fifty feet of the old house when Mandie suddenly stopped and pointed. "The house!" she exclaimed. "It's sitting on a rock pile!"

"Do you think this is the rock pile on the map?" Sallie asked as they walked around the house.

"It's the only one I can see anywhere," Joe said.

"I wonder why someone would build a house on a rock pile," Mandie said.

"Gotta have sumpin' fo' de house to sit on," Liza remarked. She held on to Snowball and followed the others.

"It is rock all the way around," Mandie noted as they came back to the front.

"We should knock on the door and see if anyone lives here," Sallie suggested.

"It looks empty, but I'll go see," Joe offered. As he put his foot on the first step to the front porch, a shot rang out above their heads.

A gruff voice yelled from inside the house. "That's fur 'nuff! Don't come no further! Whadda you want?"

Joe jumped backward.

Mandie reached to join hands with him and Liza as Joe grabbed Sallie's hand. Quickly, Mandie whispered, "What time I am afraid, I will put my trust in Thee."

They were all afraid to move. Their hearts pounded. Liza squeezed Snowball so hard he pushed his claws into her dress in fright.

The man inside the house yelled again. "I said whadda you want?"

"We're looking for a rock pile," Joe began.

"Rock pile?" the man yelled back.

The front door creaked noisily open. A dirty, bearded man stood there pointing a rifle at the young people. "What're you talkin' 'bout? A rock pile?" He looked from one to another. For some reason he singled out Liza in the group. "You there, what are y'all after?" he asked.

"Why, we's jes' after a rock pile, a 'simmon tree, and a . . . a . . . dendrum bush," Liza told him in a trembling voice. She tried to hide behind Mandie.

"What kind of dad-blame nonsense is that? I wanta know," he yelled.

"We were just measuring some distances and—"

"Measuring distances for what?" the old man interrupted, still pointing the rifle at them.

"We were just wondering how far it is from here to my house," Mandie spoke up.

"And where's your house at?" the man asked, spitting tobacco juice out into the yard near them.

Liza whispered in Mandie's ear. "Nasty, ain't he?"

Mandie jerked on her hand to shut her up. "My house is my Uncle John Shaw's house in Franklin right over that way," she told the man, waving her hand to the left.

"John Shaw, huh? He your uncle you say?"

"He was my father's brother," Mandie explained.

"I know all about them Shaws. What are you doin' this fur from home?" the man asked.

"We were just measuring to see how far we had come," Mandie replied.

"Well, you kin jest measure right off this here land. I'm stakin' a claim to it," the old man persisted, shaking his rifle at them. "John Shaw's got 'nuff. He ain't gittin' this here land."

"You mean nobody lives here?" Joe asked.

"Jes' me," the old man said. "Me and my rifle."

"Is your name Hezekiah by any chance?" Sallie spoke up.

"Who? Hezekiah? No, by granny's, it ain't Hezekiah," the man said.

"Did you ever know anyone living around here named Hezekiah?" Mandie asked.

"No, I ain't never knowed no Hezekiah. Now git off my land, all of you, 'fore you wish you had," the man warned.

"Yes, sir. We'll go," Joe said, turning to leave. Then he looked back. "You didn't tell us your name."

"My name ain't none of your bizness," the old man yelled.

"Do you know if there are any persimmon trees growing around here?" Mandie asked.

"Persimmon trees? What would I know about persimmon trees? But I'll tell you right now. Anything growin' 'round here belongs to me. Don't let me catch you puttin' your hands on it," the old man said. "Now are you goin,' or you want me to force you off?"

"We're going," the young people all said at once. Hurrying away from the house, they ran on toward the woods, glancing over their shoulders to see if the man was following. Once inside the protection of the woods, they dropped to the ground, out of breath.

"Whew! That could have been dangerous." Joe gasped for air.

"Yes, that man is not just right, is he?" Sallie asked.

"He sure scared me," Mandie said.

"Dat man got lots of screws loose," Liza exclaimed.

Snowball left Liza's lap to crawl over to Mandie's.

Mandie took him in her arms and squeezed him. "Snowball, you'll have to stay with Liza a little longer," she said. Handing him to the Negro girl, she stood up.

Liza petted Snowball. "We ain't found no 'simmon tree yet," she complained.

"No, we still have to look for it. I'm afraid to go back toward that old man's house, so we'll have to estimate how far we've come," Mandie said.

"I'd guess we're about a hundred feet away," Joe calculated. "So if his house is where the rock pile is on the map, we should find a persimmon tree over that way about 472 feet," he said, pointing.

"We'd bettuh hurry up and git dis thing done, whatever we's doin,'" Liza said. "I don't like all dese woods."

"Let's measure from here," Joe said. "It probably won't be exactly right, but I think we'll be pretty close."

When they had measured the 472 feet, they looked all around. There was not a single persimmon tree in sight. They walked around in circles, through trees and bushes and could not find even one.

"No persimmon tree of any kind anywhere?" Mandie moaned.

"We might not be in the right spot," Joe suggested.

"Persimmon trees do not live forever," Sallie reminded them. "The persimmon tree on the map might have died or been cut down."

"Dat's right. Somebody might not like 'simmons and dey jes' cut de tree down to git rid of it," Liza added.

"Should we look for the rhododendron bush?" Mandie asked. She looked at the map. "It says here the rhododendron bush is 333 feet from the persimmon tree."

"That's not so far. Maybe if we measured 333 feet in every direction from right about here, we could find the rhododendron bush," Joe suggested.

The others agreed, but after measuring 333 feet in several directions, they could not find a rhododendron bush. Then suddenly they found themselves in dozens of rhododendron bushes. Exasperated, they looked all around them.

"We only want one rhododendron bush!" Mandie exclaimed.

"But we have dozens of them," Sallie said.

"Take dat one over there. It looks like a good one. Want me to hep you dig it up?" Liza asked, pointing to a large bush.

"No thanks. You don't exactly understand what we're doing, and it's too hard to explain," Joe told the girl.

"I do not believe any of these rhododendron bushes could be fifty years old," Sallie told them as she looked about.

"I have no idea how long they live, but you're probably right," Mandie agreed.

"Looks like we've lost out," Joe remarked.

"I'm not giving up," Mandie protested. "We'll find the hidden treasure somewhere."

"Hidden treasure?" Liza exclaimed. "Is dat what y'all been huntin' all dis time? Hidden treasure?"

Mandie and Joe exchanged glances.

"We're not sure what we're looking for," Joe told her.

"Whatever it be, it must be hid good," Liza said.

"Do you think we should go back to the house? Abraham's friend might be back by now," Sallie said.

Mandie sighed. "I hate to quit now. We don't have much time left."

"We can come back as soon as we check with Abraham," Joe suggested. "It's not all that far now that we've measured the distance and know the way."

"Reckon dem Turners done left by now?" Liza spoke up.

Everyone laughed.

"They probably have," Mandie assured her.

"Let's head back," Joe urged. He led the way, and Sallie followed right behind, but Mandie walked along by Liza.

As they made their way back down the dirt pathway, Liza pulled at Mandie's skirt. "Missy," she whispered, "sumpin' I fo'git to tell you."

Mandie frowned. "What is it, Liza?"

"Dat Missy Polly, she done been back to yo' house dis mawnin' wantin' to know what y'all doin.' She wants to go wid you wherever."

"Why didn't you tell me then?" Mandie asked.

Liza smiled. "Oh, Missy, you know why I don't tell." She lowered her voice. "Dat Missy Polly, she jes' wanta be 'round de doctuh son, dat's what she want. I tries hard to keep her 'way from de doctuh son fo' you."

Mandie laughed. Joe and Sallie turned to see what she was laughing at.

"What's going on back there?" Joe called back.

"Nothing really," Mandie replied. "Just something funny Liza told me."

As everyone trudged on, Liza bent to whisper to Mandie. "Ain't nuthin' funny. It serious."

Mandie smiled and said, "Thanks for telling me, Liza. I'll watch out."

CHAPTER SEVEN

WHO WAS HEZEKIAH?

As soon as they came within sight of the cemetery, Liza raced ahead. She didn't like being near that place. When the others came around the corner of the cemetery, they spied a horse and buggy standing at the hitching post in front of the house.

"Dr. Plumbley is at Abraham's!" Mandie exclaimed.

Joe and Sallie raced after her around the house to Abraham's little cottage. Liza, not knowing what it was all about, decided to follow. Holding on to Snowball, she caught up with them. Abraham and Dr. Plumbley were sitting and rocking on the front porch.

Mandie sat on the steps in front of the two men. "Dr. Plumbley . . ." she said, out of breath, "I'm so glad . . . we caught . . . you . . . before you left this time."

Dr. Plumbley smiled. "I believe you all have been running," he said.

They nodded, and Sallie joined Mandie on the steps. Joe put the rope and the hoe on the end of the porch and sat beside the girls.

Liza looked around. "Don't see no Turners nowhere," she muttered. "Must be gone. Snowball, we go see." She took the kitten and headed for the Shaws' house.

Mandie looked up at the big Negro doctor. "Dr. Plumbley," she began again, breathing a little easier, "Abraham said you used to live here in Franklin."

"Sure did, many years ago. I was born in Franklin and lived here with my grandparents until they died," the doctor replied. "I was twelve years old then, and I had to go to New York and live with relatives. My brother, Elijah, was luckier. Some friends here in Franklin took him into their home. He was only nine years old."

The young people looked at each other.

"What year did you leave Franklin?" Joe asked.

"I remember that very well. It was Easter Sunday, 1852, right after my grandparents' funeral. My aunt in New York had come down, and I went back with her that day," he said.

"What are y'all doin,' takin' a census or sumpin'?" Abraham spoke up.

"No," Mandie replied. "We're trying to find people who lived here in Franklin in 1850. I want to show you something." She pulled the copy of the map out of her apron pocket and spread it on the floor by the steps. "Will you look at this, Dr. Plumbley?"

Abraham and the doctor got up and sat by Mandie on the steps.

Dr. Plumbley's face lit up as he read the map. "Where did you get this?" he asked.

"We found it in the attic tacked to the back of an old sideboard. Did you know my aunt, Ruby May Shaw, who drew this map?" Mandie held her breath, awaiting his answer.

Dr. Plumbley looked at her and smiled sadly. "Yes, I knew Ruby. She was like an angel on earth. She was so good and kind." He pulled out a handkerchief and dabbed the corner of his eye.

"You did!" Mandie exclaimed.

Sallie and Joe crowded closer.

Dr. Plumbley pointed to Hezekiah's house on the map. "That's where my grandparents' house was. I lived there."

"You lived there?" Sallie cried.

"Did you ever know anyone named Hezekiah?" Joe asked.

"I sure did. I knew him well. I am Hezekiah," Dr. Plumbley said.

All three young people bombarded him with questions.

"But Abraham said your name was Samuel," Mandie argued.

"My name is also Hezekiah—Samuel Hezekiah Plumbley. Everyone else called me Samuel, but Ruby found out my other name was Hezekiah, and it fascinated her. She insisted on calling me Hezekiah."

Mandie reached for the doctor's big black hand and squeezed it. "Oh, Dr. Hezekiah, I'm so glad to meet you and to find out that you really knew my father's little sister!" she exclaimed.

"And I'm delighted to meet Ruby's niece," Dr. Plumbley replied, putting his other hand on top of hers.

"Do you know anything about this map?" Sallie asked the doctor.

"Were you with Ruby when she buried whatever this treasure is?" Joe asked.

"No, to everything. This is the first time I ever saw or heard of a map," Dr. Plumbley said.

"Was your house on the main road way down yonder?" Mandie questioned. "There's a sign there now saying Fine Food Since 1852."

"Right on that spot," he said. "I haven't been to Franklin in a long, long time, but I rode down that way yesterday. That big road has been cut through since we lived there."

"Was your house the one that burned down?" Sallie asked.

Dr. Plumbley nodded. "Yes. My grandparents died in the fire," he said softly. "It was Good Friday, and I was at the church services. Grandma was sick, and Grandpa was too feeble to get her out when the roof caught fire. Nobody lived close by, and I wasn't there to help. If I had been, I might have been able to rescue both of them."

Everyone was silent, sharing the doctor's sadness.

Dr. Plumbley wiped his eyes. "They say the Lord knows best," he continued. "I was in His house of worship when it happened, and my brother was with me."

"Where were your parents?" Joe asked.

"My grandparents were the only parents I ever knew. My ma ran off with some man after I was born, and my pa didn't want me or my brother. He left us with my grandparents. Neither my ma nor my pa was ever heard of again," Dr. Plumbley explained.

"Dr. Plumbley, you don't know anything about the rest of this map, do you?" Mandie asked. "Do you know where the rock pile, persimmon tree, and rhododendron bush are?"

Dr. Plumbley inspected the map again. "No, I'm sorry. I don't know where those things could be," he said. "The house, though, I believe, is where Ruby's little girlfriend Patricia lived."

"Uncle Ned said he thought her friend lived there. He said her father worked for my grandfather," Mandie said.

"Yes, everybody called the man Scoot. I don't know what his given name was. They moved away right after your grandfather closed the mine," the doctor recalled.

"Did you know that my Uncle John has reopened the mine?" Mandie asked.

"You mean that?" Dr. Plumbley looked shocked. "When your grandpa closed it, he said it would never be opened again."

"I know," Mandie replied. "But we wanted to hunt for rubies, so Uncle John got it fixed up. And then there was this man who said he wanted to buy it."

"Buy it? But your grandpa closed it because some of your grandma's ancestors are buried there," the doctor told her.

"You are so right," Joe said. "If we could have met up with you before we got involved in that mine, things would have turned out better."

"Uncle Ned knew about the burial grounds, but he wouldn't tell anybody," Mandie explained. "He said the Cherokees have different customs from the white people. But then I'm part Cherokee myself," she said proudly.

"When you mentioned Uncle Ned, are you talking about the old Indian who lived with your grandparents at one time?" the doctor asked.

Mandie smiled. "I certainly am. In fact, Sallie is his granddaughter."

Dr. Plumbley reached for Sallie's hand and smiled at here. "I loved your grandfather when I was a youngster. He was always so kind to everybody, and he knew everything. All the children loved him."

Sallie nodded. "They still do. I think I have a wonderful grandfather."

"He's visiting the Shaws right now," Joe informed him.

"But we have to go home tomorrow," Sallie said. "I live with my grandparents over at Deep Creek. Did you also know my grandmother, Morning Star?"

"Of course," the doctor replied. "But she couldn't speak English at all, so we weren't well acquainted."

Mandie laughed. "She still can't speak much English, but she's trying real hard to learn."

"And you, young lady," Dr. Plumbley said to Mandie, "I understand you are Mr. Jim Shaw's daughter."

Mandie nodded.

"I left Franklin before your father was ever born, but I've kept in touch with friends here, and I know about him. In fact, your Uncle John was only about four years old when I left. Seems a hundred years ago, doesn't it, Abraham?"

"Now we ain't dat old, Samuel. I be sixty-one come December, and you be one year younger than me," Abraham replied. "You jes' looks 'round, and you be seein' lots o' older people. Why, we jes' middle-aged, me and you."

"You'll probably live to be a hundred, Abraham." Dr. Plumbley laughed.

Joe shuffled his feet impatiently. "Dr. Plumbley, do you have any idea what Ruby might have buried?" he asked, anxious to continue their search.

"No, sorry. I never heard about this map. You say you found it tacked on the back side of an old sideboard in the attic? That puzzles me because Ruby said she had a trunk in the attic where she locked away her secrets and treasures. She wore the key to the trunk on a ribbon around her neck."

"We did find it on the back of the sideboard—when Uncle John was moving some furniture out of the attic," Mandie said.

Joe's eyes grew wide. "Have y'all been through all the trunks in the attic?" he asked.

"Goodness, no." Mandie replied. "There are trunks on top of trunks up there."

"It would take a long time to go through all of them because the furniture would have to be moved around to get to some," Sallie explained.

"After all these years that trunk may have been thrown out," the doctor said.

"No, I wouldn't think so. Uncle John says that he can't remember anybody ever cleaning out the attic," Mandie answered. "We found a wardrobe stuffed full of dolls that belonged to Ruby and some old important papers that Uncle John didn't even know were there."

"Tell us about Ruby," Sallie said, looking up at the big Negro doctor.

"Ruby was a beautiful little girl, dark hair and eyes, and a big smile that absolutely lit up her face," Dr. Plumbley told them. "She liked to wear ruby-colored clothes and ribbons in her hair because that was her name. I think she was named Ruby because her papa discovered rubies in the mine the day she was born. He thought the sun rose and set in her. He was so proud of her."

"Uncle Ned said he wouldn't ever mention her name again after she got killed," Mandie said, "and that he wouldn't allow anyone else to mention her name around him."

"That's right. It just broke his heart. Even though he had John, and then later Jim, he was never as attached to them as he was to Ruby," the doctor explained. "But then she was his firstborn, and she was also the only girl."

"Uncle Ned said my grandfather just grieved himself to death after Ruby was killed," Mandie recalled. "And then my grandmother died soon after my father was born."

"I knowed yo' pa, Missy," Abraham spoke up. "I lived right here when he was bawn, and I stayed right here while he growed up."

Again Joe seemed anxious to get back to the subject of Ruby's treasure. "Dr. Plumbley, we were down in the old newspaper building Friday, going through old newspapers," he said. "We found the story about Ruby's death in one of the papers. Do you remember who the Negro boy was who found her after her pony threw her?"

A deep sadness covered Dr. Plumbley's face. "That Negro boy was . . . me," he said slowly. "I was—"

"You were the one who found her?" Mandie interrupted.

Dr. Plumbley nodded. "I was going over to your grandpa's house to get some eggs. He kept a lot of chickens, and he gave my grandmother all the eggs she wanted. I went out of my way to go past the ruby mine because I always liked to look around there when I got the chance. I was walking along the path when I heard a great commotion ahead of me.

"Then I heard an animal whining. I ran and ran until I came to the bend in the path where it goes around that huge oak tree. There I found little

Ruby." His voice broke. "She must have been thrown from her pony up against that big oak. It was a terrible sight. I've never gotten over it."

"Wasn't she used to riding?" Mandie asked quietly. "Or was the pony a new one for her?"

"Ruby rode like a streak of fire from the time she could sit up straight on a pony." Dr. Plumbley smiled sadly. "Your grandpa always said she rode like a real Indian papoose. And she had had that pony a long time. It was a beautiful Shetland." He paused a moment. "After the accident your grandpa ordered the pony shot, but Uncle Ned arranged for one of the young Indians from his village to take the pony away. He told your grandpa it had been shot and buried."

Mandie looked quickly at Sallie. "That sounds like your grand-father—soft-hearted for animals. But I've never known him to cover up the truth like that."

"You do not understand," Sallie replied. "It would have been cruel to kill the pony. My grandfather forgave the poor animal. Besides, no one knew what caused the pony to throw her. It might not have been the pony's fault."

"I understand," Mandie agreed. "I would have done the same thing. Dr. Plumbley, was Ruby already dead when you found her?"

"I think so. It must have been instant death. The commotion I heard must have been the pony throwing her off. When I found her, her neck was broken." He wiped his eyes with his handkerchief. "Even though I'm supposed to be a big, strong man now that I'm a doctor, I still feel shivers go over me when I remember little Ruby lying there. I remember thinking, she's too good to remain on this earth. God wants her home with his other little angels."

"Abraham, you didn't know her, did you?" Joe asked.

"No, I was too young when I left here. When I come back later all dis done happened," the gardener replied. "I does know, though, old Mistuh Shaw, he never smiled no mo.' He not innerested in nuthin' no mo.'"

"I ran like crazy," Dr. Plumbley continued his recollections. "Old Mr. Shaw was the first one I found here in the yard, so he's the one I had to tell. He was carrying the eggs in from the barn, and when I told him what happened, he went wild. He threw those eggs everywhere and ran back the way I had come."

Everyone sat silent for a moment.

"How long are you going to be here?" Mandie asked hesitantly.

"I don't know," the doctor replied. "My brother is still sick, and I took a little vacation to come down here and doctor him. So I'll be around until he mends."

"What I really meant was how long are you going to be here at Abraham's house today?" Mandie asked.

"If he'll give me something to eat, I might stay for supper. That is . . . if he asks me." Dr. Plumbley grinned at his friend.

"You knows I'll give you sumpin' to eat. I can cook jes' as good as any woman, jes' 'bout," Abraham said.

"Except for one, right, Abraham?" Mandie teased.

Abraham frowned. "What you talkin' 'bout, Missy?"

"The one you haven't talked to for forty years," Mandie replied.

Abraham got up from the steps, dusted off the seat of his pants, and sat down in a rocking chair. "I ain't been knowin' no woman forty years," he said.

"I know what she's talking about, Abraham," Dr. Plumbley said. "I think it's time you brought Jenny home."

"Who's Jenny?" the old man asked stubbornly.

"Just think how nice it would be to have a woman in the house," the doctor told him.

"Look who's talkin.' You didn't git married yo'self till 'bout three year ago, after you done got to be a old man," Abraham replied.

"Why, you just said a while ago that we aren't old," Dr. Plumbley teased. "You well know I couldn't get married when I was young. I had to work very hard to get an education so I could go to medical school. I didn't have time or money to support a wife and family."

Liza came across the yard to Abraham's front porch. "Miz 'Lizbeth she say fo' y'all to git yo'selves in de parlor," she told the young people.

"All right," Mandie replied. "What does she want? Do you know?" She stood up, folded the map, and put it in her apron pocket.

"She say de Turners dey done gone. You come home now," Liza repeated.

The young people exchanged glances.

"We weren't waiting for the Turners to leave, Liza. It was you who didn't want to see them," Mandie reminded her.

"Is anyone else there?" Joe asked.

"Nope. Jes' Miz 'Lizbeth, Mistuh John, and dat Injun man," Liza replied.

Mandie turned to the Negro doctor, who was now standing on the porch. "Could you come over to the house with us and meet my mother and Uncle John. You said you know Uncle Ned already."

The doctor looked at his friend. "Abraham, what time are you going to have dinner?"

"Whenever you come back," he answered.

"I won't be gone long," Dr. Plumbley promised.

Mandie led the way back to the house and into the parlor. Grasping Dr. Plumbley's big hand, she stepped forward. "Mother, Uncle John, this is Abraham's friend, Dr. Samuel Hezekiah Plumbley from New York," she announced. "Uncle Ned, you already know him from way back, remember?"

Uncle Ned stood, looked the doctor over, and put his hand on the big man's shoulder. "This young Samuel Plumbley?" the Indian asked as he studied the smiling black face.

"That's me," Dr. Plumbley said, putting an arm around the Indian's shoulders. "You don't know how glad I am to see you again."

"Friend of Ruby," Uncle Ned said, a little excited, which was unusual for him. He turned to John and Elizabeth. "Friend of Ruby," he repeated.

Uncle John stood and gripped the doctor's hand. "You were a friend of my little sister's?"

"Yes, sir, I knew Ruby," Dr. Plumbley replied.

Uncle John introduced Elizabeth.

"How do you do, Dr. Plumbley? Please sit down," she invited.

The young people sat and listened as the adults discussed the same things they had been talking about.

Uncle John was happy to find a friend of his sister's, and Uncle Ned was delighted to see the small boy, now grown big and tall, who had known his dear little papoose, Ruby.

CHAPTER EIGHT

THE SECRET HIDING PLACE

As soon as the excitement subsided, Mandie asked her mother if she and her friends could look in the attic for the trunk that belonged to Ruby.

"A trunk?" Elizabeth questioned.

"Dr. Plumbley told us Ruby had a special trunk she kept all her secrets and treasures in," Mandie explained. "And she wore the key around her neck."

"Are you giving up on the map search?" Uncle John asked.

"Oh, no, sir," Mandie replied. "But we're at a dead end right now. I thought we might find something in Ruby's trunk."

"Go ahead and look, dear—all of you. But don't waste the rest of the day up there, and do be careful moving things around. Some of that furniture is heavy," Elizabeth cautioned.

The young people raced upstairs. When they reached the attic, they again despaired at the sight of so many pieces of furniture, boxes, trunks, and other discards.

"Let's start with the easy ones," Mandie said. "The trunks near the door are easier to get to."

She led the way and the three of them began opening trunks and searching the contents. As they worked their way deeper into the attic, they found trunks packed with old clothes, books, shoes, papers, dishes, blankets, linens, and even baby clothes.

"Look!" Mandie exclaimed, picking up a piece of white cloth. "Somebody's baby diaper!" She held it up for the others to see. "It'd be fun to know whose it was, wouldn't it?"

"Yes, it would be, but it could also be embarrassing," Sallie said.

"It might have been your Uncle John's when he was a baby." Joe laughed. "I'd hate for somebody to find a diaper I used to wear."

"And here are some booties, and bonnets, and sweaters. They're all white, so I don't know whether they were for a girl or a boy," Mandie said.

"My mother told me that when she was a baby everything was always white, whether it was for a girl or a boy," Joe said.

Mandie was still poking into the trunk when she felt something metal deep down below the clothes. Pushing things aside, she withdrew a large framed portrait of a baby dressed in a long white dress, lying in the arms of a beautiful young woman."I've found something wonderful!" she exclaimed. "Just wonderful!"

Sallie and Joe rushed to her side to see what it was.

"It's just a portrait of a baby and its mother," Joe said.

"But look at the face of the mother." Sallie pointed.

Joe's eyes grew wide. "That is the same lady that is in the portrait hanging in the library."

"It's my grandmother! It is!" Mandie cried. "I wonder which baby this is."

"Leave that trunk open, Mandie, and after we get through, we can take the picture downstairs and see if your uncle knows who the baby is," Sallie told her.

"I hope he does," Mandie said. Placing the portrait on top of the baby clothes, she left the trunk open and continued on to the next trunk. "Sallie, your grandfather would probably know better than Uncle John because he saw all of them when they were babies."

"Yes, he would," Sallie agreed.

Joe opened another trunk and found some old decaying clothes. "What good is all this old stuff up here?" he asked. "Why don't you throw it out?"

"I think it ought to be cleaned out up here, too. I'll ask Uncle John about it when we have time to do it one day," Mandie said, opening a trunk that was almost empty.

Sallie, in the far corner, was bent over a large trunk. "I think I have found something," she called.

Mandie and Joe hurried to look. The trunk was full of a little girl's clothes, many of which were ruby-colored.

Mandie gasped. "These are Ruby's clothes!" She reached to pull some of the garments out of the trunk and then suddenly withdrew her outstretched hands. "How can I go through those things?" She shivered. "It's all so sad. Ruby seems so real to me now." Mandie's blue eyes filled with tears.

Joe patted her softly on the shoulder. "Maybe we should forget the whole thing . . ."

"Oh, no," Mandie protested. "We have to see if there is anything here that will help us find the treasure. It's just so sad."

"Want me to look?" Joe offered.

Mandie nodded as she stared at the things in the trunk.

"I will help you, Joe," Sallie volunteered.

Joe carefully removed the first garment. It was a ruby-red riding outfit. He shook out the wrinkles and handed it to Sallie, who placed it carefully on a nearby table.

One after another, Joe removed the contents of the trunk. Sallie put them in a neat pile on the table. There was not a thing in the trunk but clothes.

"Don't you think there must be another trunk?" Joe asked. "A rich girl like Ruby would have had a lot more clothes than this, wouldn't she?"

Mandie nodded and her voice trembled as she spoke. "But you know, when people die, you usually give their clothes to the needy. There may not be any more."

"Let's keep looking," Joe said. He and Sallie replaced the garments in the trunk and continued on.

They found lots of old clothes but no more that could have belonged to a ten-year-old girl.

"Didn't they wear funny-looking clothes back in the old days?" Joe asked as they searched a trunk of long dresses with hoops and ostrich feathers.

"We think they're funny, but to them that was the latest style," Mandie said. "I suppose years from now people will look at our old clothes and laugh at them." She began to brighten a little. "I'd like to know what the clothes will look like then. I imagine the dresses will be shorter and not so full because everything shrinks with time. Things get smaller and thinner."

"I had never thought about that, but it is true," Sallie agreed.

"We'd better hurry. The day is going by fast," Joe reminded the girls.

They went through every trunk that they could find and finally plopped down on an old settee.

"There just aren't any more of Ruby's things here, at least not in a trunk," Joe said.

"What about something other than a trunk?" Mandie asked, looking around.

"It would take hours and hours to go through all the furniture up here," Sallie said.

"Maybe we could search the furniture near the trunk that has Ruby's clothes in it," Mandie suggested. "When people brought things up here, they would put the things together that they brought up at one time, wouldn't they?"

"You mean if they cleaned out one room downstairs and brought all the furniture up here, they would place it all together?" Joe asked.

"Yes, more or less, depending on how much room they needed for it," Mandie replied.

"Maybe," Joe said.

"But we moved the furniture all around up here when we selected pieces for the Burnses' house," Sallie reminded them.

"That's right. We also decided that the oldest furniture was in that corner over there—" Mandie pointed. "—Because it would have been the first put in here, remember? It's also the hardest to get to."

"I suppose we could look in all the furniture in that corner," Joe said. He made his way over to it, stepping over boxes and sliding over the tops of chests.

Mandie and Sallie joined him. They opened dressers, looked in wardrobes and boxes, and were almost finished when Uncle Ned appeared at the doorway. He stood there watching them.

"That furniture older than Ruby," he called across the attic to them. "Not Ruby's. Belong to her grandma, grandpa."

"My great-grandparents? My goodness, it must be old!" Mandie exclaimed.

"Old. Older than me," Uncle Ned replied. "Furniture of Ruby still in Ruby's room."

"Ruby's room?" Mandie asked. The three waded through furniture, boxes, and trunks to get to Uncle Ned.

"She still has a room?" Sallie asked.

"Ruby's room on second floor near Papoose's room," Uncle Ned replied.

"Let's go see it. Show us which room it is," Mandie said excitedly.

"This girl has been dead fifty years, and she still has a room?" Joe said, unbelieving.

Uncle Ned led the way down the stairs to the second floor. He passed Mandie's room, went on down the hallway to the end, and opened the door. "This Ruby's room," he said, waiting for the young people to enter.

The room did not look like it belonged to anybody. It had an empty feeling about it even though it was full of mahogany furniture. There were no personal articles sitting around and no personal pictures or decorations on the walls.

Mandie walked over to the huge wardrobe and flung open the doors. It was empty. Sallie opened drawers in a chest of drawers. They were empty. Joe checked the dresser. It was empty, too.

The young people looked at each other and then at Uncle Ned.

"When Ruby die, Talitha take everything out of this room except furniture. She give it all away. Shut door, never use room," Uncle Ned explained.

"My Grandmother Talitha did that? Then she took everything out before Uncle John was old enough to remember," Mandie reasoned. "And he would have no memories of this room. He may have thought it was just another guest room."

"Is there anything at all in any of the drawers or anywhere?" Joe asked.

"No, not in drawers, not in furniture," Uncle Ned told them. "Ruby had secret hiding place. Talitha never found."

"Do you know where it is?" Mandie asked.

"I not like to bother. Just way Ruby left it," the old Indian said.

"My grandfather, you must tell us what you know," Sallie pleaded.

"How do you know about it when her mother didn't even know?" Joe asked.

"Ruby tell me secrets," Uncle Ned said sadly. "She show me secret place."

"And when she died, you didn't tell her parents about the secret place?" Mandie asked.

"Ruby tell me secret. I never tell secret," Uncle Ned replied. "Secret not to be told."

"My grandfather, please tell us," Sallie begged. "Ruby is long dead."

"Please," Mandie said. "We won't tell anyone else if you don't want us to."

"The secret place may have something in it about the treasure map," Joe suggested. "Do you know what's in it?"

Uncle Ned shook his head. "No, I never bother," he repeated.

"Is it in this room?" Mandie persisted.

"Are we near it?" Sallie asked.

Joe scratched his head. "Is it in the secret tunnel in this house?"

Uncle Ned hesitated for several moments then walked over to the tall fireplace with a huge mantlepiece. The fireplace was ornate and made in sections of marble with fancy brass strips running between and around the edges. He paused for a moment, and a sad expression flitted across his old wrinkled face.

Taking a deep breath, Uncle Ned reached up to the marble section on the left end. Carefully tugging away at the heavy marble, he managed to lift it up, disclosing a hollow space beneath it in the mantlepiece.

The young people hovered near, watching and waiting. They were all too short to see inside the space.

Joe reached for the tall footstool by the high, four-poster bed, and brought it over to the mantlepiece. Mandie stepped up on it and still had to tiptoe to see inside the section of marble.

"Uncle Ned, can I take things out so we can see what it is?" Mandie asked.

Uncle Ned nodded. "Can look but must put back."

Mandie carefully took a large white feather out of the opening and held it up for the others to see. "I wonder where this came from?" she asked. "It must be something special."

"Special school play. Ruby Indian in play," Uncle Ned informed them.

"She was half Indian," Joe remarked.

Mandie gave the feather to Sallie to hold, then turned back to the secret hiding place. A moment later she withdrew a thick cloth draw-string bag from inside. "Look!" she cried. Quickly untying the string, she stretched the top open and took out an exquisite necklace made of rubies. "Oh, look! This must be worth a fortune!" she exclaimed, dangling the necklace for the others to see.

"Yes, father of Ruby give to her when Ruby born. Belong to his mother," the Indian explained. "Was Ruby's most treasured thing."

"This was my great-grandmother's!" Mandie said, examining the necklace in awe. "We should tell Uncle John about this."

"Tell me about what?"

Everyone turned to see Uncle John standing in the open doorway.

"I was looking for y'all and heard you talking in here," he said.

Uncle Ned sighed. "Ruby have secret treasure place." He pointed to the opening in the mantlepiece.

Uncle John walked over to where Mandie stood on the footstool. "Why, the mantlepiece opens up. Did you know about this, Uncle Ned?"

"Yes, Ruby show me. This Ruby room. Promise never tell about place, but now Ruby gone," he said sadly.

"This was Ruby's room? I never knew," Uncle John said.

Mandie handed him the ruby necklace. "Uncle Ned told us that your father gave this necklace to Ruby when she was born. It was his mother's, your grandmother's."

"My grandmother's?" Uncle John turned the necklace over in his hands. "This is beautiful! And it has been here ever since Ruby died?"

"Yes," Uncle Ned answered. "I never bother. I not know what in hiding place."

Mandie reached into the hole again and pulled some papers from the opening. They were drawings Ruby had made of the house, animals, and unrecognizable people. The last thing Mandie found was a tiny locket on a long gold chain.

"A locket!" Mandie gasped. She quickly stuck her fingernail in the catch. As the locket came open, cameo pictures of a man on one side and a woman on the other appeared.

"Uncle John!" Mandie quickly held out the locket to him. "Your mother and father?"

John looked closely at the pictures. "Yes, it is, Amanda."

"Oh, Uncle John," Mandie said excitedly. "Could I wear the locket sometime when I'm all dressed up for something special?"

"We'll see," Uncle John said. "I think all of these things are special, but the necklace and the locket especially need to go in my safe."

"You right, John Shaw," Uncle Ned said sadly. "Ruby not ever coming back."

"You kept your promise to her, Uncle Ned. And I think she would be glad you showed us the hiding place. These things are too precious to leave in a place like that." Uncle John put his arm around the old Indian's shoulders.

Uncle Ned looked down at the floor and Mandie detected tears in his eyes. Uncle Ned never cries, she thought. He must have loved Ruby a lot.

She jumped down from the footstool and took his wrinkled hand. "Uncle Ned, Ruby is not ever coming back, but I am here. I'm still your Papoose, remember?"

Uncle Ned squeezed her hand. "Yes, you always my Papoose. Remember, I promise Jim Shaw I watch over Papoose after he go to happy hunting ground," he said in a shaky voice. "So many already gone to happy hunting ground."

"Maybe I'll be around for a while, Uncle Ned. I'm only twelve years old, you know." Mandie smiled up at him.

Sallie gave her grandfather a hug. "I am not quite one year older than Mandie," she said. "And I hope to grow up, and get married, and have many little papooses for my grandfather to love."

Uncle Ned returned her hug.

"Well, it seems I got left out of all this," Joe teased. "I think we'd better be going, though, or the day will be gone."

"Let's go back up to the attic," Mandie suggested. "Uncle John, come with us. I have something I want to ask you about."

"Yes, go to attic," Uncle Ned said quickly. "More things belong to Ruby in wardrobe with dolls. Come," he said, leading the way to the attic. Taking them directly to the huge wardrobe, he indicated the big drawer at the bottom.

"That's the drawer where we found the map, remember?" Mandie said.

Joe pulled the drawer out.

"It looks like a lot of papers to me," Uncle John said.

"Under papers," Uncle Ned directed them. "Under papers."

The young people quickly began removing papers and envelopes and finally came to a small Bible at the bottom.

When Mandie picked it up and opened it, a paper fell out. "Why, it's a copy of the treasure map," she said.

"And the Bible belonged to Ruby, didn't it?" John asked.

The old Indian nodded.

Mandie turned the map over and read out loud a handwritten note on the back, " 'Had to tack the other copy of my map behind the sideboard for the time being because I lost the key to my trunk. I must remember that the rhododendron bush is the one growing near the huge rock.' "

"More clues," Joe said.

"What else is in the drawer?" Sallie asked.

Mandie sorted through various cards and letters addressed to Ruby, several school books, pencils, hair ribbons. "Uncle Ned, how did you know about all this?" she asked.

"I put there. All I could save. Father of Ruby not want to see anything belong to her. I hide all this," he replied.

"Let's take that copy of the map back downstairs and show it to Dr. Plumbley," Joe suggested. "That is, if he's still here."

"He's still here," Uncle John said. "I came up to find y'all to say good-bye to him."

"Come on," Mandie urged, taking the map with her as she led the way downstairs. "Maybe he can help us figure out this note."

"I hope so, but I doubt it," Joe said.

"Yes, things have changed so much since then," Sallie added.

Uncle Ned followed last with a bowed head and stooped shoulders. "Samuel Plumbley know much," he muttered to himself.

CHAPTER NINE

MORE CLUES

Halfway down the attic steps Mandie stopped. Uncle John was right behind her. "I forgot to show you something, Uncle John," she said. "Let's go back for just a minute. Uncle Ned, you, too. Joe and Sallie, you know what it is. We'll catch up with you downstairs in a minute."

"Don't take too long," Joe told her as he and Sallie went on down.

Mandie took Uncle John and Uncle Ned straight to the trunk where she had found the baby clothes. She picked up the portrait and held it up for them to see. "Look what I found in this trunk. It must be your mother, Uncle John, and either you, or my father, or Ruby as a baby," she said.

"I've never seen that before," Uncle John said. "But yes, that's definitely my mother."

"Uncle Ned, do you know which baby it is?" Mandie asked.

The old Indian moved closer to look. "That is Ruby. I here when man paint picture. These baby clothes belong to Ruby. Talitha save. Hope she have other little girl to wear clothes. But only boys, Jim and John."

"Why did she put this portrait in the trunk? Why isn't it hanging somewhere?" Uncle John asked.

"Father want everything of Ruby taken away—everything. I take things, hide in wardrobe. Talitha hide clothes here—this and other trunk. Everything else give away," Uncle Ned replied.

Uncle John put his arm around Mandie as he held the portrait on top of the baby clothes. "Where shall we hang this?"

"In the library," Mandie said quickly, "where my grandmother's portrait is."

"I'm not sure we can find enough wall space in the library to hang this there," Uncle John said.

"All we have to do is move my grandmother's portrait to one end of the fireplace and hang this one at the other end," Mandie suggested. "I believe they're the same size."

"Now why didn't I think of that?" Uncle John asked. "We'll do that before you go back to school. Let's just leave it here for now. I imagine Dr. Plumbley is getting impatient with us by now. He was getting ready to leave."

"Oh, no!" Mandie exclaimed as she rushed ahead of them down the stairs. She still had the copy of the map in her hand that they had found in Ruby's Bible.

In the parlor Joe and Sallie were trying their best to keep Dr. Plumbley talking so he wouldn't leave until Mandie got there. Elizabeth watched in amusement nearby.

"Here's Mandie now with the other copy of the map, Dr. Plumbley," Joe said as Mandie came through the doorway.

Uncle John and Uncle Ned followed her into the room and sat down near Elizabeth.

"I have it," Mandie said, waving the paper in the air as she hurried forward to sit on a chair near the doctor. "Read the note on the back, Dr. Plumbley. Do you have any idea where this huge rock is that she said is near the rhododendron bush?"

Dr. Plumbley examined the paper, then handed it back to Mandie. "There are lots of rocks around this neck of the woods. And there are quite a few that a ten-year-old child would call huge."

"Do you remember any special rock that Ruby knew about?" Joe asked.

"Maybe one that was a little different?" Sallie added.

Dr. Plumbley thought for a minute and then shook his head. "No, I'm sorry. I can't remember any special rock offhand," he said, "and I'm afraid I'm going to have to be leaving." He stood.

All the young people jumped up.

"Dr. Plumbley, please go with us to look for this rock," Mandie begged.

"You know the area better than we do," Joe said.

"And you lived not far from the buried treasure, according to Ruby's map," Sallie said.

Dr. Plumbley laughed and looked at the adults, who were watching him. "What am I going to do with these young people? There are three against one," he said, shaking his head.

Uncle John laughed. "I'd say you'll have to give in to their wishes, or you'll never have another day's peace until you return to New York," he said.

"They can be persistent," Dr. Plumbley admitted.

"Sallie and Joe have to go back to school tomorrow, and I have to go Wednesday. We don't have much time. Please help us," Mandie pleaded.

"With you helping we could find this thing in no time, whatever it is," Joe said.

Dr. Plumbley looked from one to another of the young people. "Just what is it you want me to do?" he asked.

"Go with us to the place where your house used to be, and help us find the rock pile, persimmon tree, and rhododendron bush that are on the map," Mandie answered. "They're all near where you lived."

"And if I don't go?" the doctor asked.

"We won't get another holiday until Christmas. We'll have to wait until then to finish searching," Joe said.

"But that buried treasure has been in that spot for fifty years. It will stay there a little while longer, I'm sure," the doctor said, smiling.

"We do not know that it has been there for fifty years. Someone else may have already found it. We will not know until we find the place on the map," Sallie said.

"Why, even the spot may be gone," Dr. Plumbley reasoned. "Things may be so changed we'll never find it."

"Then you'll go with us?" Mandie asked.

Dr. Plumbley threw up his hands and laughed. "I surrender," he said. "Lead the way."

"Thank you!" Mandie grinned.

Joe and Sallie echoed her gratitude.

"Amanda, don't y'all be gone too long," Elizabeth said, as the group started to leave the room.

"We'll be back soon, Mother," Mandie replied.

"Wish us luck," Joe said, laughing.

"I hope you find whatever it is," Uncle John called to them.

As they went out the parlor door, Dr. Plumbley spoke to Mandie. "I must tell my friend that I'll be back soon. Remember, he's cooking supper for me."

"And we need to get his hoe and rope again," Joe said.

"The quickest way is through the kitchen," Mandie said, leading the way down the hall. "Come on."

As they entered the kitchen, Jenny stood at the table peeling potatoes. She looked up.

Mandie walked over to her and introduced Jenny to Dr. Plumbley as Abraham's wife.

Dr. Plumbley extended his hand. Jenny ignored the gesture and rushed over to the sink. "Y'all be on yo' way. I'se got a meal to cook."

"It was nice meeting you, Jenny. I hope I see you again sometime," Dr. Plumbley said.

Mandie quickly headed out the back door. "I don't think she was very nice to meet," she whispered to Sallie.

When they were all outside, Snowball came running to Mandie in the yard. She picked him up and carried him with her to the gardener's house.

Abraham sat on the front porch, rocking. " 'Bout time you come back, Samuel," Abraham fussed.

"I'm not back yet. You see, these nice young people have asked me to go on a treasure hunt with them. I just wanted to let you know I'll be back soon," Dr. Plumbley replied.

"Well, if you ain't back soon, I'll eat without you," Abraham warned.

Joe picked up the hoe and the rope from the end of the porch. "May we borrow these again, Abraham?" he asked.

Abraham nodded his head but said nothing.

"Do you want to go with us?" Mandie invited.

"I ain't gwine nowhere. And if y'all agwine, well, git!" Abraham snapped.

"Oh, you're grouchy just like Jenny," Mandie teased, petting Snowball in her arms.

"Dat Jenny ain't got nuthin' to do wid me, grouchy or not. Now git!" He rose and opened the front screen door. "And hurry back, Samuel, if you wants any supper."

"I sure do want some supper, so I'll be back soon," the doctor promised.

Using the hoe like a walking stick, Joe led the way across the road past the cemetery to the dirt pathway.

"I've been down this pathway many a time," Dr. Plumbley remarked, looking around as they walked along. "But, my, how things have changed! This path used to be much bigger, wide enough for buggies and wagons to go down it. And now it has just about disappeared under all these weeds and bushes."

"Wait till you see what we have to go through," Mandie warned.

"Joe had to chop out a pathway where it had all grown up," Sallie said.

When they came to that particular place, Dr. Plumbley couldn't believe all the trees growing there.

"This was wide open cow pasture when I left here forty-eight years ago," Dr. Plumbley said. "Guess I am getting old, no matter what Abraham says."

"I hope things haven't changed so much that you can't recognize these other places on the map," Mandie said.

"We'll see," the doctor answered.

When they came to the end of the path, they stopped to look across the road at the house with the sign Fine Food Since 1852.

"My grandparents' house was right where that big fine house sits now. It was only an old four-room house, two rooms downstairs and two upstairs. They were upstairs when the fire happened," Dr. Plumbley said softly, staring at the boardinghouse. "If they'd been downstairs, someone might have been able to save them. But the roof caught fire and that house went up like a bunch of kindling. If they could have only lived until I was grown and educated, I could have done so much for them."

Mandie took the doctor's big hand in hers. "But Dr. Plumbley, you probably wouldn't have gone to New York and become a doctor, would you?"

"Maybe. You see, I lived with my aunt in New York. Her husband died, leaving her with some money they had saved. She wanted me to have it to use toward my education. I did repay her, though. I insisted on that."

"Well, what do we do now?" Joe asked.

"If you don't mind, I'd like to go over there and look around," Dr. Plumbley said.

"Come on. We've been inside and met Mr. Jud Jenkinson, the man who owns it now," Mandie said.

"Not inside. I'd just like to look around the yard," the doctor said.

They crossed the road and followed Dr. Plumbley around the house to the back yard. He stood there, looking about. The young people silently watched and waited.

"There it is!" the doctor exclaimed, pointing downhill and walking ahead. "It's still here."

They followed as he came to stop by a straggly old apple tree.

The doctor reached to touch the limbs. "The frost has already got the leaves, but this is the apple tree I remember," he said. "I used to swipe the apples and take them down there to eat." He pointed downhill to a small creek. "My grandmother always wanted to save them for pies and applesauce. And if she caught me, it was too bad. I wouldn't be able to sit down for a week." He laughed.

The young people smiled at each other.

"What did she whip you with that hurt so bad?" Mandie asked.

"She didn't do it. She'd get my grandpa to take his old leather razor strop and just about wear it out on me," the doctor said. "It sure hurt, but she knew what she was doing. She was teaching me to distinguish right from wrong. She was a good woman."

"Was your house in exactly the same spot as this one?" Joe asked.

"As far as I can tell, according to the well over there, our house was sitting directly behind this one," he said. "But then this big road has been cut through here, so it's hard to tell for sure. Things don't look the same."

"If this road wasn't here, what kind of a road did you have then?" Mandie asked.

"Just the dirt path we came down from the cemetery. It curved past our house and dead-ended into the creek down there," the doctor said. "This new road cut into part of it."

Mandie perched Snowball on her shoulder and held up the copy of the map. "You see, according to this, we have to count 936 feet to a rock pile. It looks like it goes back that way at an angle." She pointed.

Dr. Plumbley looked at the map and then at the direction Mandie was pointing. "That could be an awfully wide area," he said.

"We went that way and found an old house built on top of a rock pile," Joe said.

"And a terrible man camping out in it with a rifle," Sallie added.

"A man with a rifle?" the doctor asked, alarmed.

"We can stay far enough away from it so the man won't see us," Joe said.

"Well, let's hope he doesn't see us," Dr. Plumbley said. "Are you using that rope to measure off the distances?"

"Yes," Mandie replied.

"Then let's get started," Dr. Plumbley urged. "Here, let me take one end."

Soon they came within sight of the old house. Pointing through a small opening in the trees, Joe said, "That's the house over there on the rock pile."

Dr. Plumbley looked where Joe was pointing. "I don't remember that place being there. It might have been, but I don't remember it."

"Then maybe it is sitting on the rock pile that Ruby put on the map," Mandie said.

"It could be," the doctor agreed.

"If you think it is, then we should measure 572 feet and find a persimmon tree," Mandie reasoned.

"Only we looked for a persimmon tree and could not find a single one," Sallie said.

"Trees do die sometimes, and people do cut them down, you know," Dr. Plumbley reminded them.

"Well, anyway, let's measure it again and see if we can find one," Joe suggested.

At the end of the 572 feet the young people looked around.

"This isn't the same place we came to when we measured the distance this afternoon!" Mandie exclaimed.

"No, it is not," Sallie said.

Joe shook his head. "I still don't see any persimmon trees."

"Nor do I," Dr. Plumbley said.

"Do you recognize anything around here?" Mandie asked him. Taking Snowball in her arms again, she stroked his soft white fur absentmindedly.

"Nothing looks familiar," the doctor answered.

"We must keep searching," Sallie said, looking around.

"Yes, we may be off the line of the map a little, but we can look close by for a persimmon tree," Joe agreed.

"We should mark the spot we measured to, so we will not lose it," Sallie said. She picked up a fallen limb. "I will put this right here."

After circling the area and still not finding one, they returned to the spot Sallie had marked.

"There could have been a persimmon tree around here back then," Dr. Plumbley told the disappointed young people. "I remember there were many of them between our house and Ruby's. But I haven't seen a single one today."

"Why don't we pretend this spot is a persimmon tree and measure 333 feet to find the rhododendron bush on the map?" Mandie asked.

"It may not come out right, but we can try it," Sallie agreed.

"Well, whatever we're going to do, let's hurry. I'm getting hungry," Joe said. "Which way do we measure?"

"That way," Mandie pointed at an angle to their left.

They came out into the same mass of rhododendron bushes they had found that afternoon.

"We've been here before," Joe said.

"I remember," Mandie agreed. "The map we just found in Ruby's Bible says the rhododendron bush is the one growing near the big rock."

"I don't see any rock. All I see is rhododendron bushes," Joe said.

Dr. Plumbley looked around. "Well, suppose we look in between all these bushes and see if we can find a rock. How about that?"

"Good idea," Mandie said.

"That's gonna take forever," Joe moaned.

"Not quite that long, Joe," Sallie teased.

They thoroughly searched beneath and around all the bushes but found nothing. Snowball struggled to get down, but Mandie held him tightly.

As they came out on the far side of the bushes, Dr. Plumbley straightened up and looked around. "Wait a minute," he said, hurrying ahead. "I believe I recognize something!"

The young people quickly followed, and they soon came out of the bushes into a clearing. There, just ahead of them, was a huge boulder.

"The rock!" Mandie cried.

They all ran to look.

"I remember this rock very well now," the doctor said. "Ruby used to bring food for my grandparents, and she would meet me at this rock. How could I have forgotten?"

"Why did she bring it here?" Mandie asked. "Why didn't she take it to your house?"

"The Shaws' cook always came with her, but they were not allowed to go to our house because my grandma had tuberculosis, and they were afraid of catching it," he explained. "We had a schedule worked out between us. I would meet Ruby and the cook here at certain times."

"Did her parents know about this?" Joe asked.

"Oh, yes. They knew. They were very kind to us and were always doing things for us. They were good people," the doctor said.

"If this is the special rock on the map, all we have to do is find the rhododendron bush that is the nearest to it," Mandie said.

They looked around and moaned. There were dozens of rhododendron bushes around the rock, any one of which could have been considered the nearest to the rock.

Joe sighed. "What are we going to do now?"

"That's a good question," Dr. Plumbley said, scratching his head.

CHAPTER TEN

THE MAP'S TREASURE

"We could dig all these bushes up and look under them," Joe suggested as they surveyed the mass of rhododendron bushes.

"My goodness, Joe, there're too many. We'd never get done," Mandie said, slowing petting her white kitten.

"We could narrow it down some," Dr. Plumbley remarked. "The small bushes must have grown up since Ruby buried her treasure."

"Would a rhododendron bush grow for fifty years?" Sallie asked. "If it was not cared for like these out here, would it not eventually die?"

Mandie and Joe shrugged.

"Sorry, I have no idea how long a rhododendron bush can live unattended," Dr. Plumbley said.

"If one did grow that long, wouldn't it be a good-sized tree by now?" Mandie asked.

"I never heard of rhododendron trees," Joe said.

Mandie looked at the map they found in Ruby's Bible. She pointed to the writing on it. "I think there is a mistake somewhere," she said. "The other map definitely said dig three feet under a rhododendron bush, and this map says dig one foot."

The others gathered around to look.

"In that case it won't take long to dig up the dirt around a few of these bushes and see if we hit something," Joe said. "One foot is not all that deep."

"But the soil washes," Sallie reminded them. "It has either washed more dirt over the place or washed dirt away from it. The land is sloped here, so I would say it washed the dirt away from it."

"You have great powers of deduction, Sallie," Dr. Plumbley said.

"She sure does," Joe agreed.

"I learn things from my grandfather," Sallie said.

"And her grandfather is the smartest man I ever knew," Mandie added.

"Since we only have one hoe, I'll start digging first," Joe volunteered. Taking the tool from Dr. Plumbley, he began walking around. "Let me find a place to begin."

Snowball again tried to wriggle free, and Mandie finally set him down.

"How about digging right here?" She indicated a place near the rock.

"All right. Here goes," Joe said, stomping the hoe into the ground.

The others stood around and watched as Joe loosened the soil among the bushes.

"Maybe we should go behind you and replant the bushes," Dr. Plumbley suggested.

"Yes, we should," Mandie agreed. "It would be a shame to dig up all these things and leave them to die."

"That's fine," Joe said, "but for goodness sakes, keep that cat away from me or he could get hurt."

Mandie bent down to call to her kitten. "Here, Snowball. Come here."

The white kitten stood there, looking at her. Then he took a flying leap into the rhododendron bushes and disappeared. Mandie and Sallie chased after him.

"Here, kitty, kitty!" Sallie called.

"Snowball! Come here!" Mandie searched underneath the bushes.

"Here he is," Joe yelled at them. Reaching down, he grabbed Snowball from under the bush he was digging up.

Mandie took her kitten and sat down on the grass nearby to hold him out of the way. Sallie joined her, and Dr. Plumbley stood, watching Joe dig.

Since Joe wasn't having any success, Dr. Plumbley finally spoke up. "How about letting me have that hoe a while, so you can rest?" he offered.

"Thanks," Joe said, handing him the tool. "All this may be for nothing. I'll start replanting the bushes."

Mandie turned to Sallie. "Would you hold Snowball for me so I can help Joe?" she asked.

"You just hold Snowball, and I will help Joe," Sallie said, getting up.

"I want to help, too, so you do a little and then hold Snowball while I do some," Mandie told her friend.

"All right," Sallie agreed.

Together she and Joe put the bushes back into the holes they had come out of and pushed the dirt up around them. Since Dr. Plumbley was using the hoe, they had to do the grimy work by hand.

Dr. Plumbley kept right on digging up bushes while they followed behind and replanted them. The doctor was bigger and stronger than Joe, so he was able to go faster.

"Let me help now, Sallie," Mandie said, getting up.

"I'm sorry my hands are so dirty for holding Snowball," Sallie said, brushing the dirt off her red skirt. She took the white kitten and sat down.

"That's all right. He'll wash himself if you hold him loose enough," Mandie said.

Sallie allowed the kitten to move about in her lap and wash his fur.

Suddenly Mandie stopped working and looked up. "Joe! I just thought of something! Whose land are we digging up? They might not like what we're doing," she exclaimed.

Joe continued with his work. "I don't know whose land this is," he answered.

Dr. Plumbley stopped digging and looked at her. "When I lived here, all this land belonged to your grandpa, Missy," he said.

"This far from the house?" Mandie asked.

"This is not really that far from your house. Your grandpa owned hundreds and hundreds of acres of land around here," the doctor said. "And he farmed most of it. There was some pastureland, but he had tenant farmers tending the land."

"Surely Ruby would bury her treasure only on their own property," Sallie reasoned.

"But I wonder if it still belongs to our family," Mandie said.

"If it does, why doesn't Mr. Shaw farm it?" Joe asked.

"Franklin has become quite a little city since I left here forty-eight years ago," Dr. Plumbley observed. "There's not as much farming being done. There are a lot of businesses here now."

"Your uncle is so rich that he probably does not need to grow crops," Sallie said to Mandie.

"He could grow crops and give them away if he doesn't need anything," Mandie said with a sigh. "I suppose there are a lot of decisions to make and problems to solve when you get rich."

Dr. Plumbley continued to dig. "I wouldn't know about that," he said, laughing. "I've never been rich. I have enough income from my practice now to live on, but I'll never be rich."

"Yes, Mandie," Joe teased, "you're the only rich one here."

"I'm not rich, Joe Woodard," Mandie objected. "My uncle might be, but I'm not. I don't want to be rich," she said emphatically.

"I would like to be rich so I could help other people," Sallie said.

"I would like to be rich so I wouldn't have to work anymore," Joe said.

"You don't work, Joe. You go to school," Mandie argued.

"When I grow up I'll have to work," Joe told her. He stood a bush in its original hole and helped her push the dirt around it.

As Mandie knelt there helping Joe, she felt someone behind her. She quickly turned around to look, but there was no one in sight.

Sallie saw her reaction, and she, too, looked around.

She didn't see anyone, either.

They looked at each other in silent understanding. Then there was the noise of a twig snapping in the nearby bushes. Joe and Dr. Plumbley heard it, too.

"Must be an animal or something," Mandie said, breaking the silence.

"I do not think so," Sallie said, still watching the bushes behind them. She stood up and Snowball escaped from her arms, bounding off into the bushes.

Mandie turned to chase him. "Snowball, come back here!" she called as she and Sallie followed the kitten into the bushes.

Joe and Dr. Plumbley went on with their work. Mandie bent down to look beneath the bushes. Suddenly she came upon a pair of worn boots in front of her. She raised up and came face to face with the man who was camping out at the old farmhouse. He looked wild, and his rifle was pointed straight at her.

"I done told y'all to stay away from here. I'm staking a claim," he told her in a slurred voice.

"We didn't go near your house on the rock pile," Mandie told him. Slowly backing up toward the area where Joe and Dr. Plumbley were working, she bumped into Sallie, who had been close behind her.

They grabbed each other's hands and tried to move backward, but the bushes were too thick. They got tangled in weeds and briars.

"I done told y'all to stay away from here," the man repeated. "I'm staking a claim."

Sallie whispered in Mandie's ear. "He has been drinking spirits."

Mandie was really frightened then. People sometimes went crazy like that. "We'll go, mister. We're going right now. I've lost my kitten, but as soon as we find him, we'll leave," she promised.

He just stood there pointing the rifle at them. Then suddenly he screamed in pain. Snowball had run up his back and was sticking his claws through the man's clothes. The man turned and twisted, trying to reach the kitten on his back.

The girls couldn't run away and leave the kitten.

Mandie began to yell. "Help, Joe! Help quick!"

"Help!" Sallie hollered.

Instantly Joe and Dr. Plumbley came running through the bushes.

Joe recognized the man and realized what was going on. Jumping behind the man, he grabbed the rifle. Then Dr. Plumbley knocked the man down with his fist.

"What are you doing here?" Joe demanded, holding the rifle over the man.

"Who are you, mister?" Dr. Plumbley asked.

The man didn't answer but lay there rubbing his jaw.

Snowball, frightened with all the commotion, ran to his mistress. Mandie picked him up and held him tightly.

"He's the man who was camping out in the old house on the rock pile," Joe explained. Glaring down at the man, he demanded, "I asked you a question, mister. What are you doing here?"

"I wanta know what y'all doin' on my land," the man said, managing to get to his feet.

"This is not your land," Joe told him.

"Yes it is, too," the man insisted. "Been abandoned by the Shaws all these years. I done staked a claim on it. Y'all git off my land."

"Mister, you had better get one thing straight," Dr. Plumbley said, shaking his fist in the man's face. "This is not your land and never has been, and if you don't get off of it in about one minute, I'll bust you good next time."

The man, who was much smaller than the doctor, began to tremble. "I'll go," he said, "but I'll need my rifle. I can't live without it to hunt with."

Joe held the gun tighter. "If I give you back the rifle, you'll shoot us all."

"I won't harm you," the man promised.

"You just get out of here," Dr. Plumbley ordered. "We'll take your rifle over to the boardinghouse when we get ready to leave. You can pick it up there. Now go, man!"

"I'm goin.' I'm goin' right now," the man mumbled. He turned and stumbled into the bushes.

"He had been drinking, hadn't he?" Mandie asked Joe as they walked back to the area where they were digging up bushes.

"He sure smelled like it. Ugh!" Joe made a nasty face. "But that cat . . ."

"It wasn't Snowball's fault this time," Mandie protested, hugging her kitten. "I know he ran away, but Sallie and I both felt someone watching us. That man was already there."

"Yes, the kitten may have saved your lives by attacking that man," Dr. Plumbley agreed. "He is one smart cat."

"Well, anyhow, we'd better get on with our work," Joe said, reaching for a bush to put back into place.

Once more Snowball escaped from Mandie's arms and ran straight to the hole and started scratching, throwing dirt all over Joe.

"Hey, Mandie, get that cat out of the way!" Joe hollered.

"All right." Mandie hurried to pick up Snowball. The kitten tried to resist her. "I'm sorry he kicked dirt all over you, Joe." She looked down at the hole he was going to put the bush in and blinked.

"Wait!" she cried. Stooping down beside the hole, she dug at the dirt with her hand. "There's something here!"

Joe quickly picked up the hoe and removed more dirt. Sallie and Dr. Plumbley crowded in to see what was going on.

With a clank, the hoe struck something. Joe dropped the tool and swept the dirt away with his hand, uncovering the top of a ceramic jar.

"We've found it! We've found it!" Mandie jumped up and down.

"Yes, we have!" Sallie exclaimed.

Dr. Plumbley wiped the perspiration from his face. "Thank goodness!" he said.

Joe carefully pulled the jar from the hole in the ground. It came out whole except for the bottom, which had cracked off. He gently laid the jar down in front of Mandie. Everyone sat down to see what it was.

Mandie dusted off the dirt. "A cookie jar!"

"Be careful. It's broken," Sallie cautioned.

Removing the lid, Mandie pulled out a faded piece of paper, which was wedged inside the jar.

Joe watched breathlessly as Mandie unfolded the paper. "I'll just give up if that's another map telling us to go somewhere else," he moaned.

The handwriting was dim, and the paper was crumbling. They all leaned over it as Mandie read aloud, " 'Hezekiah and his grandparents are so poor. I know my father helps them, but I want to do my share, too.' "

Mandie looked up at the doctor in amazement.

"Keep reading," Joe urged.

Mandie continued. " 'Hezekiah wants to grow up and become a doctor, and I think he would make a good one. I want to help him. My father has so much money. We need to give a lot of it away. I found this ruby myself in my father's mine. Hezekiah wouldn't be able to get his education here in the South, but the ruby must be worth enough money to pay for a doctor's education in New York City. So I'll hide it here until Hezekiah is old enough to go up North and learn to be a doctor. "For unto whomsoever much is given, of him shall be much required." Luke 12:48.' " Mandie's voice broke as she finished reading.

Tears flowed down Dr. Plumbley's black face. Everyone was silent for a moment.

"But where is the ruby?" Joe asked.

Mandie bent to look into the hole in the ground. Something glittered in the sunlight that filtered through the trees. She reached down and lifted the bottom of the ceramic jar, which held a huge ruby.

Mandie trembled as she reached for Dr. Plumbley's hand and tried to press the ruby into it. Her blue eyes clouded with tears. "It's yours, Hezekiah," she whispered hoarsely.

"No, no, Missy," the doctor protested. He pushed the stone back into her hand. "I can't take that."

"But it was Ruby's, and she wanted to give it to you," Mandie said, still offering the ruby to him. "I wish you could have had it before now to pay for your education."

"It would not have been possible for me to take it back then, either, Missy," he explained. "That is too valuable for someone to give away. You must give it to your uncle." He took a handkerchief out of his pocket to wipe his eyes.

"But it's not my uncle's," Mandie insisted. "It was Ruby's. She said in the note that she found it herself and that she was saving it for you. You have to take it, please."

"Missy, I don't want to argue about it. Let's just give it to your uncle and let him decide what to do with it," the doctor said.

"I know what he'll decide," Mandie said. "He'll do what Ruby planned to do with it. I'll give it to him and you'll see."

Dr. Plumbley rose and went back to working. "If we hurry and get those bushes replanted, I might get back in time for supper with Abraham," he said.

"Don't worry about supper," Mandie told him. "If it's too late to eat with Abraham, I'm sure my Uncle John will ask you to eat with us. And Jenny cooks wonderful meals."

Dr. Plumbley stopped for a moment. "What are we going to do about Jenny and Abraham?" he asked. "Do y'all have any suggestions about how we can get those two silly fools back together? They are absolutely wasting their lives by staying angry with each other."

"If they have been angry for forty years, I do not see a chance to bring them back together," Sallie said.

"Maybe we could work on Jenny if you would work on Abraham, Dr. Plumbley," Mandie suggested. "He's your friend, and he might listen to you."

"I don't know," the doctor said. "We've known each other ever since we were born, I suppose. But even though we did stay in touch through the mail, we've been separated a good many years. And Abraham's always been stubborn."

Joe helped the doctor replant another bush. "Why don't we just tell them both what we think of them for their childish nonsense?" he said. "I believe in coming out with it, whatever it may be."

"I would think that might cause them to become more stubborn if we criticized them," Sallie cautioned.

"We could try. If that didn't work, we could think up something else," Mandie said. "Maybe Uncle John knows more about it than Abraham told us."

"Yes, let's do talk to your uncle," the doctor agreed. "This worries me because I think so much of Abraham."

"My grandfather probably knows all about it, but he never tells any of his secrets unless he is forced to," Sallie reminded them.

"He might tell us something about this situation," Dr. Plumbley said.

Joe stepped back and surveyed their work. "Looks good as new again," he announced. "I don't think we harmed the plants any."

"I think they will be all right," said Dr. Plumbley. "Now, we must take the rifle back to the boardinghouse."

"I forgot about that," Joe groaned. "And here I am, starving to death." He picked up the rifle where he had laid it.

"I'm anxious to show the ruby to Uncle John and Mother." Mandie held Snowball tightly as she put the ruby and the note in her pocket.

Dr. Plumbley picked up the hoe. "I'll carry this," he offered.

Heading back the way they had come, they crossed the road again and went inside the boardinghouse. Jud Jenkinson stood behind the counter in the store.

"Well, hello, young folks. Glad to see you again," he greeted them.

Mandie introduced Dr. Plumbley. "He lived in the house that burned down here before yours was built. His grandparents died in that fire."

Jud came out from behind the counter to shake hands with the doctor. "I'm pleased to make your acquaintance," he said. "Do you still live around here, Doctor?"

"No, I've been in New York ever since my grandparents died," Dr. Plumbley replied. "I have my own medical practice up there. I'm just visiting my brother, Elijah Plumbley. He lives about ten miles down the main road from town."

"I believe I've heard of him," Jud said. "If you've been gone all these years, you probably found everything a lot different here in Franklin."

"Just about everything." Dr. Plumbley laughed.

"We've come to ask a favor, Mr. Jenkinson," Joe said, laying the rifle on the counter. "This belongs to a wild man who says he's staking a claim to that old house on the rock pile across the road a ways. He threatened us with the gun for being on the land." Joe's voice squeaked a little. "We managed to take the gun away from him, and we told him we'd leave it here. Would you mind giving it to him if he comes looking for it?"

"Why, I'll be glad to," Mr. Jenkinson agreed. "But if you're talking about property within three miles of here across the road, it all belongs to the Shaws. Didn't you know that, Miss Mandie?"

"No, I don't know anything about Uncle John's property," Mandie answered. "But Hezekiah—Dr. Plumbley here—said it used to be my grandfather's."

The man nodded.

"Thanks, Mr. Jenkinson," Joe said. "We have to be going now. That delicious smell of food from your kitchen makes me hungry, and it'll be suppertime by the time we get back to Mandie's house."

"You're welcome. Y'all come back to see me," Mr. Jenkinson called to them as they left.

Mandie set Snowball on her shoulder. "Now we have three things to ask Uncle John about," she said: "the ruby, this crazy man, and Jenny and Abraham."

They hurried along the dirt path back to Uncle John's house.

"I hope he has all the answers," Joe said.

"If he does not know, my grandfather will know all about those things," Sallie promised.

"If he'll tell," Mandie added.

CHAPTER ELEVEN

OTHER PEOPLE'S BUSINESS

"We found it! We found it!" the three young people cried, rushing into the Shaws' sunroom.

Uncle John, Elizabeth, and Uncle Ned halted their conversation abruptly.

"Look!" Mandie put Snowball down and hurriedly took the huge ruby out of her apron pocket. "This is what we found!" she exclaimed. "And here's the note that was buried with it." She handed the ruby and the paper to Uncle John.

The young people dropped into chairs around the room, and Dr. Plumbley sat on the settee with Uncle John and Elizabeth.

John Shaw quickly scanned the note and examined the ruby. Elizabeth read the note aloud so Uncle Ned would know what was going on. A sad expression crossed Uncle Ned's wrinkled face.

"Imagine, burying a ruby like this!" Elizabeth examined the gem, then gave it back to her husband.

"Dr. Plumbley, I believe you have just inherited what looks like a perfect ruby," John said, offering the ruby to the doctor.

Dr. Plumbley shook his head. "Oh, no, Mr. Shaw. I couldn't accept that. It wouldn't be right of me."

"Oh, nonsense!" John replied. "It plainly says here that Ruby was saving it for you. I'd like to carry out her wishes. If she had lived, I'm sure you would have had it long before now. And if my father had known about it, he would have made sure that you got it before he died."

"But Mr. Shaw, Ruby wanted to keep that for my education. Like I told these young people, I got my education years ago, and I've long since repaid my aunt who financed it. I don't need it now," the doctor insisted.

"That doesn't matter. It is yours. Ruby gave it to you. There was just a delay in your receiving it," John said, once again holding the ruby out to him.

Dr. Plumbley stood up. "I'm afraid I must be going now," he said. "Abraham is supposed to have supper ready for me. It has been a pleasure meeting all you good folks, and I hope to see you again."

"Wait, Dr. Plumbley." Mandie stood up, trying to detain him. "We haven't decided what we're going to do about Jenny and Abraham, remember?"

"And we haven't told Mr. Shaw about the crazy man yet," Joe added.

Sallie glanced at her grandfather. "Yes, we must discuss this while my grandfather is also present," she said. "He may know something."

The doctor looked into Mandie's pleading blue eyes and sat back down. "I can only stay a minute longer, or Abraham will think I'm not coming back," the doctor insisted.

Mandie returned to her chair. "First, we'll tell them about the crazy man," she began, relating their adventures with the wild man and his rifle.

Elizabeth's face showed alarm, and Uncle Ned leaned forward in concern.

"You didn't find out who the man was?" Uncle John asked with a frown.

"No, he wouldn't tell us his name," Mandie replied.

"We were so afraid of him we wanted to hurry and get away," Sallie said.

"I'm pretty sure he had been drinking," Joe explained. "He was wild. He didn't make any sense."

"He could have been dangerous," Uncle John said. "We do still own that land and also that old house sitting on the rock pile. We just haven't used it in a long time. He had no right to be on our land. There's no way he can claim it."

Uncle Ned finally spoke. "Must be man named Sod. Live in Burningtown."

"Sod?" Uncle John questioned the odd name. "I've never heard of him."

Dr. Plumbley turned to Uncle Ned. "Was his father named Lister?"

Uncle Ned nodded. "Yes, father dead long ago."

"I thought there was something familiar about him. He's about the same age I am. I remember he was always stirring up trouble among the young people," Dr. Plumbley told them. "Back then people thought he had a little something missing."

"I think I know whom you're talking about," John said. "I wonder why he thinks he can stake a claim to our property?"

"He have more missing now. Make no sense," Uncle Ned observed.

"Maybe he has also become a drunkard," Dr. Plumbley suggested. "Anyway, I think we're rid of him. I don't believe he'll be back."

"I'm glad Dr. Plumbley was with y'all," Elizabeth said. "He could have hurt you."

"Uncle John, we have something else we want to talk to you about," Mandie said, changing the subject. "Did you know that Abraham and Jenny are married?"

Uncle John nodded slowly and smiled at her.

"And that they haven't lived together in forty years?" Mandie continued.

Uncle John kept nodding. "Yes, we know all about that."

"John!" Elizabeth sounded shocked. "You mean our cook, Jenny, is married to Abraham the gardener? Why does she live here in the house with us while he stays in that cottage in the back yard? What happened?"

Mandie related what Abraham had said about the man at the stables, but Elizabeth couldn't believe the story.

"Well, I've never heard of such a silly reason to separate," Elizabeth said. "And this has been going on for forty years?"

Sallie sat up straight in her chair. "I think he is still in love with Jenny," she said.

Uncle Ned nodded. "Too stubborn to tell her."

"You're right, Uncle Ned," John Shaw agreed. "Abraham has always been a stubborn man. He always has to have things his way. My father let him run the garden whatever way he wanted to. He does a good job if you leave him alone, but don't ever tell him he's wrong about anything, especially about Jenny."

"What about Jenny?" Mandie asked. "Is she stubborn, too?"

"Well, sometimes," Uncle John said. "But you can get her to see two sides of a question most of the time."

"Then maybe we should work on her," Joe said.

Elizabeth's eyebrows shot up. "Work on her?"

"We've all decided to see if we can get them together again," Mandie said.

"Dear, don't go interfering in other's people's business," Elizabeth warned.

"We're only trying to help," Mandie replied.

"We think if one knows how the other one feels, we might be able to make them realize they're wasting their lives apart," Joe explained.

"And make them realize that they do still love each other," Sallie added.

Uncle Ned smiled. "Pray Big God help. Been tried before."

"Tried before, Uncle Ned?" Mandie asked.

"I try. Listen, but do nothing," the old Indian replied. "Too stubborn."

Dr. Plumbley stood up again. "I really must go. Abraham is probably waiting for me to eat with him."

"Won't you please take this ruby?" Uncle John tried again, standing up beside the big man. "It's rightfully yours. And it would give me great pleasure to be able to carry out Ruby's wishes."

"No, thank you, Mr. Shaw, but I couldn't accept such a gift," the doctor told him. "I appreciate your kindness, and I hope we remain friends."

"Of course we'll always be friends," Uncle John assured him. "This has nothing to do with our friendship. We want you to feel welcome at our house here at any time."

"Yes, Dr. Plumbley, you must come back to visit us," Elizabeth insisted. "It is our good fortune to know a friend of John's sister, Ruby."

"Thank you, ma'am," the doctor said. "Thank you very much. I will come again. And if y'all are ever up in New York, please let me know, and come to visit with my wife and me."

Mandie's blue eyes lit up. "Uncle John, could we go to New York one day?" she asked. "I've never been there."

Uncle John smiled down at her. "One of these days we'll just have to take a trip up there," he said.

Dr. Plumbley turned to go.

"When are you leaving town, Dr. Plumbley?" Joe asked.

"If my brother is getting along as well tomorrow morning as he has been, I plan to return to New York tomorrow," the doctor said. "I have enjoyed being with you young people especially."

"Thank you, sir," Joe said.

"We've enjoyed getting to know you, Hezekiah," Mandie said. She took his hand and gave it a squeeze.

The Negro doctor smiled with a sad expression in his eyes.

"Will you talk to Abraham?" Sallie asked.

"Yes, I will talk to him. You young people work on Jenny," he said, leaving the room. "Good night and thanks."

After seeing the doctor to the front door, Uncle John returned to the sunroom and sat down. He turned the ruby over in his hands. "What am I going to do with this?" he asked, looking at Uncle Ned.

"Maybe Elijah, brother of Samuel, need," the old Indian suggested.

"That's an idea. We'll find out what his circumstances are and see if we can help him," John agreed.

"Ruby would be disappointed if she knew Hezekiah wouldn't accept the ruby, wouldn't she?" Mandie said.

"I imagine so." Uncle John nodded. "I just wish there were some way to get him to take it."

"Ruby must have had a very warm heart to have given him something so valuable," Elizabeth remarked.

Uncle Ned smiled sadly. "Ruby good all way through," he said.

"Maybe we can figure out some way to carry out Ruby's wishes," Mandie suggested.

"But what about Jenny?" Joe asked.

Mandie walked over to her mother and put her arm around her. "Mother, is Jenny cooking supper right now?" she asked.

"Well, not exactly cooking. Since this is Sunday, she's probably warming up what was left over from our noon meal," Elizabeth replied.

"Let's go see what she's doing," Mandie told Joe and Sallie.

The three young people rose and started to leave the room.

"All of you get washed up first, so you'll be ready to eat," Elizabeth told them.

They hurried upstairs, hastily cleaned up, and raced back down to the kitchen, where Jenny was stirring two pots of food at once on the big iron cookstove. Jenny saw them come in and quickly turned back to the stove.

Joe strode up behind her, trying to look into the pots. "Jenny, something smells delicious!" he exclaimed.

"Git out of here," she snapped. "I ain't got no time fo' no foolishness."

"What we want to talk to you about is not foolishness. It's just plain common sense," Mandie said.

The cook didn't reply. She just kept stirring the pots.

"Jenny, this food smells awfully good," Joe complimented her. "Why don't you take some of this nice-smelling food to poor old Abraham out there all alone in his little house?"

"Git!" Jenny hissed.

"We don't want to git," Mandie told her. "We want to stay right here and talk to you until you get supper on the table."

"Well, you ain't, Missy," Jenny said, turning to look at her, " 'cause I'll go git Aunt Lou to git you out of here."

"You don't want Aunt Lou to hear what we're going to talk to you about, do you?" Joe asked.

"Ain't nuthin' to talk 'bout," Jenny said, still stirring the pots.

"I don't think there's been enough talking done. That's what's wrong with things now," Mandie said. "If you and Abraham had really talked things over, you wouldn't be living here alone in the house and him alone out there in the little cottage."

"Ain't none of yo' bidness." Jenny slammed a lid onto one of the pots.

"We're only trying to help you," Mandie insisted.

Sallie looked directly into Jenny's eyes. "Abraham still loves you," she said.

Jenny stopped stirring.

"He does," Sallie assured her.

Jenny slammed the lid onto another pot and said, "No, he don't!"

"But he does still love you a whole lot, Jenny," Mandie argued.

"Now, how y'all knows dat?" Jenny asked.

Joe smiled. "We have ways of finding out things."

"What ways dat be?" Jenny asked.

"We talked to Abraham," Mandie said.

"And he done tol' you dat?"

"He didn't have to say it," Mandie said. "We could tell."

Just then one of the pots on the stove started to boil over. Jenny quickly turned back to the stove and slid the pot off the burner. "Y'all gwine t' cause me t' burn up de supper, and den you won't have nuthin' t' eat tonight," she grumbled.

"We'll help you watch it," Joe said. Picking up a large spoon, he began stirring one of the pots. "Oh, Jenny, these beans are starting to stick." He grabbed a towel nearby and pulled the pot off the burner.

Mandie tried to get back to the subject. "Jenny, don't you love Abraham?" she asked. "You must have loved him when you married him."

Jenny turned around and put her hands on her slim hips. "Y'all git out of here," she demanded, "or y'all ain't gwine t' have no supper."

"You might as well give in," Joe teased. "It's three against one."

Jenny busied herself at the stove again. "Go ahaid and talk. You ain't gittin' no answers."

"Didn't you take the vows, 'till death do us part,' when you married Abraham?" Mandie persisted. "You're not living up to your part of the bargain."

"And don't blame it all on Abraham," Joe added.

"Maybe there were some misunderstandings on both sides," Mandie added.

Jenny kept stirring the pots vigorously.

"Everybody has faults," Mandie reminded her. "Nobody is perfect. So we need to forgive each other and wipe the slate clean."

Sallie rested her hand lightly on Jenny's shoulder. "Abraham is so lonely out there in that little cottage all alone," she said softly. "He does not even have anyone to talk to out there."

Jenny glanced at the Indian girl.

"Really lonely," Sallie added.

Silently, Jenny began removing the pots from the stove. Joe rushed to help her, and then she started taking dishes down from the cupboard.

"And you must be lonely all alone up there in that little room," Mandie said. "It's just not right for a man and his wife to be separated."

Jenny slammed the dishes down, but fortunately they didn't break. She turned quickly to face Mandie. "You listen here now! It better a man and his wife live apart than to live together and fuss and fight!" she said vehemently.

"Did y'all fuss and fight?" Mandie asked, taken aback.

"It was all one-sided fussin' wid dat Abraham doin' it all," Jenny replied. "I wouldn't belittle myself to fuss back. I jes' up and left."

"Then we'll have to talk to Abraham," Joe said.

"Don't do no good to talk to dat man. Too stubborn," Jenny said, taking down more dishes.

"That is what my grandfather said—that Abraham is stubborn," Sallie confirmed.

Mandie smoothed her blonde braid. "We'll have to find a way to break his stubborn streak."

"Den y'all go do dat and leave me alone," Jenny told them.

The three young people looked at each other and smiled. Maybe Jenny was listening to them after all.

"Let's run over there and see what Abraham is doing," Mandie suggested.

"Fine," Joe agreed. "As long as we get back in time for supper."

"Supper be ready in a minute," Jenny warned them.

"We'll hurry," Mandie said.

They rushed out the back door and over to Abraham's little cottage.

Abraham came to the door and allowed them to come back to the kitchen where he and Dr. Plumbley were preparing their supper. "What y'all be wantin'?" he fussed.

"We want to see Dr. Plumbley for a minute," Mandie said. She stood on tiptoe to speak into the doctor's ear. "We've been talking to you-know-who," she whispered.

Dr. Plumbley nodded and continued setting the table.

Mandie turned to the gardener. "Abraham, we've been talking to Jenny, and we found out she still loves you," Mandie said.

Abraham turned furiously, burning his finger on a pot handle. "If dat's what y'all come here fo,' " he yelled, "y'all kin jes' git back to de big house!" He stuck his finger in his mouth to cool the burn.

"That food smells good, Abraham. You must be a good cook," Joe said.

Abraham ignored the compliment.

"Jenny sure is a good cook, too," Joe continued. "The Shaws are lucky people to have her to cook all those delicious meals. She sure knows what she's doing."

"She don't know what she's doin,' " Abraham argued. "She don't know how to come in outta de rain."

"She must know something about what she's doing because she sure cooks good meals. We enjoy them," Mandie said.

"And she does still love you, Abraham," Sallie assured him.

"Love!" the gardener scoffed. "Dat woman don't know what dat word mean!"

Mandie sighed deeply. "Abraham, did Dr. Plumbley tell you about what we found this afternoon?" she asked. "You should have come with us."

"No, he ain't told me what you found," Abraham said. "You mean y'all done found sumpin'?"

"We found Ruby's treasure on the map we showed you. It was a great big ruby, a real one," Mandie explained.

"A great big ruby? What you gwine to do wid it?" Abraham asked.

"Ruby left a note that said she wanted Dr. Plumbley to have it, and Uncle John tried to give it to him, but he wouldn't take it," Mandie replied.

Abraham whirled to face his doctor friend. "Wouldn't take it?" he hollered. "Is you crazy in de haid? Why don't you take dat ruby?"

Dr. Plumbley looked up from dishing food from the pot. "I explained to Mr. Shaw that I don't need it," he said.

"Well, he don't need it neither," Abraham said. "Anybody offer me anything like dat, I takes it."

Mandie smiled at the doctor. "I don't think Abraham is the only stubborn one around here."

"Me, stubborn?" Abraham protested. "I ain't stubborn."

"You are definitely stubborn, Abraham," Mandie told him. "You're so stubborn you'd rather live alone than go tell Jenny you still love her."

Abraham thought for a moment. "She don't love me," he said. "She never did."

"You're not a mind reader," Dr. Plumbley spoke up. "How do you know what Jenny thinks? You've never asked her, have you?"

"I don't hafta aks her. I knows," Abraham muttered as he set a platter of fried chicken on the table.

"No, you don't know either. You're guessing," the doctor argued.

There was a knock at the door and Liza yelled, "Eatin' time! Eatin' time!"

"Coming!" Joe yelled back.

"We'll see you later, Abraham," Mandie said. "Good night, Dr. Plumbley."

The three young people hurried back to the house for their supper. As they entered the back door they came face-to-face with Aunt Lou.

Aunt Lou shook her big apron at them. "Y'all git in dat dinin' room," she scolded. "And don't y'all come botherin' de cook no mo.' You hear?"

"We won't," they all promised.

They met up with the adults in the hallway on their way into the dining room.

"I hear y'all have been in the kitchen bothering Jenny," Elizabeth chided. "I suppose you have also been bothering Abraham."

After Uncle John returned thanks for the food at the table, Liza placed a platter of food in front of them. "Oh, dat botherin' done Jenny good," she said. "She be in there singin' a love song. I ain't never seen her so happy."

The three young people looked at one another and grinned.

"She sho' is, and I ain't never heerd her sing like dat befo,' " the Negro girl continued. "I don't know what's goin' on, but it sho' be good."

CHAPTER TWELVE

MUCH IS GIVEN

Before sunrise Monday morning, the young people gathered in the sunroom, waiting for Jenny to prepare breakfast. Snowball didn't like the early hour, and he curled up asleep by his mistress.

Sallie sat down beside Mandie on the settee. "We must part ways today," she said sadly.

"But we can all get together for Christmas," Joe reminded her. "And that's not so long off."

"I feel as though our search was all for nothing," Mandie said with a little pout. "Dr. Plumbley won't take the ruby, and Uncle John doesn't know what to do with it."

"He'll come up with a good use for it, I'm sure," Joe said.

The young people sat silently for several moments, then Mandie spoke. "Do you reckon Abraham and Jenny will ever get together again?"

"They might if they would talk things over," Sallie said.

"But they're not even at the talking stage," Joe remarked. "They don't want to talk to each other."

"I just thought of something." Mandie changed the subject. "We promised to let Mrs. Hadley know what we found buried on the map."

"Would we have time to visit them this morning?" Sallie asked. "I do not know what time my grandfather and I will be leaving. Maybe he would ride out there with us this morning."

"My father probably won't be here until this afternoon. He has some calls to make on the way," Joe said.

"I'll ask my mother if we can go," Mandie promised.

When Elizabeth and Uncle John came downstairs for breakfast, they gave the young people permission to visit the Hadleys, provided Uncle Ned went with them. He agreed to go.

Uncle John had put the ruby away in his safe because it was too valuable for Mandie to be carrying around. But he allowed her to take the note they had found to show Mrs. Hadley.

When they arrived, they joined the Hadleys in their parlor. Mrs. Hadley read the note and listened to the three young people's account of what they found.

"What a sad story," the woman responded.

"If only we could get Dr. Plumbley to accept the ruby," Mandie said.

Mrs. Hadley gave the note back to Mandie. "But dear, you said he told y'all he didn't need it."

"My Uncle John doesn't need it either," Mandie replied.

"Think of all the good that could be done with that ruby," the woman mused. "It could feed a lot of hungry people or pay for medical treatment of sick people who can't afford a doctor, especially the Cherokees."

"We're building a hospital for the Cherokees not far from where Uncle Ned and Sallie live," Mandie told her. "We were exploring a cave and found some gold that belonged to them many years ago. They wouldn't accept the gold, so we're using it to build the hospital."

"That's a wonderful thing to do," said Mr. Hadley, who was sitting next to Uncle Ned. "So many people can't afford a doctor these days."

"My father doctors sick people whether they can pay or not," Joe spoke up. "He says God gave him his talents in medicine and that they should be put to use for the good of the people, not just for profit."

"Dr. Woodard is a fine man," Mr. Hadley said. "Are you going to study medicine, too, when you grow up?"

"No, sir, I don't think so," Joe replied. "I think I'd rather be a lawyer."

"Well, people need lawyers, too," Mrs. Hadley agreed.

Uncle Ned stood up. "Must go now," he announced.

The young people promised to visit again and rode off on their ponies with Uncle Ned.

As they approached the Shaw home, they spotted Dr. Plumbley's horse and buggy at the gate.

Mandie frowned in confusion. "I didn't think Dr. Plumbley was coming back again," she said. "I thought he was going home to New York."

"Maybe he forgot something," Sallie suggested.

"Probably came by to tell Abraham good-bye," Joe said.

They all dismounted and tied their horses to the hitching post at the gate.

"When are we leaving to go home, my grandfather?" Sallie asked.

"Eat first, then go," Uncle Ned said, starting up the walkway to the house.

The young people rushed ahead. Inside, they met Liza in the front hallway.

"In de parlor," she said, waving her hand in that direction.

They could hear Dr. Plumbley's strong voice and hurried to see why he had come back. Stopping at the doorway, with Uncle Ned behind them, they looked into the parlor.

Uncle John and Elizabeth sat on the settee. Dr. Plumbley was seated nearby. A tall, thin Negro boy, a little older than Joe, sat alone by a window.

"Come on in. This is Dr. Plumbley's brother's grandson, Moses," Uncle John said, introducing everyone.

The young people sat down near Moses.

"I thought you were leaving town this morning," Mandie said to Dr. Plumbley.

The doctor drew a deep breath. "I had planned to," he said. "But my brother Elijah crossed over in his sleep sometime during the night."

"He died?" Mandie gasped. "Oh, I'm sorry, Dr. Plumbley."

Joe and Sallie also expressed their sympathy.

"I thought he was better," Dr. Plumbley said, wiping his eyes with a handkerchief, "but I reckon the Lord thought it was time for him to go."

Moses caught his breath and looked away from the young people so they wouldn't see the tears in his eyes.

"Is there anything we can do?" Joe asked.

"No, thank you," the doctor replied. "I just came to town to make the arrangements. I'll be leaving as soon as everything is over. Moses will be alone now since both his parents are dead. So I brought him to town to see if he could stay with Abraham until I can send for him. Moses wants to study medicine."

"Why don't you take him with you when you leave?" Mandie asked.

The doctor didn't answer for a moment, and then he said, "Well, you see, it costs a lot of money to go to New York from here. And my wife and I will have to find a larger place to live. We only have one bedroom—"

"The ruby!" Mandie interrupted. "Uncle John, the ruby! We can give it to Moses!"

Uncle John smiled at her. "That's exactly what I was thinking. I'll go get it."

As he left the room, Dr. Plumbley protested. "No, no," he said. "Moses couldn't accept that ruby any more than I could."

Moses looked puzzled, and the young people explained how they came to find the ruby.

"I sho' wish I could've gone with y'all," Moses said. "Must've been a lot of fun."

"Except for the crazy man threatening us," Joe reminded him.

When Uncle John came back into the room, he walked over to Moses and showed the ruby to him. "This is what they found," he said, cradling the ruby in the palm of his hand.

Moses' eyes grew wide at the sight of the shiny red gem.

Uncle John walked over to sit beside Dr. Plumbley. "Now there's no use arguing about this," he said. "We want you to take this and use it for Moses' education. There are never enough doctors, so the money will be well spent." John held the stone out to the doctor.

"That's right," Dr. Plumbley replied. "There's no use arguing about it because we're not going to accept it." He shook his head. "There's no way we could ever pay you back, so it just wouldn't be right for us to take it."

"You could take the boy on home with you to New York now, and you wouldn't have to send for him later," John Shaw reasoned. "You could find a bigger place to live after you get him up there and put him in school."

"Mr. Shaw, you don't realize how much your family has already done for mine," Dr. Plumbley argued. "Your father practically fed and clothed my grandparents and me. And I've never been able to repay it. I can't get further indebted to the Shaw family."

"Stubborn, just like Abraham," said Uncle Ned.

"You also have the cost of your brother's funeral to pay out," John reminded him. "How do you think you're going to manage all these things without some help? You told us you only make a meager living from doctoring. This is not my help. It's Ruby helping you."

"It's not Ruby's help. She left many years ago. That stone belongs to you and nobody else," the doctor insisted.

"You're wrong. It is not mine," John replied. "I consider the note that Ruby wrote the same as a will. She willed this to you, and she would be awfully hurt if she knew you wouldn't accept it."

Dr. Plumbley stood up. "I'm sorry, Mr. Shaw. I don't look at it that way. I thank you very much, but I cannot accept the ruby. Now, I need to find Abraham and talk to him about Moses."

After the doctor and his nephew had gone, John Shaw turned to his wife. "I don't understand why he won't take this ruby," he said in frustration.

"Well, he just doesn't want it, so you can't make him accept it, John," Elizabeth said.

"I guess I should lock it up again then," John said, rising to leave the room.

Mandie looked at her friends. "Let's go outside," she suggested.

Sallie and Joe followed her out onto the front porch, and they all sat down in the big swing. For several minutes they gently rocked back and forth in the swing, talking about the ruby, Dr. Plumbley, his nephew, and the situation with Abraham and Jenny.

"Why don't we go see what Jenny is cooking for dinner?" Joe suggested. "I'm hungry."

Mandie and Sallie laughed.

"I know what you're up to, Joe Woodard," Mandie teased as they rose from the swing.

"We'd better be quiet. Aunt Lou may catch us." Joe led the way around the house to the back door, so they wouldn't have to pass the parlor, where the adults were sitting.

The three were trying to silently ease the back door open when Jenny suddenly came up behind them and pushed it open.

"Out o' my way! I'se gotta see 'bout de food befo' it burn up," Jenny fussed, rushing into the kitchen.

The three young people stood outside the back door for a moment.

"Now where has Jenny been?" Joe asked quietly.

"Probably taking the garbage out," Sallie answered.

"Or visiting Abraham?" Mandie speculated.

"Abraham? Do you think she might have been over there?" Joe asked.

"Let's go visit him," Mandie said.

They turned and walked over to the gardener's cottage, but he was nowhere to be seen. Dr. Plumbley and Moses were sitting on Abraham's porch alone.

"Is Abraham not home?" Mandie asked as she and her two friends sat down on the steps.

"No, we're waiting for him," Dr. Plumbley replied.

"Here he comes now," Joe said.

Abraham plodded across the yard from the back door of the big house, carrying a flour sack stuffed full of something. He stumbled up onto the porch, shoved the sack through his front door, and then sat down on the porch with the doctor. "I jes' heered 'bout Elijah, Samuel. I'm terrible sorry," he said. "Mr. Shaw jes' told me."

"You weren't home when we came," Dr. Plumbley told his friend, "so we went over there."

"Ain't been gone long." Abraham slowly rocked back and forth in his rocking chair. "Been over to de big house gittin' some things."

Dr. Plumbley looked at Abraham pleadingly. "I wanted to ask you if you'd let Moses stay here with you until I can send for him," he said. "I don't want him to stay alone out there in Elijah's house."

"Stay here wid me?" Abraham stopped rocking and pondered the question.

"I'll send you money for his board, of course," Dr. Plumbley said.

"Stay wid me?" Abraham repeated. "I don't think dat would work out, Samuel."

"What do you mean, Abraham? Moses is a good boy, easy to get along with," the doctor assured him.

Abraham looked directly at the boy. "I knows you's a good boy," he said. "It's jes' dat it wouldn't be—uh—convenient—uh—right now."

"Convenient? What on earth are you talking about?" the doctor asked.

The young people leaned forward, listening for his answer.

"I—uh—already have somebody gwine t' stay wid me," Abraham explained, avoiding the doctor's gaze.

"Oh, I see. I didn't know you were taking in a boarder," Dr. Plumbley said.

"Well, dadblame it, Samuel!" Abraham exploded. "Here ebrybody been preachin' to me, and when I finally gits 'round to askin' Jenny to come home, you be tryin' to give me a boarder. She wouldn't like dat."

"Abraham!" Mandie cried. "Jenny is coming home?" She jumped up and reached for the old man's hand. "I'm thrilled to death!"

"Abraham, if your wife is coming back to live with you, I wouldn't interfere with that for anything in the world." Dr. Plumbley beamed. "I'm so happy for you!"

"Let's go see Jenny!" Joe exclaimed.

The young people hurried across the yard to the big house, but as they pushed open the back door, they came face-to-face with Aunt Lou.

"Where y'all goin' in sech a all-fired hurry?" Aunt Lou demanded.

"We've got to see Jenny, Aunt Lou," Mandie answered.

The big Negro housekeeper quickly grabbed her by the shoulders and turned her the other direction. "You ain't botherin' Jenny. She got to git dat dinnuh done!" Aunt Lou scolded. "Now git goin.' "

"But we just wanted to tell her how happy we are that she is moving in with Abraham," Mandie said.

"I knows all 'bout dat," Aunt Lou said. "You tell her later."

Mandie sighed, and she and her friends walked down the hallway to the parlor, where the adults still sat talking.

"Guess what?" Mandie announced. "Jenny is moving in with Abraham."

"That's great," Uncle John replied.

"It's about time," Elizabeth agreed.

Uncle Ned grinned broadly.

"But it's not all good news," Joe said. "Abraham is not going to let Moses stay with him because Jenny won't like it."

Everyone became silent, and the three young people sat down on the settee.

"I wonder what Dr. Plumbley is going to do," Sallie said.

"He is going to have to take that ruby, whether he likes it or not," Mandie stated.

Uncle John smiled. "You're right, Amanda," he agreed. "You get him back in here while I go get the ruby."

The young people hurried over to Abraham's front porch where Abraham, Dr. Plumbley, and Moses were still sitting.

"Uncle John wants you to come back to see him for a minute, Dr. Plumbley," Mandie called up to the porch.

"Do you know what he wants? We have to be going," the doctor replied.

"He just said to ask you to come back for a minute," Mandie said. "Come on."

Dr. Plumbley and Moses followed the young people to the house and into the parlor where John Shaw sat holding the ruby once more.

"You wanted to see us about something, Mr. Shaw?" Dr. Plumbley asked.

"Yes, sit down for just a minute. I know you're in a hurry," John Shaw told him.

Everyone sat down.

John cleared his throat. "Now there is nothing left for you to do but take this ruby for Moses," he insisted. "I understand Abraham is moving Jenny in over there and can't keep the boy."

Dr. Plumbley immediately stood up. "I'm sorry, Mr. Shaw. I've already told you I couldn't do that," the doctor refused.

John also stood. "What other alternative do you have?"

"I'll figure out something, but I can't accept charity," the doctor said.

"Charity!" John bellowed. "This is something that rightfully belongs to you!"

The doctor touched Moses on the shoulder and turned toward the door.

Mandie blocked his way. "Dr. Plumbley," she said firmly, "are you going to let your pride stand in the way of Moses' education? There have been plenty of other people who have paid for someone else's education before. Why can't you take the ruby for Moses? My father used to say, 'pride goeth before a fall.' "

Dr. Plumbley did not move. "I'm sorry, Missy," he said softly.

"And remember the Bible verse Ruby wrote in her note?" Mandie continued. " 'For unto whomsoever much is given, of him shall be much required.' What if your pride keeps us from living up to that?"

Tears rolled down the doctor's black face as he reached for Mandie's small hand. "Missy, you're so much like little Ruby. That's the way she always talked," he said shakily.

Mandie held her other hand out to Uncle John for the ruby, and he gave it to her. When she pressed the gem into the doctor's big hand, he didn't refuse it this time.

Dr. Plumbley stared at it through his tears. "I may not live that long, but Moses will repay this," he promised, looking at the boy. "It will all be repaid."

"You don't pay someone back for a gift," Mandie argued. "Ruby gave this to you as a gift."

"That's right," Uncle John persisted. "If you want to show your gratitude, you just help Moses be the best doctor he can be."

Just then Liza stuck her head in the door. "Dinnuh done be ready!" she announced.

Elizabeth rose gracefully. "Dr. Plumbley, you and Moses must come on in and eat dinner with us," she said. "I know you're in a hurry, but you've got to eat somewhere."

"Yes, come on," John urged.

Dr. Plumbley put his arm around Mandie. "Thank you, Missy—little Ruby." He looked up. "Thank you all for everything," he said.

As soon as the noon meal was over, Uncle Ned motioned to Mandie. "Come. Talk. Then Sallie and I leave."

She followed him out onto the front porch. The others understood and waited inside.

As they sat down in the swing, Uncle Ned took Mandie's small white hand in his. His face was shining as he spoke to her. "Papoose do good job," he said. "Ruby be proud of Papoose."

"Thank you, Uncle Ned. When you asked me to come out here, I was wondering what I had done wrong," Mandie admitted. "What you say to me always means so much."

"See? Easy to be good Papoose," Uncle Ned told her. "Easy to be good as it is to be bad."

"I'm trying hard, Uncle Ned," Mandie said.

"Must ask Big God take care of Moses now his father gone to happy hunting ground," the old Indian said.

"Yes, let's do." Mandie looked toward the sky, holding the old Indian's hand. "Dear God, please take care of Moses and help him to become a doctor, a good doctor, God. He's going to miss his grandpa. Thank you."

"Yes, Big God. Bless Moses," Uncle Ned asked, looking upward.

"He will," Mandie promised.

"Yes, must go now," Uncle Ned said.

Mandie looked up suddenly, hearing the sound of approaching hoofbeats.

A stranger on horseback dismounted at the gate in front of them and came up the walkway to the front porch. "Good afternoon," he said, a little out of breath. "I have a message for Miss Amanda Shaw." He offered them an envelope.

Puzzled, Mandie took it. "I'm Amanda Shaw," she replied. "Thank you." What is this? she wondered.

As the man left, Mandie opened the envelope and withdrew a sheet of paper. She began reading aloud. " 'Dear Amanda, I have just learned of a great mystery here in Asheville that sounds like an adventure you would enjoy. Please hurry back in time to spend the night with me so that I may tell you about it before you have to check into school. Love always, Grandmother Taft.' "

Uncle Ned patted the top of her blonde head. "Remember. Be good Papoose. Do not get in trouble. Will see you at school first full moon," he promised.

This must be something awfully exciting for Grandmother to send me a special letter like this, Mandie thought.

She could hardly wait to return to Asheville.

MANDIE

AND THE
MYSTERIOUS
BELLS

With love
to my other granddaughter,
Jordan Leigh Leppard,
that adorable, brown-eyed dear,
who knows Mandie's story
but can't read it herself yet.

CONTENTS

MANDIE AND THE MYSTERIOUS BELLS

"Blessed are the merciful;
for they shall obtain mercy."
Matthew 5:7

CHAPTER ONE

GRANDMOTHER'S MYSTERY

As Mandie stepped off the train with Jason Bond in Asheville, North Carolina, she found her good friend Celia waiting on the depot platform.

"Celia!" she exclaimed. "How did you get here?"

"Your grandmother sent me," Celia replied. The two girls embraced each other. "You see, she asked my mother to let me come back a day early for school on account of the mystery that she wrote you about."

Mandie pulled her coat around her more tightly to keep out the cold wind. "Has she told you what it's all about yet?" she asked eagerly.

"No, she's waiting for you," Celia answered. She turned to greet Mandie's companion. "How are you, Mr. Bond?"

"Fine, little lady," Mr. Bond replied, smiling down at the girl. "Mr. and Mrs. Shaw were busy, so they sent me with Miss Amanda."

"Come on," Celia urged. "Ben is waiting with the rig over there." She led the way down the platform. "Here he comes now. Have you got all your baggage?"

"I'll get the trunk, Missy," Mr. Bond offered, hurrying to where all the luggage had been unloaded from the train.

Ben drove the rig over to pick up the baggage, and the two men loaded the trunk and the bag Mandie was carrying.

Ben smiled at Mandie. "Welcome home, Missy. We'se glad to have you back."

Mandie laughed. "Thanks, Ben, but my grandmother's house is not home," she reminded him. "My mother and stepfather, Uncle John, back in Franklin, would have a fit if they heard you call this home."

"But you lives at dat Miz Heathwoods' school back up yonder on de hill . . ." Ben looked puzzled.

"Only while school is going on," Mandie explained as they climbed into the horse-drawn vehicle.

"Den you lives different places, don't you now?" Ben shook the reins and the horses started on their way.

"Yes, I suppose so—ever since I met up with Mr. Jason here at my Uncle John's house in Franklin," Mandie said, reaching over to squeeze Mr. Bond's hand. "He's my uncle's caretaker, you know. And he helps us solve our mysteries sometimes."

"Now, Miss Amanda . . ." Jason Bond laughed. "All I really do when you're at home is try to keep up with whatever you're into next."

Ben looked at Mr. Bond and winked. "Dat's impossible, Mistuh Bond," he said. "Impossible to keep up wid dese two girls."

Jason Bond smiled.

"Well, Ben, we have a brand new mystery," Mandie announced. "And as soon as my grandmother tells us about it, we'll get right to work on it." Her blue eyes sparkled as she talked. "Grandmother sent me a message to come back to school a day early so I could spend the night with her. She said something mysterious is going on here in Asheville."

Ben grinned. "Good luck!"

"I'm thankful I have to go back home tomorrow," Mr. Bond joked.

Mandie and Celia laughed.

Ben pulled the rig up in front of Mrs. Taft's huge mansion. The girls jumped down and ran to the door.

They found Mrs. Taft sitting in the parlor by the big open fireplace, where logs blazed and crackled their own welcome. As Mandie's grandmother rose to greet them, she smoothed her faded blonde hair. She was a tall woman, and very dignified, except when she was helping her granddaughter solve mysteries.

Mandie gave her a big hug. "Tell us about the mystery, Grandmother!" she cried excitedly.

"Not until you get your coats off," Mrs. Taft replied. She turned to greet Mr. Bond, who had followed the girls into the room. "Thanks for bringing Amanda," she said.

"I was glad to do it, ma'am," Jason Bond said. "It sure feels good in here. It's gettin' purty cold out there now."

The two girls hastily removed their coats and hats and handed them to the maid who stood waiting. Mr. Bond gave the maid his coat, and she hung everything on the hall tree just outside the parlor doorway.

"I imagine it is cold out there," Mrs. Taft said. "Come on over by the fire." She turned to the maid. "Ella, we'll be ready for some hot coffee and cocoa when you finish there."

"Yes, ma'am," Ella answered from the doorway. "I'll git it right heah." She hurried on down the hallway.

"Do sit down, Mr. Bond," Mrs. Taft told the man, indicating the armchair opposite hers by the fireplace. "We'll have something to warm us up in a few minutes. Then in a little while the cook will have dinner ready."

Mr. Bond took the chair opposite Mrs. Taft as Mandie and Celia sat on footstools by the hearth.

"Where is Hilda?" Mandie asked.

"She's staying with the Smiths next door until y'all go back to school," Mrs. Taft replied. "I didn't want her involved in this adventure. You know how she is. She runs away every chance she gets, and I'm afraid one day we might not find her."

"You're a mighty good lady to give her a home," Mr. Bond remarked.

"Well, I had to," Mrs. Taft insisted. "I couldn't let her be put in some mental institution, especially since it was Mandie and Celia who found her hiding in the school attic."

"But she's getting better," Mandie reminded them. "Dr. Woodard said she is."

"Yes, she is," Mrs. Taft agreed.

"She's bound to improve now that her parents can't keep her shut up in a room like they did," Mr. Bond smiled.

"I think so, too. But now, Grandmother, please tell us about the mystery—please!" Mandie begged, clasping her small white hands around her knees.

"Well, it's like this," her grandmother began. "There's something very mysterious going on here in Asheville. The bells on our church downtown have been ringing thirteen times at the stroke of midnight."

"Do they ring thirteen times at noon, too?" Mandie asked.

"No, just at midnight," her grandmother replied. "And no one can figure out what's wrong. The bells are activated by the clock on the hour and half past the hour. Several people have examined the bells and the clock mechanism, but they haven't found a thing wrong," she explained.

"Sounds spooky," Celia whispered.

"Some folks say it's a bad omen, and the whole town is upset because no one can solve the mystery." Mrs. Taft paused for a moment. "I know you girls are good at things like this, so I thought maybe you'd like to look into it."

"Sure, Grandmother," Mandie quickly agreed. "I think we could find out what's wrong. Don't you, Celia?"

"Well, we could try," Celia replied.

"We have almost all day today, and we don't have to check into school until tomorrow afternoon," Mandie said. "Grandmother, could we all just go down to the church and look around?"

"It's too cold out there for me, but if Mr. Bond would agree to escort you two girls, you may go after we eat," Mrs. Taft promised. "You'll have to bundle up, though. There's no heat in the church except when there's a service, you know."

"Mr. Jason, will you take us, please?" Mandie begged.

"I reckon I can go with you girls, long as you don't stay too long," he replied. "Like your grandmother said, it's cold out there for these old bones."

"Thanks," Mandie said, reaching over to squeeze his hand.

"How do we get inside?" Celia asked. "Who has the key?"

"It never is locked, dear," Mrs. Taft answered, "until the sexton makes his rounds about bedtime. Then he locks the doors. But he opens them again early every morning."

As Mrs. Taft finished speaking, the church bells rang in the distance. They all listened and counted.

Mandie pointed to the china clock on the mantelpiece. "That clock says it's eleven o'clock," she said, "but the bells rang twelve times. I counted."

"I did, too," Celia agreed.

"You're right," Mrs. Taft said. "So now the bells are not correct in the daytime either. Did you count the rings, Mr. Bond? Was it twelve?"

The old man nodded. "Yes, you're right. It was twelve. Maybe the clock mechanism needs repair."

"Several workmen have examined everything, but they found nothing wrong," Mrs. Taft repeated. "Of course, they didn't tear the clock apart, from what I understand, but they did inspect all the connections between the clock and the bells. There just doesn't seem to be anything wrong."

Ella the maid entered the room carrying a large silver tray with a steaming silver coffeepot and a silver teapot of hot cocoa. She set the tray on the low table by Mrs. Taft.

"I'll pour it, Ella. Thank you," Mrs. Taft said. "Would you let us know just as soon as dinner is ready?"

"Yes, ma'am," Ella replied, leaving the room.

"I know you girls like hot cocoa," Mrs. Taft said as she leaned forward to pour for them, "but what about you, Mr. Bond? Would you care for coffee or cocoa?"

"Coffee—black, please, ma'am," he answered. "Once I got old enough to drink coffee, I've never stopped. Guess you'd call me an old coffee sot," he laughed.

Mrs. Taft passed him a cup of steaming coffee, and then poured some for herself. "I suppose I am, too," she said, sipping the hot coffee. "However, once in a great while I get a taste for hot cocoa."

Mandie warmed her hands on her hot mug of cocoa and took a drink. "Grandmother, Joe said he would be here this weekend with his father," she said. "He promised to bring Snowball with them since they'll be coming in the buggy. I didn't want to bother with Snowball on the train."

"I knew they were coming," Grandmother acknowledged. "Dr. Woodard told me when I was at your house for Thanksgiving last week. And I knew they would bring that cat of yours." She smiled and took another sip of her coffee. "Now, as soon as you girls finish your cocoa, run upstairs to your rooms and freshen up for dinner."

"Rooms?" Mandie questioned. "We only need one room, Grandmother."

"Well, I had Annie make up two rooms next to each other," Grandmother Taft explained, "but if you want to share one, that's all right. Just don't stay awake talking all night."

"We won't. Thanks," Mandie said. She and Celia quickly put their empty cups on the silver tray and jumped up. "We'll be back in a few minutes."

Grabbing their coats and bonnets from the hall tree, they headed upstairs.

The girls' baggage had been put in separate rooms, but the door between was standing open.

"I think I'll change into something more comfortable," Mandie called to Celia in the other room. She hung her coat and bonnet in the huge wardrobe.

"And warmer," Celia called back from the other room.

"I think I'll wear this." Mandie took an indigo woolen dress from the trunk and held it up for Celia to see through the doorway. "And I'll wear my wool cape with the hood so I don't have to wear a bonnet."

"Me, too," Celia said, holding up a dark green woolen dress. "And I'll wear this."

Mandie changed her clothes quickly. "Don't forget your boots," she reminded her friend.

Celia laughed. "You'd think we were going to the North Pole!"

"Well, it does seem awfully cold—a lot colder than it was at home," Mandie said. "Was it cold in Richmond?"

"I suppose so. I didn't really notice because I wasn't outdoors much, what little time I was there," Celia answered. "By the time I left your house after Thanksgiving and got home to Richmond, your grandmother had sent my mother a message asking if I could come back to school a day early and spend the night with her."

Celia finished dressing first and joined Mandie in her room. Sitting on the footstool by the warm fireplace, she straightened her stockings above the top of her shiny black boots.

"Just think," Mandie said as she shook down her long skirt which partially covered her boots, "the year 1900 will soon be gone. Thanksgiving has passed and Christmas is coming up." She turned to the tall mirror standing nearby and smoothed the long blonde braid that hung down her back.

"Time sure does fly," Celia agreed. "We're almost halfway through our first year at the Heathwoods' school, but it seems like we just started a few weeks ago."

"Maybe that's because we seem to get so many holidays," Mandie laughed. "Pretty soon we'll be getting out for Christmas."

Celia grew quiet. "It'll be the first Christmas for both of us without our fathers, won't it?" she said softly.

Mandie nodded. "I remember Christmas morning last year back there in Swain County," she said. "My father had brought in a small Christmas tree and we had decorated it. I got up so early I caught him wrapping presents by the tree, but he just laughed and said it wasn't time to get up yet. I stayed up, though, and helped him finish." She blinked back tears in her blue eyes.

"Our whole family was at our house for Christmas last year," Celia recalled. "All my aunts, uncles, and cousins—everybody. They stayed for days and days." Her eyes brightened. "My father gave me my pony for Christmas." She smiled.

"I know y'all raise horses," Mandie said, approaching a touchy subject carefully, "and you said your father was killed when he was thrown from a horse. Was it a new horse, or had y'all had it a long time?"

"He had just bought it the day before." Celia's voice quivered. "Mother sold it after it threw my father."

"I guess I was lucky that my father didn't die so suddenly," Mandie conceded. "He got a bad cold that turned into pneumonia." She drew a long breath. "He died in April, right when the weather was turning warm and the wildflowers were beginning to bloom."

A light tap on the door made the girls look up. Mandie opened the door to find Annie, the upstairs maid, standing there.

"Miz Taft, she say fo' you girls to git downstairs. Dinnuh be on de table," Annie announced.

"Thanks, Annie," Mandie smiled. "We're coming right down." As the maid left, Mandie turned to Celia. "Guess we'd better get going."

"Yes, let's hurry so we can get through dinner and go down to the church," Celia agreed.

The girls rushed through the meal as fast as they could. Mrs. Taft and Mr. Bond seemed to be in no hurry. They sat talking and sipping coffee while Mandie and Celia squirmed in their seats.

When Ella came in to refill the coffee cups, Mrs. Taft smiled at the girls. "Ella," she said, "ask Ben to bring the rig around to the front door, please. These girls seem anxious to leave."

"Let us walk, please, Grandmother," Mandie begged. "It's not far." Ella waited.

"No, it's too cold out there today," Mrs. Taft replied. "Besides, you forget that Mr. Bond's legs are not as young as yours." She looked up at the maid. "Go ahead, Ella, and tell Ben."

As the maid left the room, Mandie smiled at Jason Bond. "Sorry, Mr. Jason," she said. "I keep forgetting that you are older than we are."

Everyone laughed.

"A good bit older, young lady," Mr. Bond teased. "I know you're used to your old Indian friend, Uncle Ned, chasing around on adventures with you, but I'm just too old for that—or maybe I should say too old and too lazy."

Mandie smiled across the table at him. "We love you anyhow, Mr. Jason."

"You girls may be excused." Mrs. Taft looked amused. "Wrap up good now," she called as they hurried from the room.

Taking the steps two at a time, they stopped in their rooms only long enough to snatch up their cloaks and gloves. Mr. Bond buttoned up his warm coat and waited in the front hallway.

When they were all in the rig, Ben shook the reins and sent the horses flying. The girls squealed with delight and held on tightly. Jason Bond looked from them to Ben but didn't say a word.

Ben grinned broadly. "I loves to go fast," he explained, "but Miz Taft, she don't like it, so I'se glad to have some fun and git y'all to the church quick."

Mandie and Celia laughed, but Jason Bond just held on and looked straight ahead.

After a few minutes Ben pulled the horses up sharply in front of the big brick church and everyone lurched. Ben grinned again.

"Thanks, Ben," Mandie said, scrambling down from the rig with Celia and Mr. Bond close behind. "I guess you did get us to the church quick. That was fun!"

"Yeh, Missy," the Negro man replied. "Now, is I s'posed to wait heah or come back latuh to git y'all?"

Mr. Bond spoke up. "You'd better wait here, Ben," he said. "We won't be inside very long. You can come inside with us if you think it's too cold to sit out here."

"I be all right out heah," Ben replied, settling back in his seat.

The girls and Mr. Bond stopped to stare up at the tall steeple where the huge clock was mounted. They could faintly see the bells inside the belfry.

"Looks normal," Mr. Bond remarked.

"But it's—" The bells interrupted Mandie to ring once for one o'clock. "Well, it rang right this time," she said.

"Must be something wrong inside," Celia suggested as they started up the wide steps to the double front doors on the porch of the church.

Mr. Bond stepped ahead of the girls to open the door for them and ushered them inside.

Mandie looked around the familiar sanctuary. "This is where we go to church while we're at the Heathwoods' school, Mr. Bond," she said. "Grandmother Taft is a member here."

"Sure is a big church," the old man commented as he walked around.

"Let's go up in the gallery," Mandie suggested.

"I'll stay down here," Mr. Bond said, sitting down in a nearby pew. "Just don't get into anything up there now."

"Come on, Celia!" Mandie led the way to a door at the back of the church. Opening the door, she started up the steps to the gallery, and Celia followed.

At the top of the stairs, Mandie surveyed the rows and rows of benches. "I've never been up here before," she said.

"I don't see any bells. How do we get to them?" Celia asked.

As the girls looked around, they spotted another door at the end of the gallery. They hurried over to open it. There, high above their heads, hung the huge bells in the belfry. Heavy ropes dangled down in various places.

"How can we get up there?" Mandie asked. "There aren't any steps going up to the bells."

"It looks awfully high from down here," Celia noted.

Mandie touched the ropes carefully for fear she would cause the bells to ring. Then she saw that some of the rope was actually a rope ladder extending up into the belfry. "Here!" she exclaimed, shaking the rope. "We have to go up this ladder."

Celia looked at the rope in fright. "Go up a rope ladder? We can't do that, Mandie."

"Yes, we can," Mandie assured her. "It won't be any worse than walking over a swinging bridge, and I've done that lots of times without falling."

"But I've never been on a swinging bridge," Celia protested. "That thing will swing around and we could fall off."

"We won't if we're careful to hold on real tight," Mandie said. Quickly removing her cape and gloves, she threw them on a nearby bench and grasped the first rung of the rope ladder. "Come on."

Celia slowly removed her cape as she stood watching. "I'll get all dizzy and fall," she argued.

"No you won't," Mandie assured her. "Just don't look down. Keep looking up. Come on." She swung onto the next rung of the ladder and began to make her way up.

Celia nervously watched the ladder swing with Mandie's weight. She didn't move.

Reaching the top, Mandie stepped into the belfry and looked around at the huge bells. "Come on, Celia. You can see the whole town from up here," she called down to her friend. "You won't fall if you hold on with all your might. Come on."

"Well, all right. I'll try," Celia finally agreed. As she reached up and grasped the first rung of the ladder, it swung around and she stopped. Her heart beat wildly and her hands grew clammy.

Mandie knelt down on the floor of the belfry at the top of the ladder. "Reach up for the next rung, Celia," she called. "Keep looking up. Don't look down."

Celia took a deep breath and did what her friend said. Slowly, carefully, she made her way up the ropes. After several minutes she grasped the top rung and started to reach for Mandie's extended hand, but then she looked down. "Oh!" she gasped, shaking with fright. "Look how far it is down to the floor!"

Mandie grabbed Celia's hand and gave her such a hard pull that Celia sprawled onto the floor of the belfry beside her.

Celia closed her eyes. "I just know I'll never make it back down," she moaned.

"Come on. Get up," Mandie said, helping her to her feet. "Look outside. You can see everywhere from up here."

There were rafters running every which way. The only floor to walk on was a small piece supporting the bells, and a narrow walkway around the outer edge of the belfry. Celia held onto Mandie's hand as they carefully made their way around the narrow walkway to peer outside at the town.

"I thought you were the one who got dizzy-headed from heights," Celia reminded Mandie. "Remember telling me about the widow's walk at Tommy's house in Charleston?"

"But that was completely outside, where if you slipped, you could fall all the way down to the ground," Mandie explained. "Up here we have these walls to protect us." She pointed down to the road. "Look, there's Ben in the rig down there."

Celia quickly turned back to look at the huge bells. "Let's get this exploration over with," she begged. "Just what are we looking for anyway?"

"Anything we can find," Mandie replied. As she stepped back over to the bells, Celia followed slowly and carefully.

Mandie's eyes searched the walls of the belfry. "Where are the connections to the clock?" she wondered aloud. "Where is the clock located from here?"

"Do you think the clock on the outside is as far up as the bells are?" Celia asked. "The clock is on the front side, remember?"

Mandie turned back to the front of the belfry. "No, I believe the clock is lower than the bells."

Celia found some wires and ropes coming out of the front wall. "Here it is!" she exclaimed. "The clock is on the outside of these wires and things. See? They go on over to the bells."

"You're right," Mandie agreed, carefully moving over to examine what Celia had found.

"But how does the clock make the bells ring, Mandie?" Celia asked.

"Well, I guess it's sort of like that big grandfather clock that my grandmother has. The pendulum trips something inside the clock and makes it chime," Mandie explained, tracing the wires.

"But how does the clock know how many times to strike?" Celia was baffled.

"Oh, Celia, I don't know everything," Mandie fussed as she traced the wires. "It just does somehow. The insides are made with one notch, two notches, or whatever, I suppose, to allow the clock to strike as it rotates—or something. Anyhow, these wires do go to the bells. See?"

Celia watched as Mandie followed the length of the wires to the bells. "I don't see anything wrong with them, do you?" she asked.

"No, they're all connected," Mandie replied.

Suddenly the girls felt the floor beneath their feet tremble slightly. Then there was a hard thud from somewhere below. They grabbed each other's hand.

"What was that?" Celia gasped.

"The whole place shook!" Mandie exclaimed.

"I think we'd better go back down," Celia decided.

"Yes, I suppose we'd better for now," Mandie agreed. "But we'll have to come back later. You go down the ladder first."

Celia sat down on the floor to grasp the rope ladder swinging below. After a few tries she finally got into a position to slide down onto the first rung. She held her breath and looked up at Mandie.

"Now don't look down," Mandie cautioned her from above.

At that moment one of Celia's hands missed a rung, and she grasped wildly into the air. Her hand found a rope hanging down from above. She grabbed it and hung on with all her might. Suddenly the bells started ringing. She was so frightened she slid down the rope and landed in a heap on the floor below. When she let go, the bells stopped ringing.

"Oh, Celia, are you all right?" Mandie called to her as she quickly came down to her. "I guess that rope is there to ring the bells by hand."

"At least it gave me some way to get down," Celia answered, trying to get her breath.

Just then they heard Mr. Bond's voice. "What are you girls doing up there?" he called from below. "I think you'd better get down here fast."

"We're coming," Mandie called back.

They grabbed their cloaks and gloves, and scurried around the gallery to the steps leading down into the sanctuary.

"We still don't know what was shaking everything or what that noise was," Celia reminded her friend as they reached the bottom of the stairs.

"I know, but we'll come back and find out," Mandie promised. "Anyway, we know what everything looks like up there now. Maybe Joe can help us when he gets here this weekend."

Mr. Bond was waiting for them at the bottom of the steps. "You know you'll have the whole town here in a minute, ringing those bells that way," he scolded. "What on earth were you doing up there?"

"I'm sorry, Mr. Bond," Celia apologized. "It was my fault. I slipped on the ladder and caught hold of the extra rope. I didn't know it would ring the bells."

"What ladder?" Mr. Bond wanted to know.

Celia glanced at Mandie. "The ladder to the belfry," she answered slowly.

"Now don't you girls go climbing any more ladders while you're in my care," the old man said. "Let's go outside and get going."

"Thanks for coming with us, Mr. Jason," Mandie said as they stepped into the rig where Ben was waiting.

Ben shook the reins, and the horses started off. "Did y'all find out whut makin' dem bells ring de wrong number at de wrong time?" he asked.

"No, but we will," Mandie promised.

"You hope," Celia whispered to her friend.

As they sped around the corner in the rig, the bells on the church rang three times. Everyone looked at each other.

"They rang three times, but it is really two o'clock," Celia said.

"I have an idea someone went up there as soon as we left," Mandie whispered.

"Thank goodness they didn't come up there while we were there," Celia replied.

"But we might have caught them if they had," Mandie reminded her.

CHAPTER TWO

STRANGERS IN THE CHURCH

Mandie and Celia were awake before daylight the next morning, excited because Mrs. Taft had promised them they could go back to the church. They lay there in the warm bed discussing the mystery of the bells. The wind was blowing cold and hard outside and rattling the shutters. Annie had not yet come to start the fire in the fireplace in the room. "What are we going to do this time when we go to the church?" Celia asked.

"I thought we could just stay there a while and watch to see if anyone comes into the church, especially when the clock strikes twelve noon," Mandie replied, pushing up her pillow so she could sit up in bed.

Celia did likewise and the two tugged at the heavy quilts to cover their shoulders.

"But if somebody comes into the church, what will we do?" Celia asked.

"We won't let them see us," Mandie replied. "We'll just hide somewhere where they can't see us but we can see them."

"That'll be hard to do in that big church," Celia noted. "It's so wide open."

"There are draperies on each side of the place where the choir sits, and there's a low short curtain that runs across the platform behind where the preacher stands. The pews are so tall we might be able to hide between some of them, too," Mandie suggested.

"Well, what do we do if someone does come in?"

"We'll wait to see what they do, and then we'll just come out and ask them who they are, I suppose," Mandie answered.

"I sure hope no criminals come into the church while we're there." The way the bed was placed in the room the girls were facing the door directly. Celia was looking that way when the door softly and slowly came open. She moved closer to Mandie and gasped. As Annie appeared through the doorway, Mandie laughed and said, "It's Annie."

"Mornin,' Missies," Annie greeted them as she went over to the fireplace. "Y'all awake nice and early. I'll jes' git dis heah fire goin' now, and it'll be warm in heah in no time, it will."

"Thanks, Annie," Mandie said. "It is cold in here."

The maid quickly cleaned out the ashes and put them in the bucket on the hearth. Then, after laying kindling for a new fire, she took a match from the pocket of her long white apron and lit the wood. The fire spread quickly and the logs crackled.

"I heard my grandmother tell my mother that she was going to have that steam heat put in, Annie," Mandie said. "You know, the kind of heat that you just turn a knob on this thing standing in the room and the heat comes right out. Then you won't have to build fires in the fireplaces anymore."

"Steam heat? Whut kinda heat be dat, Missy?" Annie stooped and fanned the fire with her apron to make it burn better.

"Like they have in Edwards' Dry Goods Store downtown," Mandie replied. "You know how warm it always is in there."

"Oh, you mean dem big hot metal things whut stand up on de floor?" Annie rose from the hearth. "Well, dey ain't 'zackly magic. Dey gotta have a fire goin' somewheres to make 'em git hot."

"I know," Mandie agreed, sliding out of bed and reaching for her slippers. "But I think it's just one big fire that makes them hot, probably in the basement, so you'd have only one fire to tend to." She hurried to stand in front of the warm fireplace as she quickly put on her robe.

Celia followed. "That's the kind of heat we have at home," she said, wrapping her robe around her. "Just about everybody in Richmond has that kind of heat now, but I don't know for sure how it works."

"Well, right now we ain't got it," Annie said, turning to leave the room, "so I'se got to go build more fires."

"Don't forget, Annie. Grandmother said you could go with us to the church this morning," Mandie reminded her.

"Lawsy mercy, Missy," Annie sighed. "I don't be knowin' why y'all wants to go traipsin' down to dat spooky church. Dem spooks down there is liable to git us."

"Oh, Annie, there's no such things as spooks," Mandie replied, smiling. "You wait and see. All that trouble with the bells is being caused by some good, solid human being—not something you can't catch hold of."

"Well, I sho' hopes dem bad human bein's don't git ahold of us," Annie mumbled as she went out the door.

"I do believe Annie is afraid to go with us," Mandie said, laughing as she and Celia sat on the rug by the fire.

"But, Mandie, it could be something—or someone—we should be afraid of," Celia reminded her.

At that moment the girls heard the church bells ringing in the distance. Silently, they counted to seven, and looked at the clock on the mantel.

"Right that time," Mandie said.

"Maybe they'll quit acting crazy and ring right all the time," Celia said.

"But then we wouldn't have a mystery to solve," Mandie argued. "I'm getting hungry. Let's get dressed and go find some breakfast."

After a delicious, hot breakfast, the girls were allowed to go to the church. Ben brought the rig around to the front door, and they were soon on their way.

The wind was still blowing hard and cold. The few people they saw walking on the streets were bundled up in heavy winter clothes. Winter had arrived.

Ben coaxed the horses to a fast speed, and Annie held onto her seat in fright.

"Now, you listen heah, you, Ben," she said sternly. "Don't you go runnin' wild like dat. You liable to git us all killed."

"But de Missies, dey like ridin' fast, don't you now?" he called back to the girls.

"Not too fast, please, Ben," Celia replied.

"We don't want to scare Annie, so would you please slow down a little, Ben?" Mandie asked.

"All righty, Missy. We sho' don't wanta skeer dis old woman up heah beside me, does we now?" Ben replied, laughing as he slowed the horses.

Annie twisted around and gave Ben a mean look. "Whut old woman?" she demanded. "Ain't me. I ain't old as you are. Won't be eighteen 'til next summer."

"Well, if you ain't old, den quit actin' like you wuz," Ben replied. As he pulled the rig up in front of the church, he turned to grin at the girls. "Heah we be's," he announced.

The girls jumped down from the rig and waited for Annie. She looked back at Ben. "Ain't you comin' wid us?"

"I stays right heah," Ben replied, settling back comfortably in the driver's seat.

"He can't go in with us, Annie," Mandie told the maid. "That would be too many people to hide. There are three of us already. Come on."

As they entered the church, they looked around. There was no one in the vestibule or the sanctuary.

"Annie, we have to hide you somewhere," Mandie said, walking toward the altar. "How about standing behind those draperies up there where the choir sits?"

"Lawsy mercy, Missy. Why I got to hide?" Annie asked nervously.

"We came here to watch to see if anyone goes up there and rings the bells. We all have to hide," Mandie explained. "Come on. You can get behind those draperies. It'll be more comfortable than sitting down on the floor behind that low curtain across the platform like we're going to do."

Annie reluctantly followed Mandie and Celia to the draperies. The girls showed her how to keep herself hidden. There was even a small stool back there where she could just barely have room to sit.

The girls stepped back to look at the dark red plush draperies as they fell into folds and concealed Annie.

"Just right," Celia remarked.

"Annie, please don't make any noise or come out unless we come back there to get you," Mandie warned.

"I sho' won't, Missy. Jes' you don't fo'git and leave me heah all day," Annie answered from behind the draperies.

"We won't. We're only going to stay until the bells ring at twelve noon. Then we have to go back and get ready to check into school," Mandie explained.

The girls hurried over to the low curtain across the platform behind the pulpit. They stepped behind it and sat down on the floor.

Celia looked at the curtain in front of her, which was only a little higher than her head. "It just barely hides us," she said.

"We can peek through the holes where the curtain rings are, though. See?" Mandie said, bending forward to fit her eye to the opening for the rod. "Mandie! I just thought of something!" Celia said suddenly. "We forgot to look up in the gallery and the belfry to see if anyone was already up there."

Mandie sprang to her feet. "You're right," she said. "We need to be sure there's no one there. Let's go see."

They dropped their capes and gloves behind the curtain where they had been hiding, and started for the stairs.

"Where you two gwine now?" Annie called from behind the draperies.

"We're just going to look upstairs, Annie. We'll be right back." Mandie answered. "Please stay where you are."

"I ain't stayin' heah long by myself," Annie called back.

"We'll be back in a minute," Mandie promised.

The girls hurried to the door and raced up the stairs to the gallery. No one was there. They opened the door to look up into the belfry. No one was there, either.

"We can't see inside the whole belfry from down here," Mandie said, moving around to look upward. She grabbed the end of the rope ladder. "You stay right here. I'm going up there to look around."

"Be careful," Celia whispered, as Mandie quickly climbed up the rope ladder.

At the top Mandie walked around. "Nobody up here, either," she called. She quickly came back down the swinging rope ladder. As she let go of the last rung, she sat down hard on the floor.

"Are you all right?" Celia bent down to make sure her friend wasn't hurt.

"I'm all right," Mandie assured her. "I came down too fast, and it made the ladder swing too much. I just let go to keep from swinging around." She stood up and brushed off her skirt.

The girls again took up their watch behind the low curtains. They sat still and talked only in whispers in case someone suddenly came into the church. During a long silence, the girls were startled when Annie sneezed loudly.

"Bless you," Celia called to the maid.

"I hope you're not getting a cold, Annie," Mandie said in a loud whisper.

"I ain't got no cold yet, but I will have if I has to stay in dis cold place much longer," Annie complained. Suddenly the draperies moved, there was a loud crash, and the Negro girl fell through the opening in the draperies.

Mandie and Celia jumped up and ran to her rescue.

"I be all right." Annie got up from the floor. "Dis dadblasted stool jes' turned over. Dat's all." She set the stool upright again. "Y'all go on back and git dis over wid so's we kin go home." She returned to her hiding place.

Mandie and Celia resumed their watch from behind the low curtains.

"It won't be long till twelve o'clock, Annie," Mandie called.

She and Celia put their capes around themselves and huddled together. It was cold in the church.

Before long the huge double doors of the church made a loud squeaking noise.

"Sh-h!" Mandie whispered.

As she and Celia peered through the holes in the curtain, an expensively dressed woman appeared inside the sanctuary. A tall, neatly attired man followed her from the vestibule down the center aisle.

Mandie's heart did flip-flops as she watched and waited. Celia grabbed Mandie's hand tightly.

The couple talked in low voices as they walked down the aisle, pausing to look into each pew on both sides, making their way toward the front.

Mandie strained her ears but couldn't make out what the strangers were saying. She just hoped Annie would stay out of sight.

As the strangers neared the altar, Mandie could hear a little of what they were saying.

"I know it's got to be here," the woman said. "I was . . ."

Mandie couldn't hear the end of the sentence because the woman had leaned down between the pews.

"Well, we have to find it," the man said firmly. "If someone else finds it, that wouldn't be too good."

"Oh, dear," the woman sighed. She seemed almost in tears.

"We've got to find it," the man repeated. "You go up that aisle over there, and I'll take this one over here." He indicated the two aisles at the sides of the church.

The woman started looking in the pews on the left as the man went to the right. "If only you'd stop blaming me," she moaned.

"I know it wasn't intentional, but it was your fault," the man told the woman. "If you hadn't decided to come into this church to keep from being seen you wouldn't have lost it."

"You told me to hide and I didn't know what else to do," the woman protested.

"Well, if you had stayed in one place instead of walking around looking at all those stained-glass windows we'd know what area to search," he said. "It could be almost anywhere in here."

"I was afraid someone would come in and see me if I just sat still," the woman said. As the strangers got farther away up the aisles, Mandie couldn't make out what they were saying, but by the time they reached the back of the church, they were obviously arguing.

The man took the woman's arm and pointed to the last pew. She pulled her arm away and slid into the pew. But when the man sat down next to her, she moved away from him. Then taking a handkerchief from her purse, she dabbed at her eyes.

Mandie and Celia looked at each other. They dared not even whisper for fear of being heard. The man seemed so angry, and the woman seemed to be afraid of him. The man was doing most of the talking. Oh, how the girls wished they could hear their conversation!

Finally, the strangers got up and started back down the outside aisles. This time they moved slower, carefully bending to look at the seat of each pew and then stooping to look beneath each one. They finally met in front.

"Nothing," the woman sobbed.

"Nothing over there, either. Let's go up this center aisle once more," the man said. "And please be sure you look very carefully."

As they walked along together, the woman took the left side and the man, the right. Once in a while the man would watch the woman when she wasn't looking as though he wanted to be sure of what she was doing.

Mandie realized her foot had gone to sleep from being cramped up behind the curtain, but she dared not change positions.

Celia shivered again and wrapped her arms about herself.

The strangers finally met at the back of the church, but just as the man opened his mouth to speak, the bells started ringing in the belfry. The man grabbed the woman by the arm and pushed her ahead of him as they rushed out the doors of the church.

Mandie and Celia sat stunned for a moment, looking at each other and mouthing the numbers as the bells rang—one, two, three . . . Finally Mandie jumped up, stomping the foot that had gone to sleep, and hurriedly limped toward the stairs to the gallery. "Let's see who's in the belfry," she said.

Celia didn't seem in a hurry to run into someone up there, but she followed anyway.

As they ran up the stairs, they kept counting—out loud now. Across the gallery, they jerked open the door to the belfry.

"I'll go first," Mandie offered, grabbing the rope.

"You're not really going up there, are you?" Celia's voice quivered.

"Of course," Mandie called back.

The bells stopped after twelve rings and then sounded a weak, shaky thirteenth ring.

Mandie hurried up the ladder as Celia stood below and watched. She put her head through the opening at the top, and looked around before she got off the ladder. "There's nobody up here," she called, climbing onto the belfry floor. "I don't see a thing."

"Come on back down then," Celia hollered.

Then suddenly Mandie heard her name, "M-M-Mandie!" She looked down to see Celia frozen on the spot and white as a sheet.

A hand reached out and touched Celia on the shoulder. Celia screamed.

"Look behind you, Celia," Mandie yelled. "It's only Annie."

Trembling all over, Celia turned slightly.

Annie came around her and apologized. "I'se sorry, Missy," she said. "I didn't mean to skeer you. Y'all went and left me alone down there, and I jes' got skeered."

"Th-that's all right, Annie," Celia managed to say.

Annie looked up into the belfry just as Mandie hurried down the rope ladder. The hem of Mandie's long skirt was tucked into her waistband to keep it out of her way.

As Mandie swung onto the floor and straightened her skirt, Annie gasped. "Lawsy mercy, Missy. Miz Taft have a heart 'tack if she know you go climbin' round dat way."

"You worry too much, Annie," Mandie said. She turned to Celia. "Are you all right?"

Celia took a deep breath. "I am now," she said, her voice still trembling. "But I was sure whoever has been messing with the bells had caught me."

"I'm sorry, Celia," Mandie said. "I guess we'd better go now. We have to get to school, you know."

"Thank goodness!" Celia exclaimed.

The three made their way through the gallery to the stairs.

"I didn't see anything going on up there, but there's got to be something wrong somewhere," Mandie said.

At the bottom of the stairs, Celia stopped. "And those people who were here a while ago," she said, "I wonder who they were and what they were looking for."

"I do, too," Mandie said as they went on through the vestibule. "Have you ever seen them before, Annie?"

"Now, Missy, jes' 'cause I lives in Asheville ain't no sign I knows ev'rybody in town," Annie said, opening the front door. " 'Sides, dis be white folks' church. I goes to my own church. I don't mix wid no white folks."

Mandie and Celia looked at each other and smiled as they went on down the front steps. Ben was waiting in the rig. He saw them coming and stepped down to the road by the rig.

"Not only dat," Annie continued, "dat lady didn't look like she come from dis heah town."

"What makes you say that?" Mandie asked.

"She jes' look too high uppity," Annie replied. "You know, too fancy dressed."

"Aren't there any fancy, uppity people in this town?" Mandie teased.

"No, not de likes of huh," Annie shook her head. "I don't think she live in dis heah town."

Mandie turned to Celia. "Why don't we look around outside while we're here?"

"We should go back to your grandmother's, shouldn't we?" Celia reminded her friend.

"Ben can walk with us if you're afraid we might find somebody," Mandie suggested. Without waiting for Celia's reply, she called the Negro man, "Ben, would you walk around the church with us?"

Ben walked over to them with a puzzled look on his face. "Why, 'course, Missy."

"Dat man couldn't catch nobody fo' you," Annie said with a teasing glance at the driver. "He too slow, dat Ben is."

Ben scowled at her. "Fust you says I'm too fast, and now you says I'm too slow," he grumbled. "Woman, make yo' mind up, or ain't you got one?"

Annie ignored him and walked on around the side of the church. The girls grinned at Ben and followed the Negro girl around the building.

Thick shrubbery grew against the church, but since it was wintertime, there weren't any leaves, and they could see right through the bushes. Annie stayed ahead of the other two girls, and Ben lagged behind as they all carefully looked over the outside of the building and the yard.

When they turned the back corner and faced the rear of the church, the girls stopped in amazement then ran up to the wall. There, all over the brick, was a lot of huge, illegible handwriting, evidently written with whitewash.

"What does it say?" Celia gasped.

"I cain't read dat," Annie fussed.

Ben stared at the writing with the others. "You cain't read nohow," he mumbled.

"I don't think it says anything," Mandie decided. She brushed her hand over the mess. "It's dry now, but it either dripped and ran together, or whoever wrote it didn't know how to write."

"Who in the world could have done such a thing? Imagine messing up a church building with all that!" Celia said.

"It's probably connected with the mystery of the bells," Mandie replied.

"Missy, I think we better git goin,' " Annie spoke up.

"Let's just walk the rest of the way around the building," Mandie urged. "We can hurry."

She led the way. They returned to the front of the church without finding anything else unusual.

The girls were puzzled. What was that mess supposed to be? A message? A warning? And when did it get there? No one had mentioned that strange writing before.

The mystery was deepening.

CHAPTER THREE

APRIL'S THREAT

Later that day Ben loaded the luggage and drove the girls to school. As they rode up the half-circle graveled driveway, the huge, white clapboard house at the top of the hill came into view. Gray curls of smoke rose out of the tall chimneys. The giant magnolia trees surrounding the school were now bare.

The rig came to a halt in front of the long, two-story porch supported by six huge, white pillars. A small sign to the left of the heavy double doors read The Misses Heathwood's School for Girls. Tall narrow windows trimmed with stained glass flanked each side of the doors. Above the doors, matching stained glass edged a fan-shaped transom of glass panes.

The white rocking chairs, with their bare cane bottoms, were still sitting along the veranda behind the banisters. The green flowered cushions had been removed and taken inside for the winter. The wooden swing hung bleakly on its chains attached to the ceiling. Uncle Cal, the old Negro man who worked for the school, came out to help unload the baggage.

"Hello, Uncle Cal," Mandie greeted him as she and Celia stepped down from the rig. "Did you and Aunt Phoebe have a nice Thanksgiving?"

"Sho' did, Missy 'Manda, but we'se glad to see you back," the old man replied. "You, too, Missy," he told Celia.

"Thanks, Uncle Cal," Celia replied, tossing back her long auburn hair. "Guess what! We have another mystery to solve."

" 'Nuther mystery? I sho' hope y'all ain't aimin' to git in no mo' trouble," the old man said, reaching for a bag in the rig.

"It's about the bells in the church downtown, Uncle Cal," Mandie explained. "They're ringing the wrong time."

"Ev'rybody know dat, Missy 'Manda. De whole town mad 'bout it. Cain't set no clock by dem bells no mo.' " Uncle Cal turned to go up the front steps and Ben and the girls followed.

Celia laid her hand on Mandie's arm, and stopped her on the porch for a moment. Uncle Cal and Ben went inside with the luggage. "Mandie, I just remembered something," she said. "Remember what April Snow told us when we left school for the Thanksgiving holidays?"

"She said, 'Enjoy your holidays, because you might not enjoy coming back,' wasn't that it?" Mandie asked.

"Her exact words," Celia confirmed. "What do you think she's planning to stir up now?"

"I have no idea, but we'll be on the lookout for her this time," Mandie assured her friend. "We'll be prepared."

They went on through the double doors into the long center hallway. They stopped and looked around the wainscoted, wallpapered hallway. It was empty. Their eyes traveled up the curved staircase leading to a second-story balcony, which ran near a huge crystal chandelier. The place seemed to be deserted.

They walked on. A tall, elderly lady with faded reddish-blonde hair, wearing a simple black dress, came out of the office off the hallway.

"Hello, Miss Hope," Mandie said, hurrying to greet the lady.

"I hope you girls had a nice holiday," Miss Hope Heathwood replied, putting an arm around each girl.

"We did, Miss Hope. I know y'all did, too, with all of us noisy girls gone," Celia said, laughing.

"Oh, but we missed you lively young ladies," Miss Hope said. "You know we only had three girls here over the holidays—just the ones who lived too far away to go home. But we hardly saw them. They would show up for meal time and then disappear for the rest of the day."

"April Snow didn't go home, did she?" Mandie asked.

"No. She's around somewhere," Miss Hope said. "Now y'all get upstairs and get unpacked before time for supper." She turned back toward the office.

"Yes, ma'am," the girls replied together.

Mandie and Celia hurried upstairs to their room. They had been lucky enough to get a small bedroom together near the stairs to the attic and the servants' stairway going down. The other girls lived in rooms with four double beds and eight girls in each. Even though Mandie and Celia's room was hardly more than a large closet that could barely accommodate the necessary furniture, they were happy there.

A fire in the small fireplace warmed the room. Uncle Cal and Ben had brought up their luggage. The girls hurriedly began unpacking their trunks.

"I want to make sure that whoever wrote on the church walls is punished to the limits of the law. No one should be allowed to treat the Lord's house that way," Mandie said. "It must have been done recently, because Grandmother didn't know about it until we told her. And she always knows everything first."

"It was probably done while we were inside the church," Celia said.

"Maybe." Mandie shook out her dresses from the trunk and prepared to hang them in the huge chifforobe. With her hands full of clothes, she opened the door to the chifforobe.

A small mouse quickly jumped out, landing on her boot and causing her to drop everything.

"A mouse! Look out!" Mandie screamed.

The mouse frantically ran around in circles on the carpet, apparently looking for a way to hide.

"I'll get Uncle Cal!" Celia yelled. She almost knocked down Aunt Phoebe as she ran out the door.

The old Negro woman appeared in the doorway with a broom, and found Mandie standing up on the bed, too frightened to move.

"I wuz jes' sweepin' de hall when I hears Missy scream," Aunt Phoebe said. "Lawsy mercy, whut be de matter?"

"A mouse, Aunt Phoebe!" Mandie cried.

"It c-came out of the ch-chifforobe," Celia stuttered, watching the floor around her feet for the creature.

"I don't see no mouse, Missy. Where it be?" Aunt Phoebe asked, sweeping the broom around the room. "I don't see none. It must be done gone and hid now."

"I d-don't know, Aunt Phoebe," Mandie said, collapsing on the bed.

Aunt Phoebe picked up the clothes Mandie had dropped in a pile and laid them on a chair. She examined the chifforobe. "I don't see how no mouse could git in there," she said. "Ain't no holes or cracks in it." She closed the door to see how it fit. "Somebody musta—"

"Put it in there," Mandie interrupted. Sliding off the bed, she stood up and looked at Celia. "You know who."

"Right," Celia agreed.

"Now, who dat be wantin' to put a mouse in yo' chifforobe?" Aunt Phoebe asked.

"Can't you even guess?" Mandie asked.

"You mean dat tall, black-headed, black-eyed gal wid a Yankee mama—whut's her name?"

"April Snow," Mandie answered. "You see, she told us when we left that we'd better enjoy our holidays, because we might not enjoy coming back."

"But, Mandie, we don't know for sure that it was April," Celia reminded her.

"No, we don't. So, Aunt Phoebe, please don't tell anyone we thought it might be her," Mandie requested.

"I won't mention huh name, Missy 'Manda, but I will tell Miz Prudence dat a mouse got in yo' room," the Negro woman promised. "I'se gwine hafta put some rat poison out to git rid of it."

"Thanks, Aunt Phoebe," Mandie said with relief.

After helping the girls hang up the rest of their clothes, Aunt Phoebe hurried back into the hallway to finish her sweeping.

Mandie and Celia put their stockings and underthings in the drawers of the bureau and placed their bonnets in hatboxes on top of the chifforobe. Leaving personal belongings such as jewelry and letters in the trays of their trunks, they locked the lids.

Mandie stood up with the trunk key in her hand. "I think I'd feel safer about my trunk if I put this key on a ribbon around my neck," she said. "I can slip it under my dress. What do you think, Celia?"

"That's a good idea. I have some odd pieces of ribbon." Celia walked over to the bureau and pulled a handful of ribbons out of one of the drawers. "What color do you want?"

"Any color," Mandie said. "I think I have some extra ribbons, too."

"I have plenty here," Celia insisted. "I think you ought to take the blue one. It matches your eyes."

"But it won't show, so it doesn't matter what color it is," Mandie said, taking the blue ribbon.

"Well, you'll know what color it is anyway. I'll use the green one." Celia pulled out a bright green ribbon and carefully threaded it through the hole in her key as Mandie fixed hers. They tied the ends together, hung the ribbons around their necks, and dropped the keys out of sight inside their dresses.

"If somebody put that mouse in our chifforobe, it had to be April Snow," Mandie said, still nervously looking around on the floor.

"I think so, too, but we can't prove it," Celia agreed. "I just feel like I'm going to step on it any minute."

"Aunt Phoebe will get rid of it for us," Mandie assured her. "Let's sit down."

Sitting on the window seat, the two girls looked out at the bare limbs of the magnolia trees standing on the brown grass below.

"I'll be glad when Saturday comes," Mandie said. "Joe will be here then, and we can go back to the church."

"We can't unless we spend the weekend with your grandmother," Celia reminded her. "Miss Prudence would never let us go that far away from school."

"I thought you knew," Mandie said with a smile. "Grandmother promised to send Ben for us Friday after classes, and we won't have to come back here until Sunday afternoon."

"Oh, great!" Celia said excitedly. "We'll have all that time to work on the mystery."

The big bell in the backyard began ringing, beckoning the students to supper.

"Let's go," Mandie said, leading the way. The two girls hurried downstairs to wait in line outside the dining room door.

When Aunt Phoebe opened the French doors, the girls streamed into the dining room and took their assigned places, standing behind their chairs. No one was allowed to talk in the dining room, so they waited silently until all the girls were in. Then Miss Prudence Heathwood, the school's headmistress and sister of Miss Hope, entered from the other side of the room and took her place behind the chair at the head of the table.

As they stood there waiting, Mandie and Celia noticed that Etrulia had taken April Snow's place beside Mandie and April stood behind the chair directly across the table from them—where Etrulia ordinarily sat. They must have had permission to swap seats Mandie reasoned, because when Miss Prudence looked around the table, she did not mention the switch.

Miss Prudence picked up the little silver bell by her plate and shook it. All eyes turned in her direction.

"Young ladies, welcome back to all of you," Miss Prudence said. "I have an announcement to make. Our school is investing in those modern lights that work on electricity."

The students glanced at one another, not daring to say a word.

Miss Prudence continued. "A socket with a light bulb in it will be installed in each room. Hanging down from this socket will be a chain, which you will pull to turn the light on and off. You have all seen this kind of light downtown at Edwards' Dry Goods Store, haven't you?"

"Yes, ma'am," the girls replied almost in unison.

"Good. Then you understand what I'm talking about," she said. "Now, there will be workmen coming in tomorrow, but y'all do not have permission to carry on conversations with these men. You will stay out of whatever room they are working on until they've finished. Do you understand?"

"Yes, Miss Prudence," the girls responded all around the table.

"After the lights are installed," the headmistress continued, "there will be more workmen coming to put in one of those large furnaces in the basement. This will be connected by metal ducts to what they call a radiator in each room. The house will be heated this way, and we will discontinue fires in the fireplaces except for emergencies and special occasions. You are not to talk to these workmen either. Are there any questions?"

"No, Miss Prudence," the girls said, again quickly exchanging glances.

Although the girls were curious about these modernization efforts, they dared not question Miss Prudence. The headmistress had a way of making a person look dumb. They'd find out about all this from someone else.

"Now, young ladies," Miss Prudence said, "we will return our thanks." After waiting for the girls to bow their heads, she spoke, "Our gracious heavenly Father, we thank Thee for this food of which we are about to partake, and we ask Thy blessings on it and on all who are present. Amen. Young ladies, you may be seated now."

With the noise of scraping chairs, the girls sat down. The dining room held only half of the students. Mandie and Celia were in the first sitting.

Mandie kept an eye on April Snow throughout the entire meal, but the girl never once looked across the table. April completely ignored Mandie and Celia, quickly disappearing as soon as the girls were dismissed.

Mandie and Celia joined the other girls in the parlor after the meal.

Mandie looked around. "April Snow isn't in here," she said quietly to Celia.

"Maybe we should go back to our room," Celia suggested. "She might be up to something."

"You're right. Let's go."

They cautiously entered their room, fearing that the mouse might be there or that April might be lurking nearby. But the room was empty.

As Mandie looked around the floor for the mouse, she noticed white powder along the mopboard. "Aunt Phoebe must have put something on the floor to kill the mouse," she remarked.

"She said she was going to put out something," Celia agreed.

The girls sat down on the window seat and looked out into the early winter darkness. The wind blew hard against the windowpane, but the fire in their fireplace kept the room cozy and warm.

"I wonder how April got Miss Prudence's permission to swap seats at the table," Mandie mused. "You know she has never allowed that before."

"At least not while we've been going to school here," Celia added.

"April must have finagled that while we were gone home for Thanksgiving," Mandie decided. "I just know she must have been the one who put the mouse in our chifforobe."

"But how would she catch the mouse in the first place?" Celia wondered aloud.

"I sure wouldn't want to catch a mouse. Ugh!" Mandie shivered at the thought. She changed the subject. "What did you think of Miss Prudence's announcement at supper?"

"It'll be nice to have lights overhead, won't it?" Celia replied. "We have that kind at home, and it makes a big difference. We'll be able to see to read better at night."

"I suppose so," Mandie answered. "We don't have electricity or radiators, you know. My Uncle John has enough money to afford it. I don't know why he doesn't get all those things done. It would be less work for everybody. Even the church downtown here in Asheville has lights run by electricity, you know."

"But they don't have heat with radiators. Remember all those iron stoves sitting around the sanctuary?" Celia said.

"I know. Maybe Grandmother would donate enough money to put in the heat someday," Mandie speculated. "I suppose sooner or later everybody will have all these new lights and heat."

"Talking about the church, do you think we'll ever find out who that man and woman in the church were?"

"Probably. If we just keep working on the mystery of the bells, I think we can solve the mystery of the strangers, too," Mandie replied, thoughtfully leaning her elbow against the window. "I'm still puzzled about that loud thumping noise and whatever made the belfry shake while we were up there. I believe everything that has happened is all connected."

"I think so, too," Celia agreed, watching her feet for any sign of the mouse.

There was a knock at the door and Aunt Phoebe came in and looked around. "Y'all ain't seen no sign of dat mouse no mo,' has y'all?"

"No, Aunt Phoebe," Mandie replied. "Maybe the stuff you put around the mopboard got him."

"Stuff 'round de mopboard?" the Negro woman asked. "I ain't put nothin' 'round de mopboard. Where?"

"That white stuff down there." Celia pointed to some of it by the bureau.

"Lawsy mercy, Missies. I ain't put dat on de flo,'" the old woman said, bending to look closely at the white powder.

"Then I wonder who did and what it is," Mandie said, stooping down beside her.

Aunt Phoebe stuck her finger in the white powder and smelled it. Straightening up, she looked on top of the bureau, picked up Mandie's powder jar and opened it. "Heah be whut dat is," she said. "Somebody done dumped all yo' bath powder on de flo.'"

"Oh, for goodness' sakes!" Mandie exclaimed. "What is going to happen next?"

"I comes to tell y'all I be up heah fust thing after y'all goes to yo' schoolrooms in de mawnin,'" Aunt Phoebe informed them. "I be gwine to put some liquid stuff dat you cain't see 'round de flo.' But it stink good, so I waits fo' y'all to leave yo' room. And jes' y'all 'member. Dis liquid stuff deadly poison."

"We'll be careful about dropping anything on the floor," Mandie promised.

"Dis stuff be dried up in no time after I puts it 'round," Aunt Phoebe told them. "Jes' leave dis white powder, and I'll clean it up in de mawnin.'"

"Thank you, Aunt Phoebe," Mandie said. "April Snow probably did it, but we don't know for sure."

"I he'p you watch out fo' dat girl," the old woman said, shaking her head as she walked out the door. "She gwine hafta stop dis nonsense."

"Maybe we ought to talk to Miss Hope about the things that are going on," Celia suggested.

"What could we say?" Mandie asked. "We don't have any proof. Let's go find April and follow her around to see what she's doing."

"That's a good idea," Celia agreed.

The two girls left their room, walking slowly down the hallways, looking about for April Snow. She was nowhere to be seen. They returned to the parlor. There she was, sitting alone in a corner, reading the newspaper while the other students sat around talking.

Mandie and Celia looked at each other, then took a seat in two vacant chairs near Etrulia and Dorothy, a girl they didn't know very well.

Etrulia turned to them and said, "We've all been reading the newspaper. They say the whole town is angry about the bells in the church downtown. And now, because the bells are ringing thirteen times, they claim something bad is about to happen."

"That's just superstition," Mandie said. "The bells couldn't cause something bad to happen just because they're ringing wrong."

"I know that," Etrulia conceded, "but you know this town is full of superstitious people. They can really get everyone wound up about something like this."

"What else does the newspaper say?" Celia asked.

"Oh, there are several articles about it," Etrulia replied. "When April finishes reading it, y'all ought to look it over. Someone has even been writing on the back wall of the church."

Mandie and Celia looked at each other.

"When does this newspaper come out? What time of day?" Mandie asked.

Etrulia looked puzzled. "I suppose it comes out in the afternoon," she replied. "At least that's when the school gets it. You know it takes hours and hours to set up the presses and print it and then deliver it. I imagine they work on it all morning and then deliver it in the afternoon. That's what my father does. He owns the newspaper back home."

"You mean whatever news the paper has in it would have been collected early in the morning in order to be out in the afternoon?" Mandie questioned her.

"As far as I know, all the news has to be in by eight o'clock in the morning in order to be printed for the afternoon," Etrulia answered. "Why are you asking all this?"

"I was just curious about when the writing on the church wall was discovered," Mandie replied. "It must have been early this morning or last night, then."

"Yes," Etrulia agreed. "I sure hope they catch whoever is doing such disgraceful things."

Mandie nodded. "I do, too," she said.

Etrulia moved on across the room with some of the other girls while Mandie and Celia talked quietly.

"So we know the writing wasn't done while we were in the church," Mandie said hardly above a whisper.

"That's right," Celia agreed. "It would have had to be a lot earlier."

"Maybe someone did it in the dark when no one could see them," Mandie suggested. "I'm just itching to solve this mystery."

"Well," Celia said with a sigh, "as soon as Friday comes, we can get started."

April laid the newspaper down and walked over to the piano as one of the girls began playing.

Mandie picked up the paper. The front page was full of news stories about the town's reactions to the bells ringing the wrong hour and the vandalism at the church. The only other news item on the front page was a story of a bank robbery in Charlotte the week before, which officials were still investigating.

So many things are happening, Mandie thought, *and they don't seem to be related at all.*

CHAPTER FOUR

CONCERN FOR HILDA

Aunt Phoebe used the rat poison in Mandie and Celia's room the next morning. As she promised, it soon dried up, and the odor went away. There was no sign of the mouse, alive or dead.

As the week dragged by, April Snow seemed to avoid Mandie and Celia, and they didn't go out of their way looking for her, either. They did, however, stay alert for any mischief she might do.

Finally, Friday came.

Mandie and Celia, with their bags nearby, sat waiting in the alcove near the center hallway of the school. They watched through the floor-length windows for Ben to come in Mrs. Taft's rig.

Mandie sprang from her chair. "I hear him coming!" she cried, grabbing her bag. "I know Ben's driving. He's just aflying."

As the rig came within sight, the girls hurried outside onto the veranda. They were so excited about leaving school for the weekend that they didn't even feel the cold north wind blowing around them. The sky was cloudy with a promise of rain or possibly snow.

Ben halted the rig in the curved driveway, and the girls ran down the steps. Joe Woodard was with him.

"Joe!" Mandie exclaimed. "I didn't think you'd be in town until tomorrow."

Joe, tall and lanky for his fourteen years, jumped down from the rig and held out Snowball, Mandie's white kitten. "Well, I could go home and take Snowball with me, and come back tomorrow," he teased.

Mandie snatched the kitten from him and cuddled it. "Now, Joe," she said, "you know I'm glad you could come today. We're just snowed under with mysteries."

Joe ran his long, thin fingers through his unruly brown hair. "Fixing to get into trouble again, are you?" he teased.

Ben put the girls' bags in the rig and everyone climbed aboard.

"No, we aren't," Mandie argued.

"Not if we can help it," Celia added.

Ben held the reins loosely in his hands and waited for a lull in the conversation. "Is y'all ready to proceed now?" he asked. "Miz Taft, she say hurry back. We better git a move on."

"Of course, Ben. Let's go," Joe said.

With a slap of the reins, the horses took off at a fast trot down the cobblestone streets toward Grandmother Taft's house.

Joe listened as the girls related what had happened since they returned to school. "And I suppose y'all want me to help solve this problem of the bells ringing wrong," he said.

Ben drew the rig up in Mrs. Taft's driveway.

Mandie smiled sweetly. "Of course," she replied, jumping down from the vehicle.

"Yes," Celia agreed, following Mandie. "Three heads are better than two."

Joe's long strides caught up with the girls as Ella, the Negro maid, opened the front door.

"Miz Taft, she be in de parlor," Ella informed them. "Ben, you take dem bags on upstairs. Miz Taft, she be in a hurry to see dese girls."

"Yes, ma'am, Miz Housekeeper," Ben replied sarcastically. He took the other bag from Joe and headed for the stairs.

Joe's father, Dr. Woodard, waited in the parlor with Mrs. Taft. After exchanging greetings, the young people sat down together on a nearby settee.

Mandie cuddled Snowball in her lap. "I'm glad y'all could come a day early, Dr. Woodard," she said.

The doctor cleared his throat. "Well, you see, your grandmother sent for me." He looked to Mrs. Taft to explain.

"Sent for you?" Mandie looked at her grandmother, puzzled.

"Now, don't get excited, Amanda," Mrs. Taft said. "But Hilda is sick. She—"

"Hilda? Sick?" Mandie interrupted. "Is it bad?"

"Amanda," Mrs. Taft reprimanded. "Please wait until I have finished talking before you get excited. Yes, Hilda is sick. She has pneumonia—"

"Pneumonia!" Mandie cried. "That's what took my father out of this world. Oh, is it bad, Dr. Woodard?" She dropped Snowball into Joe's lap and ran to stoop at Dr. Woodard's knee.

Dr. Woodard smoothed her blonde hair. "I'm afraid it could get bad," he said. He had been Jim Shaw's doctor back in the spring in Swain County.

Mandie jumped up. "Where is she?" she demanded. "Where is Hilda?"

"She's upstairs in her bedroom, dear," Dr. Woodard replied. "We've got a special nurse staying with her."

"I want to go see her," Mandie said, turning to leave the room.

"No, Amanda!" Mrs. Taft called sharply. "Hilda is not allowed to have any visitors. We don't want everyone else to catch this and come down sick, too."

With tears in her blue eyes, Mandie turned back and dropped onto the settee.

Joe reached for her hand and held it tight. "I know you're thinking about your father, Mandie," he said softly. "But don't. It won't help. It will only make it worse."

Snowball stepped over into his mistress's lap, curled up again, and began purring.

"Mrs. Taft, we were just here this past Tuesday, and Hilda was visiting with the Smiths. Did she get sick all of a sudden?" Celia asked.

"Yes, they brought her home that night, and she was running a high fever," Mrs. Taft replied. "When she didn't seem to get any better, I sent for Dr. Woodard, and he got here this afternoon."

"We've done all we can do right now," Dr. Woodard told Mandie. "We just have to pray that the Lord will heal her."

As a tear rolled down her cheek, Mandie lifted her head and began to pray softly. "Oh, dear God," she said, "please heal Hilda. She has been through so much, and now that things are getting better for her, please let her live to enjoy it."

The others joined in with their prayers. When they were finished, Mandie took Joe's handkerchief and dried her eyes.

"I remember how Hilda looked when we found her in the attic," Celia said. "She was so scared of us, and so starved-looking. Then she found out we were her friends, and she started getting better."

"The poor girl had never had any friends," Joe added. "Imagine her parents keeping her shut up in a room just because she wouldn't—or couldn't—talk."

"But she can talk," Mandie said firmly. "She is beginning to say a lot of words. She just never had a chance to learn because her parents thought she was demented."

"Well, she is not real bright, but she has more sense than people give her credit for," Dr. Woodard said. "And I can see that with the proper care and attention, like Mrs. Taft has been giving her, she could eventually lead an almost normal life."

"You'll keep watch over her, won't you, Dr. Woodard?" Mandie begged.

"I'll be here for the weekend. Then I have to go back to Swain County to see some sick folks there," the doctor replied. "But the nurse we have up there now knows what she's doing, and another nurse will relieve her at bedtime. Hilda won't be left alone."

"Thank you, Dr. Woodard," Mandie said. "Thanks to you and the Lord, she's going to pull through. I just know it."

After a short silence, Celia changed the subject. "Mrs. Taft, has anything else happened at the church since Mandie and I were there?" she asked, pushing back her long auburn hair.

"The church keeps having different people investigate, but they can't find anything wrong," Mrs. Taft replied.

"That's because there is nothing wrong with the clock or the bells," Mandie declared, straightening her shoulders. "It's just some person doing something that no one can catch them doing."

"But, Mandie, we were there when the bells rang thirteen times for twelve noon, remember? And there was no one there at all except us," Celia reminded her.

"They were just too quick for us, but we'll catch them sooner or later," Mandie predicted. "Just you wait and see."

"What about the man and the woman we saw in the church, Mrs. Taft?" Celia asked. "Did you find out anything about them?"

"No, dear," Mrs. Taft replied. "I've asked about them everywhere, but no one seems to have seen them enter or leave the church. And, according to the description y'all gave me of them, I don't believe they are people I know."

"Why didn't y'all follow them when they left the church?" Joe asked. "Or at least watch from the door when they went outside?"

"Because that was when the bells started ringing," Mandie explained, "and we had to go up to the belfry to see if anyone was up there."

"Hmm, I might as well ask," Joe said. "When do we visit the church to look for clues?"

Mandie and Celia both looked at Mrs. Taft.

"I suppose you young people could go some time in the morning after it warms up a little," she said.

"Thanks, Grandmother," Mandie said. She turned to Joe. "We'll go early enough so we'll be back in time for dinner, Joe," she added.

"Oh, good. I absolutely refuse to miss a meal, especially from your grandmother's table," Joe teased.

"I sure hope there's not any more shaking and thumping in that belfry," Celia remarked. "I don't know how we're ever going to figure out what that was. It must have been something awfully strong to shake the belfry that way."

"Either the shaking caused the thumping, or the thumping caused the shaking," Mandie figured. "It was all so fast and so close together, it must have been connected."

"That has me puzzled, Amanda," Mrs. Taft said. "That church is well built, and I can't imagine anything shaking any part of it unless it was an earthquake. But it seems no one else in town felt anything, so it couldn't have been an earthquake."

"Don't worry about it, Mrs. Taft. We'll figure it all out," Joe assured her.

Mandie gasped. "Oh, goodness!" she cried. "I just remembered something. The full moon is tomorrow, and that's when Uncle Ned promised to come to see me. He won't know I'm here and not at the school."

"Well, you could go to Aunt Phoebe's house tomorrow night and watch for him," Mrs. Taft said, "provided Joe and Celia go with you. Since Aunt Phoebe's house is right there in the backyard of the school, it ought to be safe enough, don't you think, Dr. Woodard?"

"I'm sure they'll be safe with Aunt Phoebe and Uncle Cal," the doctor answered. "They're good people."

"But Grandmother, Uncle Ned doesn't come to visit until after curfew at ten o'clock so that no one at the school will see him," Mandie explained. "He always waits under the huge magnolia tree right down below our bedroom window."

Uncle Ned was an old Cherokee friend of Mandie's father. When Jim Shaw had died, Uncle Ned had promised him he would watch over Mandie. And he kept his word. He regularly visited her and knew everything that was going on where she was concerned.

"If it's going to be late, I'll send Ben with y'all. He'll have to take y'all over there anyway. I'll tell him to wait for y'all," Mrs. Taft said.

"Grandmother, could we leave here in time to go by the church and check it out again tomorrow night before we go to Aunt Phoebe's?" Mandie begged. "Please?"

"Why, Amanda, I thought you were all going to the church tomorrow morning," Mrs. Taft replied.

"We are, but we should go to the church as many times as possible because you never know when we might find something to solve the mystery," Mandie insisted.

"Let's have one thing understood here and now, Amanda," Mrs. Taft said firmly. "You are not to go to the church without Ben or another adult with you at any time. And that applies to you, Celia. Don't you agree, Dr. Woodard?"

"Yes, ma'am," the doctor said. "There's no telling who or what you might run into at the church, and I certainly don't want Joe going there without an adult. In fact, I forbid it. Remember that, Joe."

"Yes, sir," Joe answered quickly. "I'd like to have an adult along anyway to back me up in case of trouble. These two girls wouldn't be much help if something unexpected happened."

Mandie glared at Joe. "I can remember a few times when you needed our help, Joe Woodard," she said. "Celia and I are both twelve years old, and you are only two years older."

Snowball jumped down to the floor and scampered out of the room. "I know. I know," Joe agreed. "Time about is fair enough."

"Remember the time the Catawbas kidnapped you, and—" Mandie began.

"I said, all right," Joe interrupted.

"Well, then," Mandie said, and turning to her grandmother asked, "Is it all right then for us to go to the church before we go to Aunt Phoebe's house since Ben will be with us?"

"Amanda, you know it will be dark then," Mrs. Taft reminded her. "It gets dark early now."

"But the church has those electric lights in it," Mandie persisted.

"If we can find the strings in the dark to pull them on," Celia said.

"If we light up the church, everyone in town will know it," Joe objected. "And if there's anyone messing around there, they'll run away fast."

Mandie thought for a moment. "Could we take a lantern with us, Grandmother?" she asked.

"I suppose so," Mrs. Taft agreed reluctantly. "Just don't stay out too late. Keep your visit with Uncle Ned short. And be sure you stay within sight of Ben at all times."

"Thanks, Grandmother," Mandie said. "We will. I promise."

Little did Mandie know how impossible that promise would be to keep.

CHAPTER FIVE

TRAPPED!

"You are not taking that white cat, are you?" Joe asked Mandie as the three young people put on their coats the next morning.

Mandie looked down at Snowball, who was sitting on the arm of the hall tree watching. "No, I guess not," she said. "He might get away from me and—"

"And get lost." Joe finished her sentence. "And then we'd have to go looking for him."

"All right," Mandie agreed. She turned to Celia. "Are you ready?"

"All ready," Celia replied, tying her bonnet under her chin.

Mandie stooped to look into the eyes of her kitten. "Now, Snowball, you stay here in the house," she cautioned. "Don't you dare go outside."

Snowball meowed in response and sat watching as the three young people opened the front door and went outside.

They all climbed aboard the waiting rig, Ben shook the reins, and they were off.

"Tell me again about that shaking in the belfry," Joe said.

"I think it was the floor up there," Mandie replied.

"Or was it the whole belfry trembling?" Celia asked.

"It could have been, but it seems like I felt my feet shaking," Mandie said.

Celia laughed. "I was shaking all over. That's for sure."

"You two are a big help," Joe said, exasperated. "How can I find out what caused something when I don't even know what it was?"

"We certainly don't know what it was," Mandie said.

"But if you could remember exactly what was shaking, it might help me figure out what was going on," Joe urged.

Ben pulled the rig up sharply in front of the church, and Mandie jumped down. "Anyway, here we are," she announced. "You can go up there yourself and look around."

"Yo' grandma, she say fo' me to wait right heah fo' y'all," Ben told Mandie.

"Please do, Ben," Mandie said. "If you get cold, come inside the church."

"It nice and warm under dis heah lap robe," Ben said. "I jes' wait heah."

The young people hurried inside the church and looked around the sanctuary. There was no one in sight.

Mandie led the way. "The door and steps to the gallery are right over here," she told Joe, taking off her coat. "Let's leave our coats down here. It's not that cold now, and they'll just get in the way."

After taking off their coats and leaving them on a back pew, Joe and Celia followed her up the stairs and across the balcony.

"Then this door here leads to the belfry," Mandie said, opening the door and showing Joe the bells overhead.

"And this must be the rope ladder." Joe grasped it and quickly skimmed upward.

As he swung off at the top, Mandie started climbing. Celia stayed where she was.

"Aren't you coming, Celia?" Mandie called down to her.

"I think I'll just stay down here and watch out for y'all," she replied nervously.

Mandie and Joe explored the belfry. They examined the floor and walls as well as the support the bells were anchored to. There was nothing loose.

"I know something was shaking when we were up here," Mandie declared. "I didn't imagine it."

"As far as I can tell, though, there is not even a loose board up here," Joe told her. "Could it have been the vibration of the bells ringing?"

"No, the bells weren't ringing when this happened," Mandie explained. "And don't forget, there was also a thumping noise, like something had fallen."

Joe inspected the wires to the bells. "How far away did the noise sound?" he asked.

"I suppose it could have come from downstairs in the sanctuary," Mandie reasoned. "But it sounded all muffled—a thick kind of noise. It wasn't a sharp sound."

"I think we should go back down and examine the whole church as we go," Joe suggested. "Maybe we can find something that has fallen."

"We thought the shaking and the noise must have been connected because everything happened so close together," Mandie explained, heading for the ladder. "I'm coming down, Celia," she called to her friend below. "Stay out of the way."

"All right," Celia answered. "Just don't come down too fast. You might fall."

Mandie quickly descended the rope ladder and jumped off the last rung. Joe followed.

"Did you find out anything up there?" Celia asked. She seemed relieved that she didn't have to climb the swinging ladder.

"No," Mandie replied, "but we're going to search the whole church now."

Joe looked around the balcony. "Let's begin here," he said. "Go up and down each row of benches and look for anything that might be loose or anything that might have fallen."

The three young people quickly covered the gallery and found nothing of interest.

"I guess we can go down to the sanctuary, then," Joe said, leading the way downstairs.

"Why don't we leave the sanctuary to the last and work our way through the basement first," Mandie suggested. "Then we can come back through here on the way out."

"That's a good idea," Joe agreed. "Do y'all know how to get into the basement?"

"Sure," Celia answered. "We have our Sunday school classes in the basement."

"Through this doorway here by the choir loft," Mandie said, pointing.

She opened a door to a hallway with Sunday school rooms opening off the sides and a stairway at the far end. The windows in the rooms shed a little light into the hallway.

Joe looked around. "This sure is a big church," he remarked. "They have classrooms back here and more in the basement?"

Mandie laughed. "There are a lot of good people in Asheville, so it takes a huge church to hold them," she said. "Besides, most of the people who belong to this church have a lot of money."

Joe headed down the stairs and the girls followed. At the bottom, they came to a door that opened into a hallway much darker than the one above. Since the basement was half sunk into the ground, the rooms off the hallway only had small windows near the ceiling.

"It's so dark down here I think we should all stay together," Celia suggested. There was a little quiver in her voice. "Someone could be hiding in this basement."

"You're right, Celia," Joe agreed. "Let's start on this side over here."

Starting with the first classroom on the right, they searched each room up and down the hallway.

"The only things in these rooms are a few chairs and a table," Joe observed, "so there isn't really any place for anyone to hide."

"That thumping noise could have been caused by almost anything, though," Mandie said.

They all shook a few of the chairs and tables along the way to see if any of them were wobbly. In one room they found an easel, but it seemed to be standing on strong legs. On the easel stood a piece of cardboard with a map roughly drawn on it in various colors. Nearby were several small cans of watercolor paint.

"What's down there at the end of the hall?" Joe asked, heading in that direction.

"It's the room where all the classes gather for a song every Sunday before we go upstairs for the preacher's sermon," Mandie replied.

Joe surveyed the room. In the front there was a piano with a swivel stool on claw feet. Numerous chairs filled the rest of the room. "I think we've cleared the basement," he said. "Let's see what we can find in the classrooms upstairs."

The girls followed Joe back upstairs, searching each room that opened off the hallway. At the far end they came to the pastor's study.

Joe tried the door, but it wouldn't open. He looked puzzled. "I wonder why the preacher locked his office," he said.

"He farms way out in the country," Mandie explained, "so he probably does all his pastor work in his house. As far as I know, he comes to the church only when there's a service."

"Well, he still didn't have to lock the door," Joe said in exasperation.

"Joe, this isn't Swain County, where everyone leaves their doors open and unlocked," Mandie reminded him. "This is a big city. There are all kinds of people in this town. The church doors are unlocked all day. Anyone could come in."

"Yes, even strangers, like the man and woman we saw here the other day," Celia added.

"Oh, well," Joe said with a sigh, "if we can't get inside that locked room, then neither can anyone else."

"Unless they have a key," Mandie said. "And I imagine the only people who have keys are the pastor, and the sexton, and maybe some of the deacons."

"All right, let's go," Joe said.

Inside the sanctuary they wandered toward the back. Then suddenly all three of them noticed something down at the altar.

"There's a flag or something there," Celia said, pointing.

"Or a banner." Mandie hurried forward.

Joe said nothing but took quick strides down the center aisle.

There, tied around the altar, was something that looked like a large piece of a white bed sheet with big red letters painted on it—just one word—HELP! The three young people stood there for several seconds just staring at it.

Mandie walked closer to inspect the cloth. "I'd say this is a piece of one of the choir robes," she said, feeling the material.

Joe bent to look at the lettering. "And the red paint came from the watercolors we saw by the easel in one of the rooms downstairs," he said.

"Where do they keep the choir robes?" Celia asked. "Don't the choir members take their robes home with them?"

Mandie thought for a moment. "I imagine they do most of the time, but someone could have left one in the church," she said. "Or maybe it was an extra one that no one was using."

"Should we take this thing down?" Joe asked.

"First, let's look for the rest of the robe," Mandie suggested. "It looks like that's only half of it."

"But, Mandie, we've been all over the church," Celia protested.

"I know we've been everywhere, but I don't believe this was here when we came in," Mandie argued. "We would have noticed it."

"You mean someone is here in the church?" Celia's voice was barely a whisper.

Joe puzzled over the matter. "Why would anyone put the word help on half a choir robe and hang it on the altar?"

"If we could find whoever did it, then we'd know," Mandie replied. "So I think we ought to look for that person."

"Let's stay together," Celia warned, "now that we know someone else is in the church."

The three young people again went through the entire church, finding nothing and no one.

As they returned to the sanctuary Joe spoke up. "I suppose we might as well remove that thing from the altar," he said.

But as they started down the aisle, Mandie caught her breath. "Look!" She rushed forward. "It's gone!"

Joe and Celia ran after her. Sure enough, the piece of cloth was gone. They looked all around, but there was no sign of it anywhere. Then the bells started ringing.

The young people stood still to silently count the rings. It was twelve noon, but how many times would the bells toll?

"Eleven, twelve," Mandie finished her count aloud. "It was right this time."

"We'd better go," Joe said. "Your grandmother will have dinner ready by now."

"I feel like having a good meal, myself," Mandie replied.

"Me, too," Celia agreed.

When the three returned to the rig, Ben was fast asleep under the lap robe, and they had to wake him.

The Negro driver sat up and yawned. "Y'all gone so long I jes' had to take me a nap," he said.

"Well, it's time to eat, Ben," Joe told him as the three piled into the rig.

When they got back to the house, they related their morning's adventures to Mrs. Taft and Dr. Woodard. No one had any explanations.

The conversation turned to other matters, and Dr. Woodard assured the young people that Hilda was resting comfortably—no worse, but no better than when they had left that morning.

Caught up in the excitement of their adventure, the young people counted the hours until they could return to the church that night.

When the time finally came to leave, Mrs. Taft gave the Negro driver strict instructions. "Now, Ben, you be sure you keep close tabs on these young people to see that no one harms them."

"Yessum, I will," Ben promised.

The young people didn't tell Mrs. Taft that Ben always stayed outside the church and that he even went to sleep.

It was dark when they reached the church, but the full moon shone brightly, and Joe had brought a lantern and plenty of matches to look around inside.

Ben stayed outside in the rig while the three noiselessly entered the church. Inside the vestibule, they looked around the sanctuary, which was dimly illuminated by the moonlight shining through the stained-glass windows.

Joe took charge. "Let's not light the lantern until we have to," he suggested, heading for the stairs to the gallery.

"It'll be pitch dark on the stairways and in the basement," Celia said.

"And remember, we don't have very long if we're going to get to Aunt Phoebe's house in time to see Uncle Ned," Mandie reminded him.

"Y'all come on with me upstairs," Joe said, opening the door to the gallery. "I'll run up in the belfry and check it out."

Once upstairs, the three crossed the gallery in the dim light.

Joe opened the door to the belfry. "Wait right here," he told the girls, handing Mandie the lantern.

After disappearing up the rope ladder for a few minutes, he called softly to them, telling them he was coming back down. Landing with a jump, he said, "There's nothing going on up there. Let's look through the classrooms." He took the lantern from Mandie and headed down the stairs.

They hurriedly inspected the classrooms behind the altar, then turned to go down to the basement.

Mandie stopped at the head of the stairs. "It's too dark to see, Joe," she said. "We're going to have to light the lantern."

"I guess we'd better," Joe agreed. "We don't want to fall." Taking a match from his pocket and striking it on the sole of his shoe, he lit the lantern.

The light seemed bright after their eyes had become accustomed to the darkness of the church. Joe descended the stairs first, holding the lantern high so the girls could see. At the bottom of the stairs, the hallway was even darker. Thick shrubbery outside the small, high windows in the classrooms blocked the moonlight, and the lantern light threw weird shadows.

"It's spooky down here," Celia said.

Neither Joe nor Mandie responded, but the young people stayed close together as they crept from room to room, searching for clues. They ended up at the far end of the hallway.

"Nothing," Joe said with a sigh.

Just then there was a loud banging noise overhead. The three young people froze.

Celia grabbed Mandie's hand. "W-what was th-that?" she stuttered.

"Let's go find out," Joe whispered. Leading the way back down the hallway, he pushed on the door to the stairs. It wouldn't budge. "I'm afraid someone has locked this door," he said softly.

"Oh, goodness!" Celia cried. "What are we going to do?"

Mandie tried the door, too. It was definitely locked.

"Now we know someone is in the church," Joe said, pushing hard against the door again. "And that someone has locked us in here."

Mandie's heart pounded. "What are we going to do, Joe?" she asked. "We've got to get out of here and go to Aunt Phoebe's house."

Just as Joe was about to say something, the lantern dimmed and went out. Everyone gasped.

"Don't worry," Joe said. "I have some more matches." He struck a match to relight the lantern and touched the match to the wick. The lantern sputtered and went out. He tried another match. When it did the same thing, he lit another match to examine the lantern by its light. "Oh, no!" he exclaimed. "The lantern is out of oil! I'm sorry. It's my fault. I just grabbed a lantern out of your grandmother's pantry, Mandie, and I didn't bother to see how much oil there was in it."

"Oh, Joe, we really are in trouble!" Mandie cried.

"We could try the windows," Joe suggested, turning back to a classroom.

"They have bars on the outside," Mandie explained. "And they're awfully small, anyway."

Again the banging noises began overhead. The young people huddled together in the darkness. Mandie's heart pounded so loudly that she was sure the others could hear it. Her legs buckled beneath her. All three of them plopped down on the floor by the locked door.

Then there was complete silence upstairs.

"We've got to get out of here!" Mandie cried. "There may be someone dangerous up there."

"It must be someone who has some keys," Joe said. "Otherwise, how could they lock that door?"

"These locks have a thumb latch," Mandie said nervously, "and the thumb latch on that door happens to be on the other side, so all they had to do was flip the latch to lock us in here."

Celia squeezed Mandie's hand tightly. "Oh, Mandie, whatever are we going to do?"

"Let's say our verse that always helps when we get in trouble," Mandie said.

The three young people joined hands and repeated the Bible verse that always gave them strength. "What time I am afraid," they recited, "I will put my faith in Thee."

Mandie took a deep breath and rose to her feet. "Now I won't be afraid because I know God will help us get out of this predicament somehow—" she said. "He always does."

"I wish I knew what was going on upstairs," Joe said.

"Me, too," Celia agreed. "Whoever is up there could be a dangerous character."

The three walked about, softly discussing possibilities. Mrs. Taft would be worried when they didn't return, and Uncle Ned would be waiting under the magnolia tree in the cold for nothing.

Somehow they had to get out!

CHAPTER SIX

NO WAY TO ESCAPE?

"I wish I hadn't suggested we leave our coats in the sanctuary," Mandie said, briskly rubbing her arms to warm herself. "Too bad there's nothing down here to build a fire in that big stove in the hallway."

"I'm cold, too," Celia complained, "and it's so spooky down here. What are we going to do?"

"We can't stay here all night," Joe said. "We've got to get out somehow."

Celia shivered as she paced back and forth on the cold concrete floor. "I wonder why Ben hasn't come looking for us."

"He probably fell asleep in the rig again," Mandie answered.

"Well, we've got to do something," Joe announced. "Let's try the windows. We might find some loose bars on one of them or something."

Celia looked up at the high windows. "I don't think we can reach them," she said.

"You're right, Celia," Mandie agreed. "I don't believe Joe can reach that high, either."

"I can always get taller," Joe said with a grin. He carried a chair over to the window and stood on it. "Like this," he added.

"You can just barely reach the window, Joe," Mandie argued. "Celia and I would never be able to."

"Never mind. I'll check the windows myself," Joe answered.

The windows, which were locked by spring hooks, consisted of only one small pane, and they pulled out and down from the top like a door opening sideways.

Joe pulled the first one open and reached through to the bars outside. "No luck," he said. Shaking his head, he stepped down and moved the chair below the next window.

"I wish we could find something to knock the bars loose," Mandie said, looking around in the darkness.

"There's nothing here we can use," Joe reminded her as he opened the second window. "Remember, we checked the whole place."

Celia watched Joe trying to loosen the bars. "It'd probably be easier to break the door down than to knock out any of those iron bars," she commented.

"Let's try it, Celia," Mandie said. "We can work on the door while Joe works on the windows." The girls hurried out into the hallway.

"Hey, don't go hurting yourselves now," Joe cautioned. "That's an awfully strong door."

"We'll just see what we can do," Mandie called back to him. She felt her way through the darkness to the door at the end of the hallway. Celia clutched Mandie's shoulder and followed.

When they got to the door, Mandie ran her hands around the door-knob. "Oh, shucks!" she exclaimed. "The lock is on the other side, and the door opens into the hall this way. That means we have to pull on it instead of pushing."

Celia laid her hands on top of Mandie's on the doorknob. "Maybe it'll work," she said.

The girls tried to pull together on the door, but four hands wouldn't fit. Celia let go.

Mandie grasped the doorknob tightly. "I'll have to pull by myself," she said. She pulled as hard as she could, but the door didn't even rattle. The lock held fast. As Mandie shook her aching hands in the air, Celia stepped up for a try. Nothing happened.

"Maybe Joe could pull harder on it," Mandie said. "Come on, I'm going back there to see where he is."

The girls felt their way back down the dark hallway until they came to the end room where Joe was examining a window.

"Nothing yet," Joe said to them, running his hands over the bars outside. "As far as I can tell, all these bars are bolted into the brick and cement."

"And there's no way to get one loose," Mandie added. "Celia and I couldn't budge the door, either."

"What are we going to do?" Celia fretted.

"Now, Celia, don't forget. We're going to trust in God," Mandie reminded her friend. "Remember our verse?"

"I know," Celia whispered. "I just wish we could hurry up and get out of this place."

"Joe, why don't you stop working on those windows for a minute and see if you can do anything with that door?" Mandie suggested.

Joe stepped down, preparing to go on to the next window. "I only have these two left," he said, motioning to the ones on the end. "I've examined all the windows in the other rooms. I'll see what I can do with the door as soon as I'm finished here." Stepping up onto the chair, he inspected the bars on the window above him. "Just like the rest—solid," he said, stepping down and moving to the last window.

The girls watched silently as he climbed up, opened the window, and reached out to touch the iron bars.

He turned and grinned at them. "One corner is loose," he said excitedly. "If I can manage to get another corner free, we might be able to squeeze out."

Grabbing the bars with both hands, he shook them with all his strength. The loose corner wiggled a little, but the rest of the bars stayed firmly in place.

Finally Joe gave up. "Looks like we're in here to stay unless I can get the door open," he said. Closing the window, he stepped down from the chair.

"Maybe Ben will wake up and come looking for us," Mandie said hopefully.

"I don't imagine Ben will come inside the church when there aren't any lights on up there," Joe argued. "Let me try the door."

The three felt their way through the dark hallway to the door again. Joe took hold of the doorknob with both hands and pulled with all his might. Nothing happened. He released it, took a deep breath, braced his long legs, and yanked hard. Suddenly, he fell backward, knocking the girls behind him onto the floor.

"Land sakes!" Mandie cried, getting up from the hard floor. "What happened?"

"The blasted doorknob came off," Joe said, holding the knob in his hand. He stood up. "Maybe I can put it back on."

He felt around on the door for the place where the doorknob belonged. "The spindle that holds the knobs is gone!" he exclaimed. "So the other side of the knob is gone, too."

"How are we ever going to get out of here?" Celia asked.

"This is the back of the church, and Ben is parked on the road in front, but do you suppose if we yelled loud enough he might hear us?" Mandie asked.

"We could try," Joe said.

"If we could all get up there and open a window and yell, it might work." Celia sounded hopeful.

"The room where you found the loose bar has a big table in it, remember?" Mandie reminded Joe. "We could pull it over to the window and then put chairs on top of it. Celia and I ought to be able to stand on the chairs and reach the window."

"You might be able to if the chairs are steady enough," Joe said.

The three returned to the room where the table was. They pushed the table under the window with the loose iron bar, and set two chairs on top of it.

"Are y'all sure you won't fall?" Joe asked. "You could get hurt pretty bad, you know, on this concrete floor."

"At this point we just have to take chances," Mandie said. "But we'll be careful." She raised her long skirt and jumped up onto the table. Then swinging her legs around, she scrambled to her feet. Joe held the chair while she stepped up onto the seat. She looked up. Her head almost touched the ceiling in front of the window. "Come on up, Celia."

Celia copied Mandie's antics to get up on the other chair. Joe stood between the girls to support them and opened the window.

"Well, now that we're up here, what do we yell?" Joe asked.

"Let's just call Ben," Mandie said. Raising her voice, she started yelling. "Ben! Ben! Come to the back of the church!"

Celia and Joe joined in, and the three together hollered loud enough to wake the whole neighborhood.

Joe stopped to catch his breath. "He must be able to hear all the noise we're making," he said.

"Maybe he left," Celia suggested.

"No, Grandmother gave him strict orders not to leave us," Mandie said.

"Well, he's either gone off somewhere or he's deaf," Joe decided.

All three stood quietly for a minute as they tried to look out through the thick shrubbery in front of the window.

Suddenly Mandie touched Joe's arm. "Did you see something move out there?" she whispered.

"I did!" Celia said quietly.

"Where?" Joe whispered back.

"There!" Mandie pointed through the shrubbery off to the left. "Do you suppose it's Ben?"

"I saw something move," Joe whispered.

Then the bushes quit shaking.

It must be Ben, Mandie thought. Besides, if it were someone bad, he couldn't get in any more than we can get out, she reasoned. She raised her voice again. "Ben! Ben!" she shouted. "We're in here!"

There was a quick movement in the shrubbery outside, then a familiar voice answered, "Papoose! Where Papoose?"

"Uncle Ned!" Mandie exclaimed as tears came to her eyes. "We're down here in the basement, Uncle Ned!"

Joe and Celia breathed sighs of relief along with Mandie as the old Indian moved between the bushes to the window and looked in through the iron bars.

"Papoose, Doctor Son, Papoose See," Uncle Ned called to them. (He called Celia Papoose See because he couldn't pronounce her name.) "How you get in there?" he demanded.

"Somebody locked the door, and we can't get out," Mandie explained. "Oh, Uncle Ned, you're the answer to our prayers."

"Please get us out, Uncle Ned!" Celia cried.

"Do you know where Ben is?" Joe queried.

"How did you know we were here?" Mandie asked.

"One time for each question," Uncle Ned replied. "First, must get out. Ben sleep. I get Ben." The old Indian turned to go.

"Wait, Uncle Ned," Mandie called to him. "The front door is supposed to be unlocked. We came in that way. But somebody else has been in the church. Whoever it is locked the door at the bottom of the stairs."

"I go see," Uncle Ned nodded and hurried off.

"Oh, what a relief!" Celia climbed down from the chair and sat on the table.

Mandie and Joe sat down beside her.

"I guess Ben was asleep," Joe said in exasperation. "A lot of good it did to bring him with us!"

"Let's don't make trouble for him," Mandie suggested.

"We have to tell your grandmother the truth, Mandie," Joe said.

"But we don't have to go into detail," Mandie replied. "If she knows Ben went to sleep outside and we got locked in here alone, she might not let him go with us anywhere anymore, and then we might not be able to solve the mystery."

"If he goes with us anywhere else, he should stay right along with us and not take a nap outside," Joe said.

"You're right," Mandie agreed. "Next time we'll insist on that."

In a few minutes Uncle Ned reappeared at the basement window with Ben beside him. The girls quickly took their places on the chairs with Joe steadying them.

"Door locked," Uncle Ned announced. "Must think. Other way out?"

"Lawsy mercy, Missies, how y'all git in dat place all locked up like dat?" Ben called to them.

"We don't know, Ben," Mandie told him. "Someone locked the door to the basement while we were down here."

Joe reached out to touch the iron bars on the window. "These bars are loose in this one corner," he said, pointing. "I tried to get it loose enough for us to crawl out, but I didn't have any tools."

Uncle Ned examined the bars.

Ben watched as the old Indian shook the bars and thought for a minute. "I think I got a claw hammer in de rig," Ben said. "I go see."

"Please be sure you come right back, Ben," Mandie called after him.

"Yessum, Missy. I be back in a minute," the Negro replied.

Uncle Ned looked up from his examination of the bars. "Bars stuck good in cement. Hammer break cement. Much damage."

"I think my grandmother would pay for any damage we do, Uncle Ned—I hope," Mandie answered.

Ben returned with a large claw hammer. Everyone watched as the strong old Indian banged on the iron bars. The young people shielded their eyes as bits of cement flew through the air.

Uncle Ned shook the bars and hammered again. Then he turned to Ben. "You pull. I pull," he said.

Ben understood and braced himself to yank on the bars at the same time the old Indian did.

"Away!" Uncle Ned told the young people. "Bar come loose and cement hit papooses."

The three scrambled down and crouched on the table beneath the window, waiting.

"Pull!" Uncle Ned shouted.

There was a sudden, loud, cracking noise.

"One end loose," Uncle Ned announced.

The young people stood up to look.

"Must break other end," the old Indian fussed. He picked up the hammer from the ground. "Away!" he told the young people again.

Again they sat down, waiting and listening as Uncle Ned pounded and the wall vibrated with the hard blows. Cement flew everywhere. Mandie and Celia bent their heads to keep it from getting into their eyes. Joe moved away from the window to watch, and the girls followed.

Uncle Ned dropped the hammer. "Now!" he called to Ben.

Together the two men pulled and grunted. The bars wouldn't give. Uncle Ned picked up the hammer again and gave the bars a few more hard blows. Ben helped him pull again. Suddenly the bars gave way, and the two men fell backward into the shrubbery.

Mandie jumped back up on the chair to look out the now unbarred window. "Oh, thank you, Uncle Ned!" she cried.

The old Indian stood up and came over to the window. "Small to crawl through," he said, measuring the opening with his old wrinkled hands.

"I think it might be large enough," Joe said. "I can help the girls from in here if you can help them out up there."

"I help," Uncle Ned agreed.

The three young people happily chattered about who would be the first one out; then Mandie stopped suddenly. "I just remembered something!" she exclaimed. "Our coats—they're upstairs!"

"That's right!" Celia said.

"Well, I don't know how we're going to get up there with the basement door still locked," Joe told them. "And Uncle Ned said the front door was locked, too."

"We come in," Uncle Ned offered. "We open door down there."

"But Uncle Ned," Mandie said, "the doorknob is gone on both sides, and even the spindle dropped off."

"Me see." Uncle Ned turned to Ben. "We go down there. Me go first."

"Don't get stuck, Uncle Ned," Mandie called from below.

Taking his sling of arrows and his bow from his shoulder, he pushed them through the window. "Take," he told Joe.

Joe took them and moved out of the way.

Uncle Ned squatted down and stuck his long legs through the open window. As he slid in, his broad shoulders just barely made it through the opening. Ben, whose frame was even bigger than Uncle Ned's had a harder time, but when he finally landed on the table, both men sighed with relief and looked around.

"No light?" the Indian asked.

"No, Uncle Ned," Mandie replied. "Our lantern is out of oil."

Celia touched Mandie's arm. "Aren't there any of those new electric lights down here like there are upstairs?" she asked.

"I don't know," Mandie said, looking around. "If there are, there would be a string hanging from a fixture on the ceiling."

The group searched each room for any indication of electric lights, but they found none.

"Now, why would they have electric lights upstairs and none down here?" Joe wondered.

"They haven't had the lights upstairs very long," Celia replied. "They put them in since we came to school here in Asheville, and I seem to remember something about having to raise more money to wire the basement."

Mandie sighed in disappointment. "You're right, Celia," she said. "I remember now, too."

"What do you use for light when you're in the basement at night, then?" Joe asked.

"I don't think it's ever used at night," Mandie answered. "There are so many rooms upstairs that they don't really need it."

Uncle Ned spoke up. "Where door?" he asked, putting his sling of arrows over his shoulder again.

When they showed the door to him and Ben, Uncle Ned felt around in the darkness. "Here knob hole," he said. "Notches inside."

"You see, there's no way to open it," Celia said.

"Never say no way anything," Uncle Ned replied. "Always way." He took one of his arrows from his sling, felt for the hole, and carefully inserted the tip of the arrow into it.

The young people and Ben hovered around, trying to see in the darkness. Uncle Ned slowly twisted the arrow, and they heard the click of the latch withdrawing in the lock. Carefully pulling on the door by the arrow in the lock, the old Indian gradually eased the door open.

Everyone gasped.

"But that door was locked!" Mandie exclaimed. "We couldn't turn the lock, remember?"

"It certainly was," Joe agreed. "And all Uncle Ned did was turn the latch and it opened. Someone has been playing tricks on us."

"You mean somebody locked it and then later unlocked the thumb latch on the other side?" Celia asked in disbelief.

"I guess so," Joe replied.

"Get coats," Uncle Ned urged. "Ben lock window."

Ben hurriedly latched the window as the young people started up the stairs.

Joe's foot kicked something, and he bent to pick it up. "Here's the other doorknob," he said, holding it out to Uncle Ned.

"Leave here. Must hurry," Uncle Ned urged.

When they all got upstairs, they found their coats just where they had left them in the last pew at the back of the sanctuary.

Celia hurriedly slipped into hers. "Thank goodness no one took our coats while we were trapped down there!" she exclaimed. "Oh, this feels nice and warm."

"Wait a minute," Mandie cried as Joe helped her into her coat. "If the front door is locked, how are we going to get out of here?"

They all stopped and looked at each other, realizing Mandie was right.

Joe ran to try the front door. "It's locked, all right," he said, shaking his head.

"Is door in back?" Uncle Ned asked.

"You mean a back door?" Mandie replied. "I don't know. I don't think I've ever noticed. Let's go see."

They hurried to the back.

"I know where it is," Celia suddenly remembered. "It's in the back of the pastor's study. I remember seeing it once when the door to the study was open."

"And the pastor keeps his study locked," Joe reminded them. "Why would the back door be in the pastor's study?"

"His study was probably made out of the end of the hall. See?" Mandie pointed to the room down the hall. "And the door was probably already there."

"Oh, give me a country church anytime. These city churches are made too complicated," Joe moaned.

"Must go down, out window," Uncle Ned decided.

"Now, how's we gwine do dat?" Ben asked. "I almost didn't fit through dat window a-comin' in."

Mandie smiled. "Ben, if you fit coming in, you'll fit going out," she teased.

Uncle Ned led the way back down to the basement room where he and Ben had come in. "I go first," he said. "Then Ben. Be up there, help papooses get out. Doctor son last. Help papooses up. Take coats off and push through window."

They understood his plan. The old Indian gave Joe his bow and arrows and quickly scooted through the window. Joe handed the Indian's things back to him; then Ben started through. It took some squirming and twisting, but he made it all right. The young people removed their coats and pushed them through the window to the men above.

"Mandie, you go first," Joe suggested. "Then you can help Celia get out."

"All right," Mandie agreed, climbing onto the chair to reach the windowsill.

"When I get hold of your feet and push, you grab Uncle Ned's hands up there," Joe instructed.

Mandie did as she was told and soon found her feet firmly planted on the ground outside the window. She breathed a great sigh of relief.

Celia climbed through with no problem and then Joe followed, handing Uncle Ned the worthless empty lantern. He reached back inside to slam the window shut, hoping the latch would catch. It did.

Hastily putting on their coats in the bright moonlight, the young people ran out to the rig with Uncle Ned and Ben.

Mandie looked up into the old Indian's face. "How did you know we were here, Uncle Ned?" she asked.

"I go to school. Aunt Phoebe see, tell me Papoose at Grandmother house. I tell her I go to Grandmother. Aunt Phoebe not wait for Papoose now," the Indian explained. "On way to Grandmother, I see rig in front of church. Ben sleep. I know about bells. I know Papoose near."

"Then you heard us hollering our heads off," Mandie said with a nervous laugh.

Uncle Ned reached out and took her small hand in his old wrinkled one. "Papoose, what been doing?" he asked.

Mandie and the others related the night's events to Uncle Ned as they stood around the rig. They told him about all the strange things that had been happening to them since they started investigating.

"Papooses must be careful," Uncle Ned cautioned. "Sometimes bad people 'round."

"We'll be careful," Mandie promised. "Are you coming on to my grandmother's with us now?"

"No, Papoose. Must go. Horse wait under tree." He waved his hand toward a horse tethered under a bare tree across the cobblestoned street. "I come again. Remember—Papoose must think," he said. "Always think first, then do things."

"I'll try to remember that, Uncle Ned," Mandie promised.

"I promise Jim Shaw when he go to happy hunting ground that I watch over Papoose, but Papoose must learn to watch, too," the old Indian reminded her.

"I love you, Uncle Ned," Mandie said, rising on her tiptoes to give him a quick hug. "I'll be careful."

Uncle Ned hugged Mandie in return, then hurried across the street to his waiting horse.

The young people piled into the rig. Ben picked up the reins, and they waved to the old Indian as he mounted his horse and rode away.

When the rig started off, Celia looked up at the clock in the steeple. "It's twenty minutes till eleven!" she exclaimed.

Mandie frowned at Joe. "I don't remember hearing the bells ring while we were in the church," she said, "but I know we got there before ten o'clock."

"You're right. They didn't ring," Joe said with a puzzled look on his face.

"No, they didn't," Celia agreed.

"More and more mystery," Mandie said. "We've just got to solve this thing before forty-'leven hundred more things happen."

"Well, right now I imagine your grandmother and my father are beginning to wonder where we are," Joe told her.

"I know," Mandie said. She was more worried about going back to face the adults than she was about all that had happened to them that night.

CHAPTER SEVEN

BACK TO SCHOOL

Mrs. Taft and Dr. Woodard sat waiting in the parlor when the young people returned from the church.

Hurriedly hanging their coats on the hall tree, the three went to sit on stools near the blazing fire. They were cold from the weather and the fright they had just had as well as from the ordeal of now relating their adventure to the adults. Mandie picked up Snowball, who was curled up asleep on the hearth rug, and began to pet him.

Mrs. Taft had Ella serve hot cocoa. She and Dr. Woodard listened without interrupting as the three told of the events of the night. They raised eyebrows and gasped at some parts of the story but waited until the young people had finished. Then Mrs. Taft scolded them.

"I'm sorry, Grandmother," Mandie said, "but we didn't intentionally get locked in."

"No, I don't suppose you did," Mrs. Taft answered. "However, I shall have to speak to Ben. He should have stayed right with you all."

Dr. Woodard cleared his throat. "That could have been an unsavory character who locked you in," he said. He turned to Mrs. Taft. "Do you think they should just stop all this investigating business?"

"Oh no, please!" Mandie pleaded. "We have to find out what's going on."

Mrs. Taft thought for a moment. "I suppose it would be all right if they only go in the daytime—and if Ben stays right with them. But no more night adventures."

The three young people looked at each other.

"I won't be here tomorrow night anyway," Joe conceded. "We have to go home after church tomorrow."

"And we have to go back to school tomorrow afternoon," Celia added.

"We may not have time to do anything else about the mystery now, anyway," Mandie said with a sigh.

"It's late now," Mrs. Taft said. "You all get upstairs to bed. Tomorrow is Sunday, and we all have to get up early and go to church."

The young people started to leave the room and Snowball followed.

Mandie turned quickly and ran back to Dr. Woodard. "We've been so wrapped up in what happened to us that we forgot to ask about Hilda," she said. "How is she, Doctor Woodard?"

"About the same. No better. No worse," he replied.

"Is she going to just stay that way?" Mandie asked. "Isn't she ever going to get better?"

"We hope she will, Amanda," Dr. Woodard replied. "Like I said before, it's up to the Lord."

Mandie turned to the others. "Don't forget Hilda in your prayers tonight," she said.

Early the next morning, everyone was up, rushing around to get ready for church. At breakfast, Dr. Woodard announced that there was still no change in Hilda's condition. The nurses remained at her bedside around the clock, but Mandie felt frustrated that no visitors were allowed.

As they all piled into the rig to go to church, Mrs. Taft spoke quietly to the driver. "Ben, I need to have a little talk with you sometime this afternoon," she said.

"Yessum, Miz Taft." Ben looked nervous.

Mandie leaned forward to whisper in his ear. "Don't get so worried," she said. "It's nothing really bad."

Without a reply, Ben picked up the reins and drove sedately to the church. He always left Mrs. Taft at her church and then drove on to his own down the road, picking up Mrs. Taft again after services were over.

As the group stepped down from the rig, Mrs. Taft looked back at her driver. "Now, please don't be late, Ben," she said. "We're in a hurry today."

"Yessum, Miz Taft," Ben answered, muttering to himself as he drove off.

Once inside the church, they all went to their Sunday school classes. Mrs. Taft's was at the rear of the main floor, and Dr. Woodard visited the men's class in a side room nearby. As the young people headed down to the basement for their classes, the first thing they noticed was the doorknob securely fastened to the door at the bottom of the stairs.

"I can't believe my eyes!" Mandie exclaimed in a whisper.

"It seems that whoever is doing these things around here comes back to reverse whatever happened," Joe remarked. "First the *Help!* banner and now this doorknob. . . ."

"Maybe the person is sorry afterward," Celia suggested.

"They're going to be sorry when we finally find them out," Mandie promised. "The house of the Lord is no place to play games like this."

Celia and Joe agreed.

After Sunday school, the young people went upstairs and joined Mrs. Taft and Dr. Woodard in the family pew for the preacher's message. Mandie was happy that the two big stoves in the sanctuary were roaring with fires to warm the whole room. How different from last night, she thought.

As soon as Reverend Tallant stepped up behind the pulpit, he mentioned the mysterious goings-on in the church. "We have not been able to remove the writing from the back wall of the church yet, but we should have that accomplished tomorrow," he began. "Now, however, we have another complaint. It seems that neighbors living nearby heard the organ playing here in the sanctuary along about midnight. Someone notified the sexton, Mr. Clark, and he came down, looked around, and found nothing."

The minister paused momentarily while latecomers were being seated. "Mr. Clark said he had gone through and locked the door at ten o'clock," Rev. Tallant continued. "Everything was all right then."

The three young people looked at each other.

"Ten o'clock?" Mandie whispered. "He certainly didn't check the basement then because we were locked in down there before ten, and it was twenty minutes to eleven when we got out."

Celia nodded.

"You don't know what time we got locked in," Joe whispered. "The bells didn't ring at ten o'clock, remember?"

Dr. Woodard nudged his son and shook his head.

The young people hushed.

The preacher continued speaking. " . . . and we want to ask for your prayers for little Hilda Edney, who is living with Mrs. Taft. She is very ill with pneumonia. Mrs. Tillinghast and her sister, Miss Rumler, also need our prayers at this time. They are both quite sick with the flu. Now let us pray."

Mandie bowed her head with the rest of the congregation and joined in the prayers, especially for Hilda. She was worried about her. Dr. Woodard had to leave for home after dinner, and although there were other doctors in Asheville, she trusted her friend Dr. Woodard more than them all.

At the conclusion of the service, Ben waited for them as they shook hands with the preacher at the door and stepped out onto the porch.

On the way home, the young people discussed the newest development in the church mysteries.

"So someone was playing the organ at midnight," Mandie said, trying to make some sense of it. "Well, I'd like to know how anybody got inside the church. It was all locked up when we left."

"Maybe they were able to open the window where Uncle Ned removed the bars," Joe reasoned. "Come to think of it, the preacher didn't mention that someone had torn the bars off that window."

Mrs. Taft spoke up. "That's because I spoke to him before he preached and told him what happened to y'all last night," she explained. "And I promised him I would pay for the damage."

"So, since he knew who did it, he didn't mention it," Mandie said. Suddenly she caught her breath in alarm. "I hope he doesn't think we've been doing all those other things."

"Of course not, Amanda," her grandmother assured her. "But I did tell him that y'all were trying to solve the puzzle for him."

"You told him what we were doing?" Mandie gulped.

"What else was I to say when the damage was there?" Mrs. Taft replied. "It had to be explained some way."

"You're right, Grandmother," Mandie agreed. "I hope he doesn't mind our getting involved."

Mrs. Taft smiled. "I'm sure no one will mind if y'all are able to solve this mystery," she said.

Ben pulled the rig up in front of Mrs. Taft's house and helped her from the vehicle.

As the others climbed down, Mrs. Taft spoke to the driver again. "Come to the back sitting room in about two hours, Ben," she instructed. "The doctor and Joe will be leaving as soon as we finish dinner, and then the girls have to return to school. I want to talk to you before you take them back."

"Yessum, Miz Taft," Ben replied, stepping back into the rig to move it from the front driveway. "I'll be dere."

Inside the house, Dr. Woodard headed upstairs to check on Hilda while everyone else sat in the parlor, waiting for dinner to be put on the table. Mrs. Taft was strict with her servants on Sunday. She insisted that they attend their churches, and all the cooking for Sunday was done on Saturday so that when the cook came home from church, all she had to do was warm everything and put it on the table.

Mrs. Taft sat in a big overstuffed chair in the parlor and looked lovingly at her granddaughter. "Do you and Celia have your things together to take back to school, dear?" she asked.

"Yes, ma'am," Mandie replied. "We're all ready. Are you going to send for us again next Friday?"

"If you and Celia want to come, of course, dear," Mrs. Taft answered. "You know I am always glad to have you girls here with me anytime."

"Thanks, Grandmother," Mandie said. "I'm always so happy to get out of that school, and I imagine Celia is, too."

Celia nodded.

"Especially when there's some kind of adventure going on," Joe teased.

Mandie pretended to look hurt. "You won't be able to come next weekend, will you?" she asked.

"Not unless my father has to come back," he said.

Dr. Woodard entered the room. "I still don't see any change in Hilda," he said. "I've changed the treatment a little, and I hope that will make a difference. But for now, she's just not making any progress."

"Oh, Dr. Woodard, couldn't I just open the door and peek in?" Mandie begged.

"No, I'm sorry, Amanda," he replied. "You will all have to stay away from her room for the time being."

"Will you be coming back next weekend to check on her?" Celia asked.

Mandie's eyes brightened as she looked at Joe, awaiting the answer.

"I'm not sure," Dr. Woodard said. "We'll see."

Mandie smiled at Joe. *At least he didn't say no,* she thought.

As soon as the noon meal was over, Dr. Woodard and Joe left in their buggy. Mrs. Taft retired to the back sitting room to talk to Ben.

Mrs. Taft told the Negro man to sit down. "Now, Ben, I want to know why you didn't stay right with Miss Amanda and her friends when you took them to the church last night," she began.

"I stayed in de rig, Miz Taft," Ben replied.

"But you fell asleep in the rig, and those young people were locked in the church," she scolded. "If Uncle Ned hadn't come along when he did, there's no telling when they would have gotten out."

"But, Miz Taft," Ben replied. The girls could hear him scuffing his feet nervously. "You see, it's like dis heah—I ain't s'posed to go in white folks' church."

"That's nonsense, Ben, and you know that," Mrs. Taft argued. "You know as well as I do that there's a gallery in that church where the colored people are all welcome to come and join in our services. There's no reason in this world why you can't go inside a white people's church."

"I don't go in dat gallery neither, ma'am," Ben replied. "You go to yo' church. I goes to mine. You white. I'se a Negro."

"You are not obligated to attend church with white people, Ben, but you are obligated to carry out my instructions," Mrs. Taft said firmly. "That's what I pay you for—to do what I ask you to do. Now, I don't want to hear any more nonsense. If you want to keep your job, you'll have to do whatever the job requires. Is that understood?"

"I understands, Miz Taft," Ben replied. "If you say dat's part of my job, den I does my job next time."

"Thank you, Ben. I knew I could depend on you," Mrs. Taft said. "You know it isn't long until Christmas, and I always give the pay raises at Christmas."

"Yessum, Miz Taft. You sho' does."

"You are not to let the girls out of your sight again when I have left them in your care," Mrs. Taft continued. "Not out of your sight for one minute. Can I depend on you next time they go somewhere?"

"Yessum. Yessum. You kin 'pend on me."

"Thank you. Now get the rig around to the front door," Mrs. Taft said. "It's about time for the girls to go back to school."

"Yessum."

Minutes later, the girls were reluctantly on their way back to school. When they arrived, Ben took their luggage to their room. The girls stopped to speak to Miss Hope, whom they met in the front hallway.

"I hope you young ladies had a nice weekend," Miss Hope said in greeting.

"Yes, ma'am, we did," the girls replied together. "Did you?"

"We've had a little sickness here this weekend," Miss Hope informed them. "Two of the girls came down with flu—Mamie Wright and Betty Blassingame. They both went home. Mamie just lives over in Hendersonville, and Betty lives out in the country near here, so their parents came and got them." Miss Hope looked worried. "I do hope we don't have an epidemic here in the school."

"Hilda has pneumonia. She's real bad off," Mandie told her.

"Oh, dear, I'm sorry," Miss Hope replied. "I'll be praying for her, and I'll pray that you two don't come down with it."

"Thank you, Miss Hope," the girls said.

"Hurry along, now, and get freshened up for supper," the schoolmistress told them as she continued down the hall.

As soon as the girls were sure she was out of sight, they took the steps, two at a time, up to their third-floor room.

"Well, I guess it's all lessons until Friday," Mandie said, pushing open the door to their room.

Celia followed, and both girls quickly removed their coats and bonnets and started to lay them on the bed. Instantly they jumped back and screamed.

There in the middle of the bed, on top of the counterpane, lay a dead mouse!

At the sound of their screams, Miss Prudence, who had been walking by, jerked the door open. "What are you—?" She saw the mouse, turned pale, and without a word slammed the door, running down the hallway, calling for Uncle Cal.

Mandie and Celia backed away from the bed and stood frozen there in terror.

"Sh-she's afraid of m-mice, too," Mandie managed to say.

Celia moved toward the door. "I'm g-g-getting out of here," she said, backing out of the room.

In seconds Uncle Cal appeared with a garbage bucket and a brush in his hand. "Where dat so-an'-so mouse, now, Missy?" the Negro man asked. He spotted it at once. Quickly turning the bucket sideways, he brushed the dead mouse inside. "All gone, now, Missy," he announced as he headed out the door.

Mandie's heart was pounding. "Oh, thank you, Uncle Cal," she said. "Thank you."

As he went out the door, Aunt Phoebe hurried in, carrying a clean bedspread. She quickly pulled off the one on the bed and replaced it with the one she had brought.

Mandie still trembled with fright. "Aunt Phoebe, do you suppose that's the mouse we found in the chifforobe?" she asked shakily.

Celia came back inside the room to hang up her coat.

"I don't be knowin,' Missy," the old Negro woman said, smoothing the wrinkles out of the fresh counterpane. "But I tells you one thing. Miss Prudence, she be knowin' now dat mouse was real!"

"And Miss Prudence was afraid of it, too, just like us," Celia added.

"I hope she does something about it," Mandie said. "I think someone put that thing on our bed, and I hope we find out who did it."

"We find out," Aunt Phoebe promised.

CHAPTER EIGHT

MORE TROUBLE

Days passed slowly that week for Mandie and Celia at school. They longed for Friday to come so they could return to Grandmother Taft's and continue their investigation of the mystery.

The newspaper had declared a flu epidemic in the town of Asheville. Hundreds of people were ill, and the people in the town were blaming it on the mysterious happenings at the church. The bells continued ringing thirteen at midnight and the wrong number of rings at other hours during the day.

By Thursday of that week over half of the school had come down with the flu.

Miss Prudence addressed the students at breakfast on Thursday morning. "Young ladies," the headmistress began, looking around at the girls as they stood behind their chairs, "as you know, many of our students have contracted that dreadful flu that is going around town. We don't want it to spread any further here if possible. Therefore, classes will be dismissed until the epidemic is over."

The girls all looked at each other. It was unheard of for any of the students to speak out without being asked, but this particular morning Mandie forgot about the rules and dared asked a question. "Does that mean we can all go home, Miss Prudence?"

The headmistress looked sharply at Mandie, and Mandie cringed.

"Amanda, you have not asked permission to speak," the head-mistress reprimanded. "However, since we want to get this settled as quickly as possible, I will answer your question. Yes, the girls who live near enough to come back at short notice may go home. We believe that you who are not sick are less likely to come down with this illness if you are in your own homes. Does that answer your question, Amanda?"

"Thank you, Miss Prudence," Mandie said. "Then I have permission to go to my grandmother's while classes are out?"

"That is correct," Miss Prudence replied. "But you girls who live a long distance away will have to stay here."

Celia looked at Mandie and without moving her lips, she whispered, "That means I don't get to go home. It's too far."

Mandie kept her gaze on Miss Prudence but muttered under her breath, "You can go to Grandmother's with me. We'll ask."

Miss Prudence continued, "You girls may leave the school as soon as you can make arrangements to go home. Beginning today, there will be no classes until further notice. Now let us give thanks for this food."

After breakfast Miss Prudence gave Celia permission to go with Mandie. The two girls could hardly wait for Uncle Cal to take them to Grandmother Taft's house. Hurrying to their room, they hastily threw things into bags and laid out their coats and bonnets.

"We don't know how long we'll be staying, so I guess we'd better take plenty of clothes," Mandie advised.

"Right," Celia agreed. "I'm sorry those girls are so sick, but this is good luck for us."

"I hope they all get well soon," Mandie said, dropping her school books into a bag. "I think I'll take some of my books so I can study a little now and then while we're at Grandmother's."

"That's a good idea. Then we won't get too far behind," Celia replied. She added some of her own books to her bag. "We'll be having our half-year examinations after the Christmas holidays, and that's not very far away. It seems like we've had so many holidays—and now this unexpected time out."

"We're lucky Grandmother lives right here in town," Mandie said. "All we have to do is wait for Uncle Cal to take us. And just think, we'll have a little extra time to work on the mystery."

"We won't have Joe to help us, though," Celia reminded her.

Mandie flopped down on the bed. "Well," she said, "as long as Grandmother lets Ben go with us, we can try to solve something."

"Miss Prudence told us to take our things down to the front hall, remember?" Celia prompted.

Mandie jumped up and grabbed two bags. "We'll have to make two trips," she said.

"If we put our coats and bonnets on, we won't have to carry them, and we'll have two hands free to carry the bags," Celia suggested.

"You're right," Mandie laughed. "I'm in such a hurry, I'm not thinking right."

After putting on their coats and bonnets, the girls picked up two large bags each. They made their way down the stairs to the alcove in the front hallway. Just as they sat down to watch out the window for Uncle Cal, they saw him bringing the rig up the driveway. They grabbed their bags and went outside to meet him.

"Uncle Cal, I sure hope you and Aunt Phoebe don't get that flu," Mandie told the old man.

"I do, too, Missy Manda," he replied, putting the bags in the rig. "We'se too old to git dat kind of sickness. Might be bad. Old people die easier than you young ones."

"Please be real careful, and stay away from the sick ones as much as you can," she said, as she and Celia stepped into the rig.

"We has to he'p, Missy Manda," Uncle Cal said, picking up the reins. "Dat's whut we be heah fo.' Sick folks gotta have he'p, too."

"Maybe Dr. Woodard will come to town and help doctor the sick ones," Mandie said. "Hilda is real sick, according to the note I got from Grandmother yesterday, so he'll probably come back to see her."

True to her prediction, the next day, as Mandie and Celia sat looking out Mrs. Taft's parlor window, Dr. Woodard pulled his buggy up into the front driveway. The girls jumped up and ran to the front door to greet him.

Mandie opened the door. "Oh, Joe!" Mandie exclaimed. "How did you manage to come, too?"

Dr. Woodard followed his son into the front hallway as they exchanged greetings and removed their coats and hats.

"The Swain County schools closed today," Joe explained. "The flu hasn't reached that far yet, but they hope that by closing the schools it won't spread as far if someone comes down with it."

Mrs. Taft came into the hall to greet them. "Do come into the parlor to warm yourself before you go up to see Hilda," Mrs. Taft said to Dr. Woodard.

Joe followed the others into the parlor. Making his way with his father over to the hearth where the fire was blazing, he rubbed his hands together to warm up.

Snowball, curled up asleep on the rug, opened one eye to see who was invading his place at the hearth, then dozed off again.

Mandie sat on a stool near the hearth and looked up at Dr. Woodard. "Our school is closed temporarily, too," she said. "About half of the girls have come down with the flu."

"I'm glad they closed," the doctor replied, turning to warm his back in front of the fire. "Maybe it won't spread anymore."

Mrs. Taft sat down on the settee. "Did you know how bad the epidemic was here?" she asked.

"That's why I came to Asheville," the doctor replied. "To see what I could do to help the local doctors. We're lucky in Swain County. We don't have a single case yet."

"What about in Franklin?" Mandie asked, a little worried. "Is there any flu there?"

"Not that I know of, Amanda," Dr. Woodard replied. "I don't think you have to be concerned about your mother and your Uncle John. The flu all seems to be centered right here in Asheville."

"The newspaper says people are blaming it on the goings-on down at the church," Mrs. Taft told him, "as if that could bring on an epidemic."

"People can get some funny ideas sometimes when they can't figure out what's going on," Dr. Woodard said, sitting down in an armchair nearby.

"We're going to solve the mystery," Mandie announced. "Then they'll know how crazy their idea is."

Mrs. Taft looked at her granddaughter and smiled. "I certainly hope y'all can put an end to whatever's going on, Amanda," she said, "but I think it will take some doing."

Dr. Woodard went upstairs to see Hilda. He returned a short time later, shaking his head. "She's just about the same," he reported. "The nurse said she has been able to force a few spoonfuls of broth down Hilda's throat now and then, and she has been taking water, but she seems to just lie there, unaware of what's going on around her."

The young people planned to go to the church the next morning. But it didn't work out that way.

Mandie and Celia woke early when Annie crept into the room. Trying not to disturb them, she started a fire in the fireplace. The girls, half asleep, lay there silently until Annie had left and the fire began to warm the room.

"Today's an important day," Mandie told her friend. "Let's get dressed and go downstairs. Joe may be already eating breakfast. He's always so hungry." Jumping out of bed, she reached for her clothes.

Celia stretched for a moment, then followed.

Snowball, who was curled up at the foot of the bed, leaped down to the floor to avoid being covered by the bedclothes the girls threw back. Finding a nice warm place by the fire, he curled up to go back to sleep.

Mandie laughed. "Look at Snowball," she said. "He doesn't want to get up."

"I didn't either," Celia remarked as she hastened into her clothes. "It was so warm in that bed."

When they finished dressing, the girls hurried quietly down the stairs to the breakfast room. Joe was already there, sitting at the table with a huge plate of food in front of him. But what caught their attention was the fact that the opened curtains displayed a heavy downfall of snow.

"Oh, no!" Mandie cried, rushing to look out the window.

"Oh, yes," Joe replied. "It's probably a foot deep out there already, and it just keeps coming."

Celia stood beside Mandie, surveying the white-blanketed outdoors. "We can't go out in that," she moaned.

Mandie turned away from the window to the sideboard where platters of food awaited them. "Maybe Grandmother will let us go out for a little while," she said, helping herself to the food.

"I'm pretty positive she won't," Joe disagreed, hastily eating his food. "She'll be afraid you'll get sick if you roam around in all that snow. Besides, the roads would have to be cleared off before Ben could get the rig through."

When the girls had filled their plates, they joined Joe at the table.

"What about your father?" Mandie asked. "Will he be able to get out to see the sick people?"

"He always does," Joe said. "With all the snow we have in Swain County, he knows how to manage. He leaves the buggy at home and rides his horse. That horse is used to snow, and it's easier to get around on horseback than it is to drive a buggy."

"That's an idea," Mandie said, looking up at the others. "Maybe we could ride some of Grandmother's horses to the church."

Joe looked doubtful. "I'd say that as long as it's snowing, you might as well be content to sit here in the house," he told her. "Your grandmother won't let you go out."

Joe was right. Mrs. Taft firmly told the young people there would be no traipsing around in the snow outside. She didn't want them to get sick. And they could fall and have an accident. She was responsible for Celia, too.

Dr. Woodard strapped his medical bag onto the saddle he borrowed from Mrs. Taft for his horse and carefully made his way around town visiting sick people.

The next day, which was Saturday, was still snowy and cold. The newspaper reported a long list of deaths caused by the flu epidemic. Complaints about the mysterious goings-on at the church filled the paper. People blamed the church for the town's bad luck—first the flu and now the terrible snowstorm. Some even dared suggest that the church be torn down if the members couldn't solve its troubles.

It continued to snow and snow. More and more people continued to fall ill. The young people sat in the house, fussing because they couldn't get at the mystery. Early Sunday, the snow quit, but it was almost waist-deep in places. People were out early trying to shovel the snow off the main streets in town because there were no city employees to do such a job.

One of the preacher's farmhands came by Mrs. Taft's house with the message that Rev. Tallant had come down with the flu, and there would be no service at the church that morning. The church would be unlocked, he said, for anyone wanting to go there and pray, but there would be no service. The young people stood in the kitchen listening as the man talked to Mrs. Taft and drank hot coffee.

As soon as the man left, Mandie asked her grandmother, "Could we all just go to the church, anyway, this morning?"

"Amanda, you can pray here at the house as well as you can at the church," Mrs. Taft told her.

"It's a shame that we let the weather keep us away from the Lord's house," Mandie replied.

"Amanda!" Mrs. Taft scolded. "That's only your attempt to get at the mystery."

Dr. Woodard came through the back door, stomping his feet. He unbuttoned his heavy coat. "Cold out there!" he announced, removing his coat.

"Hurry on in to the fire in the parlor," Mrs. Taft invited, "and I'll get Ella to bring you some hot coffee."

"Did you get through the roads all right?" Mandie asked eagerly.

"Well, yes, the roads are pretty clear," Dr. Woodard said. "And I noticed Ben has even cleared the driveway here. But the snow is piled up higher than my head along the sides of the road. It really snowed!"

Mandie followed her grandmother and the doctor to the parlor as Celia and Joe tagged along behind.

As the adults took chairs by the fire, Mandie sat on a stool nearby. "Grandmother," she said, "Dr. Woodard says the roads are clear. Couldn't we go to the church for a little while? Please?"

"There's no service this morning," Dr. Woodard told her. "I've just been to Reverend Tallant's. He's a sick man."

"We got that message a little while ago," Mrs. Taft said. She looked over at Mandie. "I suppose you may go if Ben goes with you all and stays right by your side. But you must promise to be gone no longer than two hours. We'll be having dinner in a little over two hours."

"I promise," Mandie said quickly. "Thank you, Grandmother."

"Thank you, Mrs. Taft," Celia echoed.

Joe stood next to his father. "Do I have permission to go, too?" he asked.

Dr. Woodard looked at the young people's happy faces. "I suppose so," he said, "but remember what Mrs. Taft told you. Stay right with Ben, and be back within two hours."

The young people hastily grabbed their coats and hats and boots. They had no idea what they would do at the church, but they were eager to get there and look around.

This time Ben stayed with them. Inside the church, he stopped at the back of the sanctuary and looked around.

There was nobody else in the church. Evidently no one had come to pray. The young people searched the church. Ben held his breath as Mandie and Joe scaled the rope ladder to the belfry.

"Lawsy, Missy!" Ben gasped. "Miz Taft'll skin you alive if she ketch you a-doin' dat."

Halfway up the ladder, Mandie called down to him. "She probably did the same thing when she was young."

When they came back down, Ben followed them back into the sanctuary.

"Let's go down into the basement," Mandie suggested.

Ben took a seat in the back pew. "I stays right heah and watch de front do,'" he said. "I lets you know if'n somebody come in dis time."

"That's a good idea, Ben," Mandie called back to the Negro driver as she and the others headed for the basement.

There was no disturbance of any kind down there and no sign of anyone else being around.

The bells started ringing. The young people stopped to count, then ran through the church and up to the belfry. As they got there, the bells gave one last ring.

"It's eleven o'clock," Celia said, following Joe and Mandie to the rope ladder. "And the bells rang twelve."

They again went up into the belfry but could find no sign of anyone having been there.

"Guess we might as well go back to your grandmother's house," Joe said.

"I suppose so," Mandie agreed. "I was hoping we'd find something else here."

In the meantime, Ben, sitting on the back pew, stretched out his long legs to get comfortable and maybe take a nap. The toe of his boot caught in a loose thread in the edge of the carpet runner that ran the length of the pew. The rug was tacked to the floor and he reached down to disentangle his shoe.

"Now whutdat?" the Negro man mumbled to himself, as he felt a lump under the carpet where it had come loose.

He withdrew his boot from the thread and felt along the carpet. Poking under it with one finger he pushed out an old dirty key. Picking it up, he examined it, but he didn't know how to read and there was some kind of writing on the key.

"Oh, well," he said to himself, tossing the key in the air and then putting it in his pocket.

He stretched his legs back out, careful not to disturb the loose carpet. But the young people were there before he had a chance to take a nap.

"We're ready to go, Ben," Mandie told him as they picked up their coats and hats. "We haven't found a thing."

Ben stood up. "Dem bars on dat window, is dey still pulled off?" he asked.

"They're still off," Mandie replied. "Grandmother promised to pay for the damages we did, but she hasn't had time yet to get them fixed, I suppose."

"I s'pose somebody could be comin' and goin' through dat window whilst dem bars ain't on it," Ben told them.

The young people looked at each other.

"You're right, Ben," Joe agreed. "It would be easy to open that spring latch on the window with a knife and then close it back. No one would know it was ever open."

"Well, we can't just sit down there by that window waiting for someone to come in," Celia argued.

"We'll do that later," Mandie said. "Right now, we have to keep our promise to Grandmother and get back."

When the young people returned to Mrs. Taft's house, the place was in an uproar.

Hilda was missing! The house was being searched thoroughly for the girl.

"What happened, Grandmother?" Mandie asked anxiously.

"It seems that the nurse dozed off because she had been on duty since Friday night. The nurse who was to relieve her was unable to get through the snow," Mrs. Taft explained. "When the nurse woke up a while ago, Hilda was gone."

"How long has she been missing?" Joe asked.

"We don't know," Mrs. Taft replied. "The nurse said she must have dozed off some time before daylight, and she didn't wake up until a few minutes ago."

"Oh, please don't let any harm come to Hilda!" Mandie prayed, looking upward as she talked to God.

The young people quickly joined in the search. Every crack and corner of the huge mansion was looked into. Every inch of the grounds and the outbuildings was searched. Hilda was nowhere to be found.

"I don't understand how she got away in the weak condition she's in," Dr. Woodard declared as they all gathered in the parlor. "This could be serious for her, I'm afraid."

The townspeople quickly heard about the missing girl and came to join the search. Hours passed. There was no trace of Hilda anywhere!

CHAPTER NINE

DISCOVERY IN THE BELFRY

After going over Mrs. Taft's entire estate without finding Hilda, the search party fanned out all across town.

It was not snowing, but the high drifts, bitter cold temperatures, and strong north wind made things more difficult. Everyone was worried about the condition of Hilda's health.

Mrs. Taft allowed Mandie, Celia, and Joe to go with Ben in the rig to help look for Hilda. They knocked on doors and got permission to search people's yards and outbuildings. As they worked their way through the streets, they found themselves near the church about dusk.

"Ben, let's go look around the church and the grounds while we're this close," Mandie suggested.

"Whatever you says, Missy," Ben agreed, turning the horses in that direction.

"Do you think she could have got this far away from your grandmother's house?" Joe asked.

"Maybe," Mandie replied. "Somebody could have given her a ride in their rig or something."

"If she got a ride, there's no telling where in the world she could be by now," Celia reasoned.

Ben stopped the rig in front of the church. "I jes' stay right heah and waits fo' y'all," he said.

"Oh, no, Ben," Mandie protested as she and the others stepped down from the rig. "Grandmother told you that you were to stay right along with us wherever we go, remember?"

"Yessum," Ben grumbled, as he reluctantly followed them up the steps.

As soon as Joe opened the door, they all felt a great warmth from inside the church. They looked around. Someone had built roaring fires in both the big stoves in the sanctuary.

"I wonder why anyone would want to build fires in here today when there's no church service," Mandie said. "It couldn't have been the sexton. He knew Rev. Tallant wouldn't be here today."

Joe shrugged. "I'm not surprised at anything that goes on in this church now," he said.

"Maybe someone came here to pray, and got cold, and decided to build the fires," Celia suggested.

Ben plopped down in the back pew. "Now, y'all go ahaid and do whatever it is you gwine do," he said. "I sits right heah."

"Well, all right," Mandie said. "We're going to search the church for Hilda. If anyone comes in or goes out, yell for us."

"I will, Missy," Ben promised. He stretched his long legs out to get comfortable as he slid down a little in the seat.

"Upstairs first," Joe suggested, leading the way to the gallery.

They looked carefully in every place where someone could possibly hide. By this time they knew every nook and cranny of the building.

Joe skimmed the ladder into the belfry. "Nothing up here," he called down to the girls.

"It seems that we never find anyone here, but we always find signs of someone having been here," Celia remarked.

"We'll catch up with someone sometime. We've got to," Mandie said. "It's impossible for anyone to keep on doing things here and not be caught."

Joe slid down the ladder, and they went back downstairs. Making their way down the side aisle, they went through the door to the classrooms.

"We can go faster if we split up," Joe told them. "You girls take the rooms on that side, and I'll go down this side."

When they found nothing there, they went on downstairs to the basement. But a quick search of all the classrooms there revealed nothing.

"I guess we'd better get going," Joe said, looking around the hallway. "We've covered the whole church except for the pastor's study, and it's still locked."

"Let's go outside and look around the grounds," Mandie suggested.

When they got back to the sanctuary, Ben had nodded off. They all laughed.

Suddenly Mandie heard something. "What was that?" she whispered, looking around quickly.

"Sounded like something moving," Joe said softly.

"It wasn't very loud, whatever it was," Celia observed.

Moving over to the center aisle, they looked around and then started up the aisle. The two big stoves standing in the middle aisle still roared away with their fires.

As they started to walk by the first stove, Mandie glanced down to the right. "Look!" she exclaimed, stooping between the pews.

Joe and Celia huddled behind her to see. There lay Hilda, all wrapped up in choir robes and a small rug.

"Hilda! Hilda!" Mandie cried, smoothing back the girl's tangled dark brown hair.

Hilda didn't move. She looked as though she were soundly asleep.

"Is she—is she—all right?" Celia asked nervously.

Joe bent down and reached for the girl's wrist. "She's alive, but just barely, I believe," he said. "And she does have a terrible fever."

"Ben! Come quick!" Mandie yelled.

Startled, Ben jumped to his feet. "Yessum, yessum, Missy," he answered. Rubbing his eyes, he quickly looked around.

"Down here, Ben," Joe called to him.

Ben hurriedly joined them and gasped when he saw Hilda lying there, so flushed and motionless.

"Quick, Ben," Joe said. "Help me get Hilda into the rig. We've got to get her back to Mrs. Taft's house and into bed fast!"

"Oh, dear Lord," Mandie prayed, "please let Dr. Woodard be there when we get back."

As Joe and Ben picked up Hilda—robes, rug, and all—the girl started mumbling with her eyes closed. "God has come," she said in a whisper. "God has come!"

Tears came to Mandie's eyes. "She's still able to speak," she cried.

The girls followed as Ben and Joe carried Hilda outside and carefully tucked her into the rig.

"This time I give you permission to drive as fast as you can," Mandie told Ben.

"Cain't go too fast, Missy," Ben replied, picking up the reins. "It be slicky on de road 'cause of de snow."

In spite of the roads, however, Ben did manage to get up some speed, and soon pulled up in Mrs. Taft's driveway.

Mandie jumped down and ran to the house. "Grandmother!" she yelled, pounding on the door.

Ella quickly opened the door, and Mandie ran right past her. "Grandmother!" she screamed. "Dr. Woodard! Come quick. We've found Hilda!"

Mrs. Taft and Dr. Woodard hurried into the hall from the parlor just as Ben and Joe were carrying Hilda into the house. Dr. Woodard directed them upstairs, and the nurse who was still there tucked the girl into bed. The young people excitedly explained where they had found her.

Mrs. Taft and Dr. Woodard listened in amazement. Then Dr. Woodard sent everyone out of the room so that he and the nurse could tend to Hilda.

"We might as well go downstairs to the parlor by the fire," Mrs. Taft told the young people. "And you still haven't even taken off your coats and hats."

The young people followed Mrs. Taft down the stairs, unbuttoning as they went. In the front hallway, they hung their coats on the hall tree, then headed into the parlor.

"At least one trip to the church did some good," Mandie remarked as they pulled stools up in front of the fire.

Snowball, who was sleeping on the rug, stretched, stood up, and jumped into his mistress's lap.

Mrs. Taft sat down in an armchair. "I can't imagine how Hilda got there," she said. "And who could have built those fires and wrapped her up in all those things?"

"Someone must have," Mandie answered. "I don't think she could have."

"I hope she's going to be all right," Celia said.

"My father will do all he can. You know that," Joe assured her. "Maybe that warm fire and all those things covering her helped."

"Grandmother," Mandie said. "Hilda kept whispering, 'God has come. God has come.' She didn't open her eyes, and she didn't even seem to know she was being moved."

"She's running a high fever, and I'm sure she's delirious, dear," Mrs. Taft explained. "We'll just have to wait for Dr. Woodard to come back down and tell us how she is."

After a while the doctor joined them in the parlor. "She's really sick," he said. "She seems to be out of her head completely."

"Let's pray for her," Mandie suggested. "God can heal her."

After they had all prayed for Hilda's recovery, they sat talking in the parlor. Dr. Woodard made repeated trips upstairs to check on the girl.

Mrs. Taft asked Annie, the upstairs maid, to relieve the nurse if she had to leave Hilda's room for any reason. She also instructed the nurse to check all the windows in Hilda's room to be sure they were locked and all the draperies drawn.

The young people talked with Mandie's grandmother long into the night. They still had no real clues in the bell mystery, and now they had Hilda to worry about. They even wondered if there could be any connection between Hilda's running away and the mysterious goings-on in the church, though it didn't seem possible.

There was no change in Hilda's condition that evening. Everybody finally got so sleepy that Mrs. Taft ordered them all to bed. Dr. Woodard promised to sleep in the room across the hall from Hilda's so he would be close in case of an emergency.

Mandie felt as though she had just gone to bed when she heard Annie steal softly into the room where she and Celia were sleeping.

As Annie knelt at the fireplace arranging the kindling for the fire, Mandie sat up and pulled the covers around her. "How is Hilda, Annie?" she asked.

Celia woke and accidentally kicked Snowball, who was sleeping at their feet on top of the quilt.

"Still de same," Annie replied. "I'se jes' been in de room to tend to de fire, and she jes' layin' still. Ain't movin' at all."

Celia sat up beside Mandie in the bed. "At least she isn't any worse then," she said.

Annie moved backward a little and fanned the fire with her big white apron to get it going.

Snowball stretched and yawned, then jumped down to take his place by the warm hearth.

Annie started to leave the room. "Yo' grandma and de doctuh, dey be in de breakfus' room," Annie informed them.

"Joe isn't up yet?" Mandie asked.

"Ain't seen him," Annie replied. "I gotta git his fire goin' now." She went out the door.

Mandie jumped out of bed. "Come on. Let's get dressed," she said. Celia followed.

The two girls shivered a little in the cold room. They quickly grabbed their clothes and stood in front of the fire to get dressed.

Snowball followed them downstairs to the breakfast room. Joe was already there.

As they went to the sideboard, Mandie whispered to Celia, "It takes a girl longer to get dressed than it does a boy."

Celia smiled.

The girls were glad to see the sun shining brightly through the windows where the curtains were pulled back. After exchanging morning greetings with Joe and the adults, Mandie and Celia filled their plates and joined the others at the table.

"I was just in to see Hilda before I came downstairs," Dr. Woodard reported, "and I'm afraid she's still not doing well at all."

The conversation turned to how the young people had found her at the church and questions about the whole puzzling situation.

"Grandmother, could we go back to the church this morning?" Mandie asked. "I'd like to see if the fire's burned out and if there's any sign of anyone there."

Mrs. Taft smiled at her granddaughter. "Amanda, you visit that church more than you visit with me," she said. "But then, I was the one who got you started in all this tomfoolery. I guess it would be all right for you to go as long as Ben goes with you."

"Thanks, Grandmother," Mandie replied.

"I suppose your school will send someone to let us know when they open back up," Mrs. Taft said.

"I don't believe they'll open up again any time soon. All the girls who didn't go home are sick in bed now," Dr. Woodard said. "I was there yesterday, and the only ones walking around were Miss Hope and Miss Prudence."

"What about Uncle Cal and Aunt Phoebe?" Mandie asked quickly.

"Oh, yes, they're all right," the doctor said.

"Well, I guess we'll have a little longer, then," Celia said.

"But we'd better use what time we have, or we'll never get this mystery solved," Joe reminded them. "You know, I have to leave when my father does."

"That won't be for some time yet son," Dr. Woodard said. "I'd say about two-thirds of the town is down with the flu."

"You young people be sure to wrap up good and wear your boots," Mrs. Taft cautioned them. "I don't want y'all getting sick."

As soon as they finished their breakfast, the young people hurried to the front hallway and put on their coats and hats. Snowball followed them and sat on the arm of the coat tree, watching.

Mandie picked him up. "I'm going to take Snowball with me this time," she decided. "He needs some fresh air."

"I sure hope he doesn't run away," Joe said warily.

Snowball seemed to be thankful to his mistress for allowing him to go. He stayed on her lap in the rig and then clung to her shoulder when they got to the church.

Inside the sanctuary, both stoves were cold. The fires had long since gone out.

Ben dropped into the back pew for his usual nap while the young people looked around. They left their coats and hats on a pew near him.

They checked all the basement classrooms and found nothing there. Then they went up into the gallery and opened the door to the belfry.

"I have an idea," Mandie said, balancing Snowball on her shoulder. "Why don't we all go up into the belfry and just stay there a while? If we're real quiet, we'll be able to hear anything that goes on, and we can watch out the windows up there for anyone coming in or out of the church."

"That's a good idea," Joe said, reaching for the rope ladder. "I'll go first. Then you come next, Celia, so I can help you off at the top. Mandie has done it so much, I don't think she needs any help."

"Well—" Celia hesitated. "I suppose I can go up if that ladder doesn't swing too much."

"I'll hold on to it by the last rung down here to steady it," Mandie promised.

Celia nodded, and Joe scrambled up the ladder, waiting at the top while Celia slowly and cautiously made her way up and Mandie held the bottom rung.

"Just don't look down, Celia," Mandie reminded her. "Keep looking up at Joe."

Celia was shaking so badly that she didn't answer. When she finally got to the top rung, Joe took her hands and swung her up into the belfry. She sat down on the floor quickly. "Oh, my legs feel weak," she gasped.

Mandie hurried after her with Snowball clinging to her shoulder. About halfway up, the kitten looked down and dug his claws into the shoulder of Mandie's heavy dress. Suddenly, he jumped off her shoulder onto the rope ladder and clawed his way up by himself. At the top, he jumped into the belfry and landed at Celia's feet.

Celia laughed nervously. "I guess I'm not the only one who is afraid of that ladder," she said, cuddling the kitten.

"Let's walk around and look outside," Mandie said as she reached the top.

Just then the bells began ringing. The three young people instantly covered their ears at the deafening sound and began counting the rings. Snowball darted about in fear.

"Eleven rings," Mandie said, uncovering her ears. "But it's ten o'clock." She reached down to pick up Snowball.

"And we stood right here watching," Joe said with a puzzled look on his face. "We know that no one else was up here ringing those bells."

Celia made her way over to the walkway around the belfry. "I thought we were going to watch outside," she said.

"We are," Mandie agreed. "I'll go over on this side, and Joe, you take that side over there. There are only three of us, and there are four sides to the steeple, but we can all watch the side where the ladder is."

They did as Mandie suggested. As Joe made his way to the other side, Snowball ran ahead of him and into an almost invisible thread of some kind. It broke.

"Look!" Joe cried, stooping to inspect the thread.

Mandie and Celia watched as he traced the piece of thread to the mechanism of the huge clock. He pulled at it, and it came free, holding a tiny magnet on the end. The girls joined him and all three excitedly examined it. At last they had a clue!

"Someone must have put that magnet on the clock to mess up the mechanism, but where did the string go from there?" Mandie asked, looking around for the other end.

They searched and searched but could not find the other piece of thread. Nor could they figure out where it had been attached. Finally they sat down on the floor, and Snowball curled up in Mandie's lap.

"Let's just have a quiet thinking session for a few minutes," Mandie suggested.

They all became silent and did not move. Even Snowball sat quietly, content in his mistress's company.

"Why didn't we find this thread before when we were up here, and why didn't all those people who examined the clock mechanism find the magnet before?" Celia asked.

"Maybe whoever put it there took it down whenever they heard somebody coming," Mandie reasoned. "But where could they be hiding?"

They were silent again.

Mandie's sharp eyes caught the slight movement of a panel in the wall. At first she thought she was seeing things, but as the panel moved, she got a quick glimpse of a pair of eyes staring right at her. She caught her breath and froze.

Joe and Celia looked toward the wall to see what had startled her.

Instantly, Joe jumped up and grabbed the moving panel. "Come on out, whoever you are!" he demanded, yanking at the piece of wood.

The girls jumped up to help. Snowball scrambled onto the floor. Joe reached behind the panel and grabbed hold of someone's shoulder.

At first the person struggled, but then he gave up. "I'm coming out," said a man's voice.

"All right. Then get out fast," Joe ordered, still holding on to the panel of wood to keep it from being pushed back into place.

Slowly, from behind the paneling, a little, old, gray-looking man appeared. He fell on his knees in front of the three young people. "I'm sorry, so sorry!" he muttered.

CHAPTER TEN

PHINEAS PRATTWORTHY

The three young people stared in amazement at the gray-haired man before them. He was clean and neatly dressed, but his coat was threadbare.

"Who are you?" Joe demanded.

"Are you the one who has been making the bells ring wrong and doing all those other things around this church?" Mandie asked, putting her hands on her hips.

The old man cowered in front of them.

"Get up," Joe demanded. "We're not going to hurt you."

The man didn't obey. Joe got hold of his shoulders and pushed him backwards so they could see his face. The man was frightened.

He had bushy gray hair, bushy gray eyebrows, a long, thin face, a long nose and a wide mouth with thin lips. His ears stuck out instead of being flat against his head. He looked to be very old and very starved. He blinked at the three of them as tears came into his gray eyes.

"How did you get behind that paneling?" Mandie asked.

"I think you'd better give us some explanations real fast," Joe told the man.

The man's lips quivered as he tried to speak.

Mandie began to feel sorry for him. "Why don't we all sit down and talk," she suggested.

The young people sat down on the floor in front of the stranger who was still on his knees.

"I-I need someone to help me," the man said uncertainly.

"Help you do what?" Mandie asked as Snowball climbed into her lap.

"I am in great trouble that is not my fault," the man replied, clasping his hands tightly.

"I'll say you're in trouble," Joe said. "Just wait until the town gets hold of you."

Mandie looked at Joe with a frown. Then she looked back at the stranger. "Why have you been messing with the bells and doing all those other things?" she asked. "You are the one responsible for the help banner on the altar, and the writing on the church wall, aren't you?"

"And tearing up the paneling to hide behind," Celia added.

"I'm sorry. I'm sorry," the man said, hanging his head. "What else can I say?"

"Who are you, and where do you live?" Joe asked.

"My name is Phineas Prattworthy," the stranger replied, choking back the tears. "I live way out yonder over the mountain."

"Then why are you hanging around the church? What are you trying to do?" Joe sounded exasperated.

"I can only explain if you promise to help me," Phineas replied.

"We can't promise to help you until we know what you've done," Mandie said.

"But I didn't do what they think I did," Phineas told them, his eyes still wet with tears. "I have been wrongly accused."

Mandie leaned forward and asked, "Accused of what?"

"The grocer down on Main Street thinks I stole some groceries from him," Phineas replied. "But I didn't. I saw the man who did it, though. He came out of the store so fast that he dropped an apple. I picked it up, and when the grocer saw me with it in my hand, he thought I was the man who stole it, but I got away before he could catch me."

"That wasn't very smart," Joe said, shaking his head. "Why didn't you just explain to the grocer what happened?"

"I tried to, but he wouldn't listen. He didn't believe a thing I said," Phineas explained.

"So you came here to this church and started doing all these crazy things?" Joe asked. "Why?"

"I was only trying to get help," Phineas said. "I waited and waited, hoping to attract someone who looked like they would help me, but no one came along who looked trustworthy." He sniffed. "This church is the only place I could find to hide in, out of the cold."

Mandie's heart went out to the man at the thought of his being so hungry and cold. "If you live over on the mountain, why didn't you just go back home?" she asked.

"I lived with my son, and he died last month," Phineas explained. "I don't have any way to make a living. We don't own the house, and with my son gone, there was no one to pay the rent or buy groceries." Nervously, he rubbed the side of his long, thin face. "I'm not begging, mind you. I'd starve to death before I'd beg for something to eat. I'm only asking for someone to help me straighten out this matter with the grocer."

Mandie reached out and took the man's hand. "Mr. Phineas, we'll help you," she promised. "I believe what you've told us. We'll see that you have a warm place to stay and some food to eat."

"Mandie!" Joe exclaimed. "You can't make promises like that. We don't know this man. We'll have to check out his story."

"But he's hungry, Joe," Celia defended Mandie's decision.

"We can at least take him home to Grandmother and let her help us decide what should be done," Mandie said.

"All right. If you insist," Joe said. "But I've still got a lot of questions." He looked directly at Phineas. "How did you get behind that paneling?"

"I worked a piece loose one day and then found that I could slide down through the wall opening into the attic," the man explained.

"Attic?" Mandie's eyes grew wide. "Does this church have an attic?"

"It certainly does," Phineas replied. "That's where I left my bag."

"We didn't find any attic," Celia remarked.

"The only other way you can get into it is through the scuttle hole in the ceiling of the gallery," Phineas told them.

"So that's why we could never catch up with you," Mandie reasoned. "You hid in the attic."

The man nodded. "I saw and heard you three come into the church several times. One time I was in such a hurry to get through the paneling I fell all the way through to the attic. It made such a noise and everything shook so, I just knew you girls would find me that day."

The three people quickly looked at each other.

"So that solves that mystery," Mandie said, with a sigh. "And I suppose you wrote on the wall at the back of the church, too."

"I used whitewash which was supposed to be removable but I couldn't wash it off. It just got all blurred instead," Phineas said.

"And you put the magnet on the clock, too, I suppose," Joe said.

"You see, I used to be in the clock business long years ago. I knew I could control the mechanism with a magnet and I could withdraw it whenever I wanted to. I figured someone would come investigating the bells ringing and maybe they could help me but, like I said, I haven't seen anyone who looked trustworthy," Phineas explained with a sigh.

"And you locked us in the basement and then unlocked the door later. And you put that 'Help' banner on the altar and then took it away. Why did you do things and then reverse what you did?" Mandie asked.

"I guess I just had a guilty conscience," the old man said. "I needed help but I decided the altar was not the place to put such a thing so I took it away. And I had been outside the church and didn't realize y'all were in the basement when I locked that door. Then I heard you down there and had to come back and unlock it."

"Well, why were you locking the basement door anyhow?" Celia asked.

"I had thought I could sleep in the pastor's study on his settee that night and I wanted to be sure the basement was locked off in case anyone came prowling around. Then I found out the pastor's door was locked after all," Phineas said. "I hope you will all forgive me."

"But if you've been here hiding all this time, how could you live without any food?" Joe asked.

"Well, to begin with, I had the apple that man dropped, and then I had to look in trash cans," he told them.

Mandie and Celia cringed.

"The restaurant down on Patton Avenue throws out a lot of good food," he explained. "When I discovered that, I just went behind their building whenever I got hungry and helped myself. I don't eat much anyway."

Tears clouded Mandie's eyes to think of this poor man having to eat out of trash cans! She jumped up, dumping Snowball onto the floor, and grabbed the man's hand to help him up. "Come on," she said. "We're going to my grandmother's."

Joe looked at her with concern. "If you say so," he said.

Phineas seemed to have a bad leg. He was limping.

"Can you get down the rope ladder?" Mandie asked.

"Oh, sure," he answered. "All I have to do is slide."

"I'll go first," Joe offered. He still didn't trust the stranger.

Celia went down next, then Phineas.

As Mandie followed, Snowball fought against going down the ladder. He kept jumping off Mandie's shoulder into the belfry. After three tries, Mandie gave him a little swat and said, "Now you look here, Snowball! We are going down that ladder, and you might as well behave!"

Joe, watching the scene from below, climbed halfway up the ladder and reached for the kitten. "Give him to me," he told Mandie. "I can slide down with one hand."

Snowball squealed with anger as Joe grabbed him and held him tightly in one hand while he made his way down with the other. The kitten squirmed and tried to scratch as Joe landed below.

Mandie jumped off at the bottom and reached for the kitten. "Thanks, Joe," she said.

"Watch out," he warned her. "This cat is mad, and he's trying to scratch."

Mandie held the kitten tightly in both hands. He hushed his loud meowing and cuddled in her arms.

Joe shook his head in disgust, and the young people and Phineas headed downstairs.

As they approached Ben in the sanctuary, the Negro man stood up, looked at the stranger and asked, "Who dat be whut y'all got dere?"

"This is who we've been looking for all this time," Joe answered. "He's the answer to the mystery."

Ben just stood there with his mouth open.

"Come on, Ben," Mandie said. "We're taking him home to Grandmother."

After they were all in the rig, Ben flicked the reins and coaxed the horses to a fast pace. When the Negro driver pulled the rig into Mrs. Taft's driveway, Phineas Prattworthy looked amazed.

"Your grandmother lives here?" he asked.

Mandie climbed down from the rig. "Yes, my grandmother is Mrs. Taft," Mandie explained. "Come on."

Phineas stepped down beside her. "I know who Mrs. Taft is," he said. "I had no idea you were talking about her when you mentioned your grandmother."

"You know her?" Mandie asked, petting Snowball.

The others got down from the rig and stood around, listening.

"I knew your grandfather, Mr. Taft," Phineas told her.

Joe urged them all to go into the house. "I'm cold and hungry," he complained.

Inside, they left their coats in the hallway and ushered Phineas into the parlor where Mrs. Taft sat reading by the fire. Snowball jumped down and ran off down the hallway. Mrs. Taft rose quickly and stared at the man.

Phineas spoke first. "How are you, Mrs. Taft?" he asked, nervously.

"Phineas!" Mrs. Taft exclaimed, hurrying over to greet the man. "It is Phineas, isn't it?"

"Yes, ma'am. I'm Phineas Prattworthy," he replied.

"Where in the world have you been all these years, and where did these young people meet up with you?" Mrs. Taft asked. "Please come and sit down."

Mandie and her friends sat down, speechless, on low stools in front of the fireplace.

Phineas took the chair opposite Mrs. Taft. "Well, I fell on some hard times after y'all left Franklin, and I came over to the mountains to live," he said. "The tax man took all my property."

"You mean you lost that great big beautiful home?" Mrs. Taft looked deeply concerned. "Oh, Phineas, how sad."

"My wife died suddenly with the fever right before we had to vacate the property," Phineas continued.

"Phineas, I'm so sorry," Mrs. Taft said.

The man fidgeted nervously. "I just had one son, Paul, you know, so he and I rented a small farm up in the Nantahala Mountains. We couldn't make much of a living out of it, but we didn't starve," he said with a weak smile. "Then I had a stroke and was helpless for a long while. I'm not much good anymore. About the time I was beginning to walk again, Paul came down with the flu and died."

"I'm so sorry," Mrs. Taft said again. "But just saying I'm sorry won't help. What can I do for you?"

"Grandmother," Mandie jumped into the conversation, "we found Mr. Phineas hiding in the church. He's the one who has been messing up the bells and everything."

Mrs. Taft looked shocked. "Phineas! You were doing that?"

"Yes, ma'am," he replied. "I'm afraid I'm guilty."

As he retold the story, Mrs. Taft sat staring at him in amazement.

"I can't explain why I did all those strange things at the church," he said. "I just almost went crazy not knowing what to do to get somebody to help me."

"I just can't believe that anyone could accuse you of such a thing," Mrs. Taft exclaimed. "Well, we'll just have to get this all straightened out. I'm well acquainted with Mr. Simpson, the grocer, and I think he'll understand when we tell him the story."

Dr. Woodard joined the others in the parlor after having made rounds in town and checking on Hilda. "Phineas!" he exclaimed in surprise. "How did you get here? The last time I saw you was when I doctored you for that stroke—about a year ago, wasn't it?"

The story had to be told again, and Dr. Woodard listened attentively. When Phineas told the doctor that he didn't know why he did such strange things in the church, Dr. Woodard looked thoughtful.

"There are a lot of things that can cause a person to behave abnormally," the doctor told him. "Losing your wife, your son, and your house, and having that stroke all in such a short period of time was a lot for a person to bear. And then being unjustly accused and malnourished and living without any heat in that church most of the time—it's no wonder something snapped."

"Then I'm not crazy?" Phineas asked.

"Not likely," Dr. Woodard replied. "I think once we get this thing cleared up and get you well fed and cared for, you'll be back to your old self again."

Mandie smiled at Joe and Celia, satisfied that she had done the right thing in bringing Phineas to see her grandmother.

"That grocer may give you a fight, though," Dr. Woodard added.

Mrs. Taft spoke. "I told Phineas we would get this all straightened out for him. We'll just go talk to Mr. Simpson."

"I'm afraid that won't work, Mrs. Taft," Phineas said. "I tried to talk to him, and he wouldn't listen at all. He has his mind made up and won't change it."

"We'll see that he changes it, won't we, Grandmother?" Mandie said.

"Yes, we will," Mrs. Taft said confidently. "We'll have something to eat in a little while, and then we'll just go visit Mr. Simpson."

Mandie turned to Dr. Woodard. "How is Hilda this morning, Doctor?" she asked.

"I was just upstairs when y'all came in," Dr. Woodard replied. "She is still just lying there. That bout in the snow and the church certainly didn't help her condition."

Mandie explained to Phineas. "Our friend Hilda ran away from here yesterday," she said. "She's a girl my grandmother has living with her. Hilda has been real sick with pneumonia, and then suddenly she disappeared out of her bed. We finally found her in the church late yesterday afternoon. Did you happen to see her?"

"That must be the girl I saw come into the church in her nightclothes," Phineas replied quickly. "She was mumbling something to herself and then lay down on the floor. I thought she went to sleep. I found some old choir robes in a box in the attic and a little rug that was behind the altar, and I tried to wrap her up."

"Are you the one who started the fires in the stoves, then?" Mandie asked.

"Yes," Phineas answered. "It was so cold in the church I was afraid she would die. Then I remembered seeing the woodpile out behind the church, so I just gathered in enough wood and got the stoves going to keep her warm."

"Oh, how can we thank you, Mr. Phineas! You probably saved Hilda's life," Mandie told him.

"Hilda's not right mentally, Phineas," Dr. Woodard explained. "And she's always running off somewhere."

"I had no idea who she was, but she looked like she needed help," Phineas agreed.

"The Lord will bless you for your kindness, Phineas," Mrs. Taft said.

"Imagine that," Joe said with a little laugh. "He was the one who covered up Hilda and started the stoves. One more piece of the mystery solved."

Ella came in to announce that the noon meal was on the table.

After a leisurely meal, Mrs. Taft announced that she was going to visit Mr. Simpson, the grocer, and the young people could go with her if they wished.

Mandie, Celia, and Joe excitedly put on their wraps in the front hall.

"After a busy morning tending to the sick, I think I need a couple hours of rest," the doctor said. "And Phineas ought to stay here out of sight until we're sure Mr. Simpson won't cause trouble."

"I'll stay here and soak up some of that warmth from the fireplace if it's all right with you, Mrs. Taft," Phineas added.

Mrs. Taft agreed.

Ben drove the rig sedately down the streets of Asheville. With one hand he kept flipping the key he had found in the church. He had no idea as to what it unlocked, or who had lost it, but somehow the key fascinated him. When he got a chance he would ask Missy Manda to tell him what the writing on it said.

He pulled the rig up in front of Mr. Simpson's grocery store. Mrs. Taft asked him to wait there for them.

Inside the grocery store Mr. Simpson, an overweight, bald-headed man in his middle forties, came forward to greet Mrs. Taft.

"This is a pleasure, Mrs. Taft," he said. "What can I do for you today?"

"We seem to have a problem that I think you can help us with," she replied. Then she explained the situation with Phineas Prattworthy. "He isn't guilty," she concluded.

"Oh, Mrs. Taft, I beg your pardon, but he is," the grocer protested. "Why, he was in here not more than ten minutes ago, stealing canned beans. I saw him."

"Ten minutes ago?" Mandie spoke up. "Mr. Simpson, it couldn't have been Mr. Phineas. He has been with us at my grandmother's house for the last three hours at least."

"That's right," Mrs. Taft confirmed. "We just left him there with Dr. Woodard."

"Please tell me, what does this Phineas Prattworthy look like?" the grocer asked.

"He has a bad leg from a stroke about a year ago, and—" Mrs. Taft began.

"That's the one. He limped," the grocer interrupted. "I'm sorry, Mrs. Taft, but if you don't bring him in, I'll have to ask the sheriff to come out to your house and get him."

"Oh no, you won't," Mrs. Taft replied angrily. "You are not going to have Phineas Prattworthy arrested—not while he's in my house."

Joe stepped forward. "Mr. Simpson, there is definitely a mistake here," he told the grocer. "Mr. Prattworthy did not steal from you. It must be someone who looks like him."

"I don't have to identify him," Mr. Simpson argued. "I know him by his limp, and he's a stranger in this town."

Several other customers in the store edged closer to listen to the conversation.

"You have caused Mr. Prattworthy much distress by your false ac-cusations. Why, he had to hide in the church to keep you from putting him in jail," Mrs. Taft said.

"Yes, you told me he had been doing all that damage at the church—ringing the bells wrong and writing all over the walls," Mr. Simpson shot back. "That proves that the man is deranged."

The other customers gasped.

"Phineas Prattworthy is not deranged any more than you are, Mr. Simpson," Mrs. Taft snapped. "You drove him to do all those things."

"I can only say that unless you bring him down here first thing in the morning, I'll ask the sheriff to go to your house after him," Mr. Simpson threatened. "Now, I'm sorry, but I have customers to wait on."

"I'll get the best lawyer in the state and sue you for false accusations if you press any charges against Mr. Prattworthy," Mrs. Taft promised. She turned to go. "Just be sure you remember that, Mr. Simpson."

The young people followed Mrs. Taft back out to the rig, Mandie took her grandmother's hand. "You were great in there, Grandmother," she said with admiration. "You handled it just the way I'd have done."

Mrs. Taft smiled and patted Mandie's hand. "I know, Amanda, dear," she said, stepping up into the rig. "You're so much like I was when I was your age."

The young people climbed into the rig.

"Now what are we going to do?" Joe asked as Ben picked up the reins.

"We're going to find the real crook," Mrs. Taft replied.

"But how?" Celia asked.

"It was probably some poor farmer around here who didn't have any money to buy food," Mrs. Taft reasoned. "I don't know any other reason a person would steal food from a grocer. I'm not sure how we'll find him, but we will."

When they returned to Mrs. Taft's house, they found Dr. Woodard asleep on the settee in the parlor, but there was no sign of Phineas Prattworthy.

"Sh-h-h!" Mrs. Taft whispered. "The doctor needs his rest. Don't wake him."

After quickly checking the front part of the house, they still couldn't find Phineas.

Annie met them in the hallway and told them what had happened. "Dat man whut was heah," Annie began, "he say tell you, Miz Taft, he have to go find de crook. He say you unnerstand."

Mrs. Taft let out a big sigh. "Thank you, Annie," she said. "I know what he meant." Looking at the young people in disappointment, she said, "Now, why did he do that? The law may very well catch him if Mr. Simpson tells the sheriff who he thinks has been stealing from him. Oh, dear!"

"We'll just have to go find Phineas," Mandie said.

"I doubt that we could find him," Joe remarked. "He's pretty good at hiding."

Annie spoke up again. "Miz Taft," she said, "dat Injun man whut Missy know, he be in de sunroom."

"Uncle Ned!" Mandie cried, hurrying to the sunroom. "He'll help us find Phineas."

CHAPTER ELEVEN

THE ROBBER!

Uncle Ned, as always, agreed to help Mandie and her friends. He knew Phineas Prattworthy and he listened carefully as Mrs. Taft explained the whole story with occasional interruptions from Mandie, Joe, and Celia.

"Must help find," Uncle Ned said as Dr. Woodard came into the sunroom.

"Yes, I agree," said Dr. Woodard. "After all, Hilda might have died from the cold if Phineas hadn't done what he did for her."

"But, Dr. Woodard, I don't think he's guilty anyway," Mandie remarked. "We can't let an innocent man be prosecuted."

"Of course not, Amanda," Dr. Woodard replied.

"We find," Uncle Ned assured them. "Go now."

"I know we will find him with you helping us, Uncle Ned," Mandie told the old Indian, as they sat in the warmth from the fireplace. "Grandmother, may we go with Uncle Ned?"

"Amanda I just don't know," Mrs. Taft replied. "Evidently there is a robber involved in this, and he could be dangerous."

"Please, Grandmother," Mandie begged. "We'll stay right with Uncle Ned," she promised.

"Well, I suppose so," Mrs. Taft said uncertainly.

"Thanks," Mandie said.

"May I go, too?" Joe asked his father.

"I suppose if you stay right with Uncle Ned, it'll be all right," Dr. Woodard agreed.

"Thanks Dad," Joe said, grinning.

Mrs. Taft looked at the old Indian. "I'll send Ben with y'all, too," she said. "He can help see that the young people don't get into any trouble."

Uncle Ned nodded in agreement.

"And be back before dark," Mrs. Taft said to the young people.

They all nodded as Uncle Ned motioned for them to go. "Must go while trail fresh," he said.

The young people bundled up and followed the old Indian through the snow with Ben bringing up the rear. Ben didn't seem very happy to be involved in the hunt.

Uncle Ned traced Phineas's tracks in the snow through the yard, into the back, across the surrounding property, and into the main road. There, the tracks disappeared. The snow had been shoveled from the dirt road, and dozens of wagon wheels, horses, and footprints had marked the road.

"Maybe he went back to the church," Mandie suggested.

"He could have," Joe agreed. "We didn't tell Mr. Simpson that he had been hiding in the church—just that he had been ringing the bells and doing all that other crazy stuff. I don't believe Mr. Simpson would look for him there."

Uncle Ned nodded. "We look," he said.

Inside the church, the young people led the way, explaining to Uncle Ned what had happened there. They took him up to the gallery and showed him the rope ladder to the belfry. The old Indian was as agile as the young people as he scaled the rope ladder. Ben refused to go up.

In the belfry, Joe showed Uncle Ned the loose paneling.

"He said he hid in the attic, remember?" Mandie reminded Celia and Joe. "We never did go into the attic. Maybe he's there now."

"How can we get into the attic?" Celia asked nervously.

"He told us he could slide down through the wall behind this loose paneling into the attic," Joe said, shaking the panel in the wall.

Uncle Ned stood there looking and listening. "No other way?" he asked.

"Well, yes. He said there's a scuttle hole in the ceiling of the gallery," Mandie recalled.

"We see." Uncle Ned went back down the rope ladder, and the young people followed.

When they reached the gallery, they found Ben stretched out on one of the benches.

"Big help he is," Joe teased.

Ben got up sheepishly and joined the others.

Uncle Ned immediately spotted the trapdoor in the ceiling, but it was too high for them to reach.

"Need ladder," Uncle Ned said, looking around.

"There isn't a ladder in the building," Joe told him. "We've been through the whole church several times, and I don't remember seeing one anywhere."

"Then we get table, stack, reach," Uncle Ned decided.

The young people understood what the old Indian meant. If they brought the table and chairs up from the basement that they had used to open the basement window, they could probably reach the ceiling.

Ben was put to work helping. It was a job to get the big table up the stairs from the basement and then on up the narrow stairs to the gallery, but they finally made it.

Straddling the table over the bench directly under the scuttle hole, they put a chair on top of the table. The ceiling in the gallery was low. Joe and Uncle Ned could both reach the trapdoor by standing on the chair.

"I'll go up there," Joe volunteered.

Uncle Ned nodded and stood holding the chair for the boy to step on. The girls held their breath as they watched. Ben stood back, watching as he flipped the key in his hand.

Joe had trouble trying to slide the trapdoor open. It refused to budge.

"Get chair. I help push," Uncle Ned told them.

Joe jumped down and hurried to the basement to bring up another chair. He placed it beside the other chair on top of the table.

"Ben, you'll have to hold the chairs this time. Uncle Ned is going to stand up on one and me on the other," Joe told the Negro man.

"All right," Ben agreed. He started to put the key in his pocket as he stepped forward to help. The key slipped out of his hand and went flying between the benches, making a loud rattling noise.

Ben stooped to look around. "I jes' lost day key whut I found in dis chouch de other day."

Mandie quickly asked, "You found a key? In this church? When?"

Ben, down on his knees, looking under the benches, raised his head to answer. "Missy, I find dat key de day y'all make me come inside de church, de fust time. It be on de flo' right under my foot where I set."

Mandie said, "Come on, let's help Ben find his key. He found it here in this church, and you remember the man and woman were looking for something they had lost."

The young people quickly covered the floor. Uncle Ned, watching, bent to pick up something at his foot.

"Key," he told the young people, and he handed the key to Mandie.

Mandie squinted to read the faint printing on the key while the others crowded around to see.

"It says Property of National something or other, Charlotte, North Carolina, I think," Mandie said. "What's that other word there?"

"That's a *k* on the end of the word," Celia determined.

Joe looked closer. "Bank!" he exclaimed. "Property of National Bank of Charlotte, North Carolina."

The girls gasped. Uncle Ned nodded in understanding, but Ben looked confused.

"If dat key be de property of de bank, den I'll jes' send it back to 'em," he said innocently.

"Ben, don't you know what you've found?" Mandie asked. "This must be what the man and woman were looking for here that day we hid behind the curtains."

Celia's eyes grew wide. "And if this is what they lost—"

"Those people must be connected with that bank robbery in Charlotte," Joe interrupted.

"You mean they were bank robbers?" Celia asked.

Mandie looked up at Ben. "Can I keep this key?" she asked.

"Sho,' Missy," he replied. "Don't belong to me."

Mandie put the key in her pocket. "Uncle Ned, we need to get in touch with this bank in Charlotte," she said.

"We see, Papoose," the Indian agreed. "Now we go in attic. Be dark soon."

"You're right, Uncle Ned," Joe said, climbing up on one of the chairs. "We have to hurry."

Uncle Ned stepped up on the other chair. Ben held the chairs steady while Uncle Ned and Joe pushed on the trapdoor overhead. After several hard blows, it finally moved, and they were able to slide it back, uncovering a square hole in the ceiling.

Joe swung up inside the hole, and they could hear him walking around in the attic. "The place is pretty empty," he called down to them. "I see Mr. Prattworthy's bag over there and some odds and ends, but there's nobody up here."

"Come," Uncle Ned called to him. "We go." Joe came back down, and they closed the trapdoor and returned the table and chairs to the basement.

As they left the church, Uncle Ned asked Ben to drive them out of town toward the mountains. "Robber not stay in town. Phinny he go, too," the old Indian decided.

They all nodded. The robber wouldn't want to be seen around town, so he would most likely hide out in the country somewhere. Phineas knew that, too.

As they rode along the bumpy, snow-covered country road, they kept watch for anything unusual. There were very few buildings on the road, a few tumbled-down barns, some rough country houses, an old deserted church building, and a school. They stopped at all these places and quickly searched them.

"Uncle Ned, it's going to be dark soon," Celia reminded him.

"One more place. Then go back," Uncle Ned replied.

"Oh, I do hope we can find him," Mandie said.

"Just hope the robber doesn't find him first," Joe cautioned. "The robber must know what's going on in town."

They came to a narrow dirt road branching off the one they were traveling on. Uncle Ned motioned for Ben to pull up on the side road. "Stop there," he said.

Ben did what he was told and brought the rig to a stop. The side road was too narrow, and the snow was too deep for the rig to go down it anyway.

"Come. We walk," Uncle Ned ordered.

They all piled out of the rig onto the frozen snow.

"What's down this road?" Mandie asked.

"Old ground camp for church," the Indian replied, leading the way.

Mandie laughed. "Oh, you mean a campground for the church."

"No more. Church no more use." Uncle Ned adjusted his bow and sling of arrows on his shoulder.

The young people walked carefully on the frozen snow to keep from sliding down.

Ben trudged along behind them, mumbling to himself. "Dem hosses dey gwine be froze to death 'fo' we gits back," he fussed.

"You put their blankets on them," Joe said. "They'll be all right."

"Not fo' long," Ben argued.

In a little while Uncle Ned stopped for the others to catch up with him. He held up his hand. "Quiet," he said softly. "Not far."

Everyone hushed and cautiously followed the old Indian.

As they came around a curve, a large, old dilapidated building came in sight. Several smaller structures sagged nearby, but no one seemed to be anywhere around.

Again Uncle Ned held up his hand for them to stop. He motioned for them to hide behind a cluster of huge tree trunks nearby, then sniffed the air. "Smoke," he whispered.

There was a loud scuffling noise from somewhere behind the big building. Uncle Ned motioned for them to creep forward and stay out of sight. He slipped around the corner of the building. The noise got louder.

They heard a man's loud voice. "That's what you're going to get for snooping in other people's business," he yelled.

There was a loud crack of a whip.

Uncle Ned took an arrow from his sling and softly crept toward the back of the building. The young people stayed right behind him, and Ben brought up the rear.

As they reached the corner, they saw Phineas. He was sitting, tied up, on the snow-covered ground, and a strange man with a gun strapped to his waist raised a horse whip, ready to strike.

Uncle Ned quickly pulled back his bowstring and let his arrow fly. The arrow whizzed overhead and stuck in the tree trunk just over the stranger's head. The man whirled quickly and reached for his gun, unable to see them hiding around the corner. He looked at the arrow embedded in the tree.

"Indians!" the stranger shrieked.

"These woods are full of Indians, mister," Phineas told him as he wiggled to get free of the ropes. "Great big, strong Cherokee Indians."

"Then we'd better leave," the stranger said anxiously.

In the meantime, Uncle Ned had raced around the building to the opposite corner, and at that moment he shot another arrow above the man's head.

"Looks like they've got us surrounded," Phineas warned. "No way we can get out of here."

"We have to leave," the man insisted, nervously eyeing the second arrow. "Those Cherokee Indians are dangerous."

"You leave. I'll stay right here," Phineas offered. "Those Cherokees are my friends."

"If I leave, you're going with me," the stranger ordered. "And if they're your friends, you can see that no harm comes to us when we leave. Otherwise, you are going to be greatly harmed by me."

Uncle Ned raced back to the corner where the others were watching through the bushes.

The stranger stepped toward Phineas. He had a limp! *So this is the man who stole from the grocer,* Mandie thought. Phineas had found him!

The old Indian motioned for the others to come near. "I go behind man. Shoot arrow," he whispered. "He turn that way. I run fast. Shoot arrow again other way. Man get all confused."

"What can we do, Uncle Ned?" Joe asked in a low voice.

"You go that way. Get help," Uncle Ned motioned toward a slight path off to the right. "Mumblehead live that way. Two minutes."

Joe understood and nodded his head. Uncle Ned slipped around the building. Joe turned to the path and spoke quietly to Ben on his way. "Stay close to the girls," he whispered. "See that they don't get hurt. I'm going for help."

Ben nodded and moved closer to the girls. Together, they watched the stranger and Phineas through the bushes while Uncle Ned moved all around, shooting arrows from different directions.

The stranger seemed more and more frightened, apparently convinced he was surrounded by a whole tribe of Indians. "Hey, you!" he shouted at Phineas. "Call off these confounded Indians. Tell them we want to leave."

Phineas wriggled on the cold snowy ground to free himself from the ropes that bound him. "Do you think they're going to let us leave when they can see you're my enemy and that you've tied me up like this?" he scoffed. "Don't forget. They're my friends. If you don't release me, they'll come and get you in a few minutes."

The stranger limped around in circles for a while, evidently trying to think of some way out of his predicament. Without a word, he pulled a knife from his belt and slashed the ropes that bound Phineas.

Limbering up his wrists and ankles, Phineas finally managed to stand up. But just then, another arrow whizzed through the air and lodged in the tree behind the stranger, clipping his hat.

"Tell them to let us leave!" the stranger yelled, stomping around on his bad leg.

Phineas looked around and then let out a loud Indian yell as Uncle Ned grabbed the stranger from behind. Suddenly, scores of Indians came out of the bushes and surrounded the stranger, taking his gun and knife away from him.

"Thank the Lord!" Phineas shouted. "And thank you, Uncle Ned!"

The girls ran forward and met Joe coming from the other side.

"Go!" an Indian voice shouted.

The young people looked up to see Ben walking toward them, his eyes wide with fright, and a young Indian brave pushing him forward with an arrow poised at his back.

Ben's legs buckled beneath him, and he fell to the ground, begging for his life. "Please, I ain't done nothin,' " he pleaded. "Please!"

Uncle Ned ran to Ben's rescue. "Redbird, leave," he commanded. "Ben friend of Papoose."

Redbird smiled and reached down to help Ben up. Ben rolled away from the young Indian, and managing to get to his feet, he ran to where Mandie and Celia were standing.

Mandie glared at the stranger. "You are the man who stole food from the grocer and caused Mr. Phineas to be blamed for it, aren't you?" she asked as Uncle Ned tied the stranger's hands behind him.

"What are you white folk doing with these Indians?" the stranger asked.

"I'm part Cherokee myself," Mandie answered, "and these Indians are my friends."

Joe stepped forward to help Uncle Ned. "Come on, mister," he said in a deep, important-sounding voice. "We've got a rig not far from here. We're taking you to town."

The stranger protested. "I've got a bad leg," he complained. "I can't walk. Besides, my horse is in that old barn over there."

"You're not riding a horse," Joe ordered. "You'd only run away. You're going in the rig with us."

Uncle Ned called to the oldest Indian there, the head of the group. "Mumblehead, get horse. Tie to rig," he ordered. "Redbird, get braves. Carry bad man to rig. Hurry!"

Mumblehead disappeared while two young Indians stepped forward and picked up the stranger, carrying him to the rig as the others followed. Soon Mumblehead returned with the horse.

"Mr. Phineas, thank goodness we found you in time," Mandie said as they walked along. "Uncle Ned always knows what to do."

"How did you find the man?" Joe asked.

"I watched the store and sure enough, he came back to steal more," Phineas replied. "He stole a bag of beans and escaped before the grocer could catch him, but I followed him. His horse had thrown a shoe, so he was trying to walk," he explained. "He couldn't go very fast. Then when he turned in here off the road, he happened to look back and see me. There weren't enough bushes for me to hide in."

"Weren't you afraid of him?" Celia asked.

"I suppose so, but I was mad, too," Phineas said, "because he was committing crimes I was being blamed for."

"I can see why Mr. Simpson thought y'all were the same person," Mandie commented. "He's short like you, and he has a bad leg."

"Well, we don't exactly look alike," Phineas protested.

They got the stranger safely secured in the rig and tied the horse behind it. Uncle Ned thanked his Indian friends and told them goodbye as he and the others drove off.

The stranger moaned and groaned all the way, and the young people kept a close watch on him.

Finally Mandie spoke up. "What's wrong with you?" she asked.

"There's lots wrong with me," the stranger replied. "This here leg has got a bullet in it, for one thing."

Mandie gasped. "A bullet?"

"Who shot you?" Joe demanded.

"I guess I might as well come clean, or I'll die from this leg," the stranger said. "My name is Kent Stagrene. I robbed that bank in Charlotte, and the guard shot me," he confessed, beginning to moan again. He bent down to hold his leg; then he looked up. "I got away with the money, though."

Mandie did some quick thinking. Taking the key Ben found out of her pocket, she showed it to the stranger. "Is this the bank?" she asked.

He reached for the key, but she held it back.

"Where did you get that?" Kent Stagrene asked angrily. "That's the key to the strongbox I took."

"Then where is the money?" Joe asked.

"I don't have it anymore," he said, turning pale. "Someone else stole it from me." Within seconds he passed out.

Uncle Ned tapped Ben on the shoulder. "We take stranger to doctor man," he said.

Ben headed for Mrs. Taft's house.

CHAPTER TWELVE

AN ANGRY MOB

By the time Ben pulled the rig into Mrs. Taft's driveway, it was pitch dark.

Ella greeted them at the front door and ran to the parlor. "They's home, Miz Taft, and they's got some man wid 'em," she reported. "Looks like he's hurt."

"Go tell Dr. Woodard," Mrs. Taft ordered, hurrying to the front hallway. "He's up in his room, getting his coat. It's so late that he was about to go out looking for them."

Uncle Ned and Ben carried the still-unconscious man through the doorway. Mrs. Taft stepped back. "Who is that?" she asked shakily. "What's wrong with him?"

"He's been shot," Joe volunteered.

Mrs. Taft began to sway slightly as though she were about to faint.

"We didn't shoot him, Miz Taft," Ben assured her. "Dis de man whut rob de bank in Charlotte. De bank guard done shot him."

Ben and Uncle Ned laid the man on the floor in the hallway.

"A bank robber!" Mrs. Taft cried.

"He need doctor man," Uncle Ned said.

Phineas and the girls gathered around Mrs. Taft.

"Thank goodness, you're back, Phineas," Mrs. Taft said.

Dr. Woodard came hurrying into the hallway, followed by Ella, who stayed to see what was going on.

"Dr. Woodard, this is the bank robber and Mr. Simpson's thief all rolled into one," Mandie explained. "He confessed everything to us."

The doctor quickly knelt down to examine the stranger's leg. "It's pretty bad," he said, looking up at Mrs. Taft. "Do you have anywhere we can put this man? Even though he is a criminal he needs medical attention fast."

"Why, yes, I suppose he can be put in an empty room in the servants' quarters. Can you get him upstairs that far? The rooms are on the third floor," Mrs. Taft answered. "He'll be away from us up there."

"We can manage," Dr. Woodard said, standing up.

"We take," Uncle Ned said and motioned for Ben to help him pick up the unconscious man.

They moved slowly up the stairs carrying the criminal. Everyone stood watching. Dr. Woodard followed, giving directions.

"Ella, show them an empty room up there and then bring some coffee and cocoa to the parlor," Mrs. Taft told the maid.

The Negro girl hurried to pass the group on the stairs to direct them to a room.

The young people and Phineas removed their outerwear and left it in the hall, then followed Mrs. Taft into the parlor.

Seated by the roaring fire in the parlor, the young people related their adventures, and Phineas filled in with his as Mrs. Taft listened. Ella brought in hot coffee and hot cocoa and served it.

"The man said his name was Kent Stagrene," Mandie said, pulling the key from her pocket. "I showed him this key that Ben found in the church. He said it belongs to the strongbox he stole from the bank. Then he said somebody else stole the strongbox from him. So I think the man and woman we saw in the church that day must be the ones who robbed him."

Everyone agreed.

Suddenly Mandie caught her breath. "Mr. Phineas!" she said excitedly. "I just happened to remember something. I'm pretty sure the newspaper said there was a reward for the capture of the robber. You can get that money!"

"I didn't capture the robber," Phineas objected. "He captured me. Y'all captured the robber."

Mrs. Taft spoke up quickly. "They're right, Phineas," she said. "You found the man and went after him. Besides, these young people don't need the money. And I'm sure you could use it to get back on your feet."

"Thank you, Mrs. Taft, but I still think they are the ones who actually captured the man," Phineas replied.

"We'll see about that," Mrs. Taft said with a twinkle in her eye.

After a while Dr. Woodard and Uncle Ned joined the others in the parlor.

"Is the robber going to live?" Mandie asked as the two men sat down.

"I think so," the doctor replied. "But he has a bad wound. He should have gotten medical help right away after it happened. Uncle Ned and Ben filled me in on all the details."

"What are we going to do with him, Dr. Woodard?" Mrs. Taft said uneasily.

"Well, we left Ben watching him for now to make sure he doesn't try to get away if he regains consciousness," the doctor replied. "But we'll have to notify the sheriff that he's here."

"Will the sheriff take him away and put him in jail?" Joe asked.

"I don't think so—not in the condition he's in," his father explained. "I imagine the sheriff will just let him stay here until he is out of danger. Then he'll move him."

"What will they do to him?" Celia inquired.

"That will be up to the bank in Charlotte," Dr. Woodard told her. "Our sheriff will probably send him back to the sheriff in Mecklenburg County."

"I never dreamed there would be so much danger," Mrs. Taft said wearily, "or I never would have agreed for these young people to go looking for Mr. Simpson's thief."

Before long, Ella appeared in the doorway to announce that supper was on the table.

In the dining room, they continued discussing the matter as they ate. The young people hardly ate anything, however, because they were too excited. Mrs. Taft said she was too nervous to eat, knowing she had a bank robber in the house. But Phineas, Dr. Woodard, and Uncle Ned made good headway into the delicious food set before them.

Mrs. Taft changed the subject. "How was Hilda when you were up there a while ago?" she asked Dr. Woodard.

"She's not doing very good," he said, shaking his head.

"Is she conscious?" Mandie asked.

"No, I don't think so," the doctor replied. "She just lies there—doesn't open her eyes or respond in any way."

Ella rushed into the dining room and ran to Mrs. Taft. "De sheriff man, he be here," she said. "He want to see you and de doctuh in de parlor."

Mrs. Taft glanced at Dr. Woodard in alarm.

The doctor took charge. "Ella, please tell him we'll be there in a few minutes."

Ella quickly left the room.

"What does he want?" Mrs. Taft asked. "Phineas, you'd better get out of sight. Mr. Simpson may have sent him for you."

Dr. Woodard laid down his napkin and stood up. "That won't be necessary, Phineas," he said. "We'll just tell him the truth. We have the man upstairs that he's looking for."

Mrs. Taft followed Dr. Woodard out of the room into the parlor. Sheriff Jones was sitting by the fire. He rose to greet them. They all sat down to talk while the young people hid outside the parlor door, watching and listening. Phineas stayed in the dining room.

The sheriff started the conversation. "Sorry to bother you, Mrs. Taft, but—"

"Did that Mr. Simpson send you here?" Mrs. Taft interrupted.

"Well, yes, ma'am, he did," the sheriff admitted. "He told me you have the man who robbed his store, right here in your house."

"Of all the nerve!" Mrs. Taft exclaimed.

"I think I can explain, Sheriff," Dr. Woodard said. "You see, Mr. Simpson thought the man stealing food from his store was a man who is a friend of ours, whom we've known for years. This man's name is Phineas Prattworthy, and he has been living over on the Nantahala Mountain. But it so happens that we know for sure that Phineas is not guilty because we found the man who really stole from Mr. Simpson. He's upstairs. I've just removed a bullet from his leg."

The sheriff looked startled. "A bullet from his leg?" he asked. "Who is this man? Did Mr. Simpson shoot him?"

"No, Mr. Simpson didn't shoot him," the doctor said. "It seems this man also robbed a bank in Charlotte and was shot by a guard."

"That bank robbery last week in Charlotte?" the sheriff asked in disbelief. "You have the man who did it right here in this house?"

"Yes, we do. That's what I've just been telling you," the doctor insisted. "And he's the same man who stole Mr. Simpson's groceries."

The sheriff jumped up. "Where is he? I need to see about moving him to the jail!" he said excitedly.

"It's impossible to move him," the doctor warned. "He let that leg get infected, and right now he's barely hanging on. But if you want to see him, I'll be glad to show you where he is."

"All right," the sheriff agreed.

When the two men made their way up the stairs, the young people came back into the parlor and sat down. Dr. Woodard and the sheriff returned a short time later.

"Are you taking that terrible man out of my house, Sheriff?" Mrs. Taft asked.

The sheriff rubbed his chin thoughtfully. "No, I'm afraid I agree with Dr. Woodard that he shouldn't be moved right now," he said. "Unless you insist that I remove him from the premises, I'll leave him here."

"He can stay here provided someone guards him at all times," Mrs. Taft decided. "I don't want him wandering all over my house."

"He's not able to do any wandering around," Dr. Woodard assured her.

"Well, I can't leave Ben in there to watch him all the time," Mrs. Taft argued. "I need Ben for other things."

"If you'll allow it, I'll send a deputy over to guard him," the sheriff offered.

Mrs. Taft looked relieved. "That will be fine," she said. "Just get him out of my house as soon as it is possible."

At that moment, they heard loud noises outside the house. Everyone looked at one another.

Mandie ran to the window and peeked through the drawn draperies. "Grandmother!" she cried. "There must be a hundred people out in your front yard!"

Mrs. Taft and the sheriff quickly joined her at the window, followed by the others.

"What do they want, Sheriff?" Mrs. Taft asked nervously.

Everyone stared out the window at the sight of people everywhere. Some had lanterns, and they were all screaming something.

The sheriff took charge. "I'll go see what's going on," he said. Heading for the hallway, he opened the front door, and the others followed, staying behind him.

As soon as the door opened, the people on the lawn surged forward. "We want him! We want him!" they cried.

The sheriff took his pistol from its holster and fired a shot into the air. The crowd hushed. His face was in full view in the lamplight from the hallway.

"This is the sheriff here," he told them. "Now, what do you people want?"

"We want that man who desecrated the house of the Lord!" one man cried.

"We want the man who brought all that bad luck to this town with all that bell ringing and writing on the church wall!" a woman yelled.

"Send him out, Sheriff. We're gonna try him here and now!" another man shouted.

"He brung the flu down on this town and caused people to die!" a woman yelled.

The sheriff stepped forward. "Now, you wait just a minute!" he hollered. "I'm the law in this town, and we're going to do things by the law as long as I'm sheriff. Now go home—every one of you!"

"We ain't going home till we git that man!" a man insisted.

The angry mob grew louder and louder, pressing closer and closer toward the house. The sheriff raised his gun and fired into the air again.

His shot was answered by another shot from the crowd. "We got guns, too, Sheriff," someone called out. "And we know how to shoot 'em!"

"I'm going to arrest all you troublemakers if you don't move on," the sheriff threatened.

"There ain't a jail big enough to hold us all," a woman yelled.

"Give us that man and we'll leave!" cried a man in front.

"We know you've got him," another bellowed. "Mr. Simpson said so."

Mandie pursed her lips at hearing this. So Mr. Simpson was the cause of this, she thought angrily.

"I'm going back inside now," the sheriff called back to the crowd. "We're having supper, and I don't want you moving any closer to this house. I'll discuss the matter with the lady of the house and let you know what she has to say." He quickly closed the door.

Before anyone could say anything, the sheriff turned to Mrs. Taft and explained. "Of course I didn't mean what I told them," he said. "I'm going for help. I left my horse in the backyard. I'll be back as fast as I can. Just don't open the door under any circumstances."

Rushing through the hallway, he headed for the back door. Everyone else looked at each other nervously.

"Let's sit in the parlor," Dr. Woodard suggested, leading the way. "The draperies are all drawn, so they can't see in."

"What are we going to do?" Mrs. Taft asked as they took seats around the room.

"Nothing," Dr. Woodard replied. "We'll just wait for the sheriff to come back."

Everyone sat silently for a few seconds and then Dr. Woodard spoke again. "I need to check on Hilda and our prisoner," he decided. "I won't be long." He stood up and left.

Mrs. Taft also rose. "I think I'll talk to Phineas," she said. "He must still be in the dining room."

"He probably is," Mandie agreed. "We told him to stay there."

When Mrs. Taft left the parlor, Uncle Ned moved nearer to Mandie. All three young people sat in silence as the noise from the crowd grew stronger.

"They judge," Uncle Ned commented. "Big Book say not judge."

Mandie could feel her anger rising. "That's right, Uncle Ned," she agreed. Suddenly she jumped up and ran to the hallway. "I'm going to tell them what I think of them."

Before anyone could stop her, she opened the door, and the angry mob became very quiet as they saw the door open.

"Please listen to me," Mandie called to the crowd from the front porch. The lamps in the hallway illuminated the area where she stood.

Joe joined her while Uncle Ned and Celia stood back, just inside the house.

When the crowd saw that it was just Mandie, they laughed at her. "Where is the woman of the house?" they yelled. "We don't talk to no young'un!"

Mandie strode to the top of the steps. "Please listen to me!" she yelled at the top of her voice. "I know a lot of you are from our church, and you claim to be Christians. Well, you're not acting Christlike tonight!"

The people nearest the house hushed to listen, and gradually the whole crowd quieted.

"The Bible says, 'Blessed are the merciful; for they shall obtain mercy,' " she reminded them. "You are not showing mercy tonight. You are not behaving at all like Christians."

"Just give us that man," a man yelled. "He's the one who brought all this trouble on our town."

"No, he didn't!" Mandie yelled back. "No human being has the power to bring curses on people, or to cause illness or anything else. You people who are Christians should know that. That's plain old superstition, and there's no place for such thinking in the minds of Christians."

"Just give us that man!" the same man hollered again.

"I want to tell you about the man who was hiding in the church," Mandie continued.

The crowd immediately hushed.

"That man is so poor and disabled that he had to eat out of trash cans," she said. "He had no one left to care whether he lived or died— no one to take care of him." She took a deep breath and went on. "He happened to see a man rush out of Mr. Simpson's store and drop an apple. When he picked it up, Mr. Simpson falsely accused him of stealing. He had done nothing wrong, but he was afraid because he had no one to turn to. He hid in the church, hoping someone would come along who would help him."

"Why didn't he ask somebody to help him?" a woman yelled.

"Because he didn't think he knew anyone in this town," Mandie answered. "He didn't know anyone he could trust. You see, he was living in the Nantahala Mountains with his son. Then his son died, and the man had a stroke and was unable to work. Besides, he's very old."

"Well, Mr. Simpson said he stole from him," a man insisted.

"Tell Mr. Simpson to step forward if he's out there with you," Mandie ordered. "We'll straighten that out right now. Where is Mr. Simpson?"

"He ain't here," a woman said.

"He can't even fight his own battles, is that it?" Mandie mocked. "He has to get the town in an uproar to fight for him?"

"Where is that man who was hiding in the church?" a woman asked.

"He's right here in this house," Mandie replied. "My grandmother has taken him into her home. Most of you know my grandmother. She would never protect a criminal. You know that."

"How do we know you're telling the truth?" someone yelled.

"Because we also have in this house, and under arrest by the sheriff, the man who did steal from Mr. Simpson. He is the same man who robbed the bank in Charlotte. He—"

The crowd went wild. "A bank robber!" they yelled. "In this house?"

Joe moved closer to Mandie and gave her a little pat on the shoulder for encouragement.

"Please let me explain! Please!" Mandie pleaded with the angry crowd.

Finally the people calmed down enough to listen.

"The bank robber was shot at the bank in Charlotte, and we found him out in the woods," Mandie explained. "Dr. Woodard is looking after him, and a sheriff's deputy will be guarding him. As soon as he is able to be moved, he will be put in jail."

An old man stepped forward within the range of the light from the hallway and spoke. "I believe you, little lady. But the man did damage to the house of the Lord, and he ought to be punished for that."

The crowd waited silently for Mandie's reply.

"But that's not for an angry mob to decide," she reminded them. "That's the business of the church members, not the whole town. And not like this."

"I guess you're right, little lady," the old man said. He turned to the crowd. "It's time we'se all in our own homes," he yelled. "Let's go!"

A loud murmuring rippled through the crowd.

"Please go home," Mandie begged. "If you're the Christians you claim to be, you'll go on home. 'Blessed are the merciful; for they shall obtain mercy.' "

One by one, the crowd turned slowly to leave. Mandie's heart was suddenly thumping wildly as she realized what she had done, standing up to this crowd. "Good night, everyone," she called with a slight quiver in her voice. "God bless you."

Several in the crowd repeated her words back to her.

Without turning around, Mandie whispered to Joe, "Joe, I can't move!" she said. "I just realized what I did! They could have mobbed us!"

Joe put his arm around her, gently turning her toward the door. "You sure had me scared to death," he said as they entered the house. "I just knew they were all going to come on into the house!"

Joe closed the door behind them.

Uncle Ned stepped forward, put his arm around Mandie, and led her into the parlor. "Papoose, I proud of you," he said. "Jim Shaw would be proud of Papoose."

Mandie collapsed on the sofa. "Thank you, Uncle Ned," she replied. "Something just came over me, and I had to speak up for Mr. Phineas. I don't know what made me do it."

When Mrs. Taft returned to the parlor with Dr. Woodard and Phineas, they were astounded to hear what had happened.

Mrs. Taft started shaking. "You could have been killed, Amanda!" she exclaimed.

"But she wasn't," Dr. Woodard reminded her. "And she has cleared Phineas's reputation." He smiled at Mandie. "I think you'd make a good lawyer, Amanda—if we had such things as women lawyers."

"No, thank you," Mandie said. "Joe is going to be the lawyer."

Celia stared at her friend in amazement. "I could never have done what you did, Mandie," she said.

By the time the sheriff returned with reinforcements, the crowd had completely dispersed, and all he had to do was leave one deputy to guard the still-unconscious prisoner.

There was no more trouble in the town, and Uncle Ned went home.

By the end of the week, Kent Stagrene, the bank robber, had regained consciousness and was well enough to be moved to the jail.

Mandie had kept the key, after showing it to the sheriff.

"I'll just keep it, Sheriff Jones," Mandie told him the day he moved Kent Stagrene from her grandmother's house. "Who knows, I might just find the box it goes to." They were alone in the front hallway.

"What if we find those people? We may need the key," the sheriff said. "Besides, that key belongs to the bank and I think we ought to return it."

"I'll bring it to you in a day or two," she said.

"Miss Amanda, I don't want you getting into any trouble with that key," Sheriff Jones said. "If word got around that you had the key, those gangsters with the strongbox might just come after it."

"But nobody knows I have it except you and my family here," Mandie said. "I promise. I'll bring it to you in a day or two. Please."

The sheriff looked into those blue eyes, so much like those of her mother whom he had once known, and finally smiled and said, "All right. Just a day or two now. Remember, no longer."

As soon as the sheriff left, Mandie hurried to find Joe and Celia. They gathered in the sunroom to talk.

"I'm going to have to give up this key," Mandie told them. "What can we do about finding that strongbox before I let the sheriff have this key?"

"Now, Mandie, you are dealing with real gangsters when you try to get involved in this," Joe warned.

"Just tell me where you think they would hide the box," Mandie insisted, ignoring Joe's warning.

Celia spoke up. "Those people may not even be in this town any longer."

"That's right," Joe agreed. "There's no way we could find that box."

"We'll see," Mandie said.

The next morning the sheriff came knocking on the door, asking for Mandie. The adults were all gone and the young people were in the parlor. Ella ushered Sheriff Jones into the room.

"Well, Miss Amanda, I guess I need that key, if you don't mind," the sheriff told her.

"Did you find the box?" Mandie asked eagerly.

"We not only found the box, we also found that man and woman who had stolen it from Kent Stagrene," Sheriff Jones explained.

"Where are they? Can we see them?" Mandie wanted to know.

"Mandie, what do you want to see those people for?" Joe asked impatiently.

"I'd like to see if they're the same people we saw in the church," Mandie said.

"They were," the sheriff confirmed. "They followed Kent Stagrene to his hiding place after he robbed the bank and were able to take the box away from him. They came on into town here with the box with the intention of staying at the hotel. When they went to register, the hotel clerk saw the box and recognized it as a bank box."

"Why didn't the clerk have them arrested?" Mandie asked.

"Well, instead of notifying my office, the clerk thought he could get a reward for himself, and he asked the strangers if they wanted to put their money box in the safe. The people suddenly decided they didn't want to register and left. The clerk followed them. The man and woman split up. The clerk tried to keep up with the man but the man was too smart for him. And the woman completely disappeared."

"You still haven't said how you know they were in the church," Mandie insisted.

"When we caught them, they said they had lost the key in the church," the sheriff explained.

"Now we know," Celia said with a sigh.

"Where were they from, Sheriff Jones?" Mandie asked.

"No place in particular," the sheriff said. "They are professional gamblers and they travel from place to place, wherever they can set up games. They just happened to be in the bank when Kent Stagrene robbed it."

"Thanks for letting me know, Sheriff," Mandie said. "And, Sheriff, would you please do me a favor? Would you give the bank Mr. Phineas Prattworthy's name as the one who captured the robber? I understand the reward offered was for capture of the robber. And Mr. Phineas needs the reward money real bad."

"There are two rewards offered, one for the man and another one for the money," the sheriff explained. "As officers of the law we can't collect rewards so we'll just turn in his name for both rewards. I'm sure he'll be hearing from the bank."

"What about the hotel clerk?" Joe asked.

"He didn't capture the money," the sheriff said. "My deputy happened to be right there when it happened and he took the money box from the people."

"Thank you, Sheriff Jones. The rewards will mean so much to Mr. Phineas," Mandie said, smiling at the law officer.

And in a few days the bank in Charlotte sent a special messenger to see Phineas Prattworthy, bringing a letter of thanks and an enormous reward.

"I still don't feel I deserve it," the old man declared as they all sat in the parlor after the messenger left. "But I do owe the church for damages because of my bad conduct."

"You'll have plenty for that and plenty left over to live on," Mrs. Taft replied.

"Thank the Lord," Mandie said softly.

Mrs. Taft offered Phineas a house and farm that she owned near Asheville. He could make a good living off of it with the help of a few hired hands, which he could now afford. He was thankful for her kindness.

The next Saturday Uncle Cal came by Mrs. Taft's house with the message that classes would resume on the following Monday.

"I'm glad to see you, Uncle Cal," Mandie told the old Negro as she and Celia stood talking to him in the front hallway, "but I was hoping we'd have a little longer out of school."

"But, Missy, all dem girls done got well now, and you gotta keep on wid dat book learnin' so you won't be ignorant," he teased.

"Aren't you coming in?" Celia invited.

"No, Missy. I got lots of calls to make to git the girls all back to school," he replied, thanking her. "But me and Phoebe, we see y'all come Monday." And with that he left.

Mandie closed the door and turned toward the parlor. "Oh, shucks!" she said.

"But, Mandie, we knew everyone was better when Dr. Woodard told us he and Joe were going home yesterday," Celia reminded her.

They both sat down near the fireplace in the parlor.

"I know," Mandie said with a sigh. "Oh, well, the house seems so empty with everyone else gone that I suppose we might as well go back to school. And we do still have a mystery back there to solve. Remember our little problems with a certain mouse?" she asked.

Celia nodded. "Oh, yes," she said. "We never did get that cleared up, did we?"

Mandie sat silently for a minute. "I just wish Hilda would get well." She sighed again.

"At least when Dr. Woodard went home, he said she was no worse," Celia reminded her. "And he has those nurses staying with her around the clock. Maybe she'll change for the better soon."

Just then there was a knock on the door, and Mandie rushed to answer it.

When she opened the door, there stood Uncle Ned, smiling down at her. "Uncle Ned, come on in," Mandie greeted the old Indian, ushering him into the parlor. "I didn't know you were coming back so soon."

"I bring message from mother of Papoose," he said, sitting by the fire to warm his hands. He smiled broadly.

Snowball, who was curled up on the rug nearby, opened one eye to look at him and then went back to sleep.

"Good news?" Mandie asked excitedly.

"Yes. Good News," the Indian replied. "Mother of Papoose say she have big surprise for Papoose for Christmas."

"Surprise for Christmas?" Mandie puzzled over the message. "Tell me what it is, Uncle Ned. Please?"

"Not know, Papoose," Uncle Ned told her. "Mother of Papoose say she not tell me so I not tell Papoose."

"You mean Mother sent you all the way over here to tell me she had a big surprise for me for Christmas, and she didn't even tell you what it is?" Mandie frowned.

"I not know surprise, Papoose," the Indian repeated.

"Not even a little teeny bit?" Mandie teased.

Uncle Ned reached over to her and patted her blonde head. "Papoose, I not know surprise. Must wait for Christmas," he said with a smile.

"Oh, no," Mandie moaned. "I'll be wondering from now until Christmas holidays what this is all about."

"So will I," Celia added.

"It must be something awfully important for her to send you, Uncle Ned," Mandie reasoned.

The old Indian grinned. "Papoose see," he said. "Wait for Christmas."

After Uncle Ned left that afternoon, Mandie paced up and down in the parlor talking through this newest mystery. Celia sat patiently by the fire, petting Snowball.

What surprise could her mother have for her that was important enough to send Uncle Ned with the message? Mandie wondered. And why didn't her mother just wait until Mandie came home for the holidays and tell her about the surprise then?

Mandie could hardly wait.

More Exciting Adventures with

Mandie!

Join Mandie, Snowball, and the whole gang as they solve exciting mysteries and learn important lessons about life, friendship, and family. *The Mandie Collection: Volume 1* includes five beloved stories:

Mandie and the Secret Tunnel
When Mandie's father dies, his Cherokee friend provides comfort, and a secret tunnel reveals Mandie's family history.

Mandie and the Cherokee Legend
Mandie investigates a Cherokee legend about long-lost gold and whether it will bring a curse to the men who find it.

Mandie and the Ghost Bandits
Mandie and her friends unravel the mystery of missing gold after a late-night train wreck and some "ghostly" robbers.

Mandie and the Forbidden Attic
Mandie explores the mysterious noises in the school attic, and the outcome is a surprise to everyone!

Mandie and the Trunk's Secret
An old trunk containing potentially dangerous papers from the past intrigues Mandie and her friends.

The Mandie Collection: Volume 1 by Lois Gladys Leppard